Heaven Lake

a novel

JOHN DALTON

SCRIBNER

New York   London   Toronto   Sydney

SCRIBNER
1230 Avenue of the Americas
New York, NY 10020

First Scribner trade paperback edition 2005

SCRIBNER and design are trademarks of Macmillan Library Reference USA, Inc., used under license by Simon & Schuster, the publisher of this work.

For information about special discounts for bulk purchases, please contact Simon & Schuster Special Sales: 1-800-456-6798 or business@simonandschuster.com

Designed by Kyoko Watanabe
Text set in Minion

Manufactured in the United States of America

3   5   7   9   10   8   6   4   2

Library of Congress Control Number: 2003059123

ISBN 0-7432-4634-9
0-7432-4635-7 (Pbk)

This book is for
Jen Jen Chang and Carlotta Dalton

Contents

PART ONE

The Volunteer

One

HE WAS UP by four A.M., such was his eagerness, and less than an hour later installed on a predawn, air-conditioned express train that hurried south from Taipei through long-drawn neighborhoods of shuttered storefronts and faintly glimmering apartment houses. What little there was to see had to be viewed through a pall of damp, grainy fog. A few slumped figures were pushing carts of refuse through the alleyways. Flocks of ragged black pigeons settled on the metal boughs of nearby utility towers. And yet for Vincent every dark or shadowed feature of the landscape held a private luster that seemed, in some contrary way, hopeful, auspicious.

At first light he put his forehead to the compartment window and watched the countryside take shape as a steady plateau of cropland and industrial parks—not curtains of bamboo, he noted, not leafy barricades of Asian jungle, just neat fields of grain and rice, just factories and warehouses separated by rows of beech trees.

Several hours into his journey he began to feel the wry pinch of his predicament, all the commonplace symbols that were unavailable to him, the railway signs, for instance, with their columns of glinting white characters he couldn't read. Nor could he make out the steward's garbled announcements over the train's PA. He leaned across the aisle and told a well-dressed, responsible-looking gentleman that he was on his way to Toulio for the first time and was unsure when to get off the train. From then on, after each announcement, he turned and sought the man's guidance. Not yet, the man said with a single, restrained shake of the head. Not yet. Not yet.

And then, finally, Toulio. This time Vincent actually understood the steward's announcement, Toulio, pronounced *Doe-lay-oh,* and, to be certain, he looked across the aisle to the gentleman and received a precise nod that might also have been a mark of personal encouragement, for Vincent, for the new ministry. The train screeched to a halt. He grappled with his backpack and duffel bag and hurried out onto the station platform.

It was by then nine-thirty on a Sunday morning. The open hall of the station was jammed with ticket buyers, the oak benches filled with travelers. Though a league of strangers inspected him from a safe distance, no one stepped forward from the crowd to greet him. He glimpsed, beyond the station's entranceway, a vibrant wedge of Toulio's town center, tall buildings and traffic, a carousel of activity both larger and more brash than anything he'd anticipated.

Outside the station he came upon three young men with their backs against the station wall. One was upright, on crutches, his legs encircled in thick metal braces. The other two were resting on the station steps. They had no braces, but their thin legs lay splayed out before them at odd angles like a clutch of toppled fence posts. They were each selling Wrigley's chewing gum, Spearmint and Juicy Fruit. Could one of them be Shao-fei? His first assumption, entirely correct as it turned out, was no, not likely. Still, he stopped and bought one pack of gum from each young man. As an act of quiet consideration, as a way of inaugurating his time in Toulio, it pleased him to meet their shy gaze and drop two coins into each of their paper boxes.

A moment later he turned his attention to the station parking lot, where a wiry boy was motioning to him from the open door of a taxi.

"Hello? Shao-fei?" He shambled forth with his heavy bags. The taxi's trunk was roped shut, and he wound up dumping the bags into the empty passenger seat. "Hello," he said again. "How are you? Thanks for getting up early. Thanks for coming out to meet me."

"You're welcome," the boy said. He wore thick-lensed glasses through which he seemed to study Vincent with a pained sobriety.

"How are you?" Vincent asked once more.

"And how are you?" the boy returned.

"Good."

"Me, too," Shao-fei replied. At once his expression grew tighter, more businesslike. "Excuse me," he said. "But I feel it's a bad way. To buy the thing. To pay the money."

"What thing?"

"The *gum*," he said. "My feeling is that it's not good because the three boys, they make you pay the too-high price."

"I paid them fifteen yuan each," Vincent said. "Is that too much?"

"You can buy the gum for ten yuan at the store."

"Well, yes, I guess I could have."

"So why did you pay the too-high price?"

Vincent, at a loss, shook his head dumbly. Already it felt as if he were tiptoeing, blindly, along a narrow ledge. "I didn't know," he replied. "My mistake." He shrugged and held out the open palms of his hands, a conciliatory gesture, a peace offering.

It seemed to work well enough. The boy's intense earnestness began to dissolve. He managed a welcoming smile of sorts. Before long they were lodged beside each other in the taxi's rear seat, inching their way between columns of idling cars and motorcycles. Vincent rolled down the window and allowed the heavy air—still humid and summerlike in mid October—to wash past him. This, his first close-up view of Toulio, proved disheartening. From the town's knotted center, its clamorous hub, arose a brand of stolid architecture, beamy department stores and offices, an actual high-rise bank—or was it a hotel?—thick-ledged and drably grand. The main avenue made sense to him only as fragments of a discordant puzzle: mirrored glass and throbbing loudspeakers, a modishness that seemed pirated, misplaced; here, a flashy music store; there, the facade of a hamburger shop litigiously similar to an American franchise. Above the avenue hung a cascade of flickering signs, a profusion of signs, so many that the great tangle of them seemed to render each, individual one meaningless. Below, on the walkways, a throng of inured pedestrians twined their way through a maze of haphazardly parked motor scooters.

All of this burdened his resolve. All of this he regarded with an ache of betrayal, though the treachery was his fault entirely. Stupid to have imagined unpaved roads and quaint hilltop bungalows when the real Toulio appeared as densely quartered as any district of Taipei.

Only a few kilometers from the town center, the tall buildings abruptly subsided, replaced by long rows of connected homes. Beyond these homes, he was relieved to see the countryside open up, flat and vigorously green, beneath a muddled, gray sky.

"A few rules of my family's house, please," Shao-fei said. "Mama asks that you eat your meals in the kitchen or in the parlor. Drinks, hot or cold, you can have upstairs in your room. But don't take the hot bath late at night. Mama must have the hot water for pulling out the chicken feathers." He paused to remove his glasses and wipe a loose strand of hair from the lens. With his glasses off, the angles of his face were less severe. Unmasked, he had a rather sweet and permanently startled face. "Lock the front door but not the back door when you come in at nighttime. Maybe you don't stay out late. Alec always stay out late, so maybe you don't have to care about the locking of the door."

Alec, Shao-fei explained, also boarded at the house. He came from Scotland and *not* from England. Alec had helped him to learn English and was, in Shao-fei's words, "a great, big brother friend." He was currently the only foreign resident of Toulio and had lived in Shao-fei's home for nearly two years. "But not all the time," Shao-fei added. "Sometimes he there, and then sometimes he go away, and then *surprise* and he comes back again, like that."

He then asked Vincent a string of polite yet tritely familiar questions, the very same questions that had been posed to him repeatedly—often by strangers—during his apprenticeship in Taipei. "Do you like Taiwan food? How tall are you? Which province in America do you come from?"

"A small town called Red Bud, in the Illinois province," Vincent answered.

"Yes," Shao-fei said, "I hear about this place before. It's a good one. I know that." He asked Vincent how old he was.

"Twenty-four."

It appeared to please him, this fact. "Yes." He grinned. "I already guess that you are twenty-four in the minute before you tell me it's true." He went on to explain that he himself was sixteen years old according to the Chinese lunar calendar, or fifteen when his age was tallied in standard years. After this, he quieted and watched the road's gravel shoulder race by. His eyelids fluttered heavily. He yawned. "Don't make the telephone call to America before you first ask Mama," he said.

"I won't," Vincent promised. He'd pried a stick of Spearmint gum from its wrapper. It seemed only courteous that he offer the boy a piece. Courteous, too, that he begin speaking in the boy's native language. "*Yao bu yao?*" he asked. Want or don't want?

"No, thank you," Shao-fei replied in English. He looked at the gum and mumbled.

"What?" Vincent asked.

"Lazy boys," he mumbled. "Make you pay the too-high price."

Shao-fei's home was set amid a circle of a half dozen other tan, two-floor houses and one corner store, an enclave connected to the main roadway by a stretch of single-lane blacktop that ran for a kilometer through open rice fields. Beside the house stood pyramids of feather-flecked wire cages. From its screened windows came the scent, not unpleasant, of chicken broth on the verge of boiling. By the time Vincent had hoisted his bags onto his shoulders, the boy had made his way to the front step and was holding open a pair of ornate sliding doors.

"Shoes, please," Shao-fei reminded him.

Without setting his bags down, Vincent stepped against the heels of his shoes and pried loose his feet. Shao-fei, already free of his sandals, shuffled barefoot across a foyer and began clambering up a railed staircase. Vincent followed. For the first time that morning he was able to look upon the boy's disfigured legs.

There was nothing frail or unusual about Shao-fei's hips and thighs. The trouble began at the kneecaps, where the legs bowed outward along the shin. Both his feet were turned inward, the right foot especially, so that it twisted around and pointed almost to the left heel. The result was a reckless side-to-side lurching. He didn't limp up the staircase, but rather tottered back and forth with such swift, careening staggers that it seemed almost possible he might topple sideways over the rail.

In the upstairs hallway, the boy halted and rapped his knuckles against a closed door. "This one belong to Alec. I'm knocking to see if he wants to come talk."

They waited. Vincent shifted under the weight of his bags. "Maybe he's not in."

"He's there inside. Listen." Shao-fei knocked once more. "Big brother?"

They heard a mattress squeak, a drawer slide open and close, then the faint click of a cigarette lighter.

"If he wants to talk, he opens the door. But now I'm thinking he's not in the right mood for talking," Shao-fei said, and continued down the hallway.

Vincent's own room contained a low bed with a mattress, a dresser, a desk, a mirror, and a chair. He didn't mind its sparseness, the humble beginnings from which future accomplishment might arise. His new room lay adjacent to Alec's. An open window allowed a thin stream of cigarette smoke, expelled from Alec's room, to slip evenly along the side of the house and enter Vincent's. Mixed with the smoke was a sweet, musky fragrance, richer and more potent than tobacco smoke alone.

"If you don't like the smell, close the window," Shao-fei suggested.

"Do you know what he's doing in there?" Vincent asked.

"Smoking."

"Do you know what it is, though?"

"Yes." Shao-fei fanned his hand across the window screen. He wrinkled his nose. "It's bad air," he said.

Bad air? Vincent believed there might be other names for it. An opiate, perhaps, a narcotic, though when he recalled the few open-air rock concerts he'd attended in college, the odor seemed closer to scented marijuana, hashish.

And yet, of course, it was not for him to say. It wasn't his home. He was a boarder in another family's house, a diminished family at that, a family of two, a fifteen-year-old boy and his mother. They were Chinese. It was not for Vincent to decide what would be tolerated under the roof of their house. *No to hot baths at night. Yes to the use of illegal drugs.* Instead, he swept the floor of his new room and stowed away his clothing. He taped twin maps of Taiwan and America to the walls. Later he joined Shao-fei in the kitchen for a dinner of boiled chicken and spiced cauliflower. It wasn't until nine o'clock that he met the boy's mother, Mrs. Chen, a ruddy, determined woman, who ushered him out to the patio that adjoined the house to warn him against changing the settings of or otherwise touching the three huge gas cauldrons she used to prepare chickens for market. Afterward she led him to the family parlor and graciously accepted his first month's rent. Before bidding him good night, she helped him place a collect call to the Good Shepherd Church office in Taipei.

In the seconds before his phone call was accepted, a sudden and wholly irrational embarrassment came over him. How strange it was in those few moments, how uncomfortable, to be himself, to be Vincent, sitting alone in another family's parlor.

It was a great relief, a great assurance, to hear Reverend Phillips's voice on the line, to hear his patient "Yes?" and then his winsome exclamation, "Ah, Vincent!"

"Hello, Reverend."

"You've arrived safely, have you? And had a look around?"

"It's a much bigger town than I thought."

"Well, yes. In America it would be a small city, wouldn't it? Ninety thousand people. I don't know if I actually heard that or if it's a guess. It's bigger, certainly, than the town you come from. Much bigger. I suppose it must be twenty times the size of . . . of Bloomfield, is it? . . . No, no. That's not it. Wait a minute. . . ."

Easy to picture the Reverend at this moment, a stout man in his late fifties, a pale, tolerant face, one eye closed in concentration. He was an articulate and precise teacher, an exacting speaker and writer of the Chinese language, and yet often the lesser details eluded him. During Vincent's month of apprenticeship in Taipei, the Reverend would periodically look him in the eye and call him Richard. "Where did we leave off yesterday, Richard?" he sometimes wondered aloud, and Vincent, who fretted over the Reverend's faulty memory, would answer patiently to the wrong name.

". . . Never mind," the Reverend said now. "I'm hopeless. You've settled in, I take it?"

"I have. My room is furnished. I should be comfortable here."

"They're good people, the Chens, willing to board a foreigner, a stranger. And Shao-fei, the boy, I met him once, a year ago. Very good-natured, bright, too, speaks some English as I remember."

"And I appreciate their help. I'm just anxious now to get accustomed to the town, to find a house for the new ministry."

"That's right. You're eager for it all to begin. I know the feeling, but I'm going to remind you that these things take time."

"Yes," he said. "Time. I know."

"I hope you do know, Vincent. No doubt you've heard me speak of these things before, but it's worth remembering, I think, especially now that you've arrived. The people of Toulio will have no particular interest in Christ or the Presbyterian faith. Most will be small-town farmers and merchants, factory workers. Not very worldly folks, maybe, yet they can spot a phony a mile away. It may sound strange, but you've got to convert the never-believers as well. I'm talking about the people who'll never become Christian, never even set foot inside your Bible study class. They've got to see you as legitimate. If you can do that, then you'll have set the stage for other volunteers who'll minister in Toulio long after you've returned to America."

"The long-range view," Vincent said and nodded to the Chens' empty parlor. "I'll try to keep things in perspective that way, especially when I run into difficulties."

"That would be a very good idea," the Reverend said. "And there will be difficulties. The difficulties of being an outsider. Plus the difficulties you'll bring upon yourself; the mistakes you can't quite keep yourself from making. But don't imagine dramatic confrontations with the towns-people. Mostly it's a matter of outlasting their ambivalence. I could say you'll win them over with your conviction or your friendliness, but really the most important thing comes down to a talent you already have, a kind of sincerity, a patience for dealing with people."

"Thank you," Vincent said. "Thank you very much." These words, though, did not convey the pride he felt or the slight flush of shame. Secretly, he'd worried that the Reverend's sporadic forgetfulness might somehow undo the entire Taiwan ministry. Now, sitting in the glow of his approval, Vincent was overcome by an ardent, full-hearted loyalty.

"I'd just begun my evening prayers when you called," the Reverend explained. "Since you interrupted, I'll invite you to join me."

Join in prayer? Is that what the Reverend meant? Vincent had never prayed over the telephone before. Yet once they started there was a charged gravity to the Reverend's words and a sense of communion between them that felt perfectly right. "Oh Lord, hear our prayers," Reverend Phillips said in an office two hundred kilometers away, and then began, as he always did, with a panoramic regard for world events: for those left homeless along the Carolina coast by a raging Hurricane Hugo; for those drowned recently in a boat collision on the Thames River in London; for Nelson Mandela, let the portents be true and his twenty-seven years of imprisonment come to an end; for the tragedy at Tiananmen Square, now four months old, for the dead and wounded students and those still hiding out. Next, he prayed for those who were ill in the parish, spoke their names and the names of more fortunate parishioners blessed with new babies. His prayers then turned to Vincent. How thankful he was for Vincent's dedication to Christ's work. How pleased he was with the progress they'd made in language and Bible study. Last, he gave thanks for that which, be it knownst or unbeknownst to each person, lay at the very center of all human lives: the sweet miracle of Christ's eternal love.

"Amen. Rest well, Vincent. A new place—it's never what you expected. It always feels odd the first few days."

"Thank you, Reverend. Good night."

"Good night," he said. "God's grace."

The final thing Vincent did that evening was set out his language books and practice speaking Chinese. He'd taken several Mandarin courses at Southern Illinois University and even after graduation stayed on for an eight-week intensive language program. Since coming to Taiwan and beginning his apprenticeship at Good Shepherd, he had studied daily, three hours in the morning at a Taipei language school, one or two hours more with Reverend Phillips, and then, companionless in his dorm room, he'd given himself over to a compulsive style of review involving flash cards and pronunciation guides. He found the written characters beautiful, but far too complex, far too tedious, to sit for hours and practice the exacting strokes. Because of this, he'd turned his attention to spoken Chinese. And the language itself, the lively falling and rising tones and the smooth, elegant cadences of spoken Mandarin, appealed to Vincent. Already he had memorized an impressive array of words and phrases. Somewhat less impressive was his ability to reproduce the language's precise tones. Fortunately, there were drills to remedy this. Tonight, for example, he brought forth his cassette player and inserted a conversation tape upon which Reverend Phillips had intoned many of the terms and phrases necessary to ministry work. On the tape the hurried rhythm of the Chinese language had been slowed and the elusive tones of each word given a clear, dulcet emphasis.

"*Shiwang,*" the Reverend said. Hope. A word that began in the high first tone and ended in the plummeting fourth. *Grace. Devotion. Joy. I place myself in Christ's loving hands. Who else but Christ knows my secret heart?*

Just before eleven P.M. he glanced up from his studies and found that a small and mostly silent crowd had come together in the lane outside a neighbor's house. The men wore white armbands. The women had covered the tops of their heads and their hair with tented, white hoods. Each member of the party brandished a pair of long sticks in his or her hands. More surprising still, a sizable bonfire blazed away in the center of the lane. Thick tongues of flame spiraled up as high as the balconies of nearby homes. From Vincent's vantage point it all appeared fairly outlandish. But what was it? Impossible to say except that, judging from the dogged conduct of the participants, an earnest ceremony of some sort was under way. A devotion? Before long the crowd convened in a circle around the fire and beat their sticks in a drubbing rhythm against the pavement. The sound was like the swift galloping of a dozen wooden-legged horses.

Granted, he was tired, too drained from his long first day in Toulio to think with any real clarity. There was no way now, it seemed, to hold back his verdict: the town was garish and strange, the Chen family woefully lax, his unseen Scottish housemate a loafer at best, at worst a drug addict. These were, he knew, uncharitable views, graceless to the core.

In bed, with the lights off, he noticed how the glint of bonfire light made the furnishings of his new room appear paltry, forlorn. He closed his eyes and listened to the steady *thrum-thrum-thrum* of sticks beating the pavement. He mouthed the name of the town. *Doe-lay-oh*. It was an odd place, truly.

He'd no more than indulged in this thought when a billow of hashish smoke, released from the room next door, drifted through his window screen and spread its cloying odor about the room.

He leaped from his bed and slammed the window shut. The sharp smack of it caused those gathered around the fire to cease their drubbing and look up.

Vincent, shirtless at the window, stared back. A deep and private reluctance gripped his heart. *Oh God,* he thought. *What strangeness.* For this he'd journeyed seven thousand miles from home? Could it be a mistake? The most extravagant of his life?

Two

THERE THEN BEGAN a time, several weeks' worth of uncharted days, when Vincent roamed the various quarters of Toulio, its labyrinthlike open markets, its unruly business district, both its shabbier and more privileged residential neighborhoods where the homes were crannied together and forked by slim, winding alleyways. He was trying to form an articulate opinion of the town, one he could set to paper and pass on to his parents and a few longtime acquaintances at St. Mark's Church in Red Bud. The shape of that opinion, though, proved to be something of a problem. Yes, the buildings were all formed of pearl-gray concrete rather than wood or brick. Yes, the traffic was unreasonably loud. But these were only the obvious differences. The real difference proved harder to detect. The real difference, Vincent believed, had something to do with the climate itself. Call it a variation of latitude, maybe, a subtle inflection in the atmosphere. Familiar objects seemed to weigh a few ounces less here. Odors were sharper. The air—how to describe it?—was oddly textured, *foreign*, its foreignness most noticeable in the scattered, coppery light of sunrise and dusk.

As for the town's citizens, he had imagined them regarding him with an air of indifference or suspicion. Much to the contrary, his presence in Toulio's markets and restaurants caused a stir. Children squealed in surprise and called out "American" or "outsider." Waiters and store clerks bristled with anticipation when called upon to serve him. Initially, they were all taken by his height. Vincent was six feet, four inches tall. When he revealed his height in centimeters, a more impressive 193, people dropped their jaws and uttered a breathy and keening exclamation, "Whaaaa!" Their attention could also turn flattering. In a darkened tea house a half-circle of rosy-cheeked housewives asked him to lean toward the window so that the sunlight would strike the blond strands of his otherwise brown hair, an effect the women described as "golden." Later, alone in his room, he looked into the mirror and examined his own green eyes, his boyish lips and chin, and understood that here, in Toulio, his bland Midwestern handsomeness had ripened into something exotic.

And were the townspeople, the Chinese, inversely exotic, attractive by virtue of their tapered eyes and sable hair? In this matter, too, he could not form a definite opinion. At times he thought the broad and rather flat composition of their faces homely—or could it be a whole new dialect of human beauty? Other such pale notions came and went. What to make of their cryptic gestures and unabashed willingness to stare? It was strange how loosed from himself he felt, how unmoored, whenever a crowd turned and made him the target of its fastidious gaze. And what a relief to sense that it was Christ drawing him back, grounding him with the consoling tenor of His voice. Not a voice of actual words—words weren't always needed to converse with Christ; often His best advice sprang from Vincent's heart as the most steadfast of intuitions. This was never more true than during moments of unforeseen distress, like the morning he'd forgotten his passport at the bank and rushed back frantically to retrieve it, or the occasions, three so far, when a perfectly agreeable meal had lain serenely in his stomach a few hours before turning traitorous. After the spell of vomiting he shuffled to his room and propped his head on a pillow. The intuition that came to him then was assuasive and confidential. Were he to give it words, they might be, *Easy now, careful with yourself,* or better yet, *We should have expected something like this. We'll know better next time.*

We. Us. Ours.

Here were the pronouns that lay closest to the intimate voice of these intuitions, the private language, as if they'd arrived together in Toulio, he and Christ, and were now both a little perplexed, a little shocked, by the things they saw.

The good news, though, the gratifying discovery was this: in the tented markets and tea houses, in the bank and convenience store, people listened to his carefully phrased Mandarin—he'd been faring better lately with the seesawing tones—and judged him fluent. Or misjudged him fluent. Upon entering these establishments he could not extract from the general whir of conversation any meaningful sequence of words. He relied instead on the outright predictability of their inquiries, the questions concerning his age and height, his country of origin and reasons for coming to Taiwan. In response he would curtsy his head in a slow, discerning nod and deliver one neatly practiced answer after another. His longest sustained conversation occurred in a motorcycle repair shop with a sprightly middle-aged mechanic who waved Vincent indoors and offered to share a pot of tea. They pulled up a pair of wicker stools and discussed, among other things, the humid fall weather and the price of American gasoline. After tea, the mechanic presented a row of second-hand motorcycles and singled out a special bargain, a restored Taitung motorbike with a patched seat and rusted fenders. Buoyed by the ease of their conversation, Vincent made an impulsive purchase. He paid the mechanic 2,500 new Taiwan dollars, less than one hundred U.S., and rode home feeling unexpectedly hopeful.

Yet still there were difficulties, though never quite the ones he anticipated. Simple things proved difficult. Pay phones were an unsolvable riddle. He did not know which of the three peculiar-size coins to use, or whether to feed the slot before or after dialing. Traffic lights were baffling, dangerous. Drivers glided impassively through both green and red signals. The lingering heat, which Reverend Phillips had compared favorably with a Midwestern summer, was actually quite worse. The blanketing humidity held constant. The sun fell at a more potent slant.

The town newspaper, he learned, contained no listings for rental properties. Houses were leased by word-of-mouth or by flyers affixed to courtyard walls. He could only squint dumbly at such flyers. And when a considerate stranger read an address aloud, he wasn't able to hold it in his head long enough to locate the neighborhood, the lane, the house number. Time and again he stopped and asked for directions.

Another stranger, a stocky woman shouldering a bag of oranges, asked him what he was looking for.

"A house to rent," Vincent replied.

She turned and pointed to the outskirts of town. "You need to find Mrs. Chen and her crippled son. She's the one who lets foreigners stay in her home."

Who else in all of Toulio understood an outsider's frustrations firsthand? Who else but the Scotsman, Alec?

At night, working his way through the Psalms, translating each line into whispered Mandarin, Vincent found himself pausing to listen for his reclusive housemate. The thick, concrete wall that partitioned their rooms allowed only dull, cloistered sounds: a muffled cough, light snores, the strum of guitar chords though never a full song. Most frequently, he heard the workings of a door latch, especially the lock mechanism sliding shut.

One afternoon he heard the turning of Alec's lock and hurried into the open hallway, where he saw a tall, bare-chested figure bent toward the door. Vincent stopped short and feigned surprise. "Hey," he said.

The Scotsman turned, raised a dark eyebrow. He mumbled something low and broadly accented, something that might have been, "Hey yourself."

"I'm Vincent Saunders. I'm rooming next door."

"Yes, you are," Alec said, and tucked a key into the waistline of a faded sarong that hung in frayed edges below his knees. He looked to be in his late twenties, his bare shoulders and arms leanly muscled, his hips narrow. He had a narrow, shrewdly alert face as well, and a slippery expression poised on the brink of either ridicule or sly humor. "I saw your shite motorbike parked round the back. You're staying on then?"

"Yes, staying here for a while. I'll be in town two years."

"Two years," he said, exaggerating Vincent's flat, Midwestern drawl. "Golly, that's a long time. Are you a Boy Scout, by any chance?"

"Excuse me?"

"A Boy Scout. I heard you were. I've seen Mormons pedaling round the streets of Taipei. They all look like Boy Scouts to me."

"I'm not—" Vincent said, and bit down on his response so that it passed through his lips in a dispirited sigh. He lowered his gaze and studied the hallway's tiled floor, a ceaseless pattern of triangles and squares. "I thought I'd say hi, thought I'd introduce myself. I'm not going to be led into an argument."

"All right then," Alec said, less self-satisfied. "Right. No arguments. We shouldn't have arguments." He surveyed the distance between his bedroom door and Vincent's. Then he shrugged and descended the staircase.

Was this an apology? Not likely. In Vincent's mind, the question of comradeship had been settled. Alec would be a hindrance rather than a confidant. Now at least a certain glum pleasure could be taken in noting how often wisps of hashish smoke trickled between their window screens. The Scotsman had a formidable habit; he smoked after waking late in the morning, once or twice more throughout the afternoon, then even more prodigiously during the night. All that ingested smoke, the steady flux of mind-deadening narcotic. It was a wonder he could think coherently, a wonder he could rise from bed and manage to meet the demands of a single day.

Yet, astoundingly, Alec did manage. In fact, he earned a living teaching English to businessmen who would assemble nightly in the Chens' downstairs parlor. These meetings were loud, sometimes rowdy affairs. The most surprising thing about them, aside from Alec smoking hash before the onset of each, was that he turned out to be a meticulous and rather severe schoolmaster. In class he spoke the stringent litany of business. "Invoice," he demanded. "Productivity, tariff, first-class, third-class, merchandise, receipt." He dropped his Scottish brogue and in a more neutral voice—the same one he'd used to mimic Vincent—overarticulated each syllable. The students trailed behind, struggling with the difficult *v*s and *th*s. He then drilled each separately, raising his voice, bullying with impatience until a student at last recited a word to his satisfaction. Far from taking offense, these same students called or dropped by during the day bearing half-understood office faxes from their American buyers. Alec translated. And while his Chinese vocabulary may not have been broader than Vincent's, his ease with the language, his unforced inflections and offhanded asides, were probably better, truer.

Twice Vincent had seen thousand-yuan bills pass between student and teacher. He tried not to dwell on it, though he would like to have known Alec's approximate salary. He would like to have known how one went about finding students and what constituted a fair price for lessons. Just lately he'd begun to feel the needling obligation of money. Not that his present finances proved insufficient; he got by well enough on the modest monthly stipend provided by the Overseas Christian Fellowship. No, the problem had to do with school debt and family duty. He'd accrued his fair share of student loans during four years of study. Most of those loans had been deferred. But in his junior and senior years he had also borrowed money from his parents and older sister, Vanessa, and later, once their budgets had been stretched thin, he'd sought help from other relatives. The amounts weren't especially large: eight hundred from a widowed older cousin, fifteen hundred apiece from his uncle Clark and uncle Hayden, both of them veteran soybean farmers. These lendings burdened him more than others because he knew they'd been scraped together, knew also that though his relatives often extolled the virtues of higher education, neither they nor their children had ever attended college. Uncle Clark, in particular, was puzzled by the unusual path Vincent had chosen upon graduation. Why the Orientals? Why not put his education degree to good use and teach at Red Bud's middle school? Or if he wanted to minister in the Church, weren't there congregations all over southern Illinois looking for help? To this Vincent could only say that he preferred to minister abroad. But even the word he'd used, *preferred*, caused Uncle

Clark, a man of frugal habits and point-blank speech, to squint and look away. *Preferred*. Why had Vincent used such a word? All he could do was stand there pink-faced, humbled, while a rift widened between himself and an uncle who had done him a sizable favor.

As for Uncle Clark's question, *Why not southern Illinois? Why not Red Bud?* any honest answer would only wound his family and friends. And it wasn't merely Red Bud's size or its population, hovering just under three thousand, or its Midwestern sparseness and dawdling pace, all of which Vincent or any other townsperson could openly poke fun at. What couldn't be said was that Red Bud's more complicated and ambitious sons and daughters always defected—to St. Louis, to Chicago or beyond. The timid and the dutiful stayed. With the exception of his sister, Vanessa, Vincent's family had stayed. His uncles Clark and Hayden stayed. His aunts and cousins stayed. His parents stayed on in a two-floor, canary yellow farmhouse, a dash of sprightly color when viewed from Route 3, but less alluring, shabbier, the closer you got to the front door. In late middle age they had surrendered a certain poise, a certain gameness for small-town life. Seven years earlier they had lost their jobs at the Singer plant, where, over the course of two decades, they had assembled air conditioners and both risen to the rank of production line supervisors. But the factory had shut down, the production moved to Asia. They'd accepted a series of lesser jobs elsewhere. Vincent's mother, Marion, now worked for minimum wage in the kitchen of a Red Bud nursing home. His father, Carl, drove to Alton, Illinois, each weekday and repaired vending machines. Evenings they sat out on the back patio drinking coffee and brooding, each in their own dissolute manner. Still, they were pleased that Vincent would be volunteering for the Presbyterian Church, that he had held firm to the faith in which he had been raised. Pleased, yet a little perplexed by his decision as well.

Why Taiwan? Why go halfway round the world? Why commit himself to something so . . . well, extreme? What couldn't be said was that if you understood the true meaning and import of Christ's Word (instead of viewing it as something less, a soothing influence, a bit of Sunday-morning consolation) then ministering in Taiwan was hardly extreme. What couldn't be said was that Vincent had long harbored the suspicion that he might be complicated and ambitious. He might have the ability to see deeply into other people's lives and offer them a love and wisdom they might not even have known they were seeking. He couldn't possibly say such things, however. Regardless of his debts, monetary or otherwise, he could not, in the months leading up to his departure, offer anyone he knew or loved an entirely truthful explanation.

There was no broaching the subject of Shao-fei's disfigured legs, either. The boy's very demeanor forbade it. Even when his stagger was at its worst, when his movements became reckless, pendular lurches, he labored not to let the strain of it show on his face. Nevertheless, his eyes sometimes teared from the physical effort. He perspired. Lips drawn to the pale of his teeth, he tottered about the house, one lopsided step after another, without ever glancing down at his wayward ankles and feet. His knees and shins were scarless. Vincent guessed the defect was congenital, possibly the result of rickets. What kept him from asking was the memory of Shao-fei meeting him at the train station, seeing the lame panhandlers and declaring them lazy. It didn't matter how his legs came to be twisted. The point was stoicism in the face of difficulty. The point was pride.

So it was startling to return home midmorning and find not only that the boy had stayed home from school, but that he'd littered the parlor floor with juice cartons and candy wrappings and cast himself adrift on his mother's sagging wicker sofa.

"Not feeling well?" Vincent asked.

The boy cringed. Clearly pained by the interruption, he lifted and resettled his head against the armrest.

"Your mother knows you've stayed home? She knows you're sick?"

"Not sick," he mumbled. "Tired."

"Tired of what?"

No answer. He let his glasses slip down his nose. A few feet away a muted television flickered. He had yet to glance in its direction.

"Tired of what?" Vincent asked again. "Tired of school?"

"Tired . . . of how long it takes."

"How long what takes?"

"Everything. Everything takes so long to happen."

Vague explanations, a lethargic manner—for a moment he thought the boy had stolen, or been given, Alec's hashish. Yet when he drew close to retrieve a cellophane wrapper from the floor, he could detect nothing remotely musky or smoke-laden wafting from Shao-fei's clothing.

"I suppose there's nothing wrong with missing a day of school," Vincent said. "As long as it doesn't become a habit."

"Habit."

"Yes. Habit. When you do something often."

"Often."

"That's right. Exercise would be a good habit. Lying, gambling would be— Is this a word game, Shao-fei? Is this a game we're playing?"

"Playing," the boy mumbled.

"If there's a problem you have, I'd be happy to listen and tell you what I think. Sit up now. Take a deep breath. At least look at me when you're speaking."

He sat and placed his feet on the floor, obediently it seemed. But then he rose and shambled out the parlor toward the staircase.

"Hold on a minute," Vincent called after him, yet by then Shao-fei had begun climbing to the second floor, hoisting himself from one step to the next with the lethargy of someone five times his age. He reached the upstairs landing and like a stunted, world-weary monarch gazed down upon his guest.

"Go away," the boy scolded, before veering into his bedroom, where he closed and locked the door behind him.

And there he remained for the rest of the morning, the afternoon, the long, eventless evening. It was puzzling, this morose behavior, this contradiction. Shao-fei was *supposed* to be good-natured; Reverend Phillips had said as much. Therefore it seemed fundamentally wrong, even a bit irritating, that he should lock himself away. Shortly after nightfall Vincent tried luring the boy from his room with the promise of a trip into town for dinner. Shao-fei did not respond. Even so, it was hard not to prowl close to his room and eavesdrop during the later hours of the night. From behind the closed door came a series of faint, spiritless exhalations that might have been the cadence of sleep or the mark of a deepening despondency.

Either way, the boy did not emerge from his room the next morning, did not shower or eat breakfast or attend school. Vincent, who hadn't slept well, sensed the situation shifting from peculiar to ominous. He summoned Mrs. Chen, easily the hardest-working person he'd ever met. She sold chickens six days a week in the town market, setting out for her stall at three A.M., returning at noon. Afternoons and evenings she blanched and defeathered the birds in her patio workshop behind the house. She, too, was denied entrance into Shao-fei's room.

"This strange mood again," she complained to Vincent. "How can I help him or send him to school if he won't open the door?"

"I believe if the boy had someone to talk to," he said, choosing his words carefully. "A man, maybe, an older friend. Boys can be shy sometimes, talking to their mothers."

He wished he'd been more direct. At the suggestion of an older friend she had brightened noticeably and recommended the Scotsman. Alec, she reported, had gone to Taipei the day before to extend his visa. When he returned home this evening, *he* should be the one to speak with Shao-fei.

Without quite realizing it, Vincent had been sentenced to a day of thankless waiting, a vigil of sorts, fitful and mostly silent, which he kept outside Shao-fei's locked door. At various times throughout the afternoon a swell of indignation would arise and crest over him. The dull hours became a tedious chore. On this account, at least, the boy had been cryptically right: things did sometimes feel as if they took forever to happen.

He was home by eight that evening, the Scotsman, in time to teach his class and afterward loiter about downstairs, the parlor radio trickling out staves of breezy, piano-rich melody. Beside his sofa chair, in a pail of chipped ice, sat several bottles of imported beer he'd brought back from Taipei. He plucked one from the ice and offered it up to Vincent, who, while not opposed to a single cold beer after dinner, refused anyway.

"Cheers," Alec said. "Cheers just the same." He took a yawning swallow and in the lull that followed bobbed one knee to the music and let his gaze wander the room. "What?" he asked, focusing on Vincent in a canny, amused way. "Still holding a grudge?"

"Maybe."

"All right, so I'm a prick then," he said cheerfully.

"You mean to say you're obnoxious. But you admit you're obnoxious, so I'm supposed to chuckle over that. I'm supposed to see it as honest."

"That's the general idea, yes."

"I'm not falling for it," Vincent warned.

"Look here, Shao-fei told me you were a missionary. Then he said you didn't like me having a smoke. So I imagined you sitting in your room listening to me and making certain judgments. Is that what you were up to?"

"I couldn't hear much."

"Did you hear me call out Margaret Thatcher's name? I do that sometimes when I'm wanking off." He grinned and waited for Vincent's reaction. "Hey," he said, "are Mormons allowed to have a wank now and then?"

Vincent shook his head and sighed.

"Don't make the long face. Tell me to fuck off if you like."

"And what good would that do?"

"No good at all. Or a world of good. Give it a try."

"I'm not the prude you think I am," Vincent said. Again a swell of bitter emotion, hard-edged and truculent. He wished—longed for—the Scotsman to be absent from the house, painlessly removed. "For the record, I'm not a Mormon or a missionary. I work for an overseas fellowship, a Presbyterian organization. I'm a volunteer."

"A volunteer?" The word had been given a droll twist.

"Whatever you might think, it's different from a missionary. Less intrusive. We're not forcing our beliefs on anyone." He made himself stop. A futile effort, trying to shape a distinction for someone whose purpose was ridicule. "About the boy," he said, changing course. "Mrs. Chen wants you to speak to him. He's stayed home from school, locked himself in his room. I'm not sure what the problem is."

"He's feeling blue," Alec said.

"Could be. It's odd, though. It doesn't seem like him."

"Oh, but it's exactly like him. He gets down and mopes about in his room and lets everything go to hell. Then he bounces back, cleans his room, cleans and mops the fucking house while he's at it. It's part of the cycle. A day or two from now he'll be shuffling off to school like a real trouper." Alec flitted his fingertips through a patch of dark hair on his chin, a scraggly, unsculpted goatee. "You thought you had him sussed out, didn't you?"

Vincent puzzled over the question a moment. "I never said I had Shao-fei figured out. I'm just surprised."

"He's bound to surprise you because he tries so hard most of the time. Twice as hard as he should. But he's strange sometimes, too. And he's clumsy in a way that's got nothing to do with his fucked-up legs. If you see him trying to cook, keep an eye on him because he's liable to burn the house down. He's hopeless on a motor scooter, really just hopeless. No control over the throttle and hand brake," Alec said. Then he drained away the last swirl of beer and rolled the empty bottle between his hands. "He's good-hearted, though, Shao-fei is. He's been level with me since the day I arrived. Try finding someone else in town who'll speak their mind to an outsider."

"He looks up to you," Vincent said. "That's why Mrs. Chen thinks it's best that you speak to him."

"How long's he been in his room?"

"Yesterday and today."

"Two days," Alec reasoned. "That's long enough. Two days for feeling blue." He uncapped another beer, took a gulp, and raised the bottle aloft. "Attention all shirkers and layabouts!" he crooned at the ceiling. "Two days is what you get! That'll be the rule from now on!"

Very early the next morning, a fraction past six, Vincent heard an alarm sound in the next room followed by a low, broguish curse. He rose from bed and leaned into the hallway. Alec was there, stumbling barefoot with his sarong gripped about his waist. He squeezed his free hand into a fist and slammed it against Shao-fei's bedroom door. "ENOUGH!" he shouted. "ENOUGH! GET YOUR ARSE OUT OF BED AND OPEN THE DOOR! You WILL go to school today! DO YOU UNDERSTAND ME!"

The bolt rattled and the door swung inward. Shao-fei emerged still heavy-lidded from sleep, fumbling with his glasses. He gaped at Alec and then ducked past him toward the bathroom. Alec followed him there and gave the bathroom door several booming pounds of the fist. "Twenty minutes and you're off to school," he threatened. "We'll make sure you get there, too." He turned toward Vincent and grinned. "Vincent will make sure. He's an early riser. He'll take you to school."

Vincent accepted the duty with a shrug. In truth, he had been on the verge of volunteering. He pulled his clothes on and waited downstairs in the foyer. Minutes later Shao-fei descended the steps dressed in his autumn uniform, a crisp white shirt reined in by dark trousers and a coal black blazer.

"Ready, Shao-fei?"

To this no answer. The boy, balanced on the downstairs landing and immersed in thought, merely lifted his eyebrows a bit and blinked sheepishly at the sound of his own name.

Should he have done more for the boy? Offered more? Vincent could not decide. He was never sure how far he should go, especially when the line between benevolence and insult varied with each person. Even with his own sister, Vanessa, he did not know. She worked in Chicago as a curator's assistant by day, a music booker by night. In the months prior to his departure she had twice driven home to Red Bud so that the two of them might discuss his decision. And yet no matter how intricate or prolonged their conversations, they arrived, always, at the same point of impasse, the same unbridgeable questions. *Did she not think that people in other countries deserved the opportunity to know the Word of God? Did she not believe that Jesus Christ was the one true Lord and Savior?* In reply she screwed tight the corners of her mouth and looked upon him with an air of magnified patience. She was twenty-nine years old, even-tempered, self-reliant, pretty. In Chicago she had friends who were playwrights and installation artists. It didn't matter what she believed or didn't believe, she said. They were talking about the course of his life. What good were divisive questions? No good at all, she said. She wouldn't answer them.

Of course, he knew all too well what her refusal implied. It saddened him. As children they'd both been more studious and devout than all their many cousins, and now, when his family came together at the dinner table and he bowed his head and asked Christ to open their hearts and minds to the wisdom of the Holy Spirit, he looked up and caught Vanessa, his only sister, gazing back at him with a great personal weariness, a smile so stagey and clenched it might as well have been a frown.

That, he supposed, was disappointing enough. Still, given her life in Chicago, he might have expected it. What was far more surprising was to see an even fiercer and more tangled resentment show itself in, of all people, Carrie Ann Whitlinger, his girlfriend, or rather former girlfriend, of nearly three years. Carrie Ann had been a Christian, albeit a Lutheran, since grade school. She had grown up in Red Bud, and he had known her, distantly, in middle and high school, where she'd been a year behind him. And then she'd shown up for Bible study at the campus ministry house his second year of college. She had a bright, celebratory spirit. It took several months for him to recognize her pixie-featured good looks and understand that a portion of her goodwill was directed personally at him. By then she had a large circle of ministry house girlfriends on whom she liked to lavish greeting cards and elaborate surprise birthday parties. Few of them knew that her mother was dead and that her father, bedridden in a nursing home, had been a lifelong alcoholic. Had they known these facts they might, like Vincent, have wondered where, beyond the expected optimism of a Christian life, her hopefulness came from.

A good many of their mutual friends had also come together during campus ministry house functions and formed romantic partnerships.

Nearly all these partnerships led to engagement and even, in a few instances, marriage before graduation. These early-marrying couples were thought to be a bit hasty, a bit old-fashioned. A public announcement of an engagement was enough for most of Carrie Ann's friends to begin sleeping over at their boyfriends' apartments, enough to begin having sex. This fact didn't stop them from taking part, along with Carrie Ann, in the "Say Yes to Self-Respect" program. Each month they visited a different high school and told their audiences of girls' health and gym classes to abstain from sex until marriage, by which they meant engagement. They were not prigs, they told the girls. They went to rock concerts. They went on romantic dates. They did not have sexual intercourse, but still they spent time alone with their boyfriends and kept them happy, satisfied.

Vincent, in private, would have agreed wholeheartedly. He was, after all, that rarest of things: a sexually fulfilled virgin. Weekends, after a movie or ministry house party, he and Carrie Ann drove northeast from Carbondale out to the miles of cropland surrounding Red Bud and parked his father's Suburban wagon in a rutted tractor path or overgrown driveway. Two rules: they would undress and lie together or on top of each other face-to-face; one of them would, at all times, keep his or her underwear on. A simple arrangement, perhaps, yet it worked surprisingly well over the course of three years. Occasionally, though, it seemed that Carrie Ann was more willing than he to take the crucial next step forward, that she wouldn't even have required an engagement announcement, that any sincere intimation he might have made regarding a future for them beyond graduation would have been enough.

In April, once his assignment from the Overseas Christian Fellowship had been confirmed, he took her to Sunday worship and then brunch, where he broke the news.

It was really something, she said, an intense pinkness rising in her cheeks. It was really amazing. They would have to have a colossal party at the campus ministry house. But she didn't understand everything exactly. Did he mean that she and Vincent would wait two years for each other? Write letters? Visit, maybe?

No, he said. It was probably best not to wait, since at the end of two years he might sign up for another assignment or return to the States and enroll in a seminary.

Her cheeks burned a shade brighter. Still, she said. It was quite an accomplishment. He should be proud. The Asian people were really very lucky to get him.

And then, thankfully, this moment of terrible awkwardness passed and they were able to finish their brunch. In the days afterward they got on with their exams and ministry meetings. Most nights they chatted on the phone. He was sometimes stung by remorse, but what could he say? He liked Carrie Ann Whitlinger enormously, yet he did not want to be her husband. He felt the same reticence toward his ministry house friends. He might someday like to be their minister, but he did not want their marriages or their lives, which he felt to be a little predictable, a little bland.

One Saturday evening a few weeks later he took Carrie Ann to dinner, and afterward, having received her permission, drove from campus out to the recently seeded fields of corn and soybeans near Red Bud. The sky was heavy and low and drizzling thick drops of rain. They locked the doors and climbed with a blanket into the bed of the Suburban. Carrie Ann had a fine, small-breasted gymnast's body and before long she was mostly unclothed and stretched out beside him. He undressed completely. Then something unprecedented: she slipped off her panties. She rooted through the pockets of her slacks and produced a condom. There in the back of his father's Suburban she raised her naked hips slightly as if waiting to be entered.

He'd never seen so fraught or complicated an offering. He couldn't possibly go through with it. And what a dire, truly unpleasant situation it was to apologize, to tell her no and then endure the aftermath.

She leaned forward on one elbow, glared at him. It was perfectly all right, she said. Her mistake. She had thought she would end things between them on a high note, but of course, well, he was really something. He was really some kind of goddamn role model for everyone, for every boy and girl. She would like to lie beside him and sing his praises, but she was sorry because she couldn't, at the moment, stand to be anywhere near him.

She crawled forward. He watched her round, pale-as-milk bottom rise up as she tumbled naked into the backseat. She unlocked and opened the door. She stepped out into the rain.

For a while no amount of coaxing or pleading would get her back inside. She marched ankle-deep through a muddy field, thought better of it, turned and came back. She slumped against the front fender and cried out. A quarter mile away cars drifted by on the highway. He waited an agonizingly long time for her distress to pass. When at last it did, she climbed into the front seat, her bare legs flecked to the knees with mud, and asked him to retrieve her clothes.

On the way back to campus she demanded to know what their three years together had been leading to. All the waiting? she said. What was it all for?

Respect, he said. Friendship. He had been changed by knowing her. Her optimism had made him a—

She stopped him with long groan of protest. That's not what she was talking about, she said. She didn't want to hear another word about optimism or eternal love or Jesus Christ. She just wanted to know what they were supposed to get out of all this anyway?

It sounded to Vincent like she was tired, extremely tired and disappointed. He told her so. He recommended that she finish her exams and then take some time off in the summer. Travel, maybe. In the fall she could come back to campus and get on with her life. Go to ministry house gatherings. Meet new people.

She snickered. Meet a boyfriend, she said. Is that what he was talking about?

Yes, he said. Eventually.

Well, maybe she would, she said. But whoever her next boyfriend turned out to be, she would not be meeting him at the campus ministry house.

Every other week Vincent received a letter from Reverend Phillips. Take your time and get to know the people and the town, the Reverend advised. Be patient. Recently the Reverend had spoken with a middle-aged couple who'd been coming to Good Shepherd for several years. The Liangs. They lived in Taipei, but Mrs. Liang had grown up in Toulio. She still kept her family's home there, still went down once a month to air the shuttered rooms and visit childhood friends. Mr. Liang taught chemistry at the National University, but when they were first married he had taught private math lessons in the Toulio house. So the third floor, the Reverend believed, had already been converted into a classroom.

The Liangs were now aware of Vincent's search for a ministry house. According to Reverend Phillips they'd been at once encouraging yet wholly noncommittal. So far they'd agreed only to pass on their Toulio address. In his letter the Reverend warned against inflated expectations.

Too late for that; Vincent's hopes took a jaunty leap. He conjured a tall, gable-roofed house, a pristine third-floor classroom, school desks set in tidy, earnest rows. Yet he knew this dream house would be troublesome to locate. Rather than meander through countless residential lanes, rather than rely on either the charity or haphazard guidance of strangers, he gave the Liangs' address to a taxi driver and followed behind on his motorcycle as the cab sprinted toward the center of town. The driver swerved right at an intersection and turned down a narrow lane that ended in a cul-de-sac. Vincent parked his cycle before a gated courtyard. The Liangs' house, he discovered, stood three doors down from the repair shop where he had purchased his motorcycle.

"Are you sure?" he asked the driver, who nodded and pocketed his fare.

The gate was not locked and Vincent stepped through it and then across a yard lined with rosebushes and mini palm trees. At the door he knocked repeatedly and waited in vain for more than ten minutes.

He returned to the gate and walked down the lane. The homes here were all older, three-story dwellings, a few of which had been converted into apartment houses. They had been built one against the other and shared a lengthy open rooftop. Upon the roof, hanging from a carousel of metal poles and slack ropes, were lines of buoyant laundry shifting beneath the wind and sun.

At the end of the cul-de-sac he came upon a group of children playing in a wide patch of dirt near the pavement's edge. He pointed back to the gated house. "Do you know who lives there?" The instant he spoke, all six children, without exception, burst into uproarious laughter.

"Is your mother home?" Vincent asked the oldest child, a girl of five or six with a dirt-streaked face.

She touched her smudged chin to her shoulder. "Ma!" she called out behind her. "Ma!" She waited for a moment and when there was no reply, she shook her head softly. The other children ceased their laughing and huddled together behind her.

"Are you an American?" the girl asked.

"Yes," Vincent answered. "I come from America but I live in Taiwan now."

"Did your mother and father make you come to Taiwan?"

"No, I wanted to come here."

"Are your mother and father American?"

"Yes."

"Do they have any Chinese babies?"

"No, they don't."

"Just American babies, right?"

"Yes, just American babies."

"A boy in my class said there are Chinese babies in America, but now I think he was lying." She raised the palm of her hand and pressed it against her lips. "He lied about other things," she mumbled through her fingers. "I think he lies all the time."

Other neighbors along the street were far less talkative. A teenaged boy loitering beside a panel truck responded to Vincent's questions with a weary shrug and blank stare. An old man crouched on the stoop of his house simply turned his head and waved him off.

None of this dampened Vincent's enthusiasm. He walked back to the Liangs' front door and knocked yet again. No answer, though, looking up at the three floors of curtained windows, he believed he'd found his ministry house.

Three

"I'M LEAVING," Alec announced to Shao-fei and Vincent a few days later, a balmy Saturday in November. "I'm going to India."

"India?" Vincent asked. "For what?"

"For a holiday," Alec said, as if the answer were obvious, as if India were a nearby resort town where he would idle away a weekend on a parasol-shaded blanket near a lake.

"When?" Shao-fei asked.

"Tomorrow evening. I take a train up north to the airport in the morning."

"No, I mean, when do you come back?"

"A month, maybe two."

"That's a long time," the boy said.

"I've heard you can stretch your money a long while in India," Vincent added encouragingly. By a long while he meant months, seasons, years. "What do we tell your students?" he asked.

"Tell them I'm on holiday, and when I come back we'll pick up where we left off. Don't get any ideas about teaching them yourself."

"I have no intention—"

"And you," Alec said, turning to Shao-fei. "Stay out of my room."

Shao-fei blinked and shook his head. "No, I don't do that."

"You may just get your hands on your mother's house keys, but think twice about it. I'll be able to tell right off if you've been inside."

"Oh, I would not . . . I won't," he said, but then a moment later accepted the accusation with a guilty shrug.

By morning the boy had grown observably anxious. He moped about while Alec packed and phoned for a taxi, and then, like a timid bellhop, carried the Scotsman's shoulder bag and camera satchel outside to the alleyway.

What followed was a curt farewell, Shao-fei glum, Alec laconic and puffing on a cigarette as the driver drew near. The taxi claimed him and sped off down the single-lane rice road. Vincent watched the departure from his bedroom window—the fields of green rice stalks, the flicker of sunlight, the receding taxi, all of it picturesque, vivid as a granted wish.

In the days that followed he settled happily into a routine of prayer and language study. The Chens' second floor, he discovered, could be exquisitely quiet. No hash fumes breached his window screen. At times he felt a twinge of guilt over how thoroughly he enjoyed the Scotsman's not being there.

Six days a week Vincent drove Shao-fei to and from school; such a routine, he hoped, might keep the boy from sliding back into melancholy. At the very least it made his attendance more regular. Vincent, meanwhile, became the dutiful chauffeur, waiting each afternoon outside the parted gates of Toulio Provincial High School while a vast throng of students, all in the same stiff-shouldered black uniform, pushed past his motorcycle. Among the crowd were fresh-faced girls with bangs and gangly boys, a few of whom had learned to slouch in their dark uniforms like Hong Kong gangsters, and Shao-fei, of course, always hurrying, always zigzagging across the school parking lot wearing his long-practiced expression of gritty resolve. The slouching boys occasionally aped his wobbly stride. He was sometimes heckled. Whenever this happened, an even greater rigorousness came over the boy. He slowed his pace, clenched his jaw, grimaced in concentration. He appeared to be counting, as meticulously as possible, the lopsided rise and fall of his own steps.

They arrived home from school one afternoon and Shao-fei, simultaneously demure and giddy, ushered Vincent into his room and had him sit on a floor pillow beside the bed.

"I have a thing to show you," he said and crawled up onto the bed, moving gingerly across the mattress to a cupboard built into the headboard. He opened the paneled door, reached inside, and pulled down a photo album.

The cover was deceiving, a light blue wrinkled pattern with three tulips circled in gold trim. Below this, in the distorted English of so many Taiwan products never sold for export, was the inscription: *Remembers given, remembers received, too heavy for your pockets to hold.* Shao-fei raised the cover, set his finger to the first page. "He is my father," the boy said.

The photograph was of a man lying on a white table surrounded by flowers and bright red banners of Chinese calligraphy. Above his head was a younger version of himself, a black-and-white photograph in a modest silver frame. In the color photo Shao-fei's father looked healthy enough except for an unusual fullness in his cheeks and the fused, bloodless quality of his lips, which confirmed Vincent's worry. He turned the page. More pictures of the same dead man, photographed on the same white table, photographed while dead.

"This is a man I call Uncle," the boy continued, pointing to a second series of photos.

This elderly man, unlike Shao-fei's father, had undergone the ravishment of disease. His eyes were sunken. His offset dentures pushed against the hollows of his cheeks. He, too, had been photographed at his funeral, a tier of flowers and banners circling his body, a similar framed black-and-white portrait above his head. Vincent flipped ahead through several blank pages, yet there was nothing else but these two sets of photographs. Two funerals. Two dead men. Their defunct bodies were the album's grand subject matter.

"Who took these pictures, Shao-fei?"

"I did," the boy replied.

And how should Vincent respond to such an admission? There was no protocol for it. He had no idea if this type of picture-taking was a common Chinese custom. But the mere fact of the album, with its flawed epigram, its neat arrangement of photos, inspired deeper and more complex sympathies. At once a powerful intuition was upon him: the boy's photographs, however strange or morbid, were really just naive attempts to document matters of faith. By sidling up close to the dead, by raising his camera, Shao-fei had tried to aim his lens straight into the afterlife.

"And what were you thinking, Shao-fei, what were you looking for when you took these pictures?"

"Looking for?"

"What idea?"

"No idea. I was being careful, holding the camera."

"Do you think maybe you were looking for God in these pictures?"

"I don't think so," the boy said after a moment or two of shy reflection. "If I were looking for God, I would go someplace else, yes? If I were looking for God, I would take my camera and go to the temple."

• • •

To the temple. A wholly practical answer.

Yet Vincent could not shake his initial intuition. The boy, whether conscious of it or not, was seeking evidence of the divine. Little wonder he sometimes grew somber and locked himself away.

And would it be wrong to direct him in his search? To help separate what was dark and misleading from that which was true?

Not wrong, surely. Not intrusive. Not when you understood, as Vincent did, that Shao-fei had already begun looking for God. Not when you saw the boy staggering recklessly down hallways and across school parking lots and you considered his disadvantage in life.

Still, it was a decidedly complicated, even delicate, matter. How to broach the subject? How to ease from the role of friend and chauffeur to the more venerable position of spiritual counselor? Beyond that there was a great deal of Christian theology to impart. Where did one begin? Even the most sensible starting point, the triune God, the Father, the Son, the Holy Spirit, would only confuse Shao-fei. After careful deliberation Vincent decided to skip it altogether.

"I am a Christian," he told the boy directly. "I believe there is one God. His name is Jesus Christ." They were sitting together at Vincent's desk. He had called Shao-fei in under the guise of an English lesson, to help the boy pronounce and understand long, multisyllable English words—*university, geography, personality*—and during the course of the lesson their conversation had strayed gradually, naturally, to the artwork and maps of Vincent's open Bible. "This book," Vincent said, leafing forward to the first Gospel of the New Testament, "contains the story of Jesus Christ. His story, His Word, the Word of God. Wherever or whenever you read this book, Jesus Christ is present." He then embarked on a simplified recounting of Christ's early life, touching briefly upon the Nativity—he would save the detailed account of Jesus' birth for an evening nearer the Christmas season—and then progressing forward in chronological order describing Christ's childhood in Nazareth. When he finished, he lowered his voice and said, "What you have to understand is that Jesus chose to be born on earth and live as a man. Because He was God, He knew ahead of time what would happen to Him. But He came to earth anyway and He did something brave and wonderful for you, for me, for everyone."

Shao-fei nodded and pinched the corner of his glasses. "What is it?"

But Vincent would not elaborate on the remark, not yet, even though the boy's question sounded utterly sincere, and it took real resolve on Vincent's part to hold back the answer. His plan was to relate New Testament stories in short installments each evening. In this way he hoped to prepare Shao-fei for the magnitude and splendor of Christ's resurrection.

And day by day, evening by evening, the boy appeared increasingly open to such a revelation. He sat and listened to stories of Mary Magdalene, of Lazarus, of the storm on the lake, of the curing of the leper. True, he sometimes asked ungainly questions: *Was Lazarus really dead? How did they know he was dead? How did they know for sure?* But he was always interested, always fully present during their conversations. Mrs. Chen, busy defeathering chickens downstairs in her patio workstation, did not seem to mind—though, in fairness, Vincent was never certain she knew the topics being discussed each evening in the second floor of her home. She, like most of the citizens of Taiwan, practiced a mixture of Buddhism and Taoism and regularly burned paper money—a representation of the real money she worked so hard for—which, she believed, would spiral upward into the heavens and supply her husband and other dead relatives with an income in the hereafter. And though the boy accompanied his mother through this ritual and others, his participation seemed, to Vincent, largely mechanical. Never once did he hear anything approaching a religious discussion between the two.

By late November he had guided Shao-fei through twelve chapters of St. Mark's Gospel plus another dozen psalms and proverbs. At about the same time a broad weather front swept across the island's western seaboard. There were several days of pounding rain, after which Toulio's muddled skyline thinned and cleared. For a week a hazeless view of Taiwan's north-to-south mountain range was possible, the peaks emerald green, regal, backed by a faultless blue sky. The view struck Vincent as a significant blessing. He tried not to be overbearing in his enthusiasm. Yet once or maybe twice that week, as they were preparing to climb aboard his motorcycle in the morning and set out for Toulio Provincial High School, he said, "Look at the beautiful day Christ has made for us, Shao-fei," and the boy, jarred from his school day routine, raised his head and took a blinking, somewhat startled survey of the sky, as if seeing beyond his small enclave for the very first time.

Riding home late one evening from a lane of food stalls named Hungry Ghost Street, Vincent felt his motorcycle shudder beneath him. The engine faltered then found its rhythm and he sped on down Toulio's main avenue, which tonight was unusually thick with pedestrians. Families had come out onto their patios and sidewalks to gather around small fires set in wrought-iron cauldrons. He watched as they leaned into the heat and nourished the flames with sheet after sheet of printed paper money. Flakes of smoldering ash rose up out of the cauldrons and flitted about overhead.

The cycle lurched again, released a long smoky cough, and died. He pulled to the curb and struggled in vain to restart the engine. When he glanced up, he found a council of onlookers had formed a ring around the motorbike. A few men edged forward to offer mechanical advice, yet as a whole the group was far more interested in his unwieldy height and the lashes of dark body hair that covered his forearms. Their close scrutiny unnerved him. *I am not a stranger here,* he wanted to explain to the crowd. *I live in the home of Mrs. Chen. I am counseling her teenaged son.* All he could do, however, was blush, step off the cycle, and begin pushing it behind a slow parade of cars and scooters.

A few blocks ahead the traffic returned to an even flow. He walked his motorcycle near the shoulder—its sluggish weight numbing his arms—until he bridged a familiar intersection and arrived at the motorcycle repair shop, now closed for the night. Three doors down his dream house, the Liang home, appeared tenantless and dark. He left the cycle perched on its stand and began pacing back to the Chens' enclave.

And yet it was a most peculiar night to be out walking. A glowing sequence of firepots illuminated the stoop of every home. He continued on, but with the passing of each firepot the journey became more awkward, more oppressive, because the family surrounding each fire would grow suddenly quiet and turn to face him. They ceased dropping paper money into the flames. Children called out "American, outsider," and hid behind their parents' legs.

He smiled and nodded to each family as he passed and stepped back into the darkness. *We should be used to this by now, shouldn't we?* he either thought or whispered aloud; amid the flutter of his nerves, he could hardly tell which.

Before turning onto the long rice road that would take him to Shaofei's home, he passed one final house, one last firepot. A woman stood near the cauldron, an infant in her arms. Another child, a toddler, clung to her dress. A small black dog sprang out of the doorway and began a high-pitched yelping.

"Quiet, little Blackie," she hushed the dog. "Quiet." She stomped her foot across the loose gravel. *"Aiya,"* she hissed at the dog, which finally cowered back to the front step. She raised a hand against the glare of the fire. "Uncle Chow?" she asked. "Is that you?"

"No," Vincent murmured. He cleared his throat. "No, it's not."

"Who are you?" She took the toddler by the hand and stepped back under the doorway.

"I'm Vincent," he said.

"Who?"

"I'm a foreign teacher," he explained. "I'm just walking home."

By now he was in the ring of firelight and could see her free hand gripping the door frame, could see the quaking anxiety in her expression. "I live up ahead," he said. "My motorcycle broke and I'm just walking home."

She appeared in no way relieved by this explanation. She barely moved. And to behold her stricken face was to know precisely the impression he'd made on her, how he must have looked stepping out of the blackness and into the circle of light, his figure harsh and ungraceful and altogether out of place. He gaped at himself a moment, through her eyes and through the eyes of each family he'd plodded past. What a crushing feeling it was. It made him want to sob or cry out—this deep pang of separateness, this stinging sense of being alone.

Four

HE RETURNED TO the repair shop the next morning. The mechanic was already at work, squatting beside Vincent's motorcycle. He held up a small brown cylinder. "Bad gas filter," he said. "Easy to replace. I checked the brakes and the rear ones are bad. I should replace them, too, yes?"

Vincent sighed and imagined his brakes failing him along the narrow and often crowded streets of Toulio. "If it's not too much trouble, not too expensive."

"No trouble," the mechanic said. "Expensive? I don't know." He fell back to work, and Vincent waited awhile beside his motorcycle until he grew bored and set out along the lane toward the cul-de-sac. Three houses down an old woman with vibrant white hair stood raking branches inside the Liangs' gated courtyard.

"Excuse me," he said. "I'm looking for a house to rent in this neighborhood. I've been told this house belongs to the Liangs. Do you know them?"

She turned and he saw he'd been wrong about her age; she had a broad, unblemished face, middle-aged rather than elderly. Her hair had misled him. She looked, with her mane of vigorous white hair, like an Eskimo, an Eskimo woman clutching a rake handle instead of a dogsled. She was not startled in the least to see a foreign man standing at her front gate. On the contrary, she appeared annoyed by the interruption.

"I don't live in this neighborhood anymore," she insisted. "I'm just visiting." She waved him off and went back to her raking. A moment later she cocked her head sideways then set her rake down and strode forward to meet him at the front gate. "I heard about you. You're a Jesus teacher," she said.

"Yes." Vincent grinned. "You're Mrs. Liang, right? You and your husband know Reverend Phillips. He's told you about me. I've been in Toulio awhile now but I haven't found a house."

"All right, all right," she said. "Come in." She opened the gate and he followed her across the courtyard. At the doorway she fumbled with the latch and said, "My husband has been a Jesus believer since he was a boy." She offered this fact rotely, as if it were of no personal interest to her.

Inside, the house smelled of stale spices and dust. The kitchen counter was lined with old preserves, strange, bloated fruits and vegetables floating in glass jars. The walls of the kitchen, living room, and hallway were piled with boxes and stacks of newspapers. She motioned him into the living room and had him sit on a low wooden sofa.

"This is our old furniture," she said. "We do have new furniture, but we keep that in our Taipei apartment. I come back to clean up sometimes. Do you understand?"

"Yes," he said.

"We live in Taipei, but this is the house where I grew up. I don't want to sell it and I don't rent it because I worry about all these old things. I know most of it is junk, but I worry somebody might throw away something important. Do you understand how I worry about that?"

"I can understand that," Vincent said. A tremor of hope rose inside him. He nodded respectfully toward this odd, surprisingly vigorous older woman.

"If I rented you the house, would you sell these old things? Would you give them away to your friends?"

"I would never do that," he said. "I don't even have any friends."

"My husband is a Jesus believer. He's been to Oklahoma to pray. He speaks English. I've tried to learn that language, but it sounds so flat. I'm going to call him right now." She picked up and dialed the phone. She cleared her throat, rested her chin against the receiver, and said, "Did you eat the boiled chicken? Did you drink all of the soup, all of it like I said?" She listened to the answer and hummed skeptically into the receiver. "Is that the truth?" she asked. She discussed a few other matters and then explained to her husband that Vincent had asked to rent the house. "Oh, he's just a boy," she told her husband. "He looks just like a boy. He's a Jesus teacher. He's promised not to sell the furniture." She passed the phone to Vincent.

The voice on the other end spoke in stiff, accented English. "And your name, please?"

"Vincent. Vincent Saunders."

"Who do you work for, please?"

"Reverend Phillips in Taipei. You know his church, Good Shepherd, right?"

The voice ignored the question. "Who does Reverend Phillips work for?"

"The Overseas Christian Fellowship."

"And who do they work for, Vincent?"

"Well," he said and tried quickly to remember the history of the fellowship, the founders and benefactors, and just as suddenly it occurred to him what the voice was after. "Jesus Christ," Vincent said. "We do the work of Jesus Christ."

"Yes, and how is Christ's work going for you in Toulio?"

"Good so far, I think. Reverend Phillips is pleased. But I need a ministry house. I need a place for Bible classes and meetings. That's my biggest problem right now."

"Yes. I hope to help you with that problem. May I speak to Mrs. Liang, please?"

Vincent handed the phone to Mrs. Liang, and she pressed it to her ear for the briefest of moments before hanging up. "All right," she said. "Follow me."

They moved across the living room and up the stairs to the second floor, which contained three bedrooms. All three rooms were furnished with beds, dressers, and tables. Vincent noticed that the walls of each room ended a foot short of the ceiling, a feature, Mrs. Liang told him, that allowed parents to listen in on sleeping children. The third floor had not been divided into rooms. It stood wide open and held a dozen or so school desks. Several faded science charts hung from the walls. A sizable water stain had flowered along one corner of the ceiling. Even without a chalkboard and in need of immediate repairs, the room seemed, to Vincent, fated for the business of serious study.

She led him up the final flight of stairs to an open-air roof, where long rows of fluttering laundry stretched away in either direction.

"Let me remind you," Mrs. Liang said, "that there are two doors to the house. One on top and one on bottom. You must remember to lock both when you leave."

"You're going to rent me the house?" Vincent asked. For weeks he'd been convinced that the Liang home would be his ministry house—and still he was amazed.

"Yes," she said. "Yes, I'm taking the train back to Taipei five days from now. This means I'm going to clean the house for five days straight. Clean and sort. I'm going to do a lot of sorting because some things have to be thrown away. Come back early Friday morning and you can help me throw things out before I leave."

"That's wonderful. Thank you so much. I'm not sure what to say except that I'll take good care of your things, very good care."

"All right," she said. "All right, enough." She began pacing down the steps.

"And how much is the rent?" Vincent called out behind her.

"My husband didn't say. I suppose there is no rent."

"That's wonderful," he said. "That's very kind."

"You could pay the electric bill. And the telephone bill. You could pay for those two things."

"Of course I could. I would be happy to pay those bills."

"Enough," she said, holding open the front door and motioning him outside. "I'll see you five days from now."

When he stepped out onto the street, he saw the mechanic circling the cul-de-sac on his motorcycle. He raced up and came to an abrupt stop beside Vincent.

"Good brakes now. See," he said and squeezed the lever. "I replaced the front and rear brakes, and the gas filter, too. It's all very good now, very safe. But it's expensive."

"How much?" Vincent asked.

"Six hundred yuan."

"That's fine," Vincent said, selecting hundred-note bills from his wallet. "That's very good."

Some twenty days after Alec's departure, Shao-fei received a scroll-shaped parcel from India. It had been mailed from Manali and contained a cluster of paper rupees, a postcard, a dozen pungent incense sticks, and, more curiously, a disposable cigarette lighter. The lighter bore a pinup-style photo of a curvaceous Englishwoman squeezed into a schoolgirl's uniform. Viewed sideways, the photo glinted—the woman curtsied and raised the rear of her tartan skirt. Her bare bottom sent Shao-fei into a fit of impish giggling.

Having an excellent holiday so far, the postcard announced. *India is bad-air paradise. Suits me well. You and Vincent would hate it here. There's snow in the hills outside Manali. Haven't seen snow in years. Nothing better than sitting on the stoop of my log hut and watching the snow fall. Sorry to say I will not be back by the 25th of December (blame the snow, the bad air, the beautiful women of India). Merry Xmas all the same.*

In addition to the parcel, the boy had been granted another kind of gift: two days off from school during which he and his classmates were expected to prepare at home for a series of late-semester exams. It was Vincent's idea that he and the boy should use these days to travel someplace quiet and scenic. Each evening they were edging closer to the Crucifixion and the Resurrection, and he hoped to reveal the tragedy and beauty of these events in a place that would startle Shao-fei's senses with its newness.

"Let's go to Kenting," he told the boy. "Have you ever seen the ocean?"

"I already go."

"How about Mount Alishan or Sun Moon Lake?"

"I already go these places," he said. "Alec brought me."

In the end they settled for an early dinner at Hungry Ghost Street and then climbed on Vincent's motorcycle and rode out to a park and temple complex built into the hills outside of town. Granted, it was not an ocean-swept beachfront or a mountain plateau, but it was still scenic in its way and neatly kept with two towering pagodas on either end of the grounds and a temple and maze of flower and water gardens set in between.

While they walked the stone pathways, Vincent gathered his thoughts and practiced inwardly the story of Christ's sacrifice. Shao-fei loped beside him, roused by the open air into an exuberant mood. At a goldfish pond he plopped down beside children half his age and churned his hands beneath the water. The sight of this pleased Vincent enormously; he'd always been fond of Shao-fei, yet never before had he felt such fostering tenderness for the boy.

At dusk they began to climb the steps of one of the high-reaching pagodas, stopping now and then to lean against the ornate guardrail and peer over the edge. Below them, the red roof of the temple arced skyward at both ends. The water gardens shimmered. Upon arriving at the top tier, they looked west to a darkened and miniaturized Toulio couched beneath a layer of smog. A dim quarter moon had settled low on the town's horizon.

"I'm going to tell you now exactly what Jesus did for us, Shao-fei, and why he loves us so much." Vincent placed his hand briefly, protectively, on the slope of the boy's neck and then set forth on a detailed recounting of the Passion, describing the great physical pain Christ experienced, how the heavy iron nails were centered and pounded into His hands, how He hung suspended from the cross, suffered, and died just like a man would die, and how He had the power to stop it all, to avoid the torment and reveal Himself to his persecutors.

Next he described the pushing back of the great stone from the tomb, and the brilliance and inspiration of the moment when Christ reappeared to Mary Magdalene and the disciples. "They were surprised to see Jesus alive," he told Shao-fei. "But they shouldn't have been. Jesus said he would die and rise again in three days. And that's exactly what he did. That's exactly what he did for you, Shao-fei. He died for you and me and everyone, and then he came back to life and gave us all another chance."

He had brought along an early Christmas gift, a paperback Chinese translation of the New Testament wrapped in bright gold paper. He took it from his book bag now and pressed it into Shao-fei's hands. "When you feel very sad," he continued, "very unhappy, you can open this book and read the Word of God. What you'll feel then is Jesus' presence, Jesus' love, a stronger and wiser love than any you've ever known. It lasts forever. I can't say it any simpler than that. It lasts forever and it inspires me, Shao-fei. Me and millions of other people all over the world."

The boy pulled the book from its wrappings. He let the pages fall open, and there in the semidark of twilight he read through several columns of characters.

"Did he really die?" Shao-fei asked.

"Yes. He really died."

"Did someone make the picture?"

"There were no cameras then."

"I know this. Did someone draw the picture, when they saw Jesus dead?"

"They did," Vincent answered, though he knew it to be a half-truth at best. There were portraits of the Crucifixion, yet they were painted hundreds of years later. Still, it was hard for him not to tell a simplified version of the truth. The boy appeared quietly dazzled by the story, the gift, the seeds of a new faith. From their perch against the rail they watched the evening light recede. The sky deepened in hue. A few stars appeared, flickered tentatively through the haze.

"It's amazing to think about," Vincent said. "Jesus' love. Everything depends on it."

Without quite looking, he sensed a change in Shao-fei's posture, a relenting sigh, a bow of agreement.

"You can feel it, can't you?" he said. "It's all right to say so if you don't." He turned and regarded the boy.

Here it was, then, the most ruminative and complicated and searching expression he'd seen from Shao-fei yet.

"Yes," the boy said. "I can."

When he arrived at Mrs. Liang's home early Friday morning, the courtyard gate and front door were both hanging open, and Vincent could see the shimmer of Mrs. Liang's white hair pass from one window to another. His motorcycle was tied down with cardboard boxes and travel bags, the sum of his possessions, which he'd managed to transfer in a single trip.

He called out "Good morning" as he entered the house. Mrs. Liang, entrenched inside a small fortress of old newspapers, grunted in reply. She stepped out and tiptoed over lesser piles of molted clothing and fractured kitchen utensils. "All these," she said, "you can carry out to the street curb and throw away. Everything else stays."

He spent the next several hours this way, throwing things out, moving furniture and wall ornaments about the living room, laboring patiently to satisfy Mrs. Liang's fickle sense of order. Beneath the staircase was a dark, restricted little room from which he gathered mops and brooms, liters of cleaning agents. Dutifully he swept and mopped the floors, scrubbed a windowpane, replaced a curtain, polished a kitchen light fixture. By noon much of the ground floor clutter had disappeared. Vincent was pleased to discover he had inherited a much larger house than he first realized.

For lunch Mrs. Liang prepared a simple dish of fried noodles and vegetables. She would not engage in conversation while they ate, but later, after she had made tea and poured it deftly into small, hand-painted cups, she raised her head from a cloud of steam and said, "You know, I would never throw away books, even books I don't like. I've read a lot of them from your country, especially the old ones. The old ones are the best, I think."

Vincent nodded in agreement. He supposed she was referring to literature, in particular, novels, which he was vaguely in favor of without having read very many.

"My favorite book is American. Have you ever read it? In Taiwan we call it *Ha-ku-bay-erh-fen.*"

Vincent mused over the title. He pronounced *Ha-ku-bay-erh-fen* out loud several times before the English title came to him. *Huckleberry Finn.* "Yes," he said. "I read it in high school."

She leaned toward him then, her voice low, the bearing of her unwrinkled face confidential. "I'm going to tell you this," she said. "I'm forty-seven years old, all my hair has been white since I was thirty-five, but I'm just like Huckleberry Finn. I'm exactly like that boy."

"Uh-huh," Vincent murmured. He sipped his tea and set the cup down on a tiny saucer, gently, respectfully.

"My sister and I grew up in this house and we had the place all to ourselves. We lived here and we grew up alone. Our parents were someplace else. I'm telling you that I'm like Huckleberry Finn because we were alone and we did whatever we wanted. Sometimes we smoked cigarettes and sometimes we stole things, little things, and the neighbors thought we were wild children, but they helped us, too. Most of the furniture here, tables and chairs, are things they gave us."

"Where were your parents? Is it all right to ask you about that?"

"Of course it's all right," she said. "They're in China. They're in the Mainland. Alive or dead, that's where they are. My father brought my sister and me to Taiwan in 1949, but he couldn't bring my mother because she was working at a factory in the north and didn't meet us in time to make the trip. My father was an officer in the Kuomintang army, and we came over with thousands of other army families after the Nationalists lost the war. I say my father was a Kuomintang army officer, but I think now that he didn't like it very much. He never talked about the war or the army, and he brought us here to Toulio, to the countryside, when he could have settled us with other army families in Taipei. He bought this house, but he hardly bought any furniture because he said it was something my mother would like to do. We were waiting for my mother to come and buy the furniture.

"We waited for three months, maybe more, and there was a letter saying my mother was on her way, but she didn't show up. And then late in 1949, in October, my father left and crossed the Taiwan Strait and went back to the Fujian Province. He said he was going to go north, to the home of my mother's family in Shandong. He said he would be back as soon as he found my mother, but of course, you know, he didn't come back. Several months later we heard that the Communists had taken all of Fujian and no one was crossing the strait anymore. There was no mail going back or forth or telephone calls. I think he knew before he left there would be trouble because he left money with the neighbors." She nodded toward the row of houses beyond her gated courtyard. "We were lucky to have honest neighbors.

"So my sister and I grew up here alone, and we stole and we misbehaved because I think we were sick from worrying about my parents. When we were older, we sent letters to my mother's home in Shandong through Hong Kong and through France, but nothing came back." She poured them both more tea and rested her hands on the table. "If you read the newspapers," she continued, "then you know that the Taiwan government is allowing a few Taiwanese people to travel in China for the first time in forty years. But only a few are going and it's all unofficial. If you're linked to the Nationalist government in any way then it's impossible to go. My husband teaches for the National Taiwan University, so it's impossible for us to go now. That may change, though."

"Is that what you want?" Vincent asked. "Are you waiting to go to the Mainland to look for your parents?"

"I don't even know. I don't even know if it's possible to find them. What do you think the chances of that are?"

"I wouldn't know. I wouldn't have any idea."

"Of course you wouldn't, but what do you think?"

"I think you should go if you have the chance. You might find them or learn something. And even if you don't, the trip might make you feel better. Or you might pray . . . to Jesus Christ, I mean. I know your husband is a believer, but you haven't said either way." He lowered his voice to what he hoped was a timbre of compassion and understanding. "By praying, we place our greatest worries, our sins, everything, in Christ's hands and it lightens us. I know that from experience."

She sat and pondered what he'd said, her lips pressed together, her gaze brimming with opinion. She was smiling as well, ever so slightly, though whatever amusement she felt appeared to be exceedingly private and weighted, too, with something bitter, something very much like resentment.

A short while later she rose without speaking and carried their lunch dishes to the kitchen sink.

He drove Mrs. Liang to the Toulio train station that evening, and though it felt odd to have her clinging to him on the motorcycle, she did not seem to notice anything unusual in his stiff demeanor or in the pedestrians who scrutinized them as they passed. While they waited for her train, she reminded him to pay the telephone and electric bills and to lock the rooftop door.

"We weren't ever really bad, my sister and I," she said. "Neither was Huckleberry Finn. We never believed in Jesus, but we weren't sinners if that's what you're thinking."

"No," he said. "I wasn't thinking that at all."

"All right then. Enough. Go home and finish cleaning the house."

For an entire week, he did just that. He started by carrying his bags up to the second floor and claiming the largest of the three bedrooms as his own. Later, he concentrated his efforts on the third-floor classroom, filling in and painting over various cracks in the walls. Loose floor tiles needed to be glued into place, and once this was completed, he spent an afternoon going from store to store until he found a suitable chalkboard, an upright, portable model with a pivoting board. It was an expensive purchase, yet he was out shopping again the next morning and returned to the Liang house, his very own ministry house, with an armful of posters and school supplies.

In America, in Red Bud, it was the week of Christmas and New Year's. Undoubtedly a party was being held in the basement of St. Mark's. Most nights the whole of his extended family, now some forty persons strong, would be meeting in the home of an aunt or uncle. Tonight, perhaps, it would be Vincent's home.

Yet to think of any of this in detail was to become paralyzed by homesickness. Therefore he poured his energies into the ministry house's newly restored classroom. He scrubbed the floor. He hung posters. He even auditioned a series of chair arrangements—half circles and three-quarter circles and diagonal lines—taking stock of each, before at last positioning the desks in four traditional rows. Afterward he practiced writing on the chalkboard, one neat line after another, lowercase, uppercase, printing, cursive, humming as he worked, turning around pointedly now and then as if to face a room full of students.

Five

He needed to advertise, needed an attractive flyer that would announce the opening of the ministry house, the extravagant but earnest offer of free English lessons followed by an hour of Bible study. The news, he imagined, would circulate among the citizens of Toulio, passing like rumor from person to person until at last reaching those few broad-minded individuals who might say to themselves, "Free English lessons? Bible study? Yes, all right then," and accept the invitation.

With Shao-fei's assistance, he created three separate designs, ruling in the borders himself, adorning the corner pieces with rosebuds and church steeples and curling strands of ivy. He leaned over Shao-fei's shoulder as the boy translated his words into Chinese characters. Afterward, he chose from among the three a flyer he could not read, but one that seemed to have the requisite balance and authority. Fifty copies later, he was rolling through the town's commercial district taping his flyers to electric poles and store windows, a strategy recommended by Reverend Phillips.

For several days he busied himself with the final preparations, working at the kitchen table or cross-legged on the living room sofa, always in earshot of the telephone. He drew up a lesson plan, mulled over the topic and direction of what would be his first Bible study. This done, he surrendered to an odd, fretful apprehension. It began with the silent telephone, a phone that would not ring with inquiries, or perhaps was incapable of ringing. He called and instructed Shao-fei to telephone the ministry house. Moments later the telephone let out a hearty clamor. Now his worry shifted to the townspeople themselves. They might simply be ignoring his flyers, in which case it was best to prepare himself for the disappointment of an empty classroom. Or they might suddenly appear Monday night as a sizable crowd outside the ministry house gates. Could he accommodate more than a dozen students, and if so, what would they expect from him? Individuals he could understand and contend with, but as an imaginary crowd, the townspeople, the Taiwanese, seemed unfathomable.

Monday evening, twenty minutes before the start of class, he discovered a middle-aged gentleman waiting at the front gate. He wore a tan safari hat and after Vincent led him inside for a tour of the ministry house, he removed the hat and stroked the bald crown of his head. He said, "My name is Mr. Yao. I am happy to meet you. I have only a little hair now." His tentative English, the peculiar order of his statements, made Mr. Yao seem eccentric. But this impression vanished once he switched to Chinese and explained that he had seen Vincent's flyers and had come to the ministry house to study English. He worked in a hardware store, and no, he did not need English for his job, but rather to help his daughter, a junior high school student, as she struggled to learn the language. Relieved by his sincerity, Vincent escorted him through the kitchen and living room and upstairs to the third floor. Mr. Yao appraised each room carefully, leaned hard into door frames and tugged on the stairway railing. "Strong, solid house," he concluded. "Not like the new ones they build north of town. You move in and they're falling down around you."

They returned to the ground floor and found two women standing inside the front doorway. They appeared to be related, cousins or sisters— or twins, Vincent realized once he noticed the sameness of their long faces, the deep-set corners of their eyes, and the way they clenched each other's hands as if to keep themselves from bolting out the door.

"It's all right," Vincent said. "Welcome. You're here for English lessons, yes?"

They nodded shyly and regarded him with the same jittery grin. Over their shoulders he could see three more potential students edging forward across the courtyard.

He led them all up the stairs to the classroom and studied their reactions as they chose seats. Though none commented outright, each appeared pleased with the accommodations. For Vincent, there was a cheerful intimacy involved in having the students present under his own roof. When he spoke to them during the minutes before class, when he asked them their names and occupations, he felt an unexpected rush of sentiment steal into his voice. "Thank you so much for coming tonight," he said. "It's wonderful to have you in our ministry house. Stop by to visit because you're always welcome." At five after seven he surveyed the occupied desks and found that he had drawn a class of nine students.

And yet in spite of the solid turnout, his first lesson was fraught with obstacles, mostly because the students' command of English varied so widely. Mr. Yao had mastered the basic sentence patterns and hoped to enliven his speech with new vocabulary, whereas the Ping twins, both secretaries in a nearby shoe factory, were absolute novices. Miss Ling, a retired English teacher, brought to class her advanced-composition book. Two uniformed clerks from the post office arrived blank-faced and empty-handed.

Even more worrying, Vincent had no handouts or conversation books to distribute, and most distressing of all, no real teaching experience. Therefore he floundered between Mr. Yao's confounding requests for definitions—he asked Vincent to please explain the meaning of the word *although*—and the silent, perplexed expressions worn by the beginners. His plan had been simply to conduct English class for fifty minutes, break for ten, and then return with a second hour of translated testimonial and repetitions of English psalms. Yet sadly, the initial meeting amounted to little more than a befuddled thirty-minute English lesson, a short, cumbersome break, and finally a hurried speech in which he made two admissions: first, that he was a practicing Christian and hoped in subsequent meetings to make the details of his faith clear to everyone; second, that he was new to teaching and had not adequately prepared for the night's lesson, though he promised to do better in the future.

If Vincent felt any singular, uncomplicated emotion two evenings later as the students filed back into the classroom, it was gratitude. Why they should return after the first, directionless meeting, even if the lesson cost nothing, made sense only as an act of charity. But here they were, settled in across four rows of school desks, looking toward him with a mild sense of expectation. He stood before the chalkboard and offered what he hoped was the smile of a seasoned educator. He then paused a moment to mentally divide the class into two halves: beginners and intermediates. Across the chalkboard, he wrote: *Mark is a man. Mark is a doctor. Mark has a wife. Mark has two sons and one daughter.*

He translated each brief sentence aloud and afterward explained a short list of interrogatives: *what, who, how many*. Next, he led them all through a litany of repetitions and then singled out the beginners for questioning.

"What is Mark?" he asked one of the Ping twins.

They replied together, "Mark is a man."

"Yes." Vincent beamed. "Very good." He nodded toward a teenaged boy seated near the chalkboard. "Who is Mark?"

"Mark is a doctor," the boy answered.

"How many sons does Mark have?" Vincent asked the beginners.

"How many daughters?" Their answers contained a lazy, slightly skewered pronunciation, yet the basic syntax was correct. "How many wives does Mark have?" Vincent asked, and the class puzzled over and then chuckled at the question.

"Mark has three wifes," the teenaged boy volunteered and then added in Chinese, "He is a very tired husband." The class, beginners and intermediates alike, laughed out loud at the boy's bravado.

Scanning the students, Vincent noticed that the two post office clerks had failed to return. Their seats were now occupied by a new, more curious pair of formally dressed businessmen. The taller, leaner of the two sat rigidly in the final desk of the third row. Dressed in a gray pin-striped suit, he pondered the boy's joke, pondered and dismissed it with a face as serious as it was handsome.

Vincent asked for the man's name in formal Mandarin.

"My family name is Gwa," the man replied. His gaze, aimed tenaciously at Vincent, exuded a charmed self-confidence. He stood and proffered his hand.

"Who is Mark?" Vincent asked.

Gwa eased back into his chair and explained in Chinese, "I think my assistant would like to answer your question. He is the one who hopes to improve his English."

Beside Mr. Gwa and also attired in a pin-striped suit sat a younger but much heavier man. Though they were dressed alike, Gwa's assistant appeared less professional, more reckless in posture and grooming. He had grown fat in a top-heavy way so that his full chest and neck forced open his shirt collar and strained against his tie. Slumped in his chair, he stole a wary, sideways glance at Vincent and then closed his eyes as if the glimpse brought back sour memories of previous teachers.

Again, Vincent asked for a name.

"Ponic," the assistant answered.

"Paul?" Vincent guessed.

"Ponic."

"Peter?"

"Ponic."

"Is it a Chinese name or an English name?"

"It's an American name. Ponic."

"Could you spell it, please?"

"P-O-N-I-C. Ponic."

"I don't think I've heard that name before."

Ponic shrugged his heavy shoulders. "I have," he attested.

"Now I'm going to ask you an English question. Who is Mark?"

Ponic's gaze floundered about the room. It skimmed the chalkboard briefly and drifted over the posters Vincent had taped to the walls. Several of the intermediates began whispering the answer from across the room. Quite suddenly, a look of sharp realization bloomed across Ponic's face. "Two sons," he proclaimed. When this brought no reaction, he added, "Three wifes," and beamed a hardy though uninfectious smile.

"It's not a problem," Vincent assured him. "Repeat after me. Mark is a doctor."

"Mark is a doctor," Ponic declared as if he had given the correct answer moments earlier but was only now being properly understood.

Once the intermediates had been questioned and the class broke for intermission, Gwa sprang up and approached Vincent with his right arm thrust forward. He did not intend to shake hands again, but instead offered a business card wedged between his fingers.

"My card," he said. "I hope you will call me often."

"Thank you."

"And your wife. Did she come with you to Taiwan or is she at home in America?"

"I'm not married."

This seemed to confirm some private assumption for Gwa. He nodded thoughtfully. "Then you came to Toulio to teach English and make money?"

"Not really. I'm a volunteer for a Christian organization."

"A Jesus teacher?"

"Yes."

"Very interesting," Gwa said. He appeared genuinely surprised. "Our town has another foreign gentleman, a Scotsman. Do you know him?"

"I do. We both rented rooms at Mrs. Chen's place."

Gwa shifted his glance appraisingly and said, "Your personality is very different from the Scotsman's, I think."

"We're very different," Vincent agreed modestly. Gwa's remark seemed to acknowledge not only that foreigners were capable of distinct personalities, but that he somehow approved of Vincent's character over Alec's.

"I'm sorry we can't stay for the second hour," Gwa said. "I know Ponic would like to, but we have a business dinner. Actually, he hopes you can teach him outside, privately."

"Privately," Vincent repeated. "Yes, I can do that." He turned his attention to Ponic, who had pulled the tie out from under his vest and was now tracing his chubby finger along the design with near cross-eyed fascination. "You're sure Ponic wants to learn English?"

"Oh, he's very excited to learn the language. It's like a new hobby for him. He wants to get started right away." Gwa pinched the corner of his broad forehead and deliberated a moment. "Maybe we can hold class on the same nights. I mean, you can finish teaching here and then come meet us at my office and we'll go someplace to study. Someplace nice. We can start two nights from now."

Vincent agreed. He jotted down directions to Gwa's office. Still, he felt obliged to remind Gwa that Ponic could study just as easily in the ministry house for free.

"I realize that," Gwa said. "But you have to understand how lucky we feel to have private lessons with an American teacher. We don't mind paying you." He offered a cordial good-bye, summoned Ponic, and together they filed out the classroom door.

Gwa had made his office in what looked to be a second-story apartment perched above Toulio's busiest intersection. Vincent had little trouble finding it because the entranceway appeared just as Gwa had described— a narrow, lighted hallway wedged between a video store and a restaurant. He squeezed his motorcycle into a row of motorbikes and scooters. Within the entranceway he found an intercom and buzzer. Once pressed, the intercom let out a hollow squeak and then Ponic's husky voice. "Stay there, stay there. We'll go out back and bring the car around." Vincent said that would be fine, though likely his reply went unnoticed. Already he could hear feet shuffling down a staircase. He moved out onto the sidewalk grinning, amused by Ponic's sense of urgency in the matter. But the grin had a deeper source as well, a calm satisfaction he had carried with him from the ministry house, where the night's Bible study class had let out a half hour earlier.

Admittedly, he'd experienced something of a breakthrough, something he had known intrinsically but until tonight had not been able to formulate into principle. Psalms, proverbs, personal testimonies, observations on faith did not quite work. Stories did. Before one could have an interest in Christian theology, one first had to have an interest in, and empathy for, Christ himself. A single well-told story—as opposed to several summarized biblical events—yielded this kind of empathy. Tonight he had related the story of Christ attending a wedding in Cana of Galilee. The apostles were present, as was Christ's mother, Mary. At some point during the celebration, she drew Christ's attention to the wine supply, which had run nearly dry and might soon dampen the guests' enthusiasm. Christ begged her not to worry and then instructed the servants to fill six stone jars with well water. Once the jars were filled and set before the guests, the chief steward sampled their contents and called the bridegroom over. "It is customary to first set out the good wine," the steward explained. "And after this has been consumed to then bring out the inferior wine. I see that you have saved the best for last."

The class murmured their approval. Mr. Yao and several of the older students even clapped and chuckled out loud at the steward's announcement. Though Vincent was pleased, it took him several minutes to understand their reaction. In the realm of miracles, changing water into wine seemed relatively minor when compared with divine acts of healing lepers or raising Lazarus from the dead. But upon further reflection, he decided the wine miracle appealed wonderfully to the Chinese code of ethics. Christ acted out of deference to his mother. The host had been spared public embarrassment; in fact, the converted wine proved superior to the original. Throughout the entire episode, Christ said little and worked discreetly behind the scenes. Yet in the students' minds, he was there at the forefront—dutiful, polite, recognizable.

Presently a lustrous charcoal gray four-door sedan pulled up to the curb. Ponic sat behind the wheel. Gwa rolled down the back window and motioned Vincent inside. The sedan was too long in the front end to be a Taiwanese or Japanese model. Vincent glanced at the front grill and saw that it was American-made, a Bonneville, a Pontiac. He laughed, delighted at the discovery. "Pontiac?" he said. "Is that your name?"

"Yes!" Ponic bellowed. He slapped his own broad chest. "Ponic, Ponic," he sang out, ecstatic at having finally been understood.

They drove five short blocks to the train station, veered left, and parked beside what was easily the largest and newest building in Toulio. It stretched some eight stories high with a festoon of electric signposts circling the lower floors like a gaudy skirt. The elevator carried them up past a department store, a sushi bar, a beauty salon—all closed for the night—and lurched to a halt on the seventh floor.

Because this was their first private English lesson, Vincent had anticipated some quaint, unhurried location, an idle restaurant or tea shop. The elevator doors slid open to reveal a spacious nightclub bustling with uniformed attendants. The lounge area resembled a furniture showroom: a dozen or more sets of opposing sofas and chairs centered around glass coffee tables. Sullen-faced businessmen attired in two- and three-piece suits presided over each circle. They sat glumly, yoked between pairs of young women who hovered over the tables bantering with one another while mixing drinks and arranging bowls of appetizers. Beyond the clink of tableware, the ebullient swirl of feminine voices, Vincent detected the more resonant strains of waltz music. He turned and saw that adjacent to the lounge lay an expansive dance hall. A line of couples advanced across the floor then ebbed apart, each pair unfurling into its own precise rotation. They, too, were dressed elegantly in suits and evening gowns, and this caused Vincent to fret over the uncomely sight of his black jeans, his tennis shoes, his shabby denim book bag.

A waiter with a crisp black bow tie led them across the lounge past circles of other businessmen who nodded respectfully toward Gwa and then blinked in surprise at the sight of his foreign guest. Gwa and Vincent were ushered onto a plush mahogany sofa near the dance floor. Opposite them, Ponic whispered a long order into the waiter's ear before settling onto an identical sofa. The waiter darted off and returned with a bucket of ice, a half dozen juice glasses, and a dark bottle of liquor.

"You have this in America?" Ponic asked, cradling the bottle with exaggerated tenderness.

"I think so, but I don't really know because I don't buy whiskey."

"It's not whiskey," Ponic protested. "It's XO from France. Much better, much more expensive." He half-filled three juice glasses and, using tongs, added three cubes to each glass. "Bottoms up," he urged Vincent.

Going down it felt smoother and less bitter than the handful of other liquors he'd tried. But a moment later a sudden liquid heat rose in his throat and filled his sinuses with heady fumes. He placed the glass back on the table, closed his eyes, and shuddered. When he opened them again, Ponic had refilled the glass.

"Again. Bottoms up."

"No, thank you. I'll drink this one slowly." It was the first of many polite refusals. The waiter brought over hard-candy sweet peas, a box of betel nuts, strips of paper-thin jerky that smelled strongly of fish, and finally, three packs of Long Life brand cigarettes. "No, thank you," Vincent said to everything except the sweet peas. The cigarettes, however, were more problematic. Gwa and Ponic seemed unwilling to believe that Vincent did not smoke. Each time they set fire to one of their own, they removed a cigarette from the pack and pressed it upon him. At a nearby table, Vincent saw a woman refuse a drink by laying one hand across the fingertips of the other, a simple time-out gesture. When Gwa again presented a cigarette, Vincent flashed a quick time-out. The cigarette was promptly returned to the pack without a single word being spoken.

"You ready to begin?" Vincent asked. He hoisted the book bag onto his lap and reached inside for a notebook. Ponic deflected the question with a skittish roll of the eyes aimed deliberately at his boss.

Gwa leaned forward and confided, "I want to explain that our plan for tonight is . . ." But here Vincent missed a word, puzzled over the phrasing, which was unusually complex and elevated. Something about Chinese custom, something about an honored teacher. In an instant he'd lost the thread of Gwa's explanation.

"I'm confused," he admitted. "Could you say it again, please, but use simpler words."

"Of course." Gwa made a small show of his patience by pausing and laying a hand to the side of his face. "This is our first lesson and we feel lucky to have such an excellent teacher. So we don't want to study tonight. We want to bring you to our favorite place and treat you to a drink or food or dancing. Whatever you want. You understand now?"

"I understand." As explanations went, this was polite, uncomplicated, and altogether evasive. It had convinced him of one thing: Ponic had no intention of learning English. He zipped shut the book bag and sat gazing out over the dance floor, mute and suspicious.

Soon they were joined by two young women who settled down breezily on either side of Ponic. Like the women at surrounding tables, they appeared to be in exceptionally high spirits. They teased Ponic by calling him "our fat uncle" and made playful attempts to pull the edges of his suit jacket over his wide, protruding belly. They were not pretty, Vincent decided, but their faces had been made up and they wore knee-length black skirts slit open on the left side so that one might think of them as sexy. Unwilling to speak directly to Vincent, they giggled, cupped their hands around their mouths, and spoke emphatically into Ponic's ear. He in turn relayed their comments.

"They say you are very handsome," Ponic reported.

Vincent gave a minimal nod. Ponic had not paraphrased their words correctly. They had actually said Vincent appeared quite tall, that his eyelashes were like a woman's, and that his nose stood very high on his face.

"They want to know if you like Chinese girls," Ponic asked.

Vincent feigned a cordial smile. "Tell your friends that I like everyone."

"Oh, they're not friends," Ponic interjected. "They're hostesses. They come to your table if you order an expensive drink." In exchange for this remark, both women slapped his forearms in mock indignation. Giddily, they declared Ponic a terrible man. Their flirtations, though relatively tame, grew more girlish at every turn. Simple gestures—lighting a cigarette, mixing a drink—were endowed with a child's naive sense of discovery. They cooed with delight upon learning that Vincent was a Jesus teacher. One of them attempted an awkward sign of the cross and managed to say "holy man" in English. Naturally, it came as a relief to Vincent when they rose suddenly from the sofa and moved on to another circle of guests. But this was only a quick shift in an apparently larger rotation. Within minutes, another pair of hostesses, equally frivolous, plopped down on the sofa, and the charade began all over again.

Gwa also seemed to have little patience with the hostesses. In response to their flirtations, he parted his thin lips and exhaled a slow, indifferent stream of cigarette smoke. Mostly he studied the dancers gliding lithely across the floor. After witnessing a particularly graceful dip or turn, he might raise one eyebrow in appreciation. When the next waltz drew to a close, he excused himself and approached a tall, sylphlike young woman in a maroon velvet gown. She had just finished the previous dance, but after a quick exchange of words allowed Gwa to lead her back onto the floor. The music commenced, and they each turned their heads aside and assumed elegant, courtly postures before stepping into the waltz. Both were remarkably fluid dancers. Gwa, who seemed especially graceful to Vincent, danced with a blissful, unconscious ease. It was hard not to admire him, in spite of his elusive answers.

"He's very good, isn't he?" Ponic remarked. "I would like to dance the same way, but I can't because I'm too fat. You know why I'm so fat?"

The hostesses giggled. Vincent shook his head.

"Every man in Taiwan has to serve two years in the army, sometimes more. If you're lucky you get sent to a base near your hometown. Most likely you go to Kinmen Island. Nothing to do there but exercise and wait for the Mainland to attack. No women, either. Before I turned nineteen, I decided I couldn't stand to be a soldier. So I ate everything I could. Mr. Gwa helped. He took me out every day for pork dumplings and banana milk shakes. It all worked too well," he said and patted his plump thighs rather sadly. "Even the army doctor who turned me down said I overdid it. And now, three years later, I still have the weight, still have the bad eating habits." He shrugged and motioned toward Gwa, who was leading his partner off the dance floor. "I think you're next," he said.

"I don't know this kind of dance," Vincent explained to Gwa. His real worry, however, was more general, that he would look clumsy dancing among the Chinese.

Gwa replied by taking his hand and pressing it into the young woman's slender palm. "You *should* know it," he chided. "You should start learning it right now."

She led Vincent to the corner of the floor and placed his right hand high on her hip near the small of her back. She began urging him forward, then left and right by gently squeezing his hand in the proper direction. A long mirror ran the length of the far wall, and in it Vincent could see himself shifting to and fro like a man on stilts, pitching and reeling while other couples breezed by.

Perhaps the most exceptional thing about the young woman he danced with was how unexceptional she found Vincent. She did not stare or giggle or flirt. She kept her head lowered and appraised his uneven footwork. "Don't shuffle," she said. "Try to relax." Though they did not dance close together, he could smell the sweet, soapy fragrance of her hair, could feel the taut curve of her back beneath the velvet evening gown.

"I'm sorry. I don't know anything about this," he apologized.

"I don't mind teaching you. I have a few minutes before I take a break. You really shouldn't wear tennis shoes to dance."

"What's your name?"

"Never mind that. Don't lean out so far."

He tried to concentrate on the tempo of the waltz, but now his heart was swelling with emotion. The suddenness and intensity of the feeling almost swayed him into believing it was love. Clutching her from a respectable distance, he tried to recall exactly whom he had been physically close to, whom he had held or touched since leaving home four months earlier. He had shaken hands with Gwa, patted Shao-fei upon the neck, had sat close to a few others as he taxied them about on his motorcycle. But this was the extent of it, except for the woman he now danced with. It seemed such a mawkish, self-pitying thing to do, to catalog the people he had touched, to think of it all that way, and he closed his eyes against the thought.

"Hey," she said. "Keep your eyes open. We're almost finished."

Vincent raised his eyelids and her handsome face shifted back into view. It was not love at all, he decided, just the same grave sense of aloneness resurfacing in another light.

At half past midnight they left the club and eased into Mr. Gwa's Bonneville. With his wrist perched atop the steering wheel, Ponic let the sedan wander along Toulio's empty avenues. Near the train station, Vincent saw a lone food vendor catering to a weary gathering of nighttime commuters. A few scattered pedestrians strolled casually past rows of shuttered storefronts. Here, in the late hours, Toulio seemed to shrug off its daylight ambitions as a clamorous, mini Taipei and revert to its true self, a lesser-sized and unhurried rural township.

They drove south past Hungry Ghost Street, past Gwa's office, and crossed over the railroad tracks. At last Ponic turned the car and parked in an alleyway beside yet another large, brightly lit establishment. Before Vincent could muster a protest, Ponic shambled outside and opened his door. "Don't tell me you're tired," he admonished Vincent. "Just come and have a look."

"Thank you, but I am tired and I'd rather not go to another bar."

"It's not a bar. It's someplace better. Come and have a look."

"He's acting too pushy, isn't he?" Gwa murmured. "I'm just dropping him off here. Come inside. It will only take a minute."

They rounded the building and came upon a striped barber's pole turning slowly inside a radiant glass cylinder. An enormous store window revealed a lobby flourishing with shrubs and miniature trees set in elaborate onyx pots. A cluster of women lounged on a cushioned bench. Above them, set high on an open terrarium, a pair of armless statuaries, naked Greek goddesses, bathed beneath a marble fountain.

They entered through sliding glass doors. Two young women stationed on either side of the entrance sang out, "Thank you for coming!" Both Mr. Gwa and Ponic were greeted by name. A curvaceously plump woman sprang up from the bench and latched on to Ponic's arm. She had a wide, heart-shaped face with deep dimples. "Why do you always come so late, Ponic?" she chided in the pleading tone of a neglected housewife. "You know I stay up late waiting for you." Her companions on the bench joined in the routine, scolding and laughing along with her.

She pulled Ponic across the lobby and up a wide staircase. As he ascended, he leaned down and called back to Vincent, "Upstairs. Come and have a look."

Vincent peered up the curve of the stair rail to a meagerly lit second-floor lounge. A glimmer of movement. A female attendant trailing something long and silklike across her shoulder and down her back . . . a man's necktie? The knowledge of where he was shamed him. He tried unsuccessfully to recall the word for prostitute. "This is a business," he said finally to Gwa. "This is a business with women."

"Yes, it is. But it begins with a massage. If you want, you can go up to the second floor and have a massage. If you like that, then you can go up to a private room on the third floor and have something more. That's how it works. I'll pay for it, you understand?"

"No, thank you."

"There's nothing to feel embarrassed about. You can always say no to something you don't like. By that I mean, maybe you only want a massage. It can stop there. Nothing more."

"I don't want a massage. I don't want anything." To underscore his refusal, he placed one hand atop the other and flashed his newly learned time-out signal.

Gwa smiled broadly at the gesture. "It's late," he said. "I'm sure you're ready to go home and sleep. Let's not wait around for Ponic. I'll drive you back to the office myself." On his way out he waved to a pale gentleman behind the cash register, a quick, pragmatic wave, perhaps an assurance that Ponic's expenses would be paid in full.

They walked to the car and drove away under the flicker of gauzy lights from nearby apartment houses. Behind the wheel, Gwa cleared his throat a few times before furrowing his brow and glancing toward his guest. "I hope you're not angry," he said.

"I'm confused," Vincent replied. And he *was* confused, queerly flustered, as if a share of the brothel's strangeness had followed them out and become a leering backseat passenger. "I don't understand why you took me there."

"Why not? Why shouldn't we?"

"I'm a Jesus teacher. It's one of the first things I told you about myself."

"Yes, but there are all types of people. All types of Buddhist monks. All types of Jesus teachers."

"I'm not *that* type. I don't think many Christians are," Vincent said. Gwa's indulgent remark had made him resentful. "Was it a joke, taking me there? Was it about having some fun with a foreign Jesus teacher?"

"No, no. You're angry and you're looking at it the wrong way. How could it be a joke?"

"To see if it would be difficult for me to decide. It wasn't difficult."

Gwa took his foot off the accelerator. The car drifted to a standstill in the darkened center of the roadway. "It's much more simple than that," he said. "You're still a young man, just like Ponic. He enjoys the girls, so I thought you might, too." Outside, a lone motorcyclist beeped twice and sped by. Gwa pulled out his wallet and from a thick fold of money selected two thousand-yuan notes. "This is for tonight's lesson. I'm sorry if Ponic and I made trouble for you."

"I didn't teach Ponic any English. Not one word." He pushed back the money and the hand that offered it.

Gwa held up the returned bills for inspection, incredulous as to how they could give offense. He folded them over and slipped them into Vincent's shirt pocket.

Vincent plucked them out and set them on the car dash.

They drove the remaining four blocks to Gwa's office in silence. The row of parked motorcycles outside the entranceway had thinned, yet several, including Vincent's own, had been knocked sideways onto the curb. Untangling them became an irksome task. Vincent grasped a sooty wheel rim. Gwa lifted a handlebar. Once righted, the cycle would not start.

"Let me try," Gwa offered. He mounted the seat, flipped the key to the off position, and turned over the engine three times. He snapped the ignition back on, kick-started once, and the cycle roared to life. "Too much gas in the line," he said, handing the cycle back to Vincent and patting him on the shoulder. "I'm going away for a few weeks, to Hong Kong for business. I hope we can meet again as soon as I get back?"

To this Vincent offered a remote "Maybe," and Gwa, still hesitant and apologetic, bid him good night before slipping into the Bonneville and driving away.

All that remained then was a quick, one A.M. ride from the center of town to the ministry house gate. Guiding the cycle out onto the empty avenue, Vincent noticed a papery knot at the base of the seat—two thousand-yuan bills, nearly eighty U.S. dollars, stuffed discreetly between the gas tank and cushion. In his mind's eye he let them flutter to the pavement. In truth he buried them deep in the pocket of his jeans.

Six

THE TELEPHONE RANG late the next morning, and the sound of it shot through the empty ministry house and gave Vincent a start. He had just finished showering, and he raced from the bathroom, a towel clutched to his waist, and snatched up the receiver.

He was greeted by a tight, raspy voice. It took him several moments to recognize the voice as Alec's, several more to realize he was not calling from India or from Shao-fei's home but from the airport outside Taipei. "I need you to drive up here," Alec whispered. "I need you to come and get me. I'm sick." He gasped between words like a winded sprinter. "I already called Shao-fei. His mother's not at home. I've not enough money for a taxi. There's no one else. I want you to rent a car," he said, but this time he spoke too suddenly, a mistake that caused him to moan into the receiver.

"It'll take me four hours to reach the airport," Vincent said. "Go to a doctor. Go to a hospital and I'll meet you there." These were, he thought, reasonable instructions. He was more than willing to proceed to a Taipei hospital, to stand by a bed rail if necessary and allow his faith and level-headedness to serve as an example.

"I can't," Alec whined. "I can't. . . . I've got something with me."

"What? You've got what with you?"

"I'm sick with something," he whispered. "I need you to come and get me. I'll beg if that's what you want."

With a thousand yuan and a cursory wave of his passport, Vincent rented a dusty Toyota Corolla and drove to the airport in just under three hours. He had no choice but to speed. The Taiwan North–South Freeway turned out to be a high-speed caravan of cars and trucks running tail to tail at a harrowing velocity. A light tap on the Corolla's brakes caused a line of vehicles to channel past him on the highway shoulder. He calculated speed and car lengths and stopping time and worried. He also fretted over what he'd surrendered in exchange for the car: one blue thousand-yuan bill, money he might, given the right circumstance, have returned to Mr. Gwa.

He found Alec in the far corner of the Chiang Kai-shek International

Airport, slumped beside a row of lockers. He appeared utterly drained, yet overwrought, too, feverishly awake. His mouth was rounded into a gulping O through which he took quick, panting breaths. He had pushed his travel bag down between his legs so that it was wedged tight against his belly and crotch. India appeared to have rid him of a few pounds, or maybe it was the new haircut, a bristling skull shave that lent his forehead and cheeks an anemic pallor.

Vincent stood there, gazing down on him, trying to remember exactly what it was that he was supposed to say. Something about personal stubbornness versus common sense, how Alec should have gone straight to a hospital, how foolish it was to drink and smoke hash and eat strange food in a country like India and not expect to get sick.

"I've done it this time," Alec panted. "Had an awful fucking time of it . . . waiting, I've been waiting and . . . I suppose I should try and stand." He pressed his back against a locker and with Vincent's aid shimmied up into a standing position. "Walking . . . I don't know," he said, looking out at the yards of checkered floor between himself and the airport exit. "You'll have to help me with that." He threw an arm over Vincent's shoulder and moved forward in a pigeon-toed shuffle.

Their progress was absurdly slow; Alec huffed and groaned with each small step. He continued to clutch the bag to his abdomen, and now the bag shifted sideways and dangled between his legs like a loose diaper. All of this made for a pathetic sight, and Vincent tried to hurry him past other travelers, more than a few of whom had caught sight of the spectacle and had swiveled about, wide-eyed, to stare.

The terminal's glass doors slid open. Outside a queue of commuters stood curbside next to a line of idling buses. Without thinking, Vincent leaned down, placed an arm beneath Alec's knees, and lifted him. The abruptness of it came as a surprise to both of them. Alec gazed up, stunned to find himself an invalid in Vincent's arms. "What . . ." he said. "Are you fucking daft?"

"Maybe I am," Vincent groaned. He shifted back and forth until Alec's weight settled between his arms, and then he pushed through the curbside line and out across the parking lot. What helped him bear the considerable weight was a burgeoning sense of distaste. Alec stank of sweat and urine and unwashed clothing. When they'd gone thirty yards and arrived at the Corolla, he propped his patient against the rear fender and stepped away.

"I can take you to an emergency room," Vincent offered. "I saw hospital markers on the highway."

"No, you won't!" Alec whispered. "Take me home . . . straight away." He crawled onto the rear seat but left his legs dangling out the door. "Home . . . all right? . . . take me home," he repeated and would not draw his legs inside until Vincent agreed.

Back on the freeway, Vincent scowled into the rearview mirror, a simmering, pointless frustration that failed to reach Alec, who lay curled up and out of view in the backseat. Now and then he groaned and begged Vincent to drive faster, but they seemed already to be traveling at a fanatical speed. A flatbed truck of grinning, red-mouthed farmers nearly cut them off, and Vincent gripped the wheel and guided them safely into the next lane. In his imagination, though, they were sent hurtling over the embankment; he saw his own fiery, twisted-metal death, and then Alec slipping free of the rear compartment and climbing up the embankment to stand unscathed at the highway's edge.

They reached Toulio by late afternoon and soon after pulled into the alleyway beside Shao-fei's home. Vincent made a stiff-legged circuit of the car and opened the rear door. Alec, crouched and haggard, raised his pale head, but seemed reluctant to crawl out. Behind them the house door sprang open. "Alec!" Shao-fei bawled. There was dread in his voice and a rush of panic in his wobbly stride.

"Christ," Alec mumbled from the backseat. "Tell him I'm all right. . . . Tell him I ate some bad food in India."

Vincent called back over his shoulder, "He's OK. He's just a little sick, just ate some bad food in India."

Shao-fei ducked his head into the car, took in the feeble sight of Alec, and released an anguished sigh. "It's not good," he lamented. He grasped a belt loop on Vincent's jeans and gave it an urgent yank. "It's not good. Let's go to a doctor."

"I *know* it's not good, but he doesn't want to go to a doctor. He won't let us take him to a doctor." He reached for Alec's arm and hoisted him from the car. His sagging weight added to Vincent's annoyance, and the boy, too, traipsing beside them, thunderstruck, cloddish, roused into an extravagant state of alarm.

In fact the whole situation now seemed overwrought and ridiculous. To allay the boy's fears he blamed the Scotsman's caterwauling moans and knee-weakening cramps on a reckless diet—spoiled fruit, an excess of curry powder. And what a struggle to drag Alec across the foyer to the stair landing, to be cautious and even-tempered, to be the governor of this particular emergency.

Halfway up the stairs Alec finally abandoned the travel bag. It slipped from between his legs to reveal a large crescent-shaped urine stain. After he'd been hustled up to the second-floor bathroom and propped against the sink, he touched the stain and shrugged. "Pissed myself on the plane . . . again in the airport . . . a bit more in the car. I'm a leaky tap," he said. His eyelids fluttered dreamily. "Listen, mate . . . would you mind . . . running downstairs . . . out to the back . . . where Mama kills the chickens . . . and bringing me a pail."

"Why?" Vincent asked. "What's going on here?"

"For fuck's sake, man, it's simple. . . . I need a pail."

"Why? For what purpose?"

"Would you mind . . . *please* . . . running out to the back—"

"All right," Vincent said, hurrying back down the stairs. He returned a minute later with an orange plastic pail, which he set at Alec's feet. "Now," he said. "Tell me what's going on."

"I've got something inside me—"

Vincent scowled. "You mean you've *put* something inside you, something illegal."

"Legal or not," Alec stammered. "Legal or fucking otherwise . . . it's got to come out." Before locking himself in the bathroom, he pitched forward and groaned deeply, a cringing, reluctant groan, full of bodily misgiving. He fumbled with the button of his trousers, on the verge, it seemed, of a dire and undetermined experiment.

Then of course, still, there was the boy, half-panicked, looking like a disgraced businessman in his rumpled school uniform. He put his face against the bathroom door frame and spoke into the crevice: "Please, Alec. Please. Let's go see a doctor." He might have kept on with his pleading, his blubbering, had Vincent not taken him by the elbow and coaxed him down the hallway into the broader confines of the boy's bedroom. Once inside Shao-fei sat slump-shouldered upon the corner of his mattress. "It's not good," he repeated. "I should call Mama at the market and tell her to come home."

"No need for that," Vincent said.

"*Aiya*," he said in wearied Mandarin, a language he rarely, if ever, used in Vincent's presence. "*Aiya*. Big brother."

"All right," Vincent said gently. "Let's not get carried away."

They were interrupted by an extended shriek of pain, one that began breathy and low and rose to a shrill crescendo. From the bathroom Alec wailed again and the effect on Shao-fei was immediate: the boy lurched, cradled his belly in his hands as if he were the one in agony. "*Aiya!* Big brother!" he wailed.

It would always be difficult to know, in the weeks and months to come, if what happened next was of genuine consequence, a crucial misreckoning, or if in his attempt to counsel the boy he had merely been clumsy in his choice of tactic: clumsiness could sometimes be overscrutinized, raised to the scale of consequence. Either way it began with a scalding sense of aggravation. Vincent was aggrieved: at Shao-fei's pining melodrama, at Alec's stupidity—no, not even that, at his very presence in the room next door, his proximity and ruinous influence.

"It's not good," the boy continued. "We should make—"

"Oh *please*," Vincent fumed. "It's not good. We've established that. I don't see how it helps to act this way, to make yourself so upset—like it's a *show* of some kind, like you're an actor." It was surprising how entitled he felt to this bitterness, this raw, parental displeasure. He cowed the boy with a sullen glance. Then he took a frowning measure of the room itself, the dresser and bed, the high cupboard where Shao-fei kept his photo album, his book of the dead. "Alec isn't going to die, if that's what you're thinking."

"I didn't say that," Shao-fei whispered.

"If you're ready to act reasonable," Vincent said. "If you're ready to do something useful, then you—then we—can take a minute and pray."

"I already tried."

Tried? There was, certainly, a point to be made about the difference between trying and doing. Yet rather than use words to belabor the point, he bowed his head demonstratively and prayed. First he strove for the aura of inner calm, a bit of sanctuary inside a droning and troubled afternoon; not so easy a thing given the hours he'd spent on the freeway, or this stifling house with its air of discord. And what was it he had hoped to pray for? For understanding. For a fraction of Christ's eternal love. From the next room came a pealing, agonized groan. The subject, he remembered now, was the Scotsman Alec, and on this topic Christ, who had been Vincent's confidant and guide and who spoke to him in the most steadfast of intuitions, seemed to be saying, *Let him learn what he must. Let him suffer a little if he has to.*

"I already tried," the boy insisted.

Jarred from his prayer, Vincent pinched the bridge of his nose and sighed. He was tired. He had not eaten all day. He said, "Maybe you prayed for the wrong thing."

"What wrong thing?"

"Look here," he said. "This is what Alec did. He went to India and brought back something illegal, drugs, hash, I guess, bad air. He put it inside him and snuck it into Taiwan. It was a dangerous thing. If anyone else had done that, we would tell the police, wouldn't we? So maybe Alec needs to feel sick for a while, so he understands what he's done. Maybe we should pray he feels every bit of this pain he's brought to himself. So that he remembers. So that he never does it again."

Shao-fei listened, held Vincent's gaze. Yet there was something starkly adult in the way he pondered and rejected Vincent's explanation, a keen faculty, an aptitude for lucid judgment. The boy said, "No," said it plainly, said it absolutely.

Vincent pretended not to know what to make of it. He hoisted an eyebrow, jutted out his lower lip as if to say, No to what? At the same time a current of anguish shot through him. He had, he felt reasonably sure, gone too far, blundered through private realms of allegiance and unweaned faith. He sat silent and perplexed for what seemed a long time. Then he rose and moved into the hallway, where he languished outside the closed bathroom door. A while later Alec's wailing tapered off. In its place came the brassy, whooshing sound of water spilling into the bathtub. He knocked and heard Alec call out for him to enter.

He stepped into a bathroom spoiled by rank odors. A thin, subdued Alec lay stretched out in the tub; his long body shone naked and gauntly white beneath the water. Within the pail, scattered like loose candy across its orange bottom, were what looked to be a dozen or so small, earthy balls wrapped in clear plastic.

"Bad air?" Vincent guessed.

"That's right. You have no idea what a relief it is to get those out of me."

"You stuck those up inside you?"

"Swallowed them. Wrapped them in condoms and swallowed all ten of them."

"You're an idiot," Vincent said. It seemed an assessment worth repeating. "You're an idiot," he said again.

Lying in the tub, Alec merely shrugged. A lazy ripple of bathwater crested up over his chin. "I'm going to need to see a doctor," he said. "I think my arse is infected."

The town clinic, a lively though joyless place, was only a few kilometers away, housed in a long building of unadorned shops and offices. They entered with their arms slung round each other's shoulders, in the manner of hobbled fugitives.

"Pure and total misery," Alec said, recounting his trip home from India. "Endless flight. Endless waiting. Outrageous pain. Like a strong hand squeezing and twisting from the inside." By now his cramps had subsided. Unable to sit, he had knelt atop the front passenger seat during the ride over.

Vincent steered him toward a column of folding chairs. "You're not out of the woods yet. The doctor will be suspicious. He'll have questions."

"Doesn't matter. What matters is ten went in and ten came out." He slouched low, reclined sideways across the laps of two chairs. "If the doctor finds anything else up my arse it will come as a shocker to both of us."

Apparently, it was Vincent's duty to join the clinic's lengthy patient line and approach the front counter. There, behind a glass divider, a trio of nurses sat and looked back at him with what appeared to be the same rueful expression. "My friend is very sick," he announced. "He needs to see a doctor."

How from this modest request could such confusion follow? A series of inscrutable forms were passed beneath the divider. He was asked to name both his own and Alec's blood type. He was then ushered down a corridor to an examination room. After a short wait a bespectacled female doctor entered and felt his wrist for a pulse.

Even after he explained the mix-up, she continued to eye him for signs of illness, to mark the steadiness of his gait as they strolled to the waiting area, where Alec lay in a knees-to-chest sidelong curl.

"Your friend. What's the matter with him?" the doctor asked.

Until that moment, he had not thought about how he would describe Alec's condition. He tried to recall the word *infection,* chided himself for letting so crucial a term slip from his memory. "It's like a stomachache," he said. "But lower."

"Lower? Lower where?"

Nearby a child whimpered. A man whose cheeks and jaw had been haphazardly bandaged craned his head their way. Several less-afflicted patients loitered close. He pursed his lips and deliberated. He had once heard Shao-fei use the common word for butt, *p'i-gu*, yet Vincent knew of nothing else more medical or dignified. "In the butt," he said at last. "My friend's butt gives him great pain."

His audience blinked. Their reaction, when it arrived, was oddly contemplative. The laughter came later, after a crafty exchange of glances all around. The doctor drew in a corner of her lip, her mouth quivering, loosening into a noticeable smirk.

The clinic provided Alec with a multicolored assortment of prescription drugs. There were antibiotics, for he was indeed infected. There was also pain medication that left him slack-limbed and grinning. The bill came to 850 yuan and Vincent gave up the second blue thousand-yuan note, money he would definitely not be returning to Mr. Gwa. They drove home and Alec lay in bed that evening improving at his own leisurely pace. Mrs. Chen brought him horrible-tasting variations of the same tofu soup. "This one's for blood," she said. "This one's for digestion." She set a pot of ginseng tea by his bedside, gazed dotingly at her patient before exiting the room.

Alec sampled each soup and grimaced. "This is God-awful. I don't suppose you'd run into town and pick me up something decent?"

"No, I don't suppose I would," Vincent said.

"Fair enough." He let his chin nod toward his chest, nearly closed his eyes. "My friend's butt gives him great pain," he recited, smiling waggishly. "That was brilliant, truly. That'll make us both famous. As if the gossips in town weren't already blathering on about us." He reached into his pillow-case and withdrew a crimped plastic bag containing his ten balls of smuggled hashish. He chose one, peeled back the condom, crumbled a portion of the gritty, black matter into the palm of his hand.

"You're not planning, surely, to use—"

"Indeed I am."

"There'll be an interaction, a reaction."

"Let's hope it's a potent one."

"Well, I'm not giving you your medication if you're going to take drugs," Vincent warned.

"Oh, fuck off," Alec said happily. He began hollowing out a cigarette, mixing the loose tobacco with crumbs of hashish.

"Why is it, do you think, that you need something like hashish in your life?"

"Shhhhhhh," he murmured. "Don't start up. I'm in no mood for your Christ stuff."

"I wasn't planning to quote Scripture."

"Lucky me." Using the tip of a chopstick, he repacked the cigarette, set fire to its blunt end. After a long-drawn inhale he presented it to Vincent, a smoldering flower pinched between his index finger and thumb. "Join me in a smoke. How about that? Join me in a smoke, and I'll bow my head and pray to Jesus."

"Not a chance."

"Right you are. And not a moment's hesitation either. Jesus will credit you for that. Right now in heaven, Vincent, the angels are strumming harps and singing your name."

It took no time at all for the hash to overwhelm him. He lolled about in bed, cupping the cigarette in his hands, knocking ashes onto the sheets. "What I am doing in this little fart of a town, I do not know. Would someone please explain it to me?" he asked, bleary-eyed. "I have fifty grams of good smoke. I could sell half and buy a plane ticket. I could go back to Manali. I could be in Kashgar, easy. I could be in fucking Turpan. Christ, think of that. Turpan to Kashgar then across into Pakistan . . ." He ranted on, planning a journey that grew increasingly complex, improbable. As Vincent rose to leave, Alec glanced up and furrowed his brow. "I guess I haven't been properly . . . grateful. But listen up, 'cause here it comes and it's sure to make your volunteer heart skip a beat. Ready? Here it comes now. Thank you."

PART TWO

Sister Gloria,
Sister Moon

Seven

Dear Vincent,

   Hope this letter finds you happy, well, secure in Christ's grace and love.

   I visited the Liangs yesterday. In fact, I arrived with a fruit basket and card bearing your name (something to keep in mind if they should call and thank you for it). I wanted to give credit to Mrs. Liang in person for trusting you with her family home. As you know, in person, Mrs. Liang is a lively and unique woman, yet somewhat difficult to read at times. Still, her charitable act speaks for itself. I suspect that the free rent has much to do with the kind of impression you made on her. Mr. Liang seems very enthusiastic about the new Toulio ministry, though lately he has not been feeling well. Headaches mostly, a tingling sensation in the feet. He's been to the hospital for tests, and thankfully nothing serious has turned up. Keep him in your prayers just the same.

   And how are you, Vincent? Did I detect a note of weariness or possibly even frustration in your last letter? As the founder of our new ministry, as our sole volunteer in Toulio, you're entitled to these feelings. You've earned them through hard work. By now I'm sure you've discovered how rewarding and sometimes frustrating that work can be. Please know how delighted I am with the progress you've made so far. Acquiring a ministry house, opening it up and establishing Bible study classes; these things are by no means small accomplishments. I have absolute faith that our new ministry is high on God's agenda, and I have equally great faith in your talent for working with the people of Toulio.

   And now some good news, a hopeful announcement. There are currently three apprentice volunteers here at the Good Shepherd Parish in Taipei. In the next month, I will send one young man north to a boys' school in Keelung, one young woman will go south to a parish in Tainan, and another young woman, Gloria Hamilton, I will send to Toulio where she will join you in establishing the new ministry. Gloria comes to us from a women's Bible college in Nebraska. Isn't this your part of the country as well?

Gloria's progress in language study, especially the written characters, has been remarkable. She is focusing her attention primarily on translation of biblical texts and has some creative ideas for spreading Christ's word among Taiwanese adolescents. Because of the common background you two share, because of your excellent spoken Chinese and Gloria's outstanding ability with the written language, I think the two of you will make an exceptional team. Gloria is eager to begin at once, but I think it's best for her to avoid the mayhem of Chinese New Year and make the trip down after the celebrations.

A brief word, however, on social decorum. Once Gloria arrives she will either rent a room from Mrs. Chen and her son or stay with you in the ministry house. Of course it will be far more convenient for her to reside there in the ministry house. As you know, groups of young men and women volunteers share living accommodations here at the Christian Outreach Parish, and several of the larger ministries on the island. The citizens of Taipei think little or nothing of this arrangement. Toulio will be quite different. There will only be the two of you and the local community will be close-knit and restrictive. Neighbors will be far more watchful and opinionated, and, I'm afraid, far more likely to engage in the type of gossip that might discredit you both as representatives of Christ. Should Gloria reside in the ministry house, it is my suggestion, my strong recommendation, that you two present yourselves as brother and sister. Think of it as a polite falsehood, a way of eliminating suspicion before it begins. Other volunteers have used this tactic in the past. The trick, they told me, is not to overemphasize the relationship, but to now and then mention your history together as siblings and let that pass among students and neighbors as fact. Mostly, it's a matter of you and Gloria sitting down and getting the details right.

That's all for now, Vincent. Once again I stress my great satisfaction with your progress in Toulio. You have every reason to feel encouraged, optimistic, blessed. Look forward to Gloria's arrival once the New Year's holidays have run their course.

Yours in Christ,
Rev. Lawrence Phillips

A week before the outset of Chinese New Year and already Vincent noticed vibrant decorations strewn from apartment balconies and store-fronts, a swelling of bright, tawdry colors. Toulio's usual bluster had also expanded, had risen sharply to a level of raucous, ear-splitting noise. Much of the racket came from loudspeakers mounted atop pickup trucks that circled endlessly throughout the town shrieking out ads for New Year's sales. They broadcast at such high volume that even shuttered inside the ministry house he was compelled to clap both hands over his ears and whisper minor curses as they passed.

There had been a change in Bible study attendance as well, a worrisome decline. Five students one lesson. Three the next. Mr. Yao told him not to worry; these desertions wouldn't be permanent. Now was the time for families to stay in and give their homes a thorough cleaning, to shop and prepare for lavish meals ahead, and—because the holidays entailed so much gambling, so much giving and receiving of money—to set their finances in order. Vincent tried to think of it all as a Chinese Christmas, but with the warm February sun and rattling skeins of firecrackers, he could not make the comparison stick.

What tempered his sense of abandonment was a string of recent telephone inquiries that had, with time and careful attention, developed into two new outside teaching jobs and the possibility of a third. The first involved private lessons with a businessman, a plastics wholesaler, who traveled frequently to the United States. He spoke English well and did not want language books or lesson plans. He wanted unrehearsed conversation. He wanted a casual speaking manner, a negligible accent—virtues that in Kansas City or Dayton would put his American clients at ease. Teaching him was a guilty pleasure. All that he required of Vincent was to show up three nights a week and talk, drink tea, eat pistachio nuts, and at the end of each hour lesson accept a crisp five-hundred-yuan bill. This salary alone, converted into traveler's checks and mailed back to Red Bud, reduced his twin debts to Uncles Clark and Hayden by a hundred dollars a month.

The second was an assignment at a local preschool. The director boasted that her children knew their ABCs, which was true, and that they could count to ten and name the days of the week, which was also true in its own muddled way. When asked to stand and recite, the children chanted, "Onesday, Twosday, Threesday, Foursday, Fivesday . . ." Charmed, Vincent agreed to conduct forty-minute lessons Saturday mornings and weekday afternoons. The children ranged in age from three to six, and like all the world's preschoolers, they exuded the same cherub-faced vulnerability. Yet Vincent's students were Chinese, alike in hair color and in the full-bodied darkness of their eyes, and then, at the same time, capable of intimate differences in gesture and voice and nuance of expression. This contradiction gave their beauty an astonishing edge. In their presence, he could admit to fatherly pangs of tenderness and not consider it an exaggeration to call what he felt love. Still, he loved them best in small groups. As a whole, they clamored around his knees, and his lessons became shouting matches with Vincent waving colored pictures in the air and pleading for order by calling out, "Apple! Boat! Carrot! Dog!"

The third inquiry had come that afternoon, seconds after Vincent plucked Reverend Phillips's letter from the screen door and set it respectfully on the glass-topped tea table beside the phone. A teacher named Jonathan Hwang had called on behalf of the Ming-da Academy, a private high school, he told Vincent, the best in Yun Lin County. Hwang spoke in clear, officious English. He had seen the flyers and wanted to know if Vincent would teach for the academy. "One class of students," Hwang emphasized. "A single class that will meet and study English conversation Tuesday and Thursday afternoons. Are you interested, sir?" Vincent said he was and agreed to an interview at the academy later that day. He flipped the envelope over and jotted down directions on its back side.

Afterward, he opened the letter and read it through without pause.

In spite of himself, he was heartened by the Reverend's words—it was, after all, a letter of steadfast assurances—though he was not truly persuaded. Yes, he had secured a ministry house and begun Bible study classes, but there were no real converts among his students. He had failed to impart an understanding of Christ that went beyond stories and psalm repetitions, had failed on a much more personal level with Shao-fei, whom he had visited once since Alec's return, visited briefly, long enough to be reminded of the boy's refusal and to sense how everything between them had become either timid or disingenuous.

Then there was Gloria Hamilton to consider, a young woman from a Bible college who could translate English into Chinese characters. In a matter of days she would travel down from Taipei and he would present her to his students, possibly to Shao-fei and Alec, as his sister. Sister Gloria. She could be any type of person at all. She could be spirited, buoyed by an effusive admiration for Christ. He had come to know several such women at the campus ministry house during his years in college. Yet she could just as easily be shy and ungainly, afflicted by some deep personal sorrow. He had known campus ministry students, men and women alike, who would weep openly during prayer sessions.

He reread the letter and, growing more apprehensive, wandered up to the second floor and into the first of two unoccupied bedrooms. Whatever kind of Gloria Hamilton he might envision, he could not imagine one that would tolerate sharing a house with Alec. He set to work sweeping the floor and wiping down the furniture. He stripped the bed of its linens and carried the blankets up to the rooftop for an airing. As he cleaned, he began to relinquish notions of what type of person she would be and to wonder, purely, what Gloria Hamilton would look like. He wondered if she would be pretty, and, in turn, if the Reverend's insistence that he call her sister meant that she was more or less likely to be attractive. More likely, he decided, though such speculation only increased his apprehension. With the bedroom cleaned and put to order and nothing else to do, Vincent found himself outside the ministry house gate, beside his motorcycle, ready for a meeting with Jonathan Hwang that was still an hour away.

He set off for the town center, allowing the cycle to edge leisurely down the main avenue and on toward the business district and open markets. He skirted a block-wide temple complex and paused to look up at the tall, sculpted walls adorned with red New Year's banners. From inside came a high, wailing song and a clash of cymbals. The celebration had spilled out the temple exits and onto the sidewalks. There, crowds of worshipers gathered around banquet tables piled with fruits and cakes and large ceramic bowls cradling cooked chickens and boiled pork roasts. They ordered and reordered their tables, shifting the food and bouquets of incense sticks about, striving for . . . what exactly? The most shapely arrangement? Some sort of godly alignment? Beside these tables were heavy, wrought-iron cauldrons ablaze with paper money. In one such cauldron, someone had offered up a miniature car, an elaborate paper and plaster-glue model. It burned inside a wreath of sputtering blue flames.

Even after five months in Toulio, most of these ceremonies remained obscure to Vincent—not harsh or bizarre or even pagan, just quietly inexplicable. What did appear obvious as he threaded his way beyond the temple and through the narrow market lanes was an implicit sense of communion among neighbors, among family. Here at a corner fruit stand, a grown daughter counted out change one-handed rather than uncurl her arm from around her mother's waist. Schoolchildren darted in and out of neighbors' doorways. Grandmothers crouched together on low wicker stools, gossiping in tight circles. Five months and Vincent had yet to see a public disturbance, a traffic quarrel, a dispute in a restaurant or market shop. He had witnessed the townspeople rising and sending their children off to school in the morning, had seen them gather for tai chi in the city park, had paced by tea houses in the evenings and heard laughter and eager conversation. He looked into their lives—sometimes into the windows of their homes—and saw an abiding kindness that made the much-talked-of hospitality of his own hometown, Red Bud, seem pale in comparison.

Time also had a way of bringing the Chinese countenance into focus. In his college Mandarin class, a student had once asked how Chinese victims of crime identified their perpetrators, how the sketch artist could delineate an individual amid such a like-featured race of people. Their teacher had balked at the question and now Vincent understood why. To know a person, even to meet him briefly, was to absorb hundreds of minute details, most of which could not be translated into simple adjectives. He had seen countless teenaged boys of Shao-fei's height, hair and eye color, but none that he mistook for Shao-fei. The same was true for Gwa and Ponic, Mr. Yao. At times there were uncanny resemblances, yet they unfolded in an unexpected direction: back to his former life in the States. In a noodle stall once, Vincent recognized a Chinese man who had the same heavy eyebrows and sedate grimace as his high school history teacher. Another time he met a woman whose nervous mannerisms appeared identical to those of a local Illinois newscaster. Most often it was the gesture itself, a one-shouldered shrug, a woman sweeping the hair from her collar, that left him with a lingering sense of the familiar.

At the town roundabout he circled twice then headed south across the railroad tracks and onto a two-lane highway. He rolled past a cluster of warehouses and small factories, a concrete fishing pond, a wide, fenced-in pasture where a hundred or more white ducks waddled atop a muddy feeding trough. It was nearly five o'clock and the early evening sky had lost its bright edge. The traffic slowed enough for Vincent to look back and see a smattering of fireworks arc above Toulio's tallest buildings and freckle the town skyline with soft bursts of light.

The Ming-da Academy was located a few kilometers beyond the city limits. Its entrance, a long sweep of blacktop lined by towering palm trees, struck him as suitably distinguished. He came to a halt at the academy gates and was waved inside by an elderly guard. Ahead loomed an immense paved courtyard at the center of which stood a tall gray statue of an army officer, most likely a general, mounted on the back of an enormous horse. He circled the statue and recognized the officer's smooth round face and balding head as that of Nationalist leader Chiang Kai-shek.

The academy office lay directly before him, a squared-off, sensible brick building that served to divide the school into two long wings. Both the east and west wings contained three tiers of open-air classrooms and appeared identical except for their respective students, who wore different-colored uniforms. Students of the east wing were dressed in maroon, while the west-wing students wore dark blue. It was not until Vincent drew closer and parked his motorcycle that he realized that the school was actually divided by gender: girls in the east, boys in the west.

Jonathan Hwang was waiting for him just inside the office doors. A slim, middle-aged man in a tan windbreaker, he nodded toward Vincent without smiling and led him up two flights of stairs to a locked classroom door. Inserting the key, he said, "This is our language laboratory."

The classroom was laid out in four long rows of consoles, each with a pair of microphones and headsets. A video projector hung from the ceiling, aimed at the classroom's glossy marker board. *Laboratory* had seemed an unnecessarily clinical choice of names, but looking over the polished vinyl consoles and complicated gadgetry, Vincent saw the sense in it.

They took seats side by side at the first console. Hwang withdrew a notepad from his jacket. "I've seen your signs around Toulio," he said. "You're an English teacher. Have you graduated from college?"

"Yes, I have."

"Would you tell me where and when?"

"Southern Illinois University in Carbondale, 1989. I graduated last spring."

Hwang scribbled on his notepad. "Do you have your diploma with you?"

"No," Vincent said. "I'm sorry. I don't."

"You won't mind if I contact, if I telephone, your university? So many foreigners come to Taiwan to teach without a college degree. Do you speak Mandarin?"

"I do, yes." By now it was a claim he could make with some confidence.

"We never, under any circumstances, speak Chinese in this room. It's bad for the students. It makes them lazy." He squinted his eyes and made a slightly dour face. "The students have asked for an American teacher. The better schools in Taipei have foreign conversation teachers and I suppose they heard about this and wanted one of their own. The principal and I have decided to allow one class to study with a foreigner. Are you interested?"

"Yes, I am," Vincent said. Hesitant to ask about salary, he asked instead which class he would teach.

"Third-year students," Hwang said. "Boys probably. We don't yet know which because"—and here his face grew more distinctly dour—"the students are having an English contest, a competition to see which class will study with you. We'll announce the winner after the New Year's holidays. You may start then." He tapped his pencil on the pad and wrote out 450 yuan per class, a sum to which Vincent nodded yes.

"Please," Hwang said. "I've seen your signs. We want you to teach English conversation. Please, no Jesus material, all right?"

Having made a promise, Vincent rode home to the ministry house and in the days that followed observed a slow parade of buses and motorbikes filing out of the countryside and into the town of Toulio. Now it was the town's population that seemed to be swelling. At Hungry Ghost Street the droves of lunchtime patrons doubled and redoubled in size. All day long the lane and cul-de-sac outside the ministry house fluttered with activity beneath a haze of gunpowder smoke. Fireworks rang out incessantly; sometimes a single skein of firecrackers would split the air for minutes at a time. Neighborhood children sprinted from house to house clutching red envelopes of money in their hands.

At night he sat on the rooftop ledge until his eyes watered and his mouth tasted coppery from the burnt sulfur hanging in the air. Again he wondered if Gloria Hamilton would be nice and then, with a shudder of self-reproach, if she would be pretty. He saw rockets hurtle upward from a nearby temple and counted out their ascent. Above him, the dark ceiling hanging over Toulio bloomed fractured canopies of orange and yellow—bright, delicate designs that would shimmer briefly and fall back to earth.

Mr. Gwa telephoned three days into the New Year's celebrations and insisted that he and Vincent share dinner that evening.

"I can't," Vincent said. "I'm very busy." In truth, he had spent the day sprawled on his bed writing letters, his nostalgia for home making him wistful and drowsy-eyed, susceptible to long naps.

"Busy doing what?" Gwa asked. "Busy teaching? You have classes during New Year?"

"No, no. Not classes. Just some things I'm doing on my own. But I can't go out. I can't teach. I should explain that I've decided not to teach private English lessons anymore. I'm sorry."

"Oh, I'm not calling about that," Gwa replied. "Ponic doesn't want to learn English. I'm sure you know that already. I'm not even bringing him."

"What's this about?"

"It's about us talking. We need to have a meeting."

"I'm not going to any bars, and I can't stay out late," Vincent said, aware of how prudish he sounded.

"Yes, that's fine. Most places are closed anyway. I'd like to come visit you. It's quieter there and we can talk. I'd like to make dinner for us."

"Make dinner? You want to cook here?"

"That's right. I want to make something called hot pot. It's a winter-time meal and I think you'll like it. It's the one thing I know I can cook well. I'll be over soon. Don't worry. I'll bring everything we need."

An hour later Gwa stepped through the front door clutching a bag of groceries and a huge saucer-shaped electric wok. He had dressed for kitchen work—exercise pants and a simple checkered shirt with the sleeves rolled up to his elbows. Without his pin-striped suit, without the middle-aged formalities of businessmen and nightclubs and gray sedans, he strolled into the kitchen looking youthful and unpretentious, much closer to Vincent's own age.

They cleared the kitchen table. The hot pot preparations seemed simple enough: a pitcher of water, a dash of vegetable oil, a can of chicken stock, each of which Gwa stirred into the wok. This done, he began chopping vegetables and meat into thin strips while Vincent set the table with bowls and soup spoons and napkins. As they worked, an ad truck passed outside the ministry house. Its squawkish blare was deafening. Vincent cringed and clasped his hands over his ears.

"How can you stand it?" he asked.

"What?"

"That horrible noise. The loudspeaker."

"Oh, I don't mind the noise. Not at all. Chinese people think it makes the atmosphere more lively, better. Like a big city is better. We don't mind being close to it."

"I thought the idea of living in a small town is to find peace and quiet."

"Your idea, maybe, not ours," Gwa said. He grinned and regarded the arrangement of dishes. Splayed across the table lay a half circle of plates piled high with mushrooms, prawns, wafer-thin slices of beef, balls of fish, spinach leaves, a mound of thin translucent noodles. "Yours to keep," he said, sweeping a hand over these ingredients and the wok, too, which churned its water in a slow boil. "Consider it all a New Year's gift."

"You shouldn't, no. The dinner's enough, more than enough. . . ." But his protests seemed only to please Gwa, who began easing the contents of each plate into the steaming water. He placed the lid on the wok and then reached into the bottom of his bag and pulled out a thick paperback book.

"It's a travel guide for the Mainland. There are some maps inside I'd like you to look at." He glanced quizzically across the table. "Curious yet?" he asked. "About this meeting? About this book here?"

"Not really," Vincent said. "I'd like to know something else, though. I'd like to know why you lied about Ponic wanting to learn English."

"It wasn't a lie," Gwa said after careful deliberation, "but a kind of excuse. An excuse to get to know you. I thought it would be the best way."

"I'm not so sure it is the best way. I think most people prefer honesty. I've been thinking about the night you took me to the bar. You paid women to come to our table and talk, to pretend they were having a good time. You paid another woman to dance with us. Later, you paid a woman to sleep with Ponic. And you paid me for some reason I don't quite understand. Not for an English lesson. But I do believe, strongly, that you can't pay people for things like that because you end up buying the opposite of what you want—not real friendship, just more pretending." He sat back in his chair, pleased at finally having articulated his resentment. If only he had not spent Gwa's thousand-yuan bills. If only he could now slide them across the table as a way of accentuating his argument.

"I'm glad you think so. Maybe I feel the same way."

"But if you really did, you wouldn't—"

"Please, I think we already agree about this. And I think I can explain about the rest, but it's a long explanation." Gwa dipped a ladle into the wok and portioned out a bowl of stew. "Try this and tell me what you think."

The hot pot stew, it turned out, was delicious, undeniably so, the broth sweet, the meat and vegetables tender. He praised it accordingly, though his praise cloaked a private reluctance—something about Gwa's unflagging poise, such a deep reserve of confidence that Vincent wanted to ally himself with it one moment, undermine it the next.

"You relax, enjoy the food," Gwa ordered, deferring his share of the meal, wedging a cigarette neatly into the corner of his mouth. He measured out a thin, accommodating smile aimed, somehow, beyond Vincent, at an imagined audience whose members were more evincibly interested. "You say I pay for everything," he began. "And I suppose that's true enough. If you're a businessman, the show of money is just as important as actually having it. I've never been to America, but I'm sure it must be the same there. Am I right?"

Vincent gave Gwa a stingy, halfhearted nod.

"I have money because I worked hard when I was your age, saved what I earned, invested some in the Taiwan stock market and got lucky. But even then, fifteen years ago, I was wise enough to understand that it was only chance, nothing else. I quit playing the stock market and invested the money in a small factory that made umbrellas. I now own that factory and several more in Toulio. One makes carrying cases for businessmen. Another makes motorcycle helmets. I'm half owner of a factory that makes tennis shoes, just like Nike shoes, but they sell for much cheaper.

"Several years back, the Mainland government decided that it was all right to allow foreign investors to start up factories in China. They wanted to make it easy, so they did away with most of the paperwork. Then another big surprise. The Taiwan government decided to allow businessmen to travel to the Mainland to look for investments. First time in forty years. I was one of those allowed to go, but I didn't get involved right away. I waited a year to make sure it was safe, and then I went over, purchased an empty warehouse, and resettled the umbrella factory in Guangdong. There were some problems with supplies in the beginning, but it's been very successful because the cost of labor is one quarter of what it is here in Taiwan. In fact, I'm shutting down the carrying-case factory here and moving it to Guangdong sometime this year." He paused to extinguish his cigarette and snatch up Vincent's soup bowl. Refilling it, he raised an eyebrow and added, "If you think I'm being unfair to my Toulio employees, then you should know this. There are plenty of jobs in Taiwan—maybe even too many—but it's very different in the Mainland, where a factory job is quite valuable. In my mind, we're all Chinese, all deserve the chance to work for a living." He set the bowl carefully on the table and in the process edged closer to Vincent. "I'm telling you all this so that I can explain an experience I had last summer when I traveled in the Mainland." He flipped open the guidebook to a large colored map and traced his finger across a series of black dots. "I visited several cities in the south—Shantou, Fuzhou, back across here to Guilin, then north to Chengdu and Lanzhou. At each place I stopped there was usually someone to meet me at the airport or train station and show me around because they hoped I would decide to start a new factory in their city. But I had already made up my mind to place my new factories together in Guangdong. I just like to travel, like to see the things I once read about when I was a boy in high school. The place I most wanted to see was in Xinjiang, the desert province in northwestern China. So, I flew from Lanzhou to Urumchi because near Urumchi, atop a desert mountain, was a place called Heaven Lake. I've read about Heaven Lake many times, so you can understand that my expectations were very high. I rode a bus for a half day to the top of this mountain and I stood on the edge of the lake and had a look. I can't really describe it except to say that everything looked impossible. The water was blue, the pine trees green. I could see mountains in the distance and the peaks were covered with white snow. But these colors were so bright and clear that they looked impossible. Five hours earlier I was in the desert and then I arrived at Heaven Lake and it seemed like an impossible change.

"So there I was. I returned to Urumchi thinking that I've had my experience, the one that will stay with me forever. That night I was very tired, but the man who was showing me around insisted that I go to have dinner at the home of his Chinese friend. Not everyone in Urumchi is Han Chinese. At least half are minorities. Uighurs. Kazakhs. The Chinese don't like living there, but in the past many of them were forced to live in Urumchi by the government and now they can't get permission to leave.

"This friend turns out to be no one special. Works in the Urumchi train station. Sweeps the floors. Unloads bags. We sit down to dinner with the man's wife and two daughters. I'm tired and don't notice much, certainly not the younger daughter, but the older daughter sits down, and I see in an instant that she is extraordinary. Tall, graceful, the most beautiful face I've ever seen." Having made this declaration, he now brought the whole of his concentration to bear on describing the young woman. He appeared to mull over and reject a number of explanations. All the while his usually stolid features—the tight set of his mouth, his uncommitted gaze—came alive with a private intensity. "Maybe she's a little like the girl we danced with at the bar," Gwa offered. "Though much more beautiful. She holds herself very well, doesn't giggle or act childish. You look in her eyes and you see that everything that is being discussed at the dinner table has already occurred to her. The only thing she doesn't seem to understand, fully, is how beautiful she is. I think she must have some notion of it, but she's stuck in a desert city instead of Beijing or Shanghai or Taipei, where her attitude would be very different." He peeled back several pages of the book and produced a photograph. "Here," he said. "I have a picture. Her name is Kai-ling."

The photo had been taken indoors, inside a bare and rather dreary living room, across a table cluttered with dirty dishes. She had turned away from the camera, possibly in shyness, and so the picture captured a long cascade of silky black hair as well as the delicate profile of her face, a cream-colored complexion, a dark and astute eye fixed on something beyond the lens's range. Vincent studied the path of her gaze, then, once more, her face. She did seem pretty, and yet the photo could not equal Gwa's reverent description.

"Yes, I see. She's very beautiful."

"Clever, too, I think," Gwa said. "I didn't talk to her during dinner. But the next afternoon I met Kai-ling and her father at the Urumchi People's Park, and there I had an opportunity to speak alone with each of them. I learned from Kai-ling that she worked as a clerk in the train station, a job she received because of her father's friend in the station office. She is twenty-seven years old, older than I thought at first. She has no boyfriend, although there are other clerks in the station office who know her and have talked to her father about marriage. She hates living in Urumchi and knows that marriage is one way to get herself out. But I understood, from talking with her, that she hopes for a marriage that will get her whole family out. It's an unlikely thing to hope for, but still she's waiting for something like that to happen.

"Next, I spoke with her father and the conversation still seems very strange to me. Understand that I am thirty-seven years old and I have never really come close to marrying. I've had opportunities, even a few girlfriends in Taipei, and of course my family wants me to marry and have children. But nothing inside me feels strong enough to say yes. So it's strange that I find myself talking to Kai-ling's father, telling him about my factories in Guangzhou, telling him about my success, telling him that I'm thinking about starting a factory in Urumchi. It occurs to me then that I'm willing to start up such a factory, although it would certainly fail, just to have a chance to marry his daughter." It appeared to embarrass him, this admission. Incredulous, Gwa threw up his hands and slumped back in his seat. Call me foolhardy, he seemed to be saying. Call me reckless. "But it's all much more complicated than that," he continued. "Because even if her father agrees to allow a marriage, there are all kinds of problems. Political problems, you understand? Taiwanese can't marry Mainland Chinese. There's no law against it, but there's no procedure, no paperwork, no communication on either side that would make such a marriage possible. A person might try bribes and favors, but one would have to appeal to both sides and it would be complicated and take a long time. Another idea is to wait. My friends in the government are saying that in a year or two the Taipei court will start issuing special identity cards, and with this card you can get a marriage certificate in the Mainland. Again it's all slow and very complicated, but only for the Taiwanese. For foreigners it's different. Americans, Europeans, Australians can marry a Mainland Chinese much more easily. They've been doing it for several years. For example, an American could travel to the Mainland and meet a Chinese woman and their requirements to marry would be much simpler—a physical exam, a little paperwork, a written release from the woman's work unit. Not so difficult, really. You understand what I'm getting at?"

Slowly, shyly, Vincent nodded. Given the circumstance, it seemed like the only safe gesture he knew.

"I should explain first," Gwa said. "It would have to be someone I trust. The same way I trust Ponic. You may not think so much of him, but I would trust him with money and the woman I plan to marry. There are a lot of foreigners in Taiwan. I've met a few here and there, several in Taipei. However, when I talk with them, I see that they're only here to make money or find women for themselves. You're different. I saw that right away. You could make a promise, and I would trust you to keep it."

Vincent felt his face redden, a blush of recognition. "I think I understand what this is all about," he said, almost giddy from the strangeness of it all. "But you have to remember that I'm a Jesus teacher."

"Yes, of course you are. I'm glad about that."

"I mean I have responsibilities."

"Of course you do," Gwa said, grinning, as if these responsibilities were not hindrances but further evidence of Vincent's rightness for the job. "I was in Hong Kong last week on business, and I was able to send a message to Kai-ling's father. I explained my idea, told him that I had someone in mind who could come to Urumchi and marry Kai-ling in my place. I would give her family a large dowry. If the father has some connections in the government, he could use them to get his family out of Urumchi. So you would take a lot of money with you. Money for the dowry. Money for yourself. You would have to be careful." He'd softened his voice to pronounce the word *careful*. His nodding glance carried an odd mingling of caution and bare hope.

"Still," Gwa continued, "the family would insist on a wedding and that might take some time. It will take time also for you both to receive a marriage certificate and for Kai-ling to be granted a Hong Kong visa. So yes, going there, having the wedding, accompanying Kai-ling out of China to Hong Kong, then back to Taiwan—a month, maybe less. Afterward you can get a divorce. I know that's a common thing for Americans, so it shouldn't be difficult. Maybe later, when you're back alone in America, you can just pretend you were never married."

"This is just crazy," Vincent said. "You can't make plans like that, without me knowing, and expect me to agree."

"I know it's a big favor to ask and so I would pay you. Would you like to know how much?"

"I don't care how much because I have other—"

"Ten thousand United States dollars. Five thousand when you leave. Five when you get back. You pay all travel expenses for yourself and Kai-ling, but in the Mainland that won't be much."

Vincent sighed in exasperation. It was a heavy, prolonged sigh and during it he had time for a fleeting consideration of what ten thousand dollars would mean. Relief from the burden of family debts. From bank debt as well. A fraction of the money, sixteen or seventeen hundred, left over. Yet he was, just lately, managing these debts well enough on his own. And he couldn't simply pick up and leave Toulio for a month, not without an honest explanation to Reverend Phillips. "I have responsibilities. I work for a man in Taipei, a respected Jesus teacher, and I've already made promises to him."

"So keep your promises. Tell your boss you're going away for a month. Tell him you're helping a friend and you'll be right back."

"It's not that simple. I've promised to *stay* in Toulio, to live here for two years, to teach Bible study classes." He halted in his list, struck by yet another obligation. "There's a second Jesus teacher coming soon. She's in

Taipei now, but she . . . my sister . . . is coming to Toulio. My sister is coming, and I have to be here to meet her at the station, to look after her because she doesn't know anyone."

"That's not a problem," Gwa reasoned. "I can help you with that. There are people in this town, people I've worked with and trust, who would be happy to . . ." And on he went, advancing his extravagant cause, meeting every objection, every muddied excuse or niggling pretense move for move with a purely reasonable solution. He pledged to look after Vincent's sister. Ponic would be her chauffeur for the month. Introductions would be made on her behalf. As for Vincent's boss in Taipei, a carefully worded request for leave time could be put forth, a donation made. Occasionally a hint of brusqueness would mar Gwa's easy answers, or his hands would squeeze shut, and he would flex his knuckles against the edge of the kitchen table. Small emblems of distress. A distracted, fidgety impatience. It was hard to know from this how he would receive a firm refusal, if he would take his answer and brood, if he would lash out.

But his very persistence, his craving to persuade, was itself a small marvel. Beneath it Vincent sensed a whole other stratum of craving—for the woman, for Kai-ling. He supposed *passion* was the word for it, though *passion* seemed overheated, disconcertingly private.

And could you stand in the way of passion?

Yes, he guessed, you could. For a hundred practical reasons, but mostly because abandoning the new ministry house, if just for a month, felt too much like outright failure.

"Even if it could all be arranged," Vincent said, "even if my boss agreed to let me go, I still wouldn't do it. I wouldn't do it because I don't feel right about it. About marrying someone I don't even know. It's such a strange—such a crazy thing to ask someone to do. I mean, what do you expect?"

Gwa's tight-lipped, afflicted answer was that he expected Vincent to think about his offer, see the sense in it, and say yes. "Say yes," he insisted, or rather demanded, as if he were speaking to a young child or an imbecile. Then he cursed and whatever frustration he'd kept in check vaulted beyond his control. His face was wrenched momentarily into a spasm of loathing—a grave, fervent-eyed, even comely loathing, but still terrible—and afterward he tried to collect himself and press on with his campaign, only to waver and loose momentum.

For some time while they talked there had been a general commotion in the lane outside the ministry house. Folk music and glad, boozy voices and now the sputtering and delayed crackle of what sounded like Roman candles.

"Fireworks," Gwa said miserably. "Tomorrow's the last day of celebrations. After that we all go back to work. A few weeks from now—first month of the lunar calendar, March of the regular one—Kai-ling turns twenty-eight. It wouldn't mean much for an unmarried man, but for a woman . . ."

"I'm sorry I can't be the one to help you," Vincent said.

"If a woman's not married by thirty, most people believe she never will be. So at twenty-eight even a beautiful woman starts to get nervous. A kind of panic sets in. She's counting the days. She could do anything, yes? Someone she would never consider marrying a few years earlier, a station clerk, say, suddenly becomes a possibility. She could make any kind of choice." Soured by disappointment, Gwa lit another cigarette, panted out its acrid fumes, wincing through the scrim of tobacco smoke whenever Vincent, in a shrinking tenor of voice, explained how sorry he was, how truly sorry.

"You're not nearly sorry enough," Gwa said. "With you I've done nothing but waste my time." He gathered up his travel book, his photograph of Kai-ling, and made ready to leave. Yet still he sat awhile longer and brooded, and when his cigarette had burned down to nothing more than a crimped filter, he glanced derisively, pointedly at Vincent, threw open the wok lid, and tossed the filter into the still-simmering hot pot stew.

Eight

SHE WAS NOT so much overweight, this Gloria Hamilton, as she was solidly, vigorously built. Vincent saw her squeezing through the revolving gate of the Toulio train station. A bottleneck of sorts had formed, caused in no small part by Gloria's mammoth orange backpack. A throng of stymied passengers began straining against the pack. It slipped free all at once, and while those behind her stumbled and regained their footing, Gloria, unfazed, walked toward Vincent in a flat, manly gait.

What he noticed first—noticed with a stab of shame, because he was never the type to ogle—were her high, cone-shaped breasts, sturdy, bullet-like humps mantled by an oversize afghan sweater that stretched down past her hips to the fringes of her knees. Her face was soft and rather expressionless—buttoned, moist lips pressed between two full and hardily scrubbed cheeks.

"I'm Vincent Saunders." He helped her settle the pack onto the station floor. His voice had faltered and he despised himself for feeling such disappointment at the sight of her.

"Thank goodness you're here waiting for me," she said.

It seemed to reach each of them then, that they were no longer scraps of anecdote and conjecture passed along by Reverend Phillips, that they were at last verifiable to each other—partners, siblings, housemates. They walked to the parking lot and she gazed out at Toulio's main avenue, its clamorous hub, no doubt reconciling her own imaginings, as Vincent once had, to the hard, glaring fact of the place.

"I don't know about this. . . ." she began. "I don't know if this is something I can actually do."

A befuddled moment passed before he understood she was referring to his rickety motorcycle and not to their assignment as volunteers. "Nothing to worry about," he assured her. "Just strap on the pack. Sit. Balance in the middle."

"I've never ridden on the back of one before," she said. "Won't I burn my legs? That's what I always hear happens the first time."

"Of course you won't. Just keep your feet on the pegs." He started the engine, perhaps with more throttle than necessary, and she took several hasty steps backward.

"No," she said. "This isn't something I'm willing to do."

And so they proceeded to the ministry house, Vincent riding ahead and leading Gloria in a taxi along streets that now, in the dinner hour, had grown uncommonly still. A few children crouched on doorsteps, gripping rice bowls and chopsticks, pedaling food into their mouths in fluid, habitual turns of the wrist. Vincent drove on, perplexed by his own rudeness. He reminded himself, once they arrived and entered the ministry house, to be courteous. He bore her weighty pack and watched as Gloria stepped hesitantly through the unfamiliar rooms. She wasn't hungry, she said. She had eaten on the train and all she wanted now was to shower and rest. He followed her up to the second-floor bedroom, pained somewhat that she hadn't commented, one way or the other, on the house or her room. He set the pack inside the doorway.

"Thank you," she said. She pulled the pack to the side of the bed. Her hands, in contrast to her sturdy physique, were slender, almost delicate. "I know it's heavy. I packed books and my calligraphy supplies. The ink blocks are especially heavy, but I have to practice, you know, practice every day and . . ." Her voice trailed off to a drowsy whisper.

"You're welcome," Vincent said. "You sleep now and maybe we'll have a look around Toulio tomorrow." He said good night and slipped back downstairs.

Later, after dinner, he settled himself on the living room sofa and placed an overseas call to Red Bud. As the operator put the call through, Vincent removed his wristwatch and set it by the phone. Ten minutes would cost him forty U.S. dollars. This was a luxury he allowed himself every two months. His mother answered. It was early morning in Red Bud, and Vincent envisioned bright sunlight spilling through the kitchen window and tinting the rim of her ceramic flowerpots. He wanted, as he had wanted during previous phone calls, to somehow seek forgiveness for having left his parents alone in their Red Bud farmhouse. Everything was fine, he assured her. This was definitely not an emergency. He was just calling to talk. Six minutes of family news. Everyone was healthy. Vanessa had gotten a full-time-job offer from a well-known Chicago museum. She was dating a nice young man from Canada, an architect. There'd been an employee caught stealing from patients at the nursing home where his mother worked. A shame, too, because the story had made the local TV news. Vincent's father had tendonitis in one knee and now wore a brace when he drove the car. At St. Mark's they were holding silent auctions each month to raise money for a new furnace. "Are you all right?" she asked. "You must get lonely over there."

Within those two words, *over there,* Vincent could feel his mother's vague conception of Taiwan, distant and otherworldly. Again he assured her he was fine. He told her of his luck with the ministry house, told her of Gloria's recent arrival in Toulio. "I'm so glad you have somebody there with you now," she said. "That makes me feel better."

Yes, he agreed. He felt better, too. He said a few hurried good-byes, love to everyone. He said he thought he would be home within a year and a half. "I love you and don't worry," he said, and set the receiver in its cradle.

In bed that night he listened to Gloria's slow breathing across the bedroom's open wall. He thought of the Bible study classes they would teach, the countless introductions to be made. *This is my sister, Gloria,* he practiced in a tepid inner voice. *Please welcome her to the ministry house.* It was not the lying that concerned him, but rather how the perception of them as brother and sister would yoke them together in people's minds. Comparisons would be made. A certain brotherly affection would be expected of him. Already he felt the squeeze of family obligation.

The next morning he woke and listened for her. There was no sound coming from her bedroom. He dressed and plodded downstairs, where he found the door to the little room beneath the staircase hanging open. Gloria was inside, kneeling before a cardboard box.

"What's going on?" Vincent asked.

She stood and squinted anxiously in his direction. "I know this will seem strange, but I'm going to make my bedroom out down here, in this room."

"What?" he asked. "How's that?"

"I need my bedroom to be here because I practice my translation at least five hours a day, sometimes more, sometimes very late at night. I need a small, closed-in place where I can't get distracted. I had a place just like this in Taipei and it worked out fine."

"There's no light or windows."

"I can get a lamp, and I prefer not to have windows. Remember what I said about distractions?"

"Distractions," Vincent said. He contemplated the room's litter. "All right, I guess. Just don't throw any of this out. The landlady is worried about that sort of thing."

"I won't," she promised.

"Are you sure about this?" he asked. "I mean, did I do something wrong?"

"I'm positive about the room and, no, you haven't done a thing wrong so far." She bent over and continued filling the box with paint cans and detergent bottles. Vincent turned and ascended the stairs. In his own bedroom, he stood baffled. Beneath him, he could hear Gloria dragging the box across the cement floor, the dull echo of her footsteps inside the dim, windowless room.

Though the New Year's holidays had passed, evidence of the celebration lingered in the town's alleyway trash heaps. Vincent, out posting more English-lesson flyers, edged past piles of frayed banners and rose-colored paper lanterns. At several street corners he waded through knee-deep drifts of burnt firecracker casings. Now and then, he paused amid the debris and wondered what, if anything, he had missed.

A week after Gloria's arrival, students began filing into the ministry house and taking seats in the third-floor classroom. As the lesson commenced, Vincent scanned the class for familiar faces. Mr. Yao had returned and brought along his teenaged daughter. The Ping twins were seated in the far corner, dressed in matching green sweaters. He estimated that he had lost nearly half of his students over the holidays, but the latest string of flyers had drawn a sizable crowd of new ones. In simple terms of attendance, he could report that the ministry house appeared to be prospering.

Earlier that afternoon he and Gloria had sat down, much like Reverend Phillips recommended, to get the details straight. He had expected a complicated rehashing of their previous lives, perhaps note-taking and memorization of important dates and places. But they had few options in the matter because Vincent had already told the class that he had grown up in Red Bud, that both parents had worked in the Singer appliance factory, and that he had one sibling, a sister, four years his senior. Gloria had no choice but to take Vincent's last name and occupy his real sister's place in his family. She did not seem to mind assuming her adoptive role or adding three years to her correct age. Even when she practiced the names of Vincent's parents, Marion and Carl, she did so easefully and with a gracious regard.

In class Vincent stood and delivered a polite introduction in formal Chinese while Gloria waited in the hallway. "It gives me great happiness to introduce you to the ministry's newest volunteer. Her name is Gloria, and I am especially pleased to have her in Toulio because," and here he held his tongue for just an instant, "she's my sister."

The students raised their voices, a collective murmur of surprise. Gloria stepped to the fore of the room and from the pocket of her plaid skirt withdrew a sheet of paper containing long, vertical lines of handwritten characters. She gazed timidly into this paper, and, after the room ebbed into silence, began addressing the class.

The words she spoke were Chinese, Vincent decided, but her pronunciation was so poor, the four tones of inflection so randomly employed, that her speech amounted to little more than an incoherent tangle of shallow mumblings and emphatic trills. She rambled on in this monologue for several minutes without lifting her eyes from the paper. The students, meanwhile, traded flurried glances or shifted uncomfortably in their seats. At last she concluded her speech, made an apprehensive survey of her audience before returning her gaze to the paper's deep folds. She turned toward Vincent with a tight, weary frown of resignation that seemed to indicate her worst misgivings about the speech had now come true.

And then a reversal of sorts, a face-saving change. Gloria turned again and pointed to the chalkboard. She stepped up to the board, fished out a piece of chalk from the tray, and began recording characters in a progression of smooth, concise strokes. She worked from top to bottom, and the characters she produced were uniformly balanced and graceful. From time to time she pressed her forehead to the slate and concentrated, but mostly she allowed her delicate hand to drift down the board transcribing unwavering lines, sweeping arcs, and apostrophe-like slashes, all from memory.

A young man seated in the front row leaned in Vincent's direction and whispered, "Clever girl, your sister."

Other pupils were equally impressed. A few studied the chalkboard and scribbled quick notations inside their notebooks. Gloria's round hips swiveled as she worked, and several of the class's older gentlemen, Mr. Yao among them, appeared to be as charmed by her robust physical qualities as by her calligraphic skill.

Mrs. Ling raised her hand and in Chinese asked Gloria how long she had been practicing her characters. Gloria listened intently to the question. Soon her eyes wandered up to the water-marked ceiling tiles, and Vincent realized she had no idea what the woman had asked.

"She asked how long you've been studying written Chinese," he offered.

Gloria erased a small corner of the board and inscribed a trio of descending characters, all three incomprehensible to Vincent. The class responded with applause.

A middle-aged housewife asked her to please describe the province of Illinois. Vincent translated the question, and Gloria wrote out a lengthy answer. He interpreted other remarks and questions, yet Gloria made no outward acknowledgment that he was speaking to her in English. She pretended as if the question, posed in Chinese, needed to linger in her brain several moments before blossoming into a sudden and perfect comprehension. Then she would turn toward the board and inscribe her answer. This caused Vincent sharp pangs of irritation. He averted his eyes to stop himself from witnessing this charade. Nevertheless, he knew that he was guilty of a similar pretense. After she wrote out a line of characters on the board, Vincent sometimes found himself bobbing his head as if he understood and agreed with her response.

They taught the class together in this somewhat odd and disjointed manner. It took time for him to translate questions, additional time for Gloria to write her reply on the board. Gradually, they fell into a more focused and organized routine. This began with simple conversation drills in which Vincent stood before the class and read aloud from the evening's lesson: *Mark went to the park with Mr. Jones on Tuesday.* The class repeated this, and he followed up with a series of questions.

"Where did Mark go? Who did Mark go with? When did they go?"

Gloria guided the class in their response, a chorus of monotone voices goose-stepping their way to the correct answer.

Mark went to the park.

Mark went to the park with Mis-ter Jones.

Mark went to the park with Mis-ter Jones on Tues-day.

After the drills, they broke for ten minutes of informal chitchat. A few students gathered around Gloria and exchanged slips of paper containing hastily written messages. When they resumed, Gloria helped lead the class in repetitions of Bible psalms. She also contributed to the second hour by recording short essays on the chalkboard. At times she labored away in a frantic pantomime, sometimes underlining or repeatedly circling a single character for special emphasis. Vincent yearned to know the content of her discourse; however, his pride kept him from revealing the full extent of his illiteracy. The only clues he had were the students' reactions— ranging from boredom to subtle skepticism to open approval—and also their sporadic questions. Mr. Yao's daughter, still in her school uniform, examined Gloria's writing and asked, "What do you mean by God's special plan for the youth of Taiwan?" This caused Gloria to produce a flood of frantically charted calligraphy. She filled one side of the board, flipped it over, and set to work on the fresh slate. Vincent, standing at the very rear of the class, shook his head in wry wonder. Look at her go, he thought. She could be putting forth any manner of opinion without him knowing. He would never have expected such a quandary, or such outright peevishness on his part. What a peculiar situation, truly. Of everyone gathered in the classroom, he was the most suspicious, the most tempted to raise his hand in dissent.

Nine

WITHOUT CHAGRIN OR even a trace of contradiction, Jonathan Hwang informed Vincent that his new class at the Ming-da Academy would be comprised of forty-two teenaged girls. "The contest and the judging were both fair," Hwang said, and then wiggled his bony fingers to suggest the fickle nature of chance. "They're meeting with the principal now. I'll send them over as soon as they finish." He made an aloof, stiff-shouldered bow and left Vincent with a key to the language laboratory.

Once inside, Vincent found the room's consoles and chairs in pristine order. He practiced writing on the glossy board with erasable markers, forming loops and squiggled lines and words, and then wiping away everything but the word *welcome,* which he underlined in red and blue. Standing at the head of the class, before a waist-high lectern, he imagined himself in a white lab coat shuffling beakers and test tubes, and with a sudden smoky fizzle, distilling verbs, nouns, adjectives.

A sparkling panel of windows ran along the laboratory's south wall, and through them he could see the sweeping Ming-da courtyard. Soon a tidy column of students advanced from the east wing, swung left, and crossed under the spindly shadow of Chiang Kai-shek. They made a procession-like turn into the main building and moments later reappeared in two parallel lines outside the laboratory door. They all wore deep maroon uniforms with gold crests sewn to their lapels, and as they waited to enter, they shifted about, eagerly straightening one another's collars and shirtsleeves.

They carried this same air of regimented discipline into the class-room, where they paired off in four long rows and took their seats while a delegated student, the class secretary, called out attendance. She then held out the attendance booklet for Vincent to sign. The class president and vice president stepped forward and presented a typed letter in English from their school principal. It stated that their class had competed in and won a school-wide English competition. The letter went on to declare them an able and worthy class that had been given the distinct privilege of studying English conversation on Tuesday and Thursday afternoons with a highly honored, foreign-born master of English.

Vincent smiled at the tone of the letter. He already suspected—from a brief but polite exchange of words with the class president—that their language ability might outrival the simple lessons he had developed for his Bible study class. He began with his now standard model sentence: *Mark went to the park with Mr. Jones on Tuesday.* The class repeated this in an eager, melodic singsong, their pronunciation exceptionally clear.

He pointed to a girl in the first seat of the first row. "Where did Mark go?" he asked.

The girl rose to her feet. She stood taller than most of her classmates and wore wire-rimmed glasses. "To the park," she replied.

"Good answer," Vincent said. "But I would like you to answer in a complete sentence. Do you understand what I mean, complete sentence?"

"Yes," she said. She gazed timidly about the room, looking to her classmates for encouragement. "Well," she began. "As you told us, Mark went to the park with Mr. Jones on Tuesday. But I think that maybe he went to one or two other areas. Perhaps he went to the cinema to see a foreign movie or perhaps he went to the zoo to see the lovely panda bears."

Vincent could hardly contain his delight. He made a great show of wadding up his lesson plan and throwing it in the waste bin. "You're too clever for that," he told the class. They applauded the announcement and favored him with bright, self-satisfied smiles. Now lessonless, he resorted to drawing a map of America on the board and then described the state of Illinois and his hometown of Red Bud. He rounded out the hour-long lesson by having each student ask him a question. They began with the standard inquiries, familiar questions that had been put to Vincent both by students in other classes and by complete strangers on trains and buses. How old are you? Are you married? How many people are in your family? Then questions of finance, which the Taiwanese considered perfectly acceptable topics of conversation. How much money do you make each month? How much is a car in America? And last, several odd queries, ones, Vincent suspected, the girls had simply translated into English from their homework assignments. Why is Taiwan the true China? How does the color red affect your mood? A student in the back row asked him to please describe the heroic natures of Chiang Kai-shek and Dr. Sun Yat-sen.

He answered all these questions with great care. He praised Taiwan and its national heroes, stated prudently that the situation in the Mainland was unfortunate. All the personal questions he answered truthfully, with the exception of those concerning his invented sister, Gloria, and his monthly salary. This he reduced to half its amount so the students would not think him too money-minded.

Before they left, he outlined a seating chart and worked his way down the long rows writing their names in the square grids. They all insisted on English names, which ranged from the customary, Sally and Christina, to the unconventional, Cookie and Snoopy. Violet proved to be a highly sought-after name. Three girls claimed it as their own, and when none of the three would accept another name, Vincent dubbed them Violet One, Violet Two, and Violet Three. At the end of the third row, a slim girl with large, sleepy eyes peered into his chart and said, "My Chinese name is Ch'iu Yüeh, which means 'Autumn Moon,' but I choose the English name Trudy because it is a lovely name and because it is a true name." Vincent penciled this in and when he lifted his eyes from the paper, she was tilting her head up toward him with a fondly amused grin.

During the course of succeeding lessons, Vincent learned that the girls were all third-year students, all either sixteen or seventeen years old. Evidently their high school had chosen a British English curriculum. Thus, their vocabulary was sprinkled with phrases such as *waiting in the queue, my auntie from Taipei,* and *my bright red jumper.* They used the word *lovely* to describe everything from fried rice to Generalissimo Chiang Kai-shek. They shared a troublesome habit of lifting large, powerfully charged words from their Chinese-English dictionaries and inserting them clumsily into otherwise plain sentences: *My plan to go to the department store was demolished by my father.*

As proficient as they were in their English speaking, there remained long, uncomfortable pauses during class conversation. They understood his questions and knew the answers, and yet when asked to stand and speak, many became paralyzed with shyness. Collectively, they put forth a restrained, virginal sense of propriety that caused them to blush over the most minor mistakes and incidents. The word *kiss* discovered in a long list of English vocabulary made their faces redden and their hands fly up and cover their mouths. Most extraordinary of all was their ability to witness a single event—a joke, a mispronounced word—and react in a strikingly similar way, often mirroring one another's exact expressions. Vincent could enter the class and cunningly pretend to trip over the lectern's wooden base and send every girl reeling with laughter. How easily amused they were, and how beautiful, too. Their hair was dark and thick; their school did not allow them to wear it long, but even short it was full and clean and, he imagined, softly textured. Their bodies were slender with delicate, narrow waists, and they were shapely and tender in a way Vincent decided he was best off not thinking about.

On one particular Tuesday afternoon, Vincent turned from writing on the chalkboard and spied a hand in the back row bouncing fervently above his dark-haired audience. He glanced at his seating chart, called out the student's name, Trudy, and she stood.

"Teacher Vincent, do you have a girlfriend?" Trudy asked.

Because many people in Toulio knew he was a single male teacher, and an enigmatic foreigner as well, this had been another common question, one he consistently responded to with a good-natured no.

"No, I don't have a girlfriend." He shrugged amiably.

"Would you say," Trudy continued, "that I have a chance to become your girlfriend?"

The other students gasped in astonishment. A few girls raised tremulous hands to their lips. Trudy's question, it seemed, was not just an off-color remark. It was a stunner, an unexpected showstopper that bore down upon the class—the girls sank visibly in their seats—and produced a blunt, unbridgeable silence. Trudy herself was absolutely beaming; she had straightened her pose, widened her already large eyes in anticipation of his reply.

Against her prompting, against the class's stunned reaction, Vincent struggled for an answer. It had to be something witty enough to lighten the oppressive climate, but also uncomplicated enough so that everyone was sure to understand. He could not think of a single response.

Finally, after far too long a pause, he said, "No, Trudy, I'm at least six years older than you and I'm also your teacher. I would say you have no chance."

Trudy, still beaming, remained undaunted by this answer. "Thank you," she said, smiling resolutely, bowing into her seat as if she'd just been granted a compliment.

After the hour had finished, the class president and vice president stayed behind in the room.

"Teacher Vincent, we apologize for our classmate," the president said. "She has a . . . a . . ."

". . . a broken thing in her mind," the vice president interjected.

"What kind of broken thing?" Vincent asked. He was curious now that the room's tension had dissipated.

The president thought hard, rubbed her index finger and thumb together as if she could produce words with this kind of friction. The vice president flipped through her dictionary. They leaned their heads together and consulted a moment.

"Don't know how to say in English," the president said.

The class met again the following Thursday, a windy, overcast shadow of a day. Vincent arrived at the academy and as he made his way across the courtyard, he heard a timorous voice call out his name. He turned and saw Trudy jogging toward him from the east wing, holding her uniform skirt against her legs so that it did not flip unexpectedly in the wind. Apparently, she had raced well ahead of her classmates in order to gain his attention before he stepped into the building. She slowed to a walk, a prettily cautious stride, and smoothed out her disheveled hair, which had been cut unevenly in ragged layers, like a farmboy's.

"Teacher Vincent," she said, out of breath and looking down at the courtyard pavement. "I'm sorry I said the thing to you on Tuesday. I said the thing so my classmates would laugh. I'm sorry your face became pink. I think I must be a very stupid girl."

Her entire manner was one of such humility and overwhelming shyness that Vincent felt immediately uneasy for her. He suspected that her classmates had put her up to this apology. Perhaps they had all confronted her after the incident and made her feel far worse than was necessary. "It's nothing. Just forget about it," Vincent consoled her. "I knew you were joking."

Her eyes remained fixed on the pavement.

"Really," he said. "There's nothing to feel bad about now."

She sighed then and lifted her head a bit, the corners of her mouth creasing outward in a faint suggestion of a smile.

In class, Vincent drilled the students on their use of comparative adjectives. *Cindy is honest, but George is more honest. Mary is the most honest of them all.* The girls chimed along. Later, as he gave instructions for an upcoming speech assignment, he observed Trudy seeking his attention with vehement waves of her hand. He wasn't yet ready to begin taking questions. Still, there was something peculiarly urgent in the way she waited for him to call on her. She held her hand high and tracked him with a tenacious gaze.

"Teacher Vincent," she said aloud, interrupting the class. She had already risen to her feet, and Vincent decided against criticizing her for the interruption and hoped instead that this was some kind of attempt to redeem herself in the eyes of her classmates. "Yes?" he asked.

She cleared her throat and said, "Mary is a splendid swimmer, but George is a more splendid swimmer. Teacher Vincent is the most splendid swimmer of them all."

"That's correct," Vincent said. "That's very good."

"Yes, it is," she agreed. "And I would very much like to see you swimming in the blue ocean. Do you know why I plan to see you swimming there?"

The class was well aware that things had gone amiss. The president and vice president exchanged pained expressions. More than a few of Trudy's classmates were trying to signal her quiet with their fingers pressed tightly against their lips.

"No, but I want you to stop—"

"Because!" she said, and the exultant pitch of her voice rang out over his. "Because I would very much like to see the lovely muscles of your body."

"All right," he sighed. "That's enough already."

"I'm thinking about you now," Trudy said, lowering her pale eyelids and bowing her head in concentration. "You're in the ocean. I see you there, all alone, and I see that you really are the most splendid swimmer."

"That's enough," Vincent ordered. "Sit down, Trudy." The forcefulness in his voice proved unnecessary. She was already stooping down, easing casually into her chair. Vincent took a moment to compose himself and then went back to discussing the short speech assignment due the following week. The girls, with the exception of Trudy, sat dumbstruck and frozen, their embarrassment, their shame, acute and, as always, shared. It wasn't until almost the end of the lesson that any kind of natural rhythm returned to the class. When the bell rang, Trudy rose and filed out the door as if nothing had happened.

Over the weekend, Vincent worried about Trudy's speech project, what her topic might be and into which distressing avenues she might digress. What stayed with him most was Trudy's remarkable composure during both her apology and her outburst. All weekend he wavered back and forth, unable to decide when she had been acting and when she had been earnest.

His anxiety turned out to be uncalled for. Trudy did not attend class Tuesday or the following Thursday. When she did not show the next week, Vincent asked the class president if Trudy was ill.

"No," the president said. "Now Trudy goes every day to the other Toulio high school."

"Why is that?"

"Well," the president said. "Please wait a minute and I'll tell you." She stepped up to the board and wrote out a single character. As if on cue, all her classmates pulled out their Chinese-English dictionaries and raced to find the translation.

Violet Two found the entry first. "Ex-pel or kick out," she reported.

"Yes," the president said. "She made big problems in one, two, three other classes. Not just your class. So the principal said good-bye, Trudy." The other girls giggled and nodded accordingly. Perhaps they had seen her expulsion coming. At the very least they appeared to relish the principal's decision. Now, they leaned back in their seats and exchanged ecstatic tidbits of gossip.

Vincent saw surprisingly little of Gloria outside the ministry classroom. They did not often go out for meals together; Gloria preferred simple noodle and rice dishes, which she prepared in the ministry kitchen. Moreover, their sleeping hours were nearly opposite. Vincent, always an early riser, was frequently in bed before eleven o'clock. As he prepared himself for sleep, he would find Gloria in the kitchen mixing a towering mug of instant coffee. She would offer a cordial good night and then retreat to her odd supply-closet bedroom. With the door closed tight, she turned on her bright work lamp. Vincent could see a narrow band of light upon the threshold. Then he heard music seeping through the thin walls. She had brought to Toulio both a tape player and a small library of cassettes, a collection of her favorite songs all recorded from the same Christian radio station in Nebraska. Between songs were snatches of recorded commentary from a silk-voiced announcer: *That was Melinda Collins Young with "My Mother's Angel Eyes" and this is the voice of faith and religious freedom transmitting out of Omaha, across the highways and byways and fields of ripe corn into your homes, into your ears, and into your hearts.*

Vincent drifted off to sleep lulled by the soft murmur of this voice, and if he woke early enough, he might shamble downstairs in the predawn darkness and find Gloria's light still on, the tape player turned down to a soft hush. He could hear her riffling through papers, the shuffle of her feet on the concrete floor. Soon, she would switch off the light and fall into bed and not emerge from her room until midafternoon. While she slept, Vincent moved about the ground floor, easing himself from one room to another with light, judicious steps.

One evening he discovered Gloria's thick-leafed artist sketchbook on the living room tea table. She was not one for leaving her things scattered about the rooms; in fact, during her first month in the ministry house, she had revealed herself to be an even more secretive and reclusive housemate than Alec. In the bathroom, she kept her soap, toothpaste, and shampoo in a waterproof box beneath the sink. Her coffee and creamer and her groceries, dry foods and perishables alike, were sequestered in various corners of the cupboard and refrigerator. She had never warned Vincent about borrowing or examining these items, but he understood, implicitly, that she regarded her possessions as separate and private.

He opened the sketchbook and peered inside.

Each page contained ten neat rows of calligraphy, ten characters per row, every character recorded with painstaking precision one hundred times. He turned a dozen more pages and was struck by the sheer ardor of Gloria's effort, her devotion to minute detail. Several pages appeared indistinguishable until closer inspection unveiled subtle differences between two seemingly identical sets of characters: an arcing tail that flourished right rather than left, three top-sided garnishing strikes instead of two.

He heard the front door swing open and the low scuffing of Gloria's footsteps on the kitchen floor. He had ample time to close the sketchbook and center it on the table, but there was still the imposing question of what exactly he was doing there on the sofa, the sketchbook the only possible object of interest within arm's length. She nodded toward him and uttered, "Hey, Vincent," as she treaded to her modest bedroom. She stopped and turned. "Hey," she said again. "Did I leave that out?"

"I guess you did," Vincent said. He picked up the sketchbook and held it out. The guilty pressure of it against his fingers caused him to admit his treachery. "I glanced through it, I mean, I hope you don't mind, but it really shows your hard work. I don't know much about writing characters, but it all seems very precise."

Gloria accepted the book, the cast of her face as unreadable as ever. She flipped through several pages examining her own calligraphy. "It's harder than it looks. It's—I'm not bragging, but I've come a long way in eighteen months. You know I'm working from the same set of primers the kids use in school. About every two months I move up to another grade level. Do you know what that means? I'm learning the same vocabulary a student in Taiwan learns in one school year, except I'm learning it in two months."

"That's terrific. And what grade are you in now?"

"Soon I'll be in the fifth grade," she said solemnly. "It takes the average foreigner five years to become fluent enough to read a newspaper. If I keep at this pace, I'll be reading newspapers in less than a year. And I'll be doing other things, too."

"Like what?" Vincent asked.

"Well, translation for one thing, and something else." She ran her fingers along the sketchbook's metal spirals. "It's a special project I'm working on in my spare time. I showed it to Reverend Phillips and he likes the idea. A lot," she added. "Do you want to see it?"

"All right."

She made a beeline for her room and returned a moment later with another sketchbook. She sat beside Vincent on the wooden sofa and in her enthusiasm leaned intrusively against his left shoulder. He could smell the perfumed scent of her hair mixed with a more earthy, metallic odor of black ink.

She placed the sketchbook on the table before him, but held her hand on the cover. "I want to explain a few things before you look," she said eagerly. "What we're doing in Taiwan is trying to bring the Word of God to as many people as we can, young or old, men or women, whomever. But I really think, Vincent, that our best chance is with the teenagers. I mean, we should try for everyone, but the odds are better with adolescents because they already like things from America—you know, movies and music, pop culture things, right?"

"Right," Vincent echoed.

"Well, one of the things they really enjoy are these things like comic books, except they're not just comic books, they're longer and more involved. They're called graphic novels and the idea came from Japan. The kids read them all the time and the bookstores in Taipei are just full of them. My idea is to create a Christian graphic novel for the youth of Taiwan."

She raised the cover to reveal a collage of neatly framed boxes. The illustrations within these boxes were as precise as her calligraphy. One displayed the outline of Taiwan drifting forlornly in the East China Sea. In the corner, a motherly faced angel gazed down on the island with gracious good intent. Every box contained a kindred symbol of Christianity, a glowing Bible or cross that radiated light into darker corners of the panel. Gloria flipped ahead to a vast and intricately designed illustration that occupied an entire page. "This is the big one," she said. "This is the one I've worked hardest on. When it's published, it'll take up two pages in the book."

Vincent's eyes descended first to the center of the drawing, a Chinese boy and girl standing beside each other with calm, purposeful expressions. One held a Bible, the other a cross. Standing behind them and resting one hand on each of their shoulders was a Caucasian woman bearing an uncanny resemblance to Gloria. It was a finely detailed likeness with one exception: instead of Gloria's true-life wooden demeanor, her cartoon twin had been granted a face of extraordinary articulation, the eyes wide and deeply etched, brimming with emotion, a smile both confident and supremely generous.

What remained of the drawing fell away into two halves. The right side featured a temple celebration that had escalated into a grimly frantic revelry of worship. Firepot flames were enhanced so that they twisted upward, casting discordant light onto garish sculptures of temple gods. The ceremony participants either paraded, Druidlike, between temple columns or stood on the periphery of the fire, their eyebrows canting downward in fierce concentration. The left half formed a mosaic of Taiwan's social ills: three prostitutes loitering outside a massage parlor, a drunken businessman slumped beside a cigarette vendor's cart, a gambler waving an angry fist at his pachinko machine. They all appeared as residents of a particularly corrupt neighborhood populated by street thugs and derelicts. On the corner of one cartoon avenue, Vincent spotted a white-robed Buddhist monk, his shoulders slumped in defeat, his forearms extended outward in tremulous self-doubt.

"Wow," Vincent whispered. His eyes drifted back to Gloria's radiant self-portrait. "This is really something, Gloria. This is, well . . . this is very strong stuff."

"You don't like it?" she asked stiffly. She shifted her weight away from him and reached out to close the sketchbook.

"It's not that," he said. "You're a really fine artist, but I've been to temples. I've seen celebrations with firepots, and it's not quite like this. I guess what I'm saying is the message is really strong."

"Well, don't you think the message *needs* to be strong?"

"I suppose you're right," Vincent conceded. He now had a taste of her contentiousness, a preview of what might easily become a strained, impersonal life with Gloria in the ministry house.

"It feels right to me. I'm not afraid to be direct with the Chinese. I think they expect that of Americans. That's why we have to be up front with these people, Vincent. We represent millions of Christians in America they're never going to meet. There's a lot of things in this town that worry me. And it's not just the gambling and all the weird stuff that goes on in the temples. Yesterday, I saw that other American guy, that friend of yours, riding around with a Chinese girl on his motorcycle."

"He's a Scotsman. His name is Alec."

"That hardly matters, because she was leaning right up against him, had her arms all over him. And that's what infuriates me, because the Chinese are going to think we're the same as him."

"Not if they get to know us."

"Well, how many of them *do* know us? We have about fifteen students coming to the house for lessons, but what about everyone else in town? That's why I think we need to make ourselves more visible. That's why I'm going to tell you about an idea I have."

Vincent closed his eyes a moment, a meditation of patience. Another idea, he thought, get ready.

"I think we should start visiting people in their homes and introducing the Word of God. I've seen the Mormons do it in Taipei and I think they've had good luck with it."

"No," Vincent said. "It's an intrusive way to try and win people over. And besides that, I'm too busy right now."

"We can go out in the afternoons before you teach. I'll set my alarm clock and start getting up earlier. Please, Vincent, I really think this can work, but I need your help." By now the irritation had seeped out of her voice, and she turned toward him, tilting her head pleadingly to one side. It was an appeal meant to be girlishly endearing, though it struck Vincent as hollow and therefore somewhat unsettling.

"No, I still don't think it's a good idea."

"Please. Let's just give it a try."

"I'm sorry."

"We'll go out one afternoon, and if it doesn't work, I won't bother you with it again, all right?"

"No, I'm afraid it's not all right."

"One afternoon. That's all I'm asking."

He shook his head and sighed.

"Please," she said. "I'm not going to let up. That's the kind of person I am. You're just going to have to say yes."

"I thought I'd made it clear how I feel about—"

"Just say yes and I'll stop all of this and we'll both feel better."

"All right . . . yes. I'll go out one time and one time only."

"Oh good, Vincent. That's so sweet of you. That's all I wanted to hear, that one little yes."

At the Ming-da Academy, Trudy's class now carried on without her. In Vincent's mind there was little difference: only the element of unsavory surprise had been eliminated. The remaining forty-one girls were as forthright as ever, their maroon jackets pressed and worn crisply across their narrow backs, their bright, untroubled faces turned toward him.

The language laboratory contained a VCR and a series of half-hour English-language programs. After viewing these, the girls were generally positive, but again their language ability outrivaled the programs' curriculum of mild cartoons and giddy puppets. Next, he rented and showed the class *E.T. the Extra-Terrestrial.* Just as he expected, they were enchanted by the homely visitor from space. Vincent paused the tape after the first half hour and stepped before the class with a prepared sheet of questions. He glanced at the seating chart and called on Cookie.

"Please describe E.T. Where does he come from and what does he look like?"

Cookie rose sheepishly to her feet. "E.T. is a man from the stars. He is a small man. He is not a handsome man. I cannot think of one thing that he looks like. He has a true and lovely heart. My classmates and I like everything about him, but there is one thing we do not like."

"What's that?"

"Teacher Vincent, we do not like you to stop the movie."

The class applauded her announcement, and Vincent set the stalled picture back into motion. Before long E.T.'s adventure on Earth took a perilous turn. When he was discovered ashen-colored and unconscious beneath a highway embankment, the entire class released a collective groan of anxiety. Later, when he died on the operating table, they were all thrown headlong into despair. Yet still, a glimmer of hope endured. A warm, pulsing light began to bloom inside E.T.'s chest.

This was a moment Vincent cherished. He was sitting opposite the class behind his desk. He was not interested in the least in watching E.T.'s resurrection or in drawing attention to its likeness to Christ's own resurrection. Instead, he studied their fascination, the fall and rise of their sentiments, watched as their unguarded expressions became charged with the naked emotional beauty women reveal only to their most intimate friends and family members. E.T. shimmered back to life and in the passing of a few heartbeats their lovely, captivated faces went from sorrow to bewilderment, to a nearly unnameable emotion that verged on reverence. At last, E.T. rose up from his sickbed, and they were swept away by wild, contagious joy.

After the movie ended, they sat stunned in their seats for a moment then collected their books and papers and filed dreamily out the door. Vincent sat at his desk and began poring over the girls' handwritten speech assignments. From the classroom next door, he could hear Jonathan Hwang leading a chorus of students through an English nursery rhyme. He also heard a polite "Excuse me" and looked up to find Trudy standing before him. She now wore a stiff black uniform, the same design and insignia that Shao-fei wore to Toulio Provincial High School.

"Teacher Vincent, I ride here to see you because I want to ask you an important question." She sat down in the empty chair beside him, quite close.

"All right," Vincent said. "Go ahead." The language laboratory was an audience of vacant chairs.

"What is your plan for Saturday afternoon?"

"Well, that's the day I grade papers and plan lessons."

"What is your plan for Sunday afternoon?"

"Well, I'm not sure now but—"

"My family," she interjected, "is excited to meet you. So they plan a lunch dinner for you. Fish, shrimp, pig's feet, good Chinese food. I think Sunday is a good day."

"That's nice of your family, but are you sure they want to have a visitor now? I mean, aren't your parents upset about you going to a different school?"

Trudy wrinkled her eyebrows at the oddness of his question. "No, my father doesn't worry about that thing. He worries about other things. He worries about having the chance to meet you. He's very excited to meet you, Vincent. Can you make the plan on Sunday?"

It was clear he should say no, should fabricate an excuse or refuse outright, and then, in the wake of days to come, recast the visit as theory. In this form, he could ponder what would have happened but didn't with equal measures of whimsy and gratitude.

"You need to tell me how to get to your house," he said.

"My father and brother and me are coming to drive you there. We have a car," she said proudly.

"Then you need to know where I live." He reached for a piece of paper.

"Oh, I already know that, Vincent. Everybody knows where you live."

Ten

EXCITED WAS NOT the first word that came to Vincent's mind when he saw Trudy's father and brother waiting for him outside the ministry house. In fact, they both appeared remarkably unexcited as they leaned against a muddied and dented sedan. They were both betel nut chewers, and every few moments they turned their heads lazily to the side and spat bloodred designs onto the pavement. Trudy stood at the front gate, dressed in a dark gray evening gown adorned with wide descending lapels the color of pearl. Her attire was graceful—Vincent had never seen her in anything except oversize school uniforms—but also oddly conspicuous beside the two men who'd arrived in threadbare field clothes.

Vincent said hello to Trudy and greeted her father and brother individually in Chinese. They did not respond with words, only minimal nods. The brother removed a filterless cigarette from his trouser pocket and waved it at Vincent.

"I don't smoke, thank you." He placed one hand respectfully atop the other.

Trudy's brother was not deterred. He was a stocky, vital-bodied young man, a more youthful, softer-faced version of the father, whose prominent features—obtrusive ears and wide nose—had become more acutely defined with age and hard work. The brother continued proffering the cigarette until Vincent took it from him and placed it in his shirt pocket, patted the pocket lightly, and said, "For later."

Both men swayed on their heels, spat again out the sides of their mouths. Strange how neither seemed to feel the need of an introduction. And it was strange, also, to be a backseat passenger in their car, the father behind the wheel, piloting down Toulio's main thoroughfare, the brother rooting about the dash for his sunglasses and barking out an occasional comment in throaty, full-volumed Taiwanese.

Trudy, perched in the far corner of the seat, held the back side of one hand to the window, tapping her fingernails against the pane.

"And how are my classmates?" she asked.

"They're just fine. We've been working on speeches and watching a movie." He said this hesitantly, hoping Trudy would not feel left out.

"You like them very much, I think."

"I do. They're a good class."

"Which classmate, do you think, is the most pretty?"

"Prettiest," Vincent corrected her mildly.

"Yes, which one?"

"I try not to think about that kind of thing. Because I'm their teacher, you understand?"

"Well, it's not me," she said, a lamentable fact, one she had to raise her dimpled chin against. "I'm not the prettiest because of my hair. My auntie cut my hair, and it looks terrible, and it also looks dreadful. But she will not cut it again. I've decided that and now it's a certain decision."

By then they had passed over the railway line and veered sharply right onto a thin-shouldered avenue that carried them away from town and toward a wide plain of cropland. Far across these fields of rice and wheat, Vincent could see the hazy outline of rising hills, and beyond the hills, a dimmer yet more imposing suggestion of high mountains curtained behind dense fog. The car turned again, this time onto a grassy drive that led up to a cluster of plain brick buildings. Vincent had first assumed Trudy lived in a small community of farmhouses, an enclave similar to Shao-fei's neighborhood. But upon closer inspection, the three low-set rectangular buildings were all connected at the corners so that they formed a rigid horseshoe. The car rolled to a stop, and the four of them stepped out and ambled toward the house.

"I didn't realize you lived on a farm, Trudy. It must be very quiet out here."

"I live here, and yes, it's quiet, but I'm not a farmer. I'm a student and all I do is study, just that, nothing else. My father and brother do the work. And my grandfather, too." She pointed to a gaunt figure of a man sheltered under a wide bamboo hat. He was squatting over what appeared to be long rows of tea leaves set out to dry beneath the mild sun.

Vincent approached the old man, leaned, and offered the most common Chinese greeting, "Have you eaten enough?"

The standard reply to this was a polite *I'm full, thank you.* Without looking up, however, the old man muttered, "Not enough, never enough." Vincent, at a loss, followed Trudy into the house.

They went first to the kitchen, where her father and brother were already at the table pouring glasses of Shao-Hsing wine, then to a small living room with a cracked cement floor. The furniture appeared deeply worn, paint peeled from the brick walls, and yet a new TV, VCR, and portable stereo stood arranged in the corner. The right and left wings of the house were packed almost to the ceiling with fertilizer bags and farming implements. The bathroom was impossibly cramped, almost phone booth–size, with only an Asian toilet and two faucets jutting from the wall. The house held a single bedroom, the family's sole room for sleeping. It contained four mats, each with its own padded quilt.

Trudy guided him through her home with a casualness that lacked any trace of embarrassment. Certainly, she must have realized the broad disparity between the way she lived and the lifestyles of people in town, her classmates, who enjoyed their own bedrooms, the luxury of modern baths. She made no excuses during the brief tour, though she giggled at the size of the bathroom and declared it "tiny-tiny." Vincent was touched by her modesty.

He was also moved by her distinct sense of etiquette at the dinner table. While the men of her family grappled with chicken and pork bones and piled them unceremoniously along the table's edge, Trudy guided her chopsticks adroitly from platter to rice bowl. She sat upright on her stool, dabbing at the corners of her lips with a paper napkin. She ignored the men's vehement belches, the loud clinking of their wineglasses, the smolderings of their cigarettes, which they smoked even as they ate. She appeared to Vincent more a visitor at the table than he, as if she had strayed from a more reputable neighborhood into this home and decided to sit calmly through a meal.

The dinner was prepared and served by an older, blank-faced woman who circled the table setting down platters of fried vegetables and noodles, boiled chicken, a pile of sand-colored prawn, a thick, spice-battered fish, a basket of dumplings, and two steaming casserole bowls, one containing pig's feet, the other, pig's intestine. They ate without conversation, although both the grandfather and father urged Vincent to sample each dish by pointing to the dish and then to Vincent with their chopsticks. The pig's feet turned out to be a pleasant surprise, tender and sweetly flavored. The strips of intestine, roughly the color and shape of cannelloni noodles, were less tasty and difficult to chew. He asked Trudy, "Does your mother always cook so many different things every meal?"

"She's not my mother," Trudy said. "She's my auntie. She doesn't live with us, but she comes to cook for us every day."

"I understand," Vincent said. He came close to asking another question, then thought better of it and went back to eating.

"If you think my mother is dead, you are not correct. But if you want to ask the question where she is, I have to give you the maybe answer. Maybe, maybe, maybe, maybe," she chanted, and the melody of her singsong caused the men to look up momentarily from their plates. "Maybe she goes away to Tainan to take care of a sick person. Maybe she works at the factory far away. Maybe she tells my father she will go shopping but doesn't come back." She covered her empty rice bowl with a napkin and leaned furtively toward Vincent. "If you come to live in this house, Vincent, your ears will hear too many *maybes*."

He gave a slow, unsettled nod, reached forward to pinch a fat dumpling. "Wouldn't your aunt like to sit down and eat with us?"

"No, because she's too busy now. She always eats after we go away."

Before long, he noticed a lull in activity at the table. The men had eased back onto their stools and surveyed the empty platters. Trudy's brother retrieved six half-liter bottles of Taiwan beer from the refrigerator and began filling a row of juice glasses. He uttered something quick and emphatic in Taiwanese. Trudy interpreted. "My brother asks the question how many Taiwan beers can you drink?"

"I don't drink much beer," he explained to the brother in Chinese. "One small glass, that's all."

The brother passed him one glass of beer and then a cigarette, which Vincent deposited in his shirt pocket.

"The correct answer is six bottles," Trudy said. "They each try to drink six bottles on Sunday because they don't work after the lunch dinner."

Vincent sipped at his own beer while the others shouted *"Kan pei,"* dry glass, and emptied theirs in a single swallow. He watched uneasily as they poured and drank another round. "Maybe your father should drive me home soon. I mean, before he finishes his six bottles."

"Smart idea," Trudy said. "But first I'd like to show you the outside of the farm. I hope we can go for a walk."

Together they rose from the table. Vincent thanked Trudy's aunt for the meal, then her grandfather, father, and brother for their hospitality. Again his politeness drew little response, and it occurred to him, not for the first time that day, how little they had in common, how priggish and strange he must appear in their eyes.

The fields surrounding her home were carpeted with fragile stalks of green wheat. Mid-March and they were already ankle-high. And it was nice, really, to be away from the muggy kitchen, revived by the crisp air, following Trudy, who had hiked up her gown several inches to better rule the placement of her slippered feet.

As soon as they passed behind the left wing of the house, she swiveled around and leaned against him. She raised her head and with closed eyes brushed her lips inexpertly over his. It was not so much a kiss as a fumbling, off-centered touching of mouths. For Vincent, the moment was at once startling and inevitable; part of him had anticipated just such a thing. Afterward, she bowed her head against his chest, and to steady himself, he ran his hand down the small of her back. There was something alluring in the easy descent of his hand, more so than the kiss, and he allowed it to settle there for some time before he pulled away.

Both then and later, he was struck by the disparity of how he should feel and how he actually felt. He should view Trudy's kiss as a calculated and consequence-laden act. Yet she had leaned so bravely into his arms and he had held her there, glad to finally indulge himself in the close warmth of another body. He should, but did not, feel guilty. The reason behind this, he decided, was that the incident had unfolded innocently enough, at least on his part, and it would stop there and not go any further. In this way, it was already evolving into memory, something he might, years later and another continent away, look back on, pleased to have embraced and kissed, even awkwardly, a Chinese girl, one among many—to have known irrefutably what it was like.

During the car ride back to town, she glanced at him across the seat and asked, "Was the kiss a good one? I mean was it correct?"

"Shhhh," Vincent whispered. "Don't talk that way in front of your father and brother."

"I think it was a good one. Good and lovely, but not great."

"Shhhhh," he repeated.

"They don't understand English. They don't understand one word." To prove her point, she leaned against the front seat and said, "Father, do your big ears hear my English words?" To her brother, who swayed drowsily against the passenger door, she chanted, "Six bottles. Six bottles on Sunday," over and over, a half dozen taunting verses, until, grim-faced and beleaguered, he sank down and covered his head in his arms.

. . .

At noon the following Wednesday the mailman dropped a postcard into the crinkled mesh of the screen door. *Each day is a blessing,* someone had charted in tall, furrowed English letters across the card's back side. Not Reverend Phillips's coiling script. The return address, in the Tienmu district of Taipei, was not Good Shepherd's. *Each day is another opportunity for God's grace. More so when we follow Christ's path and share His message of salvation. Loving God, Gentle God, let us not forget how small our sacrifices are in comparison to Your own.*

The card was unsigned, though not, Vincent felt, deceitfully so. Just a case of the author's name being immaterial to the spirit of the message. And besides, it was easy to settle on the writer's identity; he knew so few people in Taipei. He turned the card's glossy front toward the light: a reprint of a landscape in watercolors; a meandering river, pagoda-topped mountains of surpassing height and steepness.

Odd that Mr. Liang, whom he had known only as a bodiless voice on the telephone, should send him a postcard. Odd, but also moderately reassuring, this nod of encouragement, this secret communiqué.

Somewhat less assuring was a different type of artifact, which he discovered a short time later while sidling past Gloria's closed bedroom door. There, running down the door's center panel, were vertical lines of her meticulous calligraphy. He counted fourteen characters. Perhaps it should not have bothered him. Fourteen characters, each as artful and measured as any of her sketchbook work. They seemed to have the rigid bearing of a warning or perhaps some strict maxim.

In the kitchen he set to work washing and drying his leftover lunch dishes. Before he'd finished Gloria emerged from her room and stood in the kitchen entranceway, her face creased from sleep, a bath towel draped over one shoulder.

"Afternoon." She yawned. "Is it afternoon? My goodness, I keep meaning to get up earlier. I keep meaning to be ready to go out. Whenever you're ready, that is."

"What's that on your door?"

She glanced back at her own fastidious brushwork. "Oh, it's like a motto. Just some words to keep me motivated."

"What does it say?"

"It's a positive-thinking message to myself. Keep up the hard work, that sort of thing."

"Will it come off? I don't think Mrs. Liang wants us writing on the walls."

"Well, you don't know, Vincent," she said, treading barefoot past him toward the bathroom. "She might just like having it there. If she doesn't, I'll paint the door."

And so for the time being, the matter was dropped. Why argue? Why unsettle a household that was mostly even-keeled, mostly agreeable? Better to be forbearing. Better to recognize the ministry house for what it was: an enterprise of deep-seated civility and gracious routine. Welcome routine. English and Bible study classes three nights a week. A loyal company of regular attendees, devoted pupils. If not reborn, if not *changed*, they frequently appeared grateful.

A prickly circumstance then, to live inside these amenities and heed their gratitude and know this: he had kissed a student. Or more exactly: he had kissed a student and nothing disgraceful had come of it.

Each day since the kiss was proof, in its way, that the incident was as harmless as he had first taken it to be. Indeed, from Wednesday onward the progress of time only made it seem more innocuous. Thursday passed without uproar. Friday was serene and reputable. By the weekend he began to stare brazenly into the memory of the kiss and wonder if it could have been longer and more passionate, if his hand, which had settled so nimbly into the cleft of her back, could have wandered elsewhere.

Then Trudy phoned rather late Sunday evening, and at the sound of her restless greeting—had she held her breath before dialing?—all his bravado and sly musings shrank away.

"I'm just calling to talk, to speak, to converse," she said. "How are you, Vincent?"

"Fine," he said.

"I've been thinking about you. What have you been thinking about?"

Such a girlish question, full of naive expectation. It caused him to suffer a shrill pang of regret. "I don't know. A lot of things."

"Did you enjoy the lunch dinner last Sunday?"

"I did. Tell your father and brother I said thank you."

"I will, and I'll tell you something about my brother now. Something I heard and something I saw. Do you want to hear? Are you in-*ter*-rested?"

"Sure," Vincent said. "I guess so."

"Last night my brother's friends come for a visit. They are his army friends. They all finish the army together one year ago. They come here last night and drink beer and smoke cigarettes. It's late at night and I go to our bedroom to sleep, and I look around and see that my father and grandfather are sleeping, but I can still hear my brother and the army friends. I listen to them, and behind them I hear the TV and I know that they are watching a movie. A yellow movie with men and women together. It's all very interesting to me! I walk to the door and very fast I take one look and then go back to my bed. So I see this thing. I see a man kissing a woman, but not a kiss on the mouth, not like our kiss. It's a kiss on the . . ." Her voice trailed off and Vincent could hear the shuffling of pages. "Neeple," she said. "That's the correct word. I thought about the kiss last night and I thought about it while I was studying today because I remember the picture of it on the TV. It's strange to me."

"Uh-huh," Vincent mumbled. Ironically, he had sometimes day-dreamed about one of his Bible study students dropping by or telephoning with a problem. But he had not imagined this, not Trudy, not the peculiar details of her sexual curiosity.

"Don't worry. I don't want you to explain the picture. That's not why I call you. I'm telling you that it feels strange to be me and not to know. I have some ideas. I know there's places men can go and pay money to be alone with a woman, but I don't know everything they do there. Nobody in this house is talking about it, my old classmates didn't talk about it, and I don't have any friends at the new school. It's strange because there's something happening in this town. Everybody knows, but they won't tell me."

"I don't know what to tell you," Vincent said. He heard Gloria, who had summoned him to the telephone, brewing water for coffee in the next room. "I should go. I have lessons to prepare, classes tomorrow afternoon and night."

"Yes, I have class at night, too, a class to make us all ready for the college entrance exam. I finish at nine o'clock, but I already tell my family that I finish at ten o'clock. That's the way I can come and visit you tomorrow, for one hour, and then ride my bike home."

"You shouldn't do that."

"Why?"

"Because it's not a good idea."

"Oh, it's not an idea I'm talking about. It's about me coming to visit you. I'll see you at nine. You can talk about your ideas then. You can explain when you see me tomorrow."

•   •   •

All afternoon and evening the next day, while he taught at the preschool and later as he led Bible study class with Gloria at the ministry house, Trudy's impending visit surfaced in the background of his thoughts as a vague, shadowy distraction. Hunched down amid a circle of nap-dazed children, he began formulating a list of explanations. Because I am six years older than you. Because I was your teacher and you were my student. Because students place a special trust in their teachers. He continued this litany during Bible study. Leaning against a windowsill while Gloria drafted lines of characters onto the chalkboard, he lowered his head and continued. Because I am a volunteer for Christ. Because my actions, like it or not, are always a reflection on Christ. Because I have made promises . . .

Once class ended Gloria retreated to her bedroom, closed her door, and flipped on her work lamp. For the first time ever Vincent indulged in the Chinese practice of walking his students outside the ministry house to the road. He stood near the front gate and waved to them as they mounted their bikes and motorcycles and rode off. It was a cool night and he shifted for warmth inside his denim jacket.

Minutes later, Trudy came rolling out of the darkness. She had already swiveled off her seat and was balanced on one foot atop the left pedal. He marveled at the way her otherwise solemn face was lit and made pretty by anticipation. She coasted to a stop, set her bicycle against the gate, and without a word leaned into him and slipped her arms beneath the folds of his jacket. "OK, Vincent," she said. "Explain to me now."

He sighed against the welcome pressure of her body and raised his head to survey the street for possible spectators. "I'm six years older," he began in a voice already tense and uneven. "Although I'm not your teacher anymore, I still teach your classmates. And they think of me in a certain way, as a certain kind of person." He felt her nodding against his chest. "They think," he continued, "they expect . . ." but his point had turned murky, unfocused. She locked her arms behind him and squeezed, and now his own hands were making a familiar descent down the curve of her back. "There are other things, too," he said and realized that he could list them all and her only response would be to clutch him more tightly. For all her boldness, for all her odd and reckless questions, she did not know that she could simply release him and climb on her bicycle and ride away and he would immediately call after her. It seemed unfair that he knew this and she did not, and perhaps as a minor act of compensation, he leaned forward and kissed the crown of her forehead.

"We can't stand here like this," he said, looking out again over the neighborhood. He brought his lips down to her ear, whispered, told her to follow the gate down to the last building, which was an apartment house, to enter and take the stairs to the roof. He explained all of this in a breathy rush of words, as if this plan were evolving as he spoke and had not been there all afternoon and evening, cloaking itself behind his explanations, behind the safer, more routine notions of the day. They released each other, Trudy slipping back into the shadowy perimeter of the gate line, making her way toward the apartment entrance. Vincent turned and strolled across the courtyard into the ministry house. Before ascending the stairs, he called out good night to Gloria and heard a weak reply rise above the soft swell of her music. On the second-floor landing he pried off his shoes, climbed the last two flights of stairs, and delicately unlocked the door to the roof.

The long, open rooftop stretched away dim and vacant beneath a canopy of bare clotheslines. He stepped back into his shoes and wandered toward a makeshift bench—a plank balanced on two cinder blocks—set near the rail. He saw Trudy, or rather the dark silhouette of her figure, zigzagging her way between columns of laundry poles.

She stepped up close to him and peered into the lighted stairwell leading down into the ministry house. "Hello, Vincent. This is the place here?"

"Yes. Gloria is downstairs, so we have to stay up here and be quiet."

"Oh, I can be quiet," she promised, drifting into his arms and kissing the corner of his mouth.

They eased down onto the bench, and she circled her arms around his neck and settled onto his lap. He felt her parted lips on his chin sliding up and ebbing tentatively over the edge of his mouth, her breath warm and spiced with a trace of ginger. He held back his own breath for a long time, until he was light-headed with pleasure, but dizzy also with the knowledge that beneath his pious, ordinary life lay a sheltered realm of craving all his own. He felt the stark, kinetic motion of this craving travel through him. He felt it in his hand as he traced his fingers over her breast and down her slim rib cage. She shivered beneath his touch, a reflex he almost mistook for ticklishness until she grasped his hand and pressed it beneath the lapel of her uniform, wanting him to repeat the caress. He did this, and she peeled back the jacket and unbuttoned her white shirt, her fingers brushing over the lace fringes of a bra that even in the darkness appeared brash and exotic, definitely not the bra of a schoolgirl. She brought her hand up and with a single twist unfastened the bra at the center. Seven months as a stranger in a country half a world from home, and this nimble turn of the wrist, this unfastening, seemed the most generous and intimate gesture he had been offered. The cups divided sideways, an astonishing novelty, and he palmed his hand against one pale breast, small and beautifully formed.

There appeared then no other route for his mouth to take but down, across the shiny crescent of her bare collar, across the breached plain of her chest, until he placed his lips over her breast and tasted the smooth button of her nipple.

"Yes, that's correct," she whispered calmly after he'd brought his face up and pressed it against hers. "That's the way I thought it should feel. Just like that."

Eleven

AT A BUSY intersection seven blocks north of the ministry house, Gloria halted in her steps and shifted her gaze from left to right, deliberating between two unfamiliar neighborhoods. One was anchored on the edge of a steep and muddy canal, the houses old, low-set, listing together in the same weather-worn direction. On the opposite side of the avenue lay a tract of recently constructed two- and three-story homes, their large windows agleam, their high exterior walls embellished with bright white tiles.

"I guess we'll just begin here," she said, pinching the cuff of Vincent's jacket sleeve and directing him across the street to an entrance lane as trim and newly fashioned as the houses it served. She had dressed nicely, a black cowl-neck sweater tucked inside a lengthy brown pleated skirt. Her hair was held back with a silver barrette, and this caused her face to loom forward, blanched and rather severe in the strong afternoon light. Tucked beneath one arm was a thick, hard-bound Chinese translation of the Bible.

She held fast to his sleeve until they'd paced up the nearest walkway and halted before a front door comprised of copper diamonds and tinted glass. "Of course, we have to remember which neighborhoods we visit," she said, smoothing the pleats of her skirt with one hand, searching for a doorbell with the other. "I mean, people will just think we're nutty if we keep showing up at their doorstep day after day."

The door swung open and a young housewife, balanced on the threshold of a long hallway, took in the sight of them. Her face went blank, but an instant later she recovered enough to affect an interested expression and say, graciously, "Can I help you?"

"This has some information about free English lessons and Bible study classes," Vincent said, referring to one of his paper flyers. "We hope you can share it with your family and friends." *Information. Hope. Share.* Circumspect words, yet they had a way, in either language, of sounding disingenuous, inane.

She accepted the flyer with both hands. "I'll do that," she promised. "I'll show it to my husband when he comes home." She remained poised in her doorway. An odd and prolonged moment crept by and Vincent realized that he and Gloria and the housewife were all wearing the same acute grin.

"Free English lessons," she read aloud. "That's very kind of you to come to Toulio and teach people for free."

He shrugged. "It's more than that, really. We want students to come for English lessons, but we hope they'll stay after for another hour of Bible study."

"I understand. But it's still a kind offer, when you consider the expense of English lessons. My sister's children both study—" And she paused, cut short by Gloria, who reached forward and reclaimed the flyer, pried it away, and set it on the cover of her Bible. She uncapped a pen and printed out a line of descending characters.

"That's wonderful," the housewife declared. "You write your characters better than I do."

Vincent translated her praise into English. Gloria merely wagged her head and drew a circle around her message.

"Yes, I understand," the woman said, reading the characters a second time. "I only know a few things about Jesus. I'm sure you know a lot more."

Gloria's pen channeled its way across the paper: a second line took shape, an addendum, maybe, to her first declaration.

"Not tomorrow night," the woman answered. "Maybe sometime later, after I talk to my husband about it." She glanced earnestly toward Vincent. "Is your friend deaf?" she whispered.

He thought it a fitting question, yet before he could translate or answer, Gloria set pen to paper once more and produced four swift but sure-limbed characters.

The housewife inched closer, tilted her head to the paper. "It's hard to say," she reported, though something in her expression had soured—her hospitality, which had yet to appear wholly genuine, waned a shade thinner. "Nobody's ever asked me that kind of question before," she said. She turned, gazed longingly down the hallway, and pretended—Vincent was certain of it—to heed the summons of someone calling to her from within the house. She really had to go, she explained. A feeble thank-you, a hasty farewell, and they were left staring into the tinctured veneer of her front door.

Pacing down the walkway, Gloria remarked that, all things considered, they were doing as well as could be expected.

"Did you understand what she said?" Vincent asked.

"Not all of it. She sounded awfully nice, though."

"She was very nice, but we made her uncomfortable. She thought you were deaf."

"Did she?" Gloria exclaimed. "That's the funniest thing I've ever heard." She let loose a breathy chuckle deep into the open collar of her sweater.

At the next house they were met by a hunched and sulking old woman who would not accept their flyer or open her screen door more than a few grudging inches. Her next-door neighbor, a boy, came to the door clutching a video game. He received their flyer, yet soon after Vincent started to speak, the boy's timid gaze fluttered back down to the game, his thumbs languishing over the plastic buttons.

No one came to greet them at the fourth house, but Vincent heard a voice behind the door calling out for them to enter. He turned the latch and Gloria followed him down a pristine hallway and into a wide, high-ceilinged parlor, a room brimming with colorful statues and elaborate furniture. In a corner, bathed beneath the soft light of a brass floor lamp, sat the origin of the voice, a wiry-bodied old man. His hair, a fine chalky white, spilled down in girlish bangs across his forehead. "What's this? Foreign visitors?" he called out to no one in particular. "Were we expecting foreign visitors today?" A queer wavering slurred his voice, a seesawing lisp for which there were two possibilities: a palsy of some type, which had begun to corrupt his vocal cords, or alcohol. He seemed to be looking at them with a drunk's sense of inverted searching.

The parlor itself, now that Vincent took note of it, was improbably crammed with artifacts: rattan sofas and stools and hulking ceramic vases and latticework partitions and a host of other objects he could only classify as Oriental and antique. Together they formed a great bounty of personal effects resettled into a room so new he could still smell the unguent tang of fresh paint.

Then a flurry of awkwardness and miscommunication. Did the man intend that they should settle onto the rattan sofa? They had already done so. Did he mean by the bobbing tilt of his head and the faint, open-palmed leveling of his hand that they should speak to him as invited guests?

"We're stopping by every house," Vincent explained. "We have a paper with some information about free English lessons." He leaned forward and presented a flyer.

The old man gave it a heavy-lidded appraisal. "I understand this," he said, waving the paper in their direction. "What I don't understand is why I need to learn to speak a new language."

Vincent relayed this to Gloria and she frowned and reached for her pen. "Gloria," he whispered. "Please don't."

But she waved him off, retrieved the paper, and began writing out an acute and prolonged reply, a short essay. Nothing for Vincent to do then but sit humbly and struggle against his own thickening sense of disquiet. He tried focusing his attention on a tall oak table braced against the opposite wall. Set atop the table was a pyramid of rising shelves covered with a maroon satin cloth. Each shelf supported an array of small religious objects: incense sticks and burners, a line of fist-size gold plates emblazoned with a gold silhouette of Buddha, candles, short rods of wood, a pair of kidney-shaped gray stones. Perched on the topmost tier were two faded portraits, both of them men dressed in black suits and sitting on high wooden armchairs.

The old man caught him studying the portraits and grinned. "Excellent," he said. "Now walk up close and look at both paintings together."

Vincent stepped up to the table and contemplated the matched portraits. From a browsing distance they appeared identical.

"Which one looks like me?" the old man asked.

"Neither. They're both the same," Vincent said. Though how to explain the wily hope, the longing to be instructed, guided through a parable or koan, if that's what this was, and led, finally, toward some radiant understanding.

"Yes, the bodies are the same," the old man went on in his dawdling and slurred voice. "Years ago when an artist did portraits, he would paint all the bodies beforehand, and then when a customer came to his shop, he would look at the person and paint in the head. Look at the heads. One is my father and the other is my wife's father. Both my wife and I have poor eyesight and all week we've been arguing over which is my father and which is hers."

Vincent leaned toward the portraits and squinted.

"Look at the heads," the old man urged. "Look at the eyes."

A renewed focus, a closer scrutiny and, true enough, the portrait on the right revealed a pug-featured countenance, a glimmer of stilled merriment in the eyes. The face on the left was leaner and more somber, the eyes hooded with thick lids, the same caustic, intelligent gaze as the old man's.

"The left," Vincent said. "That's your father."

"Are you sure?"

"Yes. Very sure."

"Then switch them quick before my wife gets home. All week long I've sworn my father's picture was on the right."

So it was a joke, a cheery bit of marital one-upmanship and not the revelation he had hoped for. Always the fitful hope. Still, he did as he was told, and when he moved back to the sofa he saw the old man bent toward the light with Gloria's finished essay held close to his face. It was a face composed of patience and frailty and shrewd intellect, and it almost caused Vincent to step forward and intervene, to apologize in advance for whatever words Gloria had written.

"I have to ask you a question, miss," the old man said, his knobby-jointed finger sifting among the lines of her calligraphy. "Do you like fried noodles?"

She cocked her head to the side and mimicked comprehension.

"Fried noodles," the old man repeated. "Do you like them?"

She nodded yes.

"Ten years ago in Kaohsiung I worked with a foreign engineer, an Englishman and a Christian. Every day he had to remind me that Chiang Kai-shek was a follower of Jesus. But he liked fried noodles. Wouldn't eat anything else. Told me his mother used to fry noodles in butter for him back home in England. He might look at other dishes, might smell them, but for six months until the project ended he wouldn't eat anything else." The old man stretched the paper taut between his hands, then folded it and handed it back to Gloria. "I don't worship statues, and whether you think of him as true or untrue, Buddha isn't a god. You should leave now. I allowed you to sit down because I thought you might be interesting. Then I read your note and I see how much you're like the Englishman. I would say you have an excellent understanding of fried noodles."

"What did he say?" Gloria asked. "Does he want us to stay for dinner?"

"He wants us to leave," Vincent said. He turned and faced the old man. "I'm sorry. She shouldn't do that. I know it's not right."

"No, she shouldn't," he agreed. "Maybe you should take her pen away. Maybe you should teach her how to listen to Chinese."

Outside the house, having retreated shame-faced from the parlor into the overbright glower of the afternoon, Vincent braced his arms on his hips and kicked the street curb experimentally. He meant to test the tenacity of his own anger, to see if it was strong enough to wage a full-scale confrontation.

But Gloria had stepped out of the house still confused. "You apologized?" she asked. "What's that about? What did I write that made him ask us to leave?"

"He allowed us into his home," Vincent explained. "He was a little grumpy, a little odd, but I liked him. We were guests in his home and you were rude to him." He handed her the rumpled sheaf of remaining flyers. "I'm not doing this anymore," he said. "You can't argue people out of their faith and into yours by writing notes, Gloria. It won't work. You're way off course."

Had he expected breathless indignation from her? Because what he got instead was much more subdued, manageable. Her eyes grew wide and moist. She heaved her full chest as if quietly stricken, soberly taken aback. "Which is not my intention," she said, a splintered and confusing reply. Another deep breath. "To argue," she added. "To be rude wasn't my intention."

"Whatever the case, whatever your—the point is you didn't respect his beliefs. Without understanding what he believed, you made it clear that he was wrong." Or put another way, *I would say you have an excellent understanding of fried noodles.* There was a finely toothed insult hinged inside this remark. How badly he wanted her to feel the sudden chomp and damp gouge of it.

A ruddiness was flooding back into her cheeks, a flustered confidence. "I would like to know one thing," she said formidably. "I would like to know at what point you, the people of this neighborhood, the whole world"—she opened her arms and made an askew windmilling motion— "became so touchy, so awfully *sensitive,* about hearing the word of God."

This he decided to let stand. To challenge it would only enlarge their quarrel, and in the process, in the general parrying of guilt and redress, he was sure to feel the milder but still corrosive bite of his own false pieties and failed conversions. Was there any way now *not* to be a hypocrite? Indeed, if Gloria had, as he said, drifted off course, then he had strayed to what seemed the most unlikely of places—to the ministry house rooftop, where Trudy would be waiting for him tonight and he would press his mouth to her warm breasts, a daredevil act, half abject craving, half solacing comfort. Standing on this street corner, he could almost imagine himself resisting, but when the time came he would not. Somehow Gloria's behavior this afternoon made it all the more likely.

He motioned obscurely toward the intersection from which they had come. "I'll see you back at the ministry house then?" he offered.

When she did not answer, he wished her luck and set off at an almost jaunty clip.

Behind him, her voice quivered and rose an octave. "I'm not going to let myself get discouraged over a little misunderstanding."

Walking away, he wondered how, with her mute's aptitude for the spoken language, she could possibly continue, how she could negotiate an introduction, much less speak across the divides of ancestry and religion. Curiosity caused him to turn back twice: once to see her motionless at the curb, arms folded, deliberating, and then once more to see her turn and set off, resolute and alone, toward the next doorstep.

"I hate the night class," Trudy said, stepping out of the rooftop shadows and into the light of the stairwell. "It's very boring to be me sitting in that classroom. You wouldn't like it, Vincent."

He could only agree, distractedly. He'd watched her, as he had for three successive nights now, traverse the ministry house's shared roof, the dark glimmer of her wending silhouette, the promise of it, and the burden, too. Tonight she settled down on the bench, reached forward, and rubbed her thumb across the widow's peak of his forehead. No explanation as to why she'd done it. An experiment possibly, a fond and inquisitive bit of touching she'd been meaning to try. Above her loomed Toulio's murky and starless skyline, not the type that would produce a steady rain or even a light drizzle, both reasonable excuses for taking Trudy by the hand and leading her down the stairs to his bedroom. Even so, he felt the close proximity of his room—two quick flights of stairs, a right turn at the landing, a short hallway and a door, an inevitable destination. How many nights would they spend in a jumble of limbs and loosened clothing before they took that journey? A few weeks? Unlikely. Doubtful they could last a single week. Three more nights then? They could at least persevere that long, couldn't they?

Evidently not. Evidently he was already drawing her close, telling her that Gloria was downstairs studying, that the bedrooms all had open walls, that they would have to speak in their softest voices. She removed her shoes and padded down the stairs behind him.

Inside his bedroom, she went straight to his dresser and tested the weight of various objects set atop its surface. She cupped her hands around a glass dish containing coins, loose shirt buttons, a tiny silver crucifix, which she lifted up so that it swayed lopsided between her fingers. She took a framed photograph into her hands, a snapshot of Vincent, his mother, father, and Vanessa standing on the porch of their Red Bud home. She studied it for a long time, then propped it back on the dresser without asking a single question. Moving to the foot of his bed, she positioned herself before a full-length mirror bracketed to the closet door. Haltingly and by means of several flinching glances, she paused and considered her own reflection.

Then, abruptly, she turned away from the mirror and crawled across the bed onto his lap. He leaned back and flipped off his reading lamp. The room fell away into darkness. He felt the mattress sink under their combined weight. She reached forward and turned the lamp back on.

She blinked twice into the restored light and shouldered her way free of the black school jacket. The crisp white shirt, the lace bra, slid down her bare arms onto the bed. She huddled forward until her breasts dangled inches over his face.

She planned, apparently, to begin shirtless and proceed at once into some new region of naked intimacy. He closed his lips over her nipples, the taste faintly sweet, faintly salty, already familiar. She sighed encouragingly, and yet when he grew more daring, when he eased his hand beneath her pants and tried to coax the elastic waistband down over her hips, her prior boldness seemed to shrink away. She glanced back once, puzzled, toward the mirror and rolled slowly sideways onto her back near the edge of the mattress, a languid retreat that posited her beyond the mirror's reflection. Now she placed Vincent's hand between her legs and clasped her thighs against his forearm and rocked her hips against the pressure of his hand. It calmed his nerves to discover that she was mostly silent in her pleasure. She welcomed his touch, examined his face, and grinned at the obvious delight with which he touched her, though during the hurried half hour they lolled about in bed together, she made no attempt to undress him or remove more of her own clothing.

Promptly at a quarter to ten she sat up in bed and pointed to her watch and then leveled her finger at the door.

"You can whisper," he said, embarrassed by how very little they had spoken since entering the room. "I didn't mean that you shouldn't speak at all."

She did not reply. Her gaze had drifted back to the closet mirror.

"You're leaving?" he asked. "You're leaving now and coming back tomorrow?"

"It's strange to be me because I haven't seen myself without my clothes," she whispered. "Not in school. Not in my house. The bathroom there is tiny, no mirror." She scooted to the foot of the bed and stood before her own reflection. Tucking her thumbs inside the waistband of her pants, she bowed forward and slipped her pants and underwear to her ankles. She drew herself up and pivoted slightly from side to side. Vincent could see the soft, pear-shaped curves of her naked hips and buttocks, her round thighs broadened from years of powering her bicycle, and in the mirror, a frontal view that revealed a black petal of hair coiling up from between her legs.

"What do you think?" he asked. He himself was doubly astonished, first by the overwhelming similarities between her body and a white woman's, mainly Carrie Ann Whitlinger's, then by the subtle differences in coloring and shape and spirit.

She folded her arms tentatively over her breast. "I don't even know what to think," she said, turning away from the mirror, away from herself, and drawing up her panties so that they rested on the crest of her hips. She sat on the bed and leaned over Vincent to retrieve her shirt and bra. "It's not like the girls in the magazines who want to show you the underwear. It's not like the yellow movie my brother watches," she said. "It's different because I'm too much real. Too real to be in that mirror right now." She planted a slow, thoughtful kiss on his chin, rose, and with her shirttail fluttering out beneath her jacket, padded up the stairs to the ministry rooftop.

For some time he had noticed that in Toulio a small number of severely retarded or mentally ill men were allowed—if such permission could be granted—to amble about wherever they chose, regardless of their shoddy clothing or lunatic mutterings or the limb-buckling contractions that passed through their spare bodies. They tended to wander separately, though each in his own oblique orbit, around the train and bus stations. Saturday nights they found their way across town to Toulio's westernmost precinct, where each weekend a sprawling night market was heaved into being atop a weedy lot. The night market drew several thousand bargain hunters. Career beggars worked the crowds. Of these the most alarming and resourceful were several rugged amputees who had lost all their appendages, at least to the knees or elbows, and who now writhed about in the gravel pathways pulling by their teeth nylon cords attached to toy wagons. Into the wagons the sympathetic dropped fifty- and hundred-yuan bills.

The retarded or mentally ill men were never so lucky or adept. If they lagged a few paces behind the toy wagons, they might receive a compensatory bill or two, but their best prospect for reward came later, in the market's dwindling and final quarter hour, when vendors offered them bruised fruit or flattened sweet buns by the bagful. These gifts inspired a bright, shuddering joy, a crooked delight. It was almost indecent, the happiness a half dozen flecked pears or curd-filled pastries brought them. In those moments one might believe, as Vincent did, in Christ's abiding tenderness for the afflicted and feebleminded. One might believe in a pervasive, God-sent affection that trickled down into the souls of ordinary people—stinting market vendors among them—tipping the scales of their hearts subtly, graciously, toward a charitable act.

He quite liked this idea and its attendant feelings. How lucid the belief. How humble yet still ennobling. And how hard he tried to cling to this vision of Christ's grace when, for several days, a bedraggled and muttish and desperately restless man, a member of Toulio's tribe of retarded or mentally ill, took up residence along a stretch of sidewalk opposite the ministry house.

Daylight hours, the man scavenged food and slept openmouthed against a neighbor's gatepost. He ranted sometimes, though he did so in a contrite, hangdog manner. Or he lolled about the sidewalk, hands down the front of his shapeless trousers, skinny hips rising and collapsing amid the scraps of his foraged meals. Never once did he speak to passersby. Never once did he touch anyone other than himself.

Even so, rightly so, the neighborhood children acceded to him his parcel of sidewalk and played elsewhere. Trudy, walking her bicycle beside the gate line and its veiling shadow, gave him a wide berth. These and other allowances were made. And further concessions might have been granted. But very early each morning, always between four-thirty A.M. and sunrise, he began a series of long, whinnying cries. Vincent, who had worked one summer in a cousin's livery stable, thought of it as human braying. Jarred awake the first morning, he knelt before the window, located the source of the braying, and thought, rather quaintly, *poor soul.* Lights from nearby homes flickered on. For an hour the man, the poor soul, kept on with his lamentations. When he stopped, Vincent and his neighbors did their best to return to a dawn-lit and fractured sleep.

The second morning he woke to the man's braying and recognized it at once for what it was: reproof for not having offered assistance the previous morning. But what could be done? What would even the most patient and elemental explanation of Christ's love do for such a man? Surely, ailments this severe were best handled by professionals. A discreet mental health agency. If not that, then perhaps the police should be called.

The third morning it became evident, incontrovertibly clear, that someone should do something.

The fourth morning someone did.

The fourth morning the braying ceased all at once. A muffled gulp. Then scuffling. Then harsh breathing, the near-carnal breathing of fully engaged wrestlers. It was hard, given the pale five A.M. light, for Vincent to determine how many neighbors were involved. The motorcycle mechanic's pickup truck was brought around. The scuffling moved from the sidewalk to the bed of the truck. A minute or two of this and the truck carried them off—to who knew where, exactly? Maybe to a discreet mental health agency. Or the police station. Or maybe the man was, at that very moment, on his way home to a family reunion arranged by Vincent's neighbors. Each of these theories seemed feasible, relieved and grateful as Vincent was, ready to sink back into a more lavish sleep.

Except for one concern, one needling particular, it had all sorted itself out well enough. The stretch of sidewalk where the man had lain for four days was now blighted with a dark stain. An inky, maplike stain with its own opaque mainland and spindly, black fjords. Could urine permeate hard pavement? Could blood? It stank of neither, or so Vincent discovered when he bent low to sweep fruit peelings and wrappers and other debris from the sidewalk. A bucket of water made no difference. Damp or dry, shaded or sunlit, the stain endured.

Something about its spidery edges, or maybe just its persistence. To see it, for example, just before a blustery March shower, the signaling breeze, the low ceiling of rain-bloated clouds. Moments later, to see the stain windblown and pounded by rain.

It did seem, truly, that there were voids into which the light of Christ or Buddha or any other hopeful belief could not travel. There were chasms in this world that deflected any earnest attempt at faith.

And from this slippery knowledge sprang other ambiguities. Why was it that the bearing of his faith seemed to change over the course of a single day? Mornings were still best for prayer. Some ineffable quality—the softness or the sheer gleaming symmetry of morning made conversations with Christ more personal and real. In the mornings, too, he felt God's percipient gaze. Under the weight of that gaze he was duly shamed by his indiscretions with Trudy. How curious then that a long and hectic day could allay his disgrace. By nine o'clock in the evening, when he met Trudy at the rooftop door and led her down to his bedroom, the things they did together seemed less like transgressions, less like the dizzying lure of sin, and more like a rendezvous born of a thousand small but willful choices.

God of hope, God of life, You are the very breath we breathe. Blow Your Spirit into our being so that all that is dead will live again. Or so wrote Mr. Liang in another of his unsigned communiqués. Did Mr. Liang ever feel his faith dwindle over the course of an ordinary day?

Did Gloria? Impossible to know because even though they taught Bible study classes together, they never once discussed private convictions. Any variety of forthright conversation now seemed unlikely. Since their afternoon of door-to-door canvassing, they had hardly spoken at all. Yet oddly, the few times they did converse, they were enormously respectful and discreet, as though they'd forged an avowed truce, as though, by virtue of remoteness and cautious manners, they had finally learned to behave like genuine adult siblings.

One damp, stock-still Thursday evening they both stepped into the living room and grabbed their jackets at precisely the same moment. It embarrassed each of them, this coincidence. With it came the understanding that they were both headed out to dinner. No way to pretend otherwise. And so they set off on foot toward the nearest lane of food stalls, strolling dumbly and at a pricklish arm's length, a timid partnership with nothing more to talk about than the warming spring weather and the prospect of holding Bible study classes in the town park. At Hungry Ghost Street, Gloria peered into a vendor's display case, assessing mounds of squid and prawns, sea bass and tuna, and still other unidentifiable fare, a strange, spongy white flesh speckled with ash-colored dots, iced hillocks of nebulous meats and vegetables, which she heeded carefully and at length before ordering simple fried noodles.

It wasn't easy, fighting back the urge to grin virtuously or laugh out loud.

Straight-faced, he ordered a bowl of prawn and rice soup, then watched as their separate meals took shape inside a row of heat-burnished iron woks. The crowd of patrons thickened. A motorcycle passed behind him, and he felt someone cuff him sharply on the shoulder. He spun about. Three vendors down Alec rolled to a stop, parked his cycle, and ducked into the sheltered patio of his favorite food stall. He waved before sitting down and patting the empty stool beside him.

"That's Alec," Vincent said to Gloria. "I'm going to sit with him and eat. Come join us if you like."

She gazed down the lane and narrowed her eyes uncomfortably. "No. I'll eat right here," she said, though she seemed baffled or sorry by the tone of voice she'd used. "Thanks a lot," she added rather stiffly. "I mean, thanks for asking me." Her noodles were ready and she accepted the plate and sat beside the case at a wobbly little table.

"Are you sure?"

"Yes, I'm going to eat this and hurry back to the house. So much to do. One project ends and another begins."

Vincent collected his soup and carried it steaming-hot down the lane. Alec was camped on a stool chatting with the woman who owned the food stall. She laughed over some remark he'd made and bent low to thrust her hand into a tub of squirming fish. Out came a plump, charcoal-colored catfish. She set it on a wood block and with a cleaver and one fluttery-quick stroke separated its head from its body.

"How's Shao-fei?" Vincent asked, once he'd set his bowl and soup spoon to order.

Alec shrugged.

"What does that mean?"

"Shao-fei is Shao-fei is Shao-fei. He's good most of the time. Then he's down moping about and then he's up again. Right now he seems to be on the high end of the cycle."

"I should stop by and see him," Vincent said. "I've been so busy lately, but I should make the time."

The comment drew an equivocal glance from Alec. He twisted back the ring on a can of Taiwan beer. "This other person I see, this young woman, I take it she's your partner? She's the new volunteer?"

"Yes, she is."

"And she's your sister? Because that's what I've heard. That's the news that's been going round."

"That's right."

"Right that she's your sister or right that that's the news going round?"

"Right that she's my sister."

"Your actual flesh-and-blood, born-of-the-same-mother-and-father sister?"

"In a manner of speaking, yes."

"In a manner of speaking?" His smile was lavish without quite being derisive. "In a manner of speaking, I could sprout golden wings and fly off to Jupiter. So why haven't you introduced me to this sister of yours?"

"I asked her to join us."

"And?"

"She said she was in a hurry."

"Hurry? There's something more to it than that."

"She's odd sometimes," Vincent confessed. "I think maybe she has the wrong impression of you."

"How's that?"

"She saw you riding around town with a girl on the back of your motorcycle. I suppose she thinks you're up to no good."

"I probably was. What's her name, this flesh-and-blood sister of yours, this born-of-the-same—"

"All right, that's enough," Vincent said wearily.

"What's her name?"

"Gloria."

"GLORIA, MY DEAR!" he shouted up the lane. "YOU CAN COME AND RIDE ON MY MOTORCYCLE!" He grasped an imaginary set of handlebars and gave the throttle a potent turn.

Three stalls up, Gloria pivoted about in her chair and took a quick, scathing glimpse of the Scotsman. She frowned into her near-empty plate of noodles and set the plate atop the vendor's case before rising to leave. Then she turned again and looked at Vincent—an uncomfortable moment because her frown intensified.

Alec flitted his hand along the edges of his goatee and watched her go. "I've done it now, haven't I?" he lamented. "I only wanted to make a place for myself in her heart, and now I've gone and driven her away."

"She's strange," Vincent admitted again. "We've had some disagreements." He could easily have confided more. And not just about Gloria. The oddest thing has happened, he wanted to say. It started at the Ming-da Academy, with a student there, a girl who spoke out in class.

"There's bound to be disagreements, sharing accommodations the way you two do."

"I'd say she's very bullheaded about most things."

"No doubt she is."

"Very set in her ways."

"And no wonder you've introduced yourselves as brother and sister. It's the kind of lie your neighbors will be grateful for—even when they can't see a whit of resemblance. Tell me this, though: Is it difficult living under the same roof with a vibrant young woman? Are you ever tempted?"

"Hardly."

"All right, so she's not exactly a looker. But don't let that stand in your way. I have on occasions found myself off the beaten path, sharing accommodations with a young lady who is less than beautiful. I'll pass on this bit of advice."

Vincent sank his spoon in his soup and waited.

"It's like fanning the hearth fire on a cold winter's night. You don't have to stare into the embers to *stoke* the flames of love." A waggish grin, and he thrust his hips rudely against the table's edge.

In spite of himself, in spite of the garishness of the gesture, Vincent parted his lips and nearly whistled through his teeth. His chest heaved. Was it laughter? It seemed so.

"What's this?" Alec asked.

For a while at least he could hardly stop—the effusive chortling, the overbrimming sense of ridiculousness. His troubles with Gloria, his entanglement with Trudy seemed to be right there at the center of it all, a sprung coil, humming, unraveling.

Alec blinked in mock astonishment. "Don't tell me you're developing a sense of humor," he said. "The other missionaries won't stand for it. Good God, man, get ahold of yourself!"

On their tenth night together Vincent asked Trudy if she thought the things they were doing together in bed were wrong. They lay side by side, each stripped down to their underwear. Through the screened bedroom window they could hear the voices of two neighborhood girls light into song and the smack of bamboo sticks against the courtyard fence as the girls beat out the song's tempo.

"I don't know what you mean," Trudy said.

"I mean guilt and shame, religious shame. I don't know if it's something I actually feel, or something I should feel but don't."

"Feel what?" she asked, mystified. "Say that again."

"Sometimes, not always, I think that God or people in heaven are watching us and they think what we're doing together is wrong."

She held up her hands pretending to block any offending view of herself. "You mean they're watching us and they see we're not doing it the correct way." She laughed briefly, secretly. Her hands flitted down to her sides. "The gods I know don't care about that. They worry about other things."

"We lie down together in bed. We take off our clothes. We have to sneak around. Doesn't it feel wrong?"

"It's wrong if the neighbors find out. It's wrong if they tell my family," she said, rolling over and straddling him. She set the tip of her crotch against his and swayed back and forth. He had taught her to do this by guiding her into position on top of him and easing her hips into just the right motion. Lately, she was becoming something of an expert at it. "This must be right," she said, straining against him. "This must be the correct way." The rough-cut layers of her hair drifted forward and covered her eyes. She rocked faster.

"Trudy," he said, clenching her thighs and moaning. He shuddered and came beneath her and for an instant the room tilted off center, became a vivid negative of itself and revealed its dark edges. He closed and opened his eyes slowly, and the room's soft light, its evenness, shifted back into view.

She swung herself over beside him, touched the center of her panties, and then reached forward and ran her hand over his damp underwear. "What's this?" she asked.

"Oh, *please,*" he whispered.

"I have an idea. How to say in English?"

"Sperm," he mumbled.

"What?"

"Sperm," he repeated, more ashamed.

"What is it?"

"It's like a seed, a water seed. If it gets inside you, it makes you pregnant. It makes babies."

She pinched the elastic band of his underwear and pulled it down to his knees. She considered his penis gravely, curled her fingers around it while it softened in her hand. He worried that she might find the sight or feel of it unpleasant, but she leaned closer and regarded it with a deepening sense of concern.

"And this?" she said. "What's this?"

Vincent rolled his eyes and sighed.

"I know what it is," she whispered emphatically. "How to say in English?"

"Penis."

"Penis," she said, testing the word. "Penis," she said again, louder, and Vincent feared that of all the words spoken in his room, this one would have the tenacity to scale the bedroom walls, march down the stairs, and announce itself over the soft chorus of Gloria's music.

"I have an idea about this," she continued. "I have an idea that you're going to put this inside me. That's correct, isn't it? That's what people do together."

He pondered her question for a moment, wondering if confirming her theory was the same as consenting to take part in the act. Sheepishly, he reached down and restored his underwear to his waist. He nodded yes.

Beneath them they heard the front door of the ministry house swing open. He knelt on the mattress and pressed his face to the window screen. A story below, he saw Gloria pacing down the street toward the 7-Eleven, clutching her pocketbook. Out of instant coffee, Vincent surmised. What else would send her out at night? She passed Trudy's bicycle parked in a shadowy alcove and then the two girls, who immediately ended their song and huddled together whispering.

"You may as well go now, while she's out," Vincent said. He pulled a T-shirt over his head, stepped barefoot into his jeans, and waited by the door as Trudy dressed. Now and then she looked deliberately at her wristwatch, a small, knowing glance meant to emphasize the fact that he was sending her home twenty-five minutes early.

She said, "Tomorrow is Saturday. I only have classes in the morning. I finish at twelve o'clock. My father knows that, too."

He rubbed his chin against his shoulder, a partial shrug.

"I'm saying I'm not coming to visit you tomorrow because I don't have the night class. It's impossible. I don't have the night class on Sunday either."

"I understand that," he said. He moved into the hallway and motioned for her to follow. Taking her by the hand, he led her down the stairs rather than up to the roof. At the first-floor landing he asked her to wait while he went alone to the front door and made sure Gloria had not turned back. He shuffled back to the landing, reclaimed her hand, and led her past the darkened kitchen, the hallway, Gloria's bedroom door. Here he halted and took a step back so that light from the living room fell across the door and illuminated Gloria's calligraphy, her positive-thinking message.

He ran his finger down the line of characters. "What did she write here? What does it mean, exactly?"

"Hard to say. What do *you* think it means?"

"I think it says something about hard work. I'm not at all sure, though, because I can't read Chinese. That's why I'm asking you to help me."

She leaned forward and pretended to study the message. "I think you would feel sorry not to see me for two days."

"Maybe I do," he mumbled.

"Sad also. I think you would feel that way too."

"Maybe not sorry and sad. More like worried and frustrated. I want to see you, but I don't like sneaking around. I don't like how that feels."

"You sneak around inside this house. I sneak from school to here to my home, everywhere."

"Yes," Vincent admitted. "You're right about that."

"So you worry about it and now you said it and now I know. That's fine. But don't stand in your room and say nothing." She squeezed his hand fiercely, then turned her attention, this time more earnestly, to Gloria's message. "I'm not so sure about what your sister writes. The simple way to say it is, 'To work very hard, very strong, and to love Jesus very strong is the same thing.' But I think she makes a mistake."

"What mistake?"

"She puts the wrong word together with *love*. It's the word for a hot head." To demonstrate, Trudy slid her free hand across her forehead and fluttered her eyelashes.

"A temperature?" Vincent guessed. "A fever."

"Yes, maybe that. 'To work hard with a fever and to love Jesus with a fever is the same thing.'"

He shook his head. "A temperature? A fever? Like when you're sick?"

"No, the other kind."

"What other kind?"

She leaned into him and placed her hands on his hips; not the embrace of dancers, but a closer, tighter grasp meant to hold him still while she swayed against him. It was the same rhythm she had used upstairs in the bedroom minutes earlier.

"This kind," she said. "I think your sister loves Jesus very much."

Twelve

WHENEVER VINCENT thought about certain types of hypocrites—priests who molested altar boys, philandering politicians who railed against the decline of the American family, ministers' wives who slept with parishioners but continued to host church auxiliary meetings—he assumed that these covert acts turned them all into impostors. Standing alone before a crowd, surrounded by admirers, they knew precisely what they were guilty of and consequently struggled to maintain their most generous, most composed public faces.

Therefore, it surprised him to discover just how easy it was to overlook his own misconduct. At the Ming-da Academy, coaxing forty-one teenage girls through the perils of English conversation, he lost sight of his guilt and became absorbed in the exchange of questions and answers. One of the Violets might raise her hand and ask for a true story. The girls leaned forward and applauded. Inevitably, he would lapse into personal anecdotes. The class president might feign exasperation, but soon enough, like the other girls, she beamed happiness. In the midst of their devotion, Vincent felt humbled, yet somehow deserving of their affection. Never mind that he was not quite who he appeared to be. Never mind that he was secretly taking their former classmate into his bed five nights a week.

Even when he stood before his evening Bible study classes at the ministry house and said, "Jesus wants us to be the best, most honest people we can be, to use His life as an example for our own," even then, he did not feel as if he was an impostor speaking through a disguise. On the contrary, he spoke these words and others and was often moved by their grace, their kind logic, without really believing them. He continued to translate Bible stories even though he could not quite gauge their relevance. He led students in repetitions of Bible psalms fully aware that his own routine of prayer had faltered away; aware also, on a deeper level, that the pulse of his convictions, his private faith, had grown dangerously shallow, nearly unreadable.

And yet he seemed to have finally grown confident as a public speaker. At last he knew how to pause and furrow one eyebrow in contemplation, how to fold his arms and shift his gaze diplomatically about the room. His voice grew increasingly candid, steady, familiar. In an odd way it did not so much matter that the things he said were true, only that they sounded accurate. And without the constant struggle to see the truth in his faith, he could relax and concentrate more fully on his teaching. Thus, his lessons unfurled at a brisk, amiable pace. If, in the midst of it all, he was overcome by a tremor of remorse, he looked to the students themselves. They appeared to follow along respectfully, unaware of any change in their teacher. Even Gloria, waiting to fill the portable chalkboard with calligraphy, nodded her support.

It was possible, Vincent decided, to know and at the same time not know his own true intentions. It was possible for all the contradictions in his life to blur. At times he thought, I could come to believe almost anything I say or do.

On a rainy afternoon in April he rode under the anonymity of a yellow raincoat to the nearby town of Hu-wei. Gliding along the rain-slick streets, it seemed likely that he was dispelling an afternoon of boredom by taking a ride to an unfamiliar town. He went first to the town center and circled the roundabout three times. Peering out from beneath the hood of his raincoat, he saw blocks of shops and restaurants stained dark gray by the cold, unremitting rain. He pulled off and coasted down one side street and then another until he located a medicine shop. He parked the cycle and stepped inside. At the counter a young mother coddled her child and watched as the clerk measured out a bag of thick black pills. After she left, Vincent stepped up and in soft but precise Mandarin asked for a box of condoms. He had not known the Chinese word for condoms until the night before when he and Trudy had searched the dictionary for the word and then together practiced the pronunciation. As the clerk reached beneath the glass case, Vincent said, "We were in the New York airport and my wife told me to buy some then, but the plane was about to leave." He shrugged at the mayhem of international travel. Beyond the medicine shop window, he saw a throng of schoolchildren huddled under a bouquet of blue umbrellas and realized that the story he had just told was probably true for somebody somewhere. It might as well be true for him.

Back in Toulio, he rolled to a stop at the town's busiest intersection and saw Ponic standing at the curb holding open the rear door of Gwa's gray Bonneville. A moment later Gwa emerged and Vincent nearly raised his hand and called out until he remembered their last meeting and thought better of it. They both turned briefly toward the traffic. Neither noticed Vincent, a rain-coated figure huddled on a motorcycle in a river of stalled cars. After they stepped back and entered the building, Vincent tried unsuccessfully to summon the name of the woman Gwa loved. Nor could he remember the name of her hometown, a desert city, though he did remember that she lived near a mountaintop called Heaven Lake.

What he did recall most clearly was the reverent manner in which Gwa had described her. He said that he sat down at a dinner table and saw in an instant that she was extraordinary. Graceful, he had said, astute, beautiful. She radiated all these qualities without realizing their effects on other people. What would it be like, Vincent wondered, to be Gwa and have such uncomplicated desire for a woman? What would an emotion that pure, that singular, feel like?

Kneeling naked on his bed that night, he heard a heavier, more emphatic rain batter the windowpane. He rolled a condom on and divided Trudy's bare legs. Whatever had kept him from entering Carrie Ann Whitlinger did not stop him now. "Tell me if it hurts," he whispered in Trudy's ear, then eased himself inside her. All his movements were gentle, unhurried, painstakingly so, as much for his sake as her own; after all, it was astonishing to close his eyes and feel the way their bodies fit together. And Trudy, gripped, it seemed, by an equal astonishment, was pushing him over onto his back and settling down on top of him and swaying, swaying, swaying, as she had been taught to sway, her pleasure wide-eyed and a bit breathless and arriving sometime after his own pleasure had crested and fallen away.

She slid off him then, leaned forward, and touched the milky bubble on the tip of his penis. "That's the water seed," she said. "That's it right there."

Try as he might, he could not fathom her casual interest in the biological workings of sex. It wasn't enough to take part in the act itself. She wanted to witness, lights on, the preparation, the joining of their bodies, the aftermath. These were things, Vincent felt, better off viewed through the imagination, or at least as dim profiles inside an unlighted bedroom. The condom proved especially unpleasant; it seemed pragmatic and salient in all the wrong ways. Secretly, he doubted its ability to protect Trudy from pregnancy.

It rained for fourteen days straight. Be it mist or shower or downpour, water fell continuously from the muddled Taiwan sky. The locals called it the plum rains. They said, The plum rains are a little early this year. At night he met Trudy at the rooftop stairwell with a towel and dried her hands, her face, the wet strands of hair that clung to the hood of her parka. Frequently, after lovemaking, he asked her, "Did that feel all right?"

"Yes. That was good," she might say. Or she might rock her hips against his thigh and say, "I like this. Let's do this thing again."

These were never satisfactory answers because what he meant to ask, almost without knowing it, was, "Are you changed, Trudy? Are you changed by the things we do in bed together?" He wanted to know because he could not sense any particular change in himself. Clearly he was no longer a virgin, but this now seemed a distinction of little significance. Sex itself was less significant, less mysterious and forbidden, too, even while its chief pleasures grew larger and more necessary with each passing day.

At times he wondered if he was in love with Trudy's former class, all forty-one of them, but making physical love only to Trudy.

Were he not afraid of her answer, he might have asked, "Do you think we're in love? Is that what you think?" Instead he asked, "Why do you keep taking the chance of coming to see me at night?"

"Because," she said smartly, "I have to practice my English, Vincent. It's very important for my future."

"Yes, but sometimes we hardly say anything at all."

"That's not me. That's you. You like to be quiet and worry. I like to watch you. That's why I come here."

He frowned, and she raised her hand and traced the downward creases at the corners of his mouth.

"*Chou mei t'ou,*" she said. "How to say in English?"

"Frown."

"Ffrowwn," she practiced the word. "Remember when I said the bad jokes to you in class and all my classmates become upset. Remember that?"

He nodded.

"Afterward they follow me outside and sit me down and tell me that I'll become a bad woman. They all frown. They say I'll meet a bad man and he will sell me away to a sex hotel in Taipei. They say I'm crazy and I'll become a very bad sex woman. In this town, Vincent, you're either a good girl like my classmates or you're a very bad sex woman. So I've been thinking about it, and I decided I'm either crazy or I'm trying to be something in between." She wrinkled her nose and whispered, "The truth is, I'm probably crazy for trying to be something in between."

One evening, before the commencement of Bible study, he slipped out of the classroom and plodded downstairs to retrieve an extra folding chair. Passing Gloria's bedroom and yielding to a hasty intuition, he pushed open her door and made an unsettling discovery. She had filled in a wall, an entire floor-to-ceiling sweep of concrete, with calligraphy. He needed to flip on her work lamp to see the full extent of it, to see that she had started, reasonably enough, with a rendering of the two hundred or so basic Chinese strokes. This had been the pinnacle of his progress with the written language, and he understood how it would be helpful to have them charted on the wall, glancing distance from the table where she worked. From the chart and leading outward in all directions, she had inscribed vertical paragraphs of calligraphy—more positive-thinking messages?— until they touched the borders of ceiling and floor. She must have tiptoed to reach the highest corners, a sure sign of zealous commitment, but the lowermost sections of the wall would require a different, more troubling posture. She must have crouched or even lain on the cement floor to ink in the ground-level characters. His first instinct was to contact Reverend Phillips and let him know that Gloria had sequestered herself inside a windowless room and taken a manic interest in Chinese calligraphy. But almost immediately he began to doubt the precariousness of her behavior. One moment it seemed serious, even dangerous, and then a second later merely eccentric. In the flux of perspectives, how could he decide? If he could not discern his own motives and conduct, how could he possibly judge Gloria's state of mind?

The whole episode left him more tired than truly alarmed. The weariness dogged him for several days until Wednesday afternoon, a day that would prove itself as the last day of the plum rains. Trudy called while Vincent was darting about the ministry house stuffing books and papers into his bag. He had a lesson at the preschool that afternoon and he stooped beside the phone and shouldered the receiver impatiently against his chin.

"I bought you an English card letter today," she said. "But it was stolen away from me. I want to tell you what it said because I remember it exactly."

"Trudy, where are you?"

"I'm here at home."

"Why aren't you in school?"

"Oh, I *don't go* to that school anymore," she said, a tremor of wild emotion suddenly swelling her words.

"What's that?"

"I said I don't go to that school now." Her voice wavered again. He heard her take a quick, sniffling gulp of air. "I'm going to a new one in Tainan City," she tried to say brightly. "It's a school I can live at, Vincent. It's a school for girls. Just girls, nothing else."

"What?" he asked and felt his tongue go dry in his mouth. "Trudy?" He held his breath. "Trudy, are you pregnant?"

"You always worry too much," she said. "You worry about the wrong thing."

"I don't understand—"

"Shhh," she said. "Listen to this. It's about the card I bought you. It's a thing to remember. So it's important. The card said, I wish you the world's happiness of all."

"Trudy," he said, exasperated.

"I know what it said," she insisted. "I bought the card. Even though they stole it away from me, I can still tell you about it. I can at least do that." She said good-bye and hung up the phone.

He stood rooted in place. Surely the dread he felt would eventually climax and subside. When it did not, he shouldered his bag and rode panic-stricken to the preschool for his three o'clock lesson.

In the parking lot, he curbed his cycle and strolled across the lot to an old woman who was begging for change near the street corner. He had dropped coins into her bamboo hat before, but today he opened his wallet and placed a five-hundred-yuan bill into her hand. She closed her wrinkled fingers over the bill and gazed up astonished into Vincent's face.

Trudy, he decided, even though she denied it, was more than likely pregnant. Her family was sending her away to what sounded like a school for wayward girls. Giving the old woman money wouldn't change anything. He was not superstitious. But somehow it made the possibility of Trudy not being pregnant feel larger.

Inside the preschool, he stood and flashed alphabet cards at his young audience. He made only trifling demands on their attention, and soon they grew fickle and wandered toward more interesting corners of the playroom. Accordingly, his own thoughts strayed to Trudy and her pregnancy, to his outright shame at having allowed their affair to progress so far. It wasn't until almost the end of the lesson, during a long and arduous game of Hangman, that he realized he might never see her again.

That evening's Bible study drew seventeen students, their largest class ever. Because the pace of this lesson moved faster, Vincent had little time for distraction. When his mind did wander, it was merely to plan out what to do next. He had never telephoned Trudy at home and did not know her number. He would have to adopt the easiest and most frustrating of plans and wait for her to call again or visit the ministry rooftop. When class let out, he walked his students to the front gate and lingered a few uneasy minutes before mounting his motorcycle and riding to the edge of town. He crossed over the rail line and headed south along a thin road bordered by dark fields of wheat. It took several slow passes to locate the grassy drive that led up to Trudy's house. Viewed from the end of the drive, the three wings of her house stood out as a coal black silhouette. He could make out no distinguishable lights or movement, the house appearing abandoned or, more aptly, shuttered for the night. Had the lights been on, he doubted he could have summoned enough courage to go to the door and ask for her. What kind of foolish coincidence had he hoped for? Trudy out for a nighttime stroll? Trudy stationed at the front window anticipating his arrival? Even if they had managed a rendezvous, all Vincent wanted was a clear accounting of what had gone wrong. Trudy would likely want the comfort of a prolonged embrace, a poignant farewell. Prevailed upon, he would join in her commiseration, but his sentiments would be obliging and false-hearted. He turned the cycle around and headed back toward town feeling the ungainly weight of his own selfishness.

A block from home, he rounded the corner, swung past the motorcycle shop, and saw a figure leaning against the front gate. In the short time it took him to set the cycle on its stand and walk to the gate, he believed the figure to be Trudy. For a minute, maybe less, he felt enlarged by the hope that she was waiting for him with an explanation that would set to rest his worst fears.

A stocky young man in threadbare work clothes stepped away from the gate. "You know who I am?" he asked softly.

"Yes," Vincent replied. "Trudy's older brother."

"Whose brother?"

"Ch'iu Yüeh," he said. "Ch'iu Yüeh's older brother."

"Yes." He stepped closer, folded his arms, and swayed lightly to and fro on the heels of his sandaled feet. His gaze was sober, patient. He said almost shyly, "I don't even know you and now I have to ask you a question that's not very polite. It's uncomfortable for me, you understand?"

Vincent nodded.

"You've been taking her to bed with you," Trudy's brother said. It seemed less like an accusation and more like some spoken understanding between them.

"I'm sorry. Yes. I'm sorry it went that far. I hope she's not pregnant."

"She's not. We took her to the doctor this morning. She was in bed with you more than once?"

"Yes, I'm sorry. I didn't mean for that to happen."

Trudy's brother weighed this answer gravely. He ceased his swaying and settled into place, then drew his fist back and struck Vincent hard just below the cheek.

Knocked back against the gatepost, he sensed the street, the gate, the ground beneath him tilt off center. At once Trudy's brother lunged forward, and something dense and bony, an elbow, dug into Vincent's side and forced out his breath. He pitched forward and was met with another fierce punch, this one to the chin. Thrown back into the gate, he thought, in a flash of almost magisterial lucidity, This is exactly what I deserve. He has every right to do this, to make his point this way.

He looked up and saw the brother's knobby face clotted, flattened, deadened by rage. Apparently, striking Vincent had brought him no satisfaction. Vincent's own face throbbed, his ribs ached. More painful still was the awareness that someone could harbor such hatred for him. "All right," he managed to say. He waved a hand to indicate that, now that it was over, he understood and accepted his reckoning.

A fist fluttered sideways out of the darkness and cuffed him sharply on the ear and he slumped to the ground. Lying on the pavement, he felt the hard edge of a sandal needling him in the ribs. He sat up and received a much harder kick in the chest. He rose and lurched toward Trudy's brother, arms flailing out, but again a fist seemed to dart out of nowhere and glance off his brow. Then a second, more exacting blow landed squarely on the bulb of his nose. He threw his arm out, a lazy arc of a punch that died in the air. He tasted blood in his mouth, felt his own pulse in the dull throb of his lip. His left eye had gone sleepy with ache and swelling. He saw streaks of color capering about like fireflies. When he reached up to rub his eyes, he pulled back a long, slinking tendril of bloody mucus that had trailed out from one nostril. A wave of dizziness crested over him. He took a second look at the brother's outraged face, fearing the point was no longer about retribution. This might be a beating without any point at all.

He received another blow to the chest, and he stepped back and eased himself down onto the pavement. Trudy's brother knelt beside him and punched him in the face. Another punch and then a third and Vincent felt blood coursing from both nostrils.

"My father told me to bring friends because you were tall and had long arms," Trudy's brother said. "Wait till I tell him what happened." He leaned close, placed his knee beside Vincent's neck. "We should never have let a dirty motherfucker like you into our home," he said and pressed his knee over Vincent's windpipe, not long enough to deprive him of breath, just long enough to show him it was something that could be done. "You should go back to America. That would be the best thing. You might go to Taipei, but I go there sometimes and if I saw you there I would just do the same thing. I'm coming back here tomorrow and every day after that until I'm sure you're gone." He bent even closer and straightened Vincent's collar, which had folded in on itself at a slanting angle. "It hurts," he said. "I know that. But it will hurt a lot more if I see you tomorrow."

Then Trudy's brother stalked off across the lane and slipped behind the wheel of his father's car. Vincent drew himself over onto his side, curled his legs up, and watched the car roll away. At the intersection the brake lights blinked twice and disappeared into a current of glittering traffic. He pinched the ridge of his nose and waited for the blood to subside and thought, stupidly, I remember riding in the back of that car.

His head throbbed mightily. He tried to locate and name his injuries. Yet his whole body ached, and this deep ache caused an exhaustion that made all of his thoughts turn banal, elementary. He thought of rising to his feet and entering the ministry house and how that might be done. Would it be possible to catch blood in his cupped hands and still call out *good night* to Gloria in an unaffected voice? And if he made it to his room and slumped down on the bed, what then?

There were lights on in the neighboring houses, and he realized that although his beating had seemed a brutally private affair, there must have been an obvious, public commotion. Undoubtedly spectators were watching from some of those lighted windows, and he rose to his feet, mostly for their benefit. He placed a steadying hand upon the gate rail. It took several tottering steps to reach his motorcycle.

Once seated, he meant to rest for a moment, but his foot found the kick start, and the warm engine turned over easily. Before he knew it the momentum of the cycle was carrying him to the intersection and out onto the main avenue. Head down, he rode toward the outskirts of Toulio.

Of this at least he was reasonably certain: a punishment had just been meted out, a retribution that felt larger than himself or Trudy's brother and at the same time exquisitely personal. And while he was already a fervent believer in the rightness of his punishment, he could not yet piece together the precise knowledge that had been handed down.

I should never have visited her house in the first place, he thought numbly, while his bloated lips curled around each syllable. *That's where the trouble began. Or earlier. I should never have grown so fond of the Ming-da students.*

Perhaps that was it. Perhaps he had, as people liked to say, learned a lesson he would not soon forget.

Thirteen

THE CHENS' SLIDING front doors had not been latched shut for the night, and Vincent passed through them and felt his way across the darkened foyer. He ascended several steps before hearing a polite, interior voice, Shao-fei's voice, remembered from the day of his arrival. *Shoes, please.* Obligingly, he back-stepped down to the landing and pried off his tennis shoes.

Now in socked feet, he grasped the railing and took each step in a solemn one-two shuffle. Blood formed in thick droplets on the tip of his chin and he used the sleeve of his jacket to dab them away. The second-floor hallway was dark except for a soft, muted light seeping from beneath Alec's bedroom door. He knocked and waited till the door swung open.

Even Alec appeared slack-jawed at the sight of him. "Oh, for fuck's sake, Vincent. What *happened* to you?"

"Wrecked on my motorcycle," he mumbled, one hand cupped beneath his chin. "Threw me off into a ditch."

Alec studied him shrewdly. Then he pushed Vincent farther into the hallway and guided him toward the bathroom. Under the stark-white overhead light, he examined Vincent again and helped him out of his jacket then dress shirt, which he wadded up and pitched in the trash can. He ran a full sink of warm water and unwrapped a fresh bar of soap. "Wash everything you can off with the water, then soap your face up well." With one hand on Vincent's shoulder, Alec guided him, face first, into the sink.

The warm water was more soothing than painful. He lathered up his hands and with soapy fingers felt how the beating had changed the contours of his face. On the brow above his left eye he discovered a prominent knot and inch-length gash. Beneath the brow, the left eye was swollen nearly shut. The eyelid had gone heavy and dull, too fat to blink properly. He ran his fingers down along his jawline and found that his bottom lip had taken on a similar thickness. It tingled beneath his touch and jutted out with a rubbery indifference. The underside of his chin had been badly scraped, but thankfully the right side of his face, the brow, eye, and cheek, had not expanded, nor were there any sudden bumps on the slope of his nose to suggest a break or fracture.

It was not until after he rinsed and began to pat his face dry with the towel that his abrasions flared up with a shuddering sting. He sucked in his breath and sat down trembling on the rim of the bathtub.

"You all right?"

Vincent nodded gingerly. He glanced up and was struck by the sight of Alec, first stooped in the bathroom doorway, then kneeling down beside him with an open box of Band-Aids in one hand. It was a posture that seemed entirely familiar, the careful vigilance with which Alec leaned forward and unrolled three Band-Aids across the cut on his brow, and Vincent watched it all with an inverted sense of déjà vu. The difference, he realized, was that it should have been him kneeling down and offering help.

"Raise your head up a bit now."

Vincent complied and felt a prickly burn as another Band-Aid sealed the underside of his chin. He flinched and heard Alec mutter something low and broguish.

"What's that?" Vincent asked.

"Motorcycle crash, my arse," he whispered. "Hey, Boy Scout, somebody beat the shit out of you, didn't they?"

He followed Alec back to the bedroom and, after a few mild protests, accepted a T-shirt and lay down on Alec's bed. His nose still trickled blood. Alec tore the cover from a book of matches, rolled it up neatly, and placed it along the gum line beneath Vincent's upper lip. Minutes later an ice-filled towel was draped across his forehead.

He lay quietly beneath the cold compress for a half hour, listening to Alec's hot plate click and hum and heat a kettle of water into a sputtering whine. He removed the match cover from beneath his lip and rinsed his mouth with a cup of hot water. Propped up in bed, turned toward Alec, he said, "I met a girl," but his lip had thickened and this brought a slight lisp to his words. He heard himself say *girwel* and immediately his heart sank. It made what he was about to describe seem trite, patently adolescent. He cupped the palm of his hand over his swollen forehead and concentrated. "I was teaching a class at the Ming-da Academy," he said, ignoring the lisp and focusing on the words that would best convey the suddenness of Trudy's outbursts in class. He told how she had been expelled from school and how later he had unwisely agreed to visit her family. Through much of this Alec wore a narrowly patient expression, tolerant but a shade insensible, as if he were a seasoned explorer forced to listen to a tenderfoot's bland travelogue. Now and then, however, his eyes fluttered open in surprise and he blurted out a startled comment: "You're joking now! Surely," or "Fucking hell, man! What were you thinking?" Vincent shrugged off these exclamations and pressed on with the story, and as he related further incidents—the way they met nightly on the ministry rooftop and how they eventually moved downstairs to his bedroom—he was not so much ashamed of the things he had done, but shamed by how predictable it all sounded. Didn't all missionaries, all priests and volunteers, go about their work under the constant suspicion of leading shabby, covert sexual lives? Thoroughly humbled, he related the incidents of that very day, events that seemed too recent to be part of any story: Trudy's cryptic telephone call and the fight outside the ministry house gates, which, Vincent admitted, was really more of a beating than a fight.

Alec wagged his head in disbelief. "He's serious, this girl's brother? He's serious about running you out of town?"

"Very. I have no doubt."

"Good God, man! You were shagging her over there at the ministry house?"

"Well . . . yes . . . we went farther than we should have. One thing led to another. Next thing we knew her brother found out."

"How so?"

"One of the neighbors must have said something. There must have been rumors."

"There's always rumors. How did he know for sure?"

"When he showed up tonight, he asked me and I told him. I thought it was something I should go ahead and admit to."

"Are you daft?" Alec groaned. "Are you completely fucking daft? Hasn't it occurred to you that you're living in a part of the world where no one admits to anything?"

It had not occurred to Vincent, but he bowed his head eager to agree, ready to bear the shame of further mistakes. "Yes, I guess you're right."

"No guessing about it. When it comes to a family losing face, the stakes are so much higher here."

"I'd go back and deny it if I could, Alec. I'd go back and change it."

"Of course you would."

"I'm not just talking about what happened tonight. I'd go back to the start and change that. The whole thing with Trudy."

"Too bad that didn't occur to you before you got her in the sack."

"It did," Vincent said. "I was making choices all along without really knowing it. I could have stopped myself and put an end to it. I had a hundred different opportunities." He rubbed his sore jaw, dismayed. The aftermath of what he had done, the fallout, began to align itself. He felt it taking shape in a long parade of consequence that began with his resignation as a Christian volunteer. Reverend Phillips would have to be notified. An explanation would have to be tendered. "I've ruined any chance for the new ministry," he said mournfully. "Gloria. Think of that. Think of Gloria running things on her own."

"You've fucked up," Alec agreed. "No undoing it now."

The bedroom at the far end of the hallway had remained vacant for nearly five months. Vincent found very little in the simple arrangement of table, chair, dresser, and bed comforting or even familiar. Clutching a borrowed pillow and blanket, he eased down onto the bare mattress, not expecting to sleep, but ready to begin sifting through layers of error and accountability. In doing so, he might eventually work his way down to the source of it all, a flaw so crucial, so pernicious, that it would overshadow any honorable qualities he had come to trust in himself.

In his present state, he could relish such a discovery. But for all his determined brooding, his thoughts kept dissolving into recollection, most often of Trudy, or rather the spectacle of Trudy crouched half-naked upon his ministry house bed. It was an image that flaunted itself with a merciless redundancy—Trudy shouldering free of her school uniform and wordlessly taking her place on Vincent's lap—and each time he reacted with a sharp, inward cringe. The beating, he realized, had diminished her as well. In a few short hours the whole of her had been fractioned down to guilt, shame, mistake.

And here lay another dimension to his regret, because he realized that the real Trudy was likely en route to a boarding school in Tainan. If he had the energy, the stamina of conscience, he could explore in detail a separate line of consequence for Trudy. She would find herself a stranger in yet another new school. It might be years before she overcame her family's indignation. For these matters and more, he was sorry. The sharpest edge of his remorse, however, pointed in another direction—the fact that his feelings for Trudy had never evolved into love. He had felt only an undefined sense of camaraderie, taking her into his bed for an hour each night. Now that he had confessed to the affair, he was almost persuaded to look back on their behavior as lewd and unscrupulous, when in fact it may have been closer to simple friendship. She had befriended him during a difficult and lonely time for reasons he could not quite fathom, and he had never really acknowledged her affection, had never thanked her for it.

He let his eyelids drift half-shut and lay still. An aching body could sometimes be hoodwinked into sleep. He wanted to believe this so he concentrated on the unsheathed window and the soft mantle of orchid-hued darkness outside. A kilometer away the shop lights of Toulio gave off a lackluster radiance. Without meaning to, he closed his eyes and summoned the enraged face of Trudy's older brother. He felt again the heavy knee that had been pressed against his windpipe. Abruptly, he rose from the bed and stumbled toward the bathroom, where for a loathsome interval he dry-heaved into the sink. His bruised ribs ached and cut short his breath. Later, when he could stand it, he gulped down a glass of water and two aspirin and returned to bed. Once more he narrowed his eyes. A deep, mending rest seemed out of the question, but he found that if he emptied his head of thoughts and allowed his worries to wash over him, he could dwell inside a faltering version of sleep.

That version of sleep carried him through to morning and a room suffused with stark, day-sprung brightness. He slipped into yesterday's pants and socks and stood before the dresser mirror. Just as he had expected, his left eye had gone from swollen to dark purple. What he had not anticipated was how the same shade of purple would seep beneath the bridge of his nose and fan out across his right eye. He could not recall being punched in this eye, and it seemed unfair that both eyes should be ringed in dark halos. Unreasonable and undeserved and something else, something he could not place until he moved to the bathroom, took a hot shower, and toweled off before the bathroom mirror. He had been burdened with raccoon eyes. The plum-colored circles suggested animal fright and timidity, an effect that would have been comical if he had noticed it in anyone other than himself.

And so, thus burdened, he sat at the bedroom window, elbows braced atop the sill. There was no movement in the other rooms of the house. Alec had not yet risen from bed, Shao-fei was at school, Mama at the open market. Below a crew of some twenty or more rice farmers labored amid the neatly framed fields. From time to time a lone motorcyclist sailed along the blacktop lane. A languorous mood washed over him. Under its sway an hour slipped by, then most of another. All the while the farmers continued their work, halting, once the day grew warmer, to eat an early lunch and sleep in the shadowed cool of a stone wall. Presently they were rising from their nap and bowing into their ample bamboo hats and filing out into the fields once more. To watch them do so, to watch them labor in the paddies, to see them pitched forward, barefoot, trouser legs rolled up to their knees, was to know, conclusively, that he was being remiss toward his own obligations. A decision was required of him. What made the decision difficult was the conviction, perfectly false, that he had dozens of options, when the shrewdest part of his being—a voice, an intuition now singular and unassisted—knew very well he had but two.

He imagined, as scrupulously as possible, two near futures for himself. Then he chose between them.

It was exhilarating, the daring and timeliness such a choice entailed, the skydiver's sense of inevitability, and afterward he plodded downstairs hoping to mark the occasion with a cold drink or meal. No such luck. The Chens' icebox was mostly bare. He pirated a roll of English-style biscuits from the cabinet and headed for the parlor. Sitting on the wicker sofa, he broke each flat biscuit apart and passed the pieces between his bruised lips. He chewed and swallowed in a dawdling, meticulous rhythm. With the same finical patience he opened his wallet and searched through the interior pockets. He flipped past receipts and a pair of useless American dollar bills and extracted a business card, which he set on the parlor table beside the telephone. For a moment, he ignored the card and dialed the operator. He asked for an airline number and mouthed the number quietly as he hung up and dialed again. A reservations clerk answered, sweet-voiced and officious. It was Thursday and he made reservations to fly from Taipei early Saturday morning. The clerk urged him to pay in advance or risk losing his seat. He declined. In fact, all he wanted was the reservation, the barest of evidence from which he could draw confidence and build a credible story. He thanked her and wished her a good day before turning his attention back to the business card. The decipherable portion of the card contained a six-digit telephone number, which he dialed at once. The remaining characters he guessed to be Gwa's name and business address.

Five droning rings and he heard Ponic's husky greeting on the other end and said, "It's me, Vincent. The foreign Jesus teacher. You remember?"

"Yes," Ponic said dully. "I remember you."

"I wanted to call and tell you and Mr. Gwa good-bye. Because I'm leaving Taiwan. I'm leaving soon, on Saturday, and I've been calling friends and saying good-bye and I found Mr. Gwa's card and I thought I should call him, too. I wanted to say good-bye and ask him for some advice."

"He's busy," Ponic said.

"Yes, I thought he might be. So please don't bother him. Just tell him I said good-bye and that I wanted to ask about the Mainland, because that's where I'm going. My plan is to travel in the Mainland for a month and then go back to America. I wanted to know the best places—"

"All right," Ponic grumbled. "All right. Hold on a second."

The receiver was set down and Vincent could hear his story being recounted in a squawky, tin-can murmur. Next came a shuffling of chairs and feet and then Gwa's voice. "Yes, all right. What is it?" he insisted.

"I was telling Ponic that I'm leaving Taiwan. I've been calling friends, people that I've known in Toulio, and saying good-bye."

"I know that already."

"I've had some problems."

"Yes," Gwa said, testy and bored. "So?"

"I couldn't get along with the other Jesus teacher, the one I told you was my sister. She's not my sister. We were told to say so because we were living together in the same house. But we didn't get along. We had very different ideas."

"And now you're leaving. What's the point of calling me?"

"I wanted to say good-bye and ask about places to visit in the Mainland. Last time I saw you, you talked about Xinjiang, about Heaven Lake. That's where I'd like to go."

The dead-air silence between them seemed, for a moment, wintry and vast. Then, to Vincent's surprise, Gwa laughed into the receiver. "I should have known," he said, still chuckling, though with a wheezing undercurrent of bitterness. "I should have guessed it."

"Like I said, I've had some problems."

"I guess you have." It sounded then as if the phone was set aside or held against Gwa's chest while he conferred with Ponic. Gwa returned shortly to gloat. "I remember you said that it wasn't right," he boasted.

"The favor I'd asked you to do for me. You said that even if your Taipei boss allowed it, you wouldn't do it . . . because it was crazy."

Vincent held his tongue and mulled over several excuses, none of them persuasive. "I did say that," he admitted. "I won't deny it now."

"So you let two months go by and now you call because you think I still need this favor from you?"

"Yes. I thought maybe you would."

"Well, maybe I don't. Maybe Kai-ling and I have decided to wait."

"That could be—that's probably the best thing," Vincent stammered. "I guess you two didn't really know each other."

"Not wait to marry. We're certain we want to marry. We've decided to wait until our governments make it possible. I have a friend in the National Assembly who tells me that the kind of marriage certificate we need shouldn't take long. A year at the most, but more likely just six months."

"That's not a long time," Vincent said. "Six months."

"It isn't. In the letters we write each other we always say it's best to wait."

"You're probably right about that."

"Of course we are, but then—*ha*—that's easy for you to say, isn't it?"

Ha? The fretful, un-Gwa-like lilt of it, the way he'd said it, more of a queasy hitch in his throat than a laugh. It had the groaning cadence of a personal burden being stretched at the seams. By Vincent's reckoning it was the most auspicious note he'd heard so far.

"I'll tell you this," Gwa said.

"Yes?"

"When it comes to writing letters, she sometimes isn't very—how to say it best?"

"Clear?"

"Steady," he said. "Dependable. Not always dependable."

"I think I understand."

"I got a letter from her recently that wasn't so dependable, wasn't so . . . patient. And now you call."

"Yes, I did."

"*Aiyaaa,*" Gwa moaned, and what for most Chinese was a mild interjection became for Gwa a kind of rancorous curse. "I don't like the way you change your mind suddenly. I don't like it at all. Are you serious this time?"

"Yes, I am."

"How serious?"

"Very. I'm leaving for Hong Kong on Saturday morning. I have a reservation. A ticket is being held."

"Then you better come and see me right away."

"I can't do that. You'll have to come see me. I'm staying with a friend, the Scotsman, because I've had some trouble. I'm not in good shape right now. You'll understand when you get here." He gave Gwa directions and hung up and then, as an afterthought, calmly ate two more biscuits.

He had a weighty feeling, a kind of buyer's remorse, that he had just mortgaged himself to a colossal undertaking. Too late to withdraw now. Not that he wanted to. He had arrived at his decision by imagining his return to Red Bud, Illinois, with a daunting exactitude. In Red Bud there would be the gauche fact of his early return crouching behind every conversation, but first there would be the car ride home from the St. Louis airport and the dumb wonder of his pummeled face and his parents' shaken yet dissimilar reactions: his mother, Marion, and her well-meant but stifling sympathies, her alarmist remarks; his father, Carl, who would partake of his son's misfortune quietly and in bitter increments as he steered their hulking Suburban toward the state line and grew, mile by mile, more sorrowful and forlorn. Which was not to say Vincent couldn't lie low someplace until his face healed. Or that he couldn't invent an exhaustive excuse for his failure. The problem was he knew his near future in Red Bud all too well. He could imagine precisely the complexion of sultry late-spring light grazing the windows of his parents' house and the feeling that went along with it—the petty boredom, the shoddy discomfort of being a reluctant lodger in his childhood bedroom. A humiliating defeat to return to that room. (And yet, contrarily, he longed to return, to retreat, to swaddle himself in the artifacts of his childhood and to never, or at least for a very long time, attempt anything more perilous than a weekend fishing trip and a part-time job sorting prescriptions at Deterdings Drugs.) Beyond that there would be the bareness of life in Red Bud and the lean months of getting back on his feet and the many shades of malaise and remorse and falseness that would be his future temperament. There would be Vanessa, with whom he could never convincingly sidestep the truth for long. There would be his kindly but scrutinizing relatives and the half-settled debts he still owed them, and there would be the now slippery endeavor of church every Sunday morning at St. Mark's, not to mention the twice-weekly meetings of the St. Mark's auxiliary, several members of which maintained close ties to the Overseas Christian Fellowship and distant but still tenable connections to Reverend Phillips in Taipei. Finally, there was the understanding in ways both explicit and undetermined that his punishment, the parade of consequence, which started in Toulio, would follow him home.

As for his near future in the Mainland, he imagined this: a stupendously blue lake set high atop a desert mountain, an impatient bride, possibly beautiful.

Outside, a truck pulled up in the alleyway and dropped off a crate of chickens. From the parlor window he heard a delirious flutter of wings, an airy ripple of sound that seemed to jump-start his heart. He clutched the telephone and realized he had accomplished only the first of many calls. To leave Toulio, to leave responsibly, would require a myriad of excuses. He began with a quick call to the airline to purchase his ticket, then the least difficult calls: to his private students, to the plastics wholesaler and the preschool. He told the wholesaler that he was flying back home to be with his father, who was sick, seriously ill, hospitalized. By the time he contacted the preschool director and Jonathan Hwang at the Ming-da Academy, he had been bullied by a vague sense of superstition into changing his story. Instead he brought serious illness to his grandfather, now twenty years dead. He felt little compunction telling Hwang that he would miss that afternoon's class because he was rushing back to the States and might or might not return. Hwang had always suspected foreigners of shiftlessness; confirming it was sure to bring the man satisfaction.

For an anguished quarter hour he considered making two calls to Taipei, one to Mrs. Liang and her husband, which he pondered and eventually deemed unnecessary, the other to Reverend Phillips. The latter he knew to be an unavoidable call, essential, imperative, and altogether unbearable. At present he could not bring himself to make it. He doubted he would find the courage in the next two days, and so he vowed to write a letter instead, this being the Reverend's preferred means of discourse. He pledged to compose this letter with as much honesty as circumstances allowed and to mail it on his way to the airport.

He phoned and woke Gloria. She was, she explained, sleeping late because she had been up all night wondering where Vincent was. He apologized at once. He had been up all night himself, he said, with Alec, who was sick with the flu or maybe some viral infection. Alec was not any better and now they were going to the clinic. It was all fairly serious and he might be away from the ministry house another night, if that was all right. Had anybody called or come by? Still groggy from sleep, it took Gloria a moment to answer no and another to begin testing him with questions. Where had he disappeared to last night? Why hadn't he called? His head spun with possible answers and he withdrew the receiver from his ear to create space for clear thought. He looked up and saw Gwa standing in the parlor doorway, the older, business-suited Gwa, his brow furrowed, his expression ripe with puzzlement. "Excuse me, I'm looking for—" He stared at Vincent and blinked.

For an instant, Vincent forgot his own bruised face. His hand was descending with a heavy-limbed willfulness, Gloria's voice a faint, tri-fling buzz, and he set the receiver gently in its cradle. Only after he rose and greeted Gwa, ushered him into the parlor and offered him a seat, only then did he realize that his face had undermined each proper courtesy.

"You two were fighting? Your sister . . . I mean, the other volunteer did this? You two were fighting?" Gwa repeated. The corner of his mouth twitched, unsure whether or not to lapse into a grin.

"No, no. This is something else. This is another thing that happened. This happened just last night."

"Where?" Gwa asked. "Here? You were fighting with the Scotsman?"

"No. I was out with the Scotsman. We were drinking. I was drinking, too, which I shouldn't do because I'm not used to it. I got into an argument with some men, young men, the kind with the fast Japanese motor-cycles. They called me a name, something stupid, and I got angry. Maybe I didn't even hear it right."

"This happened here in Toulio?"

"Yes, at Hungry Ghost Street. It was late. Most of the shops had closed down. I was drinking and so were they and we got into a fight. It was my fault, too." He searched for a more exact term. "*Shuang fang ti ch'o,*" he said. Equal blame.

Gwa studied him cautiously. Looking at Vincent seemed to cause him distress, a tightening around the eyes.

"You have to understand, I've been ready to leave for a while now. Things haven't been right between the other volunteer and me. We believe different things and it was a mistake to put us together. And then yesterday I got in a fight. I got beat up. I feel terrible about it, but at least it's forced me to decide what I really want to do."

The distress had now gone deep, cut to the quick of Gwa's usual self-assurance. "I have business partners who tease me about being too slow, too careful with my decisions," he said. "I don't like what I'm hearing right now. It makes me feel like I'm gambling." His confidence blunted, he roosted on the edge of the sofa in a wary hunch. And yet there was an unsettled sense that his distress might not have been Vincent's fault entirely. Gwa had brought along a thick bundle of artifacts pertaining to Kai-ling: letters in their fretted envelopes; scraps of notes, some of them scrawled on airline timetables; a coverless notebook with a list of hastily scribed characters; and Kai-ling herself, or at least the elliptical profile that comprised her photograph. Given the hounded way he shuffled through these items, it appeared that she, too, was an appreciable source of worry. "I have to ask you again," he began, more plea than demand. "I have to ask one more time, if you're certain, if you're serious—"

"I'm leaving for Hong Kong in two days. Whatever you decide, Mr. Gwa, whether you need a favor from me or not, two days from now I'll be in Hong Kong ready to enter the Mainland."

"All right. Very good. I'll call Hong Kong and have word sent to Kai-ling later today. There'll be no backing out once that's happened."

"I understand."

"I believe she'll be pleased to hear it," Gwa said, sifting through her correspondence, his tone hesitant, almost bashful. "She has—for a while now, I think—been getting tired of all the waiting. It's something I see in her letters, or something I think I see. The mood changing from one letter to another."

"No reason to worry, I'm sure."

"Maybe not. But she doesn't write as often as she used to."

"That's to be expected," Vincent said, as if in the general matter of romance or the specific matter of sundered lovers he had ample expertise. "My sister—my real sister in Chicago—had a boyfriend in Germany once. They lived apart an entire year and she—"

Gwa stopped him with a raised hand. "Please. There's no connection between your American sister in Chicago and Kai-ling in Urumchi. Two different worlds. Their situations are not alike." He flipped through the bundle of artifacts, referring to the notebook and its list. The first item concerned the application for a Mainland marriage certificate. Affidavits would have to be signed. There would be physical exams and meetings with officials at Urumchi's civil affairs office, where Kai-ling would handle the negotiations and Vincent would dress well and keep quiet. Once a marriage certificate had been obtained, she could apply as his spouse for a Hong Kong visa. Gwa had a partner in Hong Kong, Mr. Wu, who would help with the process. "So much to do," Gwa mused. "But Kai-ling can begin gathering documents and filing papers right away. By the time you get to Urumchi she'll have everything in order." He pressed his thumb down the list to the next item: the dowry. The dowry could be given, Gwa explained, once Vincent and Kai-ling's father, Mr. Song, sat down to finalize the wedding plans, but the amount of the dowry, three thousand U.S. dollars, should be whispered discreetly in Mr. Song's ear soon after Vincent arrived. Gwa warned him to be careful with the money, to watch for thieves, to trust no one but Kai-ling and her family. Happily, the sum Vincent would be paid had not changed, ten thousand dollars divided into two payments. The first five thousand and the dowry money would be paid out at Mr. Wu's Hong Kong office. Vincent almost balked at this until he saw the matter from Gwa's point of view, the risk of sending a foreigner to the Taipei airport with thousands of dollars. Once in the Mainland he could, Gwa explained, travel by either plane or train, the trains, of course, being slower and less expensive. He did not have to hurry to Urumchi. Kai-ling's family would need time to prepare. But once there and married, Gwa expected them to hurry back. He glanced sharply at Vincent to emphasize this point. There was a range of smaller details Gwa rushed through—the foreigner's hotel in Urumchi where Vincent would stay, how best to change money and buy travel tickets—and Vincent sensed that he had come prepared to make a more thorough and persuasive case, but seeing Vincent's swollen lip and blackened eyes had shaken his concentration. "Just be careful," Gwa said. "Careful with the money, careful not to tell strangers what you're doing in China. Send a telex to Wu if there's any trouble. He'll know how to get in touch with me." Without quite looking at Vincent, he said, "Kai-ling and her family are going to be nervous about this. If you upset them, they'll call the wedding off. They know and trust me, so you've got to go there in my place and represent me in the best possible way. Be polite, be patient. If you have the opportunity to say something good about me, about my accomplishments—"

"I will," Vincent promised. "I'll do that, especially when I'm around her father. I'll flatter you and not feel that anything I'm saying is false."

"You understand that unless you fly, the traveling in Xinjiang, in the desert, is going to be very hard."

"I understand. I'm ready for it."

"Careful what you eat and drink," Gwa said. He consulted his list. "I'm trying to think of other things. I'm sure I'm forgetting something."

"I'll be careful. I'll be polite." He coughed nervously into his hand and in a quieter, more confidential manner said, "I'll be a gentleman. Not just while I'm in Urumchi with Kai-ling's family, but when I'm with her on the way back. I'll treat her like a sister."

"How lucky for me." Gwa laughed. "You're how old, twenty-three? Twenty-four years?"

Vincent nodded.

"And how many beautiful women have you known? Not pretty or pleasant women, the world is full of those."

"A few," Vincent said.

"Seen them or known them?"

He shrugged. "Seen them, I guess."

"Kai-ling is going to scare the life out of you, especially at first. She's not going to be friendly either. In Urumchi, they've seen plenty of foreigners, Uighurs, more Uighurs than Chinese, and white men, too, Russians from the north. The Chinese there are not impressed with foreigners, not like here in Taiwan. I'll bet there are girls in Toulio who like to smile and flirt with a tall foreign boy. Am I right?"

Vincent ignored the question, though he could not help but think of Trudy, a beseeching hand signaling him from the far side of the classroom.

"That won't happen in Urumchi. Not with Kai-ling, not with anyone. You tell me you're going to be a gentleman on the way back. I'm sure you will, but it doesn't matter how you behave. I'm not worried about it. I will tell you this, though, I'll give you some simple advice: Don't get confused. You're going to Urumchi in my place. You're representing me, my intentions to marry Kai-ling. If you get confused and start mixing up your own intentions with mine, you're going to make it very hard on yourself. Do you understand what I mean?"

"Yes," Vincent said. "I think I do."

"You'll understand much better when you get there. Do you need money for the air ticket to Hong Kong?"

Vincent said he did not. He watched Gwa rise and followed him to the foyer's sliding doors. The gray Bonneville sedan was parked in the alleyway. He could see Ponic slumped back in the driver's seat taking a nap.

"Take these," Gwa said, holding out an assortment of timetables, notes, maps. "I've written down Wu's address and phone number. Kai-ling's address in Urumchi." He pointed to Kai-ling's photograph, her astute gaze, the dark cascade of hair. "Better take this with you too," he said. "So you'll be certain. I wouldn't want you to bring back the wrong woman."

Precaution or a sly joke? Vincent couldn't tell. And the weightiness of the moment—the pact made, the deal makers going their separate ways—kept him from asking. It seemed a sign of commitment was called for, and so he took Gwa's hand, squeezing it, wanting it to be more than a shake, a confirmation, an apology, a pledge. "I know how important this is," he said, meaning that, though Gwa had never mentioned love directly, this was most certainly a matter of love, and Vincent was awed by the prospect, the responsibility of what he was about to do. In his own punctilious way, Gwa appeared equally staggered; he stepped back unsteadily to the car, waking Ponic as he opened the door and slid into the rear seat. The Bonneville started, revved, wound down to a glassy purr. Out through the enclave of houses it rolled, sunlight glinting off the rear windshield until it turned abruptly and sped down the long rice road.

Upstairs he found Alec wringing out a knot of freshly washed socks in the bathroom sink. Bare-shouldered, dressed in a sarong, Alec crossed into his bedroom, where he opened the window and laid the socks across the sill so that they dripped down the side of the house.

"I'm going to China," Vincent announced. "Can you believe it?"

"Good for you," Alec said.

"I've got a flight to Hong Kong on Saturday. You're not going to believe this, but I'm going there for a reason," he said cryptically. "I was just downstairs with a former student of mine, Mr. Gwa, a businessman. Well, I guess I need to start at the beginning." And he did, commencing with the free English lesson at which he'd first met Gwa and Ponic and then their visit to the nightclub, relishing the story as he told it because, having admitted the worst to Alec, there now existed an unwitting alliance of sorts, and an audience, too, for the news of Gwa's extraordinary proposal.

Alec sat cross-legged on his mattress and listened, first dutifully but soon with a distinguishable interest. "Wait now," he interrupted. "So you chat with the nightclub hostesses, drink their silly cognac. What else?"

"I danced a little. I didn't drink much."

"I was in no condition to dance," Alec said. "Ponic and I finished the whole fucking bottle."

Vincent grinned as if he were being teased. "You?"

"Fucking right! A month or two before you did. Got completely pissed drunk, staggered out of the nightclub, and went straight to—" He raised an eyebrow. "You went along with them to the whorehouse?"

"I had no idea that's where they were taking me. I didn't, when we got there, go upstairs."

"I did," Alec said mournfully. "Went up for a massage. Some brawny-armed wench, hands like iron vises. Then went up another floor and tried to shag her. Couldn't quite do it. Trust me, you were better off staying downstairs."

Vincent rounded his mouth into a breathless *what?* He sat down heavily on the corner of the bed and gaped at Alec. "Did Gwa offer to pay you to go to the Mainland? He didn't, did he?"

"What offer? Pay me what?"

"He has a girlfriend in the Mainland. He's in love and wants to marry her, but he can't because the government won't allow it. He wants me to go there in his place, marry her, bring her back, pay me for it."

"How's that?" Alec asked. "What's this?" he demanded.

"Gwa made the offer a while ago and I turned him down. But now this happened"—he pointed toward his scraped chin—"and I agreed to do it. There are lots of details," he explained, and began, with a sure sense of Alec's attention, to list them. Mention of Kai-ling, her beauty as described by Gwa, her family situation, the amount of the dowry, these particulars caused Alec to adopt a peculiar expression. He seemed to be smiling and grinding his teeth at the same time. Vincent's reward, the ten thousand dollars, made him scowl outright.

"Oh, fuck me! You're joking now!"

Vincent said that he was not. "I'm picking up half of it in Hong Kong and then heading to Xinjiang, to a place called Urumchi."

"Urumchi! You telling me she lives in Urumchi? I've fucking *been* to Urumchi. I should be the one going there."

"Probably," Vincent conceded. "What's it like?"

"It's like a desert shithole. Goddamn it! Why didn't he come talk to me about all this?"

"Because he took us out to test us. You understand that, don't you? Getting drunk and going upstairs at the whorehouse was probably not the right thing to do. In Gwa's eyes, I mean. I'm not judging you, Alec. I'm just saying Gwa didn't consider you right for the job."

Alec did an angry double-take, glowered back. "Well, he made a hell of a fine choice in picking you!"

It might have subverted any goodwill between them, a remark like that, with its aggrieved sarcasm and worming insult. Vincent bristled when he considered its principal insinuation—that he was too . . . what, exactly? Too lecherous? The unfairness of it! Too lecherous to be a trustworthy chaperone for Kai-ling.

They took a long, lowering measure of each other. Each seemed to reach an unfavorable verdict. Each seemed ready to level a charge, deny bail.

"I'm only saying," Alec began. "You've hardly been anywhere. You've not left Toulio in a half year."

This was, technically speaking, accurate enough. Nevertheless, he refused to verify any of it, refused even the feeblest nod of agreement.

"Am I right?" the Scotsman asked, his narrow face flushed. The brusque silence, the climate of antagonism, had appeased him somehow. "Other than Taiwan, have you ever traveled abroad?"

He sulked a long while before answering. "Not really."

"That's all I'm saying then, you lack experience."

"I know I do," Vincent snapped. It had become that petulant and childish. And such a bothersome chore as well. Was this the grunt work of friendship? The drudgery of seeing past your own chafed ego. The large effort it took to ignore most slights, real or imagined.

For a while, at least, there was a vigorous late-afternoon world outside Alec's window to distract them: schoolchildren and pushcart merchants and rice farmers stowing away their instruments. A floor below, the foyer door slid open and smacked shut.

"You'll do all right," Alec said. "You speak Chinese well enough." Just when it seemed that these were his only begrudging thoughts on the matter, he added, "You know about changing money, don't you? You know about the trouble you'll have getting train tickets?" he asked, and with that began elaborating on a host of difficulties. His advice, seasoned by experience, was easy to remember because it was all cautionary in tone. Don't do this: *get into a shoving match while standing in a queue.* Stay away from that: *Chinese officials of all manner and rank.* Don't head into the Main-land without these: *a long fucking book, a money belt, a pack of toilet paper.* He talked about travel as if it were an act of hard-nosed dedication—the last time Vincent had heard such steadfast counsel it had come, oddly enough, from Reverend Phillips—and with a fondness that caused Alec to take a deep, wistful breath and commence planning Vincent's itinerary. From Hong Kong he should take the night ferry to Guangzhou and then immediately, unless he liked belligerent crowds and eating endangered animals, head northwest to Yangshuo. Yangshuo was brilliant. Yangshuo was a must. To pass it by would be a sure sign of stupidity, and Vincent would only understand this once he arrived in the village and had his first look at the landscape.

After Yangshuo, north by bus, northwest by train across a territory so vast Vincent could barely hold it in his head. Guiyang, Chongqing, Chengdu, Lanzhou: each city sounded both anonymous and familiar. Provinces blurred. Tired, Vincent rubbed the bridge of his nose. It was something of a surprise to notice Shao-fei standing in the doorway, to real-ize he'd been listening in on them for some time. He'd also seen the violet bruises surrounding Vincent's eyes, and now the boy peeled off his glasses, as if he'd not seen a battered face, but instead a smudge on his lens that needed immediate attention. He waited as Alec extolled the fresh air and scenery of Xiahe, and when there was a lull in the conversation, he fretted the zipper of his book bag and said, "Excuse me, Alec. There's a truck out-side. It's there when I come home from school and the driver is waiting."

"Not to worry. He'll know where to unload the hens."

"No, no. There's no hens. There's a thing on the back of the truck. Would you come down, please, and talk to the driver?"

"And what thing might that be?" Alec asked. He and Vincent had both risen to their feet.

"I think it's for me," Shao-fei said glumly. "I think Mama bought me a present."

He led them down to the first floor and parted the sliding doors. Parked before the house, straddling the narrow lane, sat a flatbed truck too wide to back into the alleyway. The driver had pulled down running boards and was crouched on the truck bed unbinding straps from what appeared to be an oversize tricycle. Vincent and Alec each grabbed a rear wheel and helped him lower it down the planks onto the street. It had a curious handlebar, a curved rod attached to the lone front wheel and angling back like the tiller of a sailboat. The pedals, sprocket, and seat were mounted to the right of the frame so that the rider, in this case Shao-fei, could power the bike without having to scissor his legs around the center bar.

"It's good exercise," the driver said. "Good for the boy's legs." He sidled off the tailgate and made a wobbly circuit around the bike. "He'll need to practice, get used to the pedals, strengthen his legs." The driver moved forward three shuffling paces that made clear his own pronounced limp. "A week from now you'll go looking for the boy and can't find him. Where's he at? His mother will worry and good luck finding him because now he's able to take himself into town and back."

It seemed, to Vincent, an unlikely claim, but he was swayed into believing it, more by the driver's limp than by his testimony.

"Now, I can adjust the seat here, back and forth like this." The driver produced a wrench from his pocket and used it to guide Shao-fei over the seat, the boy easing down in halting increments as he might into a tub of untested bathwater. Across the lane several neighbors had come out to watch the proceedings and wave him on.

The driver shifted the seat forward and backward until Shao-fei's bowed feet rested atop the pedals. "I'll leave the wrench with you. Watch how I tighten this," the driver said. "After all, it's your bicycle."

"Contraption is more like it," Alec whispered to Vincent. "Mama should have sprung for a three-wheeled motorbike. There's more dignity in something like that."

Shao-fei gripped the handlebar and leveraged his weight against the pedals. The tricycle bobbed forward but did not really move until the driver got behind the rear axle and set it rolling with a forceful shove. The momentum sent Shao-fei carting down the lane, too startled to pedal, yet able, after a few provisional yanks on the tiller, to negotiate a right turn and follow the lane as it snaked behind a neighbor's house.

Alec watched him roll away, paused for a cigarette. "Look here, I've been thinking about something. An idea."

"What's that?" Vincent asked, wary of untested ideas.

"I was thinking about going along with you to the Mainland. You'd go ahead and leave the day after tomorrow, and I'd catch up to you in a week's time or less. We could meet up in Yangshuo and head north together."

"How would . . . why would you do that?"

"I'm ready for my next holiday. I've got a bit of money saved. It's not like I'd tag along the whole way. I've got a few friends in the Mainland to visit. I've no interest in going to Urumchi. When we get to Xinjiang, we'll part ways. You'll go to Urumchi and I'll stay awhile in Turpan or head up to Kashgar."

Urumchi. Turpan. Kashgar. More peculiar names and obscure routes. So many ways to get lost or otherwise go astray. His first impulse, probably worth respecting, was a resounding yes. "That sounds reasonable," Vincent said. "But what I meant to ask was, why would you want to go with me?"

Alec blew a ponderous stream of smoke on the fiery tip of his cigarette. "Maybe I like the new Vincent better."

"The new Vincent?" He had thought himself ruined, not renewed.

"The beat-up Vincent," Alec said. "You'll be easier to tolerate now that someone's gone and taken the piss out of you."

Shao-fei returned, or rather careened back into view. Head tilted, grimacing, he clenched the straight handlebar and guided the contraption in a series of near-spastic jerks. And it was a contraption. Alec, who had been right about so many things, was also right about this. It lacked dignity. For proof, one needed only to watch Shao-fei strain against the pedals, seesawing back and forth like a reckless oarsman. To see this was to understand how the tricycle exaggerated the boy's most guarded vulnerabilities, magnified and made them public.

He hit the street curb at a skewed angle. A broad lurch, a shuddering sigh. Shao-fei untangled his limbs, stood, and made a brave face for the neighbors—though the face he disclosed to Alec was far more despairing. And it was Alec, of course, who helped steady the boy as he tottered back to the house.

This left Vincent with the task of seeing the driver off and then pushing the tricycle into the alleyway. It was an odd and cumbersome vehicle, hard to steer correctly. Pushing it brought to mind his own ungainly burdens, the obligations he owed to others and should attend to without delay.

Though he did delay. The magnitude of the day's transactions had wearied him. He clambered up to the Chens' second-floor hallway and into the vacant bedroom, lay down upon the mattress, and slept an exhausted and prolonged sleep. Remorseless sleep. His body seemed to be leading him through a necessary hibernation—a gift, to sleep so soundly, his life in shambles, his most pressing obligations deferred, in particular, the explanation he still owed Sister Gloria.

Fourteen

How else could he feel but cowardly, abandoning his motorcycle two blocks away and moving from one storefront awning to the next in a succession of slinking jogs? He skirted round the motorcycle shop and took his first furtive glance at the ministry house gates. Three neighborhood children were propped against the courtyard fence, two girls and a skinny, shirtless boy, each clutching a stick of grilled squid. He did not see the beige compact belonging to Trudy's family, nor were there any skulking figures huddled beside entranceways or crouched between rows of motorbikes. As further reassurance, the children took yawning bites and chewed their squid with complacent ease.

Much of the day, his last in Toulio, had already been squandered. He'd endured a leaden morning and a stupefied afternoon sitting at the Chens' second-floor bedroom window, incapable of any determined action. He had hoped to savor this final day, to squeeze the waiting out of each hour so that what remained would be fleeting and tinged with nostalgia.

He made a leaping sprint from one side of the lane to the other, a curt, sunglass-shielded nod to the children, a hurried ramble up the walkway to the front door. In the process he overstepped two grim milestones: the retarded man's stain, blanched but still detectable, and a rust-colored spray of blood, his own, which had fallen in thick drops about the sidewalk and gateposts some forty-eight hours earlier. The combination of these markers, so ugly, so potently strange, made him want to shirk free of his obligations and flee the courtyard without ever looking back.

The ministry house curtains had been drawn tight, the ground floor draped in cool shadows. He peeled back his sunglasses and treaded lightly across the kitchen and living room floors. He expected to find Gloria shuttered inside her bedroom. After knocking, he opened the door and found her chair empty. Had she stepped out for dinner? Had he been that lucky? The happy possibility of her not being home caused him to bound up the stairs in the direction of his room. There he hoped to pack quickly, and on the way out leave Gloria something truly cowardly and evasive: a hastily improvised note, all lies and trumped-up excuses to be sure, which he would fold over and tape to her work lamp.

He had no more than settled on this course of action, when he paused between landings and listened to the squeal of a school desk being drawn across the floor above him. He took a darting glance at the ceiling, then his wristwatch. This evening's English and Bible study lessons were twenty-five minutes away. Gloria was readying the third-floor classroom. He would have to break the news there.

But first he crept into his bedroom. He had been warned to travel light and, thus cautioned, chose a smaller, nylon-strapped shoulder bag in lieu of his lumpish backpack. He tried to include only the essentials: socks and underwear and T-shirts, khaki shorts, jeans instead of dress slacks, a clutch bag of toiletries, a raincoat, an extra pair of tennis shoes, a camera, his passport and three hundred dollars in traveler's checks, pens, stationery, address book, though he did not pack one of several paperback editions of the New Testament. Each choice, he realized, each item included or left out, exemplified the type of traveler he would become.

Then, reluctantly, he wandered up to the third floor via the dusky stairwell. When he arrived at the classroom doorway, Gloria straightened up from where she had been polishing desktops and was granted an uncompromised view of his ringed eyes, bruised lips, bandaged chin and forehead.

"Oh, Vincent!" she whispered aloud. "Sweet Jesus! What did they do to you?"

He understood at once to whom she was referring. She meant the Chinese. Not the compliant students who graced their classroom, but the slippery, unknowable, poker-faced crowds who convened somewhere beyond the ministry house gates. This was a prejudice she might never outgrow, and he toyed with an explanation tailored perfectly and absurdly to her distrust. He could say that he had wandered too close to a temple celebration, say, with the awe of a true survivor, that he had been lured in, ceremonially beaten, and kicked out the other side. As a farce, it almost brought a smug grin to his lips. But he saw its paranoid consequences as well, and instead recounted the same lie he had told Gwa. A late night with Alec at Hungry Ghost Street. A run-in with a group of surly young men. Excessive drinking on both sides. Equal blame.

"I'll bet you were trying to reason with them, weren't you?"

"I don't know. It happened fast. Reason what? Reason how?"

"I'll bet you were trying to tell them some of the things that we believe. That kind of truth can frighten people, Vincent. It can make them act out."

"No, it wasn't like that. Alec and I were drinking. It was all a misunderstanding. It was all stupid choices and stupid mistakes."

"What was Alec doing out? I thought you were taking him to the clinic."

He wondered where she could have gotten such a notion and then remembered it had come from him. "Look here, Gloria." He blinked into her unwavering gaze. "I didn't know how to explain it, so I made up an excuse. Alec's not sick. This is really about something else altogether. This is really about an important decision I've made." He knew of only one protocol for breaking bad news. "Would you like to sit down?"

She folded her arms across her chest. Sedately and in reply to his question, she turned her head once to the right, once to the left.

He took a deep, wincing breath. "I'm resigning as a volunteer. I won't be living in the ministry house anymore. I won't be teaching Bible study. I'm leaving Taiwan. I'm taking a night train to Taipei and flying out tomorrow morning."

Except for the howl of an actual scream, she had the frenzied, gape-mouthed look of someone screaming. Her eyes bulged. Her jaw seemed to unhinge. He had always found it difficult to gauge her expressions, but this brand of outrage was easy to recognize. Betrayal. The knowledge of it was just now filtering its way through her body. She had been betrayed, by no less than her closest confidant, her brother in Christ.

"I'm sorry about telling you all this on such short notice, Gloria. I really am."

She'd changed her mind about sitting, had slumped into the nearest school desk. She gaped about at the classroom posters as if seeing them for the first time. She was, he understood, taking stock of her future alone in the ministry house.

"I've made some mistakes and the best thing—the only thing—I can do now is leave."

"*Why?*" she begged. "You don't think we're making a difference? You don't think we're going to convert anyone?"

"We might. I don't know. We may even be close with a few students right now. I just don't think it matters."

"You don't think it *matters*?" she sang back. An enormous well of tears trembled on the brink of her lower eyelids, took the plunge, streamed down her broad cheeks. She had attained a look of glazed suffering, none of it helpless, each plunging tear a mark of rage.

Which was not to say he didn't sympathize with Gloria Hamilton. Or that they were not bound together by a few undiluted principles. Yet how to talk about the differences? All he had were pale and contrary suspicions. He suspected they'd been naive. He suspected that as children he and Gloria had each placed exceptional credence in their God and small-town virtues and had come to Taiwan because they believed these virtues superior to any other. They had either been more gullible than most children or they had possessed a stronger aptitude for believing. And now he had to wonder if that talent for faith was worth anything at all, if it did nothing but lead you down a series of ever-narrowing pathways until the only real choice was collapse or more believing—fervent belief, belief of a hounded, even manic design that stormed against any contrary opinion.

"I think you should stay another month," Gloria said, officious despite her damp cheeks.

"I'm sorry. I can't do that."

"So we can talk it through, the reasons you don't think it matters. Stay another month and that'll give us time to sort through this whole mess."

"No, thank you."

"All right then, two weeks," she said. "That's all I'm asking. If you don't feel different about things in two weeks, you can go ahead and leave."

"There's no possibility I'll change my mind, Gloria. This isn't a decision I'm willing to bargain over."

"Let's call Reverend Phillips then. I'll cancel class and the three of us can talk this over. How would that be?"

"That would be awful. I don't want to call Reverend Phillips. I'm writing him a letter instead."

"Then I'll call him myself."

"I wish you wouldn't. I wish you'd let me tell him my own way."

"Stay seven days and I'll let you tell him whatever way you like."

He could no longer bear to listen to her out of pure obligation. He threw his bag over his shoulder and made ready to leave.

"If you walk out of this ministry house, I'll do everything I can to ruin your reputation."

"Ruin my reputation?" he repeated. Her threat unleashed in him a cool poison. He felt decidedly mean, ready to speak whatever hurtful truths the situation required. "You're amazing," he said. "Truly. I've never known anyone so selfish or single-minded. Or desperate. I mean, good God, Gloria. I've seen the insane scribbling you've done all over your bedroom walls."

She was up on her feet suddenly, pushing through a row of desks, stomping toward the door where he stood. Did she intend to attack him? No, but she did something curious and startling: jabbed her right arm out all at once, her fingers raked into a claw, and pawed at the air beside his head, an act so infantile and impulsive and outright strange that there seemed no proper way to acknowledge it had happened.

"You're awful!" she howled. "I hate you. I hate the way you give up as soon as things get difficult. I'm calling Reverend Phillips right now. I'm going to let him know what kind of nonsense you're trying to pull here."

They were both fairly belligerent after that. Anger made them thick-tongued and clumsy. Gloria lurched out the doorway and down the steps, and he followed with the frenzied notion of stopping her somehow. Plodding down the steps, it seemed terribly important that Reverend Phillips not learn of his resignation this way. In his panic he nearly stumbled into her.

She had come to a halt on the second-floor landing, and he looked over her shoulder and saw a small assembly of students waiting at the foot of the stairs. Mr. Yao was there, twining his tan safari hat nervously from one hand to the other. Miss Ling. The Ping twins as well as a few others. They had all overheard the argument and were now braced against the railing, skittish as children, pretending they had not.

More so, it seemed entirely possible that they knew what Gloria didn't. The proof? The quick, searching glances. They were as shocked as others had been by Vincent's battered face. But there was also something shrinking and wounded in their reactions. They were *shamed* by the sight of him.

In the midst of this Gloria had grown smugly self-composed. "I'm not afraid to make a scene," she warned. "I'll do it if I think I need to."

He half turned and gazed up the stairs to the rooftop door. She followed his gaze, appeared to recognize the door for what it was—an escape route, his last and best, a getaway she could do little to prevent. As a concession, or perhaps as parting advice, she said, "You can't live without Jesus Christ. Nobody can. You know what's going to happen to you, don't you?"

"No," he said. "I don't know. It'll be difficult, I'm sure."

"It's worse than that. Everything falls apart. Nothing makes sense without God."

She turned to the students, most of whom had taken an emphatic interest in the ministry house flooring and wall decorations. "Vincent has something he'd like to tell you," she announced. "He says he's leaving the Toulio ministry. I've asked him to stay. For my sake and for yours, I've pleaded. But he says we don't matter!"

He took the stairs two at a time, heart pounding as he clutched his bag and bounded up toward the open air.

Finally, beyond all recourse, a letter had to be written.

It was ridiculously late by the time he sat down to his desk. Except for the Chen household, the enclave was murky and silent. A quarter moon lay low in the sky and shed a dappled glow across the untended fields of rice. In an hour Alec would drive him to the station and he would board a three A.M. express bound for the airport outside Taipei. His compartment would likely be deserted or near-deserted, which was how he preferred it, an uncrowded, predawn train, a window seat from which he could watch Toulio lapse and recede, and a moment, invariably, when the magnitude of his failure would make itself known.

Before that moment, though, there was still the matter of the letter. He began by describing his fabricated beating at Hungry Ghost Street. Reverend Phillips was sure to hear of the incident first from Gloria, and Vincent wanted his letter to concur, at least generally, with her version of their final argument. As an explanation, it was no harder or easier to improvise than a college essay, and yet he found that a falsehood committed to word, as opposed to one spoken aloud, had a graceless, inflexible quality. Untrue words stood brittle, as if anticipating honest contradiction. And while they were no uglier than true words, they reminded him of how often he had resorted to lies recently, and how ugly this habit had become. He wondered if a true accounting of what had happened was possible, wondered if he was still capable of such a thing.

He began once more, almost as pure experiment, to write something as close as possible to the truth:

By now you've heard from Gloria Hamilton and know that I've quit the Toulio ministry and left Taiwan. This is my letter of resignation to you and the Overseas Christian Fellowship. I know that I should have come to Taipei in person, or at least called, in order to break the bad news. Even without meeting face-to-face, I can picture your disappointment. It's something I find especially hard to bear because of your generosity and the great trust involved in choosing me to establish the new ministry.

In the simplest terms, this is what happened.

While teaching at the Ming-da Academy, I became involved with a teenage girl, a student named Trudy. She made advances that any conscientious teacher would have turned down. I'm sorry to say that I did not. Eventually the relationship intensified, and again I am sorry to say that we began sleeping together. Her family became aware of this and sent Trudy to a boarding school in Tainan. They have insisted, forcefully, that I leave the country. At no time did Gloria Hamilton have any knowledge of what went on.

I have no good excuse for any of my actions, except to say that I came to Toulio expecting things to be difficult. And they were difficult, though not in ways I had imagined or ways that I could prepare myself for. I was not prepared for how lonely the experience would be.

He glanced at what he had written. It seemed an audacious thing to have put to paper, and he wanted to sign off quickly and seal it inside an envelope before changing his mind. He wrote his name but could think of no suitable closing.

Before one came to mind, he was distracted by the creak of a door hinge. There was an uneven padding of footsteps in the hallway, and then the boy, Shao-fei, ambling into Vincent's room to slouch against the windowsill. He stole a few coy glimpses of Vincent, the packed shoulder bag, the unsealed letter.

"I'd be careful in the Mainland," the boy advised.

"Careful of what?"

"The tooth doctor. If you have a tooth giving you pain, I'd be very careful. A Mainland tooth doctor will use something like this," he said and made a plierslike clamp of his thumb and forefinger.

"I'll remember that."

"The people in the Mainland, the way they act," he sighed. "A little crazy. A little dangerous. They won't like you if you're a Taiwanese. That's why I won't go there." He brushed his hand once, twice, three times along the seam of his denim pants. From under his hand came a tiny shower of sparks. Stiffly and without much conviction, he grinned at this minor prank, a trick involving a concealed cigarette lighter. "Alec will be with you in the Mainland. So maybe you feel glad about that?"

"I do, yes. He knows a lot about the Mainland. He's been there before."

"Only two times," Shao-fei said.

"Even so."

"I heard you and Alec will stay a month and then come back to Taiwan."

"I'll come back for a day or two. But I don't think I'll live in Toulio again."

He pondered this news. "I don't think Alec will live in Toulio again either. I don't think he'll come back at all."

"Is that what he told you?"

"No."

"Then why do you say it?"

"It's just a feeling I have." He focused on Vincent in a canny, speculative way, as if he were determining which thoughts he could legitimately keep to himself and which he could speak aloud. "I don't care. If he wants to stay away, he can." A pause. Another questioning glance. "The stupid prick."

It nearly jolted Vincent upright in his seat, this declaration. Stupid prick. Of which *prick* had been uttered with a calculated snicker. How easy to recognize its deliberate nature. And yet, still, Vincent was startled. He had not been paying proper attention either. The boy was cultivating a reckless appearance, his hair parted at a curious angle, the tails of his dress shirt dangling out. There was a squarish bulge in his breast pocket from which sprouted, barely, the white tip of a filtered cigarette. Not that Shao-fei appeared bold enough to smoke in his presence, but the lighter and untucked shirt and brazen language meant something—a change, a new, feckless demeanor.

A precarious demeanor, by the look of it. Though he tried to pretend differently, calling Alec a stupid prick had nearly undone the boy. He'd gone crimson-cheeked waiting to be scolded for it. "It wasn't my meaning," he conceded, "that you and Alec should move away."

"I never thought that you wanted us to leave, Shao-fei."

"Yes, but I'm sorry for the different reason."

"You don't have anything to be sorry about. Not one thing."

"I'm sorry that I don't believe in Jesus." He examined, minutely, the callused skin crosshatching his knuckles and waited for Vincent's outraged reply. "I like him, though," he offered. "I like him a lot. He has the very nice personality." These few obliging words aside, his was a tough guy's capitulation. Almost at once Shao-fei was back to flaunting his mannered smirk and raking the cigarette lighter up and down his pants leg, looking a little sheepish, perhaps, for having let down his guard.

And who could blame him for this pretense? It might well be an advantage, if he was not to be perpetually friendless and left behind, if he was not to be known as the crippled teenager riding his tricycle to town and back. To be different, to be *otherwise,* he would have to forgo his natural inclinations for gentleness and loyalty. He would have to adopt fiercer customs. He was presently doing just that, glaring at Vincent and the room's bare furnishings with a slumlord's contempt, as if a swindle had occurred, as if to say, shouldn't you already be gone?

PART THREE

Best Intentions

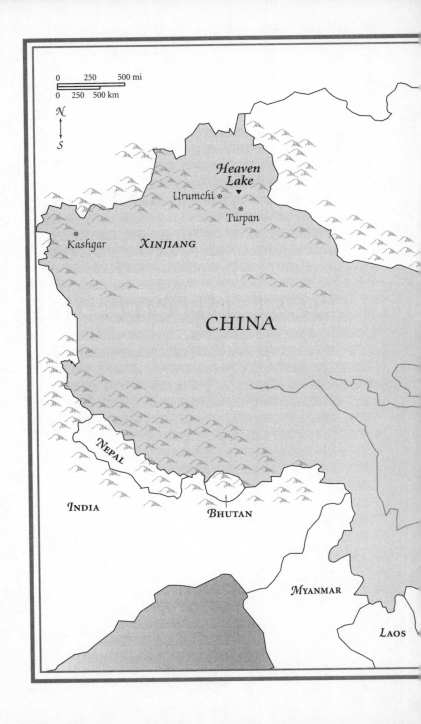

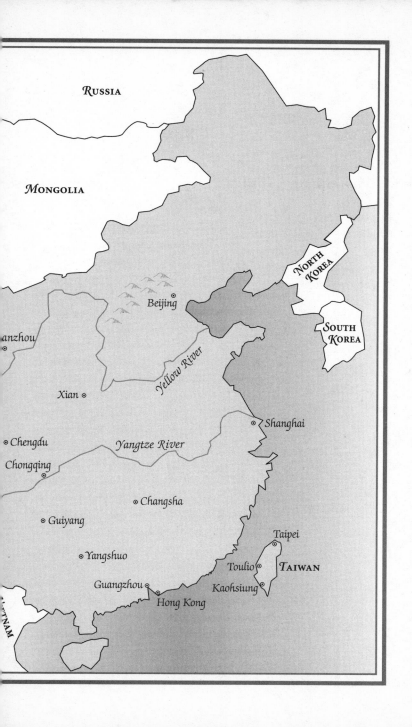

Fifteen

IT HAD COME months earlier in a letter from his mother, the actual term, *our son, the world traveler,* written without irony, written tenderly, as a proud endearment. Then, the phrase had struck Vincent as doting and naive, but sometime during his stay in Toulio, as his grasp of the Chinese language deepened, and as he learned—or was forced to learn—from his mistakes, he had felt the title gain merit and accuracy. And so he arrived in Hong Kong secretly bolstered with expatriate know-how. He cleared customs and paused on the hard, bright outer lip of Kai Tak Airport.

A gleaming shuttle bus whisked him from the airport and discharged him into what he hoped was the Kowloon district. Balanced on a street corner, he viewed six broad lanes of traffic slotted with silver-topped taxis, coach buses, city buses, red-striped minibuses. He clasped a public transport brochure beneath his chin and tried to comprehend the routes for these buses and double-decker trams and something featured prominently in swerving colored bands as an MTR.

When he looked up, he couldn't quite reconcile the broad reach of the city—the tall buildings, the windblown harbor across which lay the metropolitan sprawl of Hong Kong Island—with his own meager wish to locate Mr. Wu's office. He settled his bag onto his shoulder and plodded ahead fourteen city blocks along Nathan Road, each one traversed in a stiff-backed, decisive stride, until he glanced at a street sign, consulted his transport brochure, and discerned that he had walked thirty minutes in the wrong direction. He stepped into the shade of a hotel awning, sighed, and took a moment to forgive himself.

On the way back he slowed his pace and gaped at the mass of high-rises springing forth, shelf upon shelf, from the very rim of the sea. What startling designs these buildings assumed: many were towering, ultramodern, if not outright improbable structures composed of glass panels and spiraling steel frames. Curious, he entered the atrium of a lofty department store and discovered a computer console in lieu of a floor map. A fingertip pressed to the screen summoned layouts and instructions in Chinese and English. He took it all in, quietly impressed but also half doubting. If such technology and architecture did exist, it seemed he should have seen or at least heard about it first in America.

Back out on the wide promenades of Nathan Road, he passed store clerks and shoppers and Hong Kong professionals, Chinese men in business suits and Chinese women also in suits or blue-skirted uniforms. They conversed in Cantonese and he listened to the flourish and ripple of tones—nine tones, he knew, rather than Mandarin's four—and found no similarities, no common phrases with which he could steal inside the language. Initially he believed that the strangeness he felt in their company was due to this change in dialect. But as he strolled farther down Nathan Road, a much longer avenue than he first imagined, it became evident, oddly and emphatically clear, that no one was turning to stare at him. In Taiwan he had lived as an object of public scrutiny, and here, a mere hour's flight away, the citizens of Hong Kong were not only ignoring him in general, but failing to notice the explicit scrapes and bruises on his chin and lip, the violet crescents edging out from beneath his sunglasses. This was not to say that they weren't seeing him, because their gaze flitted over him and over a dispersion of other foreigners, and gave a slight laconic waver, the waver suggesting to Vincent—and he may have been overly sensitive in the matter—that though they did not know him personally, they knew his type and thus found him clumsy, oversized, inconsequential.

To get to Mr. Wu's office he had to first locate Kowloon Park Road—two easy right turns off Nathan Road—and then wander through a tailor's arcade of fresh suits immured in Plexiglas cases. Tucked in the rear of the arcade was an elevator that carried him three floors up to a carpeted hallway where the air-conditioning crested over him in a sudden chill wave. Ahead loomed a single office door. The placard shingled above its frame was vague, *The Tsimshatsui Business Partnership,* but inside the fluorescent lights shone with a distinct glare so that, thankfully, he did not need to remove his sunglasses. Somewhere beyond the reception desk, possibly a back office, came the shrill report of a staple gun.

A young Chinese man strode forward and Vincent turned to him expecting to be told the office was closed for the weekend and to return Monday morning. Instead the young man, who appeared quite young, nearly high school age in spite of his pressed slacks, his serious, buttoned-down oxford and tie, spoke Vincent's name and identified himself cheerfully as Donny Wu. Around him a swath of office fixtures lay in disarray: a side-ended file cabinet, a computer monitor nestled in the lap of a rolling chair.

"We're changing things over," he said. "Repainting, redoing . . . remodeling." He reached over a piled desktop, unlocked the uppermost drawer, and removed a bulging manila envelope. From the envelope Wu extracted a bundle of United States hundred-dollar bills. He began counting them in hushed but fluent English, meting each bill out to the thwack of carpet layers hard at work in the room next door. He counted out thirty, pressed his palm atop the bills, and said simply, "Dowry," then began a fresh stack. He counted out fifty more and grinned, pleased, it seemed, not with the sum of the money, but that he had depleted the envelope with neither a deficit or excess of bills.

He fingered the bridge of his nose, as if pinching an absent pair of glasses. "What next?" he said. "What now?" and stretched open his eyes, which were a dubious shade of sky blue—the result of colored contact lenses. "When do you plan to leave for the Mainland?" Donny Wu asked.

"As soon as I can get a visa," Vincent said. "I'll apply when the office opens on Monday morning. I'd like to leave Tuesday or Wednesday, whenever my visa comes back. A friend of mine has told me about a place to stay in Kowloon, the Chungking Mansions."

"Oh, the Chungking's terrible. No place to stay with this kind of money. What else do you need to do, besides the visa?"

"I need to buy some things."

"Yes, for the trip to Xinjiang. What things?"

"A money belt, for one. I'll have to hide the money on myself while I'm traveling." He regarded the second stack of hundreds. "I guess I won't need all of it. I should leave some of it here with you."

"If you want to, yes. But really, Vincent, it's better for you, more secure, if you open a bank account."

"I can do that? Here in Hong Kong?"

"You have a passport. There are many things you can do with a passport. What else do you need to buy?"

"A travel guide in English," Vincent said. "A few other things."

"Please. If you don't mind, what things?"

"I was thinking of buying a Walkman and a few cassette tapes to go with it."

"A Walkman's easy. So are the tapes and book. Is that all?"

Vincent said it was and Donny Wu seemed to withdraw from the conversation and enter a private revelry of forethought and intricate calculation. "There's a ferry that leaves from a sea terminal very close by," he said. "It leaves at nine this evening, runs all night, and arrives in Guangzhou early tomorrow morning. If I can get you a visa, if I can take you shopping and get the things you need, are you ready to leave tonight?"

He thought about it, said yes, and stowed the money in his bag. And then they were off, coiling out of the building and hurrying down Kowloon Park Road. Their first stop was a camera shop, narrow and walled in mirrors, where Donny Wu leaned across the counter and whispered a request to a female shopkeep. In response she hoisted her metal stool above her head and carried it outside to the shop entranceway. She darted inside again, slipping past them into a back room. Wu, meanwhile, had rummaged through a carousel of camera bags and from its midst untangled a nylon money belt. Vincent cinched it around his waist. He looked up to find the shopkeep at his side, cupping his elbow and guiding him out the door. She reached above the stool, above the doorway, and pulled down a powder blue backdrop. "Sit," she said, pointing at the stool.

Vincent stared back at her, dumbfounded.

"Sit," she said again. "Head up. Glasses off." She gripped a square-jawed Polaroid camera. "Visa photo," she said.

He touched the corner of his glasses and shook his head no.

"Glasses off," she repeated. "No sunglasses. No hats. Visa photo."

Gingerly, he took his place on the stool and peeled back his sunglasses. He could not quite see the clerk's reaction, shielded as she was behind her raised camera. He could only envision a face stunned and furrowed, pinched with distaste. Wu had stepped beside her and, much to his credit, looked Vincent steadily in the eyes, nurturing the same tactful grin he'd worn since they met.

"OK, ready," the shopkeep said. She did not ask him to smile.

The photo, two linked snapshots of Vincent's upraised head, took only minutes to develop. Donny Wu examined them in detail, checking and rechecking the length of each border with a transparent ruler. Vincent caught a glimpse of himself as the photos were separated and placed into a wax-lined envelope. He did not look beaten; he looked wan and feeble, soured by some foul and possibly contagious disease. Seeing them, he could not imagine officials of any nation, much less the world's most powerful communist state, granting him permission to travel in their country.

They reached the nearest Hang Seng Bank office minutes before its two o'clock Saturday closing. In line Wu produced a miniature calculator and a pad of paper. "Will you be flying from city to city in the Mainland?" he asked. "Will you be staying in nice hotels?"

Vincent pledged that he would not. The plan, he told Wu, was to travel as cheaply as possible, to arrive in Urumchi and then return to Hong Kong with most of the first five thousand dollars—money Vincent referred to with embarrassment as his fee—left over. Suddenly his proposed thriftiness sounded mercenary and, to temper any ill opinions, he admitted to being nearly broke, mentioned his school debts, plus the money he would need to purchase an airline ticket back to the States.

Wu levied one shoulder in a disinterested shrug and scribbled away on his pad. Before they reached the teller, he had sketched out an allotment of funds.

$200 in Mainland Foreign Exchange Certificates
$200 in Hong Kong dollars (visa and travel supplies)
$3,000 in traveler's checks (dowry)
$1,600 in traveler's checks (traveling expenses)
$3,000 deposited in a Hong Kong savings account

In this affair, as in others, Vincent deferred to Donny Wu's expertise and set about signing his name and recording his passport number on what seemed a boundless number of documents. When at last they were finished, he arranged the bills and traveler's checks inside his money belt and strapped it beneath his T-shirt.

He followed Donny Wu back out onto the sidewalks of Kowloon. Even here, prying his way through knots of stalled tourists, Wu prevailed as a model of cool efficiency. The calculator and pad disappeared into one trouser pocket. From the other he withdrew a cell phone upon which he made a series of brief calls, simple declarations in Cantonese that may or may not have pertained to the business at hand.

At a corner tobacco shop, he halted and asked Vincent for a red hundred-dollar Hong Kong bill. He snatched it up, hustled inside, and returned a moment later cradling a carton of Marlboro cigarettes. Without explanation, he darted off, first into one side alley then another, and finally merging onto a wide avenue Vincent recognized as Nathan Road.

They entered a tan high-rise and took a lurching elevator six floors up to the office of Ready-to-Go Travel Service. Through its locked doors of beveled glass, they could make out a cloistered and shadowy interior void of movement. At once Donny Wu began tapping doggedly on the glass with a silver coin. A short while later they were ushered inside by a stocky, middle-aged clerk.

Wu held out the cigarettes, respectfully, with both hands.

The clerk bowed his head and declined. He directed Vincent to a countertop already set with a pen and visa application. "Taking a ferry to Guangzhou," he said fondly. "When you get there, tell Old Hundred Names I said hello."

Wu pressed the cigarettes upon him again.

"I can't accept it," the clerk said. "Impossible. I've known your family too long for that. Your uncle, Wei-dong, his wife, and a second or third cousin. I can't remember which." He tugged ruefully at his cleft chin. "Not your father, of course. I never had the chance, but I wish I had. I wish we'd worked together in the Causeway Bay office. . . ."

While they exchanged pleasantries, Vincent scrolled in his name, State-side address, and passport number. He listed Guangzhou, Guilin, and Urumchi as destinations, buses and trains as means of transport. Under "purpose of visit," he skipped the box marked *business* and checked *vacation/sightseeing* instead.

". . . but I still have friends in immigration," the clerk said. "Good for a short-notice visa. Even late on a Saturday afternoon." He took Vincent's application, passport, and visa photos and clipped them together, then asked for three hundred Hong Kong dollars, double the same-day visa rate posted on a board above the counter. Wu sanctioned the price with a curt nod, and Vincent pried the bills from his money belt.

"And another hundred and ten for the ferry," the clerk whispered. He accepted the money with a creased palm thrust forward. The sudden motion of it nearly dislodged the carton of cigarettes, which had found a nesting place beneath one elbow.

They were, by Donny Wu's own admission, making excellent use of their time. He even allowed Vincent an unscheduled stop: an early dinner at a

Pizza Hut restaurant housed within a shopping mall. Wu, however, did not sit for the meal. He paced about the mall lobby instead, punching numbers on his cell phone and jotting down messages.

Afterward he escorted Vincent to an electronics store and bargained a Walkman down to half its original price. From there they proceeded several blocks to a British-style bookshop where Vincent browsed the travel shelf and chose its thickest China guide. Then, after prudent deliberation, he selected an equally thick paperback edition of a Russian novel, a famous one, which a year earlier in college he had been shamed into admitting he had never heard of.

By seven-thirty much of the evening sun had drained from the Kowloon skyline. The streets responded with flickering bursts of neon and fluorescent light, bodings of an ebullient nightlife. Vincent, who could only compare what he saw with other places he had never been, likened nocturnal Kowloon to Las Vegas, Nevada. Dark stairwells and metal-shuttered storefronts, a seediness and lost enterprise beneath the luster of electric lights, only made the comparison more appropriate. They retrieved his passport and ferry ticket from the clerk at Ready-to-Go. Hard to believe, but there stamped into the fourth page of his passport was a three-month Chinese visa.

They skirted the edge of Kowloon Park and made their way west toward the ferry terminals of Harbour City. A footbridge, a hotel alleyway, and he was following Donny Wu down a long black-topped pier out across the rippled surface of the bay. His ferry, the *Tianhu,* lay couched in mild waves, tethered by a railed walkway. Smaller vessels, some adorned with red lanterns, trolled by at a wary distance.

"You have my card," Wu said. "You can call or telex me when you get to Urumchi. The phones there may be down or there may be a long wait. A telex might be faster."

"Right," Vincent said.

"If anything happens, anything goes wrong, you contact me and I'll call Taiwan and speak to Gwa. He's nervous about this. You might send him a postcard while you're traveling. Let him know everything is fine."

"I will," Vincent said solemnly. He looked past Wu to a dark curve of shoreline fanning out toward the open sea. "I bet you've never been involved in this type of business before."

"It's like anything else," Wu said. "You're better off planning the details as carefully as you can."

"Yes, but there's something illegal about this, isn't there? Not seriously illegal. Maybe just slightly illegal. I'm not a person who usually does this kind of thing."

"Don't worry about that. It doesn't matter to me what kind of things you usually do."

There were other questions he felt the need to ask, all of them hedged around the subject of rightfulness and hinted, one way or another, at answers that absolved him of any real misdeed. And if he had further qualms, then Donny Wu, with his pressed slacks and his unshakable, somewhat impatient blue-eyed gaze, was urging him to forget them and board the ferry. He thanked Wu twice, raised his bag-laden hands in lieu of a parting handshake.

All seagoing vessels, he had heard, were prone to sudden drops and sideways lurches. On the walkway, he balanced against the rail and then paced flatfooted across the ferry's steel deck. The first-floor lounge and seating area were spacious and faultlessly clean. Other passengers had donned jackets against the brisk air-conditioning. He made a quick survey of the lower decks, which housed a floor of private cabins and, below that, four open bays of tidy bunk beds. Satisfied, he returned to the lounge, stepped outside and made his way forward to what he believed was the stern of the ship. Here, from the railing, he could view the sea terminal haloed in blue light, the long black pier, and much nearer, Donny Wu leaning against a thick piling, speaking into his cell phone.

For several minutes, while the ferry engine started, idled, and revved, he debated whether or not to wave. Only when the walkway had been withdrawn did Wu stroll toward the terminal, and Vincent stood and absorbed the fact that he had, for an afternoon and evening in Hong Kong, been chaperoned, babysat. Wu had even stayed behind in the unlikely event that his charge attempted a costly and bothersome prank: to sneak off the ferry and head to the airport with a belt crammed full of his partner's money.

Belowdeck, in the open sleeping bays, Vincent chose a lower bunk close to a lighted stairwell. In order to make room for his new purchases, he rummaged through his loaded shoulder bag and selected items for eviction—a blue raincoat, an extra pair of sneakers—which he discarded beneath the bunk. This done, he leaned back and peeled through the opening pages of his China guide. He was nearly positive that the cities of Canton and Guangzhou were one and the same. The guidebook's map proved him correct. He searched for Xinjiang, knowing it was an outlying province, but not realizing the vast quadrant of land it occupied in the country's northwest corner. For the moment he could not locate the desert city of Urumchi. He wasn't looking high enough, north enough. Urumchi, he soon discovered, lay just a few hundred kilometers from the Russian border.

Guangzhou to Urumchi. A staggering distance, really, more than three thousand and four hundred kilometers, the width of a continent. Converting such a span into actual miles only made his temples throb, his palm moisten and cleave to the page.

Sixteen

A MUDDIED SEAGULL lighting down on a pantiled roof . . . a tangle of bicycle frames strapped like a teetering crown to the cab of a market van . . . an iron kettle thrust from a third-floor window and raining water onto a box of blue and white azaleas. These were fractional glimpses of the Mainland, and Vincent could only view them by leveraging his foot to the rail and straining up off the oak-board dock. He stood a vexing twenty yards from Guangzhou proper, from the heavy yellow swing gate that would mark his official entrance into the People's Republic of China. Behind him the *Tianhu* lay moored to the paved bank of the Pearl River.

First, however, he was obliged to enter a harborside office, present his visa and declarations form, and place his bag on a long viewing table before three tight-jawed and brooding customs officials. One unfastened the zipper, reached inside, and gave the contents a bored squeeze. Vincent looked on, keenly aware that he was dealing with communists. Communists, communism, commies, he thought and sealed his lips, anxious that he might speak these words aloud. In his mind's eye he pictured a nation of people in drab gray Mao jackets, a charcoal, ruinous sky punctured by fuming smokestacks.

Yet once cleared and through the swing gate, he was reminded that he had arrived in Guangzhou on a brilliant spring day, a Sunday morning that found the citizens out en masse and filing across the Pearl River along a white stone bridge. The sunlit clarity of their procession sparked a giddy, ridiculous thrill, an apprehension that he, Vincent Saunders, had landed in China. Briefly, his own arrival seemed valiant, exotic, somehow historic in scope, and he fell in line and moved toward the city's southern bank, where the band of hundreds pouring off the bridge mixed with thousands of others already milling along the canals and market streets of Shamian Island. As he walked, he let his fingers descend to the plain of his abdomen and graze his money belt two shirts deep, thick with traveler's checks and passport.

The crowd buckled and swayed. A small girl in cloth slippers, a toddler, stepped out of her bamboo stroller and scuttled back to an asphalt abutment. At her parents' insistence, she squatted down and, through cotton pajamas slit open from zipper to rear seam, peed a warm runnel of urine onto the cobblestone sidewalk. She stood and marked its progress as it wound between stones and disappeared into a sewer grate. Vincent saw her flash a smile of tiny pearled teeth.

Unexpected as this was, it was not quite surprising enough. He was ready to be more thoroughly appalled or delighted, ready for the nation of China to define itself in some bold, heart-stopping spectacle. But so far Guangzhou remained ordinary in its fumy haze of motorbike and truck exhaust, its shrill clamor of traffic horns and keening brakes. The same peculiar odor he had noticed in nearly all Chinese cities and towns—part congealed cooking grease, part septic and subterranean—was present here, though stronger and more pervasive. Like Hong Kong, the streets were a veritable marketplace of bargain-rate commodities: latex thongs, great-bellied plaster Buddhas, laminated photos of Asian music stars, toys and carry bags all shoddily made and adorned with emblems and cartoon figures pilfered from the West. Often the vendors were bone-thin and swarthy-skinned; some actually wore blue or olive green caps and Mao jackets. A few had unfurled tattered handkerchiefs onto the sidewalk and presided over a tiny free-market inventory of candle ends, a polished door latch, a secondhand plumbing fixture.

None of these items interested Vincent personally, though he might have purchased something, a door latch, maybe, out of atonement, out of simple gratitude for being himself and not an indigent street vendor. But this would require an exchange of currency, of which there were two varieties: renminbi, otherwise known as people's money, and Foreign Exchange Certificates, which the Chinese sometimes called tourist money. He had arrived with Foreign Exchange Certificates. Even though he tendered these certificates with a patient hand, they were shunned by a street chef serving up breakfasts of peanuts and steamed buns. Another patron eyed his certificates and barked out an unintelligible question. Was it Cantonese or slurred Mandarin? He was not sure which, but as he needled through the market crowd, he was solicited, frequently, with the same blustery and muddled request.

Alec had told him—warned him—that in the matter of changing money it was best not to relinquish a bill until the changer had handed over its equivalent in renminbi. With this in mind, he held back and appraised each candidate, searching for the money changer least likely to try a swindle or lunging retreat. An elderly woman tottered forward, hindered by an arthritic limp. Her ashen hair was short-cropped and bristly, her rheumy eyes underscored by fat swells of pouched skin. "Chain geh money," she whispered in English.

He traded a crisp ten-yuan Foreign Exchange Certificate for thirteen yuan in renminbi, an apparent bargain, though the bills she returned were frayed and tissue-thin. Afterward, he opened his travel guide and consulted exchange rates. The old woman had not slighted him. More surprising yet, he learned that he had just made his first transaction on the Chinese black market. To celebrate, he purchased a bag of peanuts, then strolled along cracking their rough shells in his fist. Now and then he grinned and fancied himself mixing with the underworld.

For the time being, he thought it best to trail behind a scattering of other Caucasian tourists, most of them college-aged and saddled with nylon backpacks, in hopes that they would lead him to a moderately priced hotel. And eventually they did. But the news at the Overseas Chinese Hotel was discouraging. "No vacancies whatsoever," a young woman in a Boston University T-shirt announced to Vincent and a group of her companions waiting in the hotel lobby. He followed them several blocks to another hotel, where the same young woman entered and returned with a bleaker announcement. "Everything in Guangzhou is booked solid through the fifteenth of May," she said. "Some kind of export-business fair. The only rooms are outside the city." Her friends groaned and cursed, though the same news that spurred their frustration buoyed Vincent and caused him to improvise an alternate plan. It was not imperative that he stay overnight and tour the sights of Guangzhou. The city could be skipped over, dismissed, and he could head northwest to Guilin by train. From there he could take a bus to the much-praised town of Yangshuo, the site of his eventual rendezvous with Alec.

He set out for the Guangzhou train station along a bustling northbound avenue. At nine A.M. its cobbled promenades were still sloped in cool morning shadows. He did not mind the walking. In time he came to a demarcating intersection where the apartment houses and storefronts dropped away. Across the lane stood a grove of high sycamores. This, according to his guidebook, was a verdant corner of the enormous Yuexiu Park. He hurried forth, ready to embark on one of its winding pathways.

Halfway through the intersection, he felt a tug on the waistband of his blue jeans and looked down to discover that he had been joined by a pair of children, a boy possibly ten or eleven on his right, and on his left, a younger girl, who had pried her reedy fingers beneath the strap of his leather belt. For a moment he thought they wanted nothing more than to tug him inside the park and guide him eagerly toward a monument or pagoda, a sun-dappled fishpond he might otherwise have missed. But they were dressed in ragged clothes and tapping their chests and then knotting their free hands into cupped fists. Clearly they were not impetuous tour guides. They wanted, or rather demanded, money, and Vincent, secretly belted with a fortune in traveler's checks, was happy to give them some. He reached into his pocket and rewarded each child with a one-yuan bill. These were snatched away and stowed inside some secret fold of their clothing. Then, both at once, they thrust their small hands into his front and back pockets and claimed his remaining ten or eleven yuan in renminbi. Digging deeper still, they managed to ferret out a paper receipt from the *Tianhu* and a cloth handkerchief, which the boy shook open and tossed to the ground.

Together, the three of them had become a spectacle; he was sure of this, but when he gaped around at the throng of people lining the park entrance, he saw only a scowl from an elderly man raking the grass with his bamboo cane, a slit-mouthed hiss from a tousled mother holding a swaddled infant. The children, meanwhile, had begun to pry at the zippers of his shoulder bag. He tried a bolting escape, and they clenched his belt with both hands and shambled after him. He tried gathering their small hands in each of his own, squeezing their fingers, holding them at a distance, and then sprinting away. Yet they were quick to recover and dive for his belt. After several attempts he decided, finally, that to be successful he would have to grab one of them, most likely the boy, and throw him hard against the ground—a viable plan, perhaps, but as a public act it would be nothing less than appalling.

A jaunty young man in a starched shirt and pin-striped trousers strode by. In his raised fist he wielded a magazine rolled into a blunt, glossy club, and as he strolled past, he brought it down full-tilt, vehemently, first onto the boy's head and then onto the girl's. They both pressed their foreheads into Vincent's hips and cringed beneath the blow, and the young man hurried on, tapping his wristwatch to show this quick assault was all he had time for. The children clung to Vincent's belt gritty-fingered and dazed, and now the tousled mother reappeared, shouldering her baby and shrieking, cursing the children, he assumed, until he recognized a word, a phrase, the purpose beneath her shriek: "Stay on him! Stay on him! Stay on him!" she screamed.

Panicked, he lurched forward and entered Yuexiu Park. He feared the woman would latch on to him as well, but she was content to scuttle behind hissing, coaching the children, imploring them not to let go. He spotted a stone bench littered with food wrappers and led them all toward it and slumped down thinking that perhaps he was being mugged, mugged publicly by children.

Hunched over, travel bag shielded in his lap, he decided to wait them out. The boy and girl appeared relieved to take seats on either side of him. In other circumstances they might have been sweet-featured or even beautiful children, yet slouched against each of his shoulders their faces seemed patently slack and wearied, grim as those of weathered old men. The woman hovered over all of them, a doughy sneer, a mop of bedraggled hair. All Vincent could see of her baby was one exposed leg jutting from the swaddled blanket. She jeered instructions and the children wedged their arms between his bag and stomach. They located his money belt and groped its fat corners, though luckily they could not work their fingers beneath his shirts to pry at its zipper.

He watched a steady flux of Sunday strollers mill by on their way to a line of park vendors whose carts were laden with packaged candies, fruit drinks, warm Coca-Cola.

He was struck suddenly by a provisional hope. He turned and considered the girl, a spindly child, unquestionably the weaker of the pair. "Little sister," he said. The false tenor of the endearment pained him. "Don't worry, don't be afraid," he said and slipped his hands under her arms and wiggled his fingers along her rib cage and down to her small hips. She writhed about, pedaling her skinny legs, tossing her head from side to side, doing everything appropriate to being tickled, except, of course, laughing. He could feel a wad of bills knotted beneath the hem of her pants. He could see them half pinched into the elastic band of her underwear, and here he paused, aggrieved at how unpleasant the situation had become and how shameful the remedy.

With a single hooked index finger, he swiped his hand inside the band of her underwear and plucked out a one-yuan bill. He set off at once toward the vending carts, towing the children behind him. Bellied up tight to the glass case, he handed over his money and ordered two cans of Coca-Cola. Three paces behind, the woman let out a raucous shriek.

He popped the rings and offered them to the children. "Go ahead," he said. "Go ahead. It's all right. I know you're thirsty."

They craned their heads up at him, stunned and suspicious.

"Go ahead," he said. "Please, it's all right," and they took the cans into their gritty hands, hearing the woman shriek and knowing they should not.

The rest was surprisingly easy. They each gripped his belt with a single hand, and he batted these away and stepped back to the walkway, where the crowd was thick and idled along with a blithe, unmindful ease. Outside the park entrance he searched for a taxi, and found instead a young man offering cut-rate fares for a ride on the back of his motor scooter. "Train station," Vincent said and swung a leg across the cushioned seat.

"But you can't leave yet," the young man said. "You haven't seen all the sights of Yuexiu Park. The Five Rams. The Sun Yat-sen Memorial. The Zhenhai Tower. I can drive you round to each one."

"Already seen them," Vincent said, scanning the sidewalk for the children and the tousled mother.

"The Hall of Flowers, you've seen that?"

"Oh yes, I've seen them all and they were all very nice. Especially the flowers, all very beautiful. And now I'm ready to leave," he said. "I've seen enough."

At the Guangzhou rail station he was one in a frantic logjam of bodies straining, shoving, elbowing his way to the front counter, where he asked for sleeping-berth passage and was granted a hard-seat ticket instead. Five hours later, when his train to Guilin began to board, he became part of yet another crushing herd of travelers pressing out onto the platform and up the train's iron foot rungs and through several sections of sleeping berths. The lucky among them tumbled covetously into their reserved bunks. Goaded on from one compartment to another, he came at last to a car of rowed seats and located his own, hard seat number 16, a window-side bench.

A short while later the train lumbered forward a few hundred yards and came to a sudden halt. There it sat, well in sight of the station, for another two hours. By then much of the day's radiance had been lost. An early evening stillness spread across the rail yard. All over Guangzhou people were sauntering home to bountiful Sunday dinners, or so he imagined.

Beside him, a squat, barrel-chested man studied Vincent with a fascination that did not diminish, even as the train finally sprang into motion and rumbled north through the city's scattered outer districts. The man's stained coveralls stank of petroleum and ash. Now and then he whispered in Cantonese, and several times he pointed to the fanning bruises beneath Vincent's sunglasses.

What a nuisance, these bruises. If they were not making him feel leprous, then they were provoking all sorts of unwelcome attention.

But the man's interest only grew sharper. He mumbled and shook his bushy head as if rehearsing a complicated lecture. Then he turned and addressed Vincent, this time in accented Mandarin. They spoke Mandarin differently here, with a windy inflection, with mouthfuls of sibilant consonants. Slowly, directly, the man repeated himself. "Why did your boss beat you?" he asked.

Vincent weighed the question. There was no reason to lie, and yet a full disclosure would be exhausting, humiliating. "I was spending time alone with his sister," he said. "I shouldn't have been doing that."

The man's dark eyes flickered sympathetically. "Yes, yes, that's always the way it is. You're good enough to do sweat work six days a week, but not good enough to take a private walk with the boss's sister. Am I right?"

"Yes," Vincent said. "You are."

"I thought I was. I thought I had your story right," he said and, satisfied, eased back into his seat.

Before long they were rolling beneath a lavender twilight. The car swayed and bounced on its speeding undercarriage. Somewhere behind, in the thicket of standing passengers, a child wailed. The compartment lights would dim and waver and return to full strength. With his eyes closed, the shuddering lights made his mind unreel in a flood of disjointed imagery. He slept only for minutes at a time. In his dreams, small, gritty-fingered hands reached out to seize him.

Seventeen

THE BUS TO Yangshuo was crammed full of metal shop workers, all men, all sooty-faced and haggard from a month of what must have been grueling shifts in a shuttered-up Guilin factory. They were returning home to Yangshuo for a three-day break. Naturally enough there was talk of relaxation and fine meals and bawdy exchanges concerning forlorn wives and girlfriends. Only a few kilometers outside Guilin a gruff voice stirred from the backseats and roused them into song. This, too, may have been nothing more than a rollicking ditty, but to Vincent, who had just survived his first hard-seat train journey, it seemed cadenced in sorrow and struggle and hardships endured.

No use denying that his trip to Guilin had been a nightmare, a twenty-two-hour marathon of unremitting discomfort. And no use, either, to dwell on the wretched toilets or the day he'd spent squeezed into his seat knock-kneed and aching, a day without food, his third without bathing. Between himself and the nearest fifty passengers had been a rank proximity not unlike the reek of caged animals. A very unpleasant journey, though now that it was over he made a dogged resolution: he would never travel hard-seat again. In the future he would secure a sleeping berth. If this was not possible, he would draw from the wealth of his money belt and travel by air.

Having made a pledge, he shifted his attention outside the bus, where the countryside was doing something peculiar—soaring up suddenly into peaked hills, into shaggy pinnacles hundreds of meters tall. Days earlier Alec had called the countryside surrounding Yangshuo "Moonland," an attempt, maybe, to convey its chasmal strangeness, the spectacular mass of pinnacles rising from an otherwise level river basin. Vincent had seen this landscape before, in countless Chinese scrolls and wall hangings, the hills ink-brushed or water-colored, rearing up into such lofty, attenuated peaks that he could only suspect the artists of exaggeration. They had not exaggerated. If anything, they had failed to capture the full legion of pin-nacles, a piked, ivy-cloaked regiment bearing down on the rice meadows, the roping Li River, the slight wisp of a highway upon which Vincent now traveled.

· · ·

He saw just enough of Yangshuo screened in pale evening light, hunkered amid shaggy pinnacles, to know that he had landed in a modest little town of picturesque shops and cafés. The bus halted at the depot, discharging its band of elated metal shop workers, and then carried Vincent alone past the town center to a two-storied oblong hotel built snugly against Yangshuo's outlying hillside. The hotel receptionist, a comely and attentive young woman, smiled and with the simple conferment of a room key granted Vincent a wish he had nourished for three days: a clean, restricted room and access to a hot shower.

In the hotel baths he stood for a half hour beneath a current of steaming water. And then he slept long into the next day, awoke and dawdled about in bed, reading, while outside the late-morning sun sharpened and blanched the window curtains. Room 24 lulled him with its coziness, and frequently during the leisurely pace of the next several days he would pause and consider the beige papered walls, the neatly creased second bed, and be persuaded that he had reached a safe haven of sorts. He was fond of the hotel as well, of taking his meals alone at a corner booth in the café, fond of the front desk attendants who did not mind when twice daily he asked whether or not a Scotsman named Alec McGowan had checked in.

A deep contentment to walk the mostly vacant hallways or lie about listening to music in his room. Had he become a recluse? Was it wrong to travel to one of the most esteemed regions of China and not leave his hotel?

Perhaps, yes. But much of his reclusiveness had to do with the discouraging condition of his face. A week had passed since his beating and his bottom lip had thinned to its proper width, though there was still a fading clover-shaped bruise on the edge of his mouth, trickling down like a slosh of grape jelly. The cuts on his brow and chin had fused over nicely. Around his eyes the rings had shrunken, but they had deepened, too, into a shade of forlorn violet. On the inward corner of each eye, tiny, muddled streaks of orange and yellow were rising to the surface. He would not have thought bruised skin capable of such color.

His fourth morning in Yangshuo he wandered outside the hotel and realized he had been hiding from an imaginary crush of Yangshuo citizenry. Its true residents, mild-tempered merchants and peasant farmers, most of them women in baggy blue trousers and field jackets, did not clamor or shove one another. They strolled the town's rolling lanes at a serene pace or gathered in genial, makeshift coteries along the open riverside.

It nourished his spirit to be out in the daylight and fresh air. He strolled to Yangshuo Park and followed a rising path that coiled about the slopes and scrubby bluffs of a pinnacle named Man Hill. On the way up, he met bands of descending hikers, often tourists his own age who passed in high spirits and conversed in a varied flutter of foreign tongues. He recognized German and whispered French and an inflected English that might have been Australian or South African. Between passings, he climbed alone peering down the steep hillsides. Each clearing offered up its view, a lofty, muted green plunge to the rice fields and river basin below. A quarter hour later he rounded a jutting bend and chanced upon a group of ascending climbers, five college-aged Americans whom he tagged behind as they plodded single-file toward the summit.

The scenery prompted a few giddy remarks. "We're not in Kansas anymore," a sandy-haired young woman leading the file called back to her companions. Vincent chuckled along with them, and yet oddly, though he shared their nationality, even their slow Midwestern drawl, he did not feel capable of stepping inside their camaraderie. It was his fault, mostly, because to be adopted by this group, to be truly included in the hike and then invited to gather with them later that evening in a village restaurant, he would need to reveal a different side of himself. Mainly, he needed to shrug off his reclusiveness and prove himself interesting, to pretend as if he were perfectly content touring the hillside alone, charged with clever insights, grinning from a rich wellspring of internal contentment. It was a charade he could only maintain for seconds at a time: one moment self-possessed, at the ready with a winsome remark; the next, apprehensive, afraid the remark would be ill received or embarrassing.

Together they reached the bushy crest of Man Hill, atop which stood a small concrete pagoda. Without ever addressing his companions, without asking their names or offering his own, he lingered in their company, listening to their quips and exclamations and nodding agreeably when they arranged themselves inside the pagoda and asked him to take a group picture: three young women, two men, each of them rosy-cheeked from the climb. In the camera's viewfinder their faces shone bright and freckled and blissfully expectant, all in a way that made his heart sink. He snapped several photos, returned the camera, and watched as they began filing down the pathway. The sandy-haired young woman lagged behind to thank him.

"No problem," he said. "It's really something, isn't it?"

"Oh yes. It is. You mean the pagoda?"

"And the view. The pagoda, too. Everything. You're not really from Kansas, are you?"

"Kansas?" The very word seemed unfathomable to her.

"I'm from Illinois," he said. "I've been in Asia awhile now."

"Yes," she said. "Awhile. That's great." By then her friends had plodded a good distance ahead. She was edging down the pathway and there was a wrinkling of commiseration or maybe outright pity in her good-bye and in her parting wave. And something else as well, a cagey disdain, the longing to flee his company as if it were a great hindrance or contagious disease.

Her leave-taking sent a shudder of despair through him. His sense of aloneness was baffling. He could have sworn that he had left it in Toulio, that the origin of his loneliness had been the cloistered town itself.

By day six in Yangshuo he'd mostly given himself over, inch by fretful inch, to the conviction that Alec wouldn't be showing up.

And then at breakfast two days later, seated streetside at an outdoor café, Vincent glanced up from his travel guide and saw his former rival and housemate, Alec McGowan, coast by on a rented bicycle. He was flanked on either side by two Chinese women. Vincent recognized one of them, a comely and waifishly thin young woman, as the second-shift receptionist from his hotel. As he passed, Alec threw out his arm, grinned, and saluted in Vincent's general direction before pedaling away.

He sprang up from his table and stepped out into the open street. Already they had slipped by the town post office and were edging up the hill beyond his hotel. He waved and shouted Alec's name. When they did not turn back, he hurried to a nearby bike shop, rented a sleek, old-fashioned one-speed, and took out after them.

On the highway west of Yangshuo he rolled by other cycle-bound tourists, skirted past shifting columns of peasant farmers, veered around produce carts and lumbering water buffalo. Inevitably, the trios of cyclists he spied on the horizon, the ones he fixed his gaze upon and pedaled hard to overtake, revealed themselves close up as strangers. He rode an hour and a half farther to the riverside village of Fuli before turning back.

The desk attendant at his hotel verified that a Scotsman had checked in very late the previous night. But he was not around today, she said. He had made friends with two members of the hotel staff, a receptionist and housekeeper. This was their day off, and they had invited the Scotsman out to sightsee and play.

And what room was the Scotsman staying in?

Your room, the attendant said. Room 24.

A mistake, surely, but a quick check of Room 24 and he discovered Alec's travel bag stowed beneath the unslept-in second bed.

There was little else to do then but press on with the search. He revisited restaurants, scoured the town park. He roamed Yangshuo's crafts and antiques shops. All the while he tried to imagine Alec sightseeing or, more ambiguously, *playing* with his female hosts.

By nightfall Vincent returned to the café where he'd breakfasted and chose an outdoor seat, same table, same streetside view. He scissored spinach and sliced pork from his plate and kept an eye on the cyclists gliding off the dark roadway. Blithe chitchat drifted from nearby tables. Within the thicket of voices, he heard a familiar, quarrelsome brogue. "That's nonsense now. That's daft thinking. Good God, man, you've got to be joking!"

He discovered Alec, not in the circle of surrounding tables, but at a restaurant two doors down, where he sat hunched at the end of a long table of foreign tourists, a lively troupe of ten or more, who with their bright packs and camera bags had commandeered the front patio. He appeared to be under the sway of an ecstatic mood. For days Vincent had carried the shrouded fear of dwindling into a dismal sort of quarantine, into something like invisibility. To see Alec was to be absolved of this dread.

"Was I right or was I right?" the Scotsman nearly shouted. He'd risen to his feet and clapped Vincent hard upon the back.

"About what?"

"About Yangshuo, you dolt. About Moonland."

"You were," Vincent agreed. The presence of so many strangers at the table had made him shy. "When did you get in?" he asked. "I was looking for you."

"Last night. Snuck in late. Too late to actually sleep." He intercepted a bottle of beer and raised it, toast-style, to silence the gathering. "My mate

Vincent Saunders," he announced. "A Yank, but let's not hold that against him."

The faces that turned to regard Vincent were mostly pleasant and flushed with alcohol and blustery conversation. He caught a few of the women and a studious, freckled young man squinting at the fading bruises around his eyes.

"I should warn you all," Alec continued. "Vincent's a bare-knuckle street fighter. No teasing, no sudden movements. He's liable to react."

It made him blush, this sly wisecrack. "Not true," he insisted. He needn't have said it. Alec's wisecrack had been enough to earn a few raffish chuckles, enough to deflect any real interest in the condition of his eyes.

They took seats at the table and almost at once a bottle of beer was passed into Vincent's hands. There were cheery introductions and a slew of names to remember: Ollie from Germany, studious and freckled Paul from New Zealand, Justin or maybe Jason from Vancouver and his girlfriend, Michelle, from South Africa. At the end of the table were a trio of young women, European, one Swiss, the others possibly Dutch. He took them all in with a measured glance—a strange and almost illicit satisfaction to find that everyone present was of the same race as he.

Prior to his arrival Alec had been bandying words with a tall, bearded American named Douglas. And now the argument resumed with Douglas, the only mirthless member of their party, recounting an afternoon he'd spent in the company of several Chinese graduate students. This had happened two weeks earlier in Shanghai, and the students, who were enrolled at the Shanghai Academy of Arts, had taken Douglas and his girlfriend, Amanda, on a meandering tour of Shanghai's back alleyways. They came, eventually, to an underground coffeehouse. There, Douglas and Amanda found themselves in the midst of subversive talk. They were asked about asylum in America. Several of the students spoke of insurrection, of imminent reprisal for the massacre at Tiananmen. The workers of Shanghai, the students said, were still furious about Tiananmen, more so than the citizens of Beijing. Shanghai was bitter and vengeful. It might well be the spark that would reignite the country, or so claimed the students. And it had all sounded authentic and portentous to Douglas. He'd been glad when asked to contribute money to their cause. With the first anniversary of the massacre only fifteen days away, he believed China could erupt at any moment.

"Won't happen," Alec said. "Even if these blokes were planning something, even if they were half-serious, they wouldn't have blathered on about it to you."

Douglas, hunched over the table, let out a sour chuckle. "You've never seen people act so cautious," he pledged. He appeared quite cautious himself, peering out over the raised collar of his leather jacket, speaking in a guarded hush whenever the Chinese waiters drew near.

His girlfriend, Amanda, had taken a skittish interest in their debate. "They did seem awfully young," she said. "They all had the same trendy haircut. They all wore the same brand of sunglasses."

"Which means what, exactly?" Douglas asked.

"It means what it means."

"This isn't about fashion, Amanda."

"Of course it isn't. It's about who you're getting your information from." She was green-eyed, pale-skinned with a great mane of blond-brown hair and a spry posture that made her noticeably attractive. "I'm doubting your source, honey, not your opinion," she said. "Remember, I was there too."

"Fine," Douglas said. "Then my opinion is that there are millions of people in this country passionately devoted to the idea of democracy. And there's an intolerant government ready to flush them out of hiding and persecute them. Sparks are going to fly. It's inevitable. It's all happened before. Read your Chinese history."

"I don't think the people give a shit about democracy!" Alec blurted out. It was a typically bold declaration, and Vincent took a sly pleasure in seeing the Scotsman's glower and head-shaking disbelief aimed at someone other than himself. "Nor should they, because if they think it's the answer to their problems, then they're only fooling themselves."

Douglas grimaced and rolled his eyes, a principled man pained by the outlandishness of a radical. "I'd say you have to believe in an idea pretty strongly, pretty ferociously, to stand in front of an oncoming tank."

"Or you'd have to be out of your head with anger. Anger's the thing," Alec said. "The workers and peasants are pissed off, all right, and it's not about whatever the government decides to call itself. They're furious over other things. About a dozen of them." Not surprisingly, he was ready to list these grievances, to wrest up his fingers one at a time and call out, "Taxation, for starters. Rural peasants taxed to near starvation," then, "Food rations, all the grain and rice and meat coupons. What a great pain in the arse that must be."

Amanda, meanwhile, had scooted two seats down the table where the discourse was lighter and punctuated with infectious giggling. The burly German, Ollie, had placed one empty beer bottle atop another, balanced them mouth to mouth, with a paper receipt wedged between. The trick was to remove the paper without toppling the bottles. No one, Ollie included, seemed able to manage it, though their clumsy, whimsical attempts rendered them breathless with laughter. A young woman beside Amanda was folding her Foreign Exchange Certificates into a tiny flock of origami swans, and then Amanda herself built a wobbly teepee from discarded chopsticks. She gazed across the table to Vincent and smiled. "You're next," she said. "What's your trick? What's your hidden talent?"

"I don't have any," he said, and wished, intensely, that he did.

"How about palm reading? How about impersonations?"

"There's a thing I used to do, a thing I don't do anymore, with Bible quotes. I used to cite the quotes from memory."

"Recite Bible quotes?" She smiled again, not at all unpleasantly. "That must have made you very popular."

"No, cite the quotes, the passages. Somebody would say a line from the Bible and I would tell them exactly where it came from. John three, verse sixteen. That sort of thing."

"All right, I'll try," Amanda said. "But most of what I know from the Bible has come to me secondhand, from books and movies." She pinched her bottom lip and concentrated. "'Many are called, few are chosen,'" she offered. "Is that from the Bible?"

"It is. From Matthew twenty-two, verse fourteen."

"And this, of course. 'Though I walk through the valley of death—'"

"Psalm Twenty-three. 'The valley of the *shadow* of death.' The shadow makes it a little more . . . ominous."

The group favored him with a sprinkling of applause and a few absurd cheers, all of which pleased him more than it should have. He felt ready to demonstrate a more lavish talent, though he had no idea what it might be. ". . . and if the Mainland does erupt," Alec inveighed, somewhat drunkenly, from his corner of the gathering, "let's hope they'll be rounding up all the doom-struck, pompous foreign wankers like yourself and tossing them out on their heads."

This time Douglas bristled from the insult. He wrangled through his backpack until he'd found his hotel key, pushed back his chair as if ready to leave.

"Douglas," Amanda pleaded. "This isn't worth getting upset about. You don't have to hold it in. You can tell him to fuck off if you like. He expects it. That's the way he argues."

"Cheers," Alec said, raising his bottle to the group at large rather than Douglas, whose cheeks and forehead flared a wrathful crimson. "Cheers, cheers," he continued until everyone had finished off their beers. Then he flipped open his pack of 555s and exhibited three plump hash cigarettes with twisted ends. "Now, who'd like to walk with me down to the river pier and have a smoke?"

As it turned out, they all did, except for Douglas. They ordered another round of beer and slipped the barely chilled bottles into their pockets. Before they left Amanda draped her arms over Douglas's shoulders and tried soothing her boyfriend with a few low-muttered words and a single peckish kiss across his brow.

At night the Li River was a wide velvety curve of still-skinned water. To reach its shore, they had to descend a sequence of stone footsteps chiseled from the bank and veiled in pitch-black shadows. The pier below stretched out into a cobbled walkway, a thousand glossy-shelled river stones varnished in pale blue moonlight. They sat together in a row along the pier ledge, their legs trailing above the murky water. Alec lit the first of his hash cigarettes. Once properly kindled, it was handed to Amanda, then to Paul and on to Vincent, who did not draw it to his lips, but held the filtered end at arm's length and passed it on to Ollie. From there it made its errant way down the line into other hands and last to the three young European women. One of them, a short-haired Swiss girl with a lilting French accent, inhaled deeply and said, "Marvelous."

"Nice, isn't it," Alec said. "Got it from some Uighur hippies in Guangzhou."

"Yes, but I mean to say the river, the hills, the stars. I *marvel* at them."

One by one they craned their heads up and studied the towering pinnacles and the night sky beyond.

"It's a dream village," Amanda said.

"Yangshuo's pure genius," Alec avowed. "Yangshuo's brilliant." He leaned back on his elbows and said to Vincent, "It's nothing like the rest of China, nothing at all like where you're heading. Not just the landscape, mind you, but the pace of things, the attitude, everything."

Vincent sipped from his beer and nodded happily. He fought an odd compulsion to either lay back and sleep or to engage those around him in a sudden boisterous conversation. "I saw you ride past on a rented bike this morning. Where'd you go? I went out looking for you."

"Ha! Good thing you didn't find me. I didn't want anyone else tagging along. I'd been invited out sightseeing for the day."

"Invited by our hotel receptionist?"

"Yes, by Mei-ling and her cousin Mei-hua. Beautiful Bell and Beautiful Flower. Notice how I savor their names."

"Were they insane?" Amanda asked. "Or did they just feel sorry for you?"

"They were driven insane, slowly, by my charm and posh manners. We rode out past Fuli, took a rope ferry across the river. We're clomping round this hillside and Mei-hua—she's learning English—she says, 'Is this sunny day a delightful one for you?'"

"Oh, and you liked that, didn't you?" Amanda said.

"You bet I did. There I was pedaling round the countryside with a pair of pretty girls. I'm over the moon with happiness. 'Course I was stoned, too, but it was all very innocent. Sunshine and smiles. Very, *very* fucking delightful."

"But don't you get tired of the baby-doll antics? The pigtails? The way they cup their mouths when they giggle? They exaggerate the girlishness. I swear they do."

"It's not for me to judge."

"The miniskirts I can understand. I can see why men turn their heads."

"I wouldn't know," Alec said. "Though it sounds to me as if you're not getting enough attention."

She sat up straight and made an exasperated appeal to the other women in the group. "Did you hear that?" she asked. "Do I respond? Or do I just shove him in the river?" She tried scowling, but even in the darkness they could see the smile beneath it. "I'm serious," she said. "Do I shove him off into the river?"

No answer. The collective mood seemed to have changed from lively to quietly bemused. The last hash cigarette was lit and passed down the row. Together they lay on their backs and watched moonlight play on an exposed limestone bluff. For a long time no one in their party spoke aloud. Then Paul yawned and hugged his knees. "It's late," he said.

"How late?" someone asked.

"Very," he said, but they lounged another half hour before Alec stood and led them single-file along the cobbled pier.

The lowest steps, though darkly shadowed, were not hard to navigate. But midway up, their path crossed under the knobby belly of the riverbank, and beneath this overhang, in the absence of moonlight, they fumbled through a deep, swampy blackness. Somewhere within the midst of their rank a woman giggled.

"It's outrageous," Amanda said. "We may as well be blindfolded."

The woman giggled again, a quick, capering titter that spread from person to person until they were all doubled over, howling with laughter.

"Good God, people! Get hold of yourselves," Alec shouted.

"Whose hand is that?" Amanda asked. "Who've I got ahold of here?"

"It's me," Alec said. "But I should warn you, that isn't my thick forefinger you've got squeezed in your fist."

"It's your stubby little thumb. At least it better be."

"There's nothing stubby or little about it, woman. Feel it wiggling. That's no thumb!"

They struggled on, raking their feet blindly from one stone terrace to the next, plagued by great knee-buckling waves of laughter. Vincent laughed along with them. He could not name the source of this sudden hilarity. Maybe he was drunk, but it seemed to him something else as well, a lightness, an evaporation of the recent days he'd spent brooding and alone and half-certain that the chaos and collapse Gloria had warned of would come true. Now, though, before they reached the top of the stairs, he had time to wonder if this was what godless people did, surround themselves with friends and laugh into the darkness, into the very shadow.

With Alec there was always the hope of receiving crucial advice, some worthy parcel of travel knowledge that would stave off a costly or even calamitous mistake.

Never eat pork or chicken from a vendor's stall. Always negotiate the fare before stepping into a taxi. No good reason ever to remove your money belt: if need be you can shit, shower, and shag with it fastened round your waist. And for Christ sake, stick to a budget.

All countries will drive you broke eventually, he said. *At least in China you go broke slowly.*

True enough, because thus far China had been astoundingly cheap. Their shared double room was priced under five dollars a night. A restaurant meal rarely cost more than one or two. Alec, who was fond of converting values into both pounds and dollars, estimated the price of a warm beer at between eleven and thirteen U.S. cents. The ball of hash he had purchased in Guangzhou, so large he could not entirely close his fist around it, had cost him a scant pound and a half.

As a rule he dismissed all varieties of travel guides as false or worthless. "Pitiful," he said, though when he scooped up Vincent's copy, ready to mock its chapter on Yangshuo, he made an unexpected discovery. "By God, there's a government travel office in town," he mused. "Advance train tickets and so forth. We could set up the next leg of our trip to Chengdu. Maybe get ourselves booked into a sleeper car." They set out at once, but by the time they had located the office, a white-walled cottage on the grounds of a nearby hotel, he had already soured on the idea. His glum forecast: "We'll either be swindled or driven mad by bureaucracy."

Inside they found a pair of bored travel clerks gazing drowsy-eyed into their own maps and brochures. Yet once challenged with a complicated rail journey through three provinces, they sat upright and began consulting charts and timetables in a flurry of excitement. There would be switch-overs, they said, in Guiyang and Chongqing, forty hours of travel time, another eight hours in station layovers. They asked for passports and tourist fare up front. Though he eventually consented, Alec balked at the notion and then groused about extortion for the rest of the day. The next afternoon their tickets were hand-delivered to the hotel door. Except for a brief segment of their journey outside Guiyang, they'd been guaranteed sleeping berths the entire way. "Can you believe it?" he asked, flushed with amazement. "Well, fuck me twice for doubting."

Vincent regarded his sheaf of tickets as a small paper pledge against future hardship and therefore something of a comfort during the handful of days they remained in Yangshuo. Before long the regulars in their party began settling hotel bills, procuring tickets, and setting out, by bus or riverboat, for destinations in the Mainland and beyond. The Swiss and Dutch girls headed northeast to Shanghai. Paul set off alone for Kunming.

A few nights later those who remained, as well as a few merry newcomers, convened on the restaurant patio, a pleasant, rowdy assemblage that would be, for Vincent and Alec, a farewell gathering. Addresses were exchanged. Promises were made to look for one another at tourist sites and foreigner hotels throughout western and northern China. Douglas did not attend, yet Amanda, who arrived in fine spirits, sat chatting and sipping whiskey Cokes till midnight and beyond. As the party disbanded, she asked Alec to accompany her down to the Li River bank, where they could have a smoke and gaze up at the limestone pinnacles. "If you don't mind," she said to Vincent with a sisterly wink, a reminder that though he was in on the secret, he would not be included in their after-hours excursion.

He climbed the hill back to his hotel. He was neither drunk nor particularly tired. Rather than lie awake in bed he decided to gather his pens and stationery and sit in the hotel café. At once he set to work on letters to his parents and to Vanessa explaining that he had taken a leave of absence from the Toulio ministry and was traveling in Mainland China. He thought a long while before beginning his next task, a simple postcard he would send to Gwa via Donny Wu in Hong Kong. At last, he wrote:

> Mr. Gwa,
>
> *I am now on my way north to Chengdu having taken some time to rest and sightsee in Guangxi Province. So far I have traveled safely and guarded my possessions well. So far everything is fine. Hope to be in Urumchi in ten days' time. As I travel, I keep in mind our last meeting, your good advice, your best intentions.*

As an afterthought, he shook Kai-ling's photograph free from the folds of his stationery. A queer, almost vertiginous sense of apprehension to study her likeness: the hair; the discerning gaze; the off-focus glaze of her smooth-complected face. Even out of focus, the face shocked him with its righteousness. He was aware, perhaps for the first time, that his travels thus far had amounted to more than a panicked retreat from Toulio. He was on his way to the desert city of Urumchi to take part in a counterfeit marriage to a woman he'd never met. Astoundingly, this was something he had promised to do.

Later, just before three A.M., the hotel front door creaked open and Alec sauntered in across the lobby and took a seat beside Vincent in the café.

"So?" Vincent asked.

"A fine night on the riverbank," he answered. "Half-moon in the sky. Good smoke. Great company. Lovely company. I thought I might have had too much beer—but, good news, the pinnacles were still rising."

"Ha."

"Ha, indeed."

Kai-ling's photo lay on the table between them. Alec put his thumb on one corner, turned his wrist left, right, left again.

"That's her," Vincent said. "Gwa gave me the photo to carry along. Partly, I guess, to prove how beautiful she is, or how beautiful he *thinks* she is. You can't really tell much from the picture."

Under Alec's thumb the photo kept shifting, reeling. He scrutinized her profile from various angles. A begrudging smile formed at the corners of his lips. "Oh yes, you can," he replied. "She's a cracker, all right. She's a cracker, absolutely."

Eighteen

DAYS ON END they did nothing but ride the trains.

Folded into his third-tier bunk, Vincent discovered it was possible to lie sideways and face the cramped interior of his berth, to turn away from the commotion and plumes of cigarette smoke, and seek out a narrow sanctuary all his own. His posture—legs tucked, a fetal twisting of his head and upper back—proved fine for light, dozing naps and listening to music on his Walkman. Reading was a cumbersome experience; the book swam just several blurred inches from his nose. The bad light and hard, proximate typescript strained his eyes.

Stiff-muscled or simply bored, he would roll over for quick glimpses of the Guangxi landscape: a pea-green breadth of banking hillocks, a few hefty stone cottages graced with slate roofs. Across the compartment Alec snoozed beneath the open flaps of a history book. The remaining four bunks had been claimed by two white-shirted businessmen, a jolly, plum-faced cadre official, and, lying stock-still in the middle bunk below Alec, a tiny, wiry-haired grandmother. Every half hour, her grandson, who was berthed in the next compartment, brought her a cup of steaming water from the carriage boiler. If she complained of leg cramps, he would, without a glint of embarrassment, reach out and massage the veined and spotted flesh from her knees to her ankles.

The businessmen and cadre made benches of the two lowest bunks. Legs crossed, shirt collars loosened, they eschewed sleep in favor of loud talk and a cheerful, shoulder-to-shoulder camaraderie. In time they attracted visitors from other compartments. A parcel box was set out and topped with hot tea, sunflower seeds, and unfiltered cigarettes. Roosted above their humble feast, Vincent could see a huddle of dark, bobbing heads. He jutted an ear out to eavesdrop.

It took time to penetrate their Mainland accents, the sharp, near-whistling cadences, yet once he did, he listened and was privy to a breezy litany of complaints. The diner car food was terrible. Even so, the businessmen could only afford shitty boxed lunches. They were stashing away their food allowances. Once up north with their clients, they planned to blow it all on a lavish banquet.

"North?" the cadre stammered. "North where?"

"North of the Yangtze," a businessman countered, his voice hushed to a bosomy whisper. "North of the Yangtze, where the service is bad and the people are stupid and lazy."

The gathering thickened. Visitors from other regions of the train would—if they could slip by the hard-sleeper steward—poke their faces in and try their luck at minor, offhanded negotiations. A comrade in hard-seat had a surplus of grain coupons to trade. Any takers? A stocky teenaged boy squeezed into the compartment and wanted to know who among them was a resident of Guiyang. He had an older brother in Anshan desperate to move to Guiyang, and he hoped to find someone willing to swap housing assignments.

Later, a rumor began to circulate of a wealthy, self-made gentleman two bays down. He had declared himself a ten-thousander, a salary, Vincent understood, though he was not sure whether the amount was monthly or yearly. Eventually the man dropped by, cloaked in a Mao jacket and altogether ordinary, to verify what turned out to be a yearly earning. "Ten thousand yuan," he said without a trace of conceit. "Last two years in a row."

"How'd you do it?" someone asked.

"Raising rare birds," he answered. "Rare and colorful birds." He plucked out a brilliant saffron feather from his waistband and passed it around their circle. Even the two businessmen, who earlier had naysayed the rumor, tweaked its clear tapered quill and believed.

Just before noon a vendor passed through the carriage lugging a bin of boxed lunches. Vincent and Alec purchased one each and climbed down from their bunks to sit windowside, opposite the compartment, on two foldout cushioned seats.

"Watch this now. This is good," Alec said, after they'd finished their lunches, and, following the lead of other passengers, tossed their empty cartons out the window. He nodded at the businessmen and cadre sprawled back on their bunks, their eyelids curtained down into groggy slivers. Down the aisleway a copse of standing-room travelers bowed their heads against compartment panels and slept on their feet. "It's sleepy dream time," he said. "And all the Chairman's good little revolutionaries have settled in for a well-deserved nap." He pulled two cigarettes from his shirt pocket, one hash, the other tobacco, and lit them both.

"It's safe? Safe to smoke here?"

"Mostly. If a steward happens along, I'll flick it out the window."

"I'm wondering—I'm just curious, no attitude or anything like that. I'm wondering why you smoke hash so often."

Alec's first response was to treat the question with a brooding disdain. But then he relaxed, furrowed his goatee, took a calming glance at the passing scenery. "Fair enough," he said. "Let's say it helps me sit nicely inside my own head. Or, let's say it takes the unpleasant edge off things. Traveling's mainly unpleasant. I'm sure you've figured that out by now. Eighty percent shit, twenty percent brilliant."

"You ever consider quitting?"

"Smoking? No. Don't need to. It's not as hard on your body as alcohol. And I can go without a smoke if need be. I've done it before. Five years ago in Calcutta, I got wonked by a vegetable cart. Big, heavy fucker, out of control. No fault of mine, either. I'm standing in an open market. Next thing there's a rumbling and I'm out cold for three days. Nearly killed me. I woke up from the concussion with a cracked hip and a broken leg." He leaned toward the window and excised a deep lungful of musky smoke. He puffed on the second cigarette, waving it about to mask the odor. "So I'm three months mending flat on my arse in bed, no smoke, out of my mind with boredom. Two months more of physical rehabilitation."

"Where? Back in Scotland?"

"No, man. There in Calcutta. The hospital wasn't the horror show you'd imagine."

"But you went back home after the accident? To rest up and see your family?"

"No, didn't go back. Haven't since I left home."

"When was that?"

"Nine years ago."

"You haven't been home in nine years?"

"Don't start in with that. Don't start thinking prodigal son. I've got a perfectly reasonable family. A mother, a father, a younger sister. I left home on good terms."

"I'm sure you did. Things change, though. People grow old fast."

"I'd go back and visit if I had the cash. But I don't. Besides, I know what their lives are like. I get letters now and then. Send them some of my own. Things haven't changed much."

"I'm just saying you should, if you get the chance."

"Right," he said. "Seems you've got loads of ideas about things I *should* do."

The train swayed and lolled its sleeping passengers. Amid the relative quiet, Vincent wondered if his questions had been tainted by sanctimony. He noticed Alec listing slightly in his seat, his window-drawn gaze dolorous, glassy. He did not appear to be sitting nicely inside his own head, not with his knuckles pressed to his temple and his jaw crooked open in a disconsolate yawn.

And if this was an early sign of Alec's contempt, his browbeating displeasure, it did not reveal itself fully until later, when the others wakened from their naps and clustered around to scrutinize their two pale and lanky compartment mates.

Naturally they were curious, the businessmen and cadre and assorted visitors, who offered up cigarettes and tea before making their first hedgy attempts at conversation. The cadre wanted to know if they were American, but he, along with the businessmen, insisted on broaching his questions in fragmented, nearly impenetrable English.

"We . . . both we," the cadre said. "Both we . . . American?"

"Funny, you don't look American," Alec replied.

"You!" One of the businessmen, the livelier of the two, had managed to snare the right word. "You, both you, American?"

"Vincent here is. I'm not. I've never set foot in the god-awful country."

"American? No?" the cadre asked.

"No," Alec said. He had switched to Mandarin. "I understand you want to have a talk. That's fine with me. Let's make it easier on all of us and speak in the common language."

Except for the cadre and businessman, the other men in their carriage welcomed the change in tongue. They asked Alec where he was from. No one in their gathering had ever heard of Scotland.

"It's north of England," Alec said.

"A part of England?" someone guessed. "You're an Englishman?"

"No," he said, low and exasperated. "Scotland is different. It's not the same as England. It's a different country. A different country altogether." He seemed pained, deeply so, to have to explain, and yet he set forth like a world-weary schoolmarm indexing details of Scottish geography.

He was interrupted by the plum-faced cadre, who'd begun holding up various objects and asking for their English names. "How say English," the cadre barked, a sunflower seed wedged between his plump fingers.

"How say English," the businessman chimed in, flourishing, of all things, a wrinkled sock plucked from his tangled bedclothes.

"Sunflower seed," Alec said. "Sock."

"Sunfowler seed," they said. "Sack," they repeated while hurrying to scavenge more things for naming.

In a short while Alec's answers turned surly, ridiculous: *prick* for fountain pen, *arse-wipe* for paper napkin.

Vincent could not decide if, in the slippery chore of travel chitchat, he was faring any better. A young man his own age, a college student from Chongqing, had claimed an adjacent window stool. His hair, finely cut and recently gelled, was slicked forward into a glossy black pompadour.

He said, "In America you drink coffee, but in China we enjoy drinking tea."

"Yes, you do," Vincent said.

They sat and considered each other for a small eternity before the young man leapfrogged to the next topic.

"China is a land of many people," he said, his English as clear and precise—and as banal—as in any grammar textbook. "Some Chinese think there are too many people. There are more people in China than in America."

"Many more. Nearly a billion more," Vincent said.

"Yes, a billion more," the student said, and they locked gazes and listened to the train pound the rails in its meticulous rhythm.

And on it went, hours of extemporaneous chatter, strained or earnest or otherwise. At dusk, after another boxed meal, after a myriad of nodding introductions and names learned and obliquely forgotten, they crawled into their bunks and slept until the train arrived at Guiyang. It was a city of rain-smeared factories hampered by a starless and drizzling four A.M. sky. They took a laggard stroll through the railway station, and when they plopped down on a section of bare floor, other waylaid travelers crouched beside them, stared and asked questions. Always they were assumed to be American, and always Alec flinched from the insult.

Near sunrise they boarded a train for Chongqing and found themselves lying stuporous in the lowest bunks of another hard-sleeper bay. Around them the carriage was unnervingly alive with spirited travelers.

"Where do you come from?" their compartment mates asked, so curious and full of early-morning vigor that they parried for hip space along the edge of Vincent's bunk.

"America," he said. From across the bay he heard Alec educating his own clique of guests as to the precise locale and citizenry of Scotland.

"And your friend?"

"He's from Scotland."

"Scotland? Where's it at?"

"North of England."

"A part of England?"

"A north part, yes," he said softly. "Different country, though. Different name." He gave the same or similar answer three times more before Alec overheard him.

"A north part of what?" Alec shouted from his bunk.

"Britain," Vincent lied. He felt a flare of childish panic.

"That's not what you said. You said England, didn't you? Didn't you?"

"I was trying to think of the Chinese word for Britain. But I couldn't, so yes, I might have said England."

"You thick bastard! Fuck off!"

Vincent steadied himself for a quarrel, a lengthy, possibly harrowing one that never evolved because Alec had stopped speaking. Not to the other passengers of their compartment, but to him, Vincent. And when he thought about it, *fuck off* had been shouted in a tone of finality, at a level of utmost exasperation.

The train needled north, riding low on the flanks of steep-crested mountains. A sudden deep-welled tunnel might cocoon them in fumbling darkness and amplify each clattering gallop of the rail. During the midday siesta, Alec sat by the window and smoked. Only after he returned to his bunk did Vincent rise and take his place on the foldout stool. Each was careful not to turn or let his gaze settle on the other.

The scenery beyond their carriage took shape in a zigzag of green valleys stretching into a far and cloud-muddled horizon. Lesser slopes lay crosshatched with unpaved roads, and on these roads moved a straggling parade of mules and carts and, much more rarely, a diesel tractor spewing coal-black exhaust. Yet at all times, no matter the stage of day or the inchmeal fluctuation of scenery, Vincent saw, unfailingly, clusters of men and women or scattered individuals treading the roads or gaps between valleys. This, he thought, was what one billion one hundred and fifteen million people meant; that there would never come a moment when he would look from a train or bus window and *not* see at least one lone soul roaming the landscape.

Late in the afternoon, a few hours outside Chongqing, he swiveled around and edged toward Alec's bunk. "What's the travel time between Chongqing and Chengdu?" he asked, though he'd already gleaned the answer, eleven hours, from his travel guide.

Alec did not respond. Nor did he speak or bother to come to the window when later they crossed a wide, hueless bend of the Yangtze River and pulled into the city of Chongqing. Inside the station, they posted themselves on either end of the waiting room corridor and endured their four-hour layover privately, furtively, like opposing Cold War spies. Then, once again, they were train-bound, stretched out high and silent in their bunks, shuttling northwest across a verdant and far-reaching countryside.

Nineteen

CHENGDU LOOKED TO be a proper Chinese city: grand, hedge-lined boulevards, a well-kept city park, promenades lined with street merchants and basket weavers, a gargantuan statue of Mao Zedong holding watch before a huge and suitably imposing exhibition hall. Alec, who appeared to have an incisive grasp of Chengdu's crisscrossing lanes, led the way to the hotel district.

He chose the cavernous Chengdu Overseas Friendship Hotel. Down they went into a subwaylike portal to a subterranean main lobby where the fluorescent lights were murky and the front-desk staff appeared wan and benumbed. Alec checked in. No one there remembered him from two previous stays. He was given a receipt and told to deliver it to the third-floor key girl.

They found her at the juncture of four long corridors, a sulky, unhandsome young woman couched behind a gray metal desk. She had a phone wedged against her chin and was chatting with another key girl assigned to duty a floor below. When Alec presented the receipt and asked to have their room unlocked, she ignored him. He asked again. She talked on. He reached out with one hand and smothered the cradle switch.

"You'll be very sorry you did that," she said, not angry exactly, but with a sense of mournful foreknowledge, as if she'd gazed into the future, seen his awful punishment, and was heartsick as a result. She claimed her Peg-Board of keys and set off down the corridor in a series of plodding half steps. Vincent had never witnessed an able-bodied person walk slower or with a more irritating lack of ambition.

They were shown to a bare, high-ceilinged room, cement walls, a pair of single-mattress beds divided by a scuffed nightstand. A ceiling fan with two missing blades churned out wobbly drafts of dank air. They had still not spoken to each other, and so each, by way of a wordless, nodding agreement, took a turn showering and washing clothes in the communal bathroom while the other stayed behind in the room to guard valuables. Afterward they lay back on their mattresses and let their wet clothing drip-dry from the ends of their beds.

Their silence held a certain mild complicity, a certain shyness. By now it was mostly a matter of who would speak to the other first. Before that happened, they heard a key probing the lock from outside. The door cracked open and the key girl's pimpled forehead filled the narrow gap. A dark eye fixed its gaze on Alec.

"Close the door, you nut job!" he shouted.

The door squeezed shut. But she was back twenty minutes later leering at Alec from the open wedge of the door and moving her lips incantation-style in a whispered voice too low to actually hear.

"What's she doing?" Vincent asked.

"Who knows?" he answered. "My best guess is that she's putting a hex on me."

"A hex?"

"Fucking right. Which pisses me off because when I checked in I specifically asked *not* to have a hex put on me."

"This hotel," Vincent marveled. "I can't tell if our room is above ground or below. And the service."

"Yes, you may wonder why I keep coming back," he said. "It's the friendship. Warms my fucking heart."

By the time they reached the rail station plaza the next morning, the sun was warm and arrantly bright. They milled past bundle-laden passengers and cliques of black-market ticket scalpers whom Alec sized up from a discreet distance. Yet before he could select a scalper, they first had to settle on their next destination. He broached the subject with a hangdog air of apology.

"Look here then," he said. "I'm thinking about heading up to Xian. It's a couple of hours west of the line you'll be taking to Lanzhou. Two hours west, maybe. I'm not just thinking about it. That's what I'm going to do."

"Xian?" Vincent said.

"I know a Welsh bloke there. Married a Xian girl. He teaches English at a technical college."

"He knows you're coming?"

"No clue whatsoever." Alec grinned. "You're welcome to come along. I'll be there two days or more."

"I probably shouldn't."

"Look here," he said again. "I wouldn't mind you coming along. I was out of sorts the last few days, but I'm over that. You could come along. I'll be carrying on with this friend of mine, smoking and drinking, no doubt. But you could do other things, go to the emperor's tomb and get a look at the terra-cotta army."

"I better not," Vincent said. "They're expecting me in Urumchi. I thought I'd be farther along than Chengdu by now."

"Right then, you're sure about this?"

Vincent said that he was, though the only certain feeling he had was that of untimely abandonment. He felt the possibilities of his journey narrow, if not to the point of some dire mishap, then at least to fatigue and unmitigated boredom.

The ticket scalper Alec chose was a young man with impish smile lines creasing the corners of his eyes and a wrinkled leather cap covering his forehead at a jaunty angle, two features that implied genial honesty and a flair for big-city bartering. He promised them back-door tickets and then proceeded, literally, to the station's back wall and spoke to someone through a cracked window. An hour later they held same-day tickets in their hands.

They did not, however, have berths in the same compartment. Vincent had a hard-sleeper for the thirty-plus-hour trip to Lanzhou. Alec would hard-seat it as far as Baoji and take a connecting train to Xian. They boarded separate compartments at noon and met up again an hour later at the train's midpoint, a dining car that portioned the sleeping berths from the carriages of hard seats.

They sat together at a windowside table and played cards. The game was gin rummy. Alec furnished the deck. To ensure their place at the table, he ordered a plate of pulpy, spinachlike greens and bottles of Tsingtao beer, which he drank in measured sips at the rate of one per hour. As they played, they made provisional arrangements to meet a week later in Turpan, an oasis town in the Tarim Basin. Turpan was scorching hot during the day, Alec said, but cool enough at night. A brilliant place. If not in Turpan, he said, then they would probably catch up to each other someplace else along the line.

"Probably," Vincent said. "Or probably not. It's a big country."

"It's a *huge* country. But not when you consider the places foreign tourists tend to gather, the sites they flock to, the hotels they stay in. You'll see how it is. You'll wind up running into certain folks again and again all over China."

"And if we don't run into each other?"

"Then you go on to Urumchi and I'll take the rest of my holiday in Kashgar. I'll be staying at the Seman Hotel. Great fucking name, isn't it? The Seman. And when you finish up in Urumchi, that is, once you and Kai-ling have tied the knot and are ready to head back, you can write or telex me."

"Or maybe you could come to Urumchi early. For the wedding, I mean."

"Doubtful," Alex said. "Though it's sure to be a scene. The best thing is for you to contact me. We'll make plans then to meet up and head back to Taiwan together."

They fanned open their cards and continued the game, playing slowly and with the idle purpose of erasing long minutes from their trip. In time their scores inched past five hundred and on toward a game-ending one thousand points. By then the car had filled with dinner guests and an attendant brought them more greens and fatty pork bones and bowls of white rice. Vincent sifted through the bowl with his chopsticks, but did not eat much. Of late his appetite had grown fitful and distracted. The rare occasions he was hungry, it wasn't for box lunches or tepid railway fare.

A short while later they passed an enormous plain of meter-high maize, the long fields crisscrossed with irrigation runnels and tended by a brigade of peasant farmers in bamboo hats and blue jackets. All at once several of the bamboo hats tipped skyward and Vincent glimpsed an assortment of faces, austere or matronly or even, in a few instances, a young woman's smooth copper cheeks and dusky liquid eyes. Inside the diner car, they sat quietly as audience to this, and to the saffron-tinted sky, and to the coursing irrigation water, which was bright and dappled and seemed to draw in the evening light.

"Nice, isn't it?" Alec said.

Vincent nodded, grateful for such understatement. In this moment and others, he wanted to step down from his journey and linger over the particulars of each place. The train would not allow it.

When twilight came, they abandoned the game and gathered the stray cards from the table. The train would not arrive in Baoji until early the next morning. Rather than face the perils of his hard-seat carriage, Alec vowed to stay put and wait for the diner car attendants to run him out. He watched Vincent yawn and flutter his eyelids and said, "Go to your bunk, man. May as well. I'll see myself off the train in Baoji."

Yet Vincent stayed, at least long enough to reaffirm their plans to meet up again. The simplicity of their arrangements sparked in him an inherent distrust. He could not foresee how such a reunion—be it in Turpan or Urumchi or anywhere else along the line—would ever come to pass. He offered a sober good-bye. Before leaving, he rose and took Alec's hand in his own, shaking it clumsily for the very first time and trying to decide what exactly he meant by the gesture.

His hard-sleeper compartment was occupied by five members of a single family: a pair of fiftyish but still smooth-faced grandparents, a young married couple barely out of their teens, and sleeping in the lowest bunk, a winsome, almost regally composed three-year-old daughter. All four adults doted on the child, leveling and tucking her hand-sewn quilt, whisking away her bangs should the strands shift and sneak into the crevices of her closed eyes. Given the fastidiousness of their concern, Vincent felt bashful about removing his shoes and clambering up over the child to take his place on the third-tier bunk.

Once there, he settled into sleep, the light, easily disseyered sleep allowed by his thin-padded bunk and lurching carriage. The train's PA trumpeted out brassy march anthems, and when at ten P.M. the broadcast subsided, he woke momentarily from the absence of its squawky clatter. There were many more such wakings throughout the night, fleet recognitions of his surroundings, and then a quick dovetailing back into sleep. His dreams were similarly garbled and short-lived. In one, he returned to the Li River bank at Yangshuo and listened to Alec and freckled Paul from New Zealand as they argued perniciously and at great length over some inconsequential topic. In another, he found himself on board a hard-sleeper compartment, sitting upon a foldout stool opposite the bunks. The bay was crowded, though not with the coddled child and her two generations of doting parents. His compartment mates were instead the passengers of his trip to Guiyang three days earlier, the plum-faced cadre and two businessmen in starched white shirts and an ensemble of other men who had been visitors to their bay. While they convened in a loud, smoky huddle, Vincent glanced down the aisleway to a knot of standing-room passengers and saw a young woman, or at least her unsleeved arms and one bare, prying leg, as she tried to sunder apart the crowd and step toward him. He had a premonition then that the young woman would turn out to be Trudy and that, in the sallow and unarousing way of dreams, she would be naked.

His first concern was for her small, unshod feet padding across the grimy carriage floorboards, but when she, Trudy, drew close and took her place on the stool beside him, what pained him most was her cowed body language, the way she sat slumped and rather hollow-chested, the wings of her shoulders arcing forward as if to shield her bare breasts.

"Careful with your money," she said. "Careful what you drink, especially in the desert. Careful crossing the street. Careful what you say to people."

His only response was to reach for his travel bag and lay it across her naked lap. It was odd, though, truly. Neither the throng of passengers she had parted nor the men in his compartment took much notice of her. The shock and embarrassment of her condition was Vincent's alone to bear. Even before waking, while still swimming beneath the purled crest of the dream, he sensed his own conscience at work, burdening every nuance of Trudy's appearance with a bleak and punitive weight. Worse yet, all the while she cautioned him against danger, he was trying to think of an unobtrusive way to guide her past the businessmen and cadre and up into his sleeping berth for whatever secret gratifications they might find there.

He surfaced into the dark, constricted shell of his bunk stabbed by grief. He was bad, all right, unquestionably so, lecherous and two-faced, faulty to the core.

The carriage lights had been turned down to a dull, waxen glow. The aisleway stood open and curiously unpeopled, except for one lone windowside passenger, a woman whom he recognized as the young mother of the little girl sleeping so serenely below him.

He climbed down from his bunk and stepped into his shoes. "Excuse me," he whispered. "Is the train on time? Have we stopped in the city of Baoji yet?"

His request startled her. Perhaps she'd been kept awake wrangling, pointlessly, with her own doubts and self-dissatisfactions. "Baoji, no. Not yet," she said bashfully. "Not yet."

He pressed forward down the aisleway. A dense, soupy blackness had glazed the windows. He raised his wristwatch to an overhead bulb and saw that it was 4:20 A.M. At this hour the sleeping carriages he passed through seemed surreally tidy and subdued.

He crossed into the deserted dining car and then into the first of two hard-seat berths. A wobbling, exhausted sleep had lulled more than a few passengers from their seats onto the floor and aisleway. Their limbs had slackened and drifted during the course of sleep into odd and sometimes embarrassing entanglements. Near the fore of the car, in a gulf between hard-seats, an otherwise primly dressed old woman lay upturned and twisted, her skirt hiked up and wrapped about her legs like a scraggly diaper.

He searched for Alec and found him, not among the sprawl of slumbering bodies, but outside on the railed bridge between cars, where he was smoking and had assumed a seafarer's stance in a squall of rushing air. He nodded at Vincent's approach and stepped inside out of the wind.

"Change your mind about Xian?" he asked. He looked ready for Vincent to say yes, for the train to halt and both of them to disembark on a moment's notice.

"No, no. I'm staying on, all the way to Lanzhou. Just couldn't sleep is all. So I thought I'd get up and come find you. Thought I'd see you off when the train stops at Baoji."

"See me off?" He grinned. "You planning to wave and throw kisses?"

"'Course not, but I did want to catch you before you got off. I wanted to say a few things before we parted ways. Mostly, I guess, it's a matter of apologizing."

"No need for that, really. If it's about you telling folks I'm an Englishman, well, I'm over that. I'm not blind to the fact that I can be a moody prick at times."

"You can be," Vincent said. "You can be at times, but this is something else, and I wanted to say it now even though we'll likely meet up in Turpan in a few days or maybe some other place. Because, you know, we might not."

The carriage groaned mulishly and began banking right along an expansive bend in the track. Up ahead a string of blurry lampposts punctured the darkness. The PA crackled and a brackish voice hailed their close proximity to Baoji. Several other disembarking passengers collected their things and lined up behind Vincent. He felt elbows and parcel boxes prodding his back. "When I came to Toulio," he said. "When I first stayed at the house with you and Shao-fei, I had it in my mind that you were part of the boy's problems. A large part, a bad influence, is how I saw it. I had it in my mind then and for a long time afterward that there was some kind of competition between us. You must have noticed some of that, the righteous attitude, I mean. It must have been annoying."

"It was, but I didn't lose any sleep over it. Look here, there's no need—"

"—I've changed my opinion since, and I can say now that you showed

Shao-fei more real kindness than I ever did. That's one of those things that, well . . . the things we don't know about ourselves, the things we don't recognize. So I apologize, sincerely I do, for behaving that way."

"Understood," Alec said. "Understood. Water under the bridge."

The train slowed and now they were tunneling between columns of lampposts. They could see a rail bed strewn with garbage and hazed in early-morning ground fog, tendrils of which lapped up and crested over the station landing.

"It's a grayer, more complicated world than I ever imagined," Vincent said.

It was a peculiar comment to have voiced aloud, and Alec's cautious and bemused expression mirrored some of its oddness. "Right," he said. "No doubt. Get some sleep, man. I'll see you around, soon enough." He shuffled out onto the landing, perhaps, like Vincent, a bit humbled, a bit abashed by the exchange. The train whined and thudded to a near halt. He leapt before the carriage had entirely stilled, the first rider to debark and gain his footing, the first to cross the platform and disappear.

For Vincent much of the ensuing journey transpired as lag time, long-drawn interims of vapid idleness, spells of mind-numbing indecision. (Should he go to the carriage boiler for a cup of steaming water or stay curled, taciturn, in his bunk?) Whenever his progress north seemed markedly slow or halting, he tried to remember that beneath this heavy blanket of surplus time, beneath the boredom and pining isolation, a line of experience was taking shape. What was happening to him even in his most tedious moments was nothing less than an adventure. In the future, once he'd returned to Red Bud, it might well be the thing that distinguished him from everyone else, the one exceptional undertaking of his life.

All afternoon and evening his train crawled north through a dry and scattered countryside. The grasslands here were patchy. The shrubbery grew in knotty, misshapen clumps. From somewhere high atop the neighboring mesas the wind rolled down and swept against the train in sudden, churning gusts. When Vincent looked up from his book, he noticed that a fine layer of sand had been forced in under the compartment window frame.

He put his eyes back to the pages and did not raise them until much of the arid steppe land was behind him, and the train, having clattered its way through a long tunnel, passed into a district of smoking kilns and ramshackle brickyards. Ahead loomed a city of reedy black smokestacks. Lanzhou. No one in his compartment appeared glad to see it. Even the steward, when he sang out their approach to Lanzhou's rail station, did so in the rueful tenor of someone passing on bad news.

They'd arrived just after nine P.M.; in Lanzhou's skewed time zone this meant a late-evening, russet-colored sun still perched above the horizon. From a drove of departing passengers Vincent set forth down the platform stairs and out along a gated corridor for a close-up look at the city his guidebook deemed the most polluted in China.

It wasn't altogether dismal. Yes, there were drab warehouses and fuming smokestacks, and yes again, there was, from some unlocatable crux point of the city, a perpetual, deep-earth, industrial grind. He walked from the station to the north corner of a large open square. At an unsheltered bus stop he waited among a small troop of Lanzhou citizens, the men a swarthier, more inured variety of Mao-jacketed laborers, and several uniformed and severe-looking office women who held white handkerchiefs over their mouths and noses to filter the smoggy air. At once he became the focal point of the crowd's gaze, their listless regard, which struck him as uncannily deadpan.

A packed city bus shuttled him deeper into Lanzhou, to another cavernous and tepidly lit hotel. The elevator was under repair. He followed a key girl up an endless maze of stairs to an empty dorm on the ninth floor. Once she'd gone, he walked the long corridor listening for the murmur of other voices. No sound. He might have been the floor's only guest.

In the shower room, he opened his travel bag and made an unpleasant discovery: he'd left his laundry soap, his razor and shaving cream, on the nightstand of his Chengdu hotel room. He was momentarily stung by the loss. Yet what else could he do but pledge to guard his possessions more carefully in the future?

He stripped down and, using a plastic basin and a dollop of shampoo, scrubbed the clothes he'd worn for two days. It was all dogged, wet-fisted work. Next he washed himself and donned fresh clothing and afterward pried open the bathroom window. Outside there was cool night air to be breathed deeply and then regretted for its chemical aftertaste. Even at this height, nine stories, Lanzhou's skyline did not allow for much in the way of lucid observation. Beyond a certain smoggy middle distance, everything was clouded and insinuating, a vaporous blur from which emerged the hulking outline of something darkly girdered and murkily lit and large beyond measure—a massive oil refinery, say, or a chemical complex. He could, however, view a surrounding enclave of tenements and see, distinctly, across the alleyway to the nearest one, a huge, bunkerlike structure whose west-facing side was a checkerboard of lighted windows. Figures moved in a few of those windows. A man, for example, limped through a cluttered living room and sat at a desk. Three floors above, a woman put one hand to her hip and with the other motioned dismissively to someone in another room.

He guessed there were two hundred families in this tenement alone, five thousand people, maybe, in the entire enclave.

At this late hour, in this city of heavy industry and blighted air, it did not seem likely that any of them led happy lives. He didn't know this for certain, of course. Who could know? Still, they looked unhappy, and though it was odd and probably cruel, he rather enjoyed standing at this window, turning his gaze in the direction of other people's unrehearsed idleness and worry, their inward-looking sobriety.

Is that what he'd been gazing upon all along? Is that what travel was, when you got right down to it?

Twenty

HE WAS BACK at the Lanzhou train station by seven-thirty the next morning. At this early hour the lines to the ticket counter were but a few bodies deep. When his turn came, he huddled close to the counter bars and wished the clerk a good morning. "I'd like a ticket, please, a hard-sleeper, for the next train to—"

"Not possible."

"Excuse me?"

"Not possible."

"I haven't told you where I want to go."

"Doesn't matter." The clerk yawned. "Go ahead, tell me if you like."

"Turpan. I'd like to go to Turpan."

"Turpan then. Northwest? Into the Xinjiang desert? Are you sure?"

"I am."

"Not possible."

"Why not?" he said to the clerk, who appeared to be a woman, a tall, flat-chested woman or a short woman propped imperiously high on a stool. He could only see her dimpled chin and thin, blanched lips. "When *can* I go to Turpan? When's the next open train?"

"I sell same-day tickets. Go to Miss Lin at counter three for advance tickets. And don't try arguing with her, not with Miss Lin. She'll tell you, though, Turpan's not easy. Five days at least."

"Five days!" Vincent said, incredulous.

"Sooner maybe, it's up to Miss Lin. Try learning some manners before you visit her. Wash yourself, maybe, clean yourself up a little. She's a strict one, Miss Lin. She won't like the look of all that hair growing on the sides of your face, all that monkey hair."

He placed a hand to one thickly stubbled cheek. *Monkey hair.* Her insult struck him as weirdly appropriate, deserved. Abashed, he thought of the soap and razor he'd left behind in his Chengdu hotel room.

"Monkey hair," the clerk said. "Monkey people." She parted her lips and showed him a waxy, yellow-toothed smile. "Miss Lin," she called out. "Are we still allowing monkey people to ride the train to Turpan?"

He did not wait for an answer, just sulked his way over to the third window. When his turn came at the counter, the hilarity of the first clerk's remark had passed down an unseen line of coworkers. He heard a swell of clipped laughter in the background. "Five days," Miss Lin struggled to say between tittering giggles. "A five-day wait for all monkey people."

He strolled red-faced outside the station to walk the long perimeter of the square in search of ticket hawkers. It was still early, the square sparsely peopled, the sky semi-lit and gorged with heavy clouds. None of the shabbily dressed men he passed stepped forward to tender their services. He purchased a breakfast of steamed buns and waited. *Monkey people,* he thought. Now, a half hour after the incident, he burned with indignation.

By seven-thirty the promenades that bordered the square conveyed a great tide of day laborers, factory and refinery workers mostly, but also skirted office women and small cliques of green-suited cadre officers. A line of wildly crammed buses lurched to the curb, threw open their doors, and discharged their tousled riders. From within this harried press of human bodies, a young man sauntered forth and asked if Vincent would like to change money or buy a train ticket.

"Turpan?" the young ticket hawker repeated. "Hard-sleeper?" he said, as if these were portents of an all-too-common crime. He had an odd, laconic manner, a fidgety way of tilting his square head and sizing up the crowd around him. "Yes, then, I'll find you a ticket, all right."

He did not go to the rear of the station, as other ticket hawkers had. Rather he led Vincent onto a jammed city bus for a grinding jaunt along the eastern edge of Lanzhou. They got off and strolled to a nearby tenement. Inside lived a cousin who owed the young man certain favors. Vincent was told to wait on the street corner while the two men met and negotiated a deal. And wait he did, an hour and fifteen minutes, until the young man returned vexed and empty-handed. Another bus ride, another covert meeting, this one with a friend of a friend whose sister answered phones in the train station. The result was the same, and by noon, after several more botched contacts, Vincent dismissed his guide and headed back to the train station alone. No money had changed hands. The excursion had cost only a few yuan in bus fare, but the loss of the morning, the wasted hours and effort, had been a grievous disappointment.

There were by now other ticket hawkers roaming the open square. "Turpan, hard-sleeper," he said, to which they answered, "Yes, all right, I can, I can." He cautioned himself not to put too much faith in their promises. He tried to single out and question only those who looked streetwise and well connected. "No problem," they said. "Lanzhou to Turpan. Hard-sleeper. One ticket. No problem."

Vincent asked, "How long?"

"Lanzhou to Turpan," one of them replied. "About two days, about forty hours on the train."

"No," he said with the lowly, hangdog air of a man delayed, a man suspicious of being swindled. "How long to get the ticket?"

It would take him three days to comprehend, fully, that he was not being purposefully lied to or cheated. Unlike the station clerks, the ticket hawkers—a brusque, persistent eight of them in three days' time—were incapable of denying a request, of acknowledging the improbable or uttering a simple, unsparing "not possible." In the face of adversity, they held to their maxim of "Yes, all right, no problem." He might as well have asked for an express soft-sleeper to Iceland; surely one hawker or another would have led him down some bleached, treeless side lane of Lanzhou seeking to reclaim a favor from just the right kinsman or associate.

In the end he had no real choice but to follow them. Lanzhou was a lean, narrow-margined city, and with each futile quest he strayed farther inside its twenty-kilometer industrial corridor. Depending on the wind flow or time of day, the sooty discharge of chemical plants could either foul the open sky or slow-plunge earthward to blight entire neighborhoods of factories and apartment houses. He took special notice of the residents here. More than a few were afflicted by white, spindly skin discolorations. Even the unmarred ones coughed and held handkerchiefs to their faces. Thus, he imagined deep-festering lung ailments. When they spat onto the sidewalk, he thought of the spittle drying and releasing lethal airborne viruses.

The same open contempt he'd first encountered with the train station window clerks showed itself in all quarters of the city. At the hotel where he stayed he suffered the vagaries of ill-tempered desk attendants and key girls. In an east-end department store, where he had gone in search of laundry soap and possibly a razor, he was met by a great leaden wall of disregard. The store's goods were separated and cordoned behind dozens of individual counters, a system that precluded theft and quadrupled the number of necessary employees. Three young women were stooled behind the soap display, all of them slumped headlong and asleep against the glass countertop. He nudged their folded arms. "Off duty," muttered the first. The second complained of being sick and tired, and the third said that she would not begin her shift for another half hour. None of the three could be goaded into carrying out the lone, essential task of their profession: to reach inside the counter and hand him a box of laundry soap.

Once, on a packed city bus, a band of passengers screwed their faces up so near to his that he closed his eyes and recoiled inward. Moments later the bus jolted to a halt. Outside, two departing riders, swarthy-cheeked teenaged boys, ruffians, were jousting against each other, playing tug-of-war with a pair of socks. The socks were light brown, zigzagged with green diamonds. He gaped at the socks, which were unmistakably his own, and then down to the zipper of his travel bag and saw it splayed apart, an opening big enough to snake a hand inside and snatch the first available object.

Lanzhou, city of blowing dust and fetid air, of negligence and unanticipated hazards, of insolence and petty theft—the city itself was to blame for the loss of his socks. His grandmother had given him those socks, or at least a similar pair, and now he felt Lanzhou's sullen influence stealing shine and sweetness from his former Stateside life. For hours after the incident his indignation simmered, flared, subsided. Back at his hotel, there were other waylaid foreign tourists, each ready to recount a personal slight or peril and help fuel a burgeoning mutual resentment. Only at his calmest and most reasonable could he ponder the whirring whole of Lanzhou and know that its crude manners were not aimed discriminately at himself. If anything, it forced him to see a previously unrecognized principle of geography at work. Just as places, regions, cities differed from one another in elevation and climate and population, so, too, did they vary in terms of a distinct, self-evident, and shared sense of well-being. In this regard Lanzhou may have been the most unhappy place he had ever visited.

By day five he woke ready to strike a more potent bargain. Early that morning he telephoned the China Air office and found that it was possible to buy an air ticket at its downtown bureau, shuttle by minibus out to an airport seventy-five kilometers northwest of the city, and fly to Urumchi that very afternoon. He would be charged double the rate of a Chinese passenger, 1,040 Foreign Exchange Certificates, almost 280 U.S. dollars. In return he would arrive in Urumchi by nightfall.

He gathered his belongings and rushed to check out of his hotel. Near the front desk he was accosted by a giddily anxious young man, a ticket hawker, one of the tenacious eight he'd employed. Somehow this particular hawker had managed the insoluble feat of a hard-sleeper train ticket to Turpan. Elated, he plucked it from his shirt pocket and placed it proudly in Vincent's hands. And there it was, the prize itself, the long-awaited payoff for all his suffering and delay. Of course he considered flying anyway. What stopped him, aside from his planned rendezvous with Alec in Turpan, was a far more basic factor: the flight to Urumchi left at four o'clock; the train would start north and carry him free of Lanzhou three hours earlier.

It was a warm, clear, atypically blue-skied Monday morning, and he strolled from his hotel to the bus stop and boarded the number 10 bus to the train station. Except that it wasn't the number 10. Because he always relied on strangers to interpret signs, these sorts of mistakes happened fairly often. This particular bus shuttled him to the outskirts of the city, to a depot and mechanics' shed and a large gravel lot. No matter. He had set out well ahead of his train's departure time. When he went to the depot window, he was told that the bus he wanted, the true number 10, would begin its route in twenty minutes or less.

He stood out under a shaded eave of the depot, near a cluster of idling taxis. Just above the low rumbling of their engines he could hear a slight commotion—a few raised voices, the pebbly clink of rocks bouncing off a metal fender—and he strolled toward the rear of the gravel lot and peered into a corral of four tightly cornered buses.

A thin, slovenly woman, homely even from a distance, sat huddled against the rear tire of a bus. She held her knees to her chest and dodged a volley of plummeting rocks. The rocks, Vincent saw, had come from several corners of the enclosure at once, tossed high and with a cruel, sliding accuracy by three grim-faced bus drivers.

If he wanted to be dramatic, then what he was witnessing most resembled a public stoning. The woman sobbed in wrenching fits, a woeful outcast's misery. The three men, glumly undeterred, lobbed their stones and cursed. He understood only a few of their curses: *fuck,* used as a gibed preface to other murky words, *fucking this* and *fucking that.* By now he knew and understood the term for "whore," *biaozi,* and hated its ruthlessness, hated the dreary biblical association of whore and stone and Mary

Magdalene. One way or another, every sort of human misfortune could be linked to a Bible story. And yet, for the time being, the woman's plight did not move him toward sympathy. Ridiculous, he thought, let her suffer, the fool, and let an equal suffering befall the drivers, or the whole of Lanzhou, for that matter, each and every ignorant, flinty-eyed son of a bitch.

He did not know where this new brand of cynicism was leading him; if to a remote, closed-hearted place, then fine, he thought, so be it.

He returned to the shade of the depot. His bus, the number 10, had pulled around front and had opened its doors. He went as far as the door-way landing before turning around and plodding back across the lot into the corral of buses. He signaled to the nearest driver. "Excuse me," he said. "But is she all right? Does she need help?"

"She needs to learn a lesson," the driver said. He lobbed another stone.

"What kind of lesson?"

"She needs to learn not to sneak on our buses and sleep at night. We've warned her before. She's fucking dirty. She makes a smell in the back of the bus. A very bad smell. Look at her," he said and pointed across the lot to the woman. The sight of her cowering down, trying to curl herself within the hub of the tire, made him grin. "We're not even throwing hard," he said.

"I'd like to help her, if that's all right."

"It's not all right. We're not finished. She hasn't learned anything yet."

Vincent took a deep breath and set out across the clearing toward the woman. A sharply lobbed rock struck him in the hip and he turned to glare at the drivers. They laughed, though having received his scowl, their aim was now lower, the rocks skittering at his feet and bouncing up against his pants leg.

He knelt beside the woman. From a distance she had appeared to have the frazzled mannerisms of the retarded or mentally ill. Up close, even through a thatch of tangled hair, he could see her somber gaze and know that her faculties were intact. "Time to go," he said. He managed, despite her considerable reek, to take her by the arm and guide her to her feet. Her legs trembled. She appeared feverish, sickly. "You need to see a doctor," he said. But she would not cross the clearing until she reclaimed her belongings from the back of the bus. The climb into the rear hatch of the vehicle was too much for her. Vincent, against her protest, crawled inside and gathered together her bag and rolled blanket. At the center of the blanket lay a knot of cool, damp weight. He put the blanket in her arms and walked her across the clearing. He saw, beneath the hem of her heavy cotton skirt, that her legs and ankles were streaked in dried blood.

He nearly lost his resolve. His bus to the train station had departed. He should not have been present at this depot in the first place. Still, he hired a taxi and sat beside her during their twenty-minute ride to the clinic.

"Where are you from?" he asked her.

"Linxia," she mumbled.

"And is that where you're heading? Is that where you want to go?"

"I don't want to go anywhere," she said languidly. "I want to lie down and die."

Once summoned, the clinic nurses came right to the door of the taxi. They were, if anything, wonderfully efficient. In an instant the woman had been borne away to an examination room. Vincent sat in the waiting area with her bag and rolled blanket.

When he tried to get the nurses' attention, they shushed him and said, "Not now. You can see her in a short while." Later, once he'd explained his circumstance, they ushered him into the examination room to bid the woman farewell. By then, however, she was asleep, her crooked mouth open, her homely face slack against the sheets. Never mind, he said. He offered to pay for her expenses and her return trip to Linxia and whatever else she might require. He handed over to the head nurse the only amount that made sense, the 1,040 Foreign Exchange Certificates that he'd set aside for his air ticket to Urumchi. Given the wealth of funds still lining his money belt, it was neither a grand nor hugely generous sum; but a kind act, he hoped, a simple, decent thing. For a short while, several minutes or less, he was ecstatically happy to have done it.

Afterward he returned to the waiting area and slung his travel bag across his shoulder. Before leaving, he squatted down beside the woman's rolled blanket. He unwound the first layer, then the next.

Inside were two dead, naked infants—girls, twins, each with round bellies and thin, puckered arms. They both appeared undersized, perhaps premature. They had a stiff-limbed hold on each other, a life-seeking embrace. Their eyelids were barely parted. Their stilled gaze was the most horrendous thing he'd ever seen.

A mistake to have looked, to know how pitiless their plight, how indifferent the world's regard for them. He was not ready for such desolate knowledge. Or such burning anguish; his empty stomach clenched and heaved. He felt inwardly scalded by what he'd just learned.

Trembling, he carried the blanket into the examination room. He was late for a train, he told the nurses, but the blanket belonged to the woman, and when they were finished tending to her, they should look inside.

We'll have a look now, the head nurse said.

He placed the blanket on a table.

The nurses, who had no doubt seen their share of dead infants, were staggered by the sight. Twins! they exclaimed. Girls! They could not get over it. Nor could they determine, at first glance, when or how the babies had died. Terrible, the head nurse said. Terrible and unlucky. Twins, because they were so great a bounty, always lured misfortune. And for these two, misfortune had come for them right at the start. She reclosed the blanket. Even had they lived, she said in a sobbing breath, they would most likely not have led happy lives.

His taxi was still waiting for him outside the clinic door. He slipped inside and told the driver to hurry to the train station. But once inside Lanzhou's long industrial corridor, the traffic slowed and slowed again until they coasted at a walking pace down an avenue sided by retching chemical plants. He glanced at his wristwatch and realized that if he made his train on time, it would be by only the thinnest of margins. Outside the air blurred into a corrosive haze. People trod past looking surly and unloved, and he wondered if this was the type of place, the kind of world, that would make him pay dearly for a kind act.

Twenty-one

THE TRAINS, WHICH had often been lagging and disloyal, were now for the first time delayed in his favor. Vincent boarded late, at twenty-five minutes past one, and had no more than located his compartment and stowed his bag in the topmost bunk when the undercarriage hissed and the iron wheels screeched atop the rail.

He hurried to the carriage toilet. As soon as he shut himself inside, other waiting passengers began rattling the latch and tapping the door. The train banked right. The carriage listed to and fro. He held fast to the sink and door latch and soon he was gagging, spitting, sobbing. An implacable bleakness settled over him—he should never have looked inside the blanket. He did not have the stamina for such a sight.

He returned and took a seat by the aisle window. What to do with the wealth of hours, the forest of hours, standing between himself and his arrival in Turpan? Best not to be a strict tallier of time, he reasoned. Best not to divide the trip into careful junctures, each elapsed hour another felled tree. He unclasped his wristwatch and buried it deep in his pants pocket. Then he looked out over dry plains and mesas, mostly pastureland for distant grazing sheep. To the west rose the Qilianshan mountain range, exalted and snow-tipped. His train, however, was taking a more northerly path, and over the long course of the afternoon it roamed past the outpost town of Tianzhu and the green Wuwei Valley. After that the land grew increasingly parched, pocked with moon-crater recesses, until the pastureland turned plush only in water-cradling ravines and low-ridged oases. In between were huge flats strewn with splintered rocks and infrequent outcrops of earthen huts.

High in his bunk, he opened his Russian novel and brought the whole of his attention to bear on each word. Eventually they made sense. In time he was able to push the more desperate thoughts from his mind and fall into slumber only to awake later—much later?—to the dissolution of harsh light outside the compartment window. He wondered how much of the journey he'd escaped. At night a pall of heavy blackness pressed itself against the windows. Without any glimmering landmarks to go by, it seemed as if his carriage were hurtling across a featureless and incalculable ocean. He had not been so still, so latently inside himself, in days. When he concentrated, he could feel a muffled sort of illness ripening from within. He thought it a kind of fever, though not the kind that would bring deep, shivering sweats or delirium, not the kind that would have him blathering secrets to complete strangers. Whatever his ailment, the symptoms were far subtler than that, his temperature rising, maybe, but only by a degree or two, and a lazy inner vertigo that he felt most sharply while climbing in and out of his bunk or shuffling to the carriage boiler for a cup of hot water. He guessed the fever had been brought on by diet, by eating too little rather than eating too adventurously, and by the accruing exhaustion of prolonged travel. How stupid of him not to have taken daily vitamins from the start, or, while in Lanzhou, not to have stocked up on fruit and cool bottled water.

The following afternoon he went to the dining car for a meal and found the carriage patronless, the tables flecked with debris from what looked to have been a lively and several-coursed lunch. Even though he'd arrived late, the waiter and cooks seemed happy to serve him. They had but one remaining dish, green beans smothered in brown gravy. The waiter set it before him and hurried back to the kitchen. Vincent, however, had no real appetite for the beans. He was tired and ill, sick in a gentle, absentminded way. But eating was now a matter of sustenance, not fine flavor, and he parted his chopsticks and began dredging each bean up to his lips one at a time.

He chewed slowly, mechanically, a dozen or more beans, until he noticed that mixed within the gravy were coarse brown specks, like small rice or wheat husks. He raised the plate to his chin and realized, with an almost total lack of alarm, that these specks were actually medium-size brown ants, Chinese ants, desert ants, perhaps, dead or motionless beneath a quagmire of gravy.

From the kitchen came a sudden boom of laughter. Pots collided and rang out. He stopped scrutinizing the ants and tried wrapping his mind around several different notions at once. One: the ants had come aboard clinging to the beans and had been served to him accidentally. Two: the waiter and cooks, bigots or pranksters, had salted his beans with insects and were now huddled in the kitchen rejoicing in their stunt. Three: the ants were part of a peculiar regional recipe. Try as he might, he could not decide which was accurate. To ponder one explanation was to become convinced of its fundamental truth, but the moment he considered another possibility, he was swayed, wholly, toward a different conclusion. It seemed a dilemma he could scrutinize again and again over the course of a lifetime without ever arriving at one, irreducible answer.

Back in his hard-sleeper berth he dozed through long intervals of his journey, only to awake groggy, shaken, drained from the intensity of his sleep. His sickness, his semifever, came and went. One hour he was full of penned-in vigor and the next he was caught off guard by weakness and dull, febrile tremors. At such times he slumped down in his bunk, shunning the view from his window and allowing most of northern Gansu Province to slip by unnoticed. It was along this upland corridor that China's Great Wall came to a dry and fragmented end. Later, his guidebook confirmed that there were collapsed and half-sunken links of it between Wuwei and Zhangye, and just past Jiayuguan, a final gated watchtower. Vincent saw none of it, which, in a curious way, was in keeping with all the other renowned sites he'd failed to lay eyes upon. No Tiananmen Square or Great Hall of the People in Beijing. No Yangtze River boat ride. No amateur's survey of the terra-cotta army in Xian. Somehow he'd managed to cross the entire nation of China without viewing a single famous landmark.

The things he did look upon, usually through one corner of his compartment's dust-blotted window, the things he saw and remembered, were often elliptical still lifes, alien to him and untranslatable to others. He saw, for instance, amid a huge plain of pebbly rocks, a lone Mao-jacketed figure goose-stepping off toward a remote cabin, perhaps a surveyor's shack, which was perched kilometers away on the pale of a far-reaching plateau. It would likely take the man an hour or more to get there, but the odd and memorable thing was the way he held an open newspaper tented up over his face while pressing ahead, fully absorbed in his reading and oblivious to the heat, the graveled plateau on which he tread, the mind-bending dimensions of his own isolation.

Sometimes it seemed as if there were an infinite number of peculiarities in the world. Brown ants in his gravy. The twin babies, their tiny wrinkled expressions and their waxen limbs twined around each other's bodies. The gloomy Chengdu key girl, her listlessness and sour warnings. Not to mention the multitude of other unusual lives he'd intersected, if even briefly, during the term of his journey. His own life too—how odd that it should turn out this way.

The second night his mild fever intensified, fogging his senses and making him forgetful. More than once he woke and out of the old habit caught himself speaking to Christ, not a formal prayer, but an inward voicing of concerns. *Help me keep my strength,* he said. *Help me distinguish between those who would be my friends and those who would do me harm.*

Afterward he felt a shudder of embarrassment. To whom, exactly, or to what had he been speaking?

To nothing, probably. To nothing all along. And what he saw from his compartment window the next morning seemed like irreproachable evidence of this.

A new realm of landscape, a sky of stark and pitiless light, a ten A.M. temperature already in the low one hundreds, mound after mound of drifted sand, a stupendous, windblown emptiness.

At noon he stepped off the train into the railside village of Daheyan, a stroll of approximately one hundred yards along a main street empty and sand-scattered, ideal, he thought, for gunslingers and sombreroed layabouts. He'd been told to wait outside the town's dry-goods market for a bus to Turpan. He knew the heat would be intense. Still, he did not worry; he'd survived more than a few southern Illinois summers, famous for their heat and relentless, all-out humidity. This, at least, would be a dry heat.

Several steps into his journey, he felt the sun kindle his scalp. It came down in fluttering waves, fierce, shrewdly in sync with the plodding pulse of his days-old fever. He covered his eyes and squinted. Daheyan's main street stretched away in either direction, wide and entirely unpeopled. The few townspeople who did move about outdoors did so by skipping along from the shaded rim of one building to the next. Before long, Vincent was capering after them in the same shadows, all to avoid what was clearly an extraordinary heat. Forget shirt-drenching sweats and muggy Midwestern discomfort; this was a heat that in its full-bore intensity could make you forthwith and forever dead, turn your flesh to ash, parch your bones until the length and breadth of you was nothing more than powder-fine chalk.

He took a bus straight into the rippling, gray-floored horizon of the desert. A hundred or so meters from their course, always to the left of the bus, ran a line of cement telephone poles. The driver turned and consulted these poles whenever the tire ruts he followed ended and the path ahead became swamped with sand and gravel. And it was a wilderness of gravel—more so than crested sand dunes—a coal black, cindery variety that masked the earth around them in a carpet of broken rock. As deserts went, this one looked as if it had recently been doused in oil and set ablaze.

From the outset the bus had descended, by the slightest of gradations, into an immense basin, at the center of which lay a distant fleck of brown-green. For an hour the fleck had not grown, and then it did, all at once, opening up into fields of grain and cotton and later mud ramparts and high, trembling poplar trees. In no time at all they were wheeling past mud-brick houses and vegetable gardens. At the center of the oasis, they came to a halt before an elbow-shaped sprawl of old city blocks and mud-walled lanes. Once off the bus, Vincent was pleased to discover that he could navigate the town entirely on foot. What made this possible, aside from Turpan's neighborly size, was a network of grape trellises covering the walkways. Above him, as he walked, hung clusters of button-size early-June grapes as well as a dense mesh of sun-blocking leaves. The shade of these leaves made the tremendous heat bearable.

All around Turpan were painted signs in Arabic. Bearded Uighur men, borne up behind their donkeys on antiquated two-wheel carts, wended about the dirt lanes. In the alleys and lots behind the town's open bazaar ran hordes of half-clothed children rollicking barefoot in the dust or tun-neling like maddened pygmies beneath the legs of heat-stupored live-stock. When Vincent stopped for lunch at a tented food stall, the Uighur women who served him were middle-aged, gray-eyed, and buxom, as olive-skinned and spirited as anyone's Italian aunt. They brought him his simplest and most delicious meal in a week's time: scrambled eggs cooked with ripe tomatoes. He finished one plate and ordered another.

Of course he looked for his friend, Alec McGowan, among the groups of foreign tourists he passed. In the process he took in a number of faces that were casually familiar, men and women he had never spoken to but had seen in train station queues and hotel lobbies. But where had he seen them? Lanzhou? Chengdu? As far back as Guangzhou? Perhaps, yes. At the Turpan Guesthouse, where both his guidebook and Alec insisted he stay, he wandered out to the courtyard and chanced upon a young South African woman whose name he could not recall but who, he was sure, had been present that night at the Li River bank in Yangshuo.

They gave each other the same unsettled nod. She couldn't remember his name either, but she remembered Alec, certainly. "The errant Scotsman," she said both to Vincent and a clique of other young women gathered around the courtyard bar. "He's great fun. Loves to play host. Loves to argue. Great eyebrows," she said, mostly to the other women. "Great mouth and lips," she said. "Adorable."

And had she seen Alec anywhere in Turpan?

She hadn't. But she'd heard a report, gossip, really, that Alec, or someone like him, had been seen drunk on a train.

What train?

An eastbound train, maybe. To Zhengzhou. Or was it Beijing?

Later Vincent went to the clerk at the guesthouse's front desk and received a more definitive answer. She said she'd not seen a Scottish traveler in three weeks. To be certain, she opened her guestbook and flipped back through six pages of names and passport numbers. No one from Scotland, she said. No Alec McGowan.

It was the sort of disappointment that, if not carefully managed, could turn onerous and corrosive. He ought not to take it personally. He'd known all along—hadn't he?—that their proposed rendezvous would not come to pass. Still it made him tired, unaccountably so, weary of travel and botched plans, filled with a mopish longing for the journey to end, not just in Urumchi, but the entire expedition back to Hong Kong, back to Taipei, and then the long transpacific flight back to the United States and his inevitable return to Red Bud, Illinois.

At some point that evening during a late and solitary dinner, he made up his mind to travel by bus to Urumchi the next day. A short trip, comparatively, fewer than two hundred kilometers. An afternoon's bus ride and he'd be there. He might, at this very hour tomorrow evening, be sitting together at a table with Kai-ling and her family. Tired as he was, the thought did not excite him much. For a moment he couldn't even recall any clear attributes, any charms or praise he'd either imagined or heard spoken about Kai-ling.

Twilight in the desert transpired as a radiant and far-reaching spectacle, first the measured descent, then a clear, black-blue sky peppered with bright stars. The air cooled and stirred in gentle gusts. Walking back to the guesthouse, he passed dozens of earthen homes, thick-walled and sweltering, from which families had carried sleeping mats and bedsheets out into their yards. All of Turpan appeared to be sleeping outdoors. The children and elderly among them had already fallen asleep. Yet there were bare-chested Uighur husbands lolling about as well, and nearby, but on separate mattresses, their wives, several of whom were young and auburn-haired and swathed in multilayered white cotton gowns. A small, illicit thrill to see them, or at least the confirmation of their lean bodies turning fitfully from side to side. A bare ankle. The pearl-hued soles of their feet. It was a mistake, he knew, in any culture to ogle another man's sleeping wife. Except for a few covert glances, he kept his eyes properly averted.

Still, though, it had been enough, this small thrill, to set his expectations reeling again, to locate inside himself that instrument of pure feeling that had been lonesome and choked with disappointment and make it sing.

Twenty-two

THEY WERE MIDDLE- to late-aged women, wide in the hips and shoulders, a crowd of fifty or more, their stout bodies shrouded in velvet skirts and winding red scarves. They had broad, pale, Middle Eastern faces, their eyebrows sullied into thick, oily slashes, their ears pierced and dangling jeweled rings. They were bright-hued, vibrant in a way that made the Han Chinese women seem wispy-thin and bland in comparison. Like Vincent, these Uighur women had all purchased tickets to Urumchi and were clustered together under the shaded eaves of the Turpan bus station. They spoke what was most likely Turkish, and during the time he waited with them, they drew close, examined his sagging travel bag, clucked their tongues at his short-sleeved T-shirt, the concern of matronly aunts whose casual brooding implied that he had not prepared for the climate or the coming journey, and it was their business, their nature, to worry for him.

As a whole they were not particularly annoyed with the bus's delay. Instead they opened fat bags of linen and thread and began to sew, shrinking back with the waning shadows whenever strands of bright sunlight blanched their sandled feet. An hour passed and then another. In the interim, he sat humbly in their midst and accepted, more out of graciousness than real hunger, a slice of watermelon and a handful of crumbling rice cake. Then a bell rang out, and all at once they clutched their bags and rushed in the direction of a dust-smeared diesel bus pulling into the farthest bay. Vincent was swept along with them, out into the blistering heat, bullied inside a herd of lumbering women as they scrambled toward the bus's landing and narrow folding doors.

Pressed together as they all were, tangled in a swaying mob, they could not enter the bus. They could only surge against the landing until, one by one, women at the forefront broke free and scaled the metal steps. Yet Vincent remained lodged in the center of the maelstrom, and by the time he lunged forward and cinched a hand to the railing, dozens of feistier women had already clambered aboard. He drew himself up inside the narrow stairwell and pushed his way down the aisle. In the rear of the bus he spotted what appeared to be bundles of linen pouring through open windows. In fact these bundles were women, a bright-swaddled flow of leaner, more dexterous types, who had been vaulted up by accomplices outside the bus and were rolling headlong into the last rows of empty benches.

He would not get a seat. Midway down the aisle, he felt hands unclench his shirt and drop away. The struggling ceased. His ticket to Urumchi did not, as he thought, guarantee a journey, but was, more aptly, an invitation to join in the melee, a circus of inseverable wrangling in which the strong, the wily and dogged, prevailed. Normally he would have sulked away and grown despondent, but at present all he could muster was a mild, pointless resentment. And calm wonderment, too, because once the final seat had been occupied, the women all settled onto their benches, opened their bags of linen, and, while fishing for needle and thread, resumed their amiable chitchat. On his way out, a woman perched aisleside at the front of the bus waved a bag of rice cakes beneath his chin and urged him to take another handful.

The station clerk, grim-browed and squinting through the bars of his dark cubicle, would not refund Vincent's ticket, though he did offer the following counsel. "The women—they're not even riders. They're only holding seats for the Uighur men of Turpan. So come again tomorrow morning, but be ready. Listen for the bell. Run *ahead* of the women. Because if they grab you, if they surround you . . ." His hands fluttered up in violent pantomime. "Like wild dogs," he whispered.

Vincent loitered in the station awhile, mulling over this advice. Minutes later a stubby, skullcapped Uighur gentleman waved to him from across the station. In an instant the man shuffled forth and seized Vincent by the elbow. "To Urumchi," he said. "To Urumchi. To Urumchi you go."

"Yes," Vincent said. "To Urumchi." He nodded at the packed bus. "I wish I were going."

"To Urumchi," the man repeated. He was uncommonly short and even his voice had an odd, dwarfish timbre. "To Urumchi. On another bus."

"A today bus?" Vincent asked.

"A now bus," the man said, and led Vincent outside the station, sprinting ahead, then halting and pointing around the building's corner. "A now bus," he said, gesturing emphatically at something out of sight, something concealed and waiting in a stone-gated alley just beyond the station's east wall. And wouldn't it be absurdly appropriate, Vincent thought, after all the scuffling he'd been through, to discover another bus, clean-washed and idling and free of passengers, parked a mere hundred yards from the site of his defeat? He rounded the corner and sucked in his breath, blinking at the skullcapped little man, who had taken up a rather boastful stance at the bow of what looked to be an oversize tricycle. He raised a hand skyward and pointed vaguely toward some eastern quadrant of the oasis. "Another bus . . . a now bus," he said, and swiveled around to aim his finger at the rear of the tricycle, which had been stretched back, elongated into a steel-railed bed. In the center of the bed, perched sure-footed atop a mound of dingy hay, stood a small white-haired goat.

"To Urumchi," the man shouted. "To Urumchi you go." His enthusiasm had seized him like a fever. He bounced onto the seat and then insisted that Vincent climb up over the railing and take a place behind him on the floor of the bed. They rolled out of the alley, down one paved lane and then another. The man teetered side to side with the thrust of each pedal. Vincent gripped the rail and crouched down low, causing his T-shirt to pull away from his jeans and leave a sliver of exposed skin for the desert sun to kindle. Periodically, he felt a damp, rubbery sensation, a whiskered graze across the naked small of his back, but each time he glanced over his shoulder, he found that the goat had turned its shaggy head demurely away from him.

They did not travel far, through a market of tents and up a sandy-shouldered incline. Parked atop the rise was a long, dusty, camel-backed vehicle, which Vincent recognized as a bus once they'd drawn near. Lashed to the roof were two steep mounds of cargo, mostly wood pallets and stacks of wire caging. He stepped down from the tricycle and paced round from front bumper to end. Along the sides, gashed and dented panels had been patched over with sheets of corrugated tin. The rear hatch, the emergency door, was missing, and the resulting hole, ugly and dust-corroded, drew back inside the aisleway like a giant steel anus.

He boarded and took a seat halfway down the aisle. There were fist-size holes in the floorboard through which he could see the roadbed below.

By two-thirty in the afternoon each empty seat had found its passenger, all of them Uighur men with trickling beards, their heads wrapped in white turbans or crowned in beaded skullcaps. The driver, a chronically alert young Chinese man, throttled the engine and turned the bus north, and soon they had breached Turpan's gated ramparts and were through the nettled mouth of the oasis, where long-stretched groves of silver poplar trees shielded the roadway on both sides. The trees flickered and fell away and bronze foothills arose, steepening over the course of several kilometers into high, sun-crested bluffs.

Passengers on the bus's left side hid from the sunlight by draping their heads with overcoats and unfurled turbans. The shaded right side made the heat tolerable, and Vincent, who had chosen a right-side seat, was struck by his good fortune. He craned his head around to grin at those behind him. They were mostly stony-postured old men, a few of whom had riffled open copies of the Koran and were mouthing the words with cracked lips. A sudden buckle or dip in the roadway below would send a quaking shudder along the spine of the vehicle. The rear benches heaved. Riders were vaulted aloft. Even in midair, launched in unison toward the bus's domed ceiling, they held their bearing of austere, old-world solemnity.

Vincent dozed from time to time, and when he grew thirsty he pulled a small cantaloupe from his bag, punctured its skin, and let the cool juice trickle into his mouth. Afterward he reached for his Walkman and listened to Bach, a perfect accompaniment because this sweet, tuneful elegance, this small astonishment of sound brought deeper nuances to the larger wonders reeling past outside his window. A young Uighur man beside him leaned close, captivated, it seemed, by the tiny sprocketed wheels turning inside the cassette player. Vincent paused the tape, lifted the headphones, and placed them over the young man's bristly ears. A thumb pressed to the play button and the young man broke into a gaptoothed, effusive grin. He cupped both earphones with his sooty hands. "It's good," he declared too loud and with a novice's amazement. "It's very big, very deep. I can hear it all around me."

Vincent felt lightened by his reaction, and when the Walkman was passed across the aisle into other hands, he grinned and nodded permission, happy to share the magic, because, in a mawkish and transient sense, the journey had made them all brothers, all nomads. He turned and gazed outside the bus, where the land had yawned open wide into a vast basin of sand and pale earth. Glinting heat caused his eyes to spasm and ache. When he turned back, the Walkman had disappeared.

He rose to his feet, still unsure as to whether or not he was being teased. "Please give back the machine," he chided. "Please give back the little music machine." He surveyed two long aisles of bowed, penitent heads. "Give back the little music machine," he repeated, more insistently, until the bus lurched and he toppled back into his seat. There he sulked, and for a long time tried unsuccessfully to compose a rebuttal. Something about respect and honor among travelers, something about the hardships of travel, the tediousness, and how music could be a diversion, a salvation. Then, stirred by righteousness, he stood again to leer at his fellow passengers, especially those cradling copies of the Koran, and shouted, "God hates a thief!"

There were no real towns between Turpan and Urumchi, only scattered clusters of tiny clay houses and canvas-topped food stalls. Homely earthen mosques sprang from flinty gardens of desolate scrub weed. The highway turned from asphalt to bleached gravel and they passed through a mining site where the excavation had cast up great dust clouds of gypsum powder. The clouds whirred in lazy arcs and settled without distinction on mounds of hulking machinery and withered underbrush. It fell in thick layers upon the backs of tethered donkeys, the same dust coating the skins of spent miners, the hair and faces of their equally wearied wives and children. Vincent saw them tottering dazed along the rutted gravel fields where they appeared not ghostlike or candescent, but as gaunt, heat-stupored infants blinking out at the world from beneath a veneer of chalk-white dust.

Later, the driver pulled the bus to the roadside and threw open its doors. They all hurried out to stretch their legs along the embankment or to relieve themselves among the knolls of rock and lumpish sand. The call to reboard sparked a shoving match and the men thronged the doorway, wrangling with one another over rows of uncontested seats. Vincent was the last to enter, and when he bounded up the stairs he smacked his forehead against a bulky and low-hanging sheet of tin metal. Both sides of the aisleway erupted in laughter. Bearded men clutched their sides and howled.

"All right," Vincent said. "Enough. Enough." He raised a hand as an appeal for quiet. The raucousness continued. He rubbed his forehead and wondered if he should use their good cheer to his own advantage. "Please," he said. "Give back the little music machine," and they threw back their heads and laughed all the louder.

· · ·

Shortly before sunset there came, from the snub-nosed prow of the bus, a loud pop, queerly wooden in tone, like a pillow-size cork jettisoned from an enormous bottle of champagne. A cloud of steam shot up and fogged the windshield. The bus rolled to a halt. The driver seized up an armful of tools and in an instant swung open the doors and leapt into the desert. They filed out after him and formed an awkward circle around the front bumper. "Not to worry," the driver called out. He had scrambled below and was probing the engine's hot underbelly. "We'll make Urumchi by nightfall."

They huddled together dumbly and watched him work. Now and then he crawled out with a fistful of clamps and bolts, a length of seared tubing, and gazed up into their skeptical faces. "Urumchi by nightfall," he repeated and slipped back beneath the engine. But increasingly, as the evening darkened and the parts he extracted grew bulkier and more intricate, they could hear him reciting "Urumchi" and "nightfall," less like a promise and more like a curse. At last his head emerged beside the balding left tire. "I can hardly see what I'm doing," he shouted. "You can't expect me to wire things together in the dark."

As if on cue, those nearest the door raced inside and claimed sleeping berths by lunging onto empty benches. Others scaled the rear of the bus and, over the driver's objections, began unlashing rolls of canvas and wood pallets. In the process they discovered a dozen or so folding cots, which were freed and dangled over the rooftop ledge. In a stroke of luck, one of these cots was batted about, dropped, and fell neatly into Vincent's outstretched arms. He broke from the mob and trundled his gift a few yards up a sandy incline and planted it on the highway's soft shoulder.

Sometime later an army truck, a long-railed transport bearing rows of anonymous PLA soldiers, raced by in a flurry of road dust. Then two diesel semis running nose to end thundered past and sped into the deepening twilight. And with that, the highway emptied itself of wide, lumbering vehicles. In their place an occasional donkey cart would roll out of the shadows or clusters of strolling bodies, families, sometimes knots of Uighur men, though where in the murky expanse of desert they had come from Vincent could not tell.

Meanwhile, other stranded passengers had placed their cots in a half circle along the bus's starboard side. A roll of canvas was unfurled and draped across the earth. Someone set a wood pallet ablaze, and spurred by the flicker and ribboned curl of flame, the men eased down and removed their boots. They spoke together in a surprisingly gentle mélange of Turkish and Chinese. At times their voices did harshen and escalate, though never, it seemed, into full-blown argument, just mild jeers or teasing mixed with bouts of adolescent jostling, all of which Vincent, ten paces removed from the cusp of their circle, found vaguely distracting.

He lay flat on his back, shuttered between the cot's creaking rods, his travel bag a leaden, sagging pillow. Beneath him the desert floor gave off a dry, muted heat. He was neither hungry nor tired. The day's journey seemed to have stifled the need for food and rest. Overhead, though, the Xinjiang sky was all icy, stellar appetite. He'd never seen the cosmos shine quite so vividly, the stars themselves sharp-edged and winking.

From the bus came a sudden shriek of laughter and then a gravelly swirl of footsteps. A moment later he found his view of the night sky hindered by five broad-shouldered Uighur men. They bent down and studied the length of him, from the crown of matted hair on his forehead to his sneakered feet jutting over the cot's far end. Like the others, they were bearded and skullcapped, though he could not recall seeing any of them on the bus, certainly not the one closest, the one on his right whose thick neck and face were blighted with odd pouches of skin. Or lobes, Vincent noticed, slightly larger and more spherule than earlobes, but hanging nonetheless from the scruff of his neck, from the woolly underside of his chin, and most prominently below the left eye, where a single bulbous teardrop of flesh dangled against the slope of his cheek.

They shifted about, muttering in Turkish, and the one closest—the one he could only think of as Mr. Teardrop—prodded Vincent's chest with a stubby finger and in gruff Mandarin said, "You there, say something to us in the common language."

He gazed up and took in the sight of their parched faces, their threadbare vests and black coats, and, clipped to the rims of their leather belts, the beaded hilts of their sheathed daggers. "I'm very tired," he said. "I'm resting now. I'm waiting for the bus to be fixed."

"That's good," Mr. Teardrop said. "Good and fine. Now get up. You're coming with us. We've got something to show you."

"No, thank you, please. I think I'd like to stay here and rest." Even as he spoke these words, he was being hoisted up onto his feet. The men closed in around him and began slapping dust from his shirt in a way that seemed simultaneously charitable and angry. They marched him away from the bus, away from the circle and fire and up the sandy incline toward a remote horizon ink-black and cavernous. He tried turning, wheeling about and calling out to the other passengers, signaling to the Chinese driver, in whom he still retained a sliver of confidence. At once the men clasped his arms and corralled him onward. Yet even this did not inspire panic, not yet. Instead, what had happened to him—what was happening now—felt weirdly typical, another instance, maybe, of the usual clumsiness and social confusion he'd grown accustomed to during his long journey.

"You think you're very important," Mr. Teardrop said. "You think you're very big."

"I don't," Vincent said. "I don't think that at all."

"Oh, but you do," he said, and the others began nudging him, first playfully with the open palms of their hands, then more ruthlessly with their shoulders and elbows so that he lurched back and forth inside their ring. "You do," Mr. Teardrop repeated. "We can tell by looking at you."

They continued jostling and shoving until Vincent raised an appeasing hand and said, "All right, maybe I do think that way, but only a little," and they stopped. Then he was overcome by a great, shuddering wave of panic. Why such panic should fall upon him now, in the absence of their rough play rather than during it, he couldn't begin to say. Nevertheless, several dark possibilities hovered close enough so that it felt as if a gloved fist had fixed its thick fingers around his heart. How stupid that his knees should buckle. And how terrible to stumble along with this close mindfulness of violence and death—and something more horrible still, the understanding that he might have to endure the suffering and humiliations leading to death without Christ, without even the calming certainty of eternal love.

He stifled a deep, quaking breath and, without any prompting, announced to the group, "I'm going to Urumchi to be married."

They walked a dozen mute paces up toward the crest of the rise. At last, another man, a husky voice to Vincent's left, asked, "Marry who? A white woman in Urumchi? Another foreigner?"

"A Russian?" Mr. Teardrop guessed. "A Chinese? Not a Uighur. Don't tell me she's a Uighur bride."

"No, she's Chinese. Her name is Kai-ling. She's waiting for me in Urumchi."

"That's not good either," Mr. Teardrop said. "It's best to marry your own kind."

"I know," Vincent said. "I know that. But she's very beautiful. I have a picture of her. I'm carrying it with me in my bag." He reached for his absent travel bag, ready to produce the photograph should any of them ask. But they didn't, and before long they had crested the top of the hill and were making a plodding descent down its opposite side. In the distance, he could make out a village of huddled shacks, fifty or more, most of them tin-roofed and occupying an oval cleft of land between hillsides. Wires stretched between the rooftops. Deep within the oval, someone had strung together a garland of orange lightbulbs. The result was a blurry, ill-formed halo of jaundiced light.

The desert floor beneath their feet leveled to the width of a donkey cart. Fifty yards from the village, they saw a frenzy of barking dogs, or rather sleek four-legged silhouettes darting out between houses and racing toward them in a converging pack. The men around him cursed and dropped to their knees. They were not cowering, however; they were gathering stones. Once the dogs had drawn close, the men sprang up and hurled these stones at the cluster of growling snouts. The pack dissolved and the dogs drew close again, this time separately, with their paws splayed out and their bellies pressed to the earth, inching forward to lower their muzzles and cringe before the men, to kiss their gritty boots. The men waited patiently for the ritual to end. Then they goaded Vincent on, while behind them the dogs rose and lapped eagerly at their heels.

Mr. Teardrop led them through a maze of dirt alleyways, the surrounding houses all mud-formed with irregular doors and windows. Voices called to them from earthen doorways. They stomped past tethered donkeys and caged chickens and even a small corral of goats, one of which was crippled and pulled its own deadened hindquarters along in the dirt, kept alive for kindness or cruelty's sake.

On they went, plodding along until the alleyway opened up into a shabby inner borough of sorts, and they halted before a small cubed home, its rust-scarred door a long sheet of dented tin. Mr. Teardrop gave the door several thudding pounds. "Little Lao," he called out. "Come outside, Little Lao. We've got something to show you."

While they waited, other villagers, lured by the commotion, crept from their houses and pressed up behind them. They did not all appear to be Uighur, though Vincent couldn't name their race except to say that a few looked gypsy, others Mongolian, all of them tousled and lean and squeezed by poverty. Several of the women had thick, resinous eyebrows that stretched uninterrupted across the ridge of their foreheads. Amid the shadows and burnished orange light, he couldn't decide if this was cosmetic enhancement or genetic anomaly.

"Little Lao! Little Lao!" other voices in the crowd sang out. Children, clad only in ragged underwear, pushed to the fore of the gathering.

At last the door opened, revealing a trinket-filled yet surprisingly tidy living room within. A slight middle-aged woman in a molted gray housecoat stepped forward. "Little Lao is sleeping," she said. "He's tired." She squeezed her hair, which had been swept up in a spangled net, and said, "He's got a stiff back."

Behind her, beyond the living room and across a bare dirt floor, a burlap partition shook. A groaning voice called out, "What's this about?"

Vincent heard a bed frame creak and spied, beneath the hem of the partition, two oversize loaves of fur, not shoes, exactly, but burly moccasins stitched together from animal hides. The curtains parted and a huge, hunched-over figure strode forward, head first, tunneling through the living room and out the open door. Here he paused beside his wife and stretched to full height, a timid and painful straightening of the back, which, once completed, placed his head a foot higher than the roof of his own home. He stood bare-chested, heavy-muscled, profoundly wide in the shoulders and arms, a stockiness that extended down to his legs, where the sides of his pants had been spliced apart and filled in with extra strips of linen. "It's all been settled," he complained. He had an enormous square jaw and two rather small and deeply set eyes that dwindled and quivered as they focused on the crowd. "There's nothing more to talk about. Comrade Ahmeed knew the donkey was sick when I sold it to him. I showed him the animal's bad teeth. He knew it. He only changed his story afterward!"

"Yes, I've heard," Mr. Teardrop said. "I've heard about that. But this is something else."

"We've been to the council," Little Lao continued. He wagged his head and his sleep-disheveled hair fanned out on both sides. "Comrade Ahmeed was with me. We talked it over before the section chief. It's all been settled, you understand?"

"Of course it's all been settled," Mr. Teardrop said. "Here now, this is something different." He laid a hand on Vincent's shoulder. "It's the foreigner. You see? He thinks he's very important. He thinks he's very big."

Little Lao squinted and for the first time shifted his gaze and regarded

Vincent. "A foreigner?" he said. "A Russian? No?" he said, and his broad face bloomed with comprehension. "This again? All right then, all right. Let's be quick about it." And with that, he turned and presented his naked back.

For a while yet Vincent could make no sense of it. A back?—undeniably broad, hairless, bronze-skinned. It wasn't until he was seized by Mr. Teardrop and spun about that he understood. What they wanted, what they had snatched him from his cot and marched him panic-stricken to their village to do, was to stand back-to-back with Little Lao. He did precisely as they wished, stood tall, put his heels to Little Lao's moccasins. Their backs touched. He felt hands being stacked atop his head.

Mr. Teardrop called out, "Little Lao is seven . . . no, eight hands bigger than the foreigner." Around them the crowd received the news with a rowdy cheer.

"You have brothers this big? Friends this big in your own country?" Mr. Teardrop asked.

"No," Vincent said. True enough: by his estimate Little Lao was somewhere between six feet eleven inches and seven feet one inch tall. He would, in any city of the world, have towered over the heads of ordinary men. "No one as big as Little Lao," he announced. Again the villagers cheered and beamed a desperate sort of joy. Dogs barked and chased their own fluttering tails. Children romped about in their ragged underwear.

Then he was surrounded by Mr. Teardrop and his four companions and marched through the alleyways and outside the village. The dogs followed at their heels until some unseen border had been breached, and they barked and growled and considered the men enemies. Vincent plodded along, giddy and dazed. In time they climbed without speaking to the crest of the slope and down its other side, where gradually they drew close and could see the bus and weakening fire.

Twenty paces before the bus and the circle of men they chanced upon Vincent's travel bag, which had been ransacked and tossed away like so much rubbish. He peered inside and tallied the items stolen: his guidebook and Kai-ling's photograph, which had marked its pages, his camera, his pens, even his tangle of dirty undergarments. Aside from a few scrawled notes and rolls of film, he'd been left with a sock and his Russian novel.

A stranger had crawled onto his cot, and Mr. Teardrop and the men seized him as he slept, by the shoulders and ankles, and after two accelerating swings flung him to the ground. They guided Vincent down in his place. Mr. Teardrop grinned and bent low. "Good and fine," he said. "Go to Urumchi. Tell your Chinese bride, tell her family and friends that you have walked to our village and stood beside the biggest man in China."

He assumed, when prodded awake by the driver at daybreak, that there remained several hundred kilometers of shifting highway, hours of jouncing bench time, separating himself from the city of Urumchi. What had happened to him the night before could only have happened deep within the confines of a remote wilderness, far between townships or cities, far from any settlement of right-minded people.

The bus engine turned, revved into a sputtering half-life. Hustled on board with the other passengers, he sat numbed, peering out to the north at lofty, dawn-lit mountains, a banked chain of them, velvety turquoise in color and mounded ponderously one upon the other. The bus lurched ahead and soon they were wheeling across an expansive reach of level brown plains, some of it dry, unquartered pastureland for sheep and goats, most of it rock-strewn, ungrazeable, endless. Then a few vaporous smokestacks sprang up reedlike in the distance. The highway widened into a gate-lined city boulevard. Forty-five minutes after they'd set out, they had entered the margins of a sprawling industrial precinct and were mired in heavy traffic.

Urumchi looked to have appropriated exactly nothing from the dun-hued plains upon which it was settled. It was instead a city of broad avenues and drab, block-style architecture imported from provinces a thousand miles east. Why it should have existed on this particular stretch of meadowland, or existed at all, seemed to Vincent's travel-weary mind a great mystery.

The bus set him free a block past the Urumchi train station. Before stepping off, he turned and gave his fellow passengers, *his brothers,* a castigating glance. Was it his imagination or did they flinch a little? At the very least they seemed to slink back in their seats and urge the bus onward, bashfully, as if taking leave of a witless comrade who they'd swindled in a game of cards.

On foot he found himself in a larger and more crowded metropolis than he'd first imagined. He'd read that a million people had chosen or been forced to settle here, a fair portion of them Uighurs, though the majority of the faces he encountered while walking about downtown were dour, resolute, bitterly Chinese.

What marked his arrival, what linked itself permanently in his mind whenever he thought of Urumchi thereafter, was a street act he came upon on an open promenade near the hotel where he would stay. The act consisted of a gaunt, nappy-haired trainer and five monkeys. The monkeys were of a white-and-brown-haired variety, leaner and shorter-armed than chimps, which made them appear more humanlike when standing upright on their legs. They were staging a sidewalk comedy of sorts. Two of the monkeys had been dressed in red robes as emperor and empress. The others crawled forward on their stomachs to kowtow at the emperor's feet. Each act of prostration elicited a howl of laughter from the crowd. Yet to make the monkeys lie prostrate, the trainer first had to prod them with a long wire charged by a cluster of nine-volt batteries.

They were already jittery animals, high-strung, birdlike in their movements. They had each torn patches of fur from their own hides. Two of them bled from what was either the anus or vagina. Touching the wire to their skin only magnified their frenzy, made them, for a second or two, rabidly hysterical. They bared their long incisors, shrieked, and in the worst instances, lunged forward and sank their teeth into one another's limbs.

Vincent found it a gruesome event to have witnessed. The children in the crowd seemed to share this opinion; more than a few hid their faces against their parents' thighs. The adult audience, however, roared out their gruff laughter, as striking and raw in its way as the collared monkeys themselves. Hearing it, he could not entirely trust the strangers around him. If they could ignore this small but obvious bit of ruthlessness, what other cruelties might they be willing to overlook?

He checked into the Hong Shan Guesthouse and set to work making himself presentable. To that end he took a long lukewarm shower, scrubbing every inch of his skin and hair. He did the same to his clothes and then had to stand about much of the afternoon in a guesthouse towel while his dress shirt and trousers—his only outfit now—dried from the windowsill of his room.

There were other chores, certainly—the shopping he meant to do, for clothes, for the hard-to-find razor and shaving cream and deodorant. A few minutes out in Urumchi's formidable late-afternoon heat and he was persuaded to return to his room and wait for the cool drafts and slackening warmth of evening.

He slept deeply and well and woke with a clear mind. It was eight P.M. The other two beds in his room were not yet occupied, so he could sit without feeling foolish and practice the things he might say to Kai-ling and her parents, Mr. and Mrs. Song. *How happy I am to finally meet you,* he said. *It was a long journey, yes, thank you. Very long and very . . . Many things happened. I saw many things.*

In the windows of the guesthouse lobby he caught a reflection of himself looking thin and travel-worn yet also, perhaps, a shade adventurous with his tan and wispy half beard. He regretted his wrinkled dress shirt, but at least he was clean. At least he was no longer burdened with swollen lips and plum-colored rings around his eyes.

He ate lamb kebobs for dinner, and though the meat was tender and spicy, he lost his appetite for it halfway through. His body, alive with an unusual vitality, seemed not to require any nourishment. When he rose to leave, several ragged men, who'd been crouched against the restaurant wall, hurried over to his plate and finished what he could not.

A bright, dusky sky was beginning to fold itself over the city's tallest buildings. He hailed a motorized pedicab and handed the driver a creased card upon which, three and a half weeks earlier, Gwa had written Kai-ling's address. Sitting behind the driver, on a cushioned seat, in a carriage of sorts with decorated side and rear windows, made this last and shortest leg of his trip feel unnaturally processionlike. At the end he expected to be dropped off before a multifloored tenement. But the driver sped past the blocks of high apartment buildings and motored on to an outlying district, drearier than any tenement quarter, and parceled into tracts of identical brick-and-earth homes.

The streets here were unusually narrow, the bungalow-size houses built flush one against the next, their roofs a shared tangle of sheet metal and twisted vent pipes. Split-trousered toddlers stumbled between doorways. Each lane seemed to have its own scrappy mongrel dog ready to howl and spin frantically as the pedicab neared. They stopped at the foot of one such lane. "Fifth house on the right," the driver said, taking his fare and tip and refusing to either wait or return in an hour's time. Yet he refused with such glaring cheerfulness that when he turned his pedicab and sped away, Vincent nearly hoisted an arm to wave good-bye.

From there it was a short stroll along a lane fouled with the excrement of children and dogs. Five doors down was a house like any other, only this one matched the address Gwa had written out and belonged to Kai-ling's family, the Songs, and therefore to Kai-ling as well. Kai-ling's house. Kai-ling's muddied thongs beside the front step. Kai-ling's dusty and crumbling door stoop. Kai-ling's wind chime gone dented and gray from the heat and measureless desert wind. Kai-ling, whom he would marry, but not truly, not legitimately. Standing there at the end of his journey, it all seemed so sudden and absurd that he chortled out a weird, honking laugh, one that would have embarrassed him had anyone been close enough to hear. He glanced both ways up and down the empty lane.

Then he raised his hand and knocked upon her door.

PART FOUR

The Goat Herder

Twenty-three

HE WAS CURIOUS-LOOKING, this gentleman who, having taken his time to unlock and draw back the front door, shuffled out and stood befuddled on the crumbling stoop of the house. His tufted eyebrows tilted up. He had a high-cheeked face set atop a long and jutting neck, the face eccentrically composed and vulnerable to any number of droll comparisons. A bird? A shorthaired cat? Or better yet, a turtle—a tortoise, the pensive sort whose gaze was heavy-lidded and noticeably myopic? The man's expressions were so distinct and slow to evolve that Vincent had time to observe each one catch hold and break across his face: the surprise, the confusion, the recognition, in that order. "Oh heavens," the man who could only be Mr. Song said quietly. "You're here. You've come to Urumchi."

"I'm Vincent, yes. I'm happy to finally meet you."

"And Mr. Gwa has sent you here, hasn't he?"

"Yes. I'm here because of Mr. Gwa."

"Heavens, yes. Of course you are. We got letters from Mr. Gwa telling us you were on the way. We knew. We told ourselves it was only a matter of days, didn't we?" There were several huddled figures standing behind him inside the doorway. "He's arrived!" Mr. Song called out to them. He pried back the door further and ushered his guest into a pitchy, windowless living room.

It was a low-ceilinged room as well, which meant Vincent had to slouch down and fumble a bit toward the living room table. Once there and settled, his vision cleared and he took in the bare brick interior, two conjoined rooms several paces wide and meagerly furnished. In lieu of bedrooms were four thin, plastic-covered sleeping mats, stacked in a corner. Atop the mats stood a pyramid of bags and paper boxes. For all Vincent knew they held the entirety of the family's clothing and bedsheets. Nails had been driven into the clay mortar between bricks. From every inch of the bare walls hung dozens of homey essentials: a pencil sharpener, a pair of scissors, a ball of coarse twine, a cluster of hair curlers. Each object had been used and then put back in its original box or cellophane wrapping and hung from the wall, a painstaking thriftiness that struck him as overly prudent and a trifle sad.

In addition to Mr. Song he glimpsed two women who'd retreated to the next room and were pretending to rinse dinner dishes while peering in at their visitor. Mr. Song introduced the older of the two as his wife, and the younger, a wary and somewhat disheveled woman, as his second daughter. Next he introduced his older daughter, Kai-ling. Vincent had not noticed her upon entering, but there she was, stationed on the opposite side of the table, seated sideways in a pose queerly, even uncannily similar to Gwa's photograph, now lost, which Vincent had carried across six provinces and at times held just inches before his eyes and studied with a jeweler's finicky interest. A jeweler's skepticism as well.

He turned, glimpsed the actual Kai-ling once, quickly, and nodded hello. He turned back to Mr. Song. "I'm very glad . . ." he said and could neither remember or invent whatever followed.

"Glad of what?" Mr. Song asked.

"Glad of . . ." He touched the corner of his forehead and concentrated.

"Glad to finally arrive?" Mr. Song offered.

"Yes, I'm glad for that, and . . . glad to finally meet everyone." He nodded to the women in the kitchen.

"It's a long trip," Mr. Song said. "You came by train, yes? How many days?"

"I don't know how many days. I haven't stopped to count them yet."

"You've just arrived then? Oh! My manners. Have you eaten? You look tired."

"I've eaten. I'm full," he said.

But this answer didn't discourage Mrs. Song from venturing forth from the kitchen to ask again, once, twice, three times, "Have you eaten?"

He was full, thank you, he said, as many times as she asked.

Unconvinced, she returned to the scuffed pantry in her kitchen, promising fruit snacks, promising hot green tea.

"Which green tea?" Mr. Song inquired. "Wait, wait now," he said. "Let me help sort it out." Even his deep-lunged sighs took forever to accomplish. He rose slowly and ambled into the next room, where there were more wrapped utensils hanging from the walls. A mostly amicable debate began over what variety of green tea to use and which kettle and teacups to drink from.

Vincent felt the desertion keenly. Was there a way to call his host back to the table? He was aware of a tingling heat rising in his cheeks. There was a particular kind of remark that could be made in this situation; he tried in vain to intuit what it might be. At last he did the one sensible thing he could think of, swiveled around and faced his only companion at the table, looked upon her wholly and without pause.

She was, by any standard, a lovely woman. And not a general or exemplary loveliness either. Whatever it was that had made her father eccentric, tortoiselike, had been tempered in his older daughter, made female and softened into an expression of beauty that was tender and generous and still somehow hugely potent—the welling up of a vibrant inner life. That inner life had not found its way into Gwa's photograph. Nor had the silky sheen of her complexion. Nor the long neck with its tapered throat to consider—who would have thought the delicate inflection at the base of the neck, that smooth hollow could inspire in him such nervous timidity?—and the eyes, not heavy-lidded like her father's, but equally large and discriminating and capable, it seemed, of a great depth and intricacy of emotion. Just holding her gaze this way, steadfast and deliberate, felt like a conspicuous act of daring. Were it not for the hundred cheap trinkets hanging from the bare walls of her home or the piles of excrement outside her doorstep, he might not have been able to do it.

"When I came in on the bus this morning," he said, "we passed the train station. That's where I thought you might be, working inside the station." He waited for her response and wilted a little when none came. He'd intended the remark as a question, as a conversation starter.

"The train station," he began again. "What kind of work do you do there?"

Another formidable silence, though in the midst of this one she seemed to peer back at him from across the divide and decide in favor of a reply.

"Office work," she said at last. "Paperwork."

"Paperwork. Yes, I see," he said, mulling it over as if she'd described the most complex and extraordinary of professions.

"I keep track of the luggage and parcels," she said, more generously. "I check and double-check receipts each morning and afternoon. I work with two other girls. We take turns listening to people complain. The job would be awful if it weren't for them. The two girls, I mean. Not the people . . ." She shook her head. She'd gotten ahead of herself, and it was a surprise to see her coloring deepen into something almost like a blush. "But I know the train routes," she continued. "I know ahead of time what trains are likely to get delayed. What train did you take into Xinjiang?"

"I'm not sure. It left Lanzhou about noontime. Three, maybe four days ago."

"One car of soft-sleepers or more?"

"Just one, I think."

"That's at least a number one hundred or higher. It might have been the 301. It starts in Xian. I know a few lady stewards who work that route. Now then, if you'd been in their car and told them you knew me, they would have looked after you. Maybe they would have brought some fresh fruit to your compartment."

"Yes," he said. "Maybe." He was grinning without quite meaning to, cheered by the directness of her attention.

"And where else? What other trains? What other cities?"

"Lanzhou. Chengdu for a day. And before that Chongqing. Guilin. Yangshuo. Two weeks in Yangshuo."

She had not heard of it and said so. "Why not east?" she asked. "Beijing? Why not Shanghai?"

"It wasn't on the way. And the crowds."

"Crowds? Why should that matter? Shanghai's the center."

"The center of what?"

"Of *everything*," she said. "All the best things come from Shanghai. The clothes. The magazines."

"You've been there?"

"I haven't yet. But I will." It was a pledge that caused them both to exchange a brief, comprehending glance, a recognition that he had come to take her back to Taiwan, and she would not, or not likely, be able to visit Shanghai. "About the trains," she said. "Did you travel in the soft-sleeper carriages?"

"No. I rode in hard-sleepers mostly. Hard seats once. But it was difficult getting tickets."

"It always is. The clerks are terrible. I know. You have to learn to be pushy."

Just then her mother shouted instructions from the kitchen. In response Kai-ling rose and retrieved a box from atop the sleeping mats. Inside were six henna-colored teacups. She began wiping them down with a cloth and arranging the cups on a tray. To watch her do this was to marvel all over again. Her lean, articulate hands. Her pale face. The contrasting eyes, full and dark.

A few blustery kettle whistles and Mrs. Song entered the room carrying the hot kettle, her back and shoulders slumped, a fiftyish woman, her face stark and slightly dwindled, pared down in the way of the elderly. Beside her was Mr. Song, engrossed in his canisters of tea, and beside him his younger daughter, dressed badly in a peach-colored pantsuit, and—the comparison had to be made—discernibly less attractive, less vibrant, more plain-featured than her sister, Kai-ling.

It appeared the Songs had done their best to make an occasion of his arrival. The green tea Mr. Song had chosen, and which had to brew a quarter hour before serving, was earthy and potent but still smooth. Mrs. Song put forth small saucers of dried plums and candied peas, a smattering of pistachio nuts, several stringy and salt-laden rice snacks. The feast of conversation was somewhat harder to muster, partly because any question posed to Mr. Song—about his duties at the train station, or the number of years he'd spent in Urumchi—he turned aside with a laconic reply and a taut expression that was either a sign of great bashfulness or reticence. "Tiresome," he said of his work. "A very long time," he said of his years in Urumchi.

All the same they showed an appreciable interest in Vincent, or at least in the route he had taken to Urumchi across the nation of China. He listed once more the cities he'd passed through, starting with Guangzhou, taking his time to recall the pertinent details of each place. He talked at length about Yangshuo. He tried to describe the legion of towering pinnacles. He tried to speak vividly of the landscapes he'd seen from the compartment windows of trains. As he spoke, he was aware of other voices coming from just beyond the shared outer wall of the Songs' living room. Another family, a few unseen yards away, was also engaged in conversation, possibly over dinner or tea. A woman's voice said, quite clearly, "It's their own fault, isn't it, for not taking the boy to a better doctor." A short while later came an improbably loud and sustained belch, which neither the unseen family nor the Songs chose to acknowledge.

"But it's a good way to sightsee," Vincent said. "In a train you can sit by the window and look everything over." Should he continue? It felt as if he'd been talking all evening. Mr. Song, who had made a few terse but interested comments, now had his thick eyebrows raised in anticipation of what might come next. His daughters, though, had not spoken at all, perhaps out of deference to their father. And yet there was an essential difference in the quality of their attention: Kai-ling's had been constant, almost studious; her sister's thinly polite. As for Mrs. Song, she'd been occupied with the demands of tea service, forever heating and adding water to the kettle and dipping its snubby spout to the rim of a teacup whenever anyone drained away more than a mouthful of tea.

"An enormous country. A beautiful country," Vincent said, truthfully, and then observed the family's satisfaction, which was humble and righteous and hardly at all different from the blushing pride of the citizens of Red Bud, who expected similar praise from their foreign visitors. "And Turpan, too," he said. "I mean the trees. The grapevines. I didn't know the desert could be so beautiful."

Mr. Song pursed his lips thoughtfully. "I've heard they grow very sweet watermelons in Turpan."

"Delicious watermelons," Vincent said, as if he'd actually eaten one.

And there were grander compliments he might have invented, vaulting comparisons that favored China over America. If only the hardships and indignities he'd suffered during his journey hadn't kept surfacing in his mind. There had, he admitted, been a few delays in Lanzhou. And his bus from Turpan had broken down and he'd had to spend a night in the desert. When? they asked. Just the night before, just twenty-four hours earlier. Nothing serious, he said. Why then the unbecoming urge to confess to them, to confess to Kai-ling, that he'd been snatched from his cot and marched away to a village where the atmosphere was sinister and the practices absurd, where he'd been frightened to death, more so even, frightened beyond death? Of course it had all ended foolishly. Though at the very worst of it, at his most desperate, he'd thought of her, hadn't he?

"And then you arrived in Urumchi?" Mrs. Song said, less a question and more a signpost guiding him to the conclusion of his story.

Yes, he had, he said. He'd arrived safely that morning. He'd rested. He had found his way to their home. Now it was late, eleven-thirty P.M. Was that too late by Urumchi standards? He saw a flicker of gratitude in Mrs. Song's eyes when he began making the amenities leading to his farewell, and realizing then, too late, that if their tea conversation had seemed lopsided and incomplete, perhaps it was because he'd not mentioned his benefactor, Mr. Gwa, once.

"Please, you shouldn't leave now," Mr. Song insisted. "It's not too late."

But Vincent expected just this sort of gracious protest, and he rose to thank them for their kindness and wish them good night. They rose too, and followed him outside to see him off; he'd anticipated this as well. What he hadn't expected was that Kai-ling would accompany him farther, would walk with him unchaperoned half the length of their meager lane, while her parents and sister watched from the stoop of her house. There was something striking in the moment. Kai-ling, of course, was striking, a head taller than most Mainland women and lean and official in the rail clerk's uniform she still wore. Walking beside her felt like a rare privilege of courtship he hadn't quite earned.

"A right and a left and two rights," she said, crooking her arms to indicate the series of lanes he must follow to reach the main road. "You're staying at the Hong Shan, yes? Four kilometers from the roundabout, a two-yuan fare. Excuse me, but there's a question I have to ask," she said in the same spry breath. An air of frankness had come over her, an openness of expression that he hoped was the start of a free-speaking affinity between them. "Did you bring something with you this evening?"

For an instant his mind went blank. Then he remembered the money belt tied around his waist. Reaching down, feeling the thick lump of it beneath his shirt, brought a sweet, reviving jolt of relief. "I have, yes. I have the money Mr. Gwa gave me," he whispered back. "I'll speak to your father—"

"No, no. When you come to visit a home, a Chinese home, it's best to bring something with you. A gift."

"A gift?" he said. "Yes, of course."

"You could bring a canister of tea for my father. Fruit. Apples. You could buy a box of fruit and bring it when you come here again tomorrow evening."

"Of course," he said once more, though it pained him enormously, much more than he let on, to be reminded of what he'd forgotten, to understand that he had slighted Mr. and Mrs. Song, both of whom had shown him such courtesy and trust. And the confounding thing was he'd *known* about this sort of gift giving. Ten months now he'd lived on the cusp of Chinese society. He'd *known*. It had only slipped his mind because he'd been so absorbed in his own arrival, so indulgent in the difficulties he'd endured, as if he'd been set loose without water in the desert and had crawled into Urumchi on his hands and knees.

"There are stores near your hotel," she continued. "Bakeries and fruit stands. There are department stores not far from the Hong Shan, if you needed to buy clothes for yourself. Or barbershops if you thought you needed your hair cut. It's all right that you didn't bring anything tonight. You didn't know."

"I should have. I'm sorry."

"It doesn't matter," she said, and while he could tell, from her forth-right expression, that it did matter, that an essential rule of etiquette had been overlooked, it seemed just as likely that she'd only mentioned it for her parents' sake and not her own, and with the blunder behind them now, he'd been forgiven, unconditionally pardoned. "It's settled then," she said. "Let's not talk about it again."

Twenty-four

Early the next morning he made his way across town to the city's main telegraph office. With an attendant's help he managed to telex Donny Wu in Hong Kong, a simple dispatch saying he'd arrived in Urumchi and met with Kai-ling and her family. Then he waited for a reply. When it came, some twenty minutes later, it was typed in English and bore Gwa's name.

HAPPY TO KNOW YOU'VE ARRIVED. MY WARMEST REGARDS TO MR. AND MRS. SONG. HAS IT BEEN DECIDED YET ON WHICH DAY THE WEDDING WILL BE HELD?

A worthy question, one he hadn't been bold enough to ask the previous night. And for the time being other matters claimed his attention. There was shopping to do, of course. Certainly, he had the money. Yet none of Urumchi's downtown department stores stocked razors or shaving cream. He went to the Uighur bazaar and found a young, clean-shaven clerk who sold, among other items, hairbrushes and lathering soaps and old-fashioned wood-handled straight razors. As it happened, it was the bazaar's larger-size Uighur clothing—the sturdy brown field trousers and stiff white-cotton dress shirts—that fit him best. He capped off the day's shopping with a trip to the barbershop, where a brawny assistant slap-massaged Vincent's neck and shoulders. His scalp was kneaded and pinched like so much untanned animal hide. "Short on the sides, long on the top and back," he said to the barber. To no avail. The end result was the same bristly, bowl-shaped crop he saw on countless Urumchi factory workers.

It all had a pronounced effect upon his appearance: the new clothing and haircut and, later, the shaving away of his patchy beard. A small part of him mourned the change. In the course of several hours he'd gone from looking scruffy and intrepid to something else altogether—a field hand, guileless and Amishlike in his white and black Uighur clothing. Or, more aptly given his smoothly shorn boy-face, a field hand's apprentice.

He gaped at himself and nearly laughed. Was this the same boy-face he'd brought with him to Toulio all those months ago? To think of it now, to think of the Bible study classes he had stood before, how ready he'd been to disseminate advice to the needy and forlorn.

What could he possibly have thought to accomplish with a face like that?

He began making regular visits to the Song household, arriving just after they'd finished their dinner at nine o'clock and staying no longer than an hour. This, too, he understood, was part of the charade: that the neighbors should see him calling upon the Songs each evening. A month from now, when the family's older daughter was gone from the neighborhood, his open courting of her would be proof that she'd left under mostly honorable circumstances. All the better that he came bearing gifts: a cordoned box of apples in the beginning, and later, in no particular order, strings of hot chilies and dried mushroom caps, knobs of ginger root, a pair of ten-pound Hami watermelons, scented soaps for the ladies and Indian tea for Mr. Song, never the same favor twice so that once his first few days in Urumchi had passed, he began purchasing gifts that were probably too everyday or trite—canned pineapple or rice—or, in the case of a sketchbook and accompanying ink brushes, too specialized for a family he knew little about.

Always the entire family came to the door, welcomed him inside, thanked him profusely for the gifts. He was too kind, too generous, they said, and while the words they used to thank him were often the same each evening, he had to look closely to notice that the spirit behind their gratitude could differ slightly, more earnest and lively when he brought mushroom caps or watermelons or scented soaps, and less so when he arrived with a burlap sack of uncooked rice. They seemed very much in favor of his haircut and cleanly shaved cheeks. Mr. and Mrs. Song could not stop nodding in approval. With Kai-ling he had to make do with a brief, appreciative glance until tea was served and she, setting out teacups before each drinker, leaned close and whispered, "So much better."

Initially they liked hearing about whatever it was he had done with his day. The dullness of his routine was part of the fun, and they teased him gently about the narrow range of the meals he ate in the Uighur bazaar: eggs and tomatoes for breakfast; lamb kabobs for lunch; at dinner a pile of spicy, finger-thick Uighur noodles. His Uighur clothing was another source of amusement. Had he not been to the department stores and seen the recent fashions from Shanghai? He had, he said. But he preferred clothing that was sturdy and fit well. They smiled indulgently at this, an oddly privileged smile, he thought, for a family who owned little clothing and whose taste in fashion so exceeded their means to afford it.

And after that what was there to talk about? What could he, who would never truly become their son by marriage, share with the Songs, who would never be his in-laws? At times the lulls in their tea conversation could be vacuous. He found he could sit and simply grin at Mr. and Mrs. Song or Kai-ling through the longer interludes. The younger daughter was another matter. Over the course of several visits, she'd mostly edged away from their tea circle and now passed her time in a corner of the living room squinting at a newspaper through a pair of thick, folksy reading glasses. Perhaps there was some sourness or trouble with her. Perhaps it was a case of thinly veiled jealousy. Whenever he glanced her way, he had a hunch—so potent it had to be accurate—that she was exasperated with her older sister's fine looks and good fortune.

His third evening in the Song house he took a calming sip of tea and broached the topic of a wedding. "All the things we have to do," he began. "The details. The expense," he said, and almost at once Mrs. Song and Kai-ling rose up with their teacups and moved to the kitchen so that there was the illusion, albeit clumsily arranged, that he and Mr. Song had found themselves in a moment of relative privacy.

"So much to plan," Mr. Song said. "So much to pay in advance."

"I know. But Mr. Gwa has given me money, dowry money."

"He's too kind."

"Yes, he is. He gave me three thousand United States dollars. I have the money with me in traveler's checks."

Mr. Song's heavy eyelids squeezed nearly shut. He stared down at his own knobby hands, reached for a pencil and scrap of paper. "United States dollars?" he mumbled. "Traveler's checks?"

"That's right. Three thousand dollars. That's a little more than eleven thousand Foreign Exchange Certificates."

"It can't be!" he whispered.

"We're ten-thousanders!" one of the women in the kitchen, Mrs. Song or Kai-ling, whispered back. "Ten-thousanders! Can you believe it?"

"Hold on," Mr. Song said. He was looking at a figure he'd scrawled on the piece of paper. "What's this last zero here? It can't be right, can it?"

"It's correct," Vincent said. "It's eleven thousand." He knew it to be an extraordinary sum by Mr. Song's standards, many times more, perhaps ten times more, than he earned each year unloading bags at the Urumchi train station. Should he tell Mr. Song to think of it as a timely lesson in relative economics? Such lessons were often ridiculous or cruel.

The very next evening he arrived with an unwieldy bundle of Foreign Exchange Certificates packed into his money belt. He had converted them from traveler's checks earlier that day. The total came to 11,130 yuan in certificates. When the Songs converted them to renminbi, the amount would rise considerably.

The sheer size and weight of the bundle appeared to stagger Mr. Song. A wary look came over him, as if this impossibly large dowry would now have to be safeguarded from his eavesdropping neighbors. *Eleven thousand one hundred and thirty certificates.* He mouthed the amount rather than speak it aloud. "It's very generous," he whispered. "You can tell Mr. Gwa I said so."

The other arrangements were easier to talk about after that. Mrs. Song and Kai-ling had already decided to hold the celebration in the lane outside their house. Most of the guests would be their neighbors, of course; the most loyal among them would help sweep the lane and set out the banquet tables. And where would the ceremony itself take place? Why, here in the living room, Mrs. Song said, and directed Vincent's gaze to the family shrine, a dusty and undersize three-tiered stand containing photographs and engraved placards. Over the next several evenings she and Kai-ling compiled a guest list and argued the faults and merits of what seemed a hundred menu items. Vincent was happy to let them do it. He declared all of their choices excellent. He promised to wear whatever color and type of suit they thought best. His most pressing concerns, however, lay with the various legal documents necessary for their marriage certificate application, and on that score Kai-ling's efforts thus far appeared to have been scattered and halfhearted. She said her work unit superiors were happy to provide her with a written release for the application. And did she have this release? No, not yet, she said. But she'd gathered together her birth certificate and residence permit and had helped her parents compose a letter of consent. She had learned the names of several top-quarter civil affairs officers who might help expedite their paperwork. And yet she hadn't bothered filing or even securing the paperwork in advance. When pressed, she admitted she hadn't even applied for a passport.

Her laxness in the matter came as a rankling disappointment. At the very least it would add several weeks to Vincent's stay, at worst a month or more. Just thinking about it made him wince and sigh. They would have to file the paperwork right away, he chided her. The very next day.

"Yes, yes," she agreed. "Tomorrow morning. First thing."

When he asked her why she hadn't done it, she, who normally wore such a savvy, composed countenance, gave him what was either the most bashful or equivocal look he'd seen from her yet. "Until you arrived," she said by way of explanation, "nothing was certain. I wasn't completely sure I'd be leaving Urumchi."

"And you're sure now?" he asked.

She gave him an elegant and unfaltering nod of commitment.

He talked of other arrangements with Mr. and Mrs. Song and drank more tea. Yet for the remainder of the evening, whenever she looked his way, there was a glimmer of imploring apology in her dark eyes. He chose not to acknowledge it. Several times she glared at him from across the table. A persistent glare, a pouting curl to her lip. It wasn't fair, she seemed to be saying. He'd been forgiven for his faulty etiquette. Shouldn't she be granted a prompt and equal pardon?

She came to the Hong Shan early the next morning still seeking that pardon. "You'll be nicer to me today, won't you?" she asked right away, and when he relented and said he would, she seemed almost to blush with relief. She had not worn her rail clerk's uniform but instead came dressed in a white blouse and white stockings and a knee-length navy blue skirt. Her face was lightly powdered, her hair held back in a shiny ivory-colored clip. It pained him to see her this way, because she looked so lovely, because her white blouse had sailor's pleats and puffed sleeves, and he had grown up in a small town pining for the nice girls in his Sunday school and 4H club meetings, and here, a decade and thousands of miles away from that life, here amid the rush of Urumchi's dissolute and unlovely workaday commuters, here was Kai-ling, pressing a cloth binder to one skirted thigh and radiating wholesomeness.

It changed everything somehow to see this new facet of her and to know how eagerly she'd sought his pardon. It made treading after her through rush-hour crowds and lurching traffic a dangerous endeavor. A strange shiver of devotion passed through him and then a corresponding swell of protectiveness. Not that Kai-ling appeared to need much protection. Away from her cramped home, in the bright, daylit glare of windows and hard pavement, she was a preoccupied and unflappable member of the public. She led him in a brawling charge up into the stairwell of a gorged city bus, all for what was only the first leg in a circuitous itinerary of stops. To a gift shop for candied fruit slices. To a men's store for a tie that matched his white Uighur dress shirt. To a police station where she filed the paperwork necessary for a passport. To a government building that was not the civil affairs office but another bureau, the hallways of which were lined in elongated Peg-Boards, each board overflowing with requests for housing assignments or residency changes, and she read through the latest postings, scoffing at each one. To a hospital examination room where a harried intern studied the whites of their eyes, listened to their hearts, drew vials of blood, and charged them twenty-five yuan each to sign separate certificates of health. Then on to the train station, a ten-minute visit to the back room—she was, after all, on duty that day—time enough to introduce Vincent to her coworker and best friend, Miss Wang, who sized Vincent up and turned to Kai-ling with a winking grin. "Just your luck, Kai-ling," Miss Wang said. "You get a husband all the way from America and he dresses like a Uighur goat herder."

In the lobby of the civil affairs building he steeled himself for an atmosphere of glum autocracy, for inquisition-style desk talk with disobliging, hard-line officers of the Communist Party. The cadre they ended up speaking to was much milder than that, though the real surprise was Kai-ling, who, in his company, grew meek and vulnerable, nearly voiceless in her girlish and blushing esteem. They were told that permission for a Chinese-foreign marriage would not be easy, and she crossed her arms shyly over her chest and agreed, beholden to him, if for nothing else than his honesty in the matter. She was fortunate, she admitted, to get such good advice. She'd known to look for him, Mr. Zhang, wasn't it? That's who everyone told her to come see. Not that the others weren't fine as well, but with Mr. Zhang you knew you'd get an honest answer, knew you'd have someone to file your papers on time and keep a close watch over your case.

Vincent was tempted to think of her behavior as flirtatious, but that wasn't it, really. It wasn't a circumstance in which her prettiness was the sole measure of influence. She had sized Mr. Zhang up for what he was, a middle-aged bureaucrat, a father, likely, or at least a man who thought of himself as something of a benevolent patriarch. Thus, when he sat at his desk before them and prepared their application, she received his instructions and often mundane advice with a daughter's shy thankfulness. Vincent's tasks were relatively easy: show his passport and visa, sign an affidavit of marriageability, which would be forwarded to the U.S. embassy in Beijing. Mr. Zhang hardly spoke to him during the process, rarely, if ever, looked him in the eye. In the end the only item their application lacked was a set of photographs featuring the marrying couple together. Kai-ling began to fret over the omission. Soon enough Mr. Zhang intervened on her behalf, borrowed a Polaroid camera from a coworker and had them pose as a couple before a portrait of paramount leader Deng Xiaoping.

It seemed only right, under the circumstances, that she should tilt her head against his shoulder and he, in response, should position an arm reassuringly behind her back. The soft fabric of her white blouse billowed against his fingertips.

He never saw the results. Kai-ling was invited to join Mr. Zhang on the other side of the desk, where they talked together privately and watched the photographs develop. Something about the snapshots appeared to bother the cadre. He sighed. He mumbled at length. Vincent felt sure that fatherly Mr. Zhang was trying to dissuade her from the marriage.

On the way out of the building Kai-ling stopped to chat with the office secretary and came away from that chat with Mr. Zhang's home address scribbled on the palm of her hand. Again they journeyed by bus across town, stopping before a hedge-lined tenement. He waited as she darted inside Mr. Zhang's tenement with the candied fruit slices. Ten minutes later she returned empty-handed.

By then it was late afternoon, the sun strong and glaring and murderously hot. So much of their day had passed in a hectic blur. There had been no time for the frank conversation they seemed perpetually on the verge of having. But when he suggested a late lunch at a quiet restaurant, she told him no thank you. She had to get back to the station office and help Miss Wang with the afternoon receipts. Still, the offer amused her.

"Why a *quiet* restaurant?" she asked.

"I don't know," he said. "Doesn't matter. Any restaurant would have been fine."

"But you said *quiet.*" Her long neck was sloped at a teasing angle, her comely face patient, discriminating. "Do you have something very serious to talk to me about?"

"No, no."

"Are you sure?"

"Yes, very sure." He raised a hand and hailed her a pedicab.

"It wasn't so bad, was it?" she said. "Following me around all day. Being the goat herder."

The goat herder? He couldn't possibly answer this. He couldn't even untangle all the intricacies of her remark, the tweaking humor of it, the self-confidence, the blurry innuendo. He the goat herder. She the goat? Plus the mingled clues to decipher in her face and in the inflection of her voice. Nothing she had said to him yet had sounded so confidential, so alive with whimsy and fondness.

He watched her climb on board the pedicab and vanish into a mire of fuming vehicles. Then he hailed his own pedicab and set out for the Hong Shan. The sky was blazing and clear. A rainless June had left the street curbs and sidewalks creviced with dust. He passed a long file of workers in orange bodysuits waiting for their shift to begin outside the gates of a huge chemical plant. The trees under which they waited, hawthorns and sycamores, were brown-leafed and sagging.

Privately he thought Urumchi an ugly city. Its older buildings all looked hard-baked and vanquished. Many of its newer constructions were still cocooned in knobby-jointed scaffolding. Not far from the merchant districts the city gave itself over, ungrudgingly, to the rigors of industry, to fortresslike petroleum refineries, to mills and chemical plants, and beyond that, to several outer boroughs ravaged by heavy machinery and thus in a near-constant state of dust-blown commotion. In this regard Urumchi appeared similar to Lanzhou, as bustling and as reckless, only much hotter and with a clear, yawning sky that pushed away clouds of smokestack soot before they could turn weighty and plummet back down upon the factories that spawned them.

And what to make of the people and their brusque manners, the dour public face everyone seemed to adopt in a crowd? Was it spitefulness or mere boredom? Between the Uighurs and Chinese he sensed an indifference so complete it could only have sprung from the most intimate and terrible of tribal dissensions. Even more worrisome, the city's stark light and smothering heat had a way of making him feel clumsy, forgetful. Along the teeming promenades he sometimes bumped into other pedestrians without thinking to excuse himself. One morning while walking near Urumchi's People's Park he accidentally stepped on a beggar woman's collection plate and sent her cache of five-fen coins skittering across the pavement. No time to apologize or help the unfortunate woman. The crowd jostled him onward. And any amends he might have made seemed, in Urumchi, flagrantly pointless. It wasn't a city that harbored much real interest in liability or personal suffering.

No surprise then that he stuck close to the Hong Shan and its blocks of nearby bazaar shops and food stalls. At its best the guesthouse could be a world unto itself, moderately cool in the blazing afternoon, far from lavish, yet still a trustworthy provider of clean bedsheets and bottled water and other ordinary comforts. The Hong Shan maintained a separate wing for foreigners, where the dorm beds were assigned in the same order as travelers checked in, sequentially and regardless of gender. Vincent could return late in the evening and find a stranger asleep in one of the room's two other beds. The remaining bed might be occupied in the wee hours of the night by a late-arriving guest. The next morning the three of them would awake groggy, disheveled, wholly unknown to one another, yet squeezed into beds an arm's length apart.

He made a point of rising at a reasonable hour and sticking to a daily routine: a short walk in the morning; breakfast, lunch, and dinner at the nearby Uighur bazaar. Between meals he played pool. There were billiard tables set up throughout the city's neighborhoods, most of them outdoors in a wide passageway between office buildings or in a restaurant courtyard set near a thicket of shade trees. The table beds were often flecked with dust cinders and leaves, the sticks warped by heat. But he tried to be up early each morning and have a table to himself, to sharpen his aptitude for distance and angles, not so much with the aim of winning, but to hold his own among the off-duty cooks and refinery workers who would command the tables later in the day.

Near the end of his third week in Urumchi he telexed a short message to Alec at the Seman Hotel in Kashgar.

DELAYS HERE IN URUMCHI. STILL A MONTH TO WAIT. MAYBE MORE. STAYING AT THE HONG SHAN. HOW ARE YOU?

He checked back at the telegraph office every day for a reply that never came.

With Gwa he never had to wait more than a half hour for a response. They telexed each other at least twice a week. On the subject of Kai-ling's delay, Gwa had the following counsel:

REMEMBER. ALWAYS BE PATIENT WITH MR. AND MRS. SONG. BUT KAI-LING CAN SOMETIMES BE LAZY, INDECISIVE. THAT'S WHY YOU HAVE TO PUSH HER IN THE RIGHT DIRECTION. DON'T BE AFRAID TO STAND UP FOR YOURSELF. DON'T BE AFRAID TO USE YOUR INFLUENCE.

All day he mulled over this advice. He sat on the front steps of the Hong Shan and watched the workday crowds file past. He read his Russian novel. He lost game after game of pool. He tried to imagine what, if any, influence he might have over Kai-ling. That evening he sat beside her and drank tea. It was a knotty sort of trick to be near her and hold in his mind the practical nature of their arrangement.

And then the next morning he awoke groggy, drained. He recognized at once the sense of fogged awareness, the dull inner trembling. His fever or semifever had returned, but he spent the morning trying to deny the fact, dressing and stepping out for his eggs and tomatoes while around him the world turned sluggish and off-kilter. By afternoon he was back in bed, chilled to the bone. His underclothes were wringing wet with sweat. Not a low-grade fever at all, he thought, a full-fledged fever, a high-temperature delirium. He set a Thermos of warm water by his bed. He took two ibuprofen capsules every four hours, which slowed the impetus of the fever and allowed him to sleep.

A funny thing, though, the way his fever would peak and break, peak and break, and in the lulls between he was often quite cozy and inclined toward wistful thinking. He could turn his most pressing dilemmas over and over in his mind like so many shiny pennies. Funny that his fever, in a roundabout way, should cause him to look upon his affections for Kai-ling in an entirely new light. Especially when he considered her age, twenty-eight years. She'd be married, legitimately, to Gwa soon enough. At that age she would probably be pregnant within the year. One child, then another, possibly a third. Lovely children. Cherished children and, unlike the twin baby girls he'd seen in Lanzhou, vibrant, alive. Kai-ling would still be beautiful, of course. Yet he had never thought to speculate on this aspect of her future, particularly the hardship of it, the bitter limits of motherhood and homemaking, not to mention an entrepreneur husband who would likely leave much of the child rearing and house chores to her. In this light it was easy to imagine the liabilities of her life with Gwa as well as the advantages. No doubt there would be days when she longed to have chosen a different path. There would be times, surely, in the years to come when she'd think back to other men she'd known and who'd been kind to her, Vincent among them, and be flooded by appreciation, by a certain retrospective longing.

Such things happened in women's lives all the time. Such moments were bound to occur.

"Ever know any foreign men?" one of her future friends, another over-taxed housewife, would ask her one evening. Their children would be running riot in the next room, their husbands across town in a nightclub or worse, inaugurating the new factory or the next big investment with a throng of simpering hostesses and a bottle of French cognac.

"I knew an American once."

"Yes? Knew him how?"

"A business partner. A friend."

"Ha! The way you said it. A friend. The look on your face."

"It's not what you think. He was younger than me by a few years. He stayed in Urumchi one summer. He helped me get to Taiwan."

"What else did he help you do?"

"Nothing! You're terrible! He was . . . When I think about it now, I was lucky, really. He was very sweet, very considerate. I was lucky he was the one to help me."

It all came down to an imagined moment in her future. He was shocked a little by how completely he was willing to dedicate himself to that moment, to have a woman so beautiful think of him that way, with gratitude and maybe something more.

By seven that evening his fever was scaling steeper, higher peaks. It was clear he would not be visiting the Songs. And no way to contact them either. No telephone. Impossible to write a note in Chinese and pay a pedicab driver to deliver it. In three weeks he had never missed a visit. Kai-ling would be suspicious. She would worry. She might very well come to the Hong Shan looking for him. When she did, he wanted her to find him flushed, his damp hair swept back, attractively delirious, if such a thing was possible. He kept his head propped up stoically toward the door and waited.

Much later that night he became conscious of hot tears springing from the corners of his eyes and rolling down his cheeks. He might have been mumbling, as people with burning fevers are prone to do. The ibuprofen no longer helped. He seemed to be generating impossible waves of heat beneath his blankets, a condition that struck him as alarming, even dangerous. He struggled to sit up. "Excuse me," he whispered to his late-arriving roommates, strangers who were little more than mounded lumps in their beds.

Neither of them stirred, much less answered back.

He had once heard that children, when perilously fevered, were sometimes placed in a tub of cold water. Why not stand beneath a cold shower then? Wouldn't that lower his body temperature just as well? Soon he was up on his feet, waltzing in sweat-soaked underclothes toward a doorway that seemed to shrink and shift before him. Somehow he managed to startle his lumpish roommates, both of them women. One had even bolted up from her mattress, a hiking boot raised like a billy club high above her head.

He swayed at the foot of her bed a moment. "Please," he managed to say.

"No fucking chance!" she warned him. "Don't even think about it."

Down the hallway he went, one plodding footstep at a time. He undressed and stumbled into the open shower bay. The cold water sent his limbs into akimbo-like spasms. He felt his body rattling, stalling, shutting down. Not such a good idea after all. A terrible idea, in fact. He put his back to the tile wall and slid down until he was curled sideways on the shower floor.

Sometime later he was found by the washroom attendant, a wiry little man who spent twelve hours every day either swabbing the squat toilets or at a folding table hawking ten-fen packs of toilet paper. Each day he sat beneath a sign that read: NOT PERMITTING YOU TO DEFECATE IN THE SHOWERS. He had the perfect pockmarked, sullen face to accompany such a sign. In three weeks' time Vincent had never seen that face assume a recognizable expression. Even now, when the attendant roused him from the shower floor and handed him his damp underclothes and money belt, he did so with the same sphinxlike vacancy of feeling he exhibited when bleach-mopping the urine trough.

From this juncture onward there was a lurching rhythm to the order of things. One moment he was in the shower bay, shivering and barefoot, the next he was wrapped in a wool blanket and shuffling forward in rubber flip-flops along a passageway he'd never seen before. And then—surprise!—he was standing alone on the empty promenade outside the Hong Shan.

A pedicab pulled to the curb. The washroom attendant was kneeling on the rear bench and helped haul Vincent into the cab. And what a perfectly tranquil time to go for a ride. A smattering of indigo light had spread across the sky. On every street and lane of Urumchi there seemed to be one in a legion of masked old women out sweeping the pavement with enormous fan-shaped brooms. The long quills of their brooms waved to him.

He had few unmuddled thoughts, but that didn't keep him from deciding upon the final thing he would say to Kai-ling before they landed in Taiwan and she began her complicated future with Gwa. *Whenever you feel things are difficult, whenever you feel alone, it may help to know that someone cares for you very much.*

Another lurch and he was sitting in a paneled examining room that was not bright or antiseptic enough to be part of a hospital. A clinic, maybe, a physician's office. And while he could not recollect a doctor being present, he recalled an injection, painless, except for the chill of the serum mixing with his overwarm blood. Someone said in English, "You have an infection and therefore a fever."

Yes, he nodded. *To work hard with a fever and to love Jesus with a fever is the same thing.*

Someone said, "Drink clear fluids, rest, take your medicine."

He began pondering this advice there in the paneled examining room and it seemed to carry him tangled and sweating back to his dorm room bed.

I have an infection, he tried to say, his fever pulsing hotter and hotter, straining toward a scorched and suffocating plateau. There was bright daylight in the dorm room window. *Better to say it simply: Please know that I'll always care for you.* If only he'd been able to leave a message at the hotel's front desk, since Kai-ling had probably stopped by to check on him on her way to work. He hated the prospect of missing her. Such a shame. They'd just recently begun to understand and be comfortable with each other.

The other two dorm beds lay empty. He was peripherally aware of the attendant beside him, holding out a cup of tepid water and a palmful of thick prescription capsules. Vincent swallowed them and slept again, and his most pressing worry upon waking was that late evening had come and he had missed another visit. He imagined the entire Song family, Mr. and Mrs. Song, even the younger daughter, feeling anxious, abandoned. Only afterward did he notice that his fever had dwindled away and that he was thirsty now, a bit hungry, and lying amid a knot of cool, clammy bedclothes.

His roommates returned, gathered their things in haste, and moved across the hall to another dorm. Judging from the tight-mouthed, heedful way they shied from his side of the room, they had gone from thinking him lecherous to thinking him contagious. He was glad to have the room to himself but too exhausted to stray from his bed. He slept soundly through much of the night. Once, when he woke, the attendant came to his bedside and brought a tall Styrofoam cup of hot, clear soup. Vincent could not hold back his gratitude. "Thank you, thank you," he said, the first and easiest Chinese words he had ever learned. "Thank you for the soup. Thank you for taking care of me."

No reply. Not even a nod, or better yet, the flicker of some gracious emotion across that pockmarked face. Nothing the man had done yet appeared rooted in the customary human sympathies. He uncapped the soup and held it out for Vincent to drink. Why had he done so? Impossible to know.

And did it really matter what impelled one person to step forward and help another? Vincent, who may just have had his life saved, thought that it did not matter at all.

He tried to stand up the following afternoon and his head swooned and a configuration of wagging sunspots coursed before his eyes. He would need time to recover from his exhaustion, a day at the very least. By evening he was steady enough to shuffle to the front desk and ask for messages. There were none. He sat in the lobby awhile and waited for Kai-ling to appear. When she did not, he wondered if illness or calamity had fallen upon the Song family just as it had befallen him.

It was a puzzle he had to wait an entire day to solve. He had to be patient, however. He had to drink three Thermoses of water, eat his meals slowly, and conserve his energy so that the next day, when evening finally arrived, he was relatively strong and clear-minded and able to board a pedicab and ride past the high tenements toward Kai-ling's neighborhood of brick and clay-earth houses. Two lanes short of her home he glanced down at his empty hands. His heart did a queer sort of double thump. It mortified him to think of how close he'd come to arriving without a gift.

Back he went through the maze of houses, past the high tenements, to the main avenue and the first roadside vendor, where he assessed a meager and dusty selection of snack foods and settled on a packet of peach candies and a two-kilogram bag of roasted peanuts.

"You're too kind," Mr. Song said at the door with flagging conviction. Rightly so. The peach candy was ordinary, the peanuts heavy and a bit stale. Otherwise the Song household was the same: Mrs. Song was wringing out a pail of laundry in the kitchen, Kai-ling doing paperwork at the table, the younger daughter glancing dubiously at him over the crimped brow of a magazine. He had to sit down for some strained chitchat to remember all over again the narrow range of subjects he and Mr. Song had to talk about.

"I was sick," he explained to Kai-ling once her father had stepped away to ready the tea service.

"Sick? Oh yes, sick. I guessed you were."

"I was weak. I wasn't able to send you a message." Not entirely true. In the labyrinth of his fever he'd sent her quite a few private communiqués.

"What message?" she asked.

"That I was sick. I wanted to tell you so you and your family didn't worry."

"Yes, I see," she said. Yet she couldn't quite rein in her smile, the forbearing sort that the sophisticated of the world bestow on the naive.

"What?" he asked.

"Well, we didn't think you'd gone anywhere," she said. "We didn't think you'd give my father an eleven-thousand-yuan dowry and then sneak out of Urumchi."

"I wouldn't do that. No, no. I had a fever. I was sick."

"I know," she said. "You told me."

At least the visit didn't turn out to be a complete loss. The Songs had two pieces of news to pass on. Kai-ling had received her passport the day before. Also, Mrs. Song, with the help of a local fortune-teller, had settled on a date for the wedding ceremony, a Saturday more than three weeks hence, the twenty-eighth of July.

"An even-numbered day," Mrs. Song explained. "Which makes it better for Kai-ling and Mr. Gwa. Luckier."

Vincent leaned against the tea table, placed a steadying hand to his forehead. A wave of exhaustion crested over him. "Yes, luckier," he agreed.

Twenty-five

SHE WANTED TO know if he owned a camera, and he thought about it a moment before answering yes. And did he like to take pictures? Kai-ling asked. Yes, he said, he did. And would he like to take pictures of her?

There wasn't a trace of flirtation in any of these questions, no peering at him coyly behind the slanting bangs of her raven hair, no lollipop wandering of her tongue from one cheek to the other. Not that he trusted her passionless sincerity much either, the way so many of her efforts and words later revealed the callow taint of self-interest. But yes, he said. If she needed him to take pictures, he would. They made plans to meet at People's Park the following day, a Sunday, which would mark both the beginning of his fifth week in Urumchi and the second Sunday of July.

For a week now there had been contradictory news from the civil affairs office. Initially, they heard that their marriage application had been approved by a chief cadre member and sent on to a regional headquarters in Lanzhou. Next they heard that this same application had been forwarded to Beijing and was languishing in the office of a well-known bureaucrat. Then a social calamity of sorts: fatherly Mr. Zhang had his secretary return a carton of cigarettes that Kai-ling had dropped off at his apartment a day earlier. The Songs were beside themselves with worry. They should have paid extra for a better brand, Mr. Song said. They should have sent a box of fruit instead. Later it was learned that Mr. Zhang not only didn't smoke but despised the habit and had once tried to ban cigarette smoking in the civil affairs office building. The Songs appeared relieved by this news. Zhang wasn't against them or the marriage certificate; he just loathed their choice of gratuity. When his secretary told Kai-ling he wasn't opposed to a glass of plum wine after dinner, she rushed out and dropped a bottle of it at Zhang's doorstep the very next morning.

Through all of it, Vincent strove to maintain a hopeful equilibrium. He followed each turn and reversal of the proceedings, sent biweekly dispatches to Gwa via Donny Wu in Hong Kong. The wedding was sixteen days away and he listened to Kai-ling and her parents add and subtract items from the menu and tally up a list of returned invitations. As in so many other matters, they had a canny interest in the hard numbers and weren't at all bashful about explaining why. Chinese guests brought envelopes of money to weddings. A well-organized ceremony could help the hosts recoup their expenses. A popular, well-attended one could even turn a profit.

On Sunday morning he circled the roundabout near his hotel and found the north gate of Urumchi's People's Park choked with visitors. The park interior was no less crowded, the winding brick footpaths full of dawdling strollers, the open lawns gathering grounds for huddles of men in bright dress shirts. Here was a sprightly attired holiday class of Urumchi's Chinese: the fastidiously clothed children, the young wives flaunting bonnet-style hats or holding up frilly-edged parasols. There was a touch of strained gentility about these Sunday pilgrims in their best adornments. Nearby roamed a few jobless Uighur men, their families at home, and they barely present, striving to appear indifferent, unenvious, while just beyond the park wall the province they had lost labored on in its flat and colorless and hard-bitten way.

Kai-ling had asked him to meet her near the lake, a silty body of water banked in stone terraces and harboring, at its far end, a marina where one could hire rowboats by the half hour. All the boats were presently out, wafting upon the rippled surface of the lake. He could see couples in each one, vivid but tastefully dressed young women, some waving to friends onshore, others turned to the fore of the boat and facing their escorts, in every case a lean young man who had rolled up his sleeves and was drafting the water in long, slow pulls of the oars. Idleness and romance, Vincent thought, not at all cynically. Their arrangement seemed to him inherently old-fashioned, charming. Wasn't it perfect in its way? Wouldn't any woman seated in such a boat be tempted to evaluate the man rowing as a possible suitor?

He did not find Kai-ling on any of the lake's stone terraces, though he did spot her higher up, on a grassy hillside overlooking the south shore, where she was one among a scattered assemblage of unpartnered men and women her own age. She had worn her white sailor's blouse again, this time matched to a pleated lavender skirt. That alone was enough to make him feel uneasy—for the rest of the day he would have to square himself against her fine looks—but she had curled her hair as well, spiraled it into the thickly coifed, finger-long coils of 1940s movie stars. She looked simultaneously button cute and coolly glamorous.

She asked to see his camera, and he knelt beside her on the grass and drew his compact one-shot from its case. "Japanese," she said, weighing it approvingly in one hand before passing it back.

"It's nothing fancy," he said. "A simple camera. Takes good pictures." He'd actually just bought the camera that morning and now raised it to his eye and captured the width of the lake in its viewfinder. A tidy, sun-dappled vista. It cheered him somehow. For the first time since recovering from his fever he felt present, physically vigorous. "Maybe we could buy time on a boat," he said. "You could ride in the back. I could row and take your picture."

She put a hand to her brow and gazed across the lake to the marina.

"You and the background," he said. "The shining water."

"Go ahead," a male voice answered.

Vincent blinked. He set his camera in his lap.

"Go ahead, if you want," said a young man seated a few meters up the hill from Kai-ling.

These things happened sometimes. In China perfect strangers sometimes foisted their opinions into otherwise private conversations.

"But I have to warn you," the young man continued, "the finished photos won't be any good at all."

"Excuse me?" Vincent said.

"Too much light. Too much light bouncing off the water. You would need a special lens."

"A special lens? Yes, thank you."

"It's nothing. No need to thank me," the young man said. He pulled up a sprig of grass and flung it teasingly onto Kai-ling's lap. She did not brush it away or turn to face him. "Ling-ling," he said to her. "Ride with him if you want. We've got time before my uncle sends the car."

Not a stranger after all. And the way he spoke, so casually, not needing to look at Kai-ling or introduce himself because they were already acquainted, already a history between them, and glancing at Vincent without a trace of embarrassment, as if he knew Vincent's story also and was merely curious to get his first, sidelong peek at the foreigner.

"I don't know," she hummed doubtfully. "We'd have to wait for a boat. Then the paddling. Then the picture-taking."

"So forget the boat ride and let him take pictures of you. He's come a long way. He brought his Japanese camera."

"All right," she conceded. "The pagoda. We'll start there, yes?" She rose and strode off in the direction of a funnel-shaped roof rising above the hill's far edge. Vincent and the young man were left crouched on the hillside, an unbroached introduction between them. "Who are you?" Vincent asked, as politely as possible.

"Wei-han," the young man said.

"You're Kai-ling's friend? You work with her?"

"A friend," he said. "And you're Vincent?" He pronounced the English consonants of Vincent's name with a studied exactness.

"I am."

"You're Ling-ling's boyfriend? Am I right?"

"You are," Vincent said, though he was shocked to hear this pretense spoken aloud.

"Or her fiancé. That's more than a boyfriend, isn't it?"

"It is, yes. We're going to be married."

"I know," Wei-han replied. "Congratulations."

They stood and followed the same course Kai-ling had taken. When they caught up to her, she was leveling her back against one of the pavilion's four stone pillars. She opened her eyes unnaturally wide and sulked her lips a bit. It took Vincent a moment to realize she was posing. He raised his camera.

"You can get closer," Wei-han said. "She doesn't mind a camera in her face."

He eased forward and snapped a photo. She held herself still, the same pose, which he puzzled over awhile until she said "more" and he squeezed the shutter twice again. He thought it a rather conspicuous activity, the taking of photographs so seemingly worshipful and private here in a public park. He worried that to passersby he would appear a tactless voyeur. Yet when they moved to other locations, a terraced cove of the lake, an ivy-backed archway, he saw camera-toting admirers trailing other young women. Several were extravagant in their posturing, versed in an array of preening flourishes: a hand cocked into a cheery gun and aimed at a flawless row of bright, white teeth, or more blatant even, a teenaged girl who clutched the floppy brims of her hat to her head and shrieked into her suitor's camera as if assailed by a gale-force wind.

Kai-ling was never so animated. It was hard, even impossible, to tell whether or not she enjoyed being photographed. Watching her, squaring her likeness inside the viewfinder, he kept skirting mutely around a half-formed, indelicate question. It was nothing so simple as How does it feel to be beautiful? No, the mystery had more to do with value and purpose. Perhaps what he intended to ask was what it *meant* to be at the center of such beauty looking out. Did it *mean* as much as he thought it did?

Wei-han hovered nearby through much of the posing, offering unhurried advice on vantage points and distance—his suggestions were, in every instance, right—and breathing words of encouragement to Kai-ling, at one point interrupting the photo-taking to laud the peacefulness of her expression. "Is it all right if I take a photo or two myself?" he asked.

Vincent agreed, released his camera, and watched Wei-han loft it a foot or more above Kai-ling's head.

"Ling-ling, up here, little rabbit."

She peered up into the lens and laughed, a silly chortle, wide-lipped and gushing. The exclusivity of it made Vincent despair.

"Now then, you two together," Wei-han said.

"I don't think so, no," Vincent said. "Just photos of Kai-ling, please." He couldn't resist Wei-han's solicitations for long, however. Standing with one arm looped behind Kai-ling, Vincent worried that the developed photograph would later make him the brunt of some smirking joke between the pair. He could imagine Wei-han, in particular, gaping at the photo and baring his teeth in an indulgent snicker.

If many of the young Chinese men Vincent met had a studious mien, then Wei-han looked like an accomplished scholar. Someone must have encouraged that even-tempered, mentoring expression because he wore it constantly. It disguised, just barely, something hard and mocking inside him. That, however, didn't concern Vincent as much as Wei-han's atypical good looks, the high, ruminant forehead, deep-lashed eyes as darkly expressive as Kai-ling's, and the shrewdly committed way he passed judgment on almost everything around him.

They took a dozen more photos of Kai-ling, and when the roll expired, the three of them began tracing the stone footpath toward the park's south gate.

"We're going for a car ride," Wei-han explained. "My uncle's in the party. He's been given a car and driver. He's sending it to the park so Kai-ling and I can take a quick ride. Would you like to come with us?"

"No, thank you."

"Why not?"

"I've—well, I've ridden in a car before."

"It's a black sedan with a driver!"

"A sedan, yes. My mother drove us to school in a sedan."

"She did?" Wei-han exclaimed, part grinning surprise, part jeering rivalry. "Ling-ling, if Vincent takes you with him to America, you could be riding in a sedan every day of your life."

"Every day?" She was strolling a few paces behind them, listening and looking fractionally uneasy. "But would I have my own driver?" she asked Vincent.

He shrugged her question away. It was almost dizzying, this heaping of pretenses, one upon the other.

"I've heard this about America," Wei-han said. "Now this is something I understand to be true. I understand that Americans marry and divorce. Marry and divorce often. So often that when a man divorces and marries again, he marries his neighbor's wife, that is, after the wife has been divorced. Then several years go by and the man gets tired of his wife and marries again, another neighbor's wife, and again."

"And again," Vincent snorted.

"Yes, and again, so that by the time you're old, you've been with most of the women in your neighborhood and most of the neighborhood men have been with—"

"It's not true."

"How is it not true?"

"It's ridiculous. Nobody marries that often. Nobody I know."

"But they divorce in America. Divorce all the time."

"No, not all the time. Half the time, maybe. Half of couples divorce. Half stay together. Stay together all their lives."

"Is that right?" Wei-han said, again the patient tutor humoring someone else's frivolous argument. "We hear such different things sometimes, about how open Americans are. Who's to say what you should believe?"

Before them lay a bordered quadrangle and waterless fountain. Again the crowds were heavy and they had to dodge a cavalcade of overdressed and pinwheeling toddlers to reach the south gate. Parked beyond the gate was a file of pedicabs and mule-drawn wagons and not a single sedan, black or otherwise, among them.

They had to wait forty minutes for the sedan and tardy driver to arrive, though at least there was satisfaction to be taken in seeing Wei-han struggle to choke back his impatience. The delay caused Kai-ling to turn sullen and bored. "It's not worth it," she said. Then a black sedan pulled to the curb, or more accurately, a black Mercedes-Benz, a diplomat's car with polished chrome hubcaps and two red-star flags sprouting cavalry-style from the front fenders. Wei-han stood beside it, beaming. He hailed the driver as comrade and slipped the man a squat pack of unfiltered cigarettes. "I'll ask again," he said to Vincent. "Join us for a quick ride. Twice around the park, that's all."

It was easier to say no than to watch such prideful gloating. And though he knew his refusal to be irrational, Vincent would not allow himself to sit inside the flagged automobile, this car more emblematic of the Communist Party than anything he'd yet seen in China. Even a short ride would involve some sort of ambiguous personal compromise. So he bowed and nodded as they climbed in and drove away. His only wish was that he had seen the sedan interior, not to ogle the upholstery, but to know whether or not some type of divider existed between the driver and the backseat.

If there was a divider, he thought, then Wei-han would try to kiss or lay his hands upon Kai-ling as they circled the park. If there was no divider, their ride would be chaste.

Either way they both probably held the furtive desire to kiss or touch. For that alone he wanted retribution, wanted them mindful of how monumentally selfish and hurtful their desire was to others, to Gwa, for example. Just to think of his benefactor's suffering: the spurned affections and diminished hopes, the devastating breach of trust. Until that moment he had never felt himself to be so unconditionally Mr. Gwa's ally.

A telex would need to be tactfully composed and sent out. *Sorry to inform you that Kai-ling appears to have a young male friend here in Urumchi, a boyfriend, I think. It's the way they behave together, more intimate than simple friends. What to do next?*

It took seven minutes, by Vincent's watch, for the sedan to circle the park and swing by without stopping, the tinted windows rolled shut and throwing back an imperious glare. Now he viewed his decision not to ride along as a mistake. Better to be there, to keep them from kissing. Just maybe he would have been able to puzzle out the extent of their attachment to each other. Even just to know how long they'd been friends. Or why she had invited both of them to the park today.

This was what he wanted to ask her when the sedan came around a second time and halted center lane so Kai-ling could get out and Wei-han could wave good-bye from the backseat. "Glad to meet you," he said to Vincent, yet he did not look truly glad, only haughty and dismissive. Nor did Kai-ling look like a young woman who'd been recently kissed. If anything, she appeared relaxed, natural in a way she hadn't while posing for photographs, restored to her essential self.

But she was also in a rush, eager to part the crowds and hurry Vincent along until they were wedged into line at the nearest bus stop. When the next bus came, she pried open a gap wide enough for them both to slip on board.

"How about the car?" he asked, once the doors had closed and they were packed in tight together.

"The best," she said. "Only top-quarter people in the party live that way. The air-conditioning. The windows. You press a button, up or down, any way you want."

"You asked Wei-han to come to the park today?"

The bus whined to a halt behind a row of stalled vehicles. "Damn," she said. "So slow."

"You wanted me to meet him?"

"I wouldn't say that." A long pause. She was examining, in scrupulous detail, the navy blue collar and ruffled pleats of her sailor's blouse. "I didn't know he was coming," she said finally. "I told him not to."

He was relieved to detect exasperation in her voice. "He seemed very knowledgeable, Wei-han. But he also seemed very . . . I don't know. Not modest enough."

"Not modest enough is right."

Just then the doors opened and the abrupt surge of bodies forced them out onto an avenue of window-fronted stores. She seized him by the wristwatch, brought it up to her chin. "*Aiya!* Twenty minutes left!" she cried. "You'll wait for me, yes, while I watch the end of my show?"

"I will," he promised with only the vaguest notion of what he had consented to. It hardly mattered anyway, as animated as Kai-ling was, as pleased as *he* was to have her soft hand cinched to his wrist and drawing him along in the wake of her peach-scented perfume. They stopped outside an electronics store. Set before them was a high, uncluttered display window, and they stood among a troupe of mostly young women and looked through the glass to four upraised televisions. All four sets flickered with the same series of commercials, hand-drawn stills of farm tractors and heavy machinery, and then the broadcast switched to a carpeted runway, a woman's narrow-toed evening sandal, a checkered green skirt and vest—a fashion program, of all things, "live or almost live," Kai-ling said, from the design schools of Shanghai.

"All I'd want from that is the shoes, nothing else," a primly dressed woman beside Vincent remarked. But then another model appeared in an evening gown, thin-strapped and ink black and like none he'd seen any woman in China wear publicly. They all hummed their approval. The more curious in the group pressed close to ogle Vincent.

"Leave him be," Kai-ling admonished them.

"But who is he?" they asked.

"My designer," she said, her fingers still light against his wrist.

"Oh!" they said. "Such a liar!"

"My personal designer, and he's come all the way from Paris to design me something special." She was able to say this in a regal tone, her lips stretched to a silly, prideful smirk, and the round of laughter she earned caught Vincent by surprise. He was amused, fondly so, to think of them all as regular viewers gathering each Sunday here on this busy street corner in Urumchi to follow fashion changes two thousand miles away. Did they measure themselves, these women of modest means, against Shanghai fashion models? He guessed that in some respects they did, just as they measured themselves surreptitiously against Kai-ling, easily the prettiest in their group.

"I'll have him start with a blouse," she continued. "Sleeves to the elbows and an open collar like this," she said, running a finger perilously low across her breasts.

"You wouldn't wear that, not on TV," they scolded her. "What else?"

"Black cotton pants, a gray sweater around my waist. Those same sandals but with higher heels."

"What else?"

"Sunglasses, round, the kind you flip up when you get to the end of the runway."

"And what else?"

The question, he knew, would always be what her beauty was worth. Worth Gwa, at least, and a privileged life far away on the island of Taiwan.

"I'm not just speaking my dreams out loud," she announced. "I rode in a cadre's sedan today. I have a designer here ready to make whatever clothes I say." And with that she stepped out before her audience, bowed, and began strolling between the creviced lines of the walkway, back and forth, heel to toe, heel to toe.

Twenty-six

HEAVEN LAKE. For many foreign visitors to the Hong Shan it was the sole reason they'd come to Urumchi, and they returned from the day-long expedition staggered by what they'd seen. Lovely mountain vistas, they said. Crisp air. Rustling pine trees. The deepest blue water. Their praise was always so similar and exultant that Vincent assumed the actual trip could only pale in comparison. And besides, he preferred the coolness of his hotel, a more secure and comfortable place to wait out the final week before his wedding. If need be, he knew enough piquant details about Heaven Lake to leave China and afterward simply fabricate a visit.

Which was a shameful thing to do, when he really thought about it: pathetic and cowardly and deeply unadventurous for someone who'd journeyed across China mostly on his own. So he'd go to Heaven Lake, then, to avoid being a liar and a coward, go reluctantly, the harrowing Turpan to Urumchi bus ride still fresh in his mind. To strengthen his resolve, he visited the Songs that evening and announced he would travel to Heaven Lake the very next morning.

That turned out to be a rather complicated mistake. The Songs' younger daughter, whom the family addressed as "Little Sister," *Mei-mei*, earned a second income selling snacks and cold drinks about town. Some of her best customers were the early-morning riders departing for Heaven Lake. She met them where they gathered, near the north gate of People's Park. Then she raced off to her regular job at an Urumchi tannery. By Mr. and Mrs. Song's way of thinking, only Mei-mei could see to it that Vincent locate the right stop and board the proper bus. They were adamant that he be at their doorstep at seven the next morning so he could follow Mei-mei on her rounds.

"Thank you. But the Heaven Lake bus stop isn't far from my hotel," he reasoned.

"She doesn't mind. Do you, Mei-mei? Get here early, though, she's out the door by seven."

"I might as well just meet her—"

"Yes, yes, but you're better off sticking beside her, don't you see? She knows all the drivers," Mr. Song promised. "She'll get you the best seat."

This was precisely the kind of overreaching Chinese courtesy Vincent considered more crippling than helpful. Kai-ling could have intervened had she not been occupied drafting a letter to one or another government official. As for Mei-mei, she didn't protest the arrangement either, though she did sigh deeply and burrow a bit further into her open newspaper.

The next morning she came bushy-haired and yawning to the front door. She dragged a long pole and two buckets out into the lane and began fastening the bucket handles and balancing her cargo of sweet drinks and rice snacks and other odds and ends. Then she hoisted the pole across one shoulder and set out along the same lanes and in the same northwesterly direction from which Vincent had arrived moments earlier.

He followed several paces behind. They were, by any measure, a gruff, taciturn pair; he inwardly bristling at the inconvenience, Mei-mei loping along sleepy-eyed, sullen, oblivious to his company. At seven A.M. the sewery fragrance of her neighborhood was much sharper. The sky was still dark except for a few purple streaks of light on the horizon. She stopped at a vendor's stall and bought ice for her bottled drinks. When she picked up the pole again, he thought her fluid, nimble-footed gait worth a cheery comment. "Well done," he remarked, the first thing he'd said to her that morning. The first thing he'd said to her ever? "I mean you carry the weight very well." At once she handed the pole to him, shrugged it mutely, humorlessly, from her shoulder onto his. He bore it a half block, the ends seesawing wildly and the weighty fulcrum of the pole digging into his shoulder. Exhausted, he hailed a pedicab and had the driver balance the pole lengthwise along its frame while he and Mei-mei rode side by side in the carriage seat all the way to the park's north gate.

He didn't require anyone's help to find the Heaven Lake bus or stand in line for tickets with the other riders, several of whom were fellow guests at the Hong Shan. And Mei-mei was either too tired or in too cheerless a mood to secure him any favors from the bus driver. Not that he expected or wanted any. On the contrary, he felt marginally beholden to her if only because they had arrived together and were acquainted through Kai-ling, and she, Mei-mei, would spend the coming day laboring for small profits while he would sightsee on a mountain lake. It was this final disparity that caused him to stoop beside her and buy a carton of citrus drink and a bag of seaweed-wrapped rice crackers he knew he'd never eat.

As always, he couldn't decide if he'd done enough or too little. Probably too little, but either way he handed over his rumpled fen notes and watched their fastidious re-counting and was puzzled, utterly, when she pulled a worn photo album from her satchel and pressed it into his hands. He lifted the cover. The first two pages were lined with paper currencies: a Japanese thousand-yen note, a ten-deutsche-mark German note, British and Irish pound notes; on the next page a French twenty-franc, a Thai fifty-baht , an Italian one-thousand-lire.

"A book of money?" he said, expectantly.

She tipped her brow a quarter inch forward, a tepid little nod that he supposed meant yes.

"Money from all around the world? From the foreigners you meet? You collect it and put it in your book?"

Another tepid nod.

He leafed through more sheets, notes from Canada, Hong Kong, Switzerland, Australia, tidily arranged but by no means an extensive collection, four and a half pages in all. He flipped back to the beginning. "An American dollar? You don't have one?"

"I don't," she said modestly. "I plan someday—"

"No dollar?"

"I hope to find an American dollar and put it here at the end of my collection."

"But I have one!"

"You do?" There was a hint of awe in her whisper.

"Yes, right here with me now." He burrowed down under his shirt and pulled his wallet from his money belt. Tucked into the wallet's inner sleeve were a pair of folded U.S. dollar bills. He gave her one and watched, a shade magnanimously, as she straightened the creases and aligned it center point on its own page.

"That's the one. I've been waiting to get this one," she said after she'd immured the dollar beneath a skin of clear plastic.

"There's other kinds, you know. Other countries. You could fill a whole book."

"Yes, I know. But this is the one that matters. Thank you."

Thirty minutes would pass before he understood. His considerable satisfaction over having supplied the long-sought jewel of her collection first had to ebb and wear thin. By then the bus was bouncing hard along the outskirts of Urumchi, swinging past a livestock market, where the shepherds and buyers were all swarthy Uighur men haggling and slouching close to one another so that they might pass yuan bills back and forth like secret handshakes.

He had to witness this furtive palming of bills to understand that he'd been swindled. To be certain, he turned to the English couple one seat behind. They, too, had purchased citrus drinks and been invited to flip through Mei-mei's album after he had. He asked them if they had seen a U.S. dollar bill inside.

"No. None at all," the woman, soft-eyed and fiftyish, replied. "She had a pound note but no dollars. And we were no help to her, poor thing. But Barry here had her write out her address. We'll send her a dollar next time we come across one."

An excellent idea, he told them. They were kind to think of it, he said, all the while fighting to contain a woozy, eruptive grin. He turned back in his seat and squared his shoulders against the bench frame. Amazing! Her ruse hadn't even required slippery fast talk. She had only to show the album and wait for him to deduce the absent American dollar. And if she could turn the scam just once every day, trading her swindled American dollar for renminbi on the black market, if she could do that plus sell a few sweet drinks and snacks then she would likely have earned a second wage equal to or greater than the one she received from the tannery each month.

He respected such cleverness and thrift. Yet she had not hesitated to use him as her dupe, which, when he thought about it, was really not so amusing. When viewed in a certain light, he had probably been a dupe for the other members of her family as well. Kai-ling was capable of her own furtive half-truths and manipulations. And weren't the succession of gifts he brought each evening just another form of extortion? It occasionally seemed so. He couldn't be certain, of course, about any of their intentions. But still there remained the nagging suspicion that one way or another, before his time in Urumchi was through, the Song family would bleed him dry.

A short while later he glanced ahead and saw that the bus had set an unswerving course for an immense range of mountains. Brilliant white snow glittered from the tallest peaks. The highest of these, he knew, was called Bogda Feng, meaning "the Peak of God," an imposing title but still less poignant, less personally significant, because it was named after another people's god and not the one he had prayed to since childhood.

In time the scrub-weed desert fell away behind them and they lumbered through a long plain of grazing meadows. Flitting above the plain was a spiral of lofting hawks, most likely a different breed from the chicken hawks of southern Illinois, but he could see their elegant forms passing close above and the beautiful trembling of their splayed wingtips.

The roadway vanished amid a dry creek bed, resumed some fifty yards later. They began the long, coiling ascent at the base of the range. At once the hillside pastureland around them intensified in color. It was a trick, he realized, of so many days in the desert that he could peer from his bus at the thickening meadows and underbrush and never remember having seen anything so perfectly green. There then came a noticeable drop in temperature, a seventy-degree mollifying coolness that signaled increased altitude and, more invigorating yet, the ascension of tall, bristling pine trees. Heaven Lake, when it came into view some fifty twisting kilometers later, was compassed by such trees. Seeing its closest shore was something of a shock: the deep-hued impossible blues and greens Gwa had spoken of, the impossible change, its unlikely size as well, spacious and shimmering and broadly recessed in places, as resplendent when viewed from afar, between gaps in its curtains of pine trees, as when seen close up. At the lake's edge lay chance configurations of boulders, dove gray, half-extruded, neatly, even beautifully embedded along the banks and jutting among hundreds of mossed tree trunks that managed to hold back, in their spidering roots, great earthy clutches of crumbling shoreline.

He had never seen anything quite like it, and again could only compare it with places he had heard of but never actually been. Heaven Lake then was a thousand acres of Canadian Rockies or Swiss Alps gathered up by an appeasing god and toted over continents and oceans to be set down here, as indemnity, maybe, for the heat and bareness of the Xinjiang desert.

The bus halted. Soft billows of chill air wafted up from the barely rippled water. They were let off, many of them to shiver, on a paved turnaround. Just up a bordered pathway stood an ornate restaurant and sleeping lodge. It was noontime. The bus would return to Urumchi at four o'clock. Vincent set off on his own, climbing a trail that began low on the banks and eventually veered upward and traced the high ridges between coves. He tasted an autumn crispness in the air, delicious to breathe. From underfoot arose the sharp scent of pine needles. His happiness at that moment, the dumb pleasure to be taken in being alive and present in these surroundings, felt clownish and oversize. He was even inanely satisfied to find dollops of fresh horse manure strewn across the trail. That would explain the distant animal neighing he had heard from time to time. Still, he had to hike farther to see a steeper, diverging trail twisting up out of the crater of the lake and charting a more ambitious track for the snow-brimmed Peak of God. When he shaded his eyes, he could identify three or four horse-bound figures poised on one of the many vertiginous ridges leading to that peak.

His was the more sensible route, an ample, well-trod path carved somewhat high into the slopes of the lake and running in a full circuit above its rugged shoreline. Already he had climbed more than a hundred yards up. When he turned back, his fellow bus riders had become a wee flock of day-trippers keeping rather timidly to the park tables and log benches below. He pressed on, the lake a blue-veneered miracle, several kilometers wide and spreading out around him into wide bays and long, fingering inlets. All this stupefying beauty! To think how long he'd put off this trip. To think that he'd squandered a month and a half in ugly Urumchi when he could just as easily have passed many of those days here.

He hiked alone for what seemed a respectable distance. Then he sat at a shaded bend in the trail and drank the last few mouthfuls of citrus drink. He checked his wristwatch. Somehow two hours had elapsed. In that time he had compassed only a third of the lake. He doubted he would make it back in time to join the others for their four o'clock departure, a prospect that did not trouble him greatly. He had in his travel bag an extra layer of sturdy Uighur clothing. If need be, he might spend the night in the lodge and return to Urumchi the following day, or the day after.

That then would be his plan. He rose and hiked onward and when later he came to the far side of the lake, arriving tired and uncertain and on the verge of turning back, there the trail dipped suddenly downward, leveling off at the banks and leading into a narrow, grass-lined valley. Anchored along the valley floor were seven teepees. He counted them dutifully as if they were anthropological discoveries of considerable importance.

A clan of brightly dressed children darted about the patchy common ground between teepees, while two adult women, crimson-cheeked from the altitude, stood in an adjoining pine grove and broke dry branches into kindling. Beyond the pines came a soft, phlegmatic bleating. When he looked through to the nearest hillside, he saw several white goats poised on the tips of boulders.

The children and women were not startled in the least to see him. He was approached, surrounded, and soon guided through the flap door of the closest teepee. Inside he knelt and listened to their consonant-rich language and beheld an ample living quarters, the walls broadened by a framework of curved branches and leather straps, the floor covered with hand-sewn rugs. Instead of cumbersome dressers or wood trunks, voluminous satchels hung from the walls and held entire wardrobes in their deep pockets. A hale-bodied young mother showed him her cookware and posed an indecipherable question. "Good, very good," he answered in Mandarin and English. She smiled vaguely, wanting, it seemed, another sort of reply, a more discerning opinion, perhaps, a resounding judgment.

Whatever the confusion between himself and them, it never strained their ease and goodwill. This was especially true of the children, who pulled him outdoors and included him in their circle of games. A lopsided playground ball was brought forth and kicked about. The slightest attention from him, the merest bit of grinning encouragement, and they would blush deeply, pleasurably, or do a few happy pirouettes atop the grass. Was it their isolation, or his, that made them seem so faultless, so pure of heart? As they played, he kept an eye on the farthest ridge, and toward evening he saw the caravan of horse riders grow larger and begin their long, circuitous descent. Over the course of the next hour he watched them disappear and reemerge, light and fleet on the straightaways, plodding and stealthy on the sharp bends and acclivities. Nearer the shoreline they loped east toward the hotel and restaurant. There, half the caravan dismounted. Those who remained gathered the free horses and galloped out the final lap above the lake. What had taken Vincent hours to hike took them a nimble fifteen minutes, and when they swooped into the valley, the first among them, a lively, mustached man in a leather coat and beret, crossed the meadow and brought himself and his line of panting horses to a sudden halt.

He was too thin-featured and green-eyed to be Chinese. He called out to the children, and they returned an exuberant reply. Then he dismounted and stretched forward as if to deliver a manly slap upon the back and placed the end of a leather cord in Vincent's hand. "You walked here, to our side, from the hotel?" the man asked. "You don't stay at the hotel? You don't like it?" He spoke a slow, inchoate form of Mandarin, and at the clipped end of each phrase he grinned handsomely. "So you can eat dinner and stay with us tonight. You've seen the inside of our homes already, yes?"

"I have, yes," Vincent said. In his hand, somehow, lay the reins to an unmanned horse, a broad-chested pinto, eyes bulging, lathered in sweat. He reached up and stroked the long ridge of its nose.

At once a demure negotiation began, Vincent insisting he pay ten yuan for his food and lodging, his host asking for less, while around them the children lined up like altar boys to receive the bridles and saddle blankets that had been stripped from the horses. His host explained that he and the other men of his camp would set out again tomorrow for the Peak of God, not to the peak itself, the very top, but to the snow line. Vincent could, if he came along, hold snow in his hands and let it melt through his fingers. Each day of the summer they led a caravan of visitors to the snow line. At the end of the summer, the families here would pack up their homes, their yurts, and move down the mountain range to the plains north of Urumchi. They had in other years been as far north as the Soviet Union, which was fine because they were Kazakh people. He said "Kazakh people" twice, once in a tenor of privilege, once more with a wavering of resignation.

The horses were set loose. Vincent thought it exquisite to watch each animal shake its dusty mane and lope off toward the lush meadow grass at the edge of the valley. A lovely sight, especially now, with the cambered light of evening falling on the settlement and imbuing the crosshatched sides and tapered roof of each yurt with a shadowed quaintness. He asked the mustached caravan leader if the horses were ever hitched at night, and whether they strayed or became lost.

"No," his host replied. "Because of the grains, a satchelful for each horse at sunset and dawn. They think with their stomachs."

"And how are they on the trails?"

"Stubborn. Mules on the way up, fat cows coming down. They only behave like horses on the final half circle around the lake. They know the distance between themselves and the valley. So they race, come alive. You know what I'm saying? You know what a horse is like?"

"I do, yes. A little."

"Each one is a stubborn child," his host said. "At the end of the summer we have to drag them away."

• • •

At least he knew he was smitten. At least he, Vincent, failed volunteer, knew he was under the sway of a peculiar exultation. Everywhere he looked there were wonders to behold: the ribboned sky at twilight; the lake, or rather the corner of it he could see, no longer blue but a perfect liquid violet. If he wasn't careful, he would convince himself that he'd arrived in paradise. He could be persuaded that the Kazakh villagers, his gracious hosts, led lives of surpassing purity and virtue.

But was it true? Perhaps not. Surely each individual in this village harbored his or her own painful flaws: women as self-serving as Kai-ling, as single-minded as Gloria; young men as faulty, as contrary, as himself.

He helped carry satchels of grain out to the horses in the meadow, the children bounding ahead of him, shouting, careening against one another, and even, in one instance, scrambling under the belly of a grazing mare. Before long they'd linked arms and formed a rough-and-tumble chain of sorts. Each time their line broke he was given pause. Each time they rose and clasped hands again he wavered on the cusp of a potent idea. It's an amazement, he decided. Everything that happens in life. The sky. The lake. The horses. The romping children. All wonders. All fractions of an entirety he used to think of as God, as Jesus Christ. Understanding that this new god would never speak to him the way he longed to be spoken to meant a lifetime of partial answers and shady intuitions. He would grow old and die without knowing. What he hadn't expected, though, what the long journey to Urumchi and then to Heaven Lake had shown him, was that you could navigate your life without knowing. Even more, you could occasionally be awed by the mystery. You could sometimes love the mystery as devoutly as the believers loved their gods.

These were the branching ruminations from which he hoped to fashion something pure and forceful, an axiom, an abiding truth, to run shouting across the meadow, *Everything is a miracle, a mystery! Everything is God!*

Not that he would actually do such a thing. He was no longer the type. And besides, the full measure of what he'd just understood couldn't be nourished for long. What a shame that the brightest spirits of his exultation had to leave him—were already leaving him. Soon he'd be his old, fretful self. The dreary underside of everything he couldn't know would clutch at him. He'd stumble. He'd make the same foolish mistakes. He might well be an advocate of mysteries and miracles, but he wouldn't be able to taste their rapture or sing their praise.

In a minute or two he would only half believe any of it.

Twenty-seven

DOWN THE SPARE lane, past crumbling door stoops and mangy dogs and piles of splintered bricks, he saw the figure of a young woman leaning from the front door of the third, fourth, no, fifth house on the right, the Songs' house. He waved. The figure darted back inside. This happened two evenings later, Vincent only a few hours off the Heaven Lake bus, time enough to shower and shave at his hotel, then off to buy a watermelon and climb with it aboard a pedicab bound for the Songs'. He assumed the figure in the doorway to be Kai-ling. He had stayed two nights at Heaven Lake, and this time his absence seemed to have made her curious.

Mr. Song met him at the door looking hangdog from the heat and his day's labor at the train station. "Come in," he said and then, shaking his head rather distractedly, muttered, "Yes, good to hear it. Good for you," as Vincent described the clean air and water, the rejuvenating aura of Heaven Lake. Mrs. Song, also blasé, half listened from the kitchen. Chaired in the corner of the living room, beneath her reading lamp, was Kai-ling's younger sister, and Vincent nodded and grinned at her, a crafty, amicable grin meant to convey that though he understood he had been swindled out of his American dollar, he was not in the least bitter about it.

"I never expected to ride through a field of snow," he said. "We went as high as the horses would take us. And the view from up there! The best view, the best scenery I think I've ever seen." He had never been more sincere in his praise of a place, and it was a shame that now, with a shared topic of conversation between them, the Songs were only wanly interested.

And Kai-ling? He had to look for her among the stacked parcel boxes and hanging bags, but there she was, mostly hidden behind the kitchen archway. Her back was to him, and he noticed the high gleam of lotion atop the calves of her legs and her pearl-colored knee-length skirt. By now he had seen most, if not all, of her wardrobe, and the skirt, he realized, was new, meaning both recently purchased and modishly fashionable in a style that most of her clothing was not. There was a corresponding blouse, bone-white, and when she turned and carried the tea set into the living room, he saw the matching belt, wide as an open hand and joined together by a huge, squared buckle. The belt was probably too large, a trifle absurd, even, but the outfit in its entirety looked nice and he told her so. At once her expression, barely composed, collapsed into sneering displeasure. It was startling, this pure and open disgust he was seeing, as if he had been lecherous or belittling, when in fact all he had said was, "A nice choice. It looks good on you."

"And what do you know about clothes?" she said. "What do you know about anything?"

He smiled on the off chance he was being teased. "What?" he asked, and quickly he considered the probable causes of her displeasure: that he had given her sister an American dollar; that this evening's house gift, a smallish Hami watermelon, was hardly extravagant or original; that he had passed two nights at Heaven Lake away from her. The last of these seemed a thinly possible explanation. Could it be that she'd missed him? Could this be the kind of covetous disdain women sometimes inflicted on their boyfriends and husbands? "What?" he said again.

"What do you know about any of us?" she said, settling into a wobbly perch on the stool beside her father. "The only reason you came to Urumchi is because Gwa paid you. Tell me, how much did he pay you?"

"What a question!" He pretended to be merrily shocked, and when this failed, he said, finally, "Not enough to make me rich, if that's what you think."

"More than my dowry?"

"What? That's not—the amount—it's not so simple. Gwa's money made your family rich. In America the same amount couldn't pay a family's bills for more than a few months. Everything's different."

"It doesn't matter. You're doing it all for money, and now I know that, and now I don't have to do anything I don't want to. I don't have to marry you at all."

"You wouldn't be marrying me," he said calmly. "You would be marrying Gwa."

"Fine then. I'm not marrying Gwa."

She reached down and knotted her hands together along the hemline of her new skirt. Beside her, Mr. Song appeared pitifully sad in his tortoiselike way. Mrs. Song and the younger sister had simply turned their attention elsewhere. The thing now, he told himself, was to remain calm, steadfastly reasonable. "What happened while I was away, Kai-ling?" he nearly whispered. "What made you so angry?"

"I'm not angry. I've thought about marrying Gwa and living in Taiwan and I don't want to do either."

"You've told Gwa this? You've written him a letter?"

"No. No time for that. You can telex him tomorrow morning."

"Hold on, now. You shouldn't talk that way unless first you think awhile. Kai-ling, what happened when I was away? What changed?"

"Nothing," she said, more agitated. "Nothing at all." She looked upon him with a scalding impatience.

"Maybe you thought about being married and moving away and you got upset. I think that happens to people sometimes, when the day of the wedding gets near."

"Tell him to forget about it. Tell him to marry a girl from his own town."

"I won't tell him anything until we talk awhile. Until we take a few days to think about this."

"A few days? The wedding is in *four* days. I'm canceling it, you understand? I'm not changing my mind."

"You might, once you calm down and think."

"I've told you what I decided! The rest I don't care! You tell Gwa whatever you want! I'm done with it, you understand? I'm done with it!"

There was an edge of breathy panic to her voice that the small house could not quite accommodate. Vincent sat biding his time until they were all composed and he could proceed with a line of argument he knew largely to be a bluff. "What then?" he asked. "You give back the dowry? Is that the idea?"

Mr. Song shifted anxiously on his stool.

Kai-ling said, "We'll give back what we haven't spent on the wedding, on my passport and the marriage certificate. We'll give back half, maybe more."

"Half," he said incredulously. "You want me to tell Gwa the wedding is canceled, then tell him you're keeping half the dowry money?"

"Less than half. I don't know exactly how much. Tell him—"

"Tell him yourself. I know Gwa. He'll come to Urumchi once he learns you've canceled the wedding. You can explain it all to him then."

She sat red-faced, pouting. "I won't be here!" she cried.

"Won't be here? Where will you be?"

"I'm going away," she said, and then, as if she'd unwittingly revealed too much, she hid her face in her hands and wailed, "I don't have to tell you or Gwa anything!"

Just then one of the house's many hanging bags slipped from its hook and clattered to the kitchen floor. A moment later Wei-han, who'd been eavesdropping from the other side of the kitchen archway, sauntered into the living room and stood guard beside Kai-ling. He had the gratified look of an emissary sent from a calmer and wiser region of the kingdom. He placed a hand on Kai-ling's shoulder. He gave her mother and father, even Mei-mei, an officious nod. "There's nothing else to say to him," he advised the Song family. "And the way he's talking. The lack of respect. For Ling-ling. And for you, too, Mr. Song. I couldn't stand still and listen to it for long."

Vincent put a hand to his forehead and groaned. It struck him then, all at once: Kai-ling wasn't having prewedding jitters. A decision had been made. The Songs and Wei-han had gathered this evening to inform him of that decision. That was what had happened. That was what was happening now. His summer in Urumchi, all the idle waiting, the lesser and greater discomforts of his journey, had become a lost venture—an acute loss with an onerous, hope-deadening sting to it. Not a complete loss, surely, he prompted himself. Couldn't he be proud of the journey even though its rationale had turned pointless? Hadn't he glimpsed something important at Heaven Lake? He could sustain such optimism for only a few moments. Then he was enraged and defeated. Before he could think of Gwa's heartache, he thought bitterly of his benefactor's money. Gwa would probably want every dollar of Vincent's fee and the Songs' dowry returned to him. "I can't believe . . ." Vincent said aloud in garrulous English. "I can't understand . . . Oh, for fuck's sake!" he said, knowing full well he was invoking both the words and glowering demeanor of an absent friend. "For fuck's sake! Be reasonable about this!"

Except for a low snicker from Wei-han, they were all shocked into muteness by the volume of his words, which he'd uttered louder and more wrathfully than he had intended.

"What did he say?" Kai-ling asked. "What did it mean?"

"He's crazy," Wei-han answered. "He's jealous. He's not making sense."

"It means you should be ashamed," Vincent said. "Ashamed to break a promise. Break a promise to a man who loves you."

"What man?" she said. "Gwa?"

"Yes, Gwa. Of course Gwa. You owe him."

"And what do I owe him?"

"The dowry money," he said. "An apology. An explanation."

• • •

That explanation was woefully long in coming. Each slim parcel of information had to be hard won through wily argument or obstinate protest. He made more than a few portentous threats: Gwa would come to Urumchi within the week; Gwa would exact payment from her family if Kai-ling was not present to repay the dowry. In time he found that she and Wei-han could be cajoled into an occasional disclosure—they were moving east, they said, together. And for this vague admission they wanted from Vincent some placating but unnamed concession. When he would give them none, the talk dissolved again into petty bickering.

Tea was made, set out, then forgotten amid a rancorous exchange. It was then or shortly after that Mr. Song, in a grievous state, tried raising his soft voice above the rancor. "I'll pay what's left of the dowry," he said twice before the others paused to listen. "I'll pay it month by month from my wages." The family rallied against him, but he would not take back the offer. "It's only right," he said to Kai-ling. "Only right if you break your promise to the man." More protests followed, yet the core of Kai-ling and Wei-han's resistance seemed to have been fractured. By midnight Vincent had what he thought was a comprehensible explanation he could pass on to Gwa.

Six months earlier a retired couple, the Wans, had received long-sought permission to move from Urumchi to an outer district of Shanghai so that Mr. Wan could spend his last few years in the vicinity of his boyhood home. They settled into a tenement house on the far southern edge of the city, so far south it was not, strictly speaking, even a district of Shanghai. A half year passed and the Wans made a decision that both Kai-ling and Wei-han considered monumentally foolish. They wanted to return to Urumchi. Mr. Wan could locate no living relatives or friends from his childhood. Mrs. Wan found the youth of Shanghai unfathomable and missed—incredibly—the stubby pastureland surrounding Urumchi and the harsh Xinjiang seasons. Their written request to relocate had been intercepted by Wei-han's uncle before it had ever been posted for the general public.

And so a long-distance barter had been arranged. Kai-ling and Wei-han would swap residency permits and housing assignments with the Wans, who would return to Urumchi and occupy the second floor of a house Wei-han now shared with an elderly aunt. Kai-ling and Wei-han would travel east and reside in a distant outer suburb of the largest metropolis in China, a city Kai-ling regarded as the very center of the civilized world.

First, however, they would marry, here in Urumchi, in two weeks' time.

These were the discernible facts of their situation. And yet they did not explain Kai-ling's change of heart. Was there a tactful way, with Wei-han present, to inquire about the more private reckonings of her decision?

He didn't think so, but he asked anyway: Had she known from the start, from the time he arrived in Urumchi? Had she known all along she wanted to marry Wei-han instead of Gwa?

At this late hour, after a night of spiteful argument, she treated his question as if it were the latest in a long series of taxing and vindictive insults. For a while it seemed she would not honor it with an answer.

The matter was personal, she said at last. She frowned. She let her head loll wearily from side to side. And besides, she added, the Chinese didn't talk cheap about their feelings the way foreigners did, but, yes, if he had to know, she and Wei-han had shared a close friendship for more than a year. Two nights ago he had come to the Song home and asked for her hand in marriage. She raised her chin and gazed up a moment at her new fiancé. For as long as she had known him, Kai-ling said, she never doubted that Wei-han would make a fine husband or that he would find a way to change their lives for the better.

Twenty-eight

HE WAS NOT, as he planned, first in line at the telegraph office the next morning. A fretful Mr. Song, dressed in his bag handler's coveralls, stood waiting for him on the topmost office step.

"So much trouble," Mr. Song said, his high-cheeked face creased into a long wrinkle of worry. "Tell Gwa I apologize. Tell him I'll pay back what's left of the dowry. Month by month. As long as it takes."

"Fine," Vincent said, though he would not include the subject of the dowry in this telex; better to break the bad news incrementally.

When the doors opened, Mr. Song wished him a sorrowful good day and trudged off to work while Vincent set to paper a message he had spent much of a sleepless night composing in his head.

> MR. GWA. TERRIBLE NEWS. I HAVE LEARNED THAT KAI-LING
> HAS A BOYFRIEND HERE IN URUMCHI, A YOUNG MAN NAMED
> WEI-HAN. LAST NIGHT SHE MADE IT CLEAR TO ME THAT THEY
> WANT TO MARRY. THE TRUTH, I THINK, IS THAT KAI-LING
> WANTS TO MOVE TO SHANGHAI, AND TO DO SO SHE IS WILLING
> TO MARRY WEI-HAN WHO HAS THE RIGHT GOVERNMENT
> CONNECTIONS. ALL NIGHT I ARGUED AGAINST HER, BUT SHE
> WOULD NOT CHANGE HER MIND. A TERRIBLE SHAME. MR.
> SONG APOLOGIZES. THE WEDDING CEREMONY WE HAD
> PLANNED IS ONLY 3 DAYS AWAY. WHAT TO DO NOW?

Gwa's reply took well over an hour. It had been, Vincent guessed, written in the aftermath of his jarring announcement and transcribed to Donny Wu over the course of one or several long-distance phone calls. For all that, it was unexpectedly collected, brief.

> DON'T ARGUE WITH HER. REASON. TELL HER OF THE LIFE
> SHE WOULD HAVE HERE IN TAIWAN. REMIND HER OF THE
> ADVANTAGES. REMIND HER OF MY BEST QUALITIES. USE YOUR
> INFLUENCE. I WILL SEND HER A PRIVATE TELEX LATER THIS

MORNING. TALK WITH HER LATER TODAY. BE REASONABLE. TRY
AGAIN.

Thus began the most peculiar and desperate phase of his summer-long
courtship, a sham courtship, though weren't the aggravations agonizingly
real? He spent much of the morning and midday studying Gwa's telex and
brooding. So many roles to play, all of them glaring and incongruent—a
family adviser, a schemer, a debt collector, a hanger-on. By late that afternoon he was playing the part of a clumsy and fainthearted sleuth spying
on Kai-ling and Miss Wang and bands of other off-duty clerks as they
filed out the back room of the rail station. To trail behind Kai-ling as she
crossed the railway plaza was to feel, concurrently, like a spurned para-
mour and the most baffled sort of secret admirer.

"Please," he said to her. She and Miss Wang and a dozen other uniformed clerks had paused at a crosswalk. He must have sounded properly
grave or pitiful because rather than berate him, which seemed to be her
first inclination, she grew flustered and hustled him out of the crowd and
away from the prying glances of her coworkers.

"Shanghai is important," he began. "I understand that. I understand
you want to live close to a place you think is exciting. And Wei-han. He's
been your boyfriend for a long time, yes? You must have feelings for him.
Now's the time to say something about those feelings."

"Not to you," she said through clenched teeth.

"Then I'll say something about Gwa. He's worked hard. He's very
respected in Toulio. People like him. And he loves you."

"Nonsense. What do you know?"

"He loves you. I say that because I've heard the way he talks about you.
He loves you because you're beautiful and clever, and if you two were
married, I think he would find other reasons to love you. He's a good
man. And you know as well as I do that he's wealthy. He can give you a
way of life, a level of living, in Taiwan that you would never have in
Shanghai. And I'll say something about Taiwan."

"An island of traitors and thieves," she groaned. "They're not even real
Chinese."

"People live better there. Better than in Urumchi, better than most of
China. I know you've heard this to be true. There's nothing that you could
see or do or buy in Shanghai that you couldn't find in the city of Taipei.

Clothes, I mean. Apartments and houses. Gwa has a sedan and a driver who would take you anywhere you want to go. You could travel if you wanted. You and Gwa would have enough money to fly anyplace in the world. You understand what I'm saying? Have you heard enough? Do you want me to tell you more?"

"No more," she said.

"Then did you receive a telex from Gwa this morning?"

"I did."

"And did you read it?"

"I read it," she said bitterly. "Now he's dreaming up feelings we never had for each other."

MR. GWA, he wrote the following morning, NO CHANGE SINCE YESTERDAY. I'M SORRY. SHE WILL NOT ACCEPT THE TRUTH OF YOUR FEELINGS OR THE ADVANTAGES OF A LIFE WITH YOU IN TAIWAN. SHE HAS ALSO SPENT AT LEAST HALF THE DOWRY MONEY. SOME ON THE WEDDING, BUT PROBABLY ALSO ON HERSELF AND HER FAMILY. MR. SONG HAS PROMISED TO REPAY THE DIFFERENCE OVER MANY MONTHS, YEARS. WHAT TO DO NEXT?

The reply:

IT'S MUCH TOO SOON TO THINK ABOUT RETURNING THE DOWRY. IT'S TIME NOW TO PREPARE FOR THE WEDDING CEREMONY. I WILL TELEX KAI-LING AGAIN TODAY. GO TO THE SONG FAMILY. DON'T ARGUE. ASK WHAT YOU CAN DO TO HELP WITH THE PREPARATIONS.

His visit to the Songs' that evening lasted all of five minutes, long enough to bestow a pricey box of enormous grapefruit upon his hosts and sit momentarily beside Kai-ling at the living room table. While the tea water heated in the next room, he asked politely if there was anything he could do to help with the preparations.

"What preparations?" Kai-ling asked.

"For the wedding ceremony on Saturday," he said, suddenly miserable.

"The wedding? There is no wedding. Have you gone crazy?"

"Gwa would like me to be prepared. Is there anything I can do?"

"Yes!" she replied. "Go back to America where you belong."

"I wish I could," he said, rising to excuse himself.

STILL NO CHANGE. SHE IS STUBBORN AND WILL NOT CONSIDER
A WEDDING BECAUSE SHE HAS FEELINGS FOR WEI-HAN OR
BECAUSE SHE DREAMS OF LIVING IN SHANGHAI. I DO NOT
EXPECT HER TO CHANGE HER MIND.

The reply:

IT'S NOT MY CONCERN WHAT YOU EXPECT. DON'T TROUBLE
THE SONGS TODAY. GO TO THEIR HOME TOMORROW. MAKE
YOURSELF READY. BE PREPARED FOR A WEDDING.

And what was the best time to arrive at a wedding that he was convinced, deep in his bones, would not take place? Twelve noon, he decided, one at the latest. As a concession to Gwa, he went first to a shop near the Hong Shan department store and donned his rented suit. He bought a flower for his lapel, yet he had not thought to buy a corresponding bouquet for the bride, and this omission inspired a flutter of anxiety on the way to the Songs' neighborhood. Once there, though, the lane, the house, the cracked stoop were as ordinary, as unadorned, as absent of festivity as ever. While the pedicab driver waited, Vincent strolled to the front door and knocked. For a long while no one answered. Then the door cracked open and Mrs. Song, roused from an afternoon nap, peered out from the living room. She had never been able to pronounce his English name. All summer long she had called him Wen-shan, a loose Mandarin equivalent. "Wen-shan," she said now. "What's wrong? What's the matter?"

"I— Would you tell Kai-ling I came by today?"

She stood looking doubtfully at the carnation in his lapel, his bow tie, his black suit jacket. "What's this?" she asked.

"Today's the day," he said.

"Stop," she said. "It's gone on too long, Wen-shan. Stop or you'll make it too difficult for any of us to bear."

•   •   •

MR. GWA. I'M VERY SORRY TO TELL YOU THERE WAS NO
WEDDING YESTERDAY. I WENT TO THE SONGS PREPARED. KAI-
LING WAS NOT EVEN AT HOME. WHAT TO DO NOW? I'VE BEEN
IN URUMCHI SO LONG.

The reply:

IT'S AS MUCH YOUR FAULT AS HERS. THE WAY YOU HANDLED IT,
GIVING HER CONTROL OVER EVERY DECISION. THE WAY YOU
REPRESENTED ME. DOUBLE THE AMOUNT OF THE DOWRY.
MAKE IT CLEAR TO THE SONGS I WILL NOT INCREASE THE
AMOUNT AGAIN.

They would not come to the door, and only when he knocked persistently
and clamorously loud did Mr. Song answer and allow Vincent to speak to
Kai-ling from the doorway. She had pulled back from her plate at the
table and was on her feet, in the act of scolding her father for opening the
door, and the look she gave Vincent, a hard and pitiless sidelong glance,
made it apparent that she loathed him. It was not too strong a word. All
the lovely features of her face were set against him.

"I have to ask," he said. "Gwa won't let me leave until I do. He says he
will increase the dowry. Increase the amount. Are you interested?"

"No," she said. "Don't come here again."

"It's the last time. Do you want to know the amount?"

"I don't want to know. Don't tell me."

"He'll double the amount. Another eleven thousand yuan."

She stormed toward him, furious, and he cringed back in time to feel
the wind rush and crash of the slammed door. This sound would startle
and sadden him a hundred times that night, because she loathed him and
because it was her final and most vehement no, and in the morning he
would have no other recourse but to pass on her refusal to his benefactor,
Mr. Gwa.

Twenty-nine

MR. GWA. KAI-LING HAS REFUSED THE OFFER. THERE IS
NOTHING MORE I CAN DO. SHE AND THE SONGS WILL NO
LONGER ALLOW ME IN THEIR HOME. IT'S TIME TO STOP. IT'S
TIME FOR ME TO RECLAIM WHAT'S LEFT OF THE DOWRY
AND RETURN TO HONG KONG. WHAT TO DO ABOUT OUR
ORIGINAL AGREEMENT?

To this there was no reply. He waited most of the morning and returned
again just before the telegraph office closed late in the afternoon. Still no
reply. Nor was there an answer the following morning. He composed
another telex.

WHY NO REPLY? NEED AN ANSWER. LEAVING URUMCHI SOON.

When this drew no response, he resolved to follow through on his
threat to leave. But when to depart? Two days, three at the most. He
reserved a seat on a flight to Guangzhou three days hence knowing all
along that without a paid ticket his reservation meant little, except as a
trifling gesture, except as a bit of saber-rattling whimsy.

The waiting was, as always, interminably real. A sweltering August day
in Urumchi could stall midmorning and stretch on for hours, for days, it
seemed, in search of purpose and direction.

The only genuine relief was reading. For several months he'd journeyed through his Russian novel at the rate of some ten pages a day,
enough to keep track of the main characters and their ever-widening circle of acquaintances. During the many idle moments of a day or even in
his scattering of languid thoughts before sleep, he might review the story
thus far and be struck by the unaccustomed sympathies he felt for the
novel's vain or anxiety-prone men, its adulterous or capricious-hearted
women, all of whom seemed to be ruled by their own brightly burning
temperaments. One afternoon, while balanced on a stair rail outside the
telegraph office, he turned the final page. He gazed up from the book

bedazzled, proud. What a substantial jolt of accomplishment to have vanquished the novel's final paragraph. And what a deep and lingering solace
to see in the novel's characters the same inner vacillation of intention and
worry, the same moment-to-moment uncertainty that he felt almost
every second of his waking life.

Books were valuable in the foreigners' wing of the Hong Shan. He had
no trouble trading his novel to a Canadian geologist for a paperback
thriller set in Hong Kong. The cover was lurid, the story more so—a tale
of corrupt power brokers and their various couplings with sultry Chinese
wives and mistresses. He read the thriller in a day and a half, though in
the end he was left with a sense of ringing hollowness because there was
no sad hope in it, nor feelings that attached themselves to any real world
he knew, Hong Kong, Urumchi, or anywhere. He longed for his Russian
novel, and when he came upon the geologist frowning over it in the hotel
lobby, Vincent proposed they reexchange the books. The man agreed,
readily. Back in his dorm room, Vincent settled on his bed, pulled back
the novel's cover, and began all over again.

He chose to do much of his waiting on the steps of the telegraph office,
closer to the source of his frustration, and where each eclipsed hour nourished his thickening sense of insult. Without meaning to, he had become
one of several regular loiterers on what was a bustling downtown street
corner. Two days in a row he spotted a dust-caked boy scrounging cigarette butts from the sidewalk crevices. Tempting as it was to presume a
feisty, precocious inner life for the boy, the presumption would not hold;
the boy was damaged, feebleminded, unapproachable. More mysterious
were two huddled and whispering Tibetan women swathed in smothering layers of red wool. They stood most of the day behind a traffic pole
waiting for something—a ride? a relative? a job offer?—that never
arrived. Mr. Song stopped by each morning on his way to work to lament
the handling of the dowry, the terrible inconvenience, Vincent's long
delay, even the day's heat, everything, it seemed, but his daughter's
unscrupulous behavior.

As for the telegraph clerks, Vincent had fallen into a bad habit of lifting his gaze beseechingly each time a clerk slipped out the office doors on
an errand. Whenever he did this, they were quick to shirk free of his gaze,
though there was something in their general manner, shy and concilia-

tory, which made him wonder if they had been following the exchange of telexes and puzzling out a sordid romance in which he was the downcast suitor.

Gwa's reply arrived late on the afternoon of the third day. A quarter hour earlier the Tibetan women had quarreled briefly and sulked away in opposite directions. Surely, there was significance in that, a personal and perhaps moral lesson Vincent was on the brink of comprehending, when a clerk darted from the office and handed him a folded telex.

The opening lines of the message, once he read them twice and thought he understood them, came as an absolute astonishment.

IF SHE IS WILLING, MARRY THE SONGS' YOUNGER DAUGHTER
AND RETURN WITH HER TO TAIWAN. THE SONGS MAY KEEP
THE ORIGINAL DOWRY. SAME AGREEMENT BETWEEN US.

At once he doubted its correctness, first literally: that letters and words had been juxtaposed in the course of transmission; then figuratively: that an incensed or distraught Gwa was playing a strange and unfunny joke. Yet the remainder of the telex, hard-bearing and practical, made the prospect of a joke seem most unlikely.

IF SHE IS NOT WILLING, COLLECT WHAT'S LEFT OF THE DOWRY
FROM MR. SONG AND RETURN IT TO DONNY WU IN HONG
KONG. YOU WILL PAY THE DIFFERENCE.

His surprise was such that he telexed back immediately and asked if Gwa was serious, if the message was real.

The reply:

OF COURSE MY OFFER IS SERIOUS. OF COURSE THE MESSAGE IS
REAL.

Of course, Vincent told himself. Of course. Of course! He hoped to energize these two words until they became the eureka cry of grave understanding. Of course Gwa would want to marry the second daughter! Why shouldn't he? That made sense! Though, in the face of everything he knew about Gwa, and the little he knew about the Songs' younger daughter, it made no sense whatsoever. It was nothing less than a jarring change of tactics, and news too incredible to contain. He longed to share it, and for that reason he sprinted from the telegraph office and hailed the first pedicab and set out for the train station and his only confidant in Urumchi, Mr. Song.

As it happened, there were several Mr. Songs employed at the Urumchi train station, but only one of them had a beautiful and locally renowned daughter working in the station office. That Song was out on platform number three unloading parcels and luggage onto a pushcart with two coworkers half his age. That Song wiped his brow with a cotton scarf and, recognizing Vincent and the likelihood of important news, stepped down from the pushcart, his odd face flushed with trepidation, as if he were steeling himself for a doctor's curing injection.

Vincent hoped it was not too great an embellishment to say, "Gwa has asked about your younger daughter. He seems to be interested in her." He hoped this was at least a reasonable conjecture drawn from a rather bareboned and wholly pragmatic telex.

"Interested?" Mr. Song asked.

"He seems . . ." Vincent continued. "He asked me if . . . to ask you and her if . . . she would agree to a marriage, a wedding, and then a trip to Taiwan."

"A marriage to Gwa?"

"Yes, he seems to want to share a life with her back in Taiwan."

"Seems?" Mr. Song said. "What did the message say?"

He translated it aloud, word by word, from the unimpassioned marriage proposal, IF SHE IS WILLING, to Gwa's telex-ending caveat, YOU WILL PAY THE DIFFERENCE. Reading it, he felt properly shamed for his exaggeration, yet Mr. Song, who'd followed each word ponderously close, was neither alarmed nor offended. "It's a surprise," Mr. Song said after a moment of earnest reflection. "But it happens this way sometimes, when there's more than one daughter in a family, both of them known for being clever and for their good looks. Two daughters," he said, as if reassuring himself. "Both of them at the right age."

But age and number of daughters had nothing to do with it, Vincent thought. Did Mr. Song, swayed by fatherly affection, consider both of his daughters equal? Equally lovely? Equally sought after?

"Of course we'll let Mei-mei choose, won't we?" Mr. Song said. "Just because Gwa makes an offer doesn't mean she has to accept it. But tell me, Vincent, why do you think he decided now to ask Mei-mei to be his wife?"

"I don't know."

"Yes, but why do you think?"

Then it was a matter of Vincent intuiting an explanation, calling it forth from a morass of opaque impulses, willing it half-formed into fruition. "To save face," he said finally. "I think while we've been getting ready for a wedding here in Urumchi, Gwa has been preparing for a wedding in Taiwan, telling his relatives and friends, his business associates. And rather than admit the broken engagement, he's willing to marry Kai-ling's sister." As an impromptu explanation, it seemed almost shockingly plausible.

"Well, yes." Mr. Song reflected. "Yes."

"It's only a guess."

"But it sounds right, doesn't it? You wouldn't know something about Gwa, some secret, and keep it from us, would you, Vincent?"

"I wouldn't. But I should say this. I think Gwa has strong feelings for Kai-ling but not for her sister."

"I know, I know. Still, I have to tell Mei-mei about the telex, don't I? I have to tell her everything you and I know about Gwa. Then she can think about it and decide, say yes or say no."

"Or you can say no for her."

"Oh, but I couldn't," Mr. Song said. The mere suggestion had caused him to shake his head and grin shyly, sadly. "You're thinking of another kind of father, Vincent. It's not a decision I can make for her."

Afterward they hurried out to the station plaza, where they hailed a pedicab and set off behind a caravan of rumbling trucks and creaking city buses. For a while they sped west, weaving in and out of traffic. Then they passed into a region of wire fences and high, fuming smokestacks. The roadside here contained no promenades or shade trees. Instead, an open drainage canal carried a slow current of heavy, rust-colored wastewater off into the desert. As they rode, Mr. Song pointed out the unvaried landmarks, the carpet works, the cement plant, the mills and refineries stationed along a wide and empty avenue that led, eventually, to the tannery where his younger daughter had been employed for the past six years.

They motored up just as the day shift was set loose and trudging en masse from the tannery's rear swing gates out beneath a tin-roofed pavilion. The workers wore goggles and gloves and nose masks and thick rubber aprons that rendered them all pear-shaped and sexless. Rotely, they began to undress, goggles in one water-filled trough, gloves and aprons in another. Twenty-some workers shed their aprons before Vincent spotted a woman, not Mei-mei, but a hunched and sad-jowled lady of fifty or more years. On her bare arms he saw more than a few examples of weirdly puckered and discolored skin. Before arriving, he had been mildly curious about the process by which hides were leached of hair and turned into leather. The drift of vaporous air from the tannery gates quelled that interest. The fumes came to him as a harshly acrid, brutally chemical reek.

It was a credit to Mr. Song that he could identify his younger daughter while she remained goggled and gloved and cloaked in her rubber apron. He called to her and waited by the troughs as she cast off her garments and washed her hands and forearms to the elbow. Once the pavilion had emptied, he stood beside her and spoke calmly for what seemed a very long while, at times shaking his head or crooking his thick eyebrows in the wake of some remark he'd made or turning back to make an inclusive gesture at Vincent, still seated in the rear of the pedicab.

In this matter, she, Mei-mei, appeared to be an exemplary listener, the ruminative sort, alert, straight-postured, keenly attentive. Throughout her father's explanation she hardly moved, except to reach in her pocket and retrieve her glasses. These she polished against the leg of her pantsuit until he finished, and then she curtsied forward a little and slid them onto her nose and nodded obligingly to him all in one deft motion.

But had she understood? Had everything been made clear? During the ride back into the city, Vincent couldn't help but recount to her the reservations he'd already made clear to her father. If not a marriage of convenience, he said, then a marriage to spare Gwa's dignity. A partnership, he said. He tried to be fair. To that end he listed the advantages as well, the same luxuries and possibilities he'd flaunted before Kai-ling a few days earlier. Yet why was it that the prospect of Kai-ling out shopping for clothes in a chauffeured sedan had seemed so apt, so inevitable, whereas with her younger sister he could barely imagine it at all?

Mei-mei, meanwhile, sat beside him on the rear bench of the pedicab and appeared to be thinking long and deeply, her arms folded across her waist, lips taut, concentrating, because there was sifting to be done through the many contrary layers of Gwa's offer.

Did she have any questions? he asked.

As it turned out, she had several. To begin with, she wanted to know if

Gwa's mother or father was sick, and whether or not she would be expected to care for them or for other sick relatives.

Gwa had not mentioned it, Vincent said. So the answer was probably no.

Would she be able to travel and sightsee on the way to Taiwan?

No, he said. Or at least not very much. They would fly most if not all the way to Guangzhou. Cross into Hong Kong. Fly to Taiwan. He'd promised Gwa they would hurry back.

How was the weather in Taiwan? Was the weather bearable?

He said it was. Hot in the summer, but the fall and spring were fine, the winter mild.

And did Gwa live near the ocean?

Yes. Near enough. An hour's drive, maybe.

And were there giant waves that sometimes came from the ocean and hit the Taiwan shore and crashed down on towns, drowning many people? She gazed at him somberly. A giant wave, she said. Then she used the Japanese word, *tsunami*. She wanted to know how often tsunamis hit the island of Taiwan, and when was the last time Gwa's hometown had been smothered by a giant wave of seawater?

A tsunami? He nearly smiled. A peculiar question to be sure, though hadn't he arrived in Toulio with his own share of peculiar notions? Toulio, he explained to her, was far enough inland and located on the island's west side. Tsunamis didn't often form in the Taiwan Strait, and if they did they wouldn't reach Toulio. So the answer was never.

She took a single day to think it over, and later Vincent asked what she had done with that day, guessing she had argued the pros and cons of such a marriage, such a life, with her parents and sister, guessing maybe she had sought counsel from a revered middle school or high school teacher. Or she had strolled to the few picturesque haunts of her childhood—that's what Vincent had done when he'd pondered whether or not to join the Overseas Christian Fellowship and move to Taiwan, that's what a thousand schmaltzy movie dramas had taught him, the means by which momentous personal decisions were made, and the Chinese, no less sentimental a people, likely observed this same ritual. Therefore, she had gone for a boat ride at People's Park. She had taken the day bus up to the pine-thick shores of Heaven Lake.

In truth, he learned, her day had been like any other: off to the Heaven

Lake bus stand to sell a few snacks and cold drinks and execute her shrewd swindle, then her usual shift weighing and soaking hides at the tannery. Afterward, she came with her father to the Hong Shan, asked for Vincent, and was directed to the courtyard next door, where he had just lost, narrowly, his fourth game of pool.

"Tell him the answer is yes," she said quietly and after a prolonged and relenting exhale, a harried exhale, as if she had been pestered by Gwa's request for far longer than a day.

There didn't seem to Vincent to be any appropriate response to this, definitely not *good* or *glad to hear it* or a dumbly patronizing *congratulations,* not under these peculiar conditions and not to the Songs' second daughter, whom, during the long term of his stay in Urumchi, he'd thought of only as Kai-ling's frumpish younger sister, if he'd thought of her at all. He didn't even know her name.

Thirty

TWELVE DAYS LATER, on the sixteenth of August, he put on a rented suit, bought a carnation for the lapel, and took a pedicab out past the high tenements to the tracts of crumbling brick and earth houses, to a narrow lane that had been swept clean and set with six round folding tables topped with red tablecloths.

A few steps shy of the Song household he paused a moment to straighten his waistcoat and practice the stately and deferential expression he hoped would see him through the long evening ahead.

A curtain of ruby-colored beads had been pinned above the front door and he edged through it and skirted by a cheery clique of guests and stood in the living room, noting how the myriad hanging bags and stacked boxes had been packed away somewhere, and how the house's cracked walls had been covered with bright red calligraphic banners. Red had become the prevailing color: red banners and scrollwork, red envelopes, red-wrapped candies, crisp red paper topping every shelf and furniture surface. The family shrine had been polished, brought forth and placed atop a red-draped end table.

"Hello, have you eaten?"

It was Mr. and Mrs. Song speaking together as a spirited chorus of two. They were both dressed in clothing a shade too festive for their age: a mint green vest for Mr. Song, a bright rose pantsuit for his wife. Mrs. Song presented Vincent with a glass of pear juice and arranged a stool for him in front of the electric fan. He must stay cool, she said. He must relax. After each remark she curtsied a little and smiled broadly. Mr. Song, too, was brimming with fatherly graciousness. He raised his woolly eyebrows and made a slow, wide-eyed inspection of Vincent's suit jacket. "A very good choice," he declared. "The color. The size. I wouldn't know how to choose one, not without my wife or daughters to tell me. But you look just right in it, Vincent. Like a magazine picture."

To this Vincent shrugged and said thank you—a complicated matter to stand in the warm glare of the Songs' enthusiasm. A portion of their eagerness, he knew, was for benefit of the invited guests. But the larger share was unquestionably real. He'd spent enough evenings with the Songs to be certain that they loved their daughters. In their own way, and under odd and diminished circumstances, they were giving their younger daughter, their Mei-mei, the best celebration they could. When he looked closely at the intensity of feeling burning beneath their eagerness, he understood that they were imploring him to do the same.

He sat with Mr. Song in the cool breeze of the fan, while Mrs. Song attended to the bride in the kitchen. Again he marveled at the change the Song household had undergone. Buzzing away in the corner was an outmoded and badly nicked television set, a decoration, Mr. Song explained, on loan for the day from a wealthier neighbor. The same was true of the fan, the box-shaped portable stereo, and a few other small appliances placed carefully around the Songs' cramped living room. It was Mr. Song's opinion that these borrowed items made the atmosphere livelier.

"Yes, maybe so," Vincent offered. "But how does the ceremony work? How . . ." he began and shook his head, confounded. "When will I know we're married?"

"Soon. Mei-mei is getting ready now. A family friend, Miss Lee, is helping with the ceremony. Don't worry, we'll start soon enough." He slipped a ring, not gold, but gold hued, gold varnished, into Vincent's hands. "You didn't think of this, did you?"

"I didn't, no." He leveled the ring atop his open palm. It seemed to have no discernible weight.

"You place it on her right hand. Her middle finger."

"Yes, but I'm trying to understand what has to happen. I mean, we begin the wedding and we're not married, and something happens— some words I need to say, maybe—and then we are."

"Don't worry about words. You don't have to say a thing. It happens when you bow your head before the family shrine and pray to our ancestors. When you finish praying you'll be married and you'll place the ring on Mei-mei's hand. Not so difficult. You see?"

"I do," he said. "Yes. I'll put the ring on her middle finger. I'll stand beside her, beside Mei-mei. Should I? It doesn't seem right, me calling her Mei-mei."

"Yes, better to call her by name."

"I will. I'll call her—it's just that I don't think I've heard anyone call her by name. All summer long I've—"

"Jia-ling," Mr. Song said. He took a wincing glance at the room's bright decorations. He sighed and lowered his eyes. "All her friends and coworkers call her by name. Her name is Song Jia-ling."

"Song Jia-ling," Vincent repeated, embarrassed, yet still relieved to have learned her name, thankful also to have understood a few provisional details of the coming ceremony.

Everything else remained half-glimpsed and indefinite. Everything else about the occasion had been cobbled together with unprecedented haste. Vincent, who'd been an agent of that haste, had spent every morning of the last week hurrying across town to the telegraph office for a daily dispatch from Mr. Gwa. Arrangements had been made. Vincent had purchased tickets on a China Air jet that would carry him and Jia-ling three thousand kilometers across the vast midriff of the nation to Changsha. From there they had reservations on a night train that would take them to Guangzhou. These were relatively simple and forthright provisions. There were, however, far more tangled matters. While he'd been away at Heaven Lake the civil affairs office had issued a marriage certificate for Vincent Saunders and Song Kai-ling. He couldn't very well go back to Mr. Zhang now and ask for another certificate to marry his new bride's sister.

It had been Gwa's idea that Jia-ling take advantage of the documents her sister had already earned, the marriage certificate, even Kai-ling's green passport with its sheaf of unstamped pages, its artless and vaguely similar passport photo. And so these documents had been express-mailed to Donny Wu, who had secured and mailed back a Hong Kong visa in record time. By these means Jia-ling would pretend to be Kai-ling just long enough to clear the varied customs and immigration stands between the Mainland and Taiwan.

Vincent, as always, had his forebodings. Privately he considered this ploy a rash course of action, lazy as frauds went, and likely to cause grave turmoil at some crucial juncture during the return trip. And yet he didn't dare object. How strenuously could he oppose an arrangement that would have them married today and flying out of Urumchi two days later?

Across the living room the clique of guests had begun to disband, the wives calling out their warm regards to the unseen bride, the men sauntering over to Mr. Song and the groom to pay their respects and dole out a ridiculous number of unfiltered cigarettes. They then followed their wives out through the beaded curtain, leaving, in their wake, an open threshold before the family shrine and a looming sense of measured quiet.

That quiet compelled Vincent to rise to his feet. The bride and her entourage were just then moving through the kitchen archway. He hadn't expected the sight of their procession to frighten him so. *Not yet, not yet,* he wanted to plead, now that she, Jia-ling, was moments away from being his contrived wife. *Not yet, Jia-ling,* he pleaded inwardly once more, and almost instantly, as if yielding to his panic, the procession halted and remained stalled for several long minutes, while Mrs. Song secured a fringed sash around the waist of the bride's dress, a pink gown complicated by too many ruffles and doily-style attachments. Holding the bride by one elbow was the family friend Mr. Song had mentioned, Miss Lee, a doughy-complected and overdressed older woman whose unhappy face sagged between bouts of manic, head-bobbing exhortations. "Very good!" she sang out suddenly. "Look at her standing tall. Back straight. Look how she fills out the dress so nice."

Though they all might have agreed with her, no one appeared quite sure how to match the fervor of Miss Lee's remark.

"A very good color," Mr. Song volunteered. "A beautiful pink."

"It's lilac," Miss Lee announced. "I know a section chief's wife who wore the very same dress."

And all the bride could do was strike an unflustered pose and endure the twin hardships of Miss Lee's shrill encouragement and her mother's finicky alterations. The gown, with its folds of lacework, took time to subdue. Once it was properly tamed, Jia-ling seemed to heave a sigh of relief. Her lips—like Miss Lee's—were gluey with wine-red lipstick. Every centimeter of exposed skin on her face and throat was deep-layered in heavy white foundation cream and then doused with powder so that this stark whiteness, along with her darkly mascaraed eyes, lent her the prescient mien of a street mime or doll—a prophet doll, glassy-featured and knowing, utterly unrecognizable as the young woman who'd once hefted a balancing pole and swindled him out of an American dollar.

"My goodness, so beautiful!" Miss Lee declared, louder than necessary and without the hint of envy that would have made her praise persuasive.

This time Vincent raised his voice to agree. To be standing as near as he was and not to have done so would have been rude. "Very beautiful," he repeated, an exaggeration, perhaps, though who could tell? Beneath the dress and makeup might have lurked a lovely young woman.

The procession surged forward again until the bride, ushered along by Miss Lee one wary footstep at a time, arrived at his side. It dawned on him then that the ceremony was a private affair restricted to the Song family and Miss Lee, and that the last members of Jia-ling's entourage, the smartly dressed man and woman latching shut and standing before the front door, this couple, these partners, were Wei-han and Kai-ling, who'd commemorated their own wedding just five days earlier in an air-conditioned banquet hall across town, a celebration to which Vincent had not been invited. Every time he thought about Kai-ling's duplicity he sighed. He sighed now. These were, theoretically speaking, his last seconds as an unmarried man, and he wasted them by turning briefly to ponder the long, smooth sweep of Kai-ling's neck and the delicate inflection at the base of her throat. A moment passed. Kai-ling glanced up and caught him looking. The result was an instantaneous change in her winsome features—a remorseless frown, an intense, brow-furrowing irritation.

Incense sticks were lit and set out in brass holders. And with that the solemnity of the wedding ceremony was upon him. The awkward riddle of it, too. Still, he knew enough to stand beside Jia-ling, to bow as she did to her parents, and then to follow along as she plucked an incense stick from the holder and turned to face the family shrine. On a lower tier sat two copper-framed photographs, presumably of Mr. Song's parents. Arrayed above were a number of smallish silver-trimmed placards, and on these were written the names of yet older relatives, four or five generations' worth.

At least he knew to lower his head at the same time and with the same slow reverence as Jia-ling. At least he knew to drop his eyelids until they were almost shut.

He did not believe it possible to commune with her long-dead relatives, nor had he prayed well, prayed honestly, in a long while; nevertheless, he promised these relatives, vowed wholeheartedly, to watch over their daughter, to accompany her, in spite of the fact that their marriage was a sham, to guard and protect her until they reached Taiwan and she was eventually partnered with her next protector, Mr. Gwa. He thought of it, perhaps rather dramatically, as a pledge of safe passage.

"Bless Song Jia-ling," Miss Lee began in a pressing and decorous voice. "Bless her wise parents and many honored ancestors. Bless the husband fate has chosen for her and bless her husband's parents and ancestors. Bless the honored guests who have come to celebrate their marriage. Bless the family Jia-ling and her husband will make. Bless the sons she will bear."

Safe passage, he pledged, and when he saw Jia-ling raise her chin and stand upright, he knew the knottiest part of the ceremony was behind them.

The thing to do then was turn and reach for her hand. Cloddishly, he seized the fingertips of her left hand, which she snatched away and replaced with her right. He slipped the ring, now blood-warm and damp with perspiration, over the knuckle of her middle finger. He held out his own hand and she compassed his finger with an identical ring.

Then there were glaring explosions of white light from the flash of a camera, Wei-han's, and the front door was thrown open and Vincent felt a panicky grip on his forearm, which turned out to be Jia-ling holding fast as they shuffled outdoors. She batted and squinted her darkened eyelids. Only then did he notice she'd not worn her folksy, thick-lensed glasses. He understood, even sympathized with, her rationale: better to be blind or near blind than to appear unlovely at your own wedding. All the same, she had accepted an unflattering dress and allowed her face to be slabbed with creams and powders. She may as well have worn the glasses, he thought, alarmed a bit by how firmly she clung to his arm, and how abruptly the narrow lane outside the Song household had become the site of a thriving celebration.

"One step down," he said, "one step more," guiding her over the same door stoop she traversed ten times a day. A congregation of some forty or more guests scrutinized their every move. Amid a galley of gas-fire woks and iron stew pots a crew of old-women cooks paused to stare at them through a mantle of steam. With so many eyes upon them, their difference in height—Jia-ling could not have been more than five feet three inches tall—seemed to him disgraceful, lurid, even. Still, he led the bride and the wedding party toward an empty banquet table at the fore of the celebration. Once seated he poured Jia-ling a glass of orange juice and himself a tumbler of beer, which he drank in a few jittery gulps. Curiously, this seemed to curry the favor of other men at surrounding tables. They grinned roguishly and saluted with raised beer glasses of their own.

Before long the old-women cooks carried over a pot of clear soup to every table. The soup was flecked with snippets of fish meat and squares of dried seaweed, a delicacy, Vincent supposed, given the distance between the wedding banquet and the nearest ocean. Next they delivered another soup containing tender balls of pork meat and then a platter of cold, ginger-spiced duck cut into finger-length slivers and steamed vegetables and plates of the same tasty scrambled eggs and tomatoes he'd been eating every day for more than two months. Both he and Jia-ling were urged to sample each course as it arrived, to pinch a spicy chicken thigh or rein in a ladleful of stewed beef ribs or lamb or gritty, underboiled sweet potatoes, the only dish he regretted trying. From the Songs, from Miss Lee, came a zealous insistence that they eat, eat quickly, so that before the meal ended they could present themselves to each table of guests as man and wife. Vincent would have preferred to stay seated, to top his rice bowl with more roast lamb and carrots, yet when the last course was served—a simple platter of quartered oranges—he was goaded up onto his feet along with Jia-ling, who again seized him by the arm. Together they turned and approached the nearest table.

It seemed then, poised before ten of the Songs' friends and neighbors, that the occasion demanded a public pronouncement, possibly a short speech. Happily this was not so. All that was required of them—beyond the general provision that he and the bride behave like bashful newlyweds— was that they join their guests in a toast. Jia-ling was handed a tumbler of dark wine from which, when called upon, she took a tiny, cursory sip. This seemed to delight everyone at the table. Vincent, already renowned as a beer drinker, was given a tumbler full of local ale and prevailed upon to down it in one, continuous swallow. He did so, twice. The admiration he earned for this was both fervid and short-lived. Always another cheery male drinker sat ready to refill his glass. When he stepped back and considered their manly ardor to match him drink for drink, and the tables yet to come, he judged it best to sip from his tumbler as Jia-ling had.

Of course, not every guest showed such open-faced conviviality. At the next table two elderly attendees, both of them women, gazed up with expressions of barely muted horror. For an instant he thought they'd caught sight of some impending calamity, a chimney fire, maybe, a rooftop assassin, when actually they were reacting to nothing more than what they must have deemed the shocking difference in race between the bride and himself. Jia-ling continued to garner praise and blessings, blessings for long life and male children. But occasionally the mention of their future children would prompt a mistimed chortle, an embarrassed pause, and in one instance a whispered joke that set half a table of guests howling and stomping their feet. He was too surprised and merry from sipping beer to take much offense. Moreover, it would have been a mistake to dwell on these slights and not acknowledge the many kind guests whose congratulations were bountiful and genuine: the impoverished widow next door whose gaping mouth was a well of bad dentistry and whose best outfit, a weirdly checkered exercise suit, was stretched and riddled with burn holes, who fought back tears while assuring Jia-ling that the color and shape of the wedding dress were wonderful, the best pink, the nicest fit, who raised a glass of orange juice to Vincent and said of Jia-ling, "I've known her since she was knee-high. They all say her element is water. Ha! They're all wrong. Not water. Not fire. Not wood. But you know her true element, don't you? That's why you chose her for your bride"; or the rowdy beer drinkers who not only believed in the false marriage but appeared glad for Jia-ling, glad for *him*, approving of the match that had been made and even a tad envious of the bride he'd won; or the dapper old gentleman, a husband of thirty years, who pulled Vincent aside and said the secret was to tell your wife how beautiful she looked each morning after she'd dressed and was ready to leave for the market, the very same man who on the subject of siring sons added, wholly in earnest, "Remember, baby girls are made from on top, but baby boys are made from behind."

These were people to be grateful for and to remember, people to sip beer with and share a gusty laugh. Remarkably, in spite of everything he'd anticipated, he was having a good time at his own sham wedding ceremony. Until now he'd not felt so agreeably at the center of this lively gathering, privy to the many nods and asides and raised glasses and off-color quips. He thanked the guests he'd just met and steered Jia-ling ahead to the next bevy of well-wishers, the two final tables, which had been claimed by a number of her fellow tannery workers and a group of her elated middle-school girlfriends. Their combined attention seemed only to embarrass her. When her schoolmates asked her how she had met her American husband, she thought a beat too long and answered, "On the bus to Heaven Lake." And would they live in Urumchi or in America? a coworker asked. She said America, then changed her reply to Taiwan, then bashfully amended it to "Taiwan first and later America, maybe."

But these laconic replies were for the benefit of her friends. She had yet to speak a word to Vincent, to utter a single question or opinion from which he might construe her view of the wedding thus far. It was entirely plausible, say, that she hated the falseness of it all, or that she'd had her feelings hurt by some essential courtesy that he, due to ignorance, had failed to carry out. She might be sneering at him secretly behind that mask of powdery cosmetics, or she might—all things being possible— have taken a maidenish pleasure in acting out the wedding.

In the end he had few means by which to know her—a blurred impression or two, a glint of wily intuition. And his intuitions could sometimes be flagrantly wrong. All along he'd been certain that Jia-ling and Kai-ling were sisters only in name. And yet, when he and the bride finished greeting the guests and returned to their table, Jia-ling curtsied down beside Kai-ling and said something lengthy and hushed into her sister's ear. Afterward both young women bit down on their lips and grinned. There were corresponding degrees of whimsy and sly kinship in their sealed smiles. Whatever had passed between them had carried an intimacy he hadn't foreseen.

Nearby a camera clicked and whirred. It was off-putting for Vincent to discover that his moment of quiet observation had been captured on film by a smirking Wei-han. The camera was set down. A wineglass raised aloft. "Congratulations," Wei-han announced, tipping his glass toward Jia-ling's chalk-white mime face, her frilly, lopsided gown, and then toward Vincent. "May you two be happy together for a hundred years," he said, a haughty blessing from a champion, a first-place finisher, to a fellow runner who'd managed merely to cross the end line.

Perhaps it was too late, too pointless, to wish him or Kai-ling genuine misfortune. Wasn't it enough to know that she was not kind, was not tender or particularly empathetic? And hadn't Vincent already invented various sad futures for the couple in Shanghai anyway? In one the vast and indifferent city would thwart their best plans and show them their true insignificance. In another they would be undone by their own vanity and lack of inner substance. He didn't necessarily believe these spiteful fantasies would come to pass. He believed them even less at this moment, lofting a glass of beer in salute to Wei-han and Kai-ling, neither of who were the type to be shamed by their hollowness or past manipulations.

"Same to you. Congratulations," Vincent said and drained his entire glass in one stinging swallow. A sharp heat tickled his throat. His eyes glazed over. Looking across the littered tabletop to the primly dressed but still resplendent Kai-ling, he had what might have been his most far-reaching intuition yet. He thought, for no good reason at all, of the night he'd spent stranded in the desert, of the stranger, the unidentified petty thief who'd ransacked his travel bag and in the process inherited Gwa's photograph of Kai-ling. A fraught gift, part boon, part burden. Such a photograph would invite serious study. Pity then its new owner and scholar, whom Vincent envisioned as a bearded Uighur man, middle-aged, beggarly, love-starved, god-fearing. It was easy to imagine this man sneaking off after evening prayer to peer at Kai-ling's likeness and from the soft-lit glaze of her handsome face and jet-black hair fashion for himself a sanctuary of undiminished loveliness and perfect compassion.

Though that, of course, was regrettable. That was folly and self-deceit, to think that if a beautiful woman turned her affections your way, you would be made whole, impervious to doubt and loneliness.

It had not been made clear what Vincent should do after the celebration, while the old-women cooks dismantled and packed away their makeshift galley, while Mr. and Mrs. Song bid farewell to Miss Lee and a jolly array of neighbors and friends, several of whom had swilled too much wine and required a steadying hand to rise from their tables. Vincent and Jia-ling were instructed to wait inside, though before they'd reached the beaded curtain a straggling drinker or two shouted out a few bawdy inducements to the groom—for husbandly strength, for wedding-night endurance.

To Vincent's ear—and to his drink-fogged mind—these remarks were a cheery puzzlement. He waved adieu to the scattering of guests. Yet once he and Jia-ling entered the relative stillness of the Song living room and sat together unchaperoned before the electric fan, the salaciousness of what had been said came back to him. He glanced at the bride and was duly abashed. Were theirs an authentic ceremony, a traditionally arranged match, this quiet recess might be the bride and groom's first juncture of real privacy, a time to speak endearments, lean close, steal a kiss, the nuptial bed looming ahead large as an ocean liner.

It was hard not to be a bit flustered by the winking ghost of that expectation. Harder yet to clear his mind and make a simple, breezy, uninsinuating comment. His head swam from the effort.

"I thought the food was very good," he said. "And so many different dishes. Very nice. Very delicious."

From Jia-ling a tepid nod, which, given her mime face, seemed magnified to the point of passionate agreement.

"I guess there'll be lots of leftovers," he said.

Through the front door curtain he spied Mr. Song stacking aluminum stools in the gathering darkness. There was something unaccountably sad about the aftermath of any celebration: the bare tabletops, the heaps of gaudy litter. More so the aftermath of the sham wedding. Perhaps it was the alcohol, lulling Vincent now into different latitudes of emotion, but suddenly he felt a great crescendo of sympathy for the bride. How sad that her wedding celebration had been only a fraction as lavish as her sister's must have been. How woeful that Jia-ling's wedding day was a fraud and her coming marriage to Mr. Gwa another kind of fraud. He was sorry for her, truly, then sorry for himself as well.

He said, "I know it wasn't easy, having to stand up in front of all those people, your neighbors, your friends, and pretend. More difficult, yes, because of me. Because of who I am."

Her stenciled eyebrows tilted upward. She appeared either genuinely astonished or genuinely annoyed. "What are you talking about?"

"Because I'm not Chinese. Because I'm a foreigner."

"And what does that matter?"

"It makes it all the more embarrassing, doesn't it? I say this so we understand each other. So we can be friends and don't have to pretend and can speak the truth to each other on the way back to Taiwan."

"The truth?"

"That's right."

"The truth, I think, is that you drank too much beer."

This was precisely the kind of honesty he could appreciate. He meant to tell her so, but he leaned back and rested his head against the banner-draped wall and before he thought of it again, an indeterminate interval of time had passed. He opened his eyes to find Mr. and Mrs. Song and a freshly scrubbed Jia-ling setting out their sleeping mats. He looked for Kai-ling. Where was she? he nearly asked. But of course she lived across town now, married into another family and on the brink of a resettled life near Shanghai.

He stood and glanced at his wristwatch: 2:16 A.M. His head throbbed dully. Worse yet, he felt stifled by the sudden smallness of the Song household.

"It's late, Vincent. You may as well stay until morning," Mr. Song said.

A sincere and kindly offer; Vincent felt bashful about refusing it. No, he'd better get back to the Hong Shan, he said. He wished the Songs good night without quite looking any of them in the eye, particularly Mr. Song, whom he liked and trusted. Where had it come from, he wondered, this palpable urge to flee a good man's dwindling family?

A bright, lemon-colored moon hung over Urumchi, which made it a degree or two easier to chart his course through the tracts of shabby brick homes. Mongrel dogs sprang from the shadowed darkness and yelped pitifully as he passed. Near the main avenue the first and only pedicab driver he encountered gazed askance at his suit and tie and, for some wholly mysterious reason, sped away. This meant a long hike north past countless blocks of gated homes and storefronts. Much of the way he walked abreast of his own branching shadow. A few destitute Uighur men called to him for spare change. He had an absurd desire to answer back, to hoist his ringed hand aloft and announce that he'd been married. When at last he reached the Hong Shan, he had to skirt by several more such slumped and destitute men crouched upon the hotel steps. One of these men mumbled to him as he climbed the steps.

"Yes, good night," Vincent answered back. He stepped inside the Hong Shan and strode as far as the front desk. There he paused and turned around. The man outside had risen from the steps and pressed himself against the Hong Shan's glass doors, and when Vincent opened those doors, the man, whose hair and eyebrows were thick with dust, craned his head inside and said, "Good God, man, didn't you hear me?"

"No," Vincent apologized.

"I said, 'About fucking time you got in.'"

At once he recognized the narrow, goateed face of Alec McGowan.

"I was wondering what kept you out so late," Alec said, squinting at Vincent's suit and his wilted carnation. "Now I know."

"Yes," Vincent said, still dumbfounded.

"You're married then?"

"I am. So to speak."

"How does it feel?"

"Strange. I'm not very good at it yet."

"And how's the new bride?"

"Fine. You only missed the celebration by a few hours."

"Good thing, too. Look at me. I'm sure to have made a scene." His hair was matted, his clothes wildly tousled. It appeared as if he'd been rolled like a breakfast pastry in copious amounts of powder-fine dust.

"You should have gotten a room," Vincent said.

"No doubt."

"They keep the showers open all night."

"Glad to hear it. The thing is, I'm a little short on cash. Have been for a while," he said, his manner unembarrassed, his stare steady and effusive, as if what he lacked were of trifling importance—bottle caps, toothpicks. "In fact," he continued, "I'm so short it's safe to say I don't have any money at all."

Which was fine with Vincent. He'd spent only a fourth of his original travel allowance. Besides, a dorm room at the Hong Shan was ridiculously cheap. And even afterward, after Alec checked in and showered and re-dressed and they went out to a bazaar stall for late-night kabobs, Vincent was glad to cover the cost of the meal and a few spare items: a pack of cigarettes and four bottles of beer, which they wrapped in paper and snuck back into their dorm room.

For the first hour, at least, he couldn't quite get over it—the incontestable sight of Alec, his lean, assuring figure, his air of sly humor, all of which brought a measure of vivified newness to the Hong Shan, to the whole of Urumchi, for that matter. An amazing thing to be awake drinking beer with his friend Alec McGowan at four-thirty in the morning!

A reminder as well that the world had its share of *pleasant* surprises. Not to mention the luxury of having so much to talk about, there being between them an eleven-week separation in which they'd each been absorbed in their separate exploits. Vincent, who secretly thought his own exploits the more remarkable, was content for now to let Alec sprawl back on the opposite bed and hold forth.

And at first it was exactly the story one might have expected. It began with Alec on an express train to Xian, where he arrived unannounced at the home of his Welsh friend. At once a party began, a reunion of two fractious citizens of the United Kingdom. A bottle of scotch whiskey was uncapped, the workday week put on hold. Too bad that on the third day of festivities his friend's Chinese wife flew into a rage and kicked them both out the door. It had taken the better part of a week and several ticklish rounds of negotiations to convince his friend's wife and indignant extended family to allow her husband back in the house.

On to Turpan, where he'd missed crossing paths with Vincent by only a few days. From there a three-day bus ride that skirted across the vast and desolate length of Xinjiang to the oasis city of Kashgar.

For a month or more Kashgar was exactly the bastion of quietude and idleness he'd hoped for: strong Uighur tea in the morning, sprawling and ancient bazaars. There was no set agenda to his holiday. One day he might lie in bed reading the entire morning and afternoon. The next he pedaled a rented bicycle to the farthermost boundary of the oasis. Evenings he walked Kashgar's mud-walled lanes and took pictures of the locals. He made friends of the staff and guests at the unfortunately named Seman Hotel. He smoked. He played cards. A privileged life, in retrospect. He'd thought of himself as a dutiful traveler. "But what's a fucking traveler anyway?" he asked.

Vincent wavered, unsure whether or not he was being tested with an actual question.

"A bystander," Alec answered. "A traveler is a bystander who's not obliged to get involved, who couldn't really get involved even if he wanted to." He'd been a bystander himself, he admitted. He'd been oblivious at times. He'd been reckless, too. One night, for example, he'd gone out drinking with several Uighur gentlemen he'd met at the bazaar. He remembered riding in a donkey cart. He remembered a campfire. There'd been some sort of corn alcohol. "It's a complete and utter blur after that," he said. "Next morning, though, I come to. There's a spotty mongrel sticking its wet tongue in my ear. I'm lying at the edge of a wheat field. There's an empty mud hut nearby. My brain's like jelly, but I've enough sense to check my pockets and belt. Passport? Yes. Money? No. None at all. All gone. I hadn't bothered to safekeep any back at the Seman Hotel either.

"It comes over me then how dire my situation is. I'm in Xinjiang, China. I'm in Kashgar, one of the most remote cities on earth. I'm penniless.

"It's a long hike back to the Seman, but even then, on the way back, I'm swamped by children and money changers. No money, I tell them. They've heard that before. Still, there's a few of them that speak decent Mandarin, and I explain that I've been robbed. No money whatsoever. They ponder that a minute. They consider the ragged and generally fucked-up state I'm in.

"This is the point where everything starts to change," he said, shaking his head at the dumb wonder of what he was about to explain. "I'm not talking about dewy-eyed charity. It's just that one of the money changers knows someone who knows someone who has a cousin who might be able to help. Off we go and on the way we stop by somebody's house for lunch. We never find the cousin. It doesn't matter, though, because by nightfall I've retrieved my things from the Seman and been given a stall to sleep in at the bazaar. And that's the way the first few days go, me being escorted around Kashgar by a band of concerned Uighur men. At first I'm looking at the problem all wrong. I'm thinking about having you wire money from Urumchi. Or worse, calling the embassy and having my family wire cash from Scotland. Before long, though, it occurs to me that from one day to the next I'm doing well enough. I'm not missing many meals. I'm pitching in and helping with some work. There's a trickle of money coming in that I spend on cigarettes for myself and my new mates. And it dawns on me, gradually, that I've stopped being an outsider, a bystander. I've stopped brooding over people from a privileged distance. I've stopped spying on them through my camera. So who needs it anyway?"

"You mean the money?" Vincent asked.

"The money and everything that goes with it!" This was his most boisterous statement yet. And at the same time it also appeared to be the last bold assertion he was willing to make that night. He sat up and lit one of the cigarettes Vincent had bought him and went on to explain how he'd understood that if he could get by a few weeks without money in Kashgar, he could do the same while moving from one city to the next. After all, there were plenty of poor Uighurs and Chinese peasants traveling about in the same situation. Thanks to the good graces of a few lorry drivers, he'd managed to recross Xinjiang Province riding high atop mounds of bundled cargo. Terrible road dust, certainly, but the trip itself was far better than some bus journeys he'd taken. And the stars at night. Well, you couldn't buy that kind of splendor.

"And how about your summer, Vincent?" he said. "How's your world? Still gray, I take it?"

"Yes. Grayer every day."

They slept deeply and late and were stirred awake midafternoon by the basso rumbling of a utility cart coasting down the hallway. Right away the many niggling demands of the new day were upon them. A shower. A meal. The matter of Alec's filthy laundry. A front-desk clerk came to the door and asked that they each pay seven yuan for another night's lodging.

Over lunch Vincent explained that he and Jia-ling would be flying to Changsha the next morning. He might be able to arrange another ticket. Would Alec like to fly with them?

Fly? Alec mused.

Or did he plan to travel across the whole of China the same way he'd traveled to Urumchi? On diesel trucks? On the good graces of strangers?

Well, it was certainly possible, Alec said. It was by no means out of the question. He thought about it awhile, his jaw set, his thumb and forefinger clamped tightly to the underside of his chin. He'd probably better fly along to Changsha, he said. He'd pay back every bit of the airfare. The train fare to Guangzhou, too. The hotel and meals.

And so it was agreed upon, though when they thought about it, the most reasonable thing was simply to advance him the money all at once.

A short while later, back in the dorm room, stuffing fourteen hundred yuans' worth of Foreign Exchange Certificates into his money belt, Alec let out a chafed groan. "Right then," he mumbled sadly. "Well, looks like I'm a tourist again."

Thirty-one

SEVERAL MINUTES INTO their flight, after a loud and shuddering take-off, fumes began pouring from the ceiling, spilling down the divider between cockpit and passenger cabin and tumbling along the aisle floor, as dreamlike as tendrils of dry ice vapor in a magic show. No doubt it should have unnerved him, this vapor, plus the rumors he'd heard about China's sole airline, how the pilots were ill-trained, how the jetliners had come secondhand from the Soviet Union, outdated models even the gloom-loving and incautious Russians refused to fly in.

Vincent swiveled about and took measure of his fellow air travelers. Alec, some twelve rows back, had closed his eyes and gone into a medita-tive trance. Other veteran flyers, the suited cadre members and Chinese businessmen, for example, batted lightly at the thickening mist with newspapers and magazines. A pair of blank-faced stewardesses doled out juice cartons and airline trinkets.

Beside him Jia-ling had tightened every muscle in her body, had locked her knees against the forward seat, bracing for what must have seemed like the imminent unraveling of the aircraft. How to explain vapor? Was it just a queer side effect of the cabin pressurizing? And how to explain mild turbulence?

"Small bumps in the air," he said to her. "Nothing to worry about. Normal. It gets better, smoother, the higher we go."

She clenched her teeth and nodded with the whole of her rigid body.

His own calmness in the face of her panic came as a rather pleasant surprise. Below him, viewed through two panes of window glass, the Bogda Shan range had dwindled away to little more than pallid mounds of grainy earth. It would take five short hours to fly southeast across the Middle Kingdom, a journey that had lasted weeks by train and bus, and all he could think of on this return trip were the things that would *not* happen to him: the tickets he would not stand in line for, the horrendous public toilets he would not visit, the pickpockets and wretched poor, the odd and isolated strangers who would not frighten him, the scores of open gawkers he would not stand before. If the plane did fail or come apart, as Jia-ling feared it might, it would almost be worth it.

A stewardess leaned over them. Carrot juice? A logoed key chain?

Jia-ling refused both. She'd refused nearly every courtesy offered to her that morning. She'd entered the airport a few paces ahead of her family and, in lieu of a suitcase, lugged a cord-bound parcel box the length of the terminal. From the start she'd worn a half-stricken scowl of determination. Her departure from her family had been like no farewell Vincent had ever seen—the way they'd quarreled until the very end and pouted in operatic turns and plagued one another with desperate advice, all, ostensibly, because Jia-ling had failed to pack a raincoat.

"On purpose you forgot," her frantic mother had scolded her. "Because you don't like clips. You like buttons."

Jia-ling: "I don't care about buttons. The coat's too heavy. It makes me sweat."

Mrs. Song: "It needs to be heavy. It's a different rain in Taiwan. Heavy rain! Isn't it?"

Mr. Song, a man wholly, utterly miserable: "It is," he sighed.

Kai-ling: "Stupid! Stupid! Stupid! The way you like everyone to worry about you!"

Jia-ling: "Shut up."

Kai-ling: "Shut up yourself."

Mrs. Song: "Heavy rain gives you the worst kind of cold. You lie in bed a month. The doctors can't help you."

Jia-ling: "All right, I'll go to Taiwan and die without my raincoat."

Mrs. Song: "*Aiya!* Shut up! Shut up! The things you say! We'll send it to you. Kai-ling knows the address. She'll send it to Mr. Gwa's family. And you'll write us when you get there. You'll send us a telex."

Mr. Song: "Yes, remember."

Jia-ling: "I will."

Kai-ling, crimson-cheeked, on the brink of furious tears: "You don't have to go! You don't have to take my place!"

Jia-ling: "Shut up! I'm going! Shut up!"

Kai-ling: "Shut up yourself!"

After that they simply walked away from her family, strolled from the clamor and grief of this argument out the terminal door, across the hot tarmac, and climbed with Alec and a troupe of other passengers up the rolling staircase to the plane. During takeoff, she reached over and, without actually touching him, seized hold of his unbuttoned shirtsleeve, twisting it back and forth, inside and out, until his cuff was a wrinkly knot beneath her fingers.

They landed and changed flights in the city of Xian. This meant, among other things, a three-hour layover and a chance for Alec and Jia-ling to be formally introduced.

"Glad to meet you," Alec said, his Mandarin cordial, his contemplation of Jia-ling earnest yet touched by puzzlement or maybe even awkwardness. The afternoon before he'd gone out for a haircut and a rigorous shave, and now, without his scraggly goatee and dressed almost like Vincent in a starched white shirt and dark trousers, he made a curiously sober impression—middle-class, pragmatic, a man of mild passions.

"Thank you," she answered. "Hello."

"I've lived in Toulio for three years," he said. "Good town. Good people, most of them."

It wasn't exactly shyness that caused her to look past him. The greater part of her attention seemed to have been claimed by Xian's large, modish airport, its vaulted ceiling and long panes of tilted window glass. She watched a young woman stride by in black stockings and stiletto-heeled sandals.

"And I've met Mr. Gwa as well," Alec said.

She considered this. It didn't appear lost on her, the fact that he'd not offered an opinion of Mr. Gwa. She seemed to recognize what this meant. "They have a café here," she said. "Do I have time to drink tea?"

"Plenty of time," Vincent said.

She withdrew from their company and began pacing down the long midway. By the time she'd reached its opposite end, they'd found chairs in a waiting area.

"It's nice, isn't it?" Alec said. "The way some women walk." He was looking down the midway to where Jia-ling and several other young women were sylphlike figures amid a gallery of shops and restaurants.

"Yes," Vincent said, though he couldn't for the moment or even afterward figure out which young woman he was referring to.

"But who can say anyway?" Alec groaned absentmindedly. "I don't know what to make of it either."

"Make of what?"

"This arrangement. Tell me again, the reason you think Gwa wants to marry her."

"For face," he said and expounded on a theory that had grown increasingly vivid over the past two weeks. The people of Toulio were expecting a bride. Gwa's persevering mother had waited years for a daughter-in-law, for the promise of grandchildren. His business associates, his childhood friends, his meddling neighbors had all received invitations to an elaborate wedding ceremony. That was one pretext and the other was something he could express to Alec but never to Mr. Song: most men harbored the secret ambition of being partnered with a beautiful woman, unequivocally beautiful, as in the case of Kai-ling. In almost every circumstance they failed, which meant that either they loved women as imperfect as themselves or they believed they'd settled for less. Heartbroken and furious, Gwa had settled for Jia-ling.

"Well, yes. Could be," Alec said. He was gazing down the midway again with a slightly pained and hesitant air. "It's possible. Anything is, I suppose."

The flight to Changsha was a shorter and less rollicking affair. Jia-ling, more tranquil in her seat, managed not to cling to him—a small disappointment; her nervous grip upon his sleeve had made him feel both competent and less alone. They landed at dusk, Changsha a thousand marks of delicate window and street light on the eastern shore of the Xiang River. Vincent wrestled her weighty parcel outside to a waiting taxi and soon they were motoring along to a rail station on the eastern edge of the city. If this was her chance to sightsee, then the vistas available to her were all quite ordinary indeed: a roadway lined with shabby stone cottages, a hazy thickness to the air, columns of slow-moving freight and produce trucks, a gated industrial complex out of which stretched a long file of factory workers, young women her own age mostly, pressed together in the damp evening heat, looking put-upon, looking corralled and unlovely.

To the west the tallest buildings of Changsha glimmered against a violet sky. Vincent knew practically nothing about the city, only that Mao Zedong was born nearby and had spent a number of his early years studying in Changsha. "If we had more time," he announced, "we could visit the Mao Zedong museum."

The reaction this inspired—Jia-ling's crimped frown, Alec's head-shaking disbelief—made him chuckle. At the mention of the Mao museum, even the driver had looked up into the rearview mirror and made a sour face.

But there was a gratifying discovery to be made at the Changsha train station: Vincent and Jia-ling would be traveling soft-sleeper. Her father had reserved berths for each of them in compartments on opposite ends of the same carriage. And what luxuries to behold! The walls were paneled, the floors carpeted, the washrooms clean. A pillow and a pair of cloth slippers had been set out atop each mattressed bunk. Attendants kept the citizens of hard-sleeper and hard-seat carriages from wandering in and crowding the aisleway. The one downside: his friend Alec McGowan, who'd insisted on a same-day hard-seat ticket, would not be allowed to visit them.

By nightfall their train had set out from the station and journeyed some forty kilometers into the Hunan countryside. A pale yellow moon began to climb above the horizon. He and Jia-ling sat silently beside each other in the aisle and watched its dappled light spreading across the fields and rutted lanes. He thought, optimistically, of what lay between them as a companionable silence, but in truth she was probably just reluctant to return to her compartment, which she shared with two poshly dressed middle-aged sisters from Guangzhou. The sisters' habits were cliquish and haughty. When Vincent dragged Jia-ling's parcel into their compartment, both had winced and wrinkled their noses.

Vincent had a compartment of four berths to himself, yet his allegiance in this matter was firmly with Jia-ling. "Never mind the sisters," he advised her from his windowside perch in the aisle. "What an attitude. The way they looked down at us with their dog eyes." Dog eyes? Was this the right Chinese idiom? He hoped so. Here, after all, was a topic on which he and Jia-ling could speak as confidants. Might there be others? "Great to ride in a soft-sleeper carriage, isn't it?" he declared.

"Very nice," she said.

"We'll both be able to sleep tonight, thanks to your father. By the morning we'll be in Guangzhou. By the afternoon Hong Kong, maybe."

Just then they passed through a short tunnel and he glanced at the biformed reflections they made in the carriage windows and caught her studying him. She did that sometimes, looked at the composition of his face, his brows and eyelashes, the thickening stubble along his jawline and chin.

"Are you curious about Hong Kong?" he asked.

"A little. Yes."

"You'll like it, I think. A very modern place." He allowed another sustained silence to settle between them. "What do you think you'll do in Toulio?" he said. "I mean . . . what do you expect will happen there?"

To this no answer. Or else an answer folded into the way she turned and regarded him, her eyelids at half-mast, a pure ebony glint that seemed to sink down and reside in the lower semisphere of her iris, that glint mightier than the homely glasses and imparting a potent yet always veiled opinion of the things she took in.

All their attempts to converse after that were feeble and halfhearted. He asked if she was tired and received a weak, indecipherable shrug. Was China always this hot in August? She wasn't sure, she said, but she supposed so. For dinner they each ate a carton of tepid rice and quaggy vegetables. A short while later he bid her good night and went to his compartment, where he chose a bottom bunk and slipped beneath the muslin blankets. In the moments before sleep he thought of the forceful look he'd been given. He'd pushed things too far, hadn't he? They were not confidants. And yet he'd tried to steer their conversation into the realm of her private expectations. Had she allowed it, he might have pushed farther even. He might—for no better reason than his own prying curiosity—have asked why she'd accepted Gwa's offer in the first place. Why she'd said yes.

Very late that night, sometime after the train had crossed into Guangdong Province, they passed into a monsoonlike storm. Within his soft-sleeper compartment the effect was almost quaint, a faint throbbing on the carriage rooftop barely louder than the whirring of the overhead air conditioner. He pulled back the lace curtain and found the window glazed with rain. Then a peel of lightning, a white-veined brightness, and a railside fruit orchard flared into view. The orchard floor lay glutted in streaming water, and he made out a plow ox leashed to a tree trunk and a ponchoed orchard worker, knee-deep in water, striving to unbind the leash and set the animal free. And though it must have been a difficult, even frantic, moment for the ox and orchard keeper, Vincent was frankly glad to be seeing it from his sleeper berth and to know just what his soft-sleeper ticket had bought him: a luxurious encapsulation, a welcome degree of remove. His wish then, his secret hope, was to pass from China and chaperone Jia-ling on to Taiwan at this same aloof distance.

.   .   .

He was up at dawn the next morning and out on an aisleside stool sipping tea before any other passengers had stirred from their compartments. There was an itinerary to plan, the mode of travel—train, bus, night ferry—by which they could enter Hong Kong. He worried about Jia-ling's borrowed documents and then about the hard look she'd given him the night before. A short time later the intercom sounded and the steward announced their arrival in Guangzhou twenty minutes hence. Compartment doors jolted open. Sleep-addled riders gathered up their bags and began crowding the bridgeways between cars. He sat and waited for Jia-ling. The outer districts of the city appeared and soon after the train shuddered and braked against the rail. Still she did not come out, and when they halted at the station, he finally knocked and drew back her compartment door.

She was there inside, kneeling before her parcel box, repacking the topmost layers of clothing and books and paper-swaddled odds and ends. The compartment window was open. She'd placed a few items on the sill: a paperback book, two bananas, a small, ornately carved teak box. A hand shot up from outside the train. It brushed across the spine of the book, which shifted and toppled inward. More cautiously now, the hand pinched the end of a banana, patted over and settled on the teakwood lid, wavered a second, decided, snatched the box out the open window.

"Ohhh," Jia-ling whispered.

The hand reached back in and swiped the bananas.

Vincent lunged toward the sill. "Thief," he shouted and glimpsed a boy's shirtless back burrowing beneath the undercarriage of an adjacent train. "I'll get it back," he swore. But where had the sudden bravado in his voice come from? He'd never before made—much less kept—this variety of promise. Nevertheless he elbowed his way through the carriage. Yet even after he jumped down from the bridgeway there remained another train, some twenty cars long, separating him from the thief. He circled the train's shorter end and climbed a redbrick freight platform. From the platform he spotted a boy and then three others, all of them shirtless, all of them clutching plundered booty to their bare chests and running in a gleeful zigzag toward a sagging wire fence, toward a weedy embankment and a thicket of tin-metal shacks beyond. They were yards ahead of him already, squirreling up the embankment, and the chase he gave, as far as the buckled fence, was mostly bluff. He paused and wiped sweat from his brow. Then he jogged back to let Jia-ling know that the loss of her teak-wood box would be permanent.

What she said was, "It's not important anyway." She made this remark while tying up the strings of her parcel box, her face strained and blushing and in no way reconciled to the loss. "I didn't intend for you to run wild across the tracks," she said. "Because the box and what was in it wasn't worth anything."

He knew fundamentally that she was lying, more so that she'd lost something of value, most likely a thing of personal consequence rather than an object of monetary worth. It was not just a guess based on the frailty of her expression. He *knew* her, or thought he did, at least in that one moment.

The carriage aisle had cleared, and disembarking was a matter of handing Jia-ling his shoulder bag, then gathering up her parcel box and bearing it down the carriage steps. Alec was waiting on the lip of the gangway. His clothes were disheveled, as if they'd been wadded up and slept upon. The underside of his travel bag hung wrinkled and damp.

"Miserable storm," he said. "Complete disaster. The window seals leaked. The toilet backed up. My carriage was a rolling shithole."

"Did it storm?" Vincent asked.

"Oh, fuck off."

"I must have slept through it."

"Fuck off," he repeated, only this time there was a tenor of real irritation in it, a genuine bleakness.

"Jia-ling had a wooden box of hers stolen. A minute ago. Right out through the compartment window."

"Guangzhou," Alec groused. The city itself had become an affront. "Let's check the schedules. We catch the right bus, we'll do fine. Think of this, we could have our lunch in Hong Kong."

Vincent volunteered to pay for that lunch, offered gladly, just like he planned to buy them rooms later that day in one of Kowloon's more upscale hotels. They deserved certain luxuries. He had been so frugal in his travels, and now, close to the end, he longed to be gracious.

An hour later they were settled into the plush, reclining seats of a tour bus, wheeling along a meshwork of cracked and twisting byways. The streams they crossed over were all swollen with the previous night's rain. Gradually, though, the highway widened and rolled out before them in a long, straight plane of pavement. Their bus became part of a southbound rank of potbellied cement mixers and flatbed trailers stacked high with iron rods. Sprawled upon the rods were scores of muddied construction workers sleeping shoulder to shoulder within the hard cradle of the truck bed.

Vincent couldn't stop the forward rush of his thoughts, the anticipation of arriving in Kowloon's tourist district, its latitude of privilege, its host of Western-style indulgences. A night in Hong Kong, he thought. Suddenly he was as wistful as a furloughed sailor. And then tomorrow— could it be?—they would fly to Taiwan. At the airport there would be a meeting with Gwa that might easily turn sour. But afterward Vincent could lie low for several days in a hotel. He could book a reasonably priced air ticket to America. In four short days, in a week, surely, he would be a repatriated son welcomed back into his parents' Red Bud farmhouse.

Curiously enough, the thought didn't oppress him as it once had. What before had seemed a diminished life, a life of falseness and lingering disgrace, now seemed tolerable. He still cringed at the thought of Trudy crouched upon his bed and at his own abysmal judgment in their affair— a grave mistake, yet thankfully not a tragic one. But it was possible, wasn't it, that he could return home and admit his transgressions? That's what honest adults did, after all, admitted their worst failings to those they loved and to those who deserved to know, without revealing the sordid and desperate minutiae of what had happened. A powerful relief to understand this! He couldn't have known such relief just three months earlier. And it wasn't merely the passage of time that had lessened his remorse. The hard traveling had changed him. All the lonely spying he'd done along the way had given him a certain inward perspective.

Some thirty kilometers later their caravan slowed and crept toward a sand-colored shelter of sorts, a wide, depot-style building with twin wings stretching across the roadway. Each vehicle was brought to a halt, its cargo perused by stony-faced PLA soldiers. Riders, drivers, construction laborers were sent scurrying into the depot, where they offered up documents before a council of inspectors. When their own bus was pulled over, he and Jia-ling gathered their papers and jockeyed for position in line.

"This is the border?" he asked Alec, who had found a niche several places ahead.

"Yes. The border to Shenzhen."

"To Shenzhen?"

"To the Shenzhen Special Economic Zone. Nothing to worry about. It's the unemployed Chinese they're trying to keep out, the scroungers, the desperate sort. I suppose Shenzhen's far too special for certain types."

At least the line moved quickly. Vincent showed his opened passport and skirted past the inspector's counter. He had to return, though, and stand beside Jia-ling while the inspector pondered their marriage certificate, pondered and yawned and, after a fitful examination, waved them through.

Shortly after they'd resettled on the bus, a Chinese passenger, a fortyish gentleman, stepped into the aisle to address them. He wore a dark uniform with perfect creases along the sleeves and trousers. His broad, hairless forehead was shining as if it had been recently glossed with lotion. "You are a new husband?" he said to Vincent. His English was plodding and flat. It didn't sound much like a question.

"I am," Vincent said.

"And you are a new bride?" he asked Jia-ling, who gave a hapless shrug and turned away. "You are both sad," the gentleman continued. "You are both sad to be leaving my country?"

"We are," Vincent said. He was aware of other riders listening in, and, in spite of how little they might understand, he added, for their benefit, "It's a beautiful country."

From across the aisle, from Alec, came a derisive snort.

"My country is beautiful," the gentleman said. "I saw your passport. I know your country is America. Did you know that in Chinese we call America 'the beautiful country'? So there, we both come from beautiful countries." He turned his shiny forehead toward Alec. "Are you sad to be leaving my country?"

"I'm on the brink of tears," Alec said.

"And what is the name . . . that . . . which . . . you call your own country?"

"Scotland."

The man closed his eyes and meditated on the name.

"Scotland," Alec repeated, this time in Chinese.

The man flung open his eyes. "Your country," he said, very deliberately, "is famous for . . ." He paused and searched for a word, folded his hands on the seat top and ruminated on the many possibilities. His tireless patience was remarkable. He seemed used to having an audience of listeners abide his silence. For more than a minute he searched and then he said, "Oxford University." Discovering the name delighted him. "Your country is famous for Oxford University."

Alec scowled bitterly. He heaved his chest. "I studied at Oxford University."

"Oxford. Some say it is the best university. Some say—"

"Fucking right, it's the best. I studied there. Five years. You know what I studied those five long years?"

"Ahhh." The gentleman grinned, ready to embark on another long rumination.

"I studied wankers," Alec said. "All types, all varieties. But mostly those five years I concentrated on the Chinese wanker."

"Chinese wanker?"

"Yes. Colossal fucking bore, the Chinese wanker."

"Cole-oss-el?" the man said.

"Love to hear themselves talk. Complete idiots when it comes to geography."

"Gee-og-raphy. This word I know."

"You don't know," Alec said. "Sit down. Close your eyes. Think about it."

The gentleman, still grinning, nodded and eased down into his seat.

"Fucking wankers," Alec mumbled. He lit a cigarette and let the smoke trickle from his clenched teeth.

They rode on past hillsides whose muddy slopes were being grazed by a regiment of bulldozers. In time the highway narrowed and came to a barricade. The bus stopped. An officer boarded and again they were asked to hold out their documents and passports. But this inspection was merely cursory; the officer strode the aisle, prodded beneath a seat or two for stowaways, then stepped off.

Deeper into Shenzhen the excavation grew more frenzied. Hilltops had been blanched of trees and shrubbery and then ground down to a dusty steppe. From this new plain arose a horizon-wide crop of jutting reinforcement rods, some straight, some skewed at hard angles. Once up close they saw how this multitude of rods sprang from a vast labyrinth of cement foundations, where an army of day laborers worked without hard hats or steel-toed boots, just sandals and thin trousers, a snub-nosed mallet, an occasional wheelbarrow. In spite of this, the scale and conviction of their effort seemed, to Vincent, enormous. He could imagine them, after months of hard labor, filing off to begin the next project, leaving behind a tidy maze of virgin lanes and walkways, a whole new city of pristine offices and unrented tenements.

What such a city might look like became apparent farther down the Shenzhen freeway. The buildings here had risen to ten or more stories and were netted in bamboo scaffolding. Blocks of apartment units, stores, and office high-rises had been graced with tinted windows, automatic doors, sleek silver street lamps. In the open squares lay newly fledged parks, bare of sod grass, set with benches and dry fountains. The city, as a whole, appeared overly ornate, whimsical, like a lavish amusement park a week or two shy of its grand opening.

"Some say Shenzhen is the new China." The fortyish gentleman had turned around once more, had made a lectern of his upholstered seat back. "How do you think . . . how do you feel about the new China?"

"Return of the wanker," Alec grumbled.

"I like it," Vincent said. "It's very modern."

"Very modern, yes. When Shenzhen is finished, all the many people who before left China will want to come back home. They will want to be Chinese again." He let his gaze drift over and linger on Jia-ling.

"I suppose it could happen," Vincent said.

"Some say that in twenty years, in thirty years, China will be leader of the modern world."

"Sit down, you WANKER!" Alec bellowed. True, he'd spent the night before travel-lagged and damp, and now he may have voiced his opinion with more volume and bitterness than he intended. That was one way of deciphering it. The other was to hear it as a shout of bullying menace, of mostly unwarranted insult. Both interpretations made Vincent cringe. Nearby passengers glared and turned away. The gentleman clenched his jaw and fumed. His glossy brow tightened. Before sitting, he whispered something hard and venomous in Cantonese.

With that, what remained of their ride to the Shenzhen border elapsed at a wearisome tempo. They endured much of it in silence, the last blocks of empty structures, and then, in time, Shenzhen city, also recently formed, but very much lived in, thoroughly occupied. A population of smartly dressed citizens flooded the intersections. Canopied storefronts offered up a bounty of free-market goods. Overhead loomed more piercing, multifloored office buildings, glass-fronted and stylish and sided with flashy advertisements. It was not Hong Kong, not yet, but the difference in architecture and advantage seemed at times hard to distinguish.

Which might have been the point, Vincent concluded. In seven years the border would come down and Hong Kong repatriated to the Mainland. The Shenzhen Special Economic Zone was readying itself for that day.

The bus ferried them all the way to the city's southernmost tip, to a rail station and commercial plaza and finally a huge terminal that housed the departments of customs and immigration. Minutes earlier a loaded train had arrived and set loose a tide of passengers so that presently the terminal midway was one wide, formless surge of bodies, all of them pressing forward to the customs turnstiles, where they were channeled into strictly ordered, single-file queues. The long wait was tolerable if only because it gave Vincent ample time to burrow through his money belt and organize his currency receipts and declaration form. Time also to worry. What to do if Jia-ling's borrowed documents were discovered and she was not allowed to pass through? What to do then? All Vincent could muster was a hastily reckoned backup plan. He gave Jia-ling 250 renminbi. They settled on a rendezvous point: Shenzhen's largest department store. If he passed and she did not, he would return the next day and they would meet up again outside the store. "Whatever happens, don't panic," he said, although Jia-ling, alert yet poker-faced, appeared more poised than he.

All about them were droves of suited Hong Kong businesspeople for whom crossing the border was a weekly or daily formality. A regiment of armed guards had been posted along the terminal corridor. The trick, Vincent thought, when it came to armed guards and customs officers was to imagine them off-duty on a Sunday morning, a kettle of simmering tea at hand, a newspaper spread across their laps.

At the turnstile Alec directed them into one of ten lines leading to ten counters manned by ten different Mainland customs officers. So began a slow advance. Few people talked above a whisper. The waiting soon grew tedious, which made it more of a shock, somehow, to see Alec take a deep breath and sidestep over and insert himself into the neighboring line. There he hung his head and gazed down at the floor. Seconds later a guard sauntered forth and jostled him back inside his original line. He was by now fourth place in the queue. Chastised, he turned back to Vincent and Jia-ling. His mouth hung slightly agape. His complexion had paled. "That wasn't very smart, was it?" he said.

"No," Vincent answered. "What's going on?"

"If I asked you to do something for me now, something odd but important, would you do it?"

"I would, yes," Vincent said.

"All we do is this, talk along just like we are, but while we're talking you pry off your shoes—don't reach down, don't even bother looking down—just pry off your shoes, and I'll pry off mine, and while we're talking we'll nudge our shoes toward each other. You'll take mine and I'll take yours. Doesn't matter if we don't quite get our heels inside. Doesn't matter if we have to shuffle a bit."

"OK," Vincent said, meaning that he understood the directions, meaning that he was dumbstruck and fearful and pausing to grapple with questions of his own.

At the fore of the line a woman who'd been balanced on the yellow floor stripe received a nod from the customs officer and moved up to the counter. Woefully, Alec stepped forward and became third in the queue. Several guards turned their heads with a mechanical exactitude to stare at him.

"Never mind," he whispered. "It wouldn't have worked anyway." He stood frozen for an interminable minute or two. The line shifted forward once more. A man and his young son stepped up to the counter together, leaving Alec alone at the head of the queue. "You know what my problem is?" he said. "I'm a moody fucking prick. I have a bad night on the train, and I lash out, make a complete arse of myself." He took a moment to grin dryly and complete a long, shuddering swallow. "I probably deserve everything that I have coming," he said.

A short time later he received the customs officer's nod and stepped up to the counter, gripping his damp travel bag at the seams. He looked like the most humbled and expectant sort of immigrant, and Vincent was so fixated on this odd likeness that he didn't, for a while, at least, consider the customs officer behind the counter—a prim, middle-aged man with a receding hairline and a brilliantly shining forehead. This man had scowled when they'd last seen him on the bus. He was scowling now, an almost genteel unhappiness, given his pressed customs uniform. His scrutiny of Alec was unconditionally stern, wrathful, though he did cast a more forgiving glance in Vincent and Jia-ling's direction.

From their vantage, a half dozen paces back from the counter behind the yellow floor stripe, it wasn't possible to hear the officer's terse questions. They could, however, hear many of Alec's replies. And he began with a lie, began by saying he'd spent the summer in Shaanxi Province, in and around the city of Xian, staying at the home of a foreign teacher. As he spoke, a guard strolled over and began to sift through his travel bag. His toothpaste, his socks and deodorant and underclothing were set out on the counter. The exhibit of personal items seemed to draw everyone's attention. All ten lines squeezed forward. Other customs officers glanced up from their stations.

"No," Alec said in answer to a hushed and unintelligible query. "No," he said once more, twice more, ten times more, until the inflection of each *no* carried an embellished patience, a slurred kindness. The guard, rooting deep in Alec's travel bag, extracted a soggy currency-exchange receipt from a Kashgar bank. It was a gift the waxy-browed officer appeared to savor, enough evidence, enough contradiction, to warrant further investigation. He waved over a company of additional guards.

"Hands off," Alec insisted. "Hands off. Now, I went to Kashgar, but most of the summer I was in Xian. I told you that, didn't I?" He glowered righteously, was, for a moment, a perfect exemplar of an honorable traveler unfairly detained.

Another hushed question from the customs officer.

"Because I'm furious," Alec said. "Because I haven't done a thing and you've got them rummaging through my bag and I'm so angry I'm shaking!"

The guards closed in around him. He made a halting gesture that was misunderstood. His arms were pinned behind his back. There was a sudden and violent flailing about, of which he was both instigator and victim. At the worst of it, with his limbs bound and his face pressed to the tile floor, he shut his eyes rather than look up into the crowd of spectators. An instant later he was dragged roughshod down a long, paneled corridor.

Then came a lengthy recess. Other customs officers appeared. Documents were handed over, explanations made. The remaining guard swept Alec's things into a box and shuttled it away. The officer behind the counter grew harried; he summoned Vincent forward, only in the next instant to motion him back to the yellow floor stripe. For a long while he did nothing but sort papers. Then he scrawled a hasty message and had it delivered to a door at the end of the corridor. He wiped his brow, peered out anxiously at the stalled line, and resummoned Vincent to the counter.

He came dragging Jia-ling's parcel box behind him. He placed his documents before the officer in three stacks: his passport and visa and declarations form, his marriage certificate, and last, Kai-ling's passport and Hong Kong visa. When he looked back, he found long files of waiting strangers staring at him.

The officer riffled through the first two stacks, reclaiming the declarations form, returning the passport and visa. He glanced briefly at the marriage certificate. Kai-ling's documents appeared to bore him. "The man from Scotland is your friend?" he asked.

"We traveled together," Vincent said. "We met on the plane from Urumchi. Urumchi is where I spent the summer. Urumchi is where I met my wife. Should I call her over?"

"Not yet. Did you go with him to Kashgar?"

"No."

"Does your friend use drugs? Does he . . . did he go to Kashgar to buy drugs?"

"No, no. He's not the type."

"Are you carrying drugs with you now?"

"No."

"What is in the box?"

"My wife's things, her clothes."

"You went to Urumchi to get married?"

"No, not at first. I was traveling in China and just went to meet her. A Chinese friend in Taiwan had introduced us, by mail. We'd written each other letters. I just went to meet her, but after I'd been in Urumchi awhile and knew her, I decided it would be very good, very nice, to be married, to marry her."

As the officer listened, he flipped through Kai-ling's passport and at the final page called Jia-ling over to the counter. "This man is your husband?" he asked her in Mandarin.

She placed her hand, her ringed finger, on the counter. "He is."

"How old is your husband?"

"Twenty-five years."

"And you?"

She gave him Kai-ling's age, twenty-eight, and added, "I'm older by three years."

The age disparity amused him somehow. "Why not marry a Chinese man? Why not marry a Chinese and stay in the homeland?" It was not a scold. He'd adopted the mildly teasing air of an older relative.

She paused to concentrate. Then she raised her eyebrows in surprise and looked at Vincent. "What do you mean?" she said. "He swore to me and my family that he *was* Chinese."

The officer took a clear, smirking satisfaction in her joke. He heaved his shoulders and sighed, and when he was finished he said to Vincent, "You like the Chinese people, I think. You understand the new China."

"I do. I try to understand. Should I wait for my friend? We were supposed to have lunch together in Hong Kong."

"Don't wait. No. You could wait a very long time." And with that he returned their documents and waved them through.

Thirty-two

TOGETHER THEY TRAVERSED a long, windowed corridor and at the far end, the Hong Kong end, they lined up and passed through yet another counter and presented their documents once more and then descended a flight of stairs to an enclosed train platform. A column of sleek rail cars sat open and ready to take in passengers. For a while he and Jia-ling stood on the platform and studied the riders inside the clean shell of the train, those who had cleared customs and in a short while would be carried south and set free to wander in one of the colony's bustling neighborhoods. The doors squeezed shut and the train lurched away.

"There's some trouble with Alec," he explained to her. "Some trouble. We'll take the next train, maybe. We'll see if he shows up by then."

"But what did he say to the officer on the bus?" she asked. "He used an English insult, yes? But which one?"

"He said the officer was very . . . boring and stupid."

"That's all? Nothing else? Nothing about the man's mother?"

"No, nothing like that."

"Nothing about the man's children? Or his ancestors?"

"No, he used an English word. *Wanker.* I don't think the officer understood it. It means . . ."

"Yes?"

"Someone who likes to . . ."

"Yes. Tell me."

". . . touch himself."

She shook her head almost reverently. "Heavens," she said. "They'll keep him locked up forever."

Twenty minutes passed and still they waited. Another train pulled in and as it began to take on riders, he climbed the stairs and moved against the ebb of departing travelers. He went as far as the exit lanes and there, peering through the back door of the long customs corridor, sensed the frailty of his circumstance, how hard it would be to reenter without creating a spectacle, without placing himself and Jia-ling under suspicion.

He surrendered and rode the train with Jia-ling into Hong Kong proper. The trip took forty minutes, and during it he had time to impro-vise a plan. If Alec was released, he would undoubtedly head straight to Kowloon, to the tourist ghetto of Tsimshatsui, where they could wait for him outside the Tsimshatsui metro station. And if he wasn't released, then Vincent's first obligation was still to get Jia-ling to Taiwan. And what then? He could fly back to Hong Kong and reenter Shenzhen. He could contact a lawyer, call the British embassy, call Alec's family in Scotland, for that matter. Better yet, he could insist on a holding-cell visit. At once he began to practice, inwardly, the sort of blustery indignation he would need to make such a demand.

In Kowloon they switched to the metro and traveled light and fast in an air-conditioned subway car beneath the hard mantle of the city. In spite of their recent emergency, it was still a pleasure to walk up out of the Tsimshatsui subway station and feel that, in some wholly preposterous way, the metropolis of Hong Kong was his to reveal to Jia-ling.

A river of vibrant and lavishly varied traffic surged in both directions along Nathan Road. High-rises skinned in gold sprang from the pave-ment hundreds of meters into the sky. Southward, through the forest of high buildings, they glimpsed sea vessels churning across Victoria Har-bour. This flash of ocean, narrow as it was, made Jia-ling turn the corners of her mouth out in a canny, closed-lip grin.

Yet for the time being they were confined to a small quadrangle of sidewalk near the subway portal. An hour passed. Vincent strolled to a nearby take-out restaurant and returned with cartons of fried rice and egg rolls. Not the banquet he'd anticipated. By two-thirty in the afternoon he began to grow discouraged. Twice he caught Jia-ling dozing on her feet. To abandon their watch at the portal seemed, depending on the moment, either entirely reasonable or the callowest sort of disloyalty. At last he had Jia-ling stand guard while he set forth in search of accommo-dations. All along he'd intended to secure rooms in a luxury hotel, a plan that dissolved once he visited the Hyatt and Sheraton and learned of their extravagant rates. He chose instead, wisely it turned out, a less opulent and therefore less pricey hotel, the Olympic, quartered behind a Nathan Road shopping arcade. The two suites he rented were clean and spacious. Each had its own bath, twin beds, a love seat and reading chair, a sliding glass door and balcony from which they could look down and contem-plate one of Tsimshatsui's lonelier back alleys.

He used the phone in his suite to call Donny Wu. Three sharp rings and the line was abuzz with Wu's assured voice backed by a cacophony of street traffic.

"We're here in Hong Kong, in Tsimshatsui," Vincent said. "Jia-ling and I both."

"So soon," Wu exclaimed. "That's very good time, Vincent. Sooner than we expected." He asked for the name of their hotel, their room numbers.

"It wasn't easy," Vincent said. "Getting here." He wasn't sure exactly what phase of the journey he was referring to.

"Never is," Wu said. "The Mainland, you know, it's always difficult." They made plans to meet the following morning in the lobby of Vincent's hotel. "I'll pass on the good news to Mr. Gwa," Wu promised and abruptly hung up.

Next Vincent phoned and made flight reservations to Taipei, standby for tomorrow afternoon, guaranteed seating late tomorrow evening. Then he returned to the portal and found Jia-ling perched near the top step scrutinizing every passenger who climbed the stairs from the subway below. Together they devised yet another contingency plan. She would go to the hotel and rest. Vincent would stand guard through the evening. But for how long? The last train from the border would arrive in Kowloon at 9:40 P.M. A loyal friend, he supposed, would wait until then.

He handed Jia-ling the key to her suite and off she went, swinging her large parcel box out in front of her, taking a few lopsided steps, swinging it again. Several foreign tourists stepped aside to observe her shambling progress. The Chinese professionals she passed, most of them suavely dressed businessmen, glanced her way and then nodded to one another, a curt and rather blasé confirmation that another up-country migrant had crossed the border and made her way here, to Kowloon, to Hong Kong, the Pearl of the Orient.

At dusk Kowloon's neon signs began to overrule the weakening daylight. A younger, more modish crowd spilled from taxis and buses. Nearby the arcade switched on its carousel of shop lights. Outside the subway portal a strong harbor breeze sent a flotsam of plastic cups and paper flyers rattling around Vincent's feet.

Why this mishmash of sensations—the fashionable crowds and crescendo of light and windblown debris—should stir in him such a jumbled mixture of hope and despair he couldn't begin to say. No other city but Hong Kong made him want so desperately to be someone else. There wasn't a remedy for this longing, either. Except, of course, the false cures, one of which was to open his money belt wide and spend his way out of this sudden and deep well of personal dissatisfaction up to a higher station in life, a grander mood, a less faltering state of mind.

In the midst of this brooding there was someone who looked a lot like Alec McGowan ascending the portal steps and moving out onto the sidewalk, albeit clumsily, along with a flood of departing subway riders. Up Nathan Road this someone went, past the Hyatt and shopping arcade and on toward Kowloon Park. Vincent tagged behind. Perhaps it wasn't Alec after all. Perhaps it was, though. But there was no wrinkled travel bag. And this someone, this stranger, was not only thinner than Alec McGowan, but older, too, with a slumped way of walking, and when he turned and looked at Vincent, he did so from behind a bruised and shrunken face.

A mistake, a stupid misjudgment. Yet for hours it cast a shroud across Vincent's spirits. He loitered about the subway portal watching a tide of strangers scale the cement steps. He tore down several flyers and on the blank back sides wrote, *Alec McGowan! We are staying at the Olympic Hotel!*, before taping them back in place. At nine-forty there was still no sign of his friend. At ten Vincent took one last look down into the well of the subway and turned back toward his hotel.

Once in his suite he put the phone receiver to his ear and dialed Jia-ling's room number. From the next suite over came the faint clamor of her telephone. A dozen rings before she picked up. He told her he'd had no luck finding Alec. And why had she waited so long to answer the phone? he asked. Had she been sleeping?

"No," she said. "It just didn't seem as if the call could possibly have been for me. Someone else maybe. Or a mistake."

"There's no mistake," Vincent replied. He said he was calling about dinner. Would she like to join him?

She would.

And when would she be ready to go?

She was ready now.

The problem, though, was that he'd planned on taking her to an expensive restaurant, and she came to her hotel door dressed in a loose blouse and a green, equally shapeless pair of cotton pants. He wondered aloud if the restaurant might have a dress code and thankfully she caught on at once, disappeared back into her room, and emerged ten minutes later dressed in a rose-colored pantsuit. He'd seen the pantsuit before. Her mother had worn it to their sham wedding. It had a trace of gold embroidery along the shoulders and looked, by even the most generous estimate, fifteen years out of date.

The surprising thing was how little this wound up mattering once they set foot in the restaurant of an enormous four-star Tsimshatsui hotel. It would have been a staggering expense to actually stay in the hotel, but the restaurant—one side with a view of the harbor, the others walled in mirrors and brass banisters—was a luxury Vincent could afford. Running the length of the floor were two prodigally set buffet counters of fresh seafood, of simmering Asian and Western cuisine. On the way to their table they strolled past a dessert cart from which arose a blue phoenix carved in glistening ice.

The sheer extravagance of their surroundings unnerved him. Not so Jia-ling, who studied everything from the hotel's marble-white grand piano to the deft folds of her tented silk napkin, and whose boundless interest was as keen as it was guileless. They went to the buffet counter and filled their plates, and at the bread table she stood and gaped at the abundance of loaved bread and dinner rolls and assorted pastries, several of which had been folded into the shapes of animals—a sleeping and tiny-pawed kitten, a swan with its long neck coiled about its body.

At times like these—and there were several during the course of dinner—a deep munificence welled up inside him. *Behold,* he wanted to say, and throw out his arms opera-style toward the counters of steamed prawn and glazed tuna and barbecued beef ribs. *Behold* the dark waters of Victoria Harbour, her first unobstructed view of the sea. *Behold* the civility among their fellow diners, the clear lack of bustle in the buffet line, the easy mingling of Chinese and non-Chinese tourists. Handsome waiters stepped forward bearing sparkling goblets of ice water. Two tables to their left, an attentive Caucasian husband served tea to his elegantly attired Chinese wife. From the hotel lobby came the tinkling of the piano, a crisp and airy scaling of notes that sounded like the most polite form of privilege he'd ever heard.

How peculiar, how fickle, the wide range of his moods. Earlier he'd been made grim by the thought of Alec's arrest, and now it was as if his friend's misfortune somehow added shine to these luxuries.

After dinner they stood before the restaurant's enormous harborside windows. From this vantage they could see vessel lights moving among the listing waves, and, much closer, a wide beachfront promenade.

"About the subway," she said while studying the dark width of the bay. "You mean to tell me that it travels under water?"

"Below the water. Below the ground, even. They dug a tunnel right under the harbor."

"Under the harbor," she repeated. "It's hard to imagine, isn't it?" She raised a finger to her lips. A studied pause. Then she looked out again at the sea, frothy and black. Beyond it lay the galvanic brightness of Hong Kong Island. "Have you ever met Gwa's mother or father?" she asked.

"I haven't, no," he said.

"I'm thinking that I should buy them each a gift, yes?"

"A gift?"

"In case I meet them tomorrow. Meet them for the first time."

"Well, yes," he said. "I guess you could."

"You guess, or do you think it's something I should do?"

He turned toward her and received yet another forceful and complicated look, though, unlike the look she'd given him the night before on the train, this was not a *hard* look. She simply gazed at him, inquiringly and unafraid, for what seemed a very long time.

"I think it's something you should do," he said. "I think it would be a good idea."

"Thank you," she said and measured out a thin, mostly agreeable smile.

"For what?"

"For what you said. For your advice."

"You're welcome," he replied, certain he was being credited for more than advice, for his confidence, maybe, for whatever unnamed assurance he'd just offered her. Even more, within their parlay of looks and counterlooks, she seemed to be telling him something in return.

Perhaps this: it was time to stop treating her arranged marriage, her future life, as if it were a great peculiarity or the direst sort of compromise. It was time to start making practical plans. No more prying questions, either. Wasn't it a form of condescension for him to ask about her private expectations? He, who was blessed with many options, to marvel at how few she really had.

Almost instantly everything was made easier, thanks largely to this understanding, this unspoken consensus. They set off at once for the shopping arcades of Kowloon. In doing so, it felt as if they were bound together, however briefly, by a sense of shared enterprise. An ordinary enterprise at that, a gift for her future in-laws. The possibilities were many: tea, boxed fruits, pottery, clothing. Certainly there were great bargains to be had. Amid Kowloon's back-lane street markets they came upon endless tables of heaped clothing and colorfully ranked electronic gadgetry. Vincent couldn't resist making certain purchases: three dress shirts, a pair of blue jeans, tennis shoes, even a patterned necktie that caught his eye. Mostly, though, he trailed behind Jia-ling as she wandered among the stalls and shops. An hour passed this way, much of it a blur of faceless shoppers and garish commerce, except for two quiet incidents, two small but noticeable happenings, both of them tenuous and puzzling and seemingly aglow with significance.

The first began with an expatriate street vendor, a dreadlocked Australian woman who'd thrown a sarong across the sidewalk and set out her stock of incense, Thai beadwork, various purses and satchels made from hemp, and a single teakwood box. The box was an odd discovery, truly, because for a few reverent minutes, while Vincent turned the box in his hands and studied the carving, it seemed largely possible that it could have been Jia-ling's box. It looked wholly the same. Improbable, perhaps, but it could have been passed along from Guangzhou rail thieves to Hong Kong–bound smugglers until, astonishingly, it found its way here to this sarong-draped patch of sidewalk. Under the sway of this belief, this hope, he bought the box and hid it in his bag of new clothing. Just a few stalls down the lane, of course, he came upon a table containing a half dozen identical teakwood boxes. After that he saw them throughout the street market, neat rows of boxes stacked upon a multitude of booths and tables. He did not point these boxes out to Jia-ling or mention the one he'd purchased. She seemed, if anything, in too dauntless a mood. And by the time the market closed at midnight she was happily in possession of two boxed gifts: perfume for Gwa's mother, a bottle of imported sake for his father.

Still, Vincent remained puzzled by how whimsical he'd been, how gullible, to have hoodwinked himself into believing something was one in a million when in fact it was merely one *of*.

The second incident concerned a request Jia-ling had made soon after they set forth from the restaurant. She wanted a photograph of herself, newly arrived in Hong Kong, which she planned to mail to her parents and friends in Urumchi. Like a postcard, she said, to give them an idea of where she was and what she was doing. She thought it best to pose before a famous landmark, and yet she found each potential site they passed, be it a temple or sea terminal or clock tower, unsuitable. Now, with the buses and subway no longer running and a peculiar wee-hour bareness to the street corners and crosswalks of Nathan Road, he followed her south once more, past the hotel they'd dined in, to the very tip of the Kowloon peninsula. There she found her landmark.

And an unlikely landmark at that, the Hong Kong Space Museum. It appeared before them like a gigantic blank globe, or small planet, even, brought down to earth and embedded amid an assemblage of monolithic outer buildings. At night the enormous honeycombed globe shone with a radiant gold light.

She chose to stand in an open plaza some twenty meters before the globe, her feet pressed together, her back regally straight, her glasses plucked from her nose and deposited in the pocket of her pantsuit. With her chin jutted out and her general tight-lipped regard, she might have been the museum's loyal night watchwoman.

Looking at her through the viewfinder of his camera, he felt the last wisp of his earlier munificence fall away. A wearisome reluctance began to squeeze his heart. She had such a misguided sense of style. There was an odd and spiteful rivalry between her outmoded rose pantsuit and the museum's ultramodern design. To make matters worse, she could not be persuaded to set aside her boxed gifts, which she insisted on holding in the crook of each arm.

Once they finished, she turned about and pondered her surroundings. "Maybe I should have stood nearer the globe," she said. "Or worn different clothes."

"It'll be fine," he assured her. "We'll develop the photos tomorrow. If you don't like them, we'll have time to take a few more."

All the way back to their hotel she walked beside him without speaking. In the panel mirrors of the hotel elevator she gaped at herself and made a sour face. "But how did I look?" she asked.

"Fine," he said after a moment's pause. "You looked just right." The elevator slid open. He walked her to the door of suite 515.

"I wore the wrong clothes," she said. "I don't look like anybody else in this city."

"Neither do I," he replied. As proof, he tugged at the sleeves of his

Uighur dress shirt and grinned self-mockingly. He thought this bit of lightheartedness the right note on which to say good night, yet when she opened the door of her suite and turned on the light, he saw that the stolid expression she'd worn much of the evening was turning inward, dissolving into a scowl of private anguish.

"Jia-ling?" he said.

Her lips trembled. She wasn't the type to sob—still she pulled the glasses from her face, pinched the ridge of her nose.

"You shouldn't let it bother you," he said. What else could he do to console her? In college he and his campus ministry house friends were forever comforting one another with chaste hugs. He was ready to do so now, yet nothing about her guarded demeanor looked open to an embrace. "Once you've settled in Taiwan, you can wear whatever clothes you like," he offered. "I'm sure Gwa—"

"It won't matter to Gwa how I dress," she said. She'd steadied herself enough to look up and hold Vincent's gaze. "Gwa's thoughts and feelings will be with my sister. I'm not complaining. I knew it before I ever agreed to go to Taiwan. I just wanted a good photo of myself to send back to Urumchi. I wanted people to see it and know that I'm a successful person."

"You are a successful person."

She winced. *By what measure?* she seemed to be asking. "I had a reputation in the tannery where I worked," she explained more urgently. "A good one. People thought I was clever. They believed I was heading toward something good. A better position. A good marriage. There were people who knew me and knew my sister and thought that I was the jewel of the family."

With her glasses off and the whole of her face lit with feeling it did not seem so outlandish a claim. Again he overcame the urge to embrace her, though he couldn't stop from reaching out to place a hand upon her shoulder. Before his hand had settled, before he'd even touched her, her entire body went rigid.

She gave him a sharp, incredulous look. "What are you trying to do?" she asked.

"Help you," he said.

"Help me what? Help me feel better?"

He nodded weakly.

"You think that's possible—to touch me and say a few flattering things and have me believe it? All summer long you sat in my home looking at my older sister like a starving man. And now you're going to say a few words and make me feel good about my situation?"

"No," he said. "Jia-ling—"

"You think I'm that stupid? That desperate?"

His face burned. "No, of course not. I'm *sorry*," he said, though the tone was wrong—angry, defeated, rather than penitent. He glanced, miserable and ashamed, up and down the empty hallway. Then he said good night and walked a few unsteady steps to the door of his suite.

Once inside he stood and put his forehead against the locked door. He felt the deep ache of embarrassment, of indignation. He shouldn't have let himself get involved. How utterly unfair that she should show him her anguish, then chastise him at the first sign of his concern. It was too much, really. To feel unexpected tenderness for a person one moment and in the next to be reminded of his own flawed judgment.

He paced the floor a few times and afterward slid open the balcony door and listened to the muffled clangor and moan of Victoria Harbour's marine traffic. There were two tall cans of imported beer in the room's minifridge. He opened one and took a hearty gulp. "Cheers," he said sourly and tilted back the can. From time to time he took a peevish glance at the wall that separated his suite from Jia-ling's. Was she miserable? He hoped so. He hoped she was wretched, collapsed on her bed, regretting the things she'd said.

A while later he weighed the half-empty beer in his hand and it came to him that if he bided his time patiently and drank his beer in even swallows, then by the time he finished his can Alec would have seen the signs posted in the subway portal and found his way here to suite 517 of the Olympic Hotel.

He sat on the bed and waited. His body seemed to be winding down, his anger a slackening pulse in his veins. He retrieved a notepad and hotel pen from the dresser and tried to compose a list of things he would accomplish a few days hence when he was home in Red Bud, Illinois.

Explain to parents.

Pay back loans.

Find a job.

Two A.M. came and passed. He allowed his eyes to squeeze shut. Soon, he thought. There will be footsteps in the hallway, a knock on the door.

Much later still, he woke and found the balcony curtains billowing faintly from a harbor breeze. His empty beer can had rolled almost to the end of the mattress. Without quite intending to, he'd managed to crawl fully clothed beneath the covers of his bed.

Several times throughout the night he woke again to the ding of the elevator sliding open and the soft plod of footsteps, though whoever made these steps passed by his door and continued down the hallway.

In the morning he woke groggy with only a half hour to shave and shower before his meeting with Donny Wu. He dressed quickly, choosing from the previous night's purchases a pale green dress shirt, which he wore straight from the package. As an afterthought, he pulled his new necktie from his bag and threaded it through his collar.

He'd almost no idea why he'd included a tie until he got to the lobby and saw an impeccably dressed Donny Wu standing at an untended stretch of the hotel front desk. He wore a gray three-piece suit, the jacket unbuttoned, a centered silk tie trailing from his neck to the folds of his vest. He was busy reading a newspaper that he'd spread open at his leisure across the mahogany countertop.

"Well?" Donny Wu offered. He stepped back and considered Vincent with a wry confidence, a businessman's aplomb, before reaching forward and shaking hands. "You've made it," he said.

"I have. Good to see you."

"Good to see *you*."

They grinned at each other warily, falsely, both of them boyish young men adorned in neckties.

There was a café adjoining the hotel lobby and Vincent nodded toward it and suggested they sit for a cup of coffee. "Or breakfast?" he said. "If you haven't eaten."

But this suggestion only caused Donny Wu to sigh ruefully. "I'd like to, Vincent. But there's no time for it. And I don't have so much to say anyway." He folded up his newspaper and tucked it under his arm. Then he gripped his vest with one hand and concentrated, as if he were a young statesman on the verge of a grave and untested address. At least he'd abandoned his blue contact lenses. His eyes this morning were naturally dark and earnest and framed by a pair of tortoiseshell glasses. "Gwa," he began. "He's still upset about the woman, the older sister."

"Kai-ling."

"That's right. He's still upset about Kai-ling. I guess he feels that you could have done better . . . or done something different. Maybe he thinks it's your mistake, your fault, partly or mostly."

"She'd made up her mind," Vincent said. "There was nothing I could do."

"I understand. But Gwa, he's upset, he's angry. You didn't bring Kai-ling back, so the way he sees it is that the agreement between you is broken. He doesn't feel that he has to pay you. So he's not paying you. Not anything. Not one more dollar."

Vincent took a deep breath. "I see."

"I'll tell you something else. He wanted to find a way to take back the money he'd already paid you, whatever was left, whatever you hadn't spent. Ha! Imagine that! It's funny to think about because the price he'd have to pay someone to collect this money was probably the same or more than whatever you had left. He changed his mind, though, Gwa did. I'll tell you why. It's one thing to go to a house or hotel room and force someone to pay back money in private. But it's another to accompany them out in public to the bank and make them close out an account. So you see the advice I gave you to keep your money in a bank was really very good, wasn't it?"

"I guess so. Yes." His face had reddened. Somehow the thought of having his money forcibly collected, the threat of it, embarrassed him deeply. "But Gwa needs to understand that there was no talking Kai-ling out of her decision. I told him that in the telex. I'll tell him again when I meet with him in Taiwan."

"No, he doesn't want a meeting."

"What?"

"He doesn't want one. It's not necessary."

"But how can that be?"

"A meeting isn't necessary because Gwa was here this morning, early. He's already met the young lady from Urumchi, Kai-ling's sister—Miss Song, is it?—and they've left together. They're on their way to Taiwan."

"Taiwan . . . how?" Vincent stammered. "On their way?"

"That's right."

"Gwa was here in Hong Kong?"

"He and his assistant have been here for a few days, waiting." Wu wrinkled his slender nose. "But I told you that yesterday on the phone, didn't I?"

"You didn't, no."

"I thought I did tell you. I thought I'd made it clear."

Once again they regarded each other, this time without grinning. Vincent made no effort to hide his skepticism. He shook his head, dismayed. Donny Wu gazed back at him, blamelessly, from behind the lenses of his new glasses.

"She left this morning?" Vincent asked, incredulous. "Early?" He could sense his pulse quicken, though not hugely, not what some called a heart-racing pulse. No, this was a subtle acceleration that felt as if it might be permanent.

"An eight-thirty flight, I believe."

"Then they're in Taipei already."

"They're in Taiwan, yes. But they flew to Kaohsiung instead. It's a shorter flight. Besides, Gwa likes the airport and the city better. There are mountains outside Kaohsiung that he likes to go hiking in. There's a buffet restaurant in the city that's one of his favorites. So he's treating Miss Song to both today, I think. A hike in the mountains. A big lunch."

"I don't understand this," Vincent said, more forcefully now. "If you knew Gwa was taking her this morning, why didn't you tell me?"

To this Wu crossed his arms and made a decidedly sullen face. Whatever modest rancor there'd been in Vincent's questions appeared not to be to his liking. He leaned against the front desk, frowning, biding his time. "Like I explained before, Gwa is still unhappy about Miss Song's sister," he said, his tone judicious, instructive. "He doesn't want to have a meeting. He doesn't want to pay you any more money. There's nothing you can do about that. But it does make your job a little easier now, doesn't it? You're in Hong Kong, after all. You can stay here and sightsee awhile. Or you can fly anywhere you like. You still have money in the bank, don't you? It could be worse, I think. So really, what more do you want?"

Vincent was pacing away toward the elevators, one of which opened in time for him to step aboard. He watched the numbers scroll upward and counted the slow-lapsing seconds between floors. In the fifth-floor hallway he found the door to Jia-ling's suite wedged open. He looked inside. What had he expected to find? Strewn clothing? An overturned desk lamp?

Instead, an amber-skinned Indian woman was at work in the bathroom channeling a mop between the sink and tub. Jia-ling's weighty parcel box was gone. Nor was there any sign of the gifts she'd bought for Gwa's parents. Beyond that the suite appeared utterly ordinary. The

Indian housekeeper, however, looked exhausted. And she had yet to vacuum the carpet and make Jia-ling's queen-size bed, which had one displaced pillow and a barely ruffled bedsheet and blanket—the mark of a person who had slept perfectly still or perhaps not at all.

For the time being even the most trifling decisions were beyond him. He should go to the front desk and pay for another night's lodging. He should reclaim his money from the bank. He should gather the clothes scattered across his hotel room floor or, at the very least, unfasten his necktie.

His thoughts zoomed. He could picture certain things—Gwa standing outside Jia-ling's suite and speaking to her through the open crevice of her door—but he couldn't decide what this meant. As an experiment, he said to himself, *So I won't be flying back to Taiwan.* Certainly, the words made sense, and yet he couldn't begin to dismantle expectations he'd built carefully over the course of a long summer.

"Well, all right," he said aloud and slapped his knee as if something significant had just been settled. *First things first.* And he hurried from the hotel out into a wickedly hot August morning. Around him the whole of Hong Kong seemed to blaze with a splintered light. He trudged a few blocks to the edge of Kowloon Park, stepped off the promenade, and took a seat on a shaded bench.

What, he wondered, had he come out here to accomplish? He hardly knew, except that he'd meant to be Jia-ling's generous guide to this city. He'd meant to see her journey through to its natural end with whatever bland courtesies and congenial farewells that might entail. He'd meant to do all this with the help of his friend Alec McGowan.

And what was he to believe in the wake of all these thwarted plans? That she'd been abducted? That she'd been taken forcefully from her hotel suite while he slept on in the room next door? That she was being held hostage until Kai-ling agreed to leave her new husband and come to Taiwan and be Gwa's wife? Such scenarios were, by turns, ominous, hysterical, possible. And they all depended on an aspect of Gwa's character that Vincent had never seen—deliberate malice, a willingness to be cruel.

The alternative was to believe, just as he'd assured Jia-ling the night before, that Gwa's interest in her as his future wife was genuine. And why shouldn't it be? Was it really so unlikely? Maybe Gwa's inclinations for finding a partner were, in the end, as practical as his telexes seemed to imply.

IF SHE IS WILLING, MARRY THE SONGS' YOUNGER DAUGHTER. Maybe he was eager for their engagement to begin. And if Vincent couldn't understand such motives, maybe it was because he couldn't understand whatever mysteries lay at the heart of an arranged marriage: the mystery of compromise and sober expectations, the mystery of an unsentimental partnership.

But he would have to decide. He would have to choose, even if both possibilities, the fearful and the rational, seemed too explicit to match the jumbled truth of what might have happened to her. Either he should be rushing off to the nearest police station to alert authorities in two countries, or he should be matter-of-factly planning his return to America. To fail to decide would mean remaining on this park bench in this same pitiful state, nothing settled, nothing accomplished.

In the midst of this anxious brooding, he turned over what seemed to be a vaguely significant notion. Donny Wu had said that Gwa was taking her hiking in the mountains outside Kaohsiung. *Hiking.* It would be their first activity together, and to Vincent it seemed both unexpected enough and ordinary enough to actually happen. Plus he could picture it in his mind: Jia-ling making her way along a winding hillside trail, a little startled by the scenery, maybe, but able to keep pace with Gwa, able to heed his remarks and respond in kind with her usual poise.

To view her with this degree of clarity was almost like making a decision. He could see her moving along the trail. He could see her forthright expression. He watched her, as if from a secret window in his mind, and it seemed as if he'd arrived at a deeply rooted conclusion. Soon he was able to rise from the bench and proceed on to the nearest Hang Seng Bank and reclaim his money. With this money he paid for another night at the Olympic Hotel. In his room he called about airfares and schedules. Later he took clothes to the laundry and turned in eight rolls of film for overnight developing. In his mind's eye he watched Jia-ling hiking in the mountains outside Kaohsiung. He believed this scenario, this version of her fate. And at the same time he doubted it entirely.

Still, the fact that he could picture her so vividly meant something, didn't it?

It cost him thirty-two U.S. dollars to apply for a same-day Mainland China visa the next morning. The lines were long and slow. Once he'd submitted his application, he went to a nearby supermarket for a few essentials. By noon he had his visa and was on board an express train bound for the Shenzhen border.

At the mainland customs counter the first officer to whom he made an inquiry looked up from behind his station with a weary shrug. He glanced at Vincent's passport and let his arm fall forward in a dismissive wave. Or else he'd motioned to an unmarked door at the end of a narrow corridor. It was hard to tell which. Nevertheless, Vincent paced to the end of the corridor and knocked on the door. A grinning, uniformed guard presented himself. He was holding what looked to be a steaming bowl of egg drop soup in his hands. Behind him a volleyball was being batted to and fro. Apparently, human liveliness was tolerated in this room, though it wasn't permitted in the customs terminal itself. And did the guards and officers gathered here know of a Scotsman named Alec McGowan? Indeed they did. Several of the guards, after all, had wrestled Alec to the floor and dragged him off to the search room by the ankles and wrists. Now they spoke of him with a cheery professional regard. He was no longer staying at customs and immigration, they said. He'd been sent elsewhere. They wrote out his new address on the back of a business card. But where was he? Vincent asked. Shenzhen City jail, they said. This was what he expected, yet to have it spoken aloud was still a shock. He carried the card outside the terminal and handed it to the first taxi driver he saw.

At once he began to square himself for the task ahead. But his taxi seemed to accomplish its journey in a single mad burst of speed. A pinwheel of shops and canopied fruit stands flitted by outside, and already the taxi was decelerating, the driver asking for his six-yuan fare. Vincent was let out before a large flag-fronted government building, one of a common class of structures that shunned Asian ornamentation in favor of bare-boned utility and forward-looking nationalism. It was almost impossible to stand before such a building and form a precise notion of what a Mainland Chinese jail would *feel* like, what flavor of desperation it might contain.

A score of uniformed policemen worked the counters of the main lobby. Suited cadre strolled the hallways. Several clusters of ordinary citizens—relatives of the incarcerated?—waited against one wall. The line Vincent was in moved quickly enough. In just a short while he had his elbows on the counter and was explaining to a patient and mostly interested young officer that his friend, the Scotsman Alec McGowan, had been arrested at the border two days earlier and brought to the city jail.

Might it be possible to visit his friend? Might it be possible to pass on a few items, a few simple things, his friend might need?

"No, I don't think so," the officer said. "I'm sorry." He appeared to mean it. "You'll have to come back during visiting hours on Sunday afternoon. You may be able to see your friend then."

But he couldn't come back on Sunday afternoon. Earnestly, he explained why. He was only in Shenzhen City for the day. Tomorrow or the day after he would be flying back to America. "If there's any way I could speak to him," he implored the young officer. "If there's any way you could think of." He pulled two cartons of cigarettes from his bag and slid them across the counter in one unwavering motion.

The officer looked upon them as if he'd been handed something antiquated and amusing—a monocle or a pocket watch. He kept them just the same.

"I would only need to talk to him for a few minutes," Vincent said.

"I understand. But there may not be anything I can do."

"Just a minute or two to make sure he's all right. And we don't even have to talk about his case. I wouldn't mind if you or another officer was present. The Scotsman and I can speak together in Chinese if you like."

"No need for that. He's already made his confession."

"To what?"

"To everything."

"Everything?"

"Everything that he did. Everything that he's guilty of."

He nodded contritely as if he understood. There was nothing to do then but join the conclave of ordinary citizens against the far wall, to stand perplexed in their midst and ponder his friend's relative guilt. He had his suspicions, of course. Yet what else could he do but wait? Occasionally the officer would rise and gaze across the lobby with a look of pointed concern. The middle and late afternoon passed this way. Once, the officer motioned Vincent over and told him that a meeting in either the cell block or visiting hall would not be possible. But Vincent stayed on anyway, and an hour and a half later at six o'clock, as a bevy of jail workers and guards were filing out the doors, the young officer rushed over and said, "All right, quickly now," and led him out a back corridor of the jailhouse. They hurried across a paved courtyard and then into the back room of what might or might not have been a police station.

Inside this back room a small band of Chinese prisoners was being videotaped by a Shenzhen City news crew consisting of a reporter and cameraman. Each prisoner was led forward in leg and wrist shackles and then handcuffed to a horizontal bar jutting from the tiled wall. The guards stepped away. A powerful lamp was turned on. For nearly two minutes the prisoner tried hiding his head in his arms while the reporter cajoled him to show himself and the cameraman veered about in pursuit of the best angle. Vincent observed the videotaping of three prisoners, each of them gangly and demure, and then he turned and noticed that the young officer was gone and a shackled Alec McGowan was in line waiting to go before the camera.

There had been many times before they were friends and even a few afterward when Vincent had been an audience to the Scotsman's recklessness and overindulgences and had wished that events would turn in such a way so that Alec would be handed down a swift, ineluctable lesson. Seeing him now cured Vincent forever of this particular desire. All the banalities of incarceration appeared, in this instance, to be true. Alec's face was slack and stubbled. His clothes sagged. He looked utterly hopeless. Goaded forward to be videotaped, he worked his shackled legs in a dawdling two-step that was all the more unnerving because it mirrored, in every nuance, the slumped and lagging gait of the sickly stranger Vincent had misidentified outside the Tsimshatsui subway portal. What could account for such a striking similarity? Vincent did not know, but it was startling nonetheless, the strange and secret channels by which life seemed to cross-reference itself.

Once he'd been cuffed to the bar, Alec, who had no relatives in the greater Shenzhen viewing area, peered undaunted into the round lens of the video camera. In his own wordless and glum manner, he seemed to be nodding to whoever might be on the other side of that lens, tipping his head forward ever so slightly to concede what was most likely a moot point in an altogether piddling disagreement. *Very well,* he seemed to be gesturing over and over again. *Have it your way.* It wasn't until the bright lamp was switched off that he turned and with a drawn expression noticed Vincent.

Two stools were shuttled across the room. Alec, still handcuffed to the wall, was permitted to sit. A guard summoned Vincent forward and searched the contents of his shopping bag. A pen and bottle of vitamins were tossed aside. Alec would be allowed to keep a pad of paper and a carton of cigarettes on the condition that the carton be opened and a pack given to each of the guards and news crew. They would all have a smoke, the guard said, setting fire to Alec's cigarette. After that they would return to the jailhouse.

Vincent took a seat on the second stool. "Are you all right?" he said. It was at once the most practical and the most useless thing he could think to ask. Perhaps it was fitting that he received no answer. "Someone knows you're here?" he tried again. "Someone at your embassy, maybe? You've called someone?"

There was a reply this time, though it was indecipherable. Alec's voice had ebbed down into a new low-toned and garbled register.

"Speak up, Alec. It does no good to mumble."

He cleared his throat and blinked his eyes dully. Vincent had to lean forward to make sense of his words and learn the discernible facts. Yes, Alec said. The British embassy had been contacted. Word had been sent to his family in Scotland. In a few days an attaché would travel down from the consulate-general in Guangzhou to see him. He'd already spoken briefly to the attaché over the phone.

"What did he say?"

"Nothing useful."

"He must have said something."

"He said that if what I liked to do was smoke hashish, I should have gone to Amsterdam or stayed put in my Glasgow flat and smoked till I was blue in the face." He bit down dryly on the filter of his cigarette. "And he was right, too. Entirely so."

"You say that because you were carrying hash in your shoes?"

"Sixty grams of it. Thirty grams flattened into the bottom of each shoe." He shook his head and an eddy of astonishment passed across his face. "The things I do, Vincent. The sheer stupidity."

"It's not so bad, maybe. People do worse."

"And if they get caught, they pay for it, too. I'll pay for it, won't I?"

"You never know the way a thing will turn out," Vincent said.

"I have a pretty good idea. I met an Australian bloke in Taipei once. Forty years old, a wife in the Philippines, kids, too. Loved to smoke. I heard several months later that he got picked up carrying hash out of the Mainland. I don't know how much he had. Heard it was taped inside his money belt. He got six years in a Mainland prison. He's still somewhere in China, the dumb bastard, serving the time. I'll get six years at least."

"You don't know that for certain."

"I do, though. I have a dark feeling about it." He released a long, trembling breath. "I keep trying to sort out what's happened to me," he said. "I still don't know what to make of it. Maybe it's not the hash—smoking it or even hiding it in my shoes—that's so bad. It's taking the small view of my life, the shitty and senseless view, and thinking that the risks I take are worth it." He wagged his head. "Here's a question," he said, as if a new thought was just now coming to him unbidden. "Do you think people can change?"

"Of course. Absolutely."

"No, that's the cheery bullshit answer. That's the Sunday-morning-sitting-in-a-church-pew answer. I don't think they can change. But that's not what I really meant to ask you. What I meant to ask was, do you think I'm the type of person who can survive something like this?"

"I think you are. You survived a month in Xinjiang without money, didn't you? You made it all the way from Kashgar to Urumchi without a single yuan in your pocket."

He thought about this at some length. "I did," he said finally. "I'm a complete fucking idiot, but at least I'm not the sort to worry much about being uncomfortable." He took the last draw on his cigarette and was able for the first time to glance at Vincent with any real force of spirit. "I always was a tourist, though. I was never anything but. The whole time I was in Kashgar and all the while when I was traveling to Urumchi, I had the hash in my shoes. It was as good as money. I could easily have gone to any foreigners' hotel and sold it and been on my merry way."

The guards crossed the room then, helped him to his feet, unhitched him from the wall. His wrists were cuffed together once more. He raised them in an awkward sort of salute. "I couldn't think of another person in all of China who would bother to come find me here. Except for the Boy Scout. Who else but you, Vincent?"

"I can make a phone call or write a letter if you like. If there's someone you want me to contact."

"No need," he said. "There's nothing to say anyway."

"All right then."

"You may as well go on the rest of the way to Taipei with Jia-ling."

"She's already in Taiwan." He sighed. "I don't know what happened exactly. I think . . . or at least it seems . . ." He took note of the guards' growing impatience and shrugged off the rest of his explanation. "It's become an ordeal," he said.

"Yes?" Alec replied. He looked too weighed down by his own ordeal to show much in the way of surprise. Still, he managed a nod of commiseration.

"I'm told she went hiking with Gwa yesterday in the mountains outside Kaohsiung."

Alec appeared to ponder this a moment. But if he had an opinion, Vincent never learned what it was. All six prisoners were being corralled together, pressed into a two-columned regiment of gangly men and then goaded down the hallway back toward the jailhouse from which they'd come. Vincent called out a few bland assurances: "Wait and see, Alec. It'll get better, I think."

To no avail. The jangling of their chains was impossibly loud, and Alec, the last in their group to step from the building, did not answer back or turn around.

Vincent returned to Kowloon in time to look westward through the confluence of tall buildings and see the gauzy remains of what had probably been a radiant sunset. Above him the city skyline had turned a dusky violet. All along Nathan Road a thousand jutting signs began to flicker and hum until they were shining forth together in a great, rippling constellation. Once more a forceful urge came over him to be somebody else—there was a multitude of people out strolling the wide promenades and therefore innumerable choices—and yet, regardless of this yearning, he was still himself, still Vincent Saunders from Red Bud, Illinois. He dined alone at a cramped little table in a tiny pizzeria and mulled over doubts and worries that were irrevocably his own. Afterward he picked up his laundry and newly printed photographs and went back to his suite at the Olympic Hotel.

Throughout the remainder of his evening he sorted and arranged more than two hundred photos across the length and width of his bed. A splintered record of his journey began to take shape. The proportions were occasionally peculiar: what had been magnificent in person was sometimes unremarkable on film; what he had thought at the time was a modest and hurried little snapshot turned out to have captured an interesting motion or expression worthy of serious study. There were more than twenty photos of Kai-ling in Urumchi's People's Park. He feared they might recast some spell of longing over him, but when he flipped through them, he saw evidence of her intense self-interest betrayed in nearly every picture.

He had taken three photographs of Jia-ling. One was underexposed. In another she'd been caught blinking. He couldn't stop looking at the third. He'd never seen such open willfulness. It showed in her tightly sealed mouth, her wide-eyed and formidable gaze. Her chin was raised a degree too high. She wore her mother's pantsuit and balanced a gift box in the crook of each elbow. On her right hand he could make out the soft luster of her wedding band.

More than anything, what seized his attention was the formality of her expression. Somehow she'd managed to evoke the stern sobriety of a subject in an old-time photograph or daguerreotype. She looked historical. She looked like a pioneer on the verge of a long and difficult journey.

Each time he considered the photograph he had a different reaction. It interested him. It startled him. It galled him. Who did she think she was, acting this way, like she was one in a million when she was merely one *of*?

He kept returning to her face, her fierce sense of purpose. To see it was to wonder about its inverse, its polar opposite. At times he thought he might be looking at the most apprehensive young woman he'd ever seen.

Of all the photographs he'd studied since arriving in Asia, this one had the deepest claim on his conscience. Every time he looked at it a new suspicion took root in his thoughts.

PART FIVE

The Other Half

Thirty-three

SEVERAL TIMES THAT morning he was appraised by strangers and invariably mistaken as a newly arrived tourist. His worn travel bag probably misled people. Plus he was a foreigner, an outsider, moving among the rail station crowds and clambering up into an air-conditioned express train jammed end to end with Chinese passengers. When yet another stranger in his carriage, a scholarly young medic in a white lab coat, asked where he was from and what Taiwanese attractions he planned to see, Vincent did not feel the need to offer a correction.

"America," he said. "Red Bud. I'm on my way to Toulio."

"Toulio? No, no. There're no attractions in Toulio," the young medic insisted. "Now then, if it's history you want, stay on the train until Tainan City. You can visit an old Dutch fort if you like. But there are temples, too. Several hundred."

The train groaned against the rails. Vincent gave a somber nod and pretended to heed this advice. He had neither the interest nor stamina for a lengthy debate. He'd flown in to Chiang Kai-shek International Airport late the night before and then traveled by taxi to the city of Taoyuan, where he'd taken a room in a flashy railside hotel. But he hadn't slept particularly well. Something disagreeable in the arrangement of his bed: the garish maroon sheets, the plaster end posts shaped as snarling lion heads. The bed itself had been encompassed by three wide and unremitting mirrors. He'd tried watching TV a few minutes. At two A.M. there'd been nothing on but a starkly lit and toilsome brand of Japanese pornography.

"And if you want a vacation on the beach," the medic persisted, "go all the way south to Kenting. Good hotels. Good meals, but only if you enjoy seafood."

Vincent let his gaze wander outside to a line of scrubby beech trees wavering in the heat. "I do," he said.

By midmorning at least half of the carriage's standing-room passengers had closed their eyes and allowed the gentle listing of the train to turn their wariness inward. While they swayed on their feet, a bright August sun was steaming up the world beyond their compartment,

blanching the open fields of wheat and rice, bringing a white-hot skittering glow to the roofs of nearby factories. Over the course of several hours
the medic stood beside him and offered a few intermittent comments
regarding Taiwan's underappreciated scenery and climate. He was still
voicing these fitful remarks when they entered Yun Lin County and drew
near the town of Toulio.

At once Vincent's heart began a panicked, off-tempo thumping.
Ridiculous that it should do so; he'd lain awake much of the previous
night counseling himself in advance of this moment, and now that the
moment was at hand it seemed possible he might sink down and collapse
onto his knees. A few minutes later his carriage rumbled through Toulio's
northernmost intersection and he saw a hundred or more of the town's
good citizens lined up on either side of the gated railroad tracks. Several
fleeting resemblances leapt at him from the blur of faces. For an instant it
seemed as if his most timid female students had gathered at the crossing,
the shyest Ming-da girls, the jittery and shrinking Ping twins, all of whom
he feared meeting again because they'd once held him in high esteem and
by now had heard the rumors and had turned their anxious imaginations
loose on his private life. No doubt they'd dreamed up unseemly motives
and appetites that did not belong to him—and maybe a few immoderate
longings that did. Mostly, though, they would be shocked to the core by
the cruel difference between his public and private self. Had they cried in
disappointment, these sweet-tempered and unworldly girls and women?
A few of them probably had.

For the time being he was too deeply awash in sadness and dread to do
anything but stand rooted in the aisle. Then the train began to slow and
let out its final screeching whine. He pressed toward the carriage doors,
where he paused a moment and glanced back at the medic and received
such a scowl of judgment that it seemed to mark not only the medic's
lowly opinion of Toulio as a travel destination, but of Vincent as well.

To step out onto the platform was to be swamped by fierce sunlight
and a tide of hot, soggy air. By the time he'd reached the open hall of the
station, the sides of his dress shirt were mooned with sweat. Except for the
humidity, exactly nothing about Toulio's town center had changed in
twelve weeks' time. The walkways were, as always, a maze of rudely parked
cycles and motor scooters. Loudspeakered ad trucks circled the market
and business districts. Outside the station blank-faced young men in leg
braces sat against the wall and sold fifteen-yuan packs of Juicy Fruit and

Spearmint gum. More than a few townspeople turned their gaze his way. None of them, however, recoiled in disgust or erupted in accusation. No former students had gathered to weep over the ruins of his private life.

He hailed a taxi and let it carry him straight from the station parking lot down the town's main avenue, with its aimless clamor and cluttered shop windows, out past the tall buildings, out past the long rows of connected houses, and then onto the single-lane, blacktop rice road that took him the final kilometer of his return journey. The taxi dropped him off at the end of a short alleyway leading to the Chens' front door.

He rang the buzzer and waited. When no one came, he tried turning the door latch and found it locked. He stepped back a few paces from the house. He gazed up at the nearest window. Was it at all reasonable, this faint hunch he had that Shao-fei was at home and staring down at him from some cloaked vantage point?

His Taitung motorcycle was parked beside Alec's in the alleyway. It took a while to coax his key from the bottom of his money belt. The effort proved unnecessary. Someone had pounded screwdrivers into the ignitions of both motorcycles. To start his cycle he needed only to rotate the screwdriver handle one notch clockwise. The engine turned over on the very first kick.

He retraced the route he'd taken minutes earlier, the motorcycle running taut and powerful beneath him, running, in fact, faster and with more agility than it ever had before. Near the town center he parked and rooted through his travel bag for the teakwood box he'd bought a few days earlier in Hong Kong. A feeble pretense, perhaps, but still the only one he had. He slipped into the narrow hallway between the restaurant and video store. For fifteen minutes he stood and pressed the intercom buzzer or spoke into the intercom itself, saying the most immediate and banal things that came to his mind, "Mr. Gwa, I'd like to speak with you, please," or "Excuse me, but I have something that belongs to Jia-ling." Afterward he walked around the block and looked for Gwa's Bonneville in the back alleyway.

No luck. But maybe he could find Gwa by locating his one-of-a-kind Bonneville. And so for the next hour Vincent perused the parking lots and side lanes of certain upscale establishments: tea houses and restaurants and even a pricey hair salon. He coasted past several of Toulio's newer townhouse and apartment complexes. He saw no Pontiac Bonnevilles. All the same the steady glide of the cycle helped make the heat and muggy air tolerable. He forgot himself, forgot his troubled reputation. One meandering, hedge-lined lane wound into another. Only when he paused at a crosswalk and saw a stocky and begrimed young man in a mechanic's uniform who was not Trudy's brother but who had the same protuberant ears and wide, flaring nose, only then did he realize how razor thin was the divide between an absentminded tour of the town and a chance meeting that would surely turn dire, punishing.

Still, he could not make himself return to Shao-fei's home without first getting a glimpse of the ministry house. Yet once he neared the neighborhood and drifted past the motorcycle repair shop and snuck that glimpse, he was still not satisfied. He parked a block away and crept along the back alleyways until he emerged at the cul-de-sac. From there he stole toward the ministry house, his shoulders drawn up and his head pitched low, hastening ahead like a man caught in a blusterous downpour. And what exactly was he hurrying toward anyway? He hardly knew, except that as compulsions went, this one felt a lot like self-exorcism, or maybe just a rending need for more anguish in his life, the anguish of being denounced by Gloria one more time, the anguish of peering in the ministry house window and seeing a faithful community that had persisted, or thrived, in his absence.

Two neighborhood girls were crouched before the front gate. They had set out a pair of water-filled basins and were presently hunched forward in the heat with their arms wrist-deep in water. It appeared that they were either bathing or simply submerging an assortment of plastic dolls— bodies in one basin, heads in the other. Upon seeing Vincent both girls rose solemnly to their feet. Their eyes were open preternaturally wide, their buttoned mouths rolled into tiny Os of wonderment. A second later they turned and sprinted for home, their pigtails helicoptering out on either sides of their bobbing heads.

He crossed the courtyard and found that a sizable clutch of mail had accumulated in the ministry house screen door: bills and government notices, several envelopes bearing his mother's spare handwriting, four or five postcards from Mr. Liang in Taipei, one of which read, *God of mystery and of light, give us the assurance of Your presence and the comfort of Your love.*

He gathered up the mail and tried peering through a kitchen window. Was this a homecoming that required a knock or a key? He used the key and pushed his way into a living room that was cool and stale-smelling and entirely dark except for a few thin slivers of curtain light. Several sharp tugs on the cord of a nearby desk lamp did nothing to alter the darkness, nor did flipping the wall switch in the kitchen. He riffled through a scattering of mail on the kitchen counter as well as the bundle of letters in his hands and discovered three months' worth of unpaid power and telephone bills.

It astonished him, the lack of human presence, the cavernlike murkiness of what had once been a moderately well-attended ministry house. Amazing that he had done this, that a personal flaw of his had slipped beyond his grasp and had brought this about.

He opened a curtain and made his way toward the stairs. Gloria's bedroom door hung open by a few inches. When he pushed it farther in, it thumped against an unseen barrier—a capsized chair, as it turned out, and a writing desk that looked to have been hastily cleared of ink brushes and sketch pads. For a scalding moment, though, he thought he'd bumped against something far worse, something grisly and immeasurable and with enough dark sovereignty to cast a pall of regret over the rest of his life.

His heart drumming away again, he climbed the stairs to the second floor. Everything in his bedroom was layered in a thin film of dust, but the room itself was cool and tranquil and otherwise unchanged. He stood and considered the dozens of modest possessions he thought he'd given up for good: his language books, his family snapshots. In that instant he decided he didn't have the will or energy to go out again that day and face the townspeople of Toulio. He wouldn't be returning to Shao-fei's home either. He would reside here in the ministry house. But for how long? Until it proved unfeasible. Or until he had an opportunity to speak with Jia-ling.

He was tired enough to fall into bed and sleep. First, he trudged downstairs and relocked the front door. Wearily, he rummaged about for some blunt object he might wield in self-defense. Nothing useful presented itself. At last he settled for a hefty iron wok ladle, which he waved lazily through the air a few times and then placed at the ready in an umbrella stand by the door.

He climbed to the top of the stairs and made sure the door to the roof was secure. On the way back down he made the mistake of looking in on the third-floor classroom. To see the tidy rows of school desks was to imagine, vividly, the earnest faces of his former students and feel the long shadow of his own hypocrisy. At once he plodded down to his bedroom and, without bothering to turn his pillow or pull back the covers, lay down atop the dust-laden bedspread.

For the second time that day he was awash in dread, though if the first instance had been born of irrational panic, then what he felt now was a gloomier and more reasoned trepidation. He should not have returned. He was not welcome in this town. He would not go unnoticed for long. Furthermore, the most elemental modes of investigation were largely beyond his ability. The ministry house, for example, did not at present have phone service, but even if it did, he'd never learned Gwa's first name and therefore could not pick up the receiver and ask an operator for his home phone number. He couldn't read a telephone directory or write up a notice to place in the local newspaper. Of all the acquaintances he'd made since first coming to Toulio, he couldn't think of a single person whom he could go to for help and who would welcome him without embarrassment or misgiving.

And yet these obstacles might all be overcome if only he had a clear notion of what he intended to do. But even his intentions were hopelessly naive: he wanted to find Jia-ling, he wanted to return to her a teakwood box that was never hers in the first place, he wanted to ask if she was all right and be assured that, yes, in fact, she was. Before leaving he wanted to see in her a newfound thankfulness for his honesty and concern, a newfound esteem.

By late evening there was barely enough window light to navigate the ministry house's pitch-dark hallways and stairwell. If he had any hopes for dinner, he had better rise from his bed now and make his way down to the first floor. Yet he couldn't bring himself to move. Evidently, as far as dinner was concerned, he had no hopes whatsoever. He closed his eyes and lost himself in the womblike security of his unlit bedroom. He tried to imagine a new day edging toward him across the shadowed horizon of the earth. *Another day,* he thought drowsily. *Get ready.* After a while he slept. Much of the night passed in a series of long, doleful naps. In between these naps he lay in the darkness and tried to gauge the true extent of his resolve and found that his hopes beat so wanly in his heart that he could hardly measure them at all.

But he rose the next morning anyway, rose sluggishly and thick-tongued and with an abiding conviction that whatever his present life was leading to, it was not so much a wealth of sustained happiness or pinnacle of accomplishment as a circuitous and impossible striving toward a destination that couldn't be reached. The thought was oddly satisfying. It might have been his first truly adult understanding. Maybe the successful lives were those that were gracefully endured. And assuredly, there were other adults in Toulio who knew this all too well, men and women right now rising from their beds, prepared to press on with another day because, in the final and deepest analysis, what other worthwhile choice was there?

Standing in line at the telephone office later that morning, he inadvertently locked gazes with a diffident and rail-thin young woman whom gradually he recognized as the assistant director of the Toulio preschool where he'd taught English for four months. He nodded hello. She had never been an effusive person and judging from the flagging steps she took across the lobby toward him, she was in no great hurry to begin a conversation. She folded her skinny arms across her stomach and asked how his grandfather was doing.

"Fine," he said and remembered her name. "He's much better, Miss Yang. He's out of the hospital now."

"And you're back in Toulio?"

"I am."

She looked toward the lobby exit. "I better get going," she said. "It's a busy time of the year for us."

A busy time? August? He had almost no idea what she was referring to or implying. In the wake of her departure he tried to determine how much hidden knowledge had been braided into her remarks, her slack demeanor. If she was truly aware of what he'd done, then she most likely wouldn't have crossed the lobby to speak to him. And yet if she wasn't aware, why hadn't she raised the possibility of him returning to teach at the preschool?

At least there was no such guesswork when it came to the biting regard his ministry house neighbors had for him. By far the worst were the moody elderly citizens of his neighborhood who passed much of their days stooled or crouched upon the patios of their homes, and who, with a peevish glance or a jowly shake of the head, could muster a lifetime's worth of sullen umbrage. He recalled once having a score of nodding acquaintances. Now the families along his block were loath to nod or wave in his direction. The motorcycle mechanic did not invite him to sit for tea. The young husbands and single men, who might best have understood his circumstance, appeared pained or quietly unnerved by his presence. To the children he was something of a lurching boogeyman. Often they gathered at the ministry house gate and could be counted on to flee from him in a great burst of foot tramping and shrieking that sounded more rapturous than afraid.

It was all dispiriting enough to make him lock the door and clamber up to the sanctuary of his second-floor bedroom. Once inside he lay down and tried not to recall the silent coupling he and Trudy had done upon this very bed. He sometimes cringed. He slept more than he should have. But he was not entirely without discipline. During the daylight hours he gathered together the makings of a new flyer, one whose characters were copied meticulously from an English-Chinese dictionary. He had no idea how to write her name. Once it was finished, he hoped the flyer would read, PLEASE HELP ME FIND THIS YOUNG WOMAN FROM MAINLAND CHINA. Below that her photograph. Below that the word REWARD and the ministry house phone number. Yet it was no use posting the flyers until he had a working telephone. As it turned out, paying one's overdue electric and phone bills did not necessarily mean a prompt resumption of service.

Three times each day—at midmorning, at late afternoon, and at evening before dinner—he rode downtown and spoke courteously into the intercom leading to Gwa's office. Each time he was answered by a wash of empty static. He took his dinners in a quiet restaurant and afterward searched for Gwa's Bonneville outside a series of nightclubs and karaoke bars. Then he returned to a ministry house that, after nightfall, appeared as murky and unkempt as an ancient shipwreck. In order to journey between rooms he had to light a candle and ignore the branching silhouettes that sprang up and flitted across the walls of the house.

Two days later, while in the midst of his morning visit to Gwa's office, he stepped away from the intercom and wrinkled his nose at an unbidden and whimsical idea. He paced back to his parked motorcycle and from the rear basket removed the teakwood box. A few days earlier he'd wrapped it in brown paper to keep it from being scratched. Now he placed it beneath one arm and, after a moment of silent consideration, entered the video store adjacent to Gwa's office. A petite young woman with hennaed hair sang out hello. He showed her the wrapped box and explained how it was that for three days he'd been stopping by Gwa's office each morning, afternoon, and evening trying to deliver the parcel. Was there a Taiwanese holiday he hadn't heard about? Was Gwa on vacation? He'd been told Gwa lived nearby. Did she, by any chance, know his home address or phone number?

In fact she knew both. In fact Gwa had rented movies from her just four or five days earlier. She looked into her computer monitor and scanned through a list of store patrons, reading out a six-digit phone number and then a rather complicated street address. She watched him mouth the numbers, the street name. "My bad manners," she cooed. "Here, I'll write it down for you."

Outside he showed the slip of paper to a taxi driver and, much to the driver's puzzlement, followed behind on his motorcycle as the taxi weaved its way north through a sequence of roundabouts and bustling lanes. As he rode, Vincent was almost painfully aware of his clammy grip on the throttle and front brake. He'd never known his palms to sweat so profusely. At the same time his mouth had gone dry. Rows of houses reeled past him. When he concentrated, he recognized the neighborhood. The previous March he and Gloria had gone door to door among these newly fashioned and multifloored private homes canvassing for Bible study students. Had they gone a few blocks deeper into the neighborhood, they might eventually have wound up here, at this very street corner, where the taxi had just now pulled over and the driver was pointing toward a three-story house glazed in bright white tiles.

A child answered the door, a boy of four or five years. He had a giddy, enraptured look about him, as if he'd been interrupted deep in the forest of his private game play. He gaped at his foreign visitor and instantly his inflated surprise became part of his game. He staggered back a few steps, reached for an invisible weapon, which he flailed about a few times, then fell and lay motionless atop the entranceway.

"Is this the Gwa home?" Vincent asked over the boy's crumpled form. "The Gwa family?"

The boy stirred. He began pulling himself across the tiled floor toward the rear of the house, leaving the door wide open and a steady crest of air-conditioning wafting over the threshold. A short while later, a smartly dressed, slim-figured woman appeared in the hallway. She came to the door with a bundle of stamped letters in her hand. "Can I help you?" she asked.

"Is Mr. Gwa home?"

"He's not—You are? I'm sorry. You know Hong-lin?"

"I think so, yes. I know a Mr. Gwa. He has an office downtown. He owns an American car, a large one, and has a friend who's very . . ."

"Yes, yes. Ponic."

"I'm Vincent. I met Mr. Gwa last fall. I taught him English conversation."

"English conversation?" She had a generous, almost perfectly formed smile. "I bet he didn't do very well, did he?"

"Not very well, no."

"I know a little English from high school and college. But he won't learn from me. No patience for it."

"Do you know where I can find him?"

"You should have come by yesterday morning, before he left on business. He'll be gone awhile. Four days in Hong Kong, more if he has to visit his factories in the Mainland."

"And you're his wife?" he said, straining to grin. "The handsome little boy who answered the door is your son?"

"Yes, that's right."

Before he could fathom what that meant, whether it enlarged or diminished his chances of finding Jia-ling, before he could grow incensed at having been lied to, he was struck by how irrefutably attractive the woman standing before him was. It had snuck up on him, her beauty, and now to feel the sudden pounce of it was to envy Gwa more and notice how familiar his wife's fine looks were, how much in terms of her expressive eyes and round chin and long neck she looked like Kai-ling. Not that they were identical, of course, but they were sisters in a kind of regal, large-eyed Chinese beauty. For a moment he couldn't get over it. Was that what desire did to married men? Inured them to their wives' loveliness and sent them out into the world yearning for other women who were not their wives yet looked the same?

"I've been searching for a girl I know," he managed to say. "I met her while traveling in the Mainland this summer. Her name is Song Jia-ling." He pulled the photo from his shirt pocket and held it out for inspection. "Have you seen her?"

"I haven't."

"She, Jia-ling, is from Urumchi, in Xinjiang. Mr. Gwa knows her. He . . . It's a long story."

"Yes?"

"He paid me to bring Jia-ling from Urumchi to Hong Kong. Before that he . . . a year ago maybe. It's confusing to try and explain it."

"You mean she's an employee. You mean to say she's a worker in Hong-lin's Guangdong factories."

"No. I don't think so. What I think happened was—"

"Wait," she said. "Wait a minute." She turned and paced to the end of the hallway and looked in on her son. She called out a gentle warning. "Not on the stairs. No, not on the table either." She stood there for a minute and did nothing but watch him play. When she came back, she was wringing her hands together, blinking unsteadily. "That's all I want to hear," she said.

"Excuse me?"

"It's too much, you understand? I don't want to think about this while my husband is away. I'll call you, maybe, if I find anything out." She glanced at his flyer and jotted down his phone number.

"Thank you," Vincent said. "But couldn't—"

"No, no," she said. "And don't expect me to call. There's probably nothing to worry about anyway, no good reason for me to talk to Hong-lin about this." She surveyed the photograph one more time. "She looks exactly like the kind of girl he would hire for his Guangdong factories. Exactly. She's probably there right now, working away."

"I don't think so," Vincent said.

"She's lucky to have a job," Gwa's wife said, stepping back and leaning on her front door until it swung soundly shut.

He rode straight home to the ministry house and after checking the phone for a dial tone—a test he performed twenty or more times a day—he began an absentminded pacing of the first floor. A host of extravagant conspiracies presented themselves. He dismissed them one at a time. An hour passed in which he reached no conclusion and accomplished nothing; he'd never felt quite so useless. The waiting was now interminable, worse even than in Urumchi because that was killing time and this was time slowed to a snail's speed and yet still somehow outpacing him. This was time with its own private agenda of regret and worry.

At four o'clock when he checked the phone there was, miraculously, the tunneling electric hum of a working connection. Instantly he was off to the copiers. A hundred copies later he made his way through an unruly Wednesday-evening rush hour affixing his flyers to every window front and utility pole in sight. How good it felt to do something so practical.

The solace of it stayed with him all the way through dinner and back to the ministry house, where, in the last grainy light before nightfall, he sat in the living room and studied Jia-ling's photograph once more.

It wasn't determination at all, he decided, while scrutinizing the stern face she'd made for the camera. She was merely peering ahead to her new life and bracing herself for the hardships to come. She'd always had a potent gaze. When he looked back over his long summer in Urumchi, he seemed to remember a number of incidents in which she'd revealed her judgment as astute, exceptional. It seemed as if he'd recognized this and other qualities right from the start.

But had he really? Perhaps not.

He considered her photograph again. It was a perpetual struggle keeping her life-size, real, when her absence made everything about her profound.

Late that night the phone rang, once, twice, five times, before he fumbled downstairs in the darkness and snatched up the receiver.

On the other end soft static, a hushed breath.

"Hello? Hello?" he said, once in Chinese, once in English. "If it's you . . ." he said.

The line clicked off and hummed and he was left to consider the possibilities.

It was Gwa, who had never wanted a wife at all, only a mistress, calling to check on Vincent from some seedy hotel room or secret apartment.

Or: Gwa's wife, too distraught by Vincent's suggestions to sleep, ready to hear a complete explanation, and then at the last moment deciding against it.

Or: Trudy's older brother, lit by six half-liter bottles of beer, at this moment behind the wheel of his father's sedan, veering drunkenly toward the ministry house, ready to make good on his threat.

Or: Jia-ling, who had managed a few desperate seconds alone with a telephone, long enough to hear Vincent's voice and Gwa's approaching footsteps.

Or: Jia-ling, who had always known she would be a mistress, never a wife, a compromised Jia-ling, calling to check in on her former chaperone whom she now thought of as either stupid or woefully naive.

So many contrary possibilities. He'd not seen her in six days. It worried him. So much could happen in a day.

He woke the next morning, his fourth in Toulio, assailed by his most urgent and darkly plausible fear yet. It had sprung, in part, from a bleak source: the pornographic film he'd seen in his Taoyuan hotel room. He'd only watched a few minutes, enough, days later, to insinuate a connection, a credible one when he remembered the film's climate of gloomy sexual coercion and then recalled the visit he and Gwa and Ponic had made many months ago to a Toulio house of prostitution. During that visit Gwa had offered to treat them to a massage or time alone with a prostitute. Vincent had declined. Ponic had accepted, leaving Gwa to settle with the cashier. But he had not gone to the register and handed over the money. He had not paid.

Was it unreasonable to believe that he had not paid because he was one of the establishment's owners?

Was it paranoid to think that here was a ruthless way for Gwa to recoup his five thousand dollars?

He could not shake the notion, once fully formed, from his head. It was his surest hunch, his most pressing intuition. And if it seemed vaguely outlandish then the X-rated film he'd seen made clear the dark vocations that were sometimes forced upon a woman. In the film a willowy and tired-looking Japanese housewife crouched in a shower stall and pretended to masturbate. There were faint abrasions along her thighs and kneecaps. What was horrible and therefore memorable was her utter lack of enthusiasm, a personal detachment that might have been bearable, or merely strange, in a plusher setting or with other bored performers. But she was alone in a mildewed shower stall, her knees apart, her fingers laboring away, her spirit elsewhere.

Thirty-four

HE PUT ON his cleanest and best dress shirt and then he rode out beyond the rail station, beyond a new supermarket and sports shoe store, out to an otherwise ordinary neighborhood of family row houses that happened to accommodate a small enclave of entertainment establishments for men. The largest of these was a newish, four-floored structure with one long window. Except for its red and white barber pole and oversize neon sign, it might have been a simple warehouse or gymnasium. Vincent parked in the gravel lot beneath a sun that was bright and rackingly hot. He'd arrived a little after one P.M.—a ludicrous time of day to visit a whorehouse.

There was unfeigned surprise in the faces of the two young female greeters who curtsied to him at the door. "Welcome to our leisure club," they warbled. Unsure where to direct him, they deferred to the man behind the cash register, a pale gentleman with long, expertly trimmed sideburns. This gentleman then rounded the counter and in the prim, expectant way of someone directing a lost tourist said, "Yes? Good afternoon."

"I'd like to spend some time with one of the girls here."

The man crossed his arms and indulged in a moment of mulish rumination. "All right," he said warily.

"There's a girl I saw here before," Vincent continued, recalling the plump, spirited woman who had teased Ponic and pulled him up the stairs. "I don't know her name, but she was a little bit fat and had a round face, a face shaped like a heart." He thought this a dubious point of reference, but the man appeared to apprehend it at once. He strolled to a nearby door, cracked it open, and called out for Miss Ying-ying.

Nearby the terrarium gurgled and rained water on its marble-breasted statuaries. Vincent took a seat on the cushioned bench. Some ten minutes later, Ponic's lady friend Miss Ying-ying entered the lobby dressed in a black knee-length skirt and a silvery blouse. She looked to be in her middle to late thirties and was, at first glance, exactly the type of woman he might have hoped to find here, breezy and efficient and good-humored. Apparently, she had not been told her client was a foreigner, and so for just an instant her lined eyebrows shot up and her powdered cheeks went slack before, admirably, she reclaimed her good graces and was able to smile and ask, "Do I know you?" without sounding the least bit shocked or aloof.

"No, but I saw you when I was here before."

"You were with another girl?"

"I was with a friend, just . . . looking." He lowered his voice to a whisper. "I'd like to speak with you in private."

She nodded as if she understood him perfectly. Up the stairs they went to a carpeted salon bathed in gauzy red lamplight. A line of reclining chairs, barber's chairs, ran from the stair rail to the far wall, where a large, intricately molded plaster dragon shot a tongue of electric fire toward the ceiling. In one of the center chairs lay a businessman, his suit jacket off, his collar unfastened. Two women labored over his body, one behind the recliner kneading his scalp, the other rubbing down his sturdy calf and thigh muscles. His eyelids were pared down to blissful slivers.

"No, thank you," Vincent said to the offer of a reclining chair ratcheted up and folded out until it was nearly level. "Not necessary." He grinned. Hadn't he learned by now how useless such protests were? Several pairs of hands guided him down stomach-first onto the chair. From behind, an unseen Miss Ying-ying sank her fingers into the small of his back and twisted his muscles, his very bones, with a flinty strength he could not possibly have readied himself for. "Oh sweet Jesus," he moaned in agony, while the owner of a second pair of hands, a stout, late-middle-aged, sour-faced woman, violated the muscles and tendons of his upper shoulders. There was a sense of ruthless collaboration in their labor. The driving strength of their arms bore down on him and made it hard to fill his lungs with air. As a result, his most ragged and desperate pleas for release came out sounding, even to his own ears, like soft whimpers of contentment.

And on it went. His masseuses never seemed to tire or falter. At last he was allowed to lurch sideways and roll onto his back. It came as only a mild surprise to discover that Miss Ying-ying was nowhere in sight. The person who all along had been kneading his lower back was actually another woman of late middle age, equally brawny in the shoulders, equally glum-faced. Were they former prostitutes, these women? Was their homeliness and bearish strength meant to make the anticipated services of Miss Ying-ying seem like the favors of a goddess? He could not decide. Besides, both women had set to work upon him again, the first squeezing his thighs, the second raking her oversize knuckles across his chest. He could only lie back and yield to their authority. There seemed to be a measure of retribution in the wiry vigor of their hands. It felt like a punishment he partially deserved.

A short while later Miss Ying-ying reappeared at his side. She was clad in an entirely new outfit: a full-length patterned skirt with a long slit up one side, and a knitted top through which he could see the faint shimmerings of a red brassiere. Another layer of cosmetics had been applied to the mostly unremarkable features of her rotund face. She was not remotely goddesslike. Still, she took his hand and helped him down from the chair, a small kindness for which he was grateful. "Just one floor up to my room," she explained patiently. "Can you make it?"

He said he could, though his first teetering steps felt as if he were trying to make his way, dazed and slack-limbed, across a river of blood-warm water.

He clung to the rail and followed her up the stairs. At the summit of the third floor he paused and considered the hallway before him, a long, uncarpeted corridor off of which stemmed twenty or more identical doors. The view momentarily staggered him. He'd come this far on the basis of a nagging hunch. And yet only now, seeing this collection of sealed doors, did he feel the grievous possibility, even probability, that Jialing was locked away behind one of them.

To think that all along his entire summer in Urumchi had been leading here. To think that he'd received money and had played a substantial role in it.

Miss Ying-ying's room was the fourth on the left. He'd not expected such a wealth of personal artifacts, stacked trays of jewelry and beadwork, hampers of folded scarves. Her bed was professionally large, and, like the hotel room he'd stayed at in Taoyuan, there were half-frosted mirrors reflecting onto the mattress. A fanning row of sandals and evening slippers compassed three-quarters of the room. An entire wall was devoted to upper and lower racks of her meticulously hung clothing.

"The other time I came here I was with two friends of mine," Vincent began. "One of them was Ponic. You know him, I think. Maybe he's a friend of yours."

"Ponic," she said with what might have been a derisive curl to her lips. He couldn't tell. She was turned away from him, bent down, rifling through a wood trunk at the foot of the bed.

"The other was Mr. Gwa, one of your bosses, or one of the owners here." She stood abruptly and made a rather woozy gesture toward her wall of clothing. "The bottom rack I paid for myself," she said. "But the top rack—most of the top rack—are gifts from boyfriends of mine." She reached out and drew back one of several indistinguishable black gowns. "It's widely known around here that this is a gift from Ponic. Do you think I get tired of wearing it?" she asked, her cheeks dimpled in a coy grin, her brows and eyes arched into such a pantomime of whimsy that he had no idea what was being implied. "So here," she said, holding forth a scroll-shaped object that she'd pulled from the trunk. "Take a look at this and tell me what you think."

In his hands lay a sizable sheaf of rolled papers. Each one contained column after column of free-flowing calligraphy. He shuffled through the first seven or eight pages. Viewed together they seemed to have the loose confidentiality of a private journal or diary. Because of this he pretended to study them modestly. He nodded. He praised the brushwork. When he looked up, he found that she had removed her blouse and skirt and was arranging them on plastic hangers.

"No, no," he said. "The reason I came here . . . what I wanted . . . I can't read," he blurted out. He had almost no notion of what he was trying to say. And by the time he figured it out, she had pulled on a bright green tank top and was stepping into yet another skirt, this one denim with jeweled buttons at the hip. She hadn't been undressing at all. She was merely changing outfits one more time.

"That's all right," she said and sat beside him on one corner of the bed. "I don't mind reading it aloud." She reclaimed the papers and then took several protracted breaths that she blew out through her rounded lips in a series of light huffs, as if she were extinguishing a candle or drying her painted fingernails.

"One day—" she began, and immediately stopped herself. Before commencing again, she tried on several ponderous expressions. "One day a sad gray cloud followed me home from the mountainside," she said. "Everywhere I went the cloud hovered over me. Looking up, I could not see the shining sun. I could not see the singing, happy birds. I could not see the deep blue of the sky. The cloud was always with me. But what could I do?" She raised her eyes from the manuscript and gave him a barbed, rhetorical look. "I told myself to think of the birds that fly happily above the clouds. I told myself to think of the wind that blows the clouds away. But I tried and tried and still it was useless. What the birds can do, I can't do. What the wind can do, I can't . . ."

He leaned back on his elbows. Inwardly, he reviewed what he'd seen of her body a few moments earlier, her squatty haunches and languishing breasts housed in red lingerie, her pale, paunchy belly. For all he knew she had a body little different from most women of her age. And yet he couldn't help thinking of the multitude of customers—hundreds? thousands?—she'd had over the years, and how the wages of her working life were somehow writ large upon her flesh.

". . . days I wandered lost and alone with the gray cloud always above my head. No one would walk with me. The children would not play at my side. The flowers . . ."

Which, when he thought about it, was a truly terrible direction to let his mind roam. Her tired flesh. Especially while she was divulging her most private and tenderhearted secrets. And yet he could swear that her story, her essay—what the hell could it be?—was at least partially responsible. It drove him to the direst sort of distraction. He stole a sidelong glance and found that she had conquered only two of the manuscript's twenty or more pages.

". . . because one person cannot carry the burden of all the sorrow in the world. I knew then that I had to go back to the mountainside at night. I had to stand alone and raise my arms to the beautiful moon. O beautiful moon, I asked, did you hear the sound of the wind blowing gently? Did you hear the sound of the leaves falling from the tree? Did you hear—"

"I do," he said. "I hear it. What you're describing in your writing, in your . . ."

"Poem."

"Poem, yes. And I want to hear the rest of it. But I came to talk about something else, and I have to speak about it now, please."

She set the sheaf of papers in her lap.

"It's about a girl I'm looking for. A Mainland girl. Her name is Song Jia-ling. She may have been brought here last week." He reached in his pocket for Jia-ling's photograph.

Miss Ying-ying gave it at best a passing, indifferent inspection.

"If you know anything at all, I'd be very grateful."

This time she allowed a second, longer glance, an irksome reconsideration. "What is she standing in front of?"

"It was taken in Hong Kong. She's standing in front of the space museum."

"Who does she think she is?" Miss Ying-ying asked sourly. "An astronaut?"

"She came to Toulio last week with Ponic and Mr. Gwa, one of the bosses here. If you know anything, I'd be happy to buy you a present, a new dress, maybe." He pulled a blue thousand-yuan bill from his wallet.

"Ha!" she snorted. "You wouldn't know what to buy. And you couldn't get anything nice unless you paid three thousand or more."

Obediently, he withdrew two more thousand-yuan bills. He knew of no way to bargain in the face of twenty closed doors.

Her red-rimmed smile was disconcertingly wide, sycophantic. "How lucky I am to be your friend!" she exclaimed, taking the bills and folding them beneath the hemline of her skirt. "And the girl in the picture, you're looking for her because you knew her in the Mainland? You were her customer there?"

"No, no. She wasn't . . ." He glanced fleetingly at the mirrors surrounding Miss Ying-ying's bed. "It's a lot to explain, but I'm looking for her because—"

"She's your little girlfriend!" Miss Ying-ying tittered.

"I want to make sure she's safe."

"She's your little sweetheart! You have tender feelings for her, yes?"

He disavowed any such thing. He wasn't ready to make such admissions, not here, in a whore's room.

"Well, I can only tell you what I know," Miss Ying-ying said.

"Anything at all."

She studied the photo, hummed awhile, handed it back. "Don't know her. Haven't seen her. Good-bye," she said. "Pay the man downstairs at the counter."

The insult of what she'd done, the sting, was quick to reach him. He was thunderstruck, then angry. "You can't do that," he sputtered.

Her manner was oddly commiserative. "I know," she said. "I know." By then she had left the bed and sashayed a few paces to an intercom box near the door. Her hand flew up and slapped the buzzer. "ROOM FORTY-TWO!" she sang out. "The foreigner is giving me trouble!"

From the floor above came a squeal of jostled furniture. He heard a rumbling, first overhead, then in the stairwell, a stampede of feet that seemed to gather weight and number as it cornered the landing and moved toward her room.

"She was here, your girlfriend," Miss Ying-ying said. "But we had to throw her out. She kept pulling up her dress and humping everything in sight. Chairs. Doorknobs. The stair rail."

"Shut up," he said.

"Blind old men," she said. "Dogs in the alleyway."

The four men who barged in her room were of a thin, rascally variety. He'd expected rugged bouncers or bodyguards, but these men were much older and had the sallow skin and jaundiced eyes of lifelong drinkers. What was their position here? Whorehouse layabouts? Still, they were full of quick, disruptive energy and brawling insults. They railed against him in drink-slurred Taiwanese. When he shook his head dumbly, they resorted to the one English vulgarity, perhaps the one English word, they knew. "FOK, FOK, FOK," they shouted and marched him from her room, down the stairs, past the second-floor salon—several recently arrived patrons sat up in their barber chairs and scowled at his bad etiquette—down to the lobby and around the terrarium, goading him along with their bony elbows and sodden breath, still shouting, "FOK, FOK, FOK, FOK, FOK."

The pale gentleman with long sideburns summoned him to the counter and demanded one thousand yuan for the massage, two thousand for the services of Miss Ying-ying. Fuming, Vincent counted out the bills. The two young greeters sang out their farewell, "Thank you for your visit!" His escorts gathered behind him and he was pushed rudely out the door into a sweltering afternoon, where he stood and tallied the cost of his visit—220 U.S. dollars—and tried to sift through the paltry scattering of knowledge he'd received in return.

By his reckoning more than a dozen other leisure clubs were scattered about Toulio, many more in the neighboring towns of Yun Lin County, hundreds in and about Taipei. If he was to be thorough, if he was to determined to pursue his dark hunch to its ultimate end, he would have to visit each one. He would have to look for her in a thousand doorways.

And if she'd not been sold into prostitution, then what other service might she have been forced into? The grudging and secondary services of a mistress? Or sweatshop work in one of the Toulio factories Gwa still owned? And wasn't it time to seek help in finding her? This might well have been the most excruciating dilemma of all—whether or not to go to the police. He'd wavered on many issues before, but never with such seesawing trepidation. To think what a reliable officer of the law might accomplish: Gwa's business office or factory could be searched; Ponic could be tracked down and brought in for questioning. Yet conversely, any decent officer would have questions regarding Vincent's culpability in the matter. How serious a crime was international marriage fraud? Serious enough, he supposed. It would be a ticklish matter to explain. Or did the real ticklishness arise from Vincent's own sullied reputation in town? Before an officer investigated a claim of a missing young Mainland woman, might that officer first want to know if the rumors concerning Vincent and a local high school girl were true?

His bleakest fear was that it didn't matter in the least if the police were involved because Jia-ling had never come to Toulio. Gwa had never brought her here. She was still in Hong Kong, where the prospect of finding her would be incalculably remote.

An intense fatigue came over him. Some regions of speculation, it turned out, were best left unexplored. He had to be similarly cautious when it came to the hours he spent alone in the ministry house. The isolation sometimes weighed on him. He was prone to sudden mumblings and odd little customs. For a day following his trip to the leisure club, he had a habit of saying aloud, "Thank you for your visit!" three times in a row in Chinese. He was still compulsive about checking the phone for a dial tone. Stranger yet, he had a considerable urge to break apart the clumps of melted candle he burned for light at night and put them in his mouth. More than once he gave in to the urge. And did this mean he was going crazy? He didn't think so. Nevertheless, he was keenly aware of his compulsions and he understood that if his seclusion were to continue for days, for weeks, especially in such unwelcome surroundings, the experience would ultimately reshape his demeanor and temperament, would distort his inner self. He supposed he would become an eccentric. Indeed, he already seemed to have an eccentric's fussy tolerance for the musty odors and deep stillness that pervaded the ministry house, and an eccentric's jitteriness when it came to any atypical movements or noise. The soft mewling of stray cats on the rooftop unnerved him more than it should have. He suspected that the neighborhood children sometimes peered at him through the window blinds. Just the sound of their reedy voices rising over the front gate could make him flinch. Therefore he was abruptly shocked when, two evenings after his visit to the leisure club, the telephone let out an insistent racket. How altogether out of place it sounded, more so even than when it had first chimed three nights earlier. He managed to pick it up on the second ring and pronounce a mostly unflustered hello.

A low grunt of surprise answered him back. Then what seemed like a breathy fumbling for words. "Yes, please . . . who is it there?" a male voice asked in English.

"It's Vincent."

"You're there in the Toulio house?"

"I am. I'm staying here awhile."

"And how is it that . . . I thought you had gone away."

Before he could answer, something of an insurrection took place on the other end of the line. A chorus of chatty female voices prevailed upon the speaker. The receiver was bandied about. The line went dead.

After some reflection Vincent believed he had just spoken to Reverend Phillips, though by the sound of it an exhausted Reverend Phillips, a groggy, ill, or otherwise burdened Reverend Phillips.

He went to bed late that night still perplexed by the call. His dreams were blurry and uneventful. And he was roused from his sleep entirely too early the next morning by yet another curious occurrence. Nearly every light in the ministry house was aglow. It was 5:17, a truly odd time of day to have the power restored. He wandered barefoot from room to room turning off switches. Each blazing ceiling fixture and floor lamp was a small marvel. *God of mystery and light!* he thought and shuffled back to bed.

Four hours later he woke again. He'd either heard or dreamed he heard a window blind being raised. He lifted his head and listened. Downstairs in the kitchen yesterday's dishes settled into the drainer with a light clink. He then heard, unmistakably, a few faint sandal-like plops, a mild groan. A stair creaked.

A moment later a figure appeared in the second-floor hallway. Predictably, Vincent's heart began to bang away inside his chest, even though the figure was rather slight and short and crowned with bright white hair. Could it be that an elderly man or woman, perhaps one of the neighborhood's incensed grandparents, had somehow snuck in through a downstairs window ready to harangue him face-to-face, ready to drive him from the ministry house? The possibility was terrifying in its way. But, of course, no such thing had happened. He recognized the figure. She was Mrs. Liang, his landlady, who, along with her sister, had grown up parentless in this house. He'd not seen her in nearly a year, and now here she was, striding undeterred into his bedroom as he, half coiled in a bedsheet, struggled to pull a T-shirt over his head.

She surveyed the general state of the room, surveyed Vincent, and shrugged in a way that might have indicated modest disapproval. She did not at all appear pressured by the need to speak or offer a hello. She'd arrived with a satchel slung across one shoulder. She removed it, stepped out the door and into the adjoining bedroom, where he could hear her unpacking several items. A short while later she returned.

"You've told Reverend Phillips that you've come back?" she asked. "You've let him know you're staying here?"

"I'm not sure. He may know. I may have spoken to him on the phone yesterday."

"You didn't. That was my husband, Mr. Liang."

"Oh," Vincent said. "Well then, the Reverend doesn't know. I didn't tell him."

"Why not?"

"I didn't think he'd be happy to hear it."

She stood and heeded his remark, nodded ever so subtly at the trouble he'd hinted at. "And what about the paint?" she asked.

"The paint?"

"The cans of paint that were in the little room under the stairs."

"We moved them. They're in a box up on the roof."

"Then I'd like you to get the box," she explained curtly. "Carry it down from the roof. I'll meet you downstairs in the little room."

After she was gone, he dressed and did as he was told. At least the box, eroded by weather, stayed in one piece as he descended the stairs. When he arrived at the first floor, he found all the furniture that had once been inside Gloria's bedroom had been pushed out into the kitchen. Mrs. Liang was inside the little room, crouching near the floorboards, then rising to her feet, following the vertical sweep of calligraphy, craning her head up at a cluster of characters that had snuck above the margin of the wall and spilled onto the ceiling. She stepped back and tried to take in the full breadth of what had been written.

"This was your idea?" she asked.

"No, Gloria's. The other Jesus teacher."

"She thought she was clever painting words on my walls? She thought she was doing me a favor?"

He knew, without being instructed, to equip himself with a brush and open a can of paint. What, after all, could reasonably be said about Gloria Hamilton? That she'd been passionate about calligraphy and Jesus? That she'd gone too far on both counts? He raised a paint-drenched brush and blotted out a large swath of her writing. In doing so, he couldn't help but wonder what had become of its author. Impossible to know, but he doubted she'd transferred to another Taiwan ministry house. He guessed that she had instead collected her things and gone back home, back to Nebraska, where her talent for calligraphy and graphic-novel illustration would become a mere curiosity, a mere party trick at church socials and picnics. She would no doubt blame him exclusively for her early return. Of all the people who bore ill will toward him, he believed Gloria Hamilton's resentment would burn the fiercest and the longest.

There was a modest pleasure to be taken in watching wide clusters of her characters disappear beneath his brush. He covered much of the wall while Mrs. Liang supervised from the doorway. She was a soft-featured, petite woman, but when she crossed her arms and glared impatiently in his direction, he picked up the tempo of his labor. "Two coats over the writing," she said. "One coat over everything else. Ceiling and floor, too. Don't forget the door. And what exactly happened here?"

"Gloria was a very stubborn person. I guess you could say she got carried away."

"She wasn't the only one," Mrs. Liang said. "From what I've heard."

He could only manage a shirking glance back in her direction.

"I've gotten phone calls from the neighbors," she said. "I've heard the gossip. I may as well hear your version of what happened."

He went back to dabbing his brush along the crevices and high corners of the room. A small consolation to have his hands engaged in this task, while at the same time he struggled to stammer out an explanation. It was like a kind of grief, explaining himself this way, saying that he'd met a headstrong high school girl who'd not been shy about declaring her affections, and that while he'd managed to tell her no in public, he'd given her an altogether different answer in private. He spoke mostly to the wall. Yes, he said, they'd spent some time alone together here in the ministry house, in the bedroom, in the bed. That part was true, if that's what the neighbors were saying.

From Mrs. Liang came a petulant groan, half complaint, half sigh. Yes, the groan confirmed, that's what the neighbors were saying, that and more.

He said he supposed he'd done it because he'd felt alone. But wasn't it a frail excuse to face the wall and say that he'd been lonely? How puny it sounded, though when you were in the grip of it, loneliness was vast, a wide river whose dark and tumbling currents could carry you in any number of directions.

If Mrs. Liang was aghast, if her earlier consternation had changed to outrage, he couldn't quite bring himself to turn around and confront her reaction. Instead he wet his brush and knelt to paint the floorboards. While he worked he tried to compose an idea, a spoken opinion, that would show he understood his own flaws and had taken appropriate measures to ensure his mistake would not happen again. Perhaps he should simply declare that in the future he would not be ruled by desire. But was this a promise that could be kept? And did he really need to make such a lofty pledge to his landlady? In the end he didn't think so. In the end the only reasonable avowals to be made were the declarations of apology. He said he was sorry and meant it. He said he'd been careless with people's trust.

"Very careless," Mrs. Liang replied. "Thank goodness Mr. Liang never heard about it."

"I should have been a better tenant. I wasn't a very good Jesus teacher either."

"I guess not," she said. "*Aiya!* You're not going to paint the floor without sweeping and mopping first, are you?"

"What?" he said. "No. I won't. I wouldn't—"

And then she was marching off impatiently to gather a mop and pail of water. When she returned, she did not like the way he was sweeping the floor and so she wrested the broom from his hands and did it herself. After that she ran a damp mop across the floor and left him to paint the remaining three walls and ceiling and floor and, last, the door panel containing Gloria's positive-thinking message. Completing this took more effort and time and paint than he might have imagined. He did not finish until after the noon hour, and when he stepped into the kitchen, he found Mrs. Liang had heated a lunch of fish soup and pork buns that she'd purchased in Taipei and brought down with her on the train. That there were two plates at the table, that a bowl of soup had been filled for him and several pork buns set aside, this courtesy, this small act of consideration, loomed suddenly, potently, large. He felt his throat constrict. He took a deep breath. "Thank you," he said and was able to stave off a deep pang of feeling that might otherwise have had him shuddering and wiping his eyes.

They sat for lunch. The few chatty remarks he made—about the August heat, the number of days he'd gone without the service of an electric fan—did not result in conversation. It was Mrs. Liang's habit to appreciate her meal in silence, to lean back in her chair and convey, in the slow lowering of her eyelids or the pursing of her lips, some secret appraisal of the food she'd just tasted. Once she'd emptied her bowl, she set out a kettle of tea water to boil on the stove and cleared her throat to speak.

"You'll be staying here awhile then?" she asked.

"If you'll let me, yes."

"And what will you do?"

Do? He wondered at the word a moment. Was there still something, some vocation, he *did*? "I won't be teaching Bible study classes," he admitted. "I came back because I'm looking for someone."

She greeted the announcement warily. Throughout their meal she'd reached across the table for sauce bottles and napkins without once consulting, or even glancing at, a stack of flyers bearing Jia-ling's photograph. She took heed of the flyers now. She leaned over them and sighed noisily. "This young woman here?"

"Yes. Her name is Song Jia-ling. I met her in the Mainland this summer, in Xinjiang. So I already know her. I know her family, too." He blinked dumbly. He wasn't at all sure where his present explanation was heading. "It's complicated," he said.

"Everything is," she replied. "But I suppose you're going to tell me about it. I suppose I'm going to hear a complicated story."

Afterward, after she'd sat drinking tea and listening impassively and forming more of her secret opinions, she directed him to the kitchen and put him to work scouring the long-dormant and now moldy refrigerator. As soon as he finished this, she sent him into the bathroom to scrub the tile work and toilet. He thought of such work as both repugnant and necessary. But was it also meant to be a form of penitence? He didn't think so, and yet, with his shirt drenched in sweat and his arm elbow-deep in the toilet, he couldn't entirely rule it out. Once he'd conquered this task, he went searching and found her tending to the mini-palms in the courtyard and chatting with a neighbor across the fence. Was there anything else? he asked. Indeed there was—a host of other domestic chores she wanted to see accomplished before she returned to Taipei the next morning. He wiped his brow and set to work mopping, washing curtains and blinds, moving furniture between rooms until the onset of evening.

They went out to dinner, not to the idle restaurant he'd been frequenting every day since his return, but straight into the crush and commotion of Hungry Ghost Street, where nearly all the vendors and cooks knew him by sight and a constant file of patrons—more than a few of them families with sons and daughters clad in the Ming-da Academy's white and blue summer uniform—paraded past the outdoor counter behind which he and Mrs. Liang sat waiting for their food. She would not allow him to lower his head or slink down on his stool. "Sit up," she insisted. "Pretend if you have to."

"And what do I pretend?" he muttered.

The answer, it seemed, was so perfectly obvious she had to scowl a bit and wag her head. "You pretend you haven't done anything wrong and they'll pretend they're not gossiping about you."

At moments like these, if he disregarded her vibrant white hair and concentrated on the spry, insistent face she'd been showing him all day, it was easy to believe she was a woman near his own age or of his own generation, with the same brisk attitudes and unfussy advice of a favorite cousin. At moments like these it was easy to believe he had gleaned an essential understanding of who she was. Why then did these understandings never seem to prevail? On the way back to the ministry house, she sat behind him on the cycle and pointed out landmarks of the small town, the Toulio village, she'd known forty years earlier. He had to concede that she had decades of life experience while he had only a modest twenty-five years. And once inside the ministry house, as he hung curtains and restocked the refrigerator, he listened in on a telephone call she made to her Taipei home and was surprised, even a bit shamed, to learn that she had worries as pressing, if not more pressing, than his own.

Throughout their day together she had not told him that her husband, Mr. Liang, was ill, perhaps seriously so, judging from the preliminary chat she had with her husband's nurse, a conversation of soft-spoken, clinically precise measurements. How many grams of wheat fiber in his afternoon tea? How many ounces of urine produced? It sounded as if these queries were part of a larger discourse that might have been going on for a long time. And when her husband was put on the line, she began at once to badger him about his evening meal. "All the soup?" she insisted. "The cabbage, too? The cabbage is part of the soup, isn't it? I don't care. It has to be eaten." She listened to his reply and a short while later relented. "I know, I know," she said, her voice as gentle now, as lenient, as it had been demanding a few moments earlier. "I'll tell the doctor and Miss Shin tomorrow. I'll make them stop."

She set the receiver against her chin and listened. "Well, yes," she said. "Busy. But it's quieter now that the classes are over and the students have gone home." She scrutinized the backs of her hands, her fingernails. "I don't know how many. More than twenty students, I think. More than I like to have stomping around the house. Yes," she said and sighed and nodded. "All right, I'll let him know." She told her husband she would see him the next afternoon and hung up the phone.

In the silence that followed she glanced pointedly across the room at Vincent.

"He's not feeling well?" Vincent inquired shyly.

"No," she said. "He hasn't felt well in a long time. Not since last New Year."

"I'm sorry to hear that."

"Yes," she said. The shrug she gave him, hapless and slight and still profoundly reluctant, was, in its way, as complete an explanation as any words she might have offered. "He says the classroom will stay cooler if you keep the rooftop door open."

"I'll remember that," Vincent said. He almost turned then and went back to sliding shelves into the refrigerator. Instead he said, "Mr. Liang seems to think that there are still Bible study classes going on here."

"He believes it, yes. Earlier in the summer, after you'd left, we got phone calls from our Toulio neighbors and he overheard a few things. He was still getting over his first surgery. So he was very distressed, very disappointed, even though he only had a faint idea that something was wrong. And when I saw how disappointed he was, I told him not to worry. It was only rumors."

"I understand. I don't blame you."

"He hadn't been able to teach classes at the university in a half year. And the idea that classes, Bible study classes, were being taught in our Toulio home was—still is—a great relief to him."

"Of course."

"So he writes his postcards. And sometimes he calls. He might still call. . . ."

"I won't tell him."

"You may have to do more than that, I think. You may have to invent a few small stories."

"I know how to do that," he admitted.

"It's very important to me that he's not disappointed."

"I understand."

"He's been a believer all his life," she said.

She barged into his room again the next morning, the hour so early, so preposterously early, that he woke reeling and dumbstruck. He could just make out Mrs. Liang's blurred likeness at the corner of his bed.

His mind was blurry as well. "All right," he answered to a question she might not even have asked. "To the airport," he said.

"Airport? What airport?" she asked.

"To the train station. I'm taking you to the train station?"

But he was wrong on this account, too. He just didn't know it yet. For the time being he rushed to dress and wash his face and before long she was ready with her satchel and they were out the door and motoring off toward the town center on his motorcycle. It was a different Toulio at 5:20 A.M. The sky was only murkily lit and the town itself was noticeably cooler, more spacious, more accommodating. At this hour there were no weighty trucks and cars clogging the main avenue. The bicyclists they glided past were all older men and women coasting along so slowly and with such a preoccupied air that they would have been a danger to themselves during the daytime rush. Two blocks before the station Mrs. Liang squeezed his shoulder and told him to veer left. He did. "Left again," she said, and they turned onto a forking lane that carried them first alongside a dry canal and then over a bridge to a hedge-lined district of older homes. A sudden clearing appeared before them, a grassy borderland to a large town park. From there they passed through a gated entrance and bounced along one of the park's gravel pathways. The pall of morning fog had still not lifted. Giant willow trees loomed obscurely from the reach of only ten or twenty yards. A deserted basketball court took shape out of what, seconds earlier, had been a haze of damp air and patchy light. She had him halt the cycle between the court and a wide, grassy meadow. A small crowd had convened upon the meadow, a gathering of some twenty late-aged women and men. By the time Mrs. Liang climbed down from the cycle and joined their ranks, the moist air had thinned by a degree or two, the sunlight had waxed a shade brighter, and he saw that he'd been wrong about the size of the crowd. Its true number might easily have been a hundred or more.

Most were dressed in sweats or running suits and had begun a slow, preliminary stretching of their arms and legs. He sat on the empty basketball court and watched them pace through various exercises: a languid bending and rising, tortoise-slow turns and pirouettes, a careful back-and-forth sweeping of their arms, as fluid and stately as any dancer's pantomime. The vast majority of those assembled were women of Mrs. Liang's age or older. Like her, they all seemed to have adopted the same pageboy haircut. They favored peach- and rose-colored sweat suits. And if he was tempted to grin—if a brigade of such women appeared mildly ridiculous, if their deep breaths and closed eyes and the flushed rapture of their faces seemed somehow indecorous to their age—then the urge to smile or laugh soon passed. In its place grew an even rarer awareness that perhaps the inner life was ageless and could reveal itself in the measured rhythms of tai chi or any other alert gesture of the body.

The exercises continued for forty minutes and then the crowd broke apart and migrated in opposite directions: the minority of men to the park benches for board games and cigarettes, the women to a tree-shaded stretch of parking lot where they began chatting in small cliques and circles. Mrs. Liang loitered among them, roaming from group to group, crouching down now and then to join a conversation and bob her white head in support or contention of what was being said. She rocked back and forth on her heels. She pulled a sheet of folded paper from her satchel and allowed it to circulate from hand to hand. Others leaned forward to examine the paper. It dawned on him eventually that she had brought along a photocopied flyer of Jia-ling and was letting it find its way, woman to woman, throughout the length and breadth of the crowd.

The news appeared to be traveling fast. In just a short while the many separate cliques had pressed together and Mrs. Liang was at the center of the gathering, speaking to a hushed and attentive audience. Several times throughout her explanation the entire confluence of women turned in unison to the basketball court and leveled their collective gaze upon Vincent. Each time this happened he blushed. They were all, it seemed, keenly interested in his story, and when one woman among them, a wrinkled and wiry-haired grandmother of at least seventy years, responded with a story of her own, the crowd clamored round to hear it. Once the old woman had finished, Mrs. Liang took her by the wrist and guided her across the court to Vincent.

The grandmother, when she arrived, wore a boggled grin and spoke Taiwanese in a shy, squeaky voice. A film of cataracts clouded most of one eye. When she looked about, she seemed to have only a tenuous grasp of where she was and who might be holding her by the arm.

"I believe we know where the Mainland girl is staying," Mrs. Liang reported.

"Yes?" he said. "And where do you think she is?"

"I don't know if you'll consider it good news or not. She's staying with the Jin family, staying with them at their home, here in Toulio."

"The Jin family? I've never heard of them."

"Mrs. Fong here is one of their neighbors. She's seen the girl walking about. Same girl as in the flyer. The rumor going around the neighborhood is that she's from the Mainland and she's staying with the Widow Jin and her son. Mrs. Fong says a wedding is being planned. The girl is a Mainland bride and is set to marry the Widow Jin's only son."

"What? What only son? What's his name?"

"It's hard to pronounce," Mrs. Liang said. "It's a clumsy name. I've never heard anything like it. Ode-dee," she tried. "Ode-deek."

"Neek!" Mrs. Fong corrected her.

"Ode-neek."

"Poe-neek," the old woman said in her creaking voice.

Vincent bowed his head in recognition. "Ponic." He sighed.

"Yes," Mrs. Liang said. "Whoever heard of such a name?"

He rode with Mrs. Liang back through the park and over the bridge and onto the forking canal road, a journey of only three or four kilometers. West of the canal they made a simple right turn and entered a neighborhood of older, unremarkable single-story homes. Each home had its own small yard. Each yard was either bare dirt and weeds or overbrimming with little flower and shrub gardens, depending, Vincent guessed, on the tastes and enthusiasms of its owners. Ponic's yard was of the bare-dirt variety, yet he had set down a swath of gravel and a line of cinder blocks and thus fashioned himself a miniature off-street parking lot. Upon the lot Mr. Gwa's gray Pontiac Bonneville sat parked several feet from the living room window.

The morning air had begun to turn humid. A swell of bright sunlight was building on the eastern horizon. He glanced at his watch. It was not yet seven o'clock. Except for a whimpering infant and a young mother hand-washing clothes on her patio, no one in the neighborhood appeared to have risen from bed. He sat on his idling motorcycle with Mrs. Liang, who had come along to read street signs and point out the Jin family home.

"What will you do?" she asked.

It seemed a decisive course of action was required of him. Too bad all he had were naive intentions. He said he would like to speak to Jia-ling. He would like to make sure she was all right. Though now, he admitted, was probably not the best time. He did not want to knock on their door so early in the morning and wake them from sleep. Better to come back in a few hours, he said. Better to speak to her when Ponic was away from home.

"You have feelings for this girl, Jia-ling?"

"I think I do, yes."

"And you didn't have feelings for her sister?"

"Not exactly. I might have thought I did, but it turned out . . . I didn't really."

"And the high school girl, the Ming-da student?"

"I didn't have feelings for her, no."

There was, surely, a look of great skepticism fixed upon Mrs. Liang's face. He was glad to be seated in front of her on the cycle and therefore not obliged to see it.

They rode to the town center and, before entering the train station, went to a vendor's cart and bought fried egg sandwiches and red paste sweet buns. They ate their breakfast sitting on a wood pew in the station, and when they finished their meal it seemed a fitting time to acknowledge all she had done for him. "Thank you," he said in a suddenly pinched voice. "For letting me stay in your house. For helping me find Jia-ling. For—"

She stopped him with a raised hand. "Enough," she said. "I don't want thank-yous."

"If not thank-yous, then what?" he asked.

She shrugged and recited a list of slightly grudging requests. She wanted her house kept clean. She wanted the bills paid on time. If he was going to leave again, she said, she wanted him to call and tell her so.

He promised to do these things and then he stood in the thickening counter line and bought her a one-way express ticket to Taipei. When he returned, she was standing at the turnstile gates looking out at the sun-streaked tracks, so deeply immersed in thought he could not quite bring himself to interrupt her.

A short while later she turned and noticed him. She measured out a kindly and reluctant smile. "Maybe it's better to let them be," she said. "If you're not sure. The match has been made. It may turn out to be a good one. And the girl, Jia-ling, she's already settled in with the Jin family."

He blinked dully at the advice he'd just been offered. "Maybe so," he said. Then she was through the turnstile and padding out across the platform, the first leg of a journey that would take her to Taipei, to her apartment, to her seriously ill husband. And Vincent was pacing away too, in the opposite direction, out into the station parking lot and a hot, plentifully bright and unavoidable August morning.

He rode to the ministry house and climbed the stairs to his bedroom. Atop his dresser sat Jia-ling's wrapped teakwood box. Just how long he might have stood there weighing the box in his hands he could not say. What a clumsy and inconsequential gift it seemed to be. Or what a considerate one. Was it possible to know which? Probably not, he guessed. Not until he understood what he meant by giving it.

He stowed it in the basket of his motorcycle and set off gliding along a series of winding lanes that took him, perhaps sooner than he would have liked, to Ponic's neighborhood. That neighborhood had roused itself from its earlier slumber. The corner shop had rolled up its gated front and set its television blaring at the highest volume. The doors of most homes, Ponic's included, had been thrown open. Occasionally a harried family man emerged from one of those doors, climbed aboard his scooter, and set off for work. Vincent observed their departures from where he sat perched on his motorcycle behind a squatty hedge. He was by no means hidden; children and whiskered old men who happened to be passing by paused to stare at him. Over the bristly top of the hedge he could see across the lane and into the Jin family home. Several shadowed figures were moving about the kitchen. It appeared that pails of water were being filled at the kitchen sink. A hand reached forward—Jia-ling's?—and collected a pile of scrub pads and washrags from the kitchen windowsill.

At ten o'clock Ponic strolled out to the Bonneville, opened the door, and hung a bundle of dry cleaning from a latch above the backseat window. He heaved his broad chest and belly, wiped his brow with the sleeve of his shirt. Then he stepped back into the house.

A short while later a produce truck rumbled by. A stray dog loped down the lane, and while it shied away from every other person it passed, it drew near Vincent and licked the underside of his tennis shoe. At the same moment a loud wail of complaint arose from inside the Jin family house. An aggrieved female voice answered back. This progressed quickly into a salvo of still louder shouts and a corresponding bray of protest and then a deep, booming crash that could only have been the shattering of something weighty and huge. As abrupt sounds went, this one happened to terrify him. For several long and possibly crucial minutes he did nothing but sit frozen behind a screen of hedge branches. *On your feet,* he commanded himself. *This isn't dangerous. It's only other people's anguish.* He managed to climb from the cycle and step to the edge of the lane.

Just then Ponic stormed from the house and climbed behind the wheel of the Bonneville. The engine started and revved to a furious howl. The sedan lurched from the gravel lot, reversing swiftly, and the resulting swerve and skid sent it careening into a pair of curbed motor scooters. What followed was a blunt, walloping crash, a sprinkling of glass, a sighing lull. A distraught Ponic staggered forth to assess the damage. The sedan's side mirror had been lopped off, its fender and door panel dented and badly scratched. He scooped up the severed mirror and stomped halfway up his gravel-strewn yard and pointed to whoever might be standing in the shaded foyer of his home. "You did this!" he cried, his beefy face a deep crimson. His neighbors, even those who'd had their scooter broadsided, would not stray from their houses to confront him. "You *made* me do this!" he revised himself. Then he turned back and climbed behind the wheel of the car again. The engine revved mightily once more and he steered the Bonneville down the lane, passing close by but never once lifting his eyes to Vincent.

In the wake of his departure the neighborhood seemed to brood in silence a moment and then, abruptly, get on with its business. Two houses down a child squealed in delight. An old man zigzagged by on a bicycle, veering around and, for no good reason, grinning at the shards of debris in the roadway. Vincent watched him ride off before striding across the lane and bare yard and approaching the Jin family home. Only once he reached the threshold did he remember the teakwood box, which he'd left in the closed basket of his motorcycle.

"Excuse me," he called out.

When no one answered, he slipped inside and took a few wavering steps across the living room. Almost immediately he felt a sogginess steal into his shoes. He frowned and looked down and discovered a floor deluged in a half-inch layer of soupy muck. The odor that rose up from the muck was horrible—stifling and feculent and brackishly thick. He nearly gagged. A few steps farther and he came upon an overturned table and then a collapsed and algae-smeared aquarium, bathtub-size, the hull of it cracked open and still trickling a rivulet of green sludge. Beyond this wreckage lay two large plastic basins, each containing fresh water and a silver-scaled dragon fish, both of them superb specimens, so large their tail fins hung over the lip of the basins and half of their side-turned bodies, gills included, rose above the waterline. They both breathed patiently or desperately—who could tell?—through one submerged gill and gaped up at him with their glassy eyes.

There was a murmuring voice issuing from the rear of the house, and he sloshed his way toward it, down a short hall and into the tiled entranceway of a kitchen. On the other side of the entranceway an old and acutely liver-spotted woman was speaking and swaying on her feet. He stepped inside without attracting her notice.

"... and no wonder, either. We ask you to do the simplest things and each time it puts you in a bad mood," the old woman, undoubtedly the Widow Jin, complained to an unseen listener elsewhere in the room. "And don't think I haven't noticed," she said. "Don't think I haven't choked on your food. You could poison us all with what little you know about cooking, what little you know about anything. Never steamed a prawn. Never scrubbed a floor or cleaned a fish tank. Because you're used to living in dirt, like an animal, and now you want us to live in dirt, like an animal. Is that what you have in mind? Is that ..."

Because she spoke in an addled croak, a very soft croak, and because her face had grown doughy and lax and could no longer hold a distinct expression, the things she said, spiteful as they might have been, seemed as trifling and weightless as air. She had already lost her claim on his attention, had become a droning hum, a bore. He stepped past her for a fuller view of the kitchen interior.

Across the room, standing before and facing the kitchen sink, was a young woman whom he recognized instantly as Jia-ling.

Her trousers and blouse were sopping wet. She was drenched in foul aquarium water. She was at the sink drying the tips of her dampened hair with a dishrag.

His first thought: She should have heeded her mother's advice and brought along her heavy raincoat. A different rain in Taiwan, her mother had said. A heavy rain. And then a great surge of relief. She was here. She was present. She may well have been tricked, swindled into a lesser arranged marriage than the one she'd been promised, but she'd not, thankfully, been kidnapped or sold into prostitution. There'd been no extravagant conspiracy. Or only a conspiracy of the most ordinary kind— a marriage, a mother-in-law, a wrecked and dirty house.

"Jia-ling," he said, and she turned around from the sink, a sodden and humbled young woman, nothing like the dauntless pioneer of her photograph, nothing like the portentous and looming figure she'd become in his imagination. Still, he believed, against considerable evidence, that he knew her.

Her reaction was an event to be carefully studied: the utter puzzlement, the mild sense of surprise, and the momentary flicker of something else—if not an equal relief, then an acknowledgment that she knew he had followed her here, from Hong Kong to Taiwan, to this very kitchen. For that she seemed to offer a fleeting pardon, a thankfulness. It transpired in an instant. As soon as it was over, he began to question whether it had existed at all.

"Are you all right?" he asked.

She nodded her damp head.

"The places I've gone looking for you," he said. "I don't know what decisions Gwa or Ponic have forced you to make. I don't know what you've had to settle for, but you don't have to stay here. I live in a house that's close by," he explained. "There's plenty of room. You're welcome to come stay there. You could take some time and decide what you want to do next. If you think about it and decide you want to go back home to Urumchi, I'll help you do it."

It took her all of five minutes to gather her things. Throughout her hurried packing, she was stepping around the Widow Jin, who continued to murmur her rambling litany of grievances. No attempt was made to appease the old woman. No one offered her an explanation or a farewell. Before long he and Jia-ling were out the door and aboard his motorcycle with her weighty parcel box balanced on the gas tank. All the way back to the ministry house he was hunched over it, angling along, peering out at the roadway ahead.

Thirty-five

SHE HARDLY MADE any noise at all, just the faint slap of her bare feet on her tiled bedroom floor, or the soft whisk of a brush in her hair, a light yawn, or the closing and stowing away of the magazines she liked to read before sleep, hushed sounds that would rise above the open divide in the wall and reach Vincent where he lay stretched out, ruminating in his own bed.

Beyond the confines of her room, over meals or house chores or sometimes when they passed in the stairway, she would make an occasional remark. "And you've never paid rent?" she marveled, peering up the stairwell to the third floor and beyond. "No rent whatsoever?" She could not get over the great size of the ministry house in relation to its scant number of occupants. She presided over other opinions and confidentialities as well, ones she most often chose not to share. Certain matters, particularly those involving her ten-day absence, could only be mentioned obliquely. She commented over breakfast one morning that she'd not been impressed by her first glimpse of Taiwan, an aerial view of smog-bound Kaohsiung, but that she'd liked the look of things better once they'd gotten in Gwa's sedan and followed the highway out into the countryside.

But hadn't they stopped for lunch in a Kaohsiung restaurant? Hadn't they gone for a hike in the mountains outside the city?

No, she reported. They'd gone straight to Toulio, straight to Ponic's home.

This seemed to Vincent a particularly heartless deception. He was both incensed and saddened on her behalf. Needlessly so, it turned out. She knew nothing of Kaohsiung restaurants and mountain hikes. Of the varied circumstances surrounding her journey to Taiwan, she would say only that Ponic and Gwa had arrived very early in the morning at the Olympic Hotel, had called her room from the hotel lobby, had brought her along for breakfast at a Tsimshatsui diner Gwa liked. After breakfast they'd had a long talk. A long talk? Vincent could well imagine the threats and coercions that comprised this talk. Yet he could not cajole her into revealing the details. Even the mildest of inquiries and she would give him a piqued stare, a sharp reminder that, though housemates, their present alliance did not extend into any true or reliable confidence.

A few days later, relaxing in the living room after dinner, he told her he'd gone to a men's leisure club, a whorehouse, looking for her. Even as he was speaking, he wondered why he needed to disclose this. To show the lengths he'd gone to, maybe. To show how worried he'd been. Too bad these rationales were all but lost on his new housemate, who sat listening to his account with a crimped frown and an escalating air of indignation.

"What?" she asked, genuinely dismayed. "But I would *never* have agreed to work in a place like that. Impossible! I would have cursed them for suggesting it. I would have walked back to Urumchi if I had to."

It was a misunderstanding that required much patience and pardon-seeking to rectify. She had disappeared from her hotel room, he explained. When he'd gone looking for her, he discovered he'd been lied to. It wasn't really such a stretch to imagine abduction, forced prostitution. Only later, once she had calmed down, did the real underpinnings of their disagreement become clear to him.

She'd known before leaving Hong Kong that her arranged marriage would be to Ponic. They had taken her out to breakfast and given her a choice. Her options had been austerely simple: Ponic or back to Urumchi. Vincent had seen her life there, not just the all-too-common poverty of her home, or the furnacelike misery of her work at the tannery, or hard-baked and pitiless Urumchi itself, but the impossibility that any of it would ever change. Ponic or Urumchi? Would Vincent, in her place, have chosen differently?

He knew this for certain: it was not his right to judge just how far her engagement to Ponic had gone. Vincent had been present in Ponic's home as she rushed to gather her things. Much of what she'd collected had come from the house's master bedroom, Ponic's bedroom. Days later she still spoke his name with what might have been an ex-lover's disdain. Certainly it saddened him to think of the compromises she might have made, but given his own indiscretions he couldn't exactly hold it against her.

Finally, there was one other, much milder conflict between them, a difference of opinion concerning a pledge that had been made to her, a promise that by agreeing to marry Ponic she would also be given work in Gwa's remaining Toulio factory. In fact, she had already been to the factory and met with the supervisor. Since then, however, her engagement to Ponic had ended. She'd moved into the ministry house on a Wednesday morning. She was to begin her first day of work at the factory the following Monday. She believed resolutely that she was still owed a job.

Vincent kept most of his misgivings to himself. Yet he couldn't help but suggest that she consider other options as well.

"What other options?" she asked.

"Well, there are certainly lots of other factories in town. Stores, too. And restaurants."

"But I already have a job!" she insisted, her voice tinged with alarm, her back, her neck, her entire demeanor rigid, obstinate.

And so on Saturday they walked up the lane to the corner repair shop and bought a secondhand three-speed bicycle from the mechanic, whose manner was aloof even as he accepted Vincent's money. Next they went to a clothing stall in the west market and purchased a required navy blue work apron. On Sunday night she boiled a meal of tofu and green vegetables and sealed it in a plastic container for the next day's lunch.

She was up very early Monday morning, loitering about the first floor of the ministry house, and then, at last, pedaling off to the factory at half past eight. After she'd gone, he went to the kitchen window every twenty minutes or so to look for her at the front gate. The morning wore on. He checked less often. Still, he waited until almost one o'clock to eat lunch, thinking she would be back and he would not be dining alone. By midafternoon he began to revise his misgivings.

She arrived home at five-fifteen; he first heard the creak of her second-hand bicycle, then the chiming thwack of its kickstand. She came through the door wearing a style of grin he'd not seen on her before, a wide, insouciant smile that reined in, barely, a large, full-spirited happiness. She was helping to make motorcycle helmets, she said. Today she had prepared the helmets for shipping, but soon she would be putting them together. She would have a workstation all to herself. She would have a cushioned chair to sit on. And the money she was making! She covered a portion of her smile with a cupped hand and whispered the amount. More than three thousand yuan per week. One hundred and twenty-five American dollars. Her Urumchi salary had just been bettered fifteenfold. The people she worked with were very friendly, she said. She only had to work half days on Saturday. And if she wanted, she was allowed to leave the factory and go shopping during her lunch hour. They really were very good helmets, she said. She put a hand to her cheek, shook her head in amazement. She had a job, she said.

Late one evening a week and a half later, Ponic came to the ministry house front door. Seen through the gray mesh of the screen and backed by grainy courtyard lamplight, he appeared neither as angry nor as heartsick as might be expected.

"We need to have a meeting," he said, almost bashfully. He sallied right to left looking past Vincent, perhaps for some sign of his truant fiancée. "I have the car here. We can go for a drive."

"To where?"

"Nowhere," Ponic said. "Just a drive."

Vincent stepped back behind the door to consult Jia-ling, who, reposed in her preferred reading chair, had overheard their exchange. Here was her chance to speak aloud any forebodings she might have, any gentle cautions or new-fledged concerns for his safety. She creased the newspaper she'd been perusing and feigned a look of extreme dull-wittedness, extreme torpor, a parody, he soon realized, of Ponic himself.

What convinced Vincent finally was seeing the Bonneville halted mid-lane before the front gate and in the rear seat a suited businessman, Gwa, blowing a fog of cigarette smoke out the open window. It wasn't enough, somehow, for Vincent to know his benefactor viewed him with contempt. He wanted to be an audience to that contempt. He wanted to hear the recriminations firsthand.

"Why are Americans so slow?" Ponic asked, as they rounded the sedan's dented and mirrorless left. "Why three months? Why not three weeks?"

"Why? I'm not sure," Vincent answered, and realized after the fact that Ponic had been referring to replacement parts.

He opened the rear door and slipped inside. He understood at once that he had to do something with the sedan's inner climate of hostility and manly affluence, had to exaggerate it in his mind until its ambience turned prankish, perfectly absurd. Only then could he relax a little and lean back into the car's busomlike upholstery.

From Gwa there came nothing remotely like a welcome, no sullen nod or incurious greeting. He sat in his tailored suit, sat listlessly in the rear seat of his one-of-a-kind chauffeured sedan, taking no discernible relish in this or any of his luxuries because of an immense personal hardship that had to be borne. He was sulking, Vincent soon realized, over lost love, over Kailing. Furthermore, he appeared angry to have had such a hardship forced upon him. And yet wasn't there something studied about the way he suffered, the way he wedged a cigarette deep into the crevice of his fingers and hung his head with a princely gloominess? Vincent would never have expected such indulgent brooding from a thirty-seven-year-old married man, a father, no less. *See what you've done,* Gwa seemed to be saying with his silence and slack posture. *See what you've cost me.*

The sedan veered left at the intersection and before long they were wending forward like a leviathan among schools of darting motor scooters. The Toulio skyline was mostly dark. They traveled north until they came to a high balustrade-lined wall that marked one end of a block-long temple complex. A ceremony of some type was in progress. Lanterns burned in its highest parapets.

"Drive around the temple a few times if you like," Gwa said moodily. His eyes, when they passed over Vincent, were beacons of glinting disappointment. "I'll let Ponic begin," he said. "He's taken some time to think about this. He's put together a list."

"I have, yes," Ponic said. He ran his plump hands indecisively along the steering wheel a moment. "First off there's the wedding portraits. We never had them taken, but I did put two thousand yuan down that I can't get back. Plus the reservations we made at the banquet hall. That may cost me too. And the car repair. The damage wouldn't have happened if she hadn't tried—on purpose—to get me so mad. Same thing with the damage in the house."

"I don't understand," Vincent said. "You want her to pay for these things?"

"Don't care who pays. As long as my mother and I receive the money."

"And what about the wedding?"

"I don't want to go through with it, not after the way she acted."

"And neither does Jia-ling. That makes it a shared decision to break it off. She doesn't want it. Neither do you."

"It's true, yes. I don't want it," Ponic conceded. "I wasn't expecting her to behave like that. All your life you hear how tender the old-fashioned Mainland girls are and how well they treat you. And then you get one and you find out it's not true." It was a discovery that still appeared to have the power to sting him. He shook his head, took a wincing glance into the rearview mirror. "There's no more old-fashioned girls," he said. "Even the Mainland girls aren't really Mainland girls anymore."

"And so it's a shared decision," Vincent repeated. "No one is at fault. Neither of you owes the other anything."

"But what about my mother? Her hopes raised up so high. Telling the neighbors one thing, and now having to make excuses. She needs more than an apology to feel right about it."

He pretended to listen to this absurdity. He pretended to think it over. Evidently, it was going to be the sort of argument in which all his opponent's complaints kept circling back around carousel-style. A wiser man would have refused to participate. Vincent pressed on anyway. There would be no payment, he explained, because Jia-ling wasn't at fault. Not for the car. Not for the fish tank. Not for the Widow Jin's disappointment. And if Ponic insisted on reparation, he might as well seek it from Mr. Gwa, since Gwa was still holding five thousand dollars that he'd failed to pay Vincent.

The remark seemed to shake Gwa from his doleful reverie. "*Would* have paid you," he said tersely. "If you'd been able to stand up and represent me the way I asked."

"I did everything your telexes asked me to do. She'd made up her mind. Surely, you can't believe it was entirely my fault."

"It's a fairly simple matter," Gwa said. "I spent time and money to have you bring Kai-ling from the Mainland to Taiwan. And when you weren't able to persuade her, Ponic thought he might like to marry her younger sister. Now both of us have nothing to show for our trouble. And where's the younger sister? She's staying with you. Is it unreasonable for me to expect my money back?"

"Your money back?" A sudden, sharp bark of laughter escaped him. In the muffled sedan interior it sounded rather squawky and hopeless. "And just how much do you expect, everything included—your money back, plus wedding expenses, plus damages? How much altogether?"

"Seven thousand American dollars," Gwa said flatly.

"You realize, don't you, how ridiculous this is? I don't have seven thousand dollars. I barely have any money left at all."

It was an excuse Gwa seemed to have anticipated. "Maybe so. But you can work. You can find a job. The younger sister is already working, isn't she? You two can make payments just like everyone else who has a debt."

"Debt? We have no debt. We don't have to pay you anything."

"You do if you want to stay in Toulio," Gwa said. "Or anywhere in Yun

Lin County. I know too many officials here. All it would take is a phone call. Not even that. Just a comment over lunch at the next mayor's conference. 'There's a Mainland girl staying in town with the foreign Jesus teacher. I heard she entered Taiwan using her sister's passport and marriage certificate.' That's a mess that would take some sorting out."

Vincent did not feel capable of a calm or reasoned response. He held his tongue and gazed out the sedan's passenger window. Through a wide portal in the temple he could see files of worshipers lighting incense sticks before an ornate cauldron, godly men and women whose lives could only be less snarled, less compromised than his own.

"Let's start with a sensible amount," Gwa said. "Three hundred American dollars the first of every month."

Vincent took a long, slow, calming breath. Inwardly, he promised himself that he would not, under any circumstances, make such payments. "I shouldn't have to pay you anything," he said. "No matter what the damages or what you first paid me to go to Urumchi. The reason I shouldn't pay is that you came to my house and lied to me, sat at my kitchen table and told me you'd never been married. I should never have gone to Urumchi in the first place. You're a man with a wife and a child and you should never have sent me."

This appeared to be a point Gwa was willing to acknowledge. He nodded in a conciliatory fashion. He heaved his shoulders. "And you fuck schoolgirls," he said and bestowed upon Vincent a sharp, leveling gaze that carried a certain grim humor, an allowance that since it was impossible to change their very natures, to be other than who they were, they might as well go ahead and admit their worst failings, they might as well laugh at what they could not change. Then he leaned back in his seat and told his driver to return to the ministry house.

They rode in silence a few kilometers. Ponic, having overheard their exchange, now appeared too bashful to look at either of them in the rearview mirror.

"I did want to ask about Kai-ling," Gwa said as they neared the ministry house front gate. "Just so I know. Just so I understand. You were afraid of her, I take it? Of how beautiful she is? You couldn't stand up to her and use your influence because of the way she looked?"

"She'd already made up her mind. By then it wasn't even a matter of influence."

"But you thought she was beautiful?"

"I did."

"Of course you did. And I'm certain it showed every time you glanced at her. Every time you were around her she thought, Oh my, look at the advantage I have. You should have been able to put her fine looks out of your mind. You take that away and what is she? Poor as dirt. Living in Urumchi. She works in a train station. She's twenty-eight and still not married. If you had quit looking at her like a princess, she would have come to her senses and gone through with the wedding."

"I don't think it's that simple. I think she had other options."

"It's exactly that simple," Gwa said. "I know your type. Always ready to get down on your knees and give a woman all the advantage. Never able to stand up for yourself. All your life you'll be like a dog begging for scraps at the table."

Whatever he might do, whatever he might eventually decide, it did him no good to pass the long, overwarm days of August and September brooding inside the ministry house. Perhaps at least in this one regard— and one regard only—Gwa had been right: perhaps Vincent did need a job. And a job might very well be possible. After all, he'd once held an assortment of private and public teaching positions. Why not make a few telephone inquiries?

He called and left several messages but did not hear back from the plastics wholesaler. This itself wasn't really a concern; the wholesaler frequently traveled abroad and was often away from home for weeks at a time. Besides, there were other options to consider. The Ming-da Academy, of course, wasn't one of them. Vincent dared not contact Johnny Hwang. But he did telephone Miss Yang at the preschool, only to learn of a startling shift in the school's policy regarding foreign teachers. The children, Miss Yang said, were at the age where they were best taught by Chinese English teachers. Foreign English teachers were too lively and unusual and as a result the children became too excited to learn. Listening to her, he felt a stabbing physical ache. Still, he managed to thank her. He managed to tell her good-bye.

Afterward he turned her excuse over and over in his mind. Its subtleties amazed him. *Too lively and unusual. Too excited to learn.* The longer he pondered her remarks, the sadder and more discouraged he became.

And yet wasn't there an obvious solution to his predicament? If he wanted to earn money, he could just as easily teach English conversation lessons in the ministry house's third-floor classroom. Flyers would need to be drawn up and posted. He would have to figure out a reasonable tuition to charge his students. Yet whenever he thought about embarking on these simple tasks, he would be seized by a reluctance so severe it felt almost like panic. Beneath it loomed the all-too-genuine possibility that his new enterprise would fail. He might not draw a single student. And there would be no way to equivocate such an outcome; he could not blame an empty classroom on chance or bad luck. It would be the town's final, censuring verdict against him.

For several days he pondered this potential failure to the point of mental stagnation, a fruitless mental wrangling, a restlessness that in the late hours of the afternoon would send him straying to the kitchen window, where he would look out at the front gate and await Jia-ling's return.

She was, if anything, a young woman who loved her job.

On the last Saturday in September she hurried home from the helmet factory with a tan envelope containing her first month's wages. At once she revealed her new bounty to Vincent. Thirteen blue thousand-yuan bills—money to repay him for her bicycle and a host of smaller expenses, money to send to her parents in Urumchi, money to open her first savings account. And still there was money above and beyond these allotments. There was money left over.

The next day she went shopping in the west market and came back with an armload of minor purchases, among them a pair of knee-length blue jean shorts and a faux designer T-shirt, both of which she donned before dinner and wore around the ministry house the rest of the evening.

The following Saturday she accompanied a group of her female coworkers to Taichung for yet another day of shopping. She returned well after nightfall in a lively mood and with a clutch of shopping bags, several of them small and logoed and bearing some sort of obscure and neatly folded garment within. She'd had her hair cut as well. The other women had taken her to a favorite Taichung salon, and the result was not so much a significant shortening or change in hairstyle as a careful reshaping of the shoulder-length hair she already had. The sides, in particular, had been trimmed in such a way that they followed the natural contours of her cheeks and jaw. She looked sleeker, somehow, livelier. She looked ready to join the ranks of a more modish and self-governing class of young women whose manners she'd been studying discreetly since leaving home six weeks earlier.

Soon there were other changes afoot, other opportunities. It turned out that many of the workers in her factory bought tickets in the underground lottery, a covert version of the legitimate Hong Kong lottery. A middle-aged secretary at the factory, a mother of three school-age children, sold these tickets and paid out in the all-too-rare event of a winner. And when she moved on to a better position at the building commissioner's office, she looked around for someone to continue selling tickets at the factory on her behalf. It was illegal, of course. No one knew whose money or authority backed the secretary. But her lottery transactions had always occurred out in the open. There'd never been an arrest. Jia-ling was the first to step forward, though she refused payment in lottery tickets and asked instead for a small percentage of each ticket sold.

And so she was launched into a second vocation. Vincent wondered sometimes if she was too money-minded, too concerned with profit. So many of her efforts were focused on securing a measure of wealth for herself. Was it greed? After some reflection he decided no, not greed, just an uncurbed determination to never again be poor.

She spent the lion's share of her new income on another personal adornment: she bought contact lenses. Her glasses, she told him, had never fit properly. For one thing they'd not been made for her. She'd bought them secondhand on the Urumchi black market. The lens prescription had been a degree or two off. And how glad she was to be rid of the thick frames. The effect on her appearance was even more striking than her haircut. At once it brought a new openness to her features. He'd once thought she had a rather squarish face, better suited for a boy, but now with her glasses gone and her eyes and nose laid bare, he saw she had the seemly face of a prudent young woman. She'd also been away from the Urumchi tannery for well over a month and there was a renewed flush of vitality to her skin. Hers may not have been a rare or notable beauty like her sister's, yet she was unquestionably lovely in her way, a knowable beauty. She seemed to him a person whose quiet appeal would not go unnoticed by the world much longer.

One evening he returned to her the teakwood box, which, in truth, had never been hers to begin with. He didn't lie about where it had come from. He said he thought she might like to have it anyway. Then he asked what she'd kept inside her original teakwood box. He asked what, if anything, had been stolen.

She was, as with other matters, evasive on the subject. "Nothing," she began. "Nothing valuable, nothing worth talking about."

He pestered her for something more, his tone good-humored. All he wanted was a clue, he said, a hint. When she refused he tried an opposite tack, insisting her denial, her secrecy, could only mean the box had contained an object of extraordinary value, and when this strategy failed, he resorted to willful silence, the implication being that this conversation, and future ones, would be made cumbersome by her secret.

In the end she relented. "Letters," she said.

"Family letters?"

Not family letters, she told him. They were letters from a boy she knew in Urumchi. He had worked selling refreshments at a number of establishments, outside the train station, for instance, or at the Heaven Lake bus stop. He had not had much schooling; his written characters were tentative, sloppy. But he had composed letters and passed them to her whenever they crossed paths as vendors. She called them letters of friendship, which Vincent knew meant letters of love, or at the very least letters of romantic intention. No wonder their theft had pained her so. It pained *him* to think of the intimacy contained in those letters and how she had safeguarded them in her teakwood box.

"It's not too late," he said, sorry to have pursued a secret this personal, this significant. "He's probably worried about you."

"He probably is," she agreed.

"You could write him a letter, so he knows you're safe and thinking about going back to Urumchi. So he knows," Vincent said. Somehow he had come to the brink of a wide, munificent emotion. He rather liked the chivalrous thrill of it, even though very little of what he'd just proposed felt particularly sincere.

She did not answer him except for a general relaxing of her careful posture, except for looking about the ministry house in what had lately become a practiced and questioning gaze.

With that the subject was dropped only to be resurrected two days later. They found themselves together in the kitchen, Vincent brewing tea, Jia-ling stowing away groceries.

"About the boy in Urumchi," she said in a pondering-aloud tone. "He knew my sister. He knew Kai-ling first. But he never wrote her letters."

He strained a layer of tea leaves, nodded.

"He wasn't shy about saying things. He wasn't shy about saying that he knew Kai-ling and me both, and he preferred his friendship with me."

"I prefer my friendship with you also." He said it barely above a whisper. The circumstance and timing felt decidedly peculiar, as if he were a stranger at a bus stop making an unbidden proposition.

"The first time you saw her, though, the first time you came to our home, the look on your face—you couldn't even speak."

There was no rebuttal for this; it was utterly, irreversibly, true. An explanation would only have muddled his position further, to say, I was *mistakenly* attracted to your sister and then later *authentically* attracted to you. Easy for her to see his oscillation as weak, his affections fleeting and insincere. Her world-weary assumption: thwarted by Kai-ling, he had settled for less.

What then to do? How to explain the twin specters of loneliness and desire? How to describe their erratic afflictions and the way love could be a mirage arising from any number of horizons?

Moreover, he was sometimes plagued by a troubling and simple equation: he had not had genuine feelings for Trudy, and therefore, as recompense, Jia-ling would not have genuine feelings for him.

Often when they were at home together it was a dizzying struggle not to make a more explicit confession of his feelings for her. He would sometimes come close to the brink of a declaration. And at the last instant he would hold back. Nothing in her posture or temperament appeared to welcome it. When she returned weary from the factory, it seemed that she could blithely shrug off any disclosure he might make. And there were other occasions when a letter from her parents or a tasty meal or a telephone call from a coworker would provoke in her a blush of contentment that would soften her prudent features and lay bare a face whose true inclinations were for guileless delight. These moments were the most precarious, the hardest to survive.

At the dinner table one evening she told him about her years in elementary and middle school, all of them unremarkable, she claimed, because in schools which promoted contests and awards she had not excelled in any subject. Rather than study she had read adventure yarns and chewed her fingernails. Thus no awards. No acclaim for Jia-ling until her first-year middle school teacher had caught her smirking and perceived an overlooked mark of distinction. "My teeth," Jia-ling said and revealed two flawlessly even, pearly-white rows, exemplars of oral hygiene. "My teacher had me stand at the chalkboard, curl back my lips. All my classmates lined up to take a look. Then students from other classes. They all filed by for inspection. There was snickering, sure. There were jokes. 'White fang,' they called me. For an hour I had to stand and show everyone my teeth." Now, at the dinner table, she parted her lips and reenacted the grimace she'd made. They both laughed.

Needless to say, he loved even this absurd, taut-lipped grimace, this smile, loved the child she had been, the childhood, which he had not properly appreciated but now adored, loved the gracious young woman who had shared an episode of her past and encouraged him to laugh. To be granted even this slim measure of intimacy, to be audience to it, thrilled him. Emboldened, he followed her to the kitchen, where they sank their plates in a well of dishwater. He saw her hands submerged in water and, on the underside of her wrist, a coin-size patch of dark, puckered skin—a chemical burn, most likely, from her days in the Urumchi tannery. Impulsively his own hand slipped beneath the surface and he touched—caressed?—her wrist. What had he meant to do? Later he would decide that his intention had been to draw her hand from the sink and observe whether she still chewed her nails. It all made sense in retrospect, though at the time his act, touching the nape of her wrist, had been much like the urge to stroke a newborn's first downy clutch of hair, spontaneity of a rapt and purposeful order. There had been nothing so rapturous in her own reaction, yet nothing shocked or cruel either. She stepped back out of reach, looked at him, then away, glumly.

That was it, he thought. He had overstepped his bounds. That touch would be the closest he would ever come. The knowledge caused his face to redden.

She seemed to notice this and on her way back to the dinner table muttered, "Such a strange boy."

And he was a strange boy, at his strangest and most bewildered when alone in the house and overcome by an intense curiosity. He sometimes turned that curiosity loose on what few possessions she'd left lying around the first floor, mainly personal artifacts, clothing. He examined her new lime green raincoat as it hung from the stand by the door. He smelled, repeatedly, the blouses she washed by hand and set out to dry in the shower stall. He did not, however, enter her closed bedroom. There was no need to, really, when he could easily place a chair to the wall, step up, and peer over the divide, taking note of what items she'd left out on the dresser. He looked for her gold wedding band: no sign of it among her brushes and bottles of lotions. She clearly wasn't wearing it on her finger any longer. Nor did he wear his. A certain pained modesty caused him to hide it each morning in the pocket of his pants.

Perched atop the chair, he looked down upon her mattress and creased pillow and then, more reluctantly, he considered the undergarments she'd hung to dry from a wire rack by the window.

There remained one additional distinction between the Song sisters, the impossible-to-mention difference in physique. Kai-ling had been a tall, willowy young woman. Jia-ling, half a foot shorter, had a rounder, better-proportioned figure, a body of taut curves, pleasing curves. The new clothes she wore about the ministry house made this all too apparent.

He nearly groaned—at the sight of her black panties and bras, at his own lack of will. He could feel his second life, his covert life, gaining momentum. It was humbling. He would have thought that by now experience would have made him a more capable and wiser governor of his longings. Regrettably, it was not so.

He was putting the chair to the wall one afternoon when he heard a sharp ringing elsewhere in the house. For a moment it seemed almost like an alarm, a warning. But it was merely the telephone. He trudged downstairs and picked up the receiver. In the seconds following his greeting there was only a low, breathy murmuring on the line.

"Hello . . . Vincent, are you there?"

"I am, yes."

"And how is the Toulio house? How is Christ's work going there?"

"It's going well, I think. Thank you for asking, Mr. Liang."

And that was mostly the extent of their conversation, a succinct and polite chat, underscored by a somewhat fogged sense of urgency, as if Mr. Liang had woken from a dream and felt compelled to call and make sure that his Toulio house still existed, that Vincent was still in it.

He called again a few days later and wanted to discuss a psalm, the Hundred and Thirty-ninth, which he'd read earlier that afternoon and had been mulling over ever since.

"It's saying the presence of Christ is inevitable," he said. "Whichever direction you travel . . . whether it's toward or away from Christ . . . the evidence is the same, isn't it, Vincent? . . . Seek and you find His spirit everywhere. Flee . . . and no matter where you wander . . . the bottom of the ocean, or farther even, to hell itself . . . and you will still know his presence . . . even there."

"Yes, even there."

"He exists in both the light and the darkness," Mr. Liang said, his voice rising an awed decibel or two. It was a level of invigoration he couldn't sustain for long. Soon his words dropped away altogether. There was no sudden gasp or fit of racking coughs. He was talking one moment, the next he released a whispered groan and at once began a series of precisely metered yet trembling breaths. Several long minutes passed, then a few more. It seemed that he had taken leave of Vincent for a while. It seemed that Mr. Liang was away, searching, as doggedly as possible, for a sanctuary of personal calm, of personal comfort. To Vincent it sounded as if the pursuit of this comfort was as serious a matter as any Bible passage they might have discussed.

And then, abruptly and without explanation, he returned.

". . . so it only makes sense that we should seek . . . rather than flee. . . . The rewards for seeking are infinite . . . and eternal, aren't they, Vincent?"

Of all the Chinese people he'd known in the last year, no one spoke his name with the same precision as Mr. Liang. *Vincent.* Every vowel and consonant softly yet flawlessly articulated. He usually called late in the afternoon. Invariably, he wanted to talk about a Bible passage or a sermon topic he'd heard on a radio broadcast the previous Sunday. He never mentioned his illness except to refer, casually, to foods he could no longer eat or to public hikes and naturalists' gatherings he could no longer attend. He still liked to write out his favorite meditations on postcards. Once, sometimes twice, a week Vincent found these postcards, these secret communiqués, waiting for him in the mesh of the ministry house screen door. And one afternoon he reached into the mesh and pulled out a communiqué by a different author—a letter from Reverend Phillips.

Dear Vincent,

As I understand it, you've returned to Taiwan and are staying in the Liangs' Toulio house, a place I still think of as our Toulio ministry house. I'm also told that you are in contact with Mr. and Mrs. Liang and have their blessing to stay as long as you like.

I'm pleased, Vincent, on both counts, pleased and relieved. If I was ever disappointed, it was only because you didn't come to Taipei and talk to me in person before resigning and leaving the country. Had you done so, I would have told you that your situation wasn't as insurmountable as you first thought. Other volunteers have made mistakes similar to your own. In each case they have found a way, through Christ's forgiveness and guidance, to start over again. Christ encourages us, each day of our lives, to start over again. Another assignment may still be possible for you elsewhere in Taiwan. I made just such an offer to Gloria Hamilton, and while she decided to return home to America, it's my sincere hope that you remain in our ministry and rediscover your life in Christ through the sharing of His Word. Trust me when I say that such rediscoveries happen every day to all of Christ's faithful.

Rev. Lawrence Phillips

With Jia-ling's help he designed a new brand of flyer. This time around there was no slipperiness, no bait and switch, only the simplest of facts, only a straightforward declaration of available services.

ENGLISH LESSONS. STUDY WITH AN AMERICAN TEACHER.
LOW RATES. ALL STUDENTS WELCOME.

Then he was out and motoring about on a busy weekday afternoon, coasting through the town's business and merchant districts, stopping every few blocks to affix a flyer to a store facade or bus stop partition. It was early October and still hot. He carried well over two hundred copies. He did not want to fail from lack of advertising. Whenever townspeople turned to stare at him, he held their gaze a moment and pretended that by now, six months after the fact, his offense, his disgrace, had paled and slipped from their memory.

Toward evening he halted at a traffic light and was distracted by a fellow motorcyclist's odd posture, the rider couched deep and sideways in the saddle, one leg shoring up the cycle's stalled weight, the other leg, with its skewed ankle and foot, curled around the frame. The rider was Shao-fei. The motorcycle belonged to Alec. In the seconds before the light changed, Shao-fei, arms stretched to the handlebars, chest squeezed against the gas tank, turned and regarded his former houseguest and spiritual counselor.

There was a newly cultivated aloofness in the boy's gaze. He blinked dully. He wrinkled his nose as if he might sneeze. All around them engines began to bay, and then the light changed and Shao-fei was wringing the throttle, letting the cycle leap ahead, riding as tight and low as a jockey on a bolting Thoroughbred.

He did not let up. Even when he gained upon columns of slower-moving vehicles, he sped crazily through their ranks rather than release the throttle or apply the brakes. It was an exuberant and perilous demonstration, though still a demonstration and performed, Vincent knew, for his benefit, as if by glancing at Shao-fei he had challenged the boy to the wildest of dares.

He would kill himself, Vincent thought, or be . . . crippled. He would be lucky to survive adolescence. He was lucky just to have reached the next intersection unscathed, lucky to have completed a veering left turn across three lanes of traffic and to have come to a graceless halt at a gas station. Vincent turned left as well and followed him right to the pump, wedged his motorcycle in close, turned off the engine.

He waited for the rapid thrumming of his heart to subside. "I don't think Alec would mind you riding his motorcycle," he said. "He'd be glad about it. I don't think he'd mind at all."

"So what if he did," Shao-fei said. "Wherever he is, he's probably drunk. He's probably sitting around smoking up his bad air."

"Maybe. Maybe not. But he'd be glad to know you've learned to ride. I think he'd want you to be careful, though."

"I don't care. I don't even think about him anymore."

"Then think about this," Vincent said.

"I know what you're going to say. Think about Jesus. Think about the way Jesus would ride a motorcycle."

Vincent might have smiled, were it not for his own culpability in the matter. Instead he lowered his voice so the station attendants would not overhear and told the boy, assured him, that his life would get better. It was probably too stagy, too prescribed a proclamation to make in public, but he made it anyway. He explained to Shao-fei that as he got older he would have a few more choices, more responsibility, too, but more choices also. If he tried, he could have most of the things he wanted. Friends, girlfriends, even.

The boy, of course, was having none of it. He beamed resentment. And why shouldn't he? He'd been subjected to Vincent's and Alec's mixed influences and mutual abandonment. Certainly, they bore some degree of blame. But how much exactly?

It was dizzying to think about, the consequences that were created by intervening too much or too little in the flow of other people's lives. There was no keeping track of it, either. Vincent felt dumbfounded in the face of such complexity.

Even so, he went on pestering the boy with what was certainly uncomplicated and probably naive advice. Your life will change, so don't put yourself in needless danger, he said. Don't drive recklessly. Be careful, Shao-fei. Take care.

There was, as always, some ground, albeit modest ground, for hope. A few townspeople had begun to notice his flyers. And while no one came by to pay for lessons in advance, the ministry house phone rang with the occasional inquiry.

It was enough to focus Vincent's desultory thoughts and energies. At once he gave himself over to long days of preparation. He cleared the classroom of furniture, swept and mopped the floor, washed the curtains, brushed another layer of white paint over the room's deepening watermark. Next he scrubbed and reordered the school desks and portable chalkboard. This done, he drew up an outline for several possible lessons. He made copies of English exercises for both novice and advanced students. While he worked, he put a sign out and left the front door open in case any interested passersby wanted to stop and ask about classes.

None did. But one of the telephone inquiries did result in a visit from a middle-aged married couple who lived in a nearby apartment building with their two young sons. Before registering their sons for lessons, they wished to meet Vincent and see the facilities. They came to the ministry house one evening, and Vincent led them up to the classroom, where he demonstrated a simple language exercise involving time of day and months of the year. When asked, he listed his credentials. The couple appeared assured, if not entirely persuaded.

He invited them to ask questions, thinking perhaps that now might be the time to discuss tuition and class schedules. But the woman had concerns that pointed in another direction. She wanted to know about the young woman they'd seen folding laundry downstairs in the living room a few minutes earlier. Who was she? Was she Vincent's wife? the woman asked.

He took a long, careful breath. This, he knew, was a matter of considerable mystery to his neighbors. He felt their curiosity, mixed with their disfavor, every time he stepped out the door. She might very well have been asking these questions on their behalf.

It was complicated, he said. He and the young woman were friends who shared the same house. Her name was Song Jia-ling and she worked at the helmet factory. They were not *together,* but he'd known her in the Mainland, and, before leaving the Mainland to come to Taiwan—here he paused and made an indistinct drifting gesture with one hand—they'd both taken part in a wedding ceremony. And so, legally speaking, he said, some people, some government officials, considered them married.

There was a certain labored courtesy in the way the couple listened to his explanation. All the while they seemed to be looking past him to the classroom's blank chalkboard. After they'd gone, he chastised himself for revealing too much. He doubted he'd ever see the couple's sons in his classroom. He doubted any right-minded person would risk the public dishonor of being his student.

And he felt no more confident about his prospects five days later, the second Monday of October, a day that was to mark the official beginning of his new enterprise. The morning was muggy and warm, the afternoon no better. Early in the evening he put a fan in the classroom window and opened up the rooftop door for a breeze. At ten till seven he peered from the third-floor window and saw exactly no one, no prospective students, no marshaling of scooters and bicycles at the ministry house front gate.

He took a seat at the head of the class and waited. At five after, he could hear Jia-ling welcoming someone at the front door. Minutes later Mr. Yao was standing in the classroom doorway, blushing slightly, holding his tan safari hat in his hands.

Beyond a simple greeting and a few chatty remarks about the weather, there was little they could say to each other. Any other topic or mention of mutual acquaintances, it seemed, would lead them into discomforting territory.

Thankfully there were soon other visitors at the classroom door: an older gentleman who'd brought along a boy, probably his grandson, and, after they'd entered and found seats, a trio of bashful nurses still wearing their hospital whites. A few minutes later a short and ruddy-complexioned mother corralled her sulking teenaged son into a front-row desk. Heartened by these arrivals, Vincent went to the window for another look. Other prospective students were curbing their scooters and making their way across the courtyard. He could hear Jia-ling directing them up the stairs, and when they stepped through the door he was pleased to welcome a group comprised of both complete strangers and several former Bible study students, including Miss Ling and her advanced-composition book. By the time the last of the late arrivers had made their way inside, he was standing beside the chalkboard looking out at a gathering of fourteen students.

The feeling this sight inspired came rushing upon him all at once. It was greater than mere surprise, mere relief. He felt he'd been pulled from a dark and tumbling current. He felt rescued.

He was thankful to have a carefully prepared lesson to fall back on. He consulted his notebook and made his introduction. There were new names to learn. He went from desk to desk asking a succession of hard-to-difficult questions in order to divide the class into beginning and advanced students, groups that henceforth would form separate classes and meet on different nights of the week. Once this was accomplished, he handed out the first lesson, a dialogue exercise depicting two travelers at a bus station. *What time do we leave?* he prompted the class. *Where are we go-ing?* The students chanted along. After that there was new vocabulary to post on the chalkboard, followed by another round of questions and then, amazingly, their time was up and they were heading downstairs, where Jia-ling would charge them 170 yuan for the hour or 150 if they paid for six lessons in advance.

He'd had almost no time to wonder what rumors his new students might have heard and what private opinions of him they might be harboring. Yet it was a good sign, surely, that eight students returned the following evening to continue on in the beginners' class. The other six arrived Wednesday evening to embark on their advanced English studies. In the end he could only conclude that some of his students, assuredly, knew what he'd done, and others, just as assuredly, had no idea whatsoever. To make matters more perplexing, he was never entirely sure into which category many of his students fell.

With his former Bible study students, however, there was sometimes a peculiar current of understanding that passed between himself and them, a sly awareness that there was more to his life than the dutiful virtues he affected while standing before the class. And there was sometimes a peculiar moment, too, that occurred at the very end of their class, a juncture in which he'd once, in a previous career, told his students to break for ten minutes and then return for an hour of Bible study. Now he merely suggested they study their vocabulary and wished them a good night.

At this moment Mr. Yao, Miss Ling, and several other students threw him an inquisitive glance, as if to say, *And?*

And nothing. He was their English teacher. He did not know which brand of guidance they should seek. He did not know or pretend to know what moved in their souls.

Thirty-six

IN EARLY NOVEMBER, after having written and mailed three polite inquiries, he returned from the grocery store one afternoon and found a letter from the British consulate-general in Guangzhou wedged into the door screen. Inside was a notice informing him that Alec McGowan had appeared before the People's Court of Guangzhou and had pled guilty to possession and attempted trafficking of fifty-seven grams of hashish. The court's panel of judges had returned a sentence of twenty-eight months to be served in a Guangdong prison.

Vincent reread the notice a half dozen times. Strange how a pronouncement like this could be both pitiless in its authority and at the same time the agent of considerable hope. Soon he set to work on a return letter, one he hoped the consulate-general would be able to forward to Alec. In the letter he advised his friend to bide his time as patiently as possible. *In twenty-eight months,* he wrote, *you will step out of prison with your whole life before you. You will still be a young man. You will still be yourself. There's much to look forward to. We may both be surprised by just how possible it is to outlive our mistakes. We may both be surprised by the lucky turns our lives will take.*

Much to look forward to? Lucky turns? The shrewder, more seasoned part of him wavered a moment over these terms. He had to wonder if he believed any of it. From what he'd seen so far of the gray and complicated world, did he actually believe there were grounds for such optimism?

As it happened, he did believe it. He could not say precisely why, except that at times, quite often, in fact, his life, regardless of what Gloria had predicted, did not seem meaningless or shameful at all, but on the contrary rich with an innate and mysterious possibility. Sometimes, if only for the flimsiest of reasons, a deep, sanctioning sense of well-being would come over him. The trick, perhaps, was to live inside that happiness as long as it lasted and when it was over to get on with the tasks at hand: all the striving and searching that had to be done, the careful truces to be made with one's aloneness and one's longings.

Or the simpler tasks even, the rising and washing and preparing of meals, the English lessons to be taught, the large, three-storied house to be kept clean and the bills to be paid on time. And the less agreeable chores as well, the least welcome of these being the visit he had to make each month to Gwa's office to pay down his debt by another three hundred dollars.

There were times, certainly, when he regarded these payments as outright thievery, outright extortion. Still, he'd made his October payment without ever mentioning it to Jia-ling. And as the most passive and inconsequential form of protest, he'd waited until today, the fifth of the month, to make his November payment. He rode to Gwa's office, parked his cycle, and took a long, steadying breath before entering the hallway. Standing before the intercom, he had a humbling realization. Didn't he make these payments willingly if only for the hapless and selfish reason of keeping Jia-ling together with him in the same house? Wasn't it a relative bargain at three hundred dollars a month?

The answer was yes on both accounts. Perhaps it was better, at least, to admit it openly to himself.

Then he pressed the intercom buzzer once and in an instant it seemed a gruff voice was booming through the intercom, "Wait, wait," and then came a romping descent down the building's inner stairwell. The door swung open. There was Ponic, interrupted at his noontime meal, stuffing the final lump of a sticky rice ball into his mouth and washing it down with a sip from a large yellowish beverage, possibly a mango milkshake. He saw Vincent and beamed a hearty brand of goodwill, his greeting deferential, his remarks chatty, generous, and—because he was not given to personal reflection and in the purest sense held no grudges—almost certainly sincere. He wanted to know how Vincent's new English school was coming along. How many students? How much money had been made? And had he been to Toulio's new American chicken restaurant? It was certainly delicious. It was certainly popular, Ponic said. Again and again he waved off the roll of money Vincent kept offering until at last some standard of decorum had been met and he took the money and slipped it into his back pocket. And how was Jia-ling? he asked, without pausing long enough to heed the answer. It wasn't disinterest or resentment exactly; it was just that he'd remembered an important bit of news. The replacement parts for the Bonneville had arrived a week earlier and had already been— He stopped himself. His face bloomed with a sharper, slyer expression. There was even bigger news, he said. Outstanding news. But should he tell? He thought about it for a fraction of a second and decided he would. "Something happened to Mr. Gwa," Ponic reported. "Something exciting and very rare. He's been away for more than three weeks checking on his factories in the Mainland. It happened that he took several days off and traveled to Shanghai and by accident found his other half."

"His other half?" Vincent asked.

"Yes. The woman he was supposed to be with all along. His other half. His true love."

Did he mean Kai-ling? Did he mean Gwa had gone to Shanghai and reunited with Kai-ling?

It had started out that way, Ponic explained. Gwa had arrived at Shanghai's central train station. He had Kai-ling's address because he'd lifted it from a letter she'd sent Jia-ling that had passed through Mr. Gwa's Toulio office. His plan was to go to Shanghai and approach Kai-ling and find a way to rekindle their relationship.

"But there was some trouble." Ponic sighed. "The bus Mr. Gwa took to his hotel got locked in traffic. An hour passed and he'd only gone a few blocks. So he sat and watched thousands of people walk by on the sidewalks. One of them was a tall, very beautiful woman. Mr. Gwa said he glimpsed her once, thought she was beautiful, and then she disappeared. The bus still wasn't moving and after another hour he became very thirsty, very impatient. He stepped off and walked down the street and entered a shop that sold tea by the canister and special herbal remedies. There was no one at the counter. He called into the back room for someone to please bring him a glass of juice. Out came a clerk, a young woman who'd started working there just the day before. She was tall, very beautiful, clever, too, and only twenty years old." Ponic grinned cannily, raised a finger for emphasis. "The very same woman Mr. Gwa had seen in the crowd an hour or so earlier."

"Yes," Vincent said wearily. "So?"

"Mr. Gwa said he knew immediately that it was more than a simple coincidence. Something extraordinary was happening, he said. She was *extraordinary*. He said he had a powerful understanding of everything she was feeling. He thanked her for the juice. They talked awhile, and he asked directions and she walked him out to the street to point the way. And he told her right then, he said, 'You realize you're going to have to quit your job and come with me. You realize I'm going to take care of you from now on.' She thought about what he said and then lowered her eyes and nodded because she understood what had just taken place."

"And what had taken place?" Vincent asked.

"She's his other half. He's hers. One half completes the other. It often happens that way. An accidental meeting. Like the way Mr. Gwa saw her from a bus window. Then fate arranges to bring two people together again. This happened six days ago. They've been together ever since."

"And Kai-ling?"

"What about her?" Ponic said. "No reason to track her down. She wasn't the other half."

"And Gwa's wife?"

"She's a wife. Not an other half."

"Then he can quit searching now," Vincent said. "Now that he's found his other half. He can stop sending foreigners to the Mainland to bring back his girlfriends."

Ponic sipped from his mango milkshake. The delicate muscles of his temples flexed in a way that insinuated serious thought. "Yes," he said. "I suppose so. No need for Mr. Gwa to look anymore. Now that he's complete."

Complete. It was a notion that, when he thought about it during the days that followed, made him smile. And cringe a bit in envy, too. Before long, however, both the folly and sting of it began to fade. Gwa's completeness, his beautiful new Shanghai lover, slipped from Vincent's mind. There were other things to take its place—the new English school, the weather, even. At long last the seasonal shift in climate arrived and produced a string of truly lovely mid-November days, mild and brightly lit days that enveloped Yun Lin County and for a few hours each morning made possible a brisk view of the nearby and usually fog-shrouded mountains. Such fine weather could not be denied. The third day of it Vincent rose early and plodded downstairs to where Jia-ling, already in her blue work apron, was packing the bag she took each day to her station at the helmet factory. It was a rare day, he said, a beautiful day, and if she had any sense she would call the factory and pretend to be sick so that the two of them could go for a ride in the mountains. He knew it to be a futile request. She said no at once. And yet her refusal carried a small reward: she smiled and appeared pleased to have been asked. He was lately gaining a fairly sure sense of what pleased her. She liked to be teased about her rigid work ethic. She liked all varieties of cake. When not working, she liked to don what little jewelry she owned, even lately her wedding band, which she wore on the second-to-last finger of her left hand, signifying neither engagement nor marriage—though what, if anything, it did signify remained a faint puzzle, one he knew better than to inquire about.

He watched her set off to work, and then he steered his motorcycle out onto the main avenue, following an eastward route that soon took him to the outskirts of town, past a scattering of much smaller roadside villages and into an open plain where the county's cropland began in earnest. This might well have been the landscape he'd imagined before ever setting foot in Toulio: the patchwork of shimmering rice fields, the clear blue breadth and width of the sky. He sped on until much of the cropland was behind him and he'd entered a lengthy orchard, where the fruit trees were spindly and dark green and bore plump tangerines a week or two shy of being ripe. By late morning he'd climbed high enough into the steepening hills to see the first of several tea plantations, the tea shrubs set in thick, curving rows, the rows covering the hillsides like enormous darkly bristled caterpillars.

He pulled to the roadside and turned off the engine. There was nothing to do then but sit awhile in the crisp air and thickening quiet and look out at the horizon.

And what could he say about the long journey he'd made? That it had been for nothing? That he'd failed at almost everything he'd set out to do? That it had changed him for the better anyway?

Afterward he started his cycle and headed back the way he'd come, back through the orchard and cropland, back, eventually, to Toulio, a town he knew and liked even though many of its manners and customs were, and would always be, beyond his reach. Even so, he knew the lanes and avenues well, at least as well as those of his own hometown, Red Bud, and was not surprised to find them jammed with lunchtime commuters. His tasks this afternoon were simple; he was a young man with errands to run. At a bookshop south of the train station he stopped and purchased an English-language newsmagazine that the shop owner had been kind enough to order on his behalf. Next he darted inside a tiny but dependable Chinese bakery and waited in line behind a young mother. Her small children, two diapered toddlers, shared the same stroller seat. They tilted their round heads up to stare at him. In the very act of greeting them, of calling them, as the Chinese preferred, *little friends,* he realized he was looking at twin baby girls.

His heart lurched through several beats. He couldn't quite sort out what he felt. Sorrow, yes, plus a shiver of dread for what he'd once seen rolled in a blanket in Lanzhou. But there was something lighter, more singular as well. These two baby girls were irrefutably beautiful, undeniably alive; even as they gaped at him, they reached to pull packages of sweet buns from the shelves.

Better to consider them a rare and cherished sight. Better to call what he felt thankfulness.

He paid for a slice of sponge cake and a loaf of French bread and turned his motorcycle toward the town center with the notion of finding a suitable place to eat lunch. At a busy intersection not far from Gwa's office he came upon the new three-floored chicken restaurant Ponic had mentioned, a veritable palace comprised of glass walls and gleaming red and white signboards. It was Toulio's first authentic, first licensed American franchise and had opened to brisk business two weeks earlier. Since then it appeared only to have grown in popularity and was, at the moment, bursting with eager lunchtime patrons, many of whom were squeezed into a wide procession stretching out the doors and occupying much of the adjacent street curb. Among the crowd were more than a few teenaged students clad in the Ming-da Academy's maroon uniform.

This, more than anything else, decided him against entering. Instead he traveled a few doors down to a pseudo-American fast food shop, its entranceway adorned with a cartoon pelican, its interior cool and mostly deserted, its owners, an older and somewhat frazzled married couple, desperately glad to have him as their customer. Was he an American? they asked. He said he was and they piled extra potato wedges on his tray and added a free side salad and plastic-wrapped cookie. Still, even with their enthusiasm and free gifts, it seemed he'd chosen the wrong restaurant, wrong because the hamburger was spongy and laced with a strange, sugary condiment, his potato wedges heavy and wet, wrong also because once he'd chosen a booth and settled down to read his magazine and eat his meal, he glanced up and spotted Trudy's brother sitting with a young woman at the back of the restaurant.

Trudy's brother had noticed him as well. He considered Vincent across the reach of several patterned tabletops, sat motionless, and stared without blinking a long moment or two. At last he seemed to arrive at some decision and turned back to the young woman he was with. They'd been lounging beside each other quite close, arms entwined, and though they were not bold enough to actually kiss in public, they returned to what they'd been doing before the interruption—a slow, close-eyed touching of their foreheads and faces, a kind of languorous nuzzling.

Vincent went back to his spongy hamburger and newsmagazine. He felt his face redden, a blush of intense, almost exuberant relief. He understood implicitly that he would not be assaulted today. He would not be punished. And he owed this particular salvation to the young woman nestled in the arms of Trudy's brother. Most likely he owed her more than that. In all probability she'd been keeping Vincent out of harm's way these past several months, just by being herself, by being a girlfriend, gentle and shy but still powerful in the way she awarded her affections. That, at least, was his sharpest and best intuition. Later when she rose and led Trudy's brother by the hand toward the restaurant doors, Vincent had to resist the urge to look up and hold her gaze and mouth the words *thank you.*

He ate what he could of his lunch and afterward bid the owners a good afternoon. Once outside the restaurant he untangled his motorcycle from a jam of parked scooters and turned toward home. The day was still lovely and clear, so flawlessly mild that he almost didn't mind the snarled lunchtime traffic. He noticed that the crowd outside the chicken restaurant had thickened. As he inched past, a few former Ming-da students— Violet Two? Snoopy?—spotted him. He tried to meet their gazes. He tried to nod like a chastened and wiser man.

There were visitors waiting for him at the ministry house front gate. He drew close and sighed upon recognizing them: Trudy's brother and his girlfriend. To acknowledge who they were, to concede the hard fact of their presence, was to feel the crumbling of his fine spirits and to know that in the realm of personal intentions, some things, perhaps most things, couldn't be accurately guessed at or predicted.

"You must be very stupid," Trudy's brother said above the steady chugging of Vincent's cycle engine. "Or a sick motherfucker." His eyes were dark and blank, his expression slack. He let a long red string of betel nut spit slide from his mouth and drip against the gatepost. "This time," he said, "it's going to be much worse for you." Then he lunged forward and thrust the hard knob of his elbow into Vincent's face.

The blow sent Vincent tumbling from the cycle onto the pavement. From his nostril came a warm runnel of blood. He looked up and caught the girlfriend smirking at him in distaste.

I haven't accomplished anything, he thought. *I haven't outlived my mistakes. It's only a matter of my punishment having been delayed until now.* He rose to his feet. He held up his fists in an unsteady semblance of someone poised to defend himself.

Another lunge. His attacker threw a hard, sliding punch that landed on Vincent's cheek. When he raised his hands to protect that cheek, he was kicked hard in the ribs. He doubled over. His reward for doing so was a thudding blow to the forehead. The hard jolt of it caused his surroundings to reel, a sensation he remembered from his previous fight, his previous beating.

But there were differences, too. This time he was being attacked in bright daylight. Children came running. Neighbors who happened to be walking or pedaling down the lane stopped to watch. He wavered under their gaze. This punishment, this lesson, felt both deserved and undeserved. Unlike during his previous beating, he longed to strike back. And if this time around he was no better at blocking punches, then at least he was beginning to throw his own with more force and accuracy. His first was a glancing blow to his opponent's shoulder. The second connected squarely against the jaw and sent Trudy's brother pitching back onto the ground. He looked up startled, then enraged. He rose, stepped back to his father's sedan. He leaned through the open passenger window. When he turned around, he was wielding a length of iron pipe.

Vincent was upon him at once—a panicked, headlong rush, yet when they collided he gripped Trudy's brother about the arms and squeezed with all his might.

Thus they staggered. They lurched. Strange croaking sounds rose from their throats. With his arms mostly pinned, Trudy's brother could only manage short, jabbing blows with the pipe. Before long it clattered to the ground. Even so, they remained bound together, staggering to and fro in a coil of limbs. It was exhausting work, this staggering. It did not seem possible that it could go on for long. And yet it did go on. Vincent could sense the crowd getting used to the spectacle. He fastened his arms around Trudy's brother and squeezed harder. Still, they were tired. Inevitably they fell, first a stumbling collision against Vincent's motorcycle, which pitched sideways to the pavement and precipitated a second, harder fall, especially for Trudy's brother, who wound up collapsing atop the cycle and bearing the full brunt of Vincent's weight.

They lay tangled together. An intense, oily heat wafted up from the motorcycle's churning engine. Trudy's brother writhed against that engine. His breath came out in a soft, keening sob. He buried his face in the crook of Vincent's shoulder. If Vincent hadn't known better, he might have thought it a type of remorse. It made for a most peculiar moment, as intimate in its way as any he'd shared with his opponent's sister.

Hands reached in to pull them from the wreckage. Vincent was helped to his feet, only to tremble and slump down cross-legged on the pavement. Trudy's brother, when separated from the engine and exhaust pipe, let out a great wail of pain. His girlfriend, no longer smirking, no longer aloof, hurried to his side. When she cried out for assistance, two men stepped forward from the crowd to help bear Trudy's brother away.

The lane seemed to be quivering beneath Vincent's body. Everything—the gateposts, the crowd, the buildings—felt as if they were leaning toward him.

"Should the police be called?" someone, a neighbor, asked Vincent.

He could not swallow air fast enough to form an intelligible answer. "No," he said at last.

"It was a private dispute? Between his family and you?"

"That's right . . . yes." He looked up. Above him hovered a council of faces whose expressions, if not exactly sympathetic, seemed to acknowledge the difficulty of his circumstances. He nodded toward those faces. Then he stood and passed through the ministry house gate. A few steps across the courtyard and he felt a grating ache in the bones of his ankle. A few steps more and he was hobbling in pain.

Once inside the ministry house he lowered the blinds and limped from one piece of furniture to the next. In the bathroom he rinsed his mouth and washed away a trail of blood that had crooked its way down his chin and throat. His upper lip had taken on a familiar thickness. There was a large red knot on his forehead. There were abrasions on his brow and cheek that might take weeks to fully heal.

He tried to climb the stairs to his bedroom. What folly that turned out to be. The instant he put weight on his ankle, his whole foot and leg thrummed with burning pain. He let out a gasp. Then he crouched at the base of the stairs. Eventually, he sat on the floor and waited for the pain to pass.

In time it did pass. But he was still reluctant to move. He sat back against the hallway wall, closed his eyes, rested.

He was roused to attention sometime later by the unlatching and swift opening of the front door. He could hear the padding of footsteps across the kitchen floor. Blinds were being raised, lights turned on. His name was being called out. Jia-ling was doing the calling.

He glanced at his watch. It was barely a quarter past two. She had no reason to be home so early. It was unprecedented. And yet there she was, one moment towering over him in the hallway, the next squatting down, peering at the abrasions on his face.

"Why are you sitting on the floor?" she asked.

"It's my ankle. It's giving me pain."

"Which one?"

"The left," he said. "I was in a fight."

But she knew that already. She told him word of his fight was traveling fast. A neighbor had come to the factory to tell her. The factory boss had given her a half hour to rush home and make sure that he was all right.

"I'm fine," Vincent said. "No reason to worry."

She did not appear at all convinced. She said she didn't like him sitting on the floor. She didn't like the look of it. "Up," she said, and, in spite of his protests, began forcing him to rise, one stage at a time, until she was under his arm supporting him as he hobbled toward the living room's wooden sofa.

There he sat and stretched out his injured leg. Gingerly, she undid the laces of his tennis shoe.

"You were fighting in the lane outside the house?"

"Yes."

"It was the second time you had a fight?"

"Yes, the second time."

"The second time," she mused. "Same place? Same young man you were fighting with?"

"Yes."

"You were fighting with the brother of a student you knew?"

He sighed plaintively. "Yes. That's right."

"A student you slept with?"

"Yes. I'm afraid so."

"This happened when you were a Jesus teacher?"

"That's right."

"Tell me, do most Jesus teachers have these kinds of problems?"

How to answer? He sometimes suspected that the desire to know God was linked inextricably to other outsize and secret desires. "Not many of them make the same mistake I did," he said. "Not many of them keep getting beaten up."

She slipped off his shoe. She coaxed his sock down, bit by bit, until it was over the heel and easy to pluck from his foot. She looked upon his swollen ankle with the same sense of frank estimation with which she'd been looking upon him—not alarm, precisely, but a deep, watchful, personal interest.

Then she stood and climbed the stairs to his bedroom and returned with an armload of pillows and blankets. She retrieved a towel and filled it with ice cubes and wrapped it around his ankle. She went to the kitchen for a bottle of cold water and fruit and a roll of English-style biscuits, all of which she placed at his side. She brought him an assortment of books and magazines. Last, she sat beside him on the sofa and told him that she was going back to work and he could call her there if the pain got worse and he thought he needed to go to the clinic. She nodded and made ready to rise and leave.

Before she did that, though, she gave him such a look, potent as always, but full of misgiving, too, full of caution, and at the same time put her hands on his forearms so that their arms were aligned and their wrists pressed together, one atop the other. She leaned toward him until her brow was touching his and her hair was framing both their faces.

"Are you discouraged?" she asked.

"I'm trying not to be."

"You wouldn't leave, would you? Because of what happened today? You wouldn't leave and go back to America without telling me?"

"I wouldn't do that, no."

"You better not," she said and squeezed his forearms fiercely. "People are just now starting to change their opinion about you."

"I doubt that," he said.

"Oh, but they are. I hear them talking. They say, 'Look at him. Always trying to do the decent thing. But always thinking about it too much.'"

"Ha," he said meekly. "You're making it up. You're putting words in their mouths. But go ahead anyway. What else are they saying?"

"They say, 'What a strange and lonely foreign boy.'"

"What else?"

"They say, 'Keep trying. You may be closer than you think.'"

. . .

For a long while after she left, he leaned back on his mound of pillows, closed his eyes, and reviewed their conversation. So much to consider: the intonation of her voice, the words themselves, what they implied, and whether their implication might be different, less auspicious, in Mandarin as opposed to English, the language he used to ponder the meaning of things. *Either way, either language, it's good,* he told himself. His heart felt swollen with possibility. *She was saying* stay. *She was saying she had strong feelings for him as well.*

It took time to recover from this astonishment. His pulse was thudding away in his veins. After he calmed himself, he readjusted the towel across his ankle. A short while later he ate half an apple and two biscuits. He could not read, however. He could not sleep. He thought about the way she'd pressed her brow against his and the way she'd run her hands across, even squeezed, the undersides of his wrists. A touch like that carried its own implication, didn't it? Doors were being thrown open to new realms of affection. And he didn't mean sexual passion exactly; he didn't mean lurid fantasies. He meant she was allowing, perhaps even encouraging, a new physical closeness, a new familiarity between them.

He thought about her touch and was astonished all over again.

Meanwhile the afternoon seemed to be drifting along, moment by moment, on its own boundless currents. Sometime later a band of neighborhood children gathered at the uncurtained living room window, where they talked in their usual reedy voices, grinned and peered in at him. "Come out!" they were saying. Were they gloating at his injuries? Who knew? If anything, they seemed to be regarding him as they might a favorite stray dog, amused, pleased, even, that he'd pulled through this latest scrape and could now oblige them by staggering out into the courtyard so they might flee in mock terror.

An ad truck passed down the lane blaring out a shrill announcement for a new perfume and cosmetics line that would be available Saturday in the town's department store. After its passing, a relative quiet settled over the lane. He could hear the neighborhood's older children—middle and high school students—arriving home from their long day of classes. It was four o'clock. He imagined her working at her station in the helmet factory. In an hour she could climb aboard her bicycle and pedal home. Until then she would likely be at her work desk fitting layers of foam padding into the inner pate of each helmet. How eager he was to know what she was thinking. Did her mind wander as she worked? Were her ruminations charged by similar astonishments and anticipations?

At ten till five the telephone let out a sudden clamor. He knew who it was, of course. He deliberated through three rings before picking up the receiver.

And was it wrong, was it obscene, to talk to a dying man while the very core of your being was alight with a wondrous new hope?

It wasn't as wrong, as incongruous, as he first feared. There was a strange symmetry between them. If he was a young man in love, then wasn't Mr. Liang his other half?

"Who is it there, please? Is it Vincent?"

"It is, yes. Hello, Mr. Liang."

"And you're there in the Toulio house?"

"I'm here, yes. I'm fine. Everything is fine."

What followed was a long, trembling sigh of relief. "I'm glad to hear that, Vincent. I'm glad to hear your voice."

"I'm glad to hear yours."

"I was trying to tell the doctor and Mrs. Liang no. But it's hard to make people understand . . . the things you don't want. I say no. I say it again and again. I had a bad day today. I almost didn't call."

"I'm sorry to hear that."

"Tell me, what will you be teaching tonight?"

"Something from Paul, I think."

"Which Paul?"

"Epistle to the Hebrews."

"Hebrews, yes. I always liked chapter four, verse twelve. *The word of God is quick and powerful . . . and sharper than any two-edged sword.*"

"That *is* good. I'll use it tonight."

"And do you think you'll have a full class?"

"I do. It's Thursday. We usually do well on Thursdays."

Then came the low groan that always preceded Mr. Liang's retreat into silence, or near silence, since it was possible to hear his dry swallowing and measured breaths. He groaned and afterward was away for some time foraging through what seemed to be a harsh and far-ranging landscape.

Vincent waited for his return. While he waited, he listened to the traffic moving along the lane outside the ministry house, and amid the rumbling of scooters and shrieking of children he heard a faintly creaking bicycle and then, more conclusively, the chiming and always hopeful thwack of its kickstand. She was at the gate. She was probably just now gathering her things from the bicycle's wire basket.

"I almost didn't call," Mr. Liang said, back from his dark sojourn. "I didn't think I should trouble you. No, it was worse than that. When I concentrated . . . I wasn't even able to picture you or the classroom . . . or anything at all about the ministry house. But then I called, and as soon as you answered . . . I began to see our Toulio house . . . very clearly. I felt better. You helped calm me, Vincent. I had a bad day. I had lost touch with God's grace. And then I called . . . and we talked about Hebrews and your Thursday night class . . . and I felt it again . . . strong as ever."

"I'm glad, Mr. Liang. I'm glad you feel better."

"I wish it could burn constantly in my heart," Mr. Liang said. "I wish I could be filled with the certainty of God's grace . . . every moment of my life."

She could be heard padding across the courtyard. In his mind's eye he watched the lithe back-and-forth swaying of her stride, watched her open the screen door and put her hand on the latch.

"Yes," Vincent said. "So do I."

Acknowledgments

The author wishes to thank James Michener and the Copernicus Society of America, the Henfield Foundation, and the Fine Arts Work Center in Provincetown for their generous support during the writing of this book.

Thanks also to friend and writer Zachary Lazar for his encouragement and seeing this novel through many drafts; to Jeff Turner for more than a decade of friendship and artistic influence; to Margot Livesey and David Carkeet for the example they've set on the page and in the classroom; to Lisa Bankoff for her keen advocacy; to Frank Conroy, Connie Brothers, Fred G. Leebron, Michael Daugherty, and James Williams for their support along the way; to my wise editor, Colin Harrison, whose attention and commitment to *Heaven Lake* have been nothing less than extraordinary.

Finally, thanks to Joan Dalton (my ally and confidante since childhood), to Jim Dalton (for my ticket to ride), to Carla Meyer (for rooting me on), and to every member of my large and generous family, the Dalton clan.

Praise for John Dalton's *Heaven Lake*

"Splendid . . . assured storytelling."

—*Newsday*

"[Dalton] has mastered the art of arriving at the universal through finely drawn particulars. . . . Serious readers who still believe in straightforward stories well told will find themselves entranced by this humbly omniscient narrator who unabashedly loves and respects his characters."

—*Elle*

"Vivid, cinematic intensity."

—*The Boston Globe*

"Sober and searching yet sublimely comic. . . . Reminiscent of the work of Graham Greene and Norman Rush, but possessing a quirky innocence and gravitas all its own. . . . Artfully pacing the series of revelations that rock the book on its way to a surprising conclusion, Dalton revises conventional assumptions about contemporary China and collective cultural views of love and marriage. . . . This could be one of the spring's—if not the year's—biggest debuts."

—*Publishers Weekly* (starred review)

"Filled with dramatic episodes and unique characters . . . an exciting page-turner."

—*Library Journal*

"Impressive . . . a beguiling story told with comic flair . . . proceeds at an exhilarating pace . . . *Heaven Lake* offers a touching meditation on the vagaries of love."

—*Los Angeles Times*

"Blossoms into an unexpectedly satisfying saga."

—*Entertainment Weekly* (A–)

"Dalton [is] both deft and generous at characterization. . . . [He is] a writer with tremendous promise. . . . *Heaven Lake* is an auspicious debut."

—*San Jose Mercury News*

"Ambitious . . . auspicious and compelling."

—*BookPage*

"Powerful and well-tuned . . . [Dalton] knows China and shows it to us with meticulousness and enthusiasm. . . . [T]he story of [Vincent's] adventures in this intriguing country captivates our attention and holds it throughout."

—*The Washington Post Book World*

"Dalton's China is closely observed and unfailingly fascinating. . . . For a novelist, *Heaven Lake* is a great place to start; for readers, it is a terrific place to end up."

—*St. Louis Post-Dispatch*

"Dalton proves that he is a fine, patient writer: attentive to psychological detail and to the compendium of small changes, quirks, decisions, and regrets that make a character a character, a plot a plot."

—*Raleigh News and Observer*

"Remarkable . . . poise and gravitas that few young American writers are likely to achieve . . . vivid and engrossing . . . a fresh comprehension of the meaning of love and faith."

—*The San Diego Union-Tribune*

"A sweeping, soul-satisfying debut." —*The Miami Herald*

"Nuanced . . . with just the right touch of wit. . . . This is a story as sensitive to the complexities and beauties of China as to the territory of the human heart."

—*The Christian Science Monitor*

"There are debuts and there are DEBUTS . . . sweeping in scope, well plotted, and filled with intricately drawn scenes and characters . . . superbly written. . . . One can enjoy Dalton's book on several levels."

—*Greensboro News and Record*

"[Dalton] clearly has an excellent understanding of Chinese culture and the way in which it can baffle and derail the unwary foreigner. Dalton artfully uses those insights to both explore the novel's deeper philosophical questions and to craft its engaging plot."

—*The Asian Review of Books*

"This is a novel of faith—in all its subtly varied forms—that keeps faith with the novelistic fundamentals of vibrant characterization, gripping narrative, and sweeping vision. Dalton marvelously captures the epic scale of China through the intimate lens of Vincent, his driven, doubting, achingly human hero. An utterly engrossing, deeply satisfying read."

—Peter Ho Davies, author of
The Ugliest House in the World and *Equal Love*

"John Dalton gives his readers a deeply satisfying story of love's disguises. So few novels succeed at being erotic as well as profound, at revealing both the divine and the profane, at reading the human heart even as it beats. *Heaven Lake* is one of them."

—Kathryn Harrison, author of
The Seal Wife, The Binding Chair, and *The Kiss*

"In this immaculately written first novel, Dalton follows a young American, Vincent, who goes to Taiwan as a Christian missionary and ends up making an epic journey to mainland China. *Heaven Lake* is large in scope, vivid in character, and beautifully plotted."

—Margot Livesey, author of *Banishing Verona*